HUNG LOU MENG, BOOK I

OR, THE DREAM OF THE RED CHAMBER, A CHINESE NOVEL IN TWO BOOKS

by

CAO XUEQIN

Translated by H. BENCRAFT JOLY

Printed on acid free ANSI archival quality paper.
ISBN: 978-1-78139-276-8
© 2012 Benediction Classics, Oxford.

Contents

PREFACE

This translation was suggested not by any pretensions to range myself among the ranks of the body of sinologues, but by the perplexities and difficulties experienced by me as a student in Peking, when, at the completion of the Tzu Erh Chi, I had to plunge in the maze of the Hung Lou Meng.

Shortcomings are, I feel sure, to be discovered, both in the prose, as well as among the doggerel and uncouth rhymes, in which the text has been more adhered to than rhythm; but I shall feel satisfied with the result, if I succeed, even in the least degree, in affording a helping hand to present and future students of the Chinese language.

H. BENCRAFT JOLY, H.B.M. Vice-Consulate, Macao, 1st September, 1891.

CHAPTER I.

Chen Shih-yin, in a vision, apprehends perception and spirituality.
Chia Yü-ts'un, in the (windy and dusty) world, cherishes fond thoughts
of a beautiful maiden.

This is the opening section; this the first chapter. Subsequent to the visions of a dream which he had, on some previous occasion, experienced, the writer personally relates, he designedly concealed the true circumstances, and borrowed the attributes of perception and spirituality to relate this story of the Record of the Stone. With this purpose, he made use of such designations as Chen Shih-yin (truth under the garb of fiction) and the like. What are, however, the events recorded in this work? Who are the dramatis personae?

Wearied with the drudgery experienced of late in the world, the author speaking for himself, goes on to explain, with the lack of success which attended every single concern, I suddenly bethought myself of the womankind of past ages. Passing one by one under a minute scrutiny, I felt that in action and in lore, one and all were far above me; that in spite of the majesty of my manliness, I could not, in point of fact, compare with these characters of the gentle sex. And my shame forsooth then knew no bounds; while regret, on the other hand, was of no avail, as there was not even a remote possibility of a day of remedy.

On this very day it was that I became desirous to compile, in a connected form, for publication throughout the world, with a view to (universal) information, how that I bear inexorable and manifold retribution; inasmuch as what time, by the sustenance of the benevolence of Heaven, and the virtue of my ancestors, my apparel was rich and fine, and as what days my fare was savory and sumptuous, I disregarded the bounty of education and nurture of father and mother, and paid no heed to the virtue of precept and injunction of teachers and friends, with the result that I incurred the punishment, of failure recently in the least trifle, and the reckless waste of half my lifetime. There have been meanwhile, generation after generation, those in the inner chambers, the whole mass of whom could not, on any account, be, through my influence, allowed to fall into extinction, in order that I, unfilial as I have been, may have the means to screen my own shortcomings.

Hence it is that the thatched shed, with bamboo mat windows, the bed of tow and the stove of brick, which are at present my share, are not sufficient to deter me from carrying out the fixed purpose of my mind. And could I, furthermore, confront the morning breeze, the evening moon, the willows by the steps and the flowers in the courtyard, methinks these would moisten to a greater degree my mortal pen with ink; but though I lack culture and erudition, what harm is there, however, in employing fiction and unrecondite language to give utterance to the merits of these characters? And were I also able to induce the inmates of the inner chamber to understand and diffuse them, could I besides break the weariness of even so much as a single moment, or could I open the eyes of my contemporaries, will it not forsooth prove a boon?

This consideration has led to the usage of such names as Chia Yü-ts'un and other similar appellations.

More than any in these pages have been employed such words as dreams and visions; but these dreams constitute the main argument of this work, and combine, furthermore, the design of giving a word of warning to my readers.

Reader, can you suggest whence the story begins?

The narration may border on the limits of incoherency and triviality, but it possesses considerable zest. But to begin.

The Empress Nü Wo, (the goddess of works,) in fashioning blocks of stones, for the repair of the heavens, prepared, at the Ta Huang Hills and Wu Ch'i cave, 36,501 blocks of rough stone, each twelve chang in height, and twenty-four chang square. Of these stones, the Empress Wo only used 36,500; so that one single block remained over and above, without being turned to any account. This was cast down the Ch'ing Keng peak. This stone, strange to say, after having undergone a process of refinement, attained a nature of efficiency, and could, by its innate powers, set itself into motion and was able to expand and to contract.

When it became aware that the whole number of blocks had been made use of to repair the heavens, that it alone had been destitute of the necessary properties and had been unfit to attain selection, it forthwith felt within itself vexation and shame, and day and night, it gave way to anguish and sorrow.

One day, while it lamented its lot, it suddenly caught sight, at a great distance, of a Buddhist bonze and of a Taoist priest coming towards that direction. Their appearance was uncommon, their easy manner remarkable. When they drew near this Ch'ing Keng peak, they sat on the ground to rest, and began to converse. But on noticing the block newly-polished and brilliantly clear, which had moreover contracted in dimensions, and become no larger than the pendant of a fan, they were greatly filled with admiration. The Buddhist priest picked it up, and laid it in the palm of his hand.

"Your appearance," he said laughingly, "may well declare you to be a supernatural object, but as you lack any inherent quality it is necessary to inscribe a few characters on you, so that every one who shall see you may at once recognise you to be a remarkable thing. And subsequently, when you will be taken into a country where honour and affluence will reign, into a family cultured in mind and of official status, in a land where flowers and trees shall flourish with luxuriance, in a town of refinement, renown and glory; when you once will have been there…"

The stone listened with intense delight.

"What characters may I ask," it consequently inquired, "will you inscribe? and what place will I be taken to? pray, pray explain to me in lucid terms." "You mustn't be inquisitive," the bonze replied, with a smile, "in days to come you'll certainly understand everything." Having concluded these words, he forthwith put the stone in his sleeve, and proceeded leisurely on his journey, in company with the Taoist priest. Whither, however, he took the stone, is not divulged. Nor can it be known how many centuries and ages elapsed, before a Taoist priest, K'ung K'ung by name, passed, during his researches after the eternal reason and his quest after immortality, by these Ta Huang Hills, Wu Ch'i cave and Ch'ing Keng Peak. Suddenly perceiving a large block of stone, on the surface of which the traces of characters giving, in a connected form, the various incidents of its fate, could be clearly deciphered, K'ung K'ung examined them from first to last. They, in fact, explained how that this block of worthless stone had originally been devoid of the properties essential for the repairs to the heavens, how it would be transmuted into human form and introduced by Mang Mang the High Lord, and Miao Miao, the Divine, into the world of mortals, and how it would be led over the other bank (across the San

Sara). On the surface, the record of the spot where it would fall, the place of its birth, as well as various family trifles and trivial love affairs of young ladies, verses, odes, speeches and enigmas was still complete; but the name of the dynasty and the year of the reign were obliterated, and could not be ascertained.

On the obverse, were also the following enigmatical verses:

Lacking in virtues meet the azure skies to mend,
In vain the mortal world full many a year I wend,
Of a former and after life these facts that be,
Who will for a tradition strange record for me?

K'ung K'ung, the Taoist, having pondered over these lines for a while, became aware that this stone had a history of some kind.

"Brother stone," he forthwith said, addressing the stone, "the concerns of past days recorded on you possess, according to your own account, a considerable amount of interest, and have been for this reason inscribed, with the intent of soliciting generations to hand them down as remarkable occurrences. But in my own opinion, they lack, in the first place, any data by means of which to establish the name of the Emperor and the year of his reign; and, in the second place, these constitute no record of any excellent policy, adopted by any high worthies or high loyal statesmen, in the government of the state, or in the rule of public morals. The contents simply treat of a certain number of maidens, of exceptional character; either of their love affairs or infatuations, or of their small deserts or insignificant talents; and were I to transcribe the whole collection of them, they would, nevertheless, not be estimated as a book of any exceptional worth."

"Sir Priest," the stone replied with assurance, "why are you so excessively dull? The dynasties recorded in the rustic histories, which have been written from age to age, have, I am fain to think, invariably assumed, under false pretences, the mere nomenclature of the Han and T'ang dynasties. They differ from the events inscribed on my block, which do not borrow this customary practice, but, being based on my own experiences and natural feelings, present, on the contrary, a novel and unique character. Besides, in the pages of these rustic histories, either the aspersions upon sovereigns and statesmen, or the strictures upon individuals, their wives, and their daughters, or the deeds of licentiousness and violence are too numerous to be computed. Indeed, there is one more kind of loose literature, the wantonness and pollution in which work most easy havoc upon youth.

"As regards the works, in which the characters of scholars and beauties is delineated their allusions are again repeatedly of Wen

Chün, their theme in every page of Tzu Chien; a thousand volumes present no diversity; and a thousand characters are but a counterpart of each other. What is more, these works, throughout all their pages, cannot help bordering on extreme licence. The authors, however, had no other object in view than to give utterance to a few sentimental odes and elegant ballads of their own, and for this reason they have fictitiously invented the names and surnames of both men and women, and necessarily introduced, in addition, some low characters, who should, like a buffoon in a play, create some excitement in the plot.

"Still more loathsome is a kind of pedantic and profligate literature, perfectly devoid of all natural sentiment, full of self-contradictions; and, in fact, the contrast to those maidens in my work, whom I have, during half my lifetime, seen with my own eyes and heard with my own ears. And though I will not presume to estimate them as superior to the heroes and heroines in the works of former ages, yet the perusal of the motives and issues of their experiences, may likewise afford matter sufficient to banish dulness, and to break the spell of melancholy.

"As regards the several stanzas of doggerel verse, they may too evoke such laughter as to compel the reader to blurt out the rice, and to spurt out the wine.

"In these pages, the scenes depicting the anguish of separation, the bliss of reunion, and the fortunes of prosperity and of adversity are all, in every detail, true to human nature, and I have not taken upon myself to make the slightest addition, or alteration, which might lead to the perversion of the truth.

"My only object has been that men may, after a drinking bout, or after they wake from sleep or when in need of relaxation from the pressure of business, take up this light literature, and not only expunge the traces of antiquated books, and obtain a new kind of distraction, but that they may also lay by a long life as well as energy and strength; for it bears no point of similarity to those works, whose designs are false, whose course is immoral. Now, Sir Priest, what are your views on the subject?"

K'ung K'ung having pondered for a while over the words, to which he had listened intently, re-perused, throughout, this record of the stone; and finding that the general purport consisted of nought else than a treatise on love, and likewise of an accurate transcription of facts, without the least taint of profligacy injurious to the times, he thereupon copied the contents, from beginning to end, to the intent of charging the world to hand them down as a strange story.

Hence it was that K'ung K'ung, the Taoist, in consequence of his perception, (in his state of) abstraction, of passion, the generation, from this passion, of voluptuousness, the transmission of this voluptuousness into passion, and the apprehension, by means of passion, of its unreality, forthwith altered his name for that of "Ch'ing Tseng" (the Voluptuous Bonze), and changed the title of "the Memoir of a Stone" (Shih-t'ou-chi,) for that of "Ch'ing Tseng Lu," The Record of the Voluptuous Bonze; while K'ung Mei-chi of Tung Lu gave it the name of "Feng Yüeh Pao Chien," "The Precious Mirror of Voluptuousness." In later years, owing to the devotion by Tsao Hsüeh-ch'in in the Tao Hung study, of ten years to the perusal and revision of the work, the additions and modifications effected by him five times, the affix of an index and the division into periods and chapters, the book was again entitled "Chin Ling Shih Erh Ch'ai," "The Twelve Maidens of Chin Ling." A stanza was furthermore composed for the purpose. This then, and no other, is the origin of the Record of the Stone. The poet says appositely:—

Pages full of silly litter,
Tears a handful sour and bitter;
All a fool the author hold,
But their zest who can unfold?

You have now understood the causes which brought about the Record of the Stone, but as you are not, as yet, aware what characters are depicted, and what circumstances are related on the surface of the block, reader, please lend an ear to the narrative on the stone, which runs as follows:—

In old days, the land in the South East lay low. In this South-East part of the world, was situated a walled town, Ku Su by name. Within the walls a locality, called the Ch'ang Men, was more than all others throughout the mortal world, the centre, which held the second, if not the first place for fashion and life. Beyond this Ch'ang Men was a street called Shih-li-chieh (Ten *Li* street); in this street a lane, the Jen Ch'ing lane (Humanity and Purity); and in this lane stood an old temple, which on account of its diminutive dimensions, was called, by general consent, the Gourd temple. Next door to this temple lived the family of a district official, Chen by surname, Fei by name, and Shih-yin by style. His wife, née Feng, possessed a worthy and virtuous disposition, and had a clear perception of moral propriety and good conduct. This family, though not in actual possession of excessive affluence and honours, was, nevertheless, in their district, conceded to be a clan of well-to-do standing. As this Chen Shih-yin was of a contented and unambitious frame of mind, and entertained no hankering after any official distinction, but day after day of his life took delight in gazing at flowers, planting bamboos, sipping his wine and conning poetical works, he was in fact, in the indulgence of these pursuits, as happy as a supernatural being.

One thing alone marred his happiness. He had lived over half a century and had, as yet, no male offspring around his knees. He had one only child, a daughter, whose infant name was Ying Lien. She was just three years of age. On a long summer day, on which the heat had been intense, Shih-yin sat leisurely in his library. Feeling his hand tired, he dropped the book he held, leant his head on a teapoy, and fell asleep.

Of a sudden, while in this state of unconsciousness, it seemed as if he had betaken himself on foot to some spot or other whither he could not discriminate. Unexpectedly he espied, in the opposite direction, two priests coming towards him: the one a Buddhist, the other a Taoist. As they advanced they kept up the conversation in which they were engaged. "Whither do you purpose taking the object you have brought away?" he heard the Taoist inquire. To this question the Buddhist replied with a smile: "Set your mind at ease," he said; "there's now in maturity a plot of a general character involving mundane pleasures, which will presently come to a denouement. The whole number of the votaries of voluptuousness have, as yet, not been quickened or entered the world, and I mean to avail myself of this occasion to introduce this object among their number, so as to give it a chance to go through the span of human existence." "The votaries of voluptuousness of these days will naturally have again to endure the ills of life during their course through the mortal world," the Taoist remarked; "but when, I wonder, will they spring into existence? and in what place will they descend?"

"The account of these circumstances," the bonze ventured to reply, "is enough to make you laugh! They amount to this: there existed in the west, on the bank of the Ling (spiritual) river, by the side of the San Sheng (thrice-born) stone, a blade of the Chiang Chu (purple pearl) grass. At about the same time it was that the block of stone was, consequent upon its rejection by the goddess of works, also left to ramble and wander to its own gratification, and to roam about at pleasure to every and any place. One day it came within the precincts of the Ching Huan (Monitory Vision) Fairy; and this Fairy, cognizant of the fact that this stone had a history, detained it, therefore, to reside at the Ch'ih Hsia (purple clouds) palace, and apportioned to it the duties of attendant on Shen Ying, a fairy of the Ch'ih Hsia palace.

"This stone would, however, often stroll along the banks of the Ling river, and having at the sight of the blade of spiritual grass been filled with admiration, it, day by day, moistened its roots with sweet dew. This purple pearl grass, at the outset, tarried for months and years; but being at a later period imbued with the essence and luxuriance of heaven and earth, and having incessantly received the moisture and nurture of the sweet dew, divested itself, in course of time, of the form of a grass; assuming, in lieu, a human nature, which gradually became perfected into the person of a girl.

"Every day she was wont to wander beyond the confines of the Li Hen (divested animosities) heavens. When hungry she fed on the Pi Ch'ing (hidden love) fruit—when thirsty she drank the Kuan ch'ou (discharged sorrows,) water. Having, however, up to this time, not shewn her gratitude for the virtue of nurture lavished upon her, the result was but natural that she should resolve in her heart upon a constant and incessant purpose to make suitable acknowledgment.

"I have been," she would often commune within herself, "the recipient of the gracious bounty of rain and dew, but I possess no such water as was lavished upon me to repay it! But should it ever descend into the world in the form of a human being, I will also betake myself thither, along with it; and if I can only have the means of making restitution to it, with the tears of a whole lifetime, I may be able to make adequate return."

"This resolution it is that will evolve the descent into the world of so many pleasure-bound spirits of retribution and the experience of fantastic destinies; and this crimson pearl blade will also be among the number. The stone still lies in its original place, and why should not you and I take it along before the tribunal of the Monitory Vision Fairy, and place on its behalf its name on record, so that it should descend into the world, in company with these spirits of passion, and bring this plot to an issue?"

"It is indeed ridiculous," interposed the Taoist. "Never before have I heard even the very mention of restitution by means of tears! Why should not you and I avail ourselves of this opportunity to likewise go down into the world? and if successful in effecting the salvation of a few of them, will it not be a work meritorious and virtuous?"

"This proposal," remarked the Buddhist, "is quite in harmony with my own views. Come along then with me to the palace of the

Monitory Vision Fairy, and let us deliver up this good-for-nothing object, and have done with it! And when the company of pleasure-bound spirits of wrath descend into human existence, you and I can then enter the world. Half of them have already fallen into the dusty universe, but the whole number of them have not, as yet, come together."

"Such being the case," the Taoist acquiesced, "I am ready to follow you, whenever you please to go."

But to return to Chen Shih-yin. Having heard every one of these words distinctly, he could not refrain from forthwith stepping forward and paying homage. "My spiritual lords," he said, as he smiled, "accept my obeisance." The Buddhist and Taoist priests lost no time in responding to the compliment, and they exchanged the usual salutations. "My spiritual lords," Shih-yin continued; "I have just heard the conversation that passed between you, on causes and effects, a conversation the like of which few mortals have forsooth listened to; but your younger brother is sluggish of intellect, and cannot lucidly fathom the import! Yet could this dulness and simplicity be graciously dispelled, your younger brother may, by listening minutely, with undefiled ear and careful attention, to a certain degree be aroused to a sense of understanding; and what is more, possibly find the means of escaping the anguish of sinking down into Hades."

The two spirits smiled, "The conversation," they added, "refers to the primordial scheme and cannot be divulged before the proper season; but, when the time comes, mind do not forget us two, and you will readily be able to escape from the fiery furnace."

Shih-yin, after this reply, felt it difficult to make any further inquiries. "The primordial scheme," he however remarked smiling, "cannot, of course, be divulged; but what manner of thing, I wonder, is the good-for-nothing object you alluded to a short while back? May I not be allowed to judge for myself?"

"This object about which you ask," the Buddhist Bonze responded, "is intended, I may tell you, by fate to be just glanced at by you." With these words he produced it, and handed it over to Shih-yin.

Shih-yin received it. On scrutiny he found it, in fact, to be a beautiful gem, so lustrous and so clear that the traces of characters on the surface were distinctly visible. The characters inscribed consisted of the four "T'ung Ling Pao Yü," "Precious Gem of Spiritual Perception." On the obverse, were also several columns of minute words, which he was just in the act of looking at intently, when the Buddhist at once expostulated.

"We have already reached," he exclaimed, "the confines of vision." Snatching it violently out of his hands, he walked away with the Taoist, under a lofty stone portal, on the face of which appeared in large type the four characters: "T'ai Hsü Huan Ching," "The Visionary limits of the Great Void." On each side was a scroll with the lines:

When falsehood stands for truth, truth likewise becomes false,
Where naught be made to aught, aught changes into naught.

Shih-yin meant also to follow them on the other side, but, as he was about to make one step forward, he suddenly heard a crash, just as if the mountains had fallen into ruins, and the earth sunk into destruction. As Shih-yin uttered a loud shout, he looked with strained eye; but all he could see was the fiery sun shining, with glowing rays, while the banana leaves drooped their heads. By that time, half of the circumstances connected with the dream he had had, had already slipped from his memory.

He also noticed a nurse coming towards him with Ying Lien in her arms. To Shih-yin's eyes his daughter appeared even more beautiful, such a bright gem, so precious, and so lovable. Forthwith stretching out his arms, he took her over, and, as he held her in his embrace, he coaxed her to play with him for a while; after which he brought her up to the street to see the great stir occasioned by the procession that was going past.

He was about to come in, when he caught sight of two priests, one a Taoist, the other a Buddhist, coming hither from the opposite direction. The Buddhist had a head covered with mange, and went barefooted. The Taoist had a limping foot, and his hair was all dishevelled.

Like maniacs, they jostled along, chattering and laughing as they drew near.

As soon as they reached Shih-yin's door, and they perceived him with Ying Lien in his arms, the Bonze began to weep aloud.

Turning towards Shih-yin, he said to him: "My good Sir, why need you carry in your embrace this living but luckless thing, which will involve father and mother in trouble?"

These words did not escape Shih-yin's ear; but persuaded that they amounted to raving talk, he paid no heed whatever to the bonze.

"Part with her and give her to me," the Buddhist still went on to say.

Shih-yin could not restrain his annoyance; and hastily pressing his daughter closer to him, he was intent upon going in, when the bonze pointed his hand at him, and burst out in a loud fit of laughter.

He then gave utterance to the four lines that follow:

You indulge your tender daughter and are laughed at as inane;
Vain you face the snow, oh mirror! for it will evanescent wane,
When the festival of lanterns is gone by, guard 'gainst your doom,
'Tis what time the flames will kindle, and the fire will consume.

Shih-yin understood distinctly the full import of what he heard; but his heart was still full of conjectures. He was about to inquire who and what they were, when he heard the Taoist remark,—"You and I cannot speed together; let us now part company, and each of us will be then able to go after his own business. After the lapse of three ages, I shall be at the Pei Mang mount, waiting for you; and we can, after our reunion, betake ourselves to the Visionary Confines of the Great Void, there to cancel the name of the stone from the records."

"Excellent! first rate!" exclaimed the Bonze. And at the conclusion of these words, the two men parted, each going his own way, and no trace was again seen of them.

"These two men," Shih-yin then pondered within his heart, "must have had many experiences, and I ought really to have made more inquiries of them; but at this juncture to indulge in regret is anyhow too late."

While Shih-yin gave way to these foolish reflections, he suddenly noticed the arrival of a penniless scholar, Chia by surname, Hua by name, Shih-fei by style and Yü-ts'un by nickname, who had taken up his quarters in the Gourd temple next door. This Chia Yü-ts'un was originally a denizen of Hu-Chow, and was also of literary and official parentage, but as he was born of the youngest stock, and the possessions of his paternal and maternal ancestors were completely exhausted, and his parents and relatives were dead, he remained the sole and only survivor; and, as he found his residence in his native place of no avail, he therefore entered the capital in search of that reputation, which would enable him to put the family estate on a proper standing. He had arrived at this place since the year before last, and had, what is more, lived all along in very straitened circumstances. He had made the temple his temporary quarters, and earned a living by daily occupying himself in composing documents and writing letters for customers. Thus it was that Shih-yin had been in constant relations with him.

As soon as Yü-ts'un perceived Shih-yin, he lost no time in saluting him. "My worthy Sir," he observed with a forced smile; "how is it you are leaning against the door and looking out? Is there perchance any news astir in the streets, or in the public places?"

"None whatever," replied Shih-yin, as he returned the smile. "Just a while back, my young daughter was in sobs, and I coaxed her out here to amuse her. I am just now without anything whatever to attend to, so that, dear brother Chia, you come just in the nick of time. Please walk into my mean abode, and let us endeavour, in each other's company, to while away this long summer day."

After he had made this remark, he bade a servant take his daughter in, while he, hand-in-hand with Yü-ts'un, walked into the library, where a young page served tea. They had hardly exchanged a few sentences, when one of the household came in, in flying haste, to announce that Mr. Yen had come to pay a visit.

Shih-yin at once stood up. "Pray excuse my rudeness," he remarked apologetically, "but do sit down; I shall shortly rejoin you, and enjoy the pleasure of your society." "My dear Sir," answered Yü-ts'un, as he got up, also in a conceding way, "suit your own convenience. I've often had the honour of being your guest, and what will it matter if I wait a little?" While these apologies were yet being spoken, Shih-yin had already walked out into the front parlour. During his absence, Yü-ts'un occupied himself in turning over the pages of some poetical work to dispel ennui, when suddenly he heard, outside the window, a woman's cough. Yü-ts'un hurriedly got up and looked out. He saw at a glance that it was a servant girl engaged in picking flowers. Her deportment was out of the common; her eyes so bright, her eyebrows so well defined. Though not a perfect beauty, she possessed nevertheless charms sufficient to arouse the feelings. Yü-ts'un unwittingly gazed at her with fixed eye. This waiting-maid, belonging to the Chen family, had done picking flowers, and was on the point of going in, when she of a sudden raised her eyes and became aware of the presence of some person inside the window, whose head-gear consisted of a turban in tatters, while his clothes were the worse for wear. But in spite of his poverty, he was naturally endowed with a round waist, a broad back, a fat face, a square mouth; added to this, his eyebrows were swordlike, his eyes resembled stars, his nose was straight, his cheeks square.

This servant girl turned away in a hurry and made her escape.

"This man so burly and strong," she communed within herself, "yet at the same time got up in such poor attire, must, I expect, be no one else than the man, whose name is Chia Yü-ts'un or such like, time after time referred to by my master, and to whom he has repeatedly wished to give a helping hand, but has failed to find a favourable opportunity. And as related to our family there is no connexion or friend in such straits, I feel certain it cannot be any other person than he.

Strange to say, my master has further remarked that this man will, for a certainty, not always continue in such a state of destitution."

As she indulged in this train of thought, she could not restrain herself from turning her head round once or twice.

When Yü-ts'un perceived that she had looked back, he readily interpreted it as a sign that in her heart her thoughts had been of him, and he was frantic with irrepressible joy.

"This girl," he mused, "is, no doubt, keen-eyed and eminently shrewd, and one in this world who has seen through me."

The servant youth, after a short time, came into the room; and when Yü-ts'un made inquiries and found out from him that the guests in the front parlour had been detained to dinner, he could not very well wait any longer, and promptly walked away down a side passage and out of a back door.

When the guests had taken their leave, Shih-yin did not go back to rejoin Yü-ts'un, as he had come to know that he had already left.

In time the mid-autumn festivities drew near; and Shih-yin, after the family banquet was over, had a separate table laid in the library, and crossed over, in the moonlight, as far as the temple and invited Yü-ts'un to come round.

The fact is that Yü-ts'un, ever since the day on which he had seen the girl of the Chen family turn twice round to glance at him, flattered himself that she was friendly disposed towards him, and incessantly fostered fond thoughts of her in his heart. And on this day, which happened to be the mid-autumn feast, he could not, as he gazed at the moon, refrain from cherishing her remembrance. Hence it was that he gave vent to these pentameter verses:

Alas! not yet divined my lifelong wish,
And anguish ceaseless comes upon anguish
I came, and sad at heart, my brow I frowned;
She went, and oft her head to look turned round.
Facing the breeze, her shadow she doth watch,
Who's meet this moonlight night with her to match?
The lustrous rays if they my wish but read
Would soon alight upon her beauteous head!

Yü-ts'un having, after this recitation, recalled again to mind how that throughout his lifetime his literary attainments had had an adverse fate and not met with an opportunity (of reaping distinction), went on to rub his brow, and as he raised his eyes to the skies, he heaved a deep sigh and once more intoned a couplet aloud:

The gem in the cask a high price it seeks,
The pin in the case to take wing it waits.

As luck would have it, Shih-yin was at the moment approaching, and upon hearing the lines, he said with a smile: "My dear Yü-ts'un, really your attainments are of no ordinary capacity."

Yü-ts'un lost no time in smiling and replying. "It would be presumption in my part to think so," he observed. "I was simply at random humming a few verses composed by former writers, and what reason is there to laud me to such an excessive degree? To what, my dear Sir, do I owe the pleasure of your visit?" he went on to inquire. "Tonight," replied Shih-yin, "is the mid-autumn feast, generally known as the full-moon festival; and as I could not help thinking that living, as you my worthy brother are, as a mere stranger in this Buddhist temple, you could not but experience the feeling of loneliness. I have, for the express purpose, prepared a small entertainment, and will be pleased if you will come to my mean abode to have a glass of wine. But I wonder whether you will entertain favourably my modest invitation?" Yü-ts'un, after listening to the proposal, put forward no refusal of any sort; but remarked complacently: "Being the recipient of such marked attention, how can I presume to repel your generous consideration?"

As he gave expression to these words, he walked off there and then, in company with Shih-yin, and came over once again into the court in front of the library. In a few minutes, tea was over.

The cups and dishes had been laid from an early hour, and needless to say the wines were luscious; the fare sumptuous.

The two friends took their seats. At first they leisurely replenished their glasses, and quietly sipped their wine; but as, little by little, they entered into conversation, their good cheer grew more genial, and unawares the glasses began to fly round, and the cups to be exchanged.

At this very hour, in every house of the neighbourhood, sounded the fife and lute, while the inmates indulged in music and singing. Above head, the orb of the radiant moon shone with an all-pervading splendour, and with a steady lustrous light, while the two friends, as their exuberance increased, drained their cups dry so soon as they reached their lips.

Yü-ts'un, at this stage of the collation, was considerably under the influence of wine, and the vehemence of his high spirits was irrepressible. As he gazed at the moon, he fostered thoughts, to which he gave vent by the recital of a double couplet.

'Tis what time three meets five, Selene is a globe!
Her pure rays fill the court, the jadelike rails enrobe!
Lo! in the heavens her disk to view doth now arise,
And in the earth below to gaze men lift their eyes.

"Excellent!" cried Shih-yin with a loud voice, after he had heard these lines; "I have repeatedly maintained that it was impossible for you to remain long inferior to any, and now the verses you have recited are a prognostic of your rapid advancement. Already it is evident that, before long, you will extend your footsteps far above the clouds! I must congratulate you! I must congratulate you! Let me, with my own hands, pour a glass of wine to pay you my compliments."

Yü-ts'un drained the cup. "What I am about to say," he explained as he suddenly heaved a sigh, "is not the maudlin talk of a man under the effects of wine. As far as the subjects at present set in the examinations go, I could, perchance, also have well been able to enter the list, and to send in my name as a candidate; but I have, just now, no means whatever to make provision for luggage and for travelling expenses. The distance too to Shen Ching is a long one, and I could not depend upon the sale of papers or the composition of essays to find the means of getting there."

Shih-yin gave him no time to conclude. "Why did you not speak about this sooner?" he interposed with haste. "I have long entertained this suspicion; but as, whenever I met you, this conversation was never broached, I did not presume to make myself officious. But if such be the state of affairs just now, I lack, I admit, literary qualification, but on the two subjects of friendly spirit and pecuniary means, I have, nevertheless, some experience. Moreover, I rejoice that next year is just the season for the triennial examinations, and you should start for the capital with all despatch; and in the tripos next spring, you will, by carrying the prize, be able to do justice to the proficiency you can boast of. As regards the travelling expenses and the other items, the provision of everything necessary for you by my own self will again not render nugatory your mean acquaintance with me."

Forthwith, he directed a servant lad to go and pack up at once fifty taels of pure silver and two suits of winter clothes.

"The nineteenth," he continued, "is a propitious day, and you should lose no time in hiring a boat and starting on your journey westwards. And when, by your eminent talents, you shall have soared high to a lofty position, and we meet again next winter, will not the occasion be extremely felicitous?"

Yü-ts'un accepted the money and clothes with but scanty expression of gratitude. In fact, he paid no thought whatever to the gifts, but went on, again drinking his wine, as he chattered and laughed.

It was only when the third watch of that day had already struck that the two friends parted company; and Shih-yin, after seeing Yü-ts'un off, retired to his room and slept, with one sleep all through, never waking until the sun was well up in the skies.

Remembering the occurrence of the previous night, he meant to write a couple of letters of recommendation for Yü-ts'un to take along with him to the capital, to enable him, after handing them over at the mansions of certain officials, to find some place as a temporary home. He accordingly despatched a servant to ask him to come round, but the man returned and reported that from what the bonze said, "Mr. Chia had started on his journey to the capital, at the fifth watch of that very morning, that he had also left a message with the bonze to deliver to you, Sir, to the effect that men of letters paid no heed to lucky or unlucky days, that the sole consideration with them was the nature of the matter in hand, and that he could find no time to come round in person and bid good-bye."

Shih-yin after hearing this message had no alternative but to banish the subject from his thoughts.

In comfortable circumstances, time indeed goes by with easy stride. Soon drew near also the happy festival of the 15th of the 1st moon, and Shih-yin told a servant Huo Ch'i to take Ying Lien to see the sacrificial fires and flowery lanterns.

About the middle of the night, Huo Ch'i was hard pressed, and he forthwith set Ying Lien down on the doorstep of a certain house. When he felt relieved, he came back to take her up, but failed to find anywhere any trace of Ying Lien. In a terrible plight, Huo Ch'i prosecuted his search throughout half the night; but even by the dawn of day, he had not discovered any clue of her whereabouts. Huo Ch'i, lacking, on the other hand, the courage to go back and face his master, promptly made his escape to his native village.

Shih-yin—in fact, the husband as well as the wife—seeing that their child had not come home during the whole night, readily concluded that some mishap must have befallen her. Hastily they despatched several servants to go in search of her, but one and all returned to report that there was neither vestige nor tidings of her.

This couple had only had this child, and this at the meridian of their life, so that her sudden disappearance plunged them in such great distress that day and night they mourned her loss to such a point as to well nigh pay no heed to their very lives.

A month in no time went by. Shih-yin was the first to fall ill, and his wife, Dame Feng, likewise, by dint of fretting for her daughter, was also prostrated with sickness. The doctor was, day after day, sent for, and the oracle consulted by means of divination.

Little did any one think that on this day, being the 15th of the 3rd moon, while the sacrificial oblations were being prepared in the Hu Lu temple, a pan with oil would have caught fire, through the want of care on the part of the bonze, and that in a short time the flames would have consumed the paper pasted on the windows.

Among the natives of this district bamboo fences and wooden partitions were in general use, and these too proved a source of calamity so ordained by fate (to consummate this decree).

With promptness (the fire) extended to two buildings, then enveloped three, then dragged four (into ruin), and then spread to five houses, until the whole street was in a blaze, resembling the flames of a volcano. Though both the military and the people at once ran to the rescue, the fire had already assumed a serious hold, so that it was impossible for them to afford any effective assistance for its suppression.

It blazed away straight through the night, before it was extinguished, and consumed, there is in fact no saying how many dwelling houses. Anyhow, pitiful to relate, the Chen house, situated as it was next door to the temple, was, at an early part of the evening, reduced to a heap of tiles and bricks; and nothing but the lives of that couple and several inmates of the family did not sustain any injuries.

Shih-yin was in despair, but all he could do was to stamp his feet and heave deep sighs. After consulting with his wife, they betook themselves to a farm of theirs, where they took up their quarters temporarily. But as it happened that water had of late years been scarce, and no crops been reaped, robbers and thieves had sprung up like bees, and though the Government troops were bent upon their capture, it was anyhow difficult to settle down quietly on the farm. He therefore had no other resource than to convert, at a loss, the whole of his property into money, and to take his wife and two servant girls and come over for shelter to the house of his father-in-law.

His father-in-law, Feng Su, by name, was a native of Ta Ju Chou. Although only a labourer, he was nevertheless in easy circumstances at home. When he on this occasion saw his son-in-law come to him in such distress, he forthwith felt at heart considerable displeasure. Fortunately Shih-yin had still in his possession the money derived from the unprofitable realization of his property, so that he produced and handed it to his father-in-law, commissioning him to purchase, whenever a suitable opportunity presented itself, a house and land as a provision for food and raiment against days to come. This Feng Su, however, only expended the half of the sum, and pocketed the other half, merely acquiring for him some fallow land and a dilapidated house.

Shih-yin being, on the other hand, a man of books and with no experience in matters connected with business and with sowing and reaping, subsisted, by hook and by crook, for about a year or two, when he became more impoverished.

In his presence, Feng Su would readily give vent to specious utterances, while, with others, and behind his back, he on the contrary expressed his indignation against his improvidence in his mode of living, and against his sole delight of eating and playing the lazy.

Shih-yin, aware of the want of harmony with his father-in-law, could not help giving way, in his own heart, to feelings of regret and pain. In addition to this, the fright and vexation which he had undergone the year before, the anguish and suffering (he had had to endure), had already worked havoc (on his constitution); and being a man advanced in years, and assailed by the joint attack of poverty and disease, he at length gradually began to display symptoms of decline.

Strange coincidence, as he, on this day, came leaning on his staff and with considerable strain, as far as the street for a little relaxation, he suddenly caught sight, approaching from the off side, of a Taoist priest with a crippled foot; his maniac appearance so repulsive, his shoes of straw, his dress all in tatters, muttering several sentiments to this effect:

All men spiritual life know to be good,
But fame to disregard they ne'er succeed!
From old till now the statesmen where are they?
Waste lie their graves, a heap of grass, extinct.
All men spiritual life know to be good,
But to forget gold, silver, ill succeed!
Through life they grudge their hoardings to be scant,
And when plenty has come, their eyelids close.
All men spiritual life hold to be good,
Yet to forget wives, maids, they ne'er succeed!
Who speak of grateful love while lives their lord,
And dead their lord, another they pursue.
All men spiritual life know to be good,

But sons and grandsons to forget never succeed!
From old till now of parents soft many,
But filial sons and grandsons who have seen?

Shih-yin upon hearing these words, hastily came up to the priest, "What were you so glibly holding forth?" he inquired. "All I could hear were a lot of hao liao (excellent, finality.")

"You may well have heard the two words 'hao liao,'" answered the Taoist with a smile, "but can you be said to have fathomed their meaning? You should know that all things in this world are excellent, when they have attained finality; when they have attained finality, they are excellent; but when they have not attained finality, they are not excellent; if they would be excellent, they should attain finality. My song is entitled Excellent-finality (hao liao)."

Shih-yin was gifted with a natural perspicacity that enabled him, as soon as he heard these remarks, to grasp their spirit.

"Wait a while," he therefore said smilingly; "let me unravel this excellent-finality song of yours; do you mind?"

"Please by all means go on with the interpretation," urged the Taoist; whereupon Shih-yin proceeded in this strain:

Sordid rooms and vacant courts,
Replete in years gone by with beds where statesmen lay;
Parched grass and withered banian trees,
Where once were halls for song and dance!
Spiders' webs the carved pillars intertwine,
The green gauze now is also pasted on the straw windows!
What about the cosmetic fresh concocted or the powder just scented;
Why has the hair too on each temple become white like hoarfrost!
Yesterday the tumulus of yellow earth buried the bleached bones,
To-night under the red silk curtain reclines the couple!
Gold fills the coffers, silver fills the boxes,
But in a twinkle, the beggars will all abuse you!
While you deplore that the life of others is not long,
You forget that you yourself are approaching death!
You educate your sons with all propriety,
But they may some day, 'tis hard to say become thieves;
Though you choose (your fare and home) the fatted beam,
You may, who can say, fall into some place of easy virtue!
Through your dislike of the gauze hat as mean,
You have come to be locked in a cangue;
Yesterday, poor fellow, you felt cold in a tattered coat,
To-day, you despise the purple embroidered dress as long!

Confusion reigns far and wide! you have just sung your part, I come on
the boards,
Instead of yours, you recognise another as your native land;
What utter perversion!
In one word, it comes to this we make wedding clothes for others!
(We sow for others to reap.)

The crazy limping Taoist clapped his hands. "Your interpretation is explicit," he remarked with a hearty laugh, "your interpretation is explicit!"

Shih-yin promptly said nothing more than,—"Walk on;" and seizing the stole from the Taoist's shoulder, he flung it over his own. He did not, however, return home, but leisurely walked away, in company with the eccentric priest.

The report of his disappearance was at once bruited abroad, and plunged the whole neighbourhood in commotion; and converted into a piece of news, it was circulated from mouth to mouth.

Dame Feng, Shih-yin's wife, upon hearing the tidings, had such a fit of weeping that she hung between life and death; but her only alternative was to consult with her father, and to despatch servants on all sides to institute inquiries. No news was however received of him, and she had nothing else to do but to practise resignation, and to remain dependent upon the support of her parents for her subsistence. She had fortunately still by her side, to wait upon her, two servant girls, who had been with her in days gone by; and the three of them, mistress as well as servants, occupied themselves day and night with needlework, to assist her father in his daily expenses.

This Feng Su had after all, in spite of his daily murmurings against his bad luck, no help but to submit to the inevitable.

On a certain day, the elder servant girl of the Chen family was at the door purchasing thread, and while there, she of a sudden heard in the street shouts of runners clearing the way, and every one explain that the new magistrate had come to take up his office.

The girl, as she peeped out from inside the door, perceived the lictors and policemen go by two by two; and when unexpectedly in a state chair, was carried past an official, in black hat and red coat, she was indeed quite taken aback.

"The face of this officer would seem familiar," she argued within herself; "just as if I had seen him somewhere or other ere this."

Shortly she entered the house, and banishing at once the occurrence from her mind, she did not give it a second thought. At night, however, while she was waiting to go to bed, she suddenly heard a sound like a rap at the door. A band of men boisterously cried out: "We are messengers, deputed by the worthy magistrate of this district, and come to summon one of you to an enquiry."

Feng Su, upon hearing these words, fell into such a terrible consternation that his eyes stared wide and his mouth gaped.

What calamity was impending is not as yet ascertained, but, reader, listen to the explanation contained in the next chapter.

CHAPTER II.

The spirit of Mrs. Chia Shih-yin departs from the town of Yang Chou. Leng Tzu-hsing dilates upon the Jung Kuo Mansion.

To continue. Feng Su, upon hearing the shouts of the public messengers, came out in a flurry and forcing a smile, he asked them to explain (their errand); but all these people did was to continue bawling out: "Be quick, and ask Mr. Chen to come out."

"My surname is Feng," said Feng Su, as he promptly forced himself to smile; "It is'nt Chen at all: I had once a son-in-law whose surname was Chen, but he has left home, it is now already a year or two back. Is it perchance about him that you are inquiring?"

To which the public servants remarked: "We know nothing about Chen or Chia (true or false); but as he is your son-in-law, we'll take you at once along with us to make verbal answer to our master and have done with it."

And forthwith the whole bevy of public servants hustled Feng Su on, as they went on their way back; while every one in the Feng family was seized with consternation, and could not imagine what it was all about.

It was no earlier than the second watch, when Feng Su returned home; and they, one and all, pressed him with questions as to what had happened.

"The fact is," he explained, "the newly-appointed Magistrate, whose surname is Chia, whose name is Huo and who is a native of Huchow, has been on intimate terms, in years gone by, with our son-in-law; that at the sight of the girl Chiao Hsing, standing at the door, in the act of buying thread, he concluded that he must have shifted his quarters over here, and hence it was that his messengers came to fetch him. I gave him a clear account of the various circumstances (of his misfortunes), and the Magistrate was for a time much distressed and expressed his regret. He then went on to make inquiries about my grand-daughter, and I explained that she had been lost, while looking at the illuminations. 'No matter,' put in the Magistrate, 'I will by and by order my men to make search, and I feel certain that they will find her and bring her back.' Then ensued a short conversation, after which I was about to go, when he presented me with the sum of two taels."

The mistress of the Chen family (Mrs. Chen Shih-yin) could not but feel very much affected by what she heard, and the whole evening she uttered not a word.

The next day, at an early hour, Yü-ts'un sent some of his men to bring over to Chen's wife presents, consisting of two packets of silver, and four pieces of brocaded silk, as a token of gratitude, and to Feng Su also a confidential letter, requesting him to ask of Mrs. Chen her maid Chiao Hsing to become his second wife.

Feng Su was so intensely delighted that his eyebrows expanded, his eyes smiled, and he felt eager to toady to the Magistrate (by presenting the girl to him). He hastened to employ all his persuasive powers with his daughter (to further his purpose), and on the same evening he forthwith escorted Chiao Hsing in a small chair to the Yamên.

The joy experienced by Yü-ts'un need not be dilated upon. He also presented Feng Su with a packet containing one hundred ounces of gold; and sent numerous valuable presents to Mrs. Chen, enjoining her "to live cheerfully in the anticipation of finding out the whereabouts of her daughter."

It must be explained, however, that the maid Chi'ao Hsing was the very person, who, a few years ago, had looked round at Yü-ts'un and who, by one simple, unpremeditated glance, evolved, in fact, this extraordinary destiny which was indeed an event beyond conception.

Who would ever have foreseen that fate and fortune would both have so favoured her that she should, contrary to all anticipation, give birth to a son, after living with Yü-ts'un barely a year, that in addition to this, after the lapse of another half year, Yü-ts'un's wife should have contracted a sudden illness and departed this life, and that Yü-ts'un should have at once raised her to the rank of first wife. Her destiny is adequately expressed by the lines:

Through but one single, casual look
Soon an exalted place she took.

The fact is that after Yü-ts'un had been presented with the money by Shih-yin, he promptly started on the 16th day for the capital, and at the triennial great tripos, his wishes were gratified to the full. Having successfully carried off his degree of graduate of the third rank, his name was put by selection on the list for provincial appointments. By this time, he had been raised to the rank of Magistrate in this district; but, in spite of the excellence and sufficiency of his accomplishments and abilities, he could not escape being ambitious and overbearing. He failed besides, confident as he was in his own merits, in respect toward his superiors, with the result that these officials looked upon him scornfully with the corner of the eye.

A year had hardly elapsed, when he was readily denounced in a memorial to the Throne by the High Provincial authorities, who represented that he was of a haughty disposition, that he had taken upon himself to introduce innovations in the rites and ceremonies, that overtly, while he endeavoured to enjoy the reputation of probity and uprightness, he, secretly, combined the nature of the tiger and wolf; with the consequence that he had been the cause of much trouble in the district, and that he had made life intolerable for the people, &c. &c.

The Dragon countenance of the Emperor was considerably incensed. His Majesty lost no time in issuing commands, in reply to the Memorial, that he should be deprived of his official status.

On the arrival of the despatch from the Board, great was the joy felt by every officer, without exception, of the prefecture in which he had held office. Yü-ts'un, though at heart intensely mortified and incensed, betrayed not the least outward symptom of annoyance, but still preserved, as of old, a smiling and cheerful countenance.

He handed over charge of all official business and removed the savings which he had accumulated during the several years he had been in office, his family and all his chattels to his original home; where, after having put everything in proper order, he himself travelled (carried the winds and sleeved the moon) far and wide, visiting every relic of note in the whole Empire.

As luck would have it, on a certain day while making a second journey through the Wei Yang district, he heard the news that the Salt Commissioner appointed this year was Lin Ju-hai. This Lin Ju-hai's family name was Lin, his name Hai and his style Ju-hai. He had obtained the third place in the previous triennial examination, and had, by this time, already risen to the rank of Director of the Court of Censors. He was a native of Kú Su. He had been recently named by Imperial appointment a Censor attached to the Salt Inspectorate, and had arrived at his post only a short while back.

In fact, the ancestors of Lin Ju-hai had, from years back, successively inherited the title of Marquis, which rank, by its present descent to Ju-hai, had already been enjoyed by five generations. When first conferred, the hereditary right to the title had been limited to three generations; but of late years, by an act of magnanimous favour and generous beneficence, extraordinary bounty had been superadded; and on the arrival of the succession to the father of Ju-hai, the right had been extended to another degree. It had now descended to Ju-hai, who had, besides this title of nobility, begun his career as a successful graduate. But though his family had been through uninterrupted ages the recipient of imperial bounties, his kindred had all been anyhow men of culture.

The only misfortune had been that the several branches of the Lin family had not been prolific, so that the numbers of its members continued limited; and though there existed several households, they were all however to Ju-hai no closer relatives than first cousins. Neither were there any connections of the same lineage, or of the same parentage.

Ju-hai was at this date past forty; and had only had a son, who had died the previous year, in the third year of his age. Though he had several handmaids, he had not had the good fortune of having another son; but this was too a matter that could not be remedied.

By his wife, née Chia, he had a daughter, to whom the infant name of Tai Yü was given. She was, at this time, in her fifth year. Upon her the parents doated as much as if she were a brilliant pearl in the palm of their hand. Seeing that she was endowed with natural gifts of intelligence and good looks, they also felt solicitous to bestow upon her a certain knowledge of books, with no other purpose than that of satisfying, by this illusory way, their wishes of having a son to nurture and of dispelling the anguish felt by them, on account of the desolation and void in their family circle (round their knees).

But to proceed. Yü-ts'un, while sojourning at an inn, was unexpectedly laid up with a violent chill. Finding on his recovery, that his funds were not sufficient to pay his expenses, he was thinking of looking out for some house where he could find a resting place when he suddenly came across two friends acquainted with the new Salt Commissioner. Knowing that this official was desirous to find a tutor to instruct his daughter, they lost no time in recommending Yü-ts'un, who moved into the Yamên.

His female pupil was youthful in years and delicate in physique, so that her lessons were irregular. Besides herself, there were only two waiting girls, who remained in attendance during the hours of study, so that Yü-ts'un was spared considerable trouble and had a suitable opportunity to attend to the improvement of his health.

In a twinkle, another year and more slipped by, and when least expected, the mother of his ward, née Chia, was carried away after a short illness. His pupil (during her mother's sickness) was dutiful in her attendance, and prepared the medicines for her use. (And after her death,) she went into the deepest mourning prescribed by the rites, and gave way to such excess of grief that, naturally delicate as she was, her old complaint, on this account, broke out anew.

Being unable for a considerable time to prosecute her studies, Yü-ts'un lived at leisure and had no duties to attend to. Whenever therefore the wind was genial and the sun mild, he was wont to stroll at random, after he had done with his meals.

On this particular day, he, by some accident, extended his walk beyond the suburbs, and desirous to contemplate the nature of the rustic scenery, he, with listless step, came up to a spot encircled by hills and streaming pools, by luxuriant clumps of trees and thick groves of bamboos. Nestling in the dense foliage stood a temple. The doors and courts were in ruins. The walls, inner and outer, in disrepair. An inscription on a tablet testified that this was the temple of Spiritual Perception. On the sides of the door was also a pair of old and dilapidated scrolls with the following enigmatical verses.

Behind ample there is, yet to retract the hand, the mind heeds not, until.
Before the mortal vision lies no path, when comes to turn the will.

"These two sentences," Yü-ts'un pondered after perusal, "although simple in language, are profound in signification. I have previous to this visited many a spacious temple, located on hills of note, but never have I beheld an inscription referring to anything of the kind. The meaning contained in these words must, I feel certain, owe their origin to the experiences of some person or other; but there's no saying. But why should I not go in and inquire for myself?"

Upon walking in, he at a glance caught sight of no one else, but of a very aged bonze, of unkempt appearance, cooking his rice. When Yü-ts'un perceived that he paid no notice, he went up to him and asked him one or two questions, but as the old priest was dull of hearing and a dotard, and as he had lost his teeth, and his tongue was blunt, he made most irrelevant replies.

Yü-ts'un lost all patience with him, and withdrew again from the compound with the intention of going as far as the village public house to have a drink or two, so as to enhance the enjoyment of the rustic scenery. With easy stride, he accordingly walked up to the place. Scarcely had he passed the threshold of the public house, when he perceived some one or other among the visitors who had been sitting sipping their wine on the divan, jump up and come up to greet him, with a face beaming with laughter.

"What a strange meeting! What a strange meeting!" he exclaimed aloud.

Yü-ts'un speedily looked at him, (and remembered) that this person had, in past days, carried on business in a curio establishment in the capital, and that his surname was Leng and his style Tzu-hsing.

A mutual friendship had existed between them during their sojourn, in days of yore, in the capital; and as Yü-ts'un had entertained the highest opinion of Leng Tzu-hsing, as being a man of action and of great abilities, while this Leng Tzu-hsing, on the other hand, borrowed of the reputation of refinement enjoyed by Yü-ts'un, the two had consequently all along lived in perfect harmony and companionship.

"When did you get here?" Yü-ts'un eagerly inquired also smilingly. "I wasn't in the least aware of your arrival. This unexpected meeting is positively a strange piece of good fortune."

"I went home," Tzu-hsing replied, "about the close of last year, but now as I am again bound to the capital, I passed through here on my way to look up a friend of mine and talk some matters over. He had the kindness to press me to stay with him for a couple of days longer, and as I after all have no urgent business to attend to, I am tarrying a few days, but purpose starting about the middle of the moon. My friend is busy to-day, so I roamed listlessly as far as here, never dreaming of such a fortunate meeting."

While speaking, he made Yü-ts'un sit down at the same table, and ordered a fresh supply of wine and eatables; and as the two friends chatted of one thing and another, they slowly sipped their wine.

The conversation ran on what had occurred after the separation, and Yü-ts'un inquired, "Is there any news of any kind in the capital?"

"There's nothing new whatever," answered Tzu-hsing. "There is one thing however: in the family of one of your worthy kinsmen, of the same name as yourself, a trifling, but yet remarkable, occurrence has taken place."

"None of my kindred reside in the capital," rejoined Yü-ts'un with a smile. "To what can you be alluding?"

"How can it be that you people who have the same surname do not belong to one clan?" remarked Tzu-hsing, sarcastically.

"In whose family?" inquired Yü-ts'un.

"The Chia family," replied Tzu-hsing smiling, "whose quarters are in the Jung Kuo Mansion, does not after all reflect discredit upon the lintel of your door, my venerable friend."

"What!" exclaimed Yü-ts'un, "did this affair take place in that family? Were we to begin reckoning, we would find the members of my clan to be anything but limited in number. Since the time of our ancestor Chia Fu, who lived while the Eastern Han dynasty occupied the Throne, the branches of our family have been numerous and flourishing; they are now to be found in every single province, and who could, with any accuracy, ascertain their whereabouts? As regards the Jung-kuo branch in particular, their names are in fact inscribed on the same register as our own, but rich and exalted as they are, we have never presumed to claim them as our relatives, so that we have become more and more estranged."

"Don't make any such assertions," Tzu-hsing remarked with a sigh, "the present two mansions of Jung and Ning have both alike also suffered reverses, and they cannot come up to their state of days of yore."

"Up to this day, these two households of Ning and of Jung," Yü-ts'un suggested, "still maintain a very large retinue of people, and how can it be that they have met with reverses?"

"To explain this would be indeed a long story," said Leng Tzu-hsing. "Last year," continued Yü-ts'un, "I arrived at Chin Ling, as I entertained a wish to visit the remains of interest of the six dynasties, and as I on that day entered the walled town of Shih T'ou, I passed by the entrance of that old residence. On the east side of the street, stood the Ning Kuo mansion; on the west the Jung Kuo mansion; and these two, adjoining each other as they do, cover in fact well-nigh half of the whole length of the street. Outside the front gate everything was, it is true, lonely and deserted; but at a glance into the interior over the enclosing wall, I perceived that the halls, pavilions, two-storied structures and porches presented still a majestic and lofty appearance. Even the flower garden, which extends over the whole area of the back grounds, with its trees and rockeries, also possessed to that day an air of luxuriance and freshness, which betrayed no signs of a ruined or decrepid establishment."

"You have had the good fortune of starting in life as a graduate," explained Tzu-tsing as he smiled, "and yet are not aware of the saying uttered by some one of old: that a centipede even when dead does not lie stiff. (These families) may, according to your version, not be up to the prosperity of former years, but, compared with the family of an ordinary official, their condition anyhow presents a difference. Of late the number of the inmates has, day by day, been on the increase; their affairs have become daily more numerous; of masters and servants, high and low, who live in ease and respectability very many there are; but of those who exercise any forethought, or make any provision, there is not even one. In their daily wants, their extravagances, and their expenditure, they are also unable to adapt themselves to circumstances and practise economy; (so that though) the present external framework may not have suffered any considerable collapse, their purses have anyhow begun to feel an exhausting process! But this is a mere trifle. There is another more serious matter. Would any one ever believe that in such families of official status, in a clan of education and culture, the sons and grandsons of the present age would after all be each (succeeding) generation below the standard of the former?"

Yü-ts'un, having listened to these remarks, observed: "How ever can it be possible that families of such education and refinement can observe any system of training and nurture which is not excellent? Concerning the other branches, I am not in a position to say anything; but restricting myself to the two mansions of Jung and Ning, they are those in which, above all others, the education of their children is methodical."

"I was just now alluding to none other than these two establishments," Tzu-hsing observed with a sigh; "but let me tell you all. In days of yore, the duke of Ning Kuo and the duke of Jung Kuo were two uterine brothers. The Ning duke was the elder; he had four sons. After the death of the duke of Ning Kuo, his eldest son, Chia Tai-hua, came into the title. He also had two sons; but the eldest, whose name was Hu, died at the age of eight or nine; and the only survivor, the second son, Chia Ching, inherited the title. His whole mind is at this time set upon Taoist doctrines; his sole delight is to burn the pill and refine the dual powers; while every other thought finds no place in his mind. Happily, he had, at an early age, left a son, Chia Chen, behind in the lay world, and his father, engrossed as his whole heart was with the idea of attaining spiritual life, ceded the succession of the official title to him. His parent is, besides, not willing to return to the original family seat, but lives outside the walls of the capital, foolishly hobnobbing with all the Taoist priests. This Mr. Chen had also a son, Chia Jung, who is, at this period, just in his sixteenth year. Mr. Ching gives at present no attention to anything at all, so that Mr. Chen naturally devotes no time to his studies, but being bent upon nought else but incessant high pleasure, he has subversed the order of things in the Ning Kuo mansion, and yet no one can summon the courage to come and hold him in check. But I'll now tell you about the Jung mansion for your edification. The strange occurrence, to which I alluded just now, came about in this manner. After the demise of the Jung duke, the eldest son, Chia Tai-shan, inherited the rank. He took to himself as wife, the daughter of Marquis Shih, a noble family of Chin Ling, by whom he had two sons; the elder being Chia She, the younger Chia Cheng. This Tai Shan is now dead long ago; but his wife is still alive, and the elder son, Chia She, succeeded to the degree. He is a man of amiable and genial disposition, but he likewise gives no thought to the direction of any domestic concern. The second son Chia Cheng displayed, from his early childhood, a great liking for books, and grew up to be correct and upright in character. His grandfather doated upon him, and would have had him start in life through the arena of public examinations, but, when least expected, Tai-shan, being on the point of death, bequeathed a petition, which was laid before the Emperor. His Majesty, out of regard for his former minister, issued immediate commands that the elder son should inherit the estate, and further inquired how many sons there were besides him, all of whom he at once expressed a wish to be introduced in his imperial presence. His Majesty, moreover, displayed exceptional favour, and conferred upon Mr. Cheng the brevet rank of second class Assistant Secretary (of a Board), and commanded him to enter the Board to acquire the necessary experience. He has already now been promoted to the office of second class Secretary. This Mr. Cheng's wife, nèe Wang, first gave birth to a son called Chia Chu, who became a Licentiate in his fourteenth year. At barely twenty, he married, but fell ill and died soon after the birth of a son. Her (Mrs. Cheng's) second child was a daughter, who came into the world, by a strange coincidence, on the first day of the year. She had an unexpected (pleasure) in the birth, the succeeding year, of another son, who, still more remarkable to say, had, at the time of his birth, a piece of variegated and crystal-like brilliant jade in his mouth, on which were yet visible the outlines of several characters. Now, tell me, was not this a novel and strange occurrence? eh?"

"Strange indeed!" exclaimed Yü-ts'un with a smile; "but I presume the coming experiences of this being will not be mean."

Tzu-hsing gave a faint smile. "One and all," he remarked, "entertain the same idea. Hence it is that his mother doats upon him like upon a precious jewel. On the day of his first birthday, Mr. Cheng readily entertained a wish to put the bent of his inclinations to the test, and placed before the child all kinds of things, without number, for him to grasp from. Contrary to every expectation, he scorned every other object, and, stretching forth his hand, he simply took hold of rouge, powder and a few hair-pins, with which he began to play. Mr. Cheng experienced at once displeasure, as he maintained that this youth would, by and bye, grow up into a sybarite, devoted to wine and women, and for this reason it is, that he soon began to feel not much attachment for him. But his grandmother is the one who, in spite of everything, prizes him like the breath of her own life. The very mention of what happened is even strange! He is now grown up to be seven or eight years old, and, although exceptionally wilful, in intelligence and precocity, however, not one in a hundred could come up to him! And as for the utterances of this child, they are no less remarkable. The bones and flesh of woman, he argues, are made of water, while those of man of mud. 'Women to my eyes are pure and pleasing,' he says, 'while at the sight of man, I readily feel how corrupt, foul and repelling they are!' Now tell me, are not these words ridiculous? There can be no doubt whatever that he will by and bye turn out to be a licentious roué."

Yü-ts'un, whose countenance suddenly assumed a stern air, promptly interrupted the conversation. "It doesn't quite follow," he suggested. "You people don't, I regret to say, understand the destiny of this child. The fact is that even the old Hanlin scholar Mr. Cheng was erroneously looked upon as a loose rake and dissolute debauchee! But unless a person, through much study of books and knowledge of letters, so increases (in lore) as to attain the talent of discerning the nature of things, and the vigour of mind to fathom the Taoist reason as well as to comprehend the first principle, he is not in a position to form any judgment."

Tzu-hsing upon perceiving the weighty import of what he propounded, "Please explain," he asked hastily, "the drift (of your argument)." To which Yü-ts'un responded: "Of the human beings created by the operation of heaven and earth, if we exclude those who are gifted with extreme benevolence and extreme viciousness, the rest, for the most part, present no striking diversity. If they be extremely benevolent, they fall in, at the time of their birth, with an era of propitious fortune; while those extremely vicious correspond, at the time of their existence, with an era of calamity. When those who coexist with propitious fortune come into life, the world is in order; when those who coexist with unpropitious fortune come into life, the world is in danger. Yao, Shun, Yü, Ch'eng T'ang, Wen Wang, Wu Wang,

Chou Kung, Chao Kung, Confucius, Mencius, T'ung Hu, Han Hsin, Chou Tzu, Ch'eng Tzu, Chu Tzu and Chang Tzu were ordained to see light in an auspicious era. Whereas Ch'i Yu, Kung Kung, Chieh Wang, Chou Wang, Shih Huang, Wang Mang, Tsao Ts'ao, Wen Wen, An Hu-shan, Ch'in Kuei and others were one and all destined to come into the world during a calamitous age. Those endowed with extreme benevolence set the world in order; those possessed of extreme maliciousness turn the world into disorder. Purity, intelligence, spirituality and subtlety constitute the vital spirit of right which pervades heaven and earth, and the persons gifted with benevolence are its natural fruit. Malignity and perversity constitute the spirit of evil, which permeates heaven and earth, and malicious persons are affected by its influence. The days of perpetual happiness and eminent good fortune, and the era of perfect peace and tranquility, which now prevail, are the offspring of the pure, intelligent, divine and subtle spirit which ascends above, to the very Emperor, and below reaches the rustic and uncultured classes. Every one is without exception under its influence. The superfluity of the subtle spirit expands far and wide, and finding nowhere to betake itself to, becomes, in due course, transformed into dew, or gentle breeze; and, by a process of diffusion, it pervades the whole world.

"The spirit of malignity and perversity, unable to expand under the brilliant sky and transmuting sun, eventually coagulates, pervades and stops up the deep gutters and extensive caverns; and when of a sudden the wind agitates it or it be impelled by the clouds, and any slight disposition, on its part, supervenes to set itself in motion, or to break its bounds, and so little as even the minutest fraction does unexpectedly find an outlet, and happens to come across any spirit of perception and subtlety which may be at the time passing by, the spirit of right does not yield to the spirit of evil, and the spirit of evil is again envious of the spirit of right, so that the two do not harmonize. Just like wind, water, thunder and lightning, which, when they meet in the bowels of the earth, must necessarily, as they are both to dissolve and are likewise unable to yield, clash and explode to the end that they may at length exhaust themselves. Hence it is that these spirits have also forcibly to diffuse themselves into the human race to find an outlet, so that they may then completely disperse, with the result that men and women are suddenly imbued with these spirits and spring into existence. At best, (these human beings) cannot be generated into philanthropists or perfect men; at worst, they cannot also embody extreme perversity or extreme wickedness. Yet placed among one million beings, the spirit of intelligence, refinement, perception and subtlety will be above these one million beings; while, on the other hand, the perverse, depraved and inhuman embodiment will likewise be below the million of men. Born in a noble and wealthy family, these men will be a salacious, lustful lot; born of literary, virtuous or poor parentage, they will turn out retired scholars or men of mark; though they may by some accident be born in a destitute and poverty-stricken home, they cannot possibly, in fact, ever sink so low as to become runners or menials, or contentedly brook to be of the common herd or to be driven and curbed like a horse in harness. They will become, for a certainty, either actors of note or courtesans of notoriety; as instanced in former years by Hsü Yu, T'ao Ch'ien, Yuan Chi, Chi Kang, Liu Ling, the two families of Wang and Hsieh, Ku Hu-t'ou, Ch'en Hou-chu, T'ang Ming-huang, Sung Hui-tsung, Liu T'ing-chih, Wen Fei-ching, Mei Nan-kung, Shih Man-ch'ing, Lui C'hih-ch'ing and Chin Shao-yu, and exemplified now-a-days by Ni Yün-lin, T'ang Po-hu, Chu Chih-shan, and also by Li Kuei-men, Huang P'an-cho, Ching Hsin-mo, Cho Wen-chün; and the women Hung Fu, Hsieh T'ao, Ch'ü Ying, Ch'ao Yün and others; all of whom were and are of the same stamp, though placed in different scenes of action."

"From what you say," observed Tzu-hsing, "success makes (a man) a duke or a marquis; ruin, a thief!"

"Quite so; that's just my idea!" replied Yü-ts'un; "I've not as yet let you know that after my degradation from office, I spent the last couple of years in travelling for pleasure all over each province, and that I also myself came across two extraordinary youths. This is why, when a short while back you alluded to this Pao-yü, I at once conjectured, with a good deal of certainty, that he must be a human being of the same stamp. There's no need for me to speak of any farther than the walled city of Chin Ling. This Mr. Chen was, by imperial appointment, named Principal of the Government Public College of the Chin Ling province. Do you perhaps know him?"

"Who doesn't know him?" remarked Tzu-hsing. "This Chen family is an old connection of the Chia family. These two families were on terms of great intimacy, and I myself likewise enjoyed the pleasure of their friendship for many a day."

"Last year, when at Chin Ling," Yü-ts'un continued with a smile, "some one recommended me as resident tutor to the school in the Chen mansion; and when I moved into it I saw for myself the state of things. Who would ever think that that household was grand and luxurious to such a degree! But they are an affluent family, and withal full of propriety, so that a school like this was of course not one easy to obtain. The pupil, however, was, it is true, a young tyro, but far more troublesome to teach than a candidate for the examination of graduate of the second degree. Were I to enter into details, you would indeed have a laugh. 'I must needs,' he explained, 'have the company of two girls in my studies to enable me to read at all, and to keep likewise my brain clear. Otherwise, if left to myself, my head gets all in a muddle.' Time after time, he further expounded to his young attendants, how extremely honourable and extremely pure were the two words representing woman, that they are more valuable and precious than the auspicious animal, the felicitous bird, rare flowers and uncommon plants. 'You may not' (he was wont to say), 'on any account heedlessly utter them, you set of foul mouths and filthy tongues! these two words are of the utmost import! Whenever you have occasion to allude to them, you must, before you can do so with impunity, take pure water and scented tea and rinse your mouths. In the event of any slip of the tongue, I shall at once have your teeth extracted, and your eyes gouged out.' His obstinacy and waywardness are, in every respect, out of the common. After he was allowed to leave school, and to return home, he became, at the sight of the young ladies, so tractable, gentle, sharp, and polite, transformed, in fact, like one of them. And though, for this reason, his father has punished him on more than one occasion, by giving him a sound thrashing, such as brought him to the verge of death, he cannot however change. Whenever he was being beaten, and could no more endure the pain, he was wont to promptly break forth in promiscuous loud shouts, 'Girls! girls!' The young ladies, who heard him from the inner chambers, subsequently made fun of him. 'Why,' they said, 'when you are being thrashed, and you are in pain, your only thought is to bawl out girls! Is it perchance that you expect us young ladies to go and intercede for you? How is that you have no sense of shame?' To their taunts he gave a most plausible explanation. 'Once,' he replied, 'when in the agony of pain, I gave vent to shouting girls, in the hope, perchance, I did not then know, of its being able to alleviate the soreness. After I had, with this purpose, given one cry, I really felt the pain considerably better; and now that I have obtained this secret spell, I have recourse, at once, when I am in the height of anguish, to shouts of girls, one shout after another. Now what do you say to this? Isn't this absurd, eh?"

"The grandmother is so infatuated by her extreme tenderness for this youth, that, time after time, she has, on her grandson's account, found fault with the tutor, and called her son to task, with the result that I resigned my post and took my leave. A youth, with a disposition such as his, cannot assuredly either perpetuate intact the estate of his father and grandfather, or follow the injunctions of teacher or advice of friends. The pity is, however, that there are, in that family, several excellent female cousins, the like of all of whom it would be difficult to discover."

"Quite so!" remarked Tzu-hsing; "there are now three young ladies in the Chia family who are simply perfection itself. The eldest is a daughter of Mr. Cheng, Yuan Ch'un by name, who, on account of her excellence, filial piety, talents, and virtue, has been selected as a governess in the palace. The second is the daughter of Mr. She's handmaid, and is called Ying Ch'un; the third is T'an Ch'un, the child of Mr. Cheng's handmaid; while the fourth is the uterine sister of Mr. Chen of the Ning Mansion. Her name is Hsi Ch'un. As dowager lady Shih is so fondly attached to her granddaughters, they come, for the most part, over to their grandmother's place to prosecute their studies together, and each one of these girls is, I hear, without a fault."

"More admirable," observed Yü-ts'un, "is the régime (adhered to) in the Chen family, where the names of the female children have all been selected from the list of male names, and are unlike all those out-of-the-way names, such as Spring Blossom, Scented Gem, and the like flowery terms in vogue in other families. But how is it that the Chia family have likewise fallen into this common practice?"

"Not so!" ventured Tzu-h'sing. "It is simply because the eldest daughter was born on the first of the first moon, that the name of Yuan Ch'un was given to her; while with the rest this character Ch'un (spring) was then followed. The names of the senior generation are, in like manner, adopted from those of their brothers; and there is at present an instance in support of this. The wife of your present worthy master, Mr. Lin, is the uterine sister of Mr. Chia. She and Mr. Chia Cheng, and she went, while at home, under the name of Chia Min. Should you question the truth of what I say, you are at liberty, on your return, to make minute inquiries and you'll be convinced."

Yü-ts'un clapped his hands and said smiling, "It's so, I know! for this female pupil of mine, whose name is Tai-yü, invariably pronounces the character *min* as *mi*, whenever she comes across it in the course of her reading; while, in writing, when she comes to the character 'min,' she likewise reduces the strokes by one, sometimes by two. Often have I speculated in my mind (as to the cause), but the remarks I've heard you mention, convince me, without doubt, that it is no other reason (than that of reverence to her mother's name). Strange enough, this pupil of mine is unique in her speech and deportment, and in no way like any ordinary young lady. But considering that her mother was no commonplace woman herself, it is natural that she should have given birth to such a child. Besides, knowing, as I do now, that she is the granddaughter of the Jung family, it is no matter of surprise to me that she is what she is. Poor girl, her mother, after all, died in the course of the last month."

Tzu-hsing heaved a sigh. "Of three elderly sisters," he explained, "this one was the youngest, and she too is gone! Of the sisters of the senior generation not one even survives! But now we'll see what the husbands of this younger generation will be like by and bye!"

"Yes," replied Yü-ts'un. "But some while back you mentioned that Mr. Cheng has had a son, born with a piece of jade in his mouth, and that he has besides a tender-aged grandson left by his eldest son; but is it likely that this Mr. She has not, himself, as yet, had any male issue?"

"After Mr. Cheng had this son with the jade," Tzu-hsing added, "his handmaid gave birth to another son, who whether he be good or bad, I don't at all know. At all events, he has by his side two sons and a grandson, but what these will grow up to be by and bye, I cannot tell. As regards Mr. Chia She, he too has had two sons; the second of whom, Chia Lien, is by this time about twenty. He took to wife a relative of his, a niece of Mr. Cheng's wife, a Miss Wang, and has now been married for the last two years. This Mr. Lien has lately obtained by purchase the rank of sub-prefect. He too takes little pleasure in books, but as far as worldly affairs go, he is so versatile and glib of tongue, that he has recently taken up his quarters with his uncle Mr. Cheng, to whom he gives a helping hand in the management of domestic matters. Who would have thought it, however, ever since his marriage with his worthy wife, not a single person, whether high or low, has there been who has not looked up to her with regard: with the result that Mr. Lien himself has, in fact, had to take a back seat (*lit.* withdrew 35 li). In looks, she is also so extremely beautiful, in speech so extremely quick and fluent, in ingenuity so deep and astute, that even a man could, in no way, come up to her mark."

After hearing these remarks Yü-ts'un smiled. "You now perceive," he said, "that my argument is no fallacy, and that the several persons about whom you and I have just been talking are, we may presume, human beings, who, one and all, have been generated by the spirit of right, and the spirit of evil, and come to life by the same royal road; but of course there's no saying."

"Enough," cried Tzu-hsing, "of right and enough of evil; we've been doing nothing but settling other people's accounts; come now, have another glass, and you'll be the better for it!"

"While bent upon talking," Yü-ts'un explained, "I've had more glasses than is good for me."

"Speaking of irrelevant matters about other people," Tzu-hsing rejoined complacently, "is quite the thing to help us swallow our wine; so come now; what harm will happen, if we do have a few glasses more."

Yü-ts'un thereupon looked out of the window.

"The day is also far advanced," he remarked, "and if we don't take care, the gates will be closing; let us leisurely enter the city, and as we go along, there will be nothing to prevent us from continuing our chat."

Forthwith the two friends rose from their seats, settled and paid their wine bill, and were just going, when they unexpectedly heard some one from behind say with a loud voice:

"Accept my congratulations, Brother Yü-ts'un; I've now come, with the express purpose of giving you the welcome news!"

Yü-ts'un lost no time in turning his head round to look at the speaker. But reader, if you wish to learn who the man was, listen to the details given in the following chapter.

CHAPTER III.

Lin Ju-hai appeals to his brother-in-law, Chia Cheng, recommending Yü-ts'un, his daughter's tutor, to his consideration.
Dowager lady Chia sends to fetch her granddaughter, out of commiseration for her being a motherless child.

But to proceed with our narrative.

Yü-ts'un, on speedily turning round, perceived that the speaker was no other than a certain Chang Ju-kuei, an old colleague of his, who had been denounced and deprived of office, on account of some case or other; a native of that district, who had, since his degradation, resided in his family home.

Having lately come to hear the news that a memorial, presented in the capital, that the former officers (who had been cashiered) should be reinstated, had received the imperial consent, he had promptly done all he could, in every nook and corner, to obtain influence, and to find the means (of righting his position,) when he, unexpectedly, came across Yü-ts'un, to whom he therefore lost no time in offering his congratulations. The two friends exchanged the conventional salutations, and Chang Ju-kuei forthwith communicated the tidings to Yü-ts'un.

Yü-ts'un was delighted, but after he had made a few remarks, in a great hurry, each took his leave and sped on his own way homewards.

Leng Tzu-hsing, upon hearing this conversation, hastened at once to propose a plan, advising Yü-ts'un to request Lin Ju-hai, in his turn, to appeal in the capital to Mr. Chia Cheng for support.

Yü-ts'un accepted the suggestion, and parted from his companion.

On his return to his quarters, he made all haste to lay his hand on the Metropolitan Gazette, and having ascertained that the news was authentic, he had on the next day a personal consultation with Ju-hai.

"Providence and good fortune are both alike propitious!" exclaimed Ju-hai. "After the death of my wife, my mother-in-law, whose residence is in the capital, was so very solicitous on my daughter's account, for having no one to depend upon, that she despatched, at an early period, boats with men and women servants to come and fetch her. But my child was at the time not quite over her illness, and that is why she has not yet started. I was, this very moment, cogitating to send my daughter to the capital. And in view of the obligation, under which I am to you for the instruction you have heretofore conferred upon her, remaining as yet unrequited, there is no reason why, when such an opportunity as this presents itself, I should not do my utmost to find means to make proper acknowledgment. I have already, in anticipation, given the matter my attention, and written a letter of recommendation to my brother-in-law, urging him to put everything right for you, in order that I may, to a certain extent, be able to give effect to my modest wishes. As for any outlay that may prove necessary, I have given proper explanation, in the letter to my brother-in-law, so that you, my brother, need not trouble yourself by giving way to much anxiety."

As Yü-ts'un bowed and expressed his appreciation in most profuse language,—

"Pray," he asked, "where does your honoured brother-in-law reside? and what is his official capacity? But I fear I'm too coarse in my manner, and could not presume to obtrude myself in his presence."

Ju-hai smiled. "And yet," he remarked, "this brother-in-law of mine is after all of one and the same family as your worthy self, for he is the grandson of the Duke Jung. My elder brother-in-law has now inherited the status of Captain-General of the first grade. His name is She, his style Ngen-hou. My second brother-in-law's name is Cheng, his style is Tzu-chou. His present post is that of a Second class Secretary in the Board of Works. He is modest and kindhearted, and has much in him of the habits of his grandfather; not one of that purse-proud and haughty kind of men. That is why I have written to him and made the request on your behalf. Were he different to what he really is, not only would he cast a slur upon your honest purpose, honourable brother, but I myself likewise would not have been as prompt in taking action."

When Yü-ts'un heard these remarks, he at length credited what had been told him by Tzu-hsing the day before, and he lost no time in again expressing his sense of gratitude to Lin Ju-hai.

Ju-hai resumed the conversation.

"I have fixed," (he explained,) "upon the second of next month, for my young daughter's departure for the capital, and, if you, brother mine, were to travel along with her, would it not be an advantage to herself, as well as to yourself?"

Yü-ts'un signified his acquiescence as he listened to his proposal; feeling in his inner self extremely elated.

Ju-hai availed himself of the earliest opportunity to get ready the presents (for the capital) and all the requirements for the journey, which (when completed,) Yü-ts'un took over one by one. His pupil could not, at first, brook the idea, of a separation from her father, but the pressing wishes of her grandmother left her no course (but to comply).

"Your father," Ju-hai furthermore argued with her, "is already fifty; and I entertain no wish to marry again; and then you are always ailing; besides, with your extreme youth, you have, above, no mother of your own to take care of you, and below, no sisters to attend to you. If you now go and have your maternal grandmother, as well as your mother's brothers and your cousins to depend upon, you will be doing the best thing to reduce the anxiety which I feel in my heart on your behalf. Why then should you not go?"

Tai-yü, after listening to what her father had to say, parted from him in a flood of tears and followed her nurse and several old matrons from the Jung mansion on board her boat, and set out on her journey.

Yü-ts'un had a boat to himself, and with two youths to wait on him, he prosecuted his voyage in the wake of Tai-yü.

By a certain day, they reached Ching Tu; and Yü-ts'un, after first adjusting his hat and clothes, came, attended by a youth, to the door of the Jung mansion, and sent in a card, which showed his lineage.

Chia Cheng had, by this time, perused his brother-in-law's letter, and he speedily asked him to walk in. When they met, he found in Yü-ts'un an imposing manner and polite address.

This Chia Cheng had, in fact, a great penchant above all things for men of education, men courteous to the talented, respectful to the learned, ready to lend a helping hand to the needy and to succour the distressed, and was, to a great extent, like his grandfather. As it was besides a wish intimated by his brother-in-law, he therefore treated Yü-ts'un with a consideration still more unusual, and readily strained all his resources to assist him.

On the very day on which the memorial was submitted to the Throne, he obtained by his efforts, a reinstatement to office, and before the expiry of two months, Yü-t'sun was forthwith selected to fill the appointment of prefect of Ying T'ien in Chin Ling. Taking leave of

Chia Cheng, he chose a propitious day, and proceeded to his post, where we will leave him without further notice for the present.

But to return to Tai-yü. On the day on which she left the boat, and the moment she put her foot on shore, there were forthwith at her disposal chairs for her own use, and carts for the luggage, sent over from the Jung mansion.

Lin Tai-yü had often heard her mother recount how different was her grandmother's house from that of other people's; and having seen for herself how above the common run were already the attendants of the three grades, (sent to wait upon her,) in attire, in their fare, in all their articles of use, "how much more," (she thought to herself) "now that I am going to her home, must I be careful at every step, and circumspect at every moment! Nor must I utter one word too many, nor make one step more than is proper, for fear lest I should be ridiculed by any of them!"

From the moment she got into the chair, and they had entered within the city walls, she found, as she looked around, through the gauze window, at the bustle in the streets and public places and at the immense concourse of people, everything naturally so unlike what she had seen elsewhere.

After they had also been a considerable time on the way, she suddenly caught sight, at the northern end of the street, of two huge squatting lions of marble and of three lofty gates with (knockers representing) the heads of animals. In front of these gates, sat, in a row, about ten men in coloured hats and fine attire. The main gate was not open. It was only through the side gates, on the east and west, that people went in and came out. Above the centre gate was a tablet. On this tablet were inscribed in five large characters—"The Ning Kuo mansion erected by imperial command."

"This must be grandmother's eldest son's residence," reflected Tai-yü.

Towards the east, again, at no great distance, were three more high gateways, likewise of the same kind as those she had just seen. This was the Jung Kuo mansion.

They did not however go in by the main gate; but simply made their entrance through the east side door.

With the sedans on their shoulders, (the bearers) proceeded about the distance of the throw of an arrow, when upon turning a corner, they hastily put down the chairs. The matrons, who came behind, one and all also dismounted. (The bearers) were changed for four youths of seventeen or eighteen, with hats and clothes without a blemish, and while they carried the chair, the whole bevy of matrons followed on foot.

When they reached a creeper-laden gate, the sedan was put down, and all the youths stepped back and retired. The matrons came forward, raised the screen, and supported Tai-yü to descend from the chair.

Lin Tai-yü entered the door with the creepers, resting on the hand of a matron.

On both sides was a verandah, like two outstretched arms. An Entrance Hall stood in the centre, in the middle of which was a door-screen of Ta Li marble, set in an ebony frame. On the other side of this screen were three very small halls. At the back of these came at once an extensive courtyard, belonging to the main building.

In the front part were five parlours, the frieze of the ceiling of which was all carved, and the pillars ornamented. On either side, were covered avenues, resembling passages through a rock. In the side-rooms were suspended cages, full of parrots of every colour, thrushes, and birds of every description.

On the terrace-steps, sat several waiting maids, dressed in red and green, and the whole company of them advanced, with beaming faces, to greet them, when they saw the party approach. "Her venerable ladyship," they said, "was at this very moment thinking of you, miss, and, by a strange coincidence, here you are."

Three or four of them forthwith vied with each other in raising the door curtain, while at the same time was heard some one announce: "Miss Lin has arrived."

No sooner had she entered the room, than she espied two servants supporting a venerable lady, with silver-white hair, coming forward to greet her. Convinced that this lady must be her grandmother, she was about to prostrate herself and pay her obeisance, when she was quickly clasped in the arms of her grandmother, who held her close against her bosom; and as she called her "my liver! my flesh!" (my love! my darling!) she began to sob aloud.

The bystanders too, at once, without one exception, melted into tears; and Tai-yü herself found some difficulty in restraining her sobs. Little by little the whole party succeeded in consoling her, and Tai-yü at length paid her obeisance to her grandmother. Her ladyship thereupon pointed them out one by one to Tai-yü. "This," she said, "is the wife of your uncle, your mother's elder brother; this is the wife of your uncle, her second brother; and this is your eldest sister-in-law Chu, the wife of your senior cousin Chu."

Tai-yü bowed to each one of them (with folded arms).

"Ask the young ladies in," dowager lady Chia went on to say; "tell them a guest from afar has just arrived, one who comes for the first time; and that they may not go to their lessons."

The servants with one voice signified their obedience, and two of them speedily went to carry out her orders.

Not long after three nurses and five or six waiting-maids were seen ushering in three young ladies. The first was somewhat plump in figure and of medium height; her cheeks had a congealed appearance, like a fresh lichee; her nose was glossy like goose fat. She was gracious, demure, and lovable to look at.

The second had sloping shoulders, and a slim waist. Tall and slender was she in stature, with a face like the egg of a goose. Her eyes so beautiful, with their well-curved eyebrows, possessed in their gaze a bewitching flash. At the very sight of her refined and elegant manners all idea of vulgarity was forgotten.

The third was below the medium size, and her mien was, as yet, childlike.

In their head ornaments, jewelry, and dress, the get-up of the three young ladies was identical.

Tai-yü speedily rose to greet them and to exchange salutations. After they had made each other's acquaintance, they all took a seat, whereupon the servants brought the tea. Their conversation was confined to Tai-yü's mother,—how she had fallen ill, what doctors had attended her, what medicines had been given her, and how she had been buried and mourned; and dowager lady Chia was naturally again in great anguish.

"Of all my daughters," she remarked, "your mother was the one I loved best, and now in a twinkle, she has passed away, before me too, and I've not been able to so much as see her face. How can this not make my heart sore-stricken?"

And as she gave vent to these feelings, she took Tai-yü's hand in hers, and again gave way to sobs; and it was only after the members of the family had quickly made use of much exhortation and coaxing, that they succeeded, little by little, in stopping her tears.

They all perceived that Tai-yü, despite her youthful years and appearance, was lady-like in her deportment and address, and that though with her delicate figure and countenance, (she seemed as if) unable to bear the very weight of her clothes, she possessed, however, a certain captivating air. And as they readily noticed the symptoms of a weak constitution, they went on in consequence to make inquiries as to what medicines she ordinarily took, and how it was that her complaint had not been cured.

"I have," explained Tai-yü, "been in this state ever since I was born; though I've taken medicines from the very time I was able to eat rice, up to the present, and have been treated by ever so many doctors of note, I've not derived any benefit. In the year when I was yet only three, I remember a mangy-headed bonze coming to our house, and saying that he would take me along, and make a nun of me; but my father and mother would, on no account, give their consent. 'As you cannot bear to part from her and to give her up,' he then remarked, 'her ailment will, I fear, never, throughout her life, be cured. If you wish to see her all right, it is only to be done by not letting her, from this day forward, on any account, listen to the sound of weeping, or see, with the exception of her parents, any relatives outside the family circle. Then alone will she be able to go through this existence in peace and in quiet.' No one heeded the nonsensical talk of this raving priest; but here am I, up to this very day, dosing myself with ginseng pills as a tonic."

"What a lucky coincidence!" interposed dowager lady Chia; "some of these pills are being compounded here, and I'll simply tell them to have an extra supply made; that's all."

Hardly had she finished these words, when a sound of laughter was heard from the back courtyard. "Here I am too late!" the voice said, "and not in time to receive the distant visitor!"

"Every one of all these people," reflected Tai-yü, "holds her peace and suppresses the very breath of her mouth; and who, I wonder, is this coming in this reckless and rude manner?"

While, as yet, preoccupied with these thoughts, she caught sight of a crowd of married women and waiting-maids enter from the back room, pressing round a regular beauty.

The attire of this person bore no similarity to that of the young ladies. In all her splendour and lustre, she looked like a fairy or a goddess. In her coiffure, she had a band of gold filigree work, representing the eight precious things, inlaid with pearls; and wore pins, at the head of each of which were five phoenixes in a rampant position, with pendants of pearls. On her neck, she had a reddish gold necklet, like coiled dragons, with a fringe of tassels. On her person, she wore a tight-sleeved jacket, of dark red flowered satin, covered with hundreds of butterflies, embroidered in gold, interspersed with flowers. Over all, she had a variegated stiff-silk pelisse, lined with slate-blue ermine;

while her nether garments consisted of a jupe of kingfisher-colour foreign crepe, brocaded with flowers.

She had a pair of eyes, triangular in shape like those of the red phoenix, two eyebrows, curved upwards at each temple, like willow leaves. Her stature was elegant; her figure graceful; her powdered face like dawning spring, majestic, yet not haughty. Her carnation lips, long before they parted, betrayed a smile.

Tai-yü eagerly rose and greeted her.

Old lady Chia then smiled. "You don't know her," she observed. "This is a cunning vixen, who has made quite a name in this establishment! In Nanking, she went by the appellation of vixen, and if you simply call her Feng Vixen, it will do."

Tai-yü was just at a loss how to address her, when all her cousins informed Tai-yü, that this was her sister-in-law Lien.

Tai-yü had not, it is true, made her acquaintance before, but she had heard her mother mention that her eldest maternal uncle Chia She's son, Chia Lien, had married the niece of Madame Wang, her second brother's wife, a girl who had, from her infancy, purposely been nurtured to supply the place of a son, and to whom the school name of Wang Hsi-feng had been given.

Tai-yü lost no time in returning her smile and saluting her with all propriety, addressing her as my sister-in-law. This Hsi-feng laid hold of Tai-yü's hand, and minutely scrutinised her, for a while, from head to foot; after which she led her back next to dowager lady Chia, where they both took a seat.

"If really there be a being of such beauty in the world," she consequently observed with a smile, "I may well consider as having set eyes upon it to-day! Besides, in the air of her whole person, she doesn't in fact look like your granddaughter-in-law, our worthy ancestor, but in every way like your ladyship's own kindred- granddaughter! It's no wonder then that your venerable ladyship should have, day after day, had her unforgotten, even for a second, in your lips and heart. It's a pity, however, that this cousin of mine should have such a hard lot! How did it happen that our aunt died at such an early period?"

As she uttered these words, she hastily took her handkerchief and wiped the tears from her eyes.

"I've only just recovered from a fit of crying," dowager lady Chia observed, as she smiled, "and have you again come to start me? Your cousin has only now arrived from a distant journey, and she is so delicate to boot! Besides, we have a few minutes back succeeded in coaxing her to restrain her sobs, so drop at once making any allusion to your former remarks!"

This Hsi-feng, upon hearing these words, lost no time in converting her sorrow into joy.

"Quite right," she remarked. "But at the sight of my cousin, my whole heart was absorbed in her, and I felt happy, and yet wounded at heart: but having disregarded my venerable ancestor's presence, I deserve to be beaten, I do indeed!"

And hastily taking once more Tai-yü's hand in her own: "How old are you, cousin?" she inquired; "Have you been to school? What medicines are you taking? while you live here, you mustn't feel homesick; and if there's anything you would like to eat, or to play with, mind you come and tell me! or should the waiting maids or the matrons fail in their duties, don't forget also to report them to me."

Addressing at the same time the matrons, she went on to ask, "Have Miss Lin's luggage and effects been brought in? How many servants has she brought along with her? Go, as soon as you can, and sweep two lower rooms and ask them to go and rest."

As she spake, tea and refreshments had already been served, and Hsi-feng herself handed round the cups and offered the fruits.

Upon hearing the question further put by her maternal aunt Secunda, "Whether the issue of the monthly allowances of money had been finished or not yet?" Hsi-feng replied: "The issue of the money has also been completed; but a few moments back, when I went along with several servants to the back upper-loft, in search of the satins, we looked for ever so long, but we saw nothing of the kind of satins alluded to by you, madame, yesterday; so may it not be that your memory misgives you?"

"Whether there be any or not, of that special kind, is of no consequence," observed madame Wang. "You should take out," she therefore went on to add, "any two pieces which first come under your hand, for this cousin of yours to make herself dresses with; and in the evening, if I don't forget, I'll send some one to fetch them."

"I've in fact already made every provision," rejoined Hsi-feng; "knowing very well that my cousin would be arriving within these two days, I have had everything got ready for her. And when you, madame, go back, if you will pass an eye over everything, I shall be able to send them round."

Madame Wang gave a smile, nodded her head assentingly, but uttered not a word by way of reply.

The tea and fruit had by this time been cleared, and dowager lady Chia directed two old nurses to take Tai-yü to go and see her two maternal uncles; whereupon Chia She's wife, madame Hsing, hastily stood up and with a smiling face suggested, "I'll take my niece over; for it will after all be considerably better if I go!"

"Quite so!" answered dowager lady Chia, smiling; "you can go home too, and there will be no need for you to come over again!"

Madame Hsing expressed her assent, and forthwith led Tai-yü to take leave of madame Wang. The whole party escorted them as far as the door of the Entrance Hall, hung with creepers, where several youths had drawn a carriage, painted light blue, with a kingfisher-coloured hood.

Madame Hsing led Tai-yü by the hand and they got up into their seats. The whole company of matrons put the curtain down, and then bade the youths raise the carriage; who dragged it along, until they came to an open space, where they at length put the mules into harness.

Going out again by the eastern side gate, they proceeded in an easterly direction, passed the main entrance of the Jung mansion, and entered a lofty doorway painted black. On the arrival in front of the ceremonial gate, they at once dismounted from the curricle, and madame Hsing, hand-in-hand with Tai-yü, walked into the court.

"These grounds," surmised Tai-yü to herself, "must have been originally converted from a piece partitioned from the garden of the Jung mansion."

Having entered three rows of ceremonial gates they actually caught sight of the main structure, with its vestibules and porches, all of which, though on a small scale, were full of artistic and unique beauty. They were nothing like the lofty, imposing, massive and luxurious style of architecture on the other side, yet the avenues and rockeries, in the various places in the court, were all in perfect taste.

When they reached the interior of the principal pavilion, a large concourse of handmaids and waiting maids, got up in gala dress, were already there to greet them. Madame Hsing pressed Tai-yü into a seat, while she bade some one go into the outer library and request Mr. Chia She to come over.

In a few minutes the servant returned. "Master," she explained, "says: 'that he has not felt quite well for several days, that as the meeting with Miss Lin will affect both her as well as himself, he does not for the present feel equal to seeing each other, that he advises Miss Lin not to feel despondent or homesick; that she ought to feel quite at home with her venerable ladyship, (her grandmother,) as well as her maternal aunts; that her cousins are, it is true, blunt, but that if all the young ladies associated together in one place, they may also perchance dispel some dulness; that if ever (Miss Lin) has any grievance, she should at once speak out, and on no account feel a stranger; and everything will then be right."

Tai-yü lost no time in respectfully standing up, resuming her seat after she had listened to every sentence of the message to her. After a while, she said goodbye, and though madame Hsing used every argument to induce her to stay for the repast and then leave, Tai-yü smiled and said, "I shouldn't under ordinary circumstances refuse the invitation to dinner, which you, aunt, in your love kindly extend to me, but I have still to cross over and pay my respects to my maternal uncle Secundus; if I went too late, it would, I fear, be a lack of respect on my part; but I shall accept on another occasion. I hope therefore that you will, dear aunt, kindly excuse me."

"If such be the case," madame Hsing replied, "it's all right." And presently directing two nurses to take her niece over, in the carriage, in which they had come a while back, Tai-yü thereupon took her leave; madame Hsing escorting her as far as the ceremonial gate, where she gave some further directions to all the company of servants. She followed the curricle with her eyes so long as it remained in sight, and at length retraced her footsteps.

Tai-yü shortly entered the Jung Mansion, descended from the carriage, and preceded by all the nurses, she at once proceeded towards the east, turned a corner, passed through an Entrance Hall, running east and west, and walked in a southern direction, at the back of the Large Hall. On the inner side of a ceremonial gate, and at the upper end of a spacious court, stood a large main building, with five apartments, flanked on both sides by out-houses (stretching out) like the antlers on the head of deer; side-gates, resembling passages through a hill, establishing a thorough communication all round; (a main building) lofty, majestic, solid and grand, and unlike those in the compound of dowager lady Chia.

Tai-yü readily concluded that this at last was the main inner suite of apartments. A raised broad road led in a straight line to the large gate. Upon entering the Hall, and raising her head, she first of all perceived before her a large tablet with blue ground, upon which figured nine dragons of reddish gold. The inscription on this tablet consisted of three characters as large as a peck-measure, and declared that this was the Hall of Glorious Felicity.

At the end, was a row of characters of minute size, denoting the year, month and day, upon which His Majesty had been pleased to confer the tablet upon Chia Yuan, Duke of Jung Kuo. Besides this tablet, were numberless costly articles bearing the autograph of the Emperor. On the large black ebony table, engraved with dragons, were placed three antique blue and green bronze tripods, about three feet in height. On the wall hung a large picture representing black dragons, such as were seen in waiting chambers of the Sui dynasty. On one side stood a gold cup of chased work, while on the other, a crystal casket. On the ground were placed, in two rows, sixteen chairs, made of hard-grained cedar.

There was also a pair of scrolls consisting of black-wood antithetical tablets, inlaid with the strokes of words in chased gold. Their burden was this:

On the platform shine resplendent pearls like sun or moon,
And the sheen of the Hall façade gleams like russet sky.

Below, was a row of small characters, denoting that the scroll had been written by the hand of Mu Shih, a fellow-countryman and old friend of the family, who, for his meritorious services, had the hereditary title of Prince of Tung Ngan conferred upon him.

The fact is that madame Wang was also not in the habit of sitting and resting, in this main apartment, but in three side-rooms on the east, so that the nurses at once led Tai-yü through the door of the eastern wing.

On a stove-couch, near the window, was spread a foreign red carpet. On the side of honour, were laid deep red reclining-cushions, with dragons, with gold cash (for scales), and an oblong brown-coloured sitting-cushion with gold-cash-spotted dragons. On the two sides, stood one of a pair of small teapoys of foreign lacquer of peach-blossom pattern. On the teapoy on the left, were spread out Wen Wang tripods, spoons, chopsticks and scent-bottles. On the teapoy on the right, were vases from the Ju Kiln, painted with girls of great beauty, in which were placed seasonable flowers; (on it were) also teacups, a tea service and the like articles.

On the floor on the west side of the room, were four chairs in a row, all of which were covered with antimacassars, embroidered with silverish-red flowers, while below, at the feet of these chairs, stood four footstools. On either side, was also one of a pair of high teapoys, and these teapoys were covered with teacups and flower vases.

The other nick-nacks need not be minutely described.

The old nurses pressed Tai-yü to sit down on the stove-couch; but, on perceiving near the edge of the couch two embroidered cushions, placed one opposite the other, she thought of the gradation of seats, and did not therefore place herself on the couch, but on a chair on the eastern side of the room; whereupon the waiting maids, in attendance in these quarters, hastened to serve the tea.

While Tai-yü was sipping her tea, she observed the headgear, dress, deportment and manners of the several waiting maids, which she really found so unlike what she had seen in other households. She had hardly finished her tea, when she noticed a waiting maid approach, dressed in a red satin jacket, and a waistcoat of blue satin with scollops.

"My lady requests Miss Lin to come over and sit with her," she remarked as she put on a smile.

The old nurses, upon hearing this message, speedily ushered Tai-yü again out of this apartment, into the three-roomed small main building by the eastern porch.

On the stove-couch, situated at the principal part of the room, was placed, in a transverse position, a low couch-table, at the upper end of which were laid out, in a heap, books and a tea service. Against the partition-wall, on the east side, facing the west, was a reclining pillow, made of blue satin, neither old nor new.

Madame Wang, however, occupied the lower seat, on the west side, on which was likewise placed a rather shabby blue satin sitting-rug, with a back-cushion; and upon perceiving Tai-yü come in she urged her at once to sit on the east side.

Tai-yü concluded, in her mind, that this seat must certainly belong to Chia Cheng, and espying, next to the couch, a row of three chairs, covered with antimacassars, strewn with embroidered flowers, somewhat also the worse for use, Tai-yü sat down on one of these chairs.

But as madame Wang pressed her again and again to sit on the couch, Tai-yü had at length to take a seat next to her.

"Your uncle," madame Wang explained, "is gone to observe this day as a fast day, but you'll see him by and bye. There's, however, one thing I want to talk to you about. Your three female cousins are all, it is true, everything that is nice; and you will, when later on you come together for study, or to learn how to do needlework, or whenever, at any time, you romp and laugh together, find them all most obliging; but there's one thing that causes me very much concern. I have here one, who is the very root of retribution, the incarnation of all mischief, one who is a ne'er-do-well, a prince of malignant spirits in this family. He is gone to-day to pay his vows in the temple, and is not back yet, but you will see him in the evening, when you will readily be able to judge for yourself. One thing you must do, and that is, from this time forth, not to pay any notice to him. All these cousins of yours don't venture to bring any taint upon themselves by provoking him."

Tai-yü had in days gone by heard her mother explain that she had a nephew, born into the world, holding a piece of jade in his mouth, who was perverse beyond measure, who took no pleasure in his books, and whose sole great delight was to play the giddy dog in the inner apartments; that her maternal grandmother, on the other hand, loved him so fondly that no one ever presumed to call him to account, so that when, in this instance, she heard madame Wang's advice, she at once felt certain that it must be this very cousin.

"Isn't it to the cousin born with jade in his mouth, that you are alluding to, aunt?" she inquired as she returned her smile. "When I was at home, I remember my mother telling me more than once of this very cousin, who (she said) was a year older than I, and whose infant name was Pao-yü. She added that his disposition was really wayward, but that he treats all his cousins with the utmost consideration. Besides, now that I have come here, I shall, of course, be always together with my female cousins, while the boys will have their own court, and separate quarters; and how ever will there be any cause of bringing any slur upon myself by provoking him?"

"You don't know the reasons (that prompt me to warn you)," replied madame Wang laughingly. "He is so unlike all the rest, all because he has, since his youth up, been doated upon by our old lady! The fact is that he has been spoilt, through over-indulgence, by being always in the company of his female cousins! If his female cousins pay no heed to him, he is, at any rate, somewhat orderly, but the day his cousins say one word more to him than usual, much trouble forthwith arises, at the outburst of delight in his heart. That's why I enjoin upon you not to heed him. From his mouth, at one time, issue sugared words and mellifluous phrases; and at another, like the heavens devoid of the sun, he becomes a raving fool; so whatever you do, don't believe all he says."

Tai-yü was assenting to every bit of advice as it was uttered, when unexpectedly she beheld a waiting-maid walk in. "Her venerable ladyship over there," she said, "has sent word about the evening meal."

Madame Wang hastily took Tai-yü by the hand, and emerging by the door of the back-room, they went eastwards by the verandah at the back. Past the side gate, was a roadway, running north and south. On the southern side were a pavilion with three divisions and a Reception Hall with a colonnade. On the north, stood a large screen wall, painted white; behind it was a very small building, with a door of half the ordinary size.

"These are your cousin Feng's rooms," explained madame Wang to Tai-yü, as she pointed to them smiling. "You'll know in future your way to come and find her; and if you ever lack anything, mind you mention it to her, and she'll make it all right."

At the door of this court, were also several youths, who had recently had the tufts of their hair tied together, who all dropped their hands against their sides, and stood in a respectful posture. Madame Wang then led Tai-yü by the hand through a corridor, running east and west, into what was dowager lady Chia's back-court. Forthwith they entered the door of the back suite of rooms, where stood, already in attendance, a large number of servants, who, when they saw madame Wang arrive, set to work setting the tables and chairs in order.

Chia Chu's wife, née Li, served the eatables, while Hsi-feng placed the chopsticks, and madame Wang brought the soup in. Dowager lady Chia was seated all alone on the divan, in the main part of the apartment, on the two sides of which stood four vacant chairs.

Hsi-feng at once drew Tai-yü, meaning to make her sit in the foremost chair on the left side, but Tai-yü steadily and concedingly declined.

"Your aunts and sisters-in-law, standing on the right and left," dowager lady Chia smilingly explained, "won't have their repast in here, and as you're a guest, it's but proper that you should take that seat."

Then alone it was that Tai-yü asked for permission to sit down, seating herself on the chair.

Madame Wang likewise took a seat at old lady Chia's instance; and the three cousins, Ying Ch'un and the others, having craved for leave to sit down, at length came forward, and Ying Ch'un took the first chair on the right, T'an Ch'un the second, and Hsi Ch'un the second on the left. Waiting maids stood by holding in their hands, flips and finger-bowls and napkins, while Mrs. Li and lady Feng, the two of them, kept near the table advising them what to eat, and pressing them to help themselves.

In the outer apartments, the married women and waiting-maids in attendance, were, it is true, very numerous; but not even so much as the sound of the cawing of a crow could be heard.

The repast over, each one was presented by a waiting-maid, with tea in a small tea tray; but the Lin family had all along impressed upon the mind of their daughter that in order to show due regard to happiness, and to preserve good health, it was essential, after every meal, to wait a while, before drinking any tea, so that it should not do any harm to the intestines. When, therefore, Tai-yü perceived how many habits there were in this establishment unlike those which prevailed in her home, she too had no alternative but to conform herself to a certain extent with them. Upon taking over the cup of tea, servants came once more and presented finger-bowls for them to rinse their mouths, and Tai-yü also rinsed hers; and after they had all again finished washing their hands, tea was eventually served a second time, and this was, at length, the tea that was intended to be drunk.

"You can all go," observed dowager lady Chia, "and let us alone to have a chat."

Madame Wang rose as soon as she heard these words, and having made a few irrelevant remarks, she led the way and left the room along with the two ladies, Mrs. Li and lady Feng.

Dowager lady Chia, having inquired of Tai-yü what books she was reading, "I have just begun reading the Four Books," Tai-yü replied. "What books are my cousins reading?" Tai-yü went on to ask.

"Books, you say!" exclaimed dowager lady Chia; "why all they know are a few characters, that's all."

The sentence was barely out of her lips, when a continuous sounding of footsteps was heard outside, and a waiting maid entered and announced that Pao-yü was coming. Tai-yü was speculating in her mind how it was that this Pao-yü had turned out such a good-for-nothing fellow, when he happened to walk in.

He was, in fact, a young man of tender years, wearing on his head, to hold his hair together, a cap of gold of purplish tinge, inlaid with precious gems. Parallel with his eyebrows was attached a circlet, embroidered with gold, and representing two dragons snatching a pearl. He wore an archery-sleeved deep red jacket, with hundreds of butterflies worked in gold of two different shades, interspersed with flowers; and was girded with a sash of variegated silk, with clusters of designs, to which was attached long tassels; a kind of sash worn in the palace. Over all, he had a slate-blue fringed coat of Japanese brocaded satin, with eight bunches of flowers in relief; and wore a pair of light blue satin white-soled, half-dress court-shoes.

His face was like the full moon at mid-autumn; his complexion, like morning flowers in spring; the hair along his temples, as if chiselled with a knife; his eyebrows, as if pencilled with ink; his nose like a suspended gallbladder (a well-cut and shapely nose); his eyes like vernal waves; his angry look even resembled a smile; his glance, even when stern, was full of sentiment.

Round his neck he had a gold dragon necklet with a fringe; also a cord of variegated silk, to which was attached a piece of beautiful jade.

As soon as Tai-yü became conscious of his presence, she was quite taken aback. "How very strange!" she was reflecting in her mind; "it would seem as if I had seen him somewhere or other, for his face appears extremely familiar to my eyes;" when she noticed Pao-yü face dowager lady Chia and make his obeisance. "Go and see your mother and then come back," remarked her venerable ladyship; and at once he turned round and quitted the room.

On his return, he had already changed his hat and suit. All round his head, he had a fringe of short hair, plaited into small queues, and bound with red silk. The queues were gathered up at the crown, and all the hair, which had been allowed to grow since his birth, was plaited into a thick queue, which looked as black and as glossy as lacquer. Between the crown of the head and the extremity of the queue, hung a string of four large pearls, with pendants of gold, representing the eight precious things. On his person, he wore a long silvery-red coat, more or less old, bestrewn with embroidery of flowers. He had still round his neck the necklet, precious gem, amulet of Recorded Name, philacteries, and other ornaments. Below were partly visible a fir-cone coloured brocaded silk pair of trousers, socks spotted with black designs, with ornamented edges, and a pair of deep red, thick-soled shoes.

(Got up as he was now,) his face displayed a still whiter appearance, as if painted, and his eyes as if they were set off with carnation. As he rolled his eyes, they brimmed with love. When he gave utterance to speech, he seemed to smile. But the chief natural pleasing feature was mainly centred in the curve of his eyebrows. The ten thousand and one fond sentiments, fostered by him during the whole of his existence, were all amassed in the corner of his eyes.

His outward appearance may have been pleasing to the highest degree, but yet it was no easy matter to fathom what lay beneath it.

There are a couple of roundelays, composed by a later poet, (after the excellent rhythm of the) Hsi Chiang Yueh, which depict Pao-yü in a most adequate manner.

The roundelays run as follows:

To gloom and passion prone, without a rhyme,
Inane and madlike was he many a time,
His outer self, forsooth, fine may have been,
But one wild, howling waste his mind within:
Addled his brain that nothing he could see;
A dunce! to read essays so loth to be!
Perverse in bearing, in temper wayward;
For human censure he had no regard.
When rich, wealth to enjoy he knew not how;
When poor, to poverty he could not bow.
Alas! what utter waste of lustrous grace!
To state, to family what a disgrace!
Of ne'er-do-wells below he was the prime,
Unfilial like him none up to this time.
Ye lads, pampered with sumptuous fare and dress,
Beware! In this youth's footsteps do not press!

But to proceed with our story.

"You have gone and changed your clothes," observed dowager lady Chia, "before being introduced to the distant guest. Why don't you yet salute your cousin?"

Pao-yü had long ago become aware of the presence of a most beautiful young lady, who, he readily concluded, must be no other than the daughter of his aunt Lin. He hastened to advance up to her, and make his bow; and after their introduction, he resumed his seat, whence he minutely scrutinised her features, (which he thought) so unlike those of all other girls.

Her two arched eyebrows, thick as clustered smoke, bore a certain not very pronounced frowning wrinkle. She had a pair of eyes, which possessed a cheerful, and yet one would say, a sad expression, overflowing with sentiment. Her face showed the prints of sorrow stamped on her two dimpled cheeks. She was beautiful, but her whole frame was the prey of a hereditary disease. The tears in her eyes glistened like small specks. Her balmy breath was so gentle. She was as demure as a lovely flower reflected in the water. Her gait resembled a frail willow, agitated by the wind. Her heart, compared with that of Pi Kan, had one more aperture of intelligence; while her ailment exceeded (in intensity) by three degrees the ailment of Hsi-Tzu.

Pao-yü, having concluded his scrutiny of her, put on a smile and said, "This cousin I have already seen in days gone by."

"There you are again with your nonsense," exclaimed lady Chia, sneeringly; "how could you have seen her before?"

"Though I may not have seen her, ere this," observed Pao-yü with a smirk, "yet when I look at her face, it seems so familiar, and to my mind, it would appear as if we had been old acquaintances; just as if, in fact, we were now meeting after a long separation."

"That will do! that will do!" remarked dowager lady Chia; "such being the case, you will be the more intimate."

Pao-yü, thereupon, went up to Tai-yü, and taking a seat next to her, continued to look at her again with all intentness for a good long while.

"Have you read any books, cousin?" he asked.

"I haven't as yet," replied Tai-yü, "read any books, as I have only been to school for a year; all I know are simply a few characters."

"What is your worthy name, cousin?" Pao-yü went on to ask; whereupon Tai-yü speedily told him her name.

"Your style?" inquired Pao-yü; to which question Tai-yü replied, "I have no style."

"I'll give you a style," suggested Pao-yü smilingly; "won't the double style 'P'in P'in,' 'knitting brows,' do very well?"

"From what part of the standard books does that come?" T'an Ch'un hastily interposed.

"It is stated in the Thorough Research into the state of Creation from remote ages to the present day," Pao-yü went on to explain, "that, in the western quarter, there exists a stone, called Tai, (black,) which can be used, in lieu of ink, to blacken the eyebrows with. Besides the eyebrows of this cousin taper in a way, as if they were contracted, so that the selection of these two characters is most appropriate, isn't it?"

"This is just another plagiarism, I fear," observed T'an Ch'un, with an ironic smirk.

"Exclusive of the Four Books," Pao-yü remarked smilingly, "the majority of works are plagiarised; and is it only I, perchance, who plagiarise? Have you got any jade or not?" he went on to inquire, addressing Tai-yü, (to the discomfiture) of all who could not make out what he meant.

"It's because he has a jade himself," Tai-yü forthwith reasoned within her mind, "that he asks me whether I have one or not.—No; I haven't one," she replied. "That jade of yours is besides a rare object, and how could every one have one?"

As soon as Pao-yü heard this remark, he at once burst out in a fit of his raving complaint, and unclasping the gem, he dashed it disdainfully on the floor. "Rare object, indeed!" he shouted, as he heaped invective on it; "it has no idea how to discriminate the excellent from the mean, among human beings; and do tell me, has it any perception or not? I too can do without this rubbish!"

All those, who stood below, were startled; and in a body they pressed forward, vying with each other as to who should pick up the gem.

Dowager lady Chia was so distressed that she clasped Pao-yü in her embrace. "You child of wrath," she exclaimed. "When you get into a passion, it's easy enough for you to beat and abuse people; but what makes you fling away that stem of life?"

Pao-yü's face was covered with the traces of tears. "All my cousins here, senior as well as junior," he rejoined, as he sobbed, "have no gem, and if it's only I to have one, there's no fun in it, I maintain! and now comes this angelic sort of cousin, and she too has none, so that it's clear enough that it is no profitable thing."

Dowager lady Chia hastened to coax him. "This cousin of yours," she explained, "would, under former circumstances, have come here with a jade; and it's because your aunt felt unable, as she lay on her death-bed, to reconcile herself to the separation from your cousin, that in the absence of any remedy, she forthwith took the gem belonging to her (daughter), along with her (in the grave); so that, in the first place, by the fulfilment of the rites of burying the living with the dead might be accomplished the filial piety of your cousin; and in the second place, that the spirit of your aunt might also, for the time being, use it to gratify the wish of gazing on your cousin. That's why she simply told you that she had no jade; for she couldn't very well have had any desire to give vent to self-praise. Now, how can you ever compare yourself with her? and don't you yet carefully and circumspectly put it on? Mind, your mother may come to know what you have done!"

As she uttered these words, she speedily took the jade over from the hand of the waiting-maid, and she herself fastened it on for him.

When Pao-yü heard this explanation, he indulged in reflection, but could not even then advance any further arguments.

A nurse came at the moment and inquired about Tai-yü's quarters, and dowager lady Chia at once added, "Shift Pao-yü along with me, into the warm room of my suite of apartments, and put your mistress, Miss Lin, temporarily in the green gauze house; and when the rest of the winter is over, and repairs are taken in hand in spring in their rooms, an additional wing can be put up for her to take up her quarters in."

"My dear ancestor," ventured Pao-yü; "the bed I occupy outside the green gauze house is very comfortable; and what need is there again for me to leave it and come and disturb your old ladyship's peace and quiet?"

"Well, all right," observed dowager lady Chia, after some consideration; "but let each one of you have a nurse, as well as a waiting-maid to attend on you; the other servants can remain in the outside rooms and keep night watch and be ready to answer any call."

At an early hour, besides, Hsi-feng had sent a servant round with a grey flowered curtain, embroidered coverlets and satin quilts and other such articles.

Tai-yü had brought along with her only two servants; the one was her own nurse, dame Wang, and the other was a young waiting-maid of sixteen, whose name was called Hsüeh Yen. Dowager lady Chia, perceiving that Hsüeh Yen was too youthful and quite a child in her manner, while nurse Wang was, on the other hand, too aged, conjectured that Tai-yü would, in all her wants, not have things as she liked, so she detached two waiting-maids, who were her own personal attendants, named Tzu Chüan and Ying Ko, and attached them to Tai-yü's service. Just as had Ying Ch'un and the other girls, each one of whom had besides the wet nurses of their youth, four other nurses to advise and direct them, and exclusive of two personal maids to look after their dress and toilette, four or five additional young maids to do the washing and sweeping of the rooms and the running about backwards and forwards on errands.

Nurse Wang, Tzu Chüan and other girls entered at once upon their attendance on Tai-yü in the green gauze rooms, while Pao-yü's wet-nurse, dame Li, together with an elderly waiting-maid, called Hsi Jen, were on duty in the room with the large bed.

This Hsi Jen had also been, originally, one of dowager lady Chia's servant-girls. Her name was in days gone by, Chen Chu. As her venerable ladyship, in her tender love for Pao-yü, had feared that Pao-yü's servant girls were not equal to their duties, she readily handed her to Pao-yü, as she had hitherto had experience of how sincere and considerate she was at heart.

Pao-yü, knowing that her surname was at one time Hua, and having once seen in some verses of an ancient poet, the line "the fragrance of flowers wafts itself into man," lost no time in explaining the fact to dowager lady Chia, who at once changed her name into Hsi Jen.

This Hsi Jen had several simple traits. While in attendance upon dowager lady Chia, in her heart and her eyes there was no one but her venerable ladyship, and her alone; and now in her attendance upon Pao-yü, her heart and her eyes were again full of Pao-yü, and him alone. But as Pao-yü was of a perverse temperament and did not heed her repeated injunctions, she felt at heart exceedingly grieved.

At night, after nurse Li had fallen asleep, seeing that in the inner chambers, Tai-yü, Ying Ko and the others had not as yet retired to rest, she disrobed herself, and with gentle step walked in.

"How is it, miss," she inquired smiling, "that you have not turned in as yet?"

Tai-yü at once put on a smile. "Sit down, sister," she rejoined, pressing her to take a seat. Hsi Jen sat on the edge of the bed.

"Miss Lin," interposed Ying Ko smirkingly, "has been here in an awful state of mind! She has cried so to herself, that her eyes were flooded, as soon as she dried her tears. 'It's only to-day that I've come,' she said, 'and I've already been the cause of the outbreak of your young master's failing. Now had he broken that jade, as he hurled it on the ground, wouldn't it have been my fault? Hence it was that she was so wounded at heart, that I had all the trouble in the world, before I could appease her."

"Desist at once, Miss! Don't go on like this," Hsi Jen advised her; "there will, I fear, in the future, happen things far more strange and ridiculous than this; and if you allow yourself to be wounded and affected to such a degree by a conduct such as his, you will, I apprehend, suffer endless wounds and anguish; so be quick and dispel this over-sensitive nature!"

"What you sisters advise me," replied Tai-yü, "I shall bear in mind, and it will be all right."

They had another chat, which lasted for some time, before they at length retired to rest for the night.

The next day, (she and her cousins) got up at an early hour and went over to pay their respects to dowager lady Chia, after which upon coming to madame Wang's apartments, they happened to find madame Wang and Hsi-feng together, opening the letters which had arrived from Chin Ling. There were also in the room two married women, who had been sent from madame Wang's elder brother's wife's house to deliver a message.

Tai-yü was, it is true, not aware of what was up, but T'an Ch'un and the others knew that they were discussing the son of her mother's sister, married in the Hsüeh family, in the city of Chin Ling, a cousin of theirs, Hsüeh P'an, who relying upon his wealth and influence had, by assaulting a man, committed homicide, and who was now to be tried in the court of the Ying T'ien Prefecture.

Her maternal uncle, Wang Tzu-t'eng, had now, on the receipt of the tidings, despatched messengers to bring over the news to the Chia family. But the next chapter will explain what was the ultimate issue of the wish entertained in this mansion to send for the Hsüeh family to come to the capital.

CHAPTER IV.

An ill-fated girl happens to meet an ill-fated young man.
The Hu Lu Bonze adjudicates the Hu Lu case.

Tai-yü, for we shall now return to our story, having come, along with her cousin to madame Wang's apartments, found madame Wang discussing certain domestic occurrences with the messengers, who had arrived from her elder brother's wife's home, and conversing also about the case of homicide, in which the family of her mother's sister had become involved, and other such relevant topics. Perceiving how pressing and perplexing were the matters in which madame Wang was engaged, the young ladies promptly left her apartments, and came over to the rooms of their widow sister-in-law, Mrs. Li.

This Mrs. Li had originally been the spouse of Chia Chu. Although Chu had died at an early age, he had the good fortune of leaving behind him a son, to whom the name of Chia Lan was given. He was, at this period, just in his fifth year, and had already entered school, and applied himself to books.

This Mrs. Li was also the daughter of an official of note in Chin Ling. Her father's name was Li Shou-chung, who had, at one time, been Imperial Libationer. Among his kindred, men as well as women had all devoted themselves to poetry and letters; but ever since Li Shou-chung continued the line of succession, he readily asserted that the absence of literary attainments in his daughter was indeed a virtue, so that it soon came about that she did not apply herself in real earnest to learning; with the result that all she studied were some parts of the "Four Books for women," and the "Memoirs of excellent women," that all she read did not extend beyond a limited number of characters, and that all she committed to memory were the examples of these few worthy female characters of dynasties of yore; while she attached special importance to spinning and female handiwork. To this reason is to be assigned the name selected for her, of Li Wan (Li, the weaver), and the style of Kung Ts'ai (Palace Sempstress).

Hence it was that, though this Li Wan still continued, after the loss of her mate, while she was as yet in the spring of her life, to live amidst affluence and luxury, she nevertheless resembled in every respect a block of rotten wood or dead ashes. She had no inclination whatsoever to inquire after anything or to listen to anything; while her sole and exclusive thought was to wait upon her relatives and educate her son; and, in addition to this, to teach her young sisters-in-law to do needlework and to read aloud.

Tai-yü was, it is true, at this period living as a guest in the Chia mansion, where she certainly had the several young ladies to associate with her, but, outside her aged father, (she thought) there was really no need for her to extend affection to any of the rest.

But we will now speak of Chia Yü-ts'un. Having obtained the appointment of Prefect of Ying T'ien, he had no sooner arrived at his post than a charge of manslaughter was laid before his court. This had arisen from some rivalry between two parties in the purchase of a slave-girl, either of whom would not yield his right; with the result that a serious assault occurred, which ended in homicide.

Yü-ts'un had, with all promptitude, the servants of the plaintiffs brought before him, and subjected them to an examination.

"The victim of the assault," the plaintiffs deposed, "was your servants' master. Having on a certain day, purchased a servant-girl, she unexpectedly turned out to be a girl who had been carried away and sold by a kidnapper. This kidnapper had, first of all, got hold of our family's money, and our master had given out that he would on the third day, which was a propitious day, take her over into the house, but this kidnapper stealthily sold her over again to the Hsüeh family. When we came to know of this, we went in search of the seller to lay hold of him, and bring back the girl by force. But the Hsüeh party has been all along *the* bully of Chin Ling, full of confidence in his wealth, full of presumption on account of his prestige; and his arrogant menials in a body seized our master and beat him to death. The murderous master and his crew have all long ago made good their escape, leaving no trace behind them, while there only remain several parties not concerned in the affair. Your servants have for a whole year lodged complaints, but there has been no one to do our cause justice, and we therefore implore your Lordship to have the bloodstained criminals arrested, and thus conduce to the maintenance of humanity and benevolence; and the living, as well as the dead, will feel boundless gratitude for this heavenly bounty."

When Yü-ts'un heard their appeal, he flew into a fiery rage. "What!" he exclaimed. "How could a case of such gravity have taken place as the murder of a man, and the culprits have been allowed to run away scot-free, without being arrested? Issue warrants, and despatch constables to at once lay hold of the relatives of the bloodstained criminals and bring them to be examined by means of torture."

Thereupon he espied a Retainer, who was standing by the judgment-table, wink at him, signifying that he should not issue the warrants. Yü-t'sun gave way to secret suspicion, and felt compelled to desist.

Withdrawing from the Court-room, he retired into a private chamber, from whence he dismissed his followers, only keeping this single Retainer to wait upon him.

The Retainer speedily advanced and paid his obeisance. "Your worship," he said smiling, "has persistently been rising in official honours, and increasing in wealth so that, in the course of about eight or nine years, you have forgotten me."

"Your face is, however, extremely familiar," observed Yü-ts'un, "but I cannot, for the moment, recall who you are."

"Honourable people forget many things," remarked the Retainer, as he smiled. "What! Have you even forgotten the place where you started in life? and do you not remember what occurred, in years gone by, in the Hu Lu Temple?"

Yü-ts'un was filled with extreme astonishment; and past events then began to dawn upon him.

The fact is that this Retainer had been at one time a young priest in the Hu Lu temple; but as, after its destruction by fire, he had no place to rest his frame, he remembered how light and easy was, after all, this kind of occupation, and being unable to reconcile himself to the solitude and quiet of a temple, he accordingly availed himself of his years, which were as yet few, to let his hair grow, and become a retainer.

Yü-ts'un had had no idea that it was he. Hastily taking his hand in his, he smilingly observed, "You are, indeed, an old acquaintance!" and then pressed him to take a seat, so as to have a chat with more ease, but the Retainer would not presume to sit down.

"Friendships," Yü-ts'un remarked, putting on a smiling expression, "contracted in poor circumstances should not be forgotten! This is a private room; so that if you sat down, what would it matter?"

The Retainer thereupon craved permission to take a seat, and sat down gingerly, all awry.

"Why did you, a short while back," Yü-ts'un inquired, "not allow me to issue the warrants?"

"Your illustrious office," replied the Retainer, "has brought your worship here, and is it likely you have not transcribed some philactery of your post in this province!"

"What is an office-philactery?" asked Yü-ts'un with alacrity.

"Now-a-days," explained the Retainer, "those who become local officers provide themselves invariably with a secret list, in which are entered the names and surnames of the most influential and affluent gentry of note in the province. This is in vogue in every province. Should inadvertently, at any moment, one give umbrage to persons of this status, why, not only office, but I fear even one's life, it would be difficult to preserve. That's why these lists are called office-philacteries. This Hsüeh family, just a while back spoken of, how could your worship presume to provoke? This case in question affords no difficulties whatever in the way of a settlement; but the prefects, who have held office before you, have all, by doing violence to the feelings and good name of these people, come to the end they did."

As he uttered these words, he produced, from inside a purse which he had handy, a transcribed office-philactery, which he handed over to Yü-ts'un; who upon perusal, found it full of trite and unpolished expressions of public opinion, with regard to the leading clans and notable official families in that particular district. They ran as follows:

The "Chia" family is not "chia," a myth; white jade form the Halls; gold compose their horses! The "A Fang" Palace is three hundred li in extent, but is no fit residence for a "Shih" of Chin Ling. The eastern seas lack white jade beds, and the "Lung Wang," king of the Dragons, has come to ask for one of the Chin Ling Wang, (Mr. Wang of Chin Ling.) In a plenteous year, snow, (Hsüeh,) is very plentiful; their pearls and gems are like sand, their gold like iron.

Scarcely had Yü-ts'un done reading, when suddenly was heard the announcement, communicated by the beating of a gong, that Mr. Wang had come to pay his respects.

Yü-ts'un hastily adjusted his official clothes and hat, and went out of the room to greet and receive the visitor. Returning after a short while he proceeded to question the Retainer (about what he had been perusing.)

"These four families," explained the Retainer, "are all interlaced by ties of relationship, so that if you offend one, you offend all; if you honour one, you honour all. For support and protection, they all have those to take care of their interests! Now this Hsüeh, who is charged with homicide, is indeed the Hsüeh implied by 'in a plenteous year, (Hsüeh,) snow, is very plentiful.' In fact, not only has he these three families to rely upon, but his (father's) old friends, and his own relatives and friends are both to be found in the capital, as well as abroad in the provinces; and they are, what is more, not few in number. Who is it then that your Worship purposes having arrested?"

When Yü-ts'un had heard these remarks, he forthwith put on a smile and inquired of the Retainer, "If what you say be true, how is then this lawsuit to be settled? Are you also perchance well aware of the place of retreat of this homicide?"

"I don't deceive your Worship," the Retainer ventured smiling, "when I say that not only do I know the hiding-place of this homicide, but that I also am acquainted with the man who kidnapped and sold the girl; I likewise knew full well the poor devil and buyer, now deceased. But wait, and I'll tell your worship all, with full details. This person, who succumbed to the assault, was the son of a minor gentry. His name was Feng Yüan. His father and mother are both deceased, and he has likewise no brothers. He looked after some scanty property in order to eke out a living. His age was eighteen or nineteen; and he had a strong penchant for men's, and not much for women's society. But this was too the retribution (for sins committed) in a previous existence! for coming, by a strange coincidence, in the way of this kidnapper, who was selling the maid, he straightway at a glance fell in love with this girl, and made up his mind to purchase her and make her his second wife; entering an oath not to associate with any male friends, nor even to marry another girl. And so much in earnest was he in this matter that he had to wait until after the third day before she could enter his household (so as to make the necessary preparations for the marriage). But who would have foreseen the issue? This kidnapper quietly disposed of her again by sale to the Hsüeh family; his intention being to pocket the price-money from both parties, and effect his escape. Contrary to his calculations, he couldn't after all run away in time, and the two buyers laid hold of him and beat him, till he was half dead; but neither of them would take his coin back, each insisting upon the possession of the girl. But do you think that young gentleman, Mr. Hsüeh, would yield his claim to her person? Why, he at once summoned his servants and bade them have recourse to force; and, taking this young man Feng, they assailed him till they made mincemeat of him. He was then carried back to his home, where he finally died after the expiry of three days. This young Mr. Hsüeh had previously chosen a day, on which he meant to set out for the capital, and though he had beaten the young man Feng to death, and carried off the girl, he nevertheless behaved in the manner of a man who had had no concern in the affair. And all he gave his mind to was to take his family and go along on his way; but not in any wise in order to evade (the consequences) of this (occurrence). This case of homicide, (he looked upon) as a most trivial and insignificant matter, which, (he thought), his brother and servants, who were on the spot, would be enough to settle. But, however, enough of this person. Now does your worship know who this girl is who was sold?"

"How could I possibly know?" answered Yü-ts'un.

"And yet," remarked the Retainer, as he laughed coldly, "this is a person to whom you are indebted for great obligations; for she is no one else than the daughter of Mr. Chen, who lived next door to the Hu Lu temple. Her infant name is 'Ying Lien.'"

"What! is it really she?" exclaimed Yü-ts'un full of surprise. "I heard that she had been kidnapped, ever since she was five years old; but has she only been sold recently?"

"Kidnappers of this kind," continued the Retainer, "only abduct infant girls, whom they bring up till they reach the age of twelve or thirteen, when they take them into strange districts and dispose of them through their agents. In days gone by, we used daily to coax this girl, Ying Lien, to romp with us, so that we got to be exceedingly friendly. Hence it is that though, with the lapse of seven or eight years, her mien has assumed a more surpassingly lovely appearance, her general features have, on the other hand, undergone no change; and this is why I can recognise her. Besides, in the centre of her two eyebrows, she had a spot, of the size of a grain of rice, of carnation colour, which she has had ever since she was born into the world. This kidnapper, it also happened, rented my house to live in; and on a certain day, on which the kidnapper was not at home, I even set her a few questions. She said, 'that the kidnapper had so beaten her, that she felt intimidated, and couldn't on any account, venture to speak out; simply averring that the kidnapper was her own father, and that, as he had no funds to repay his debts, he had consequently disposed of her by sale!' I tried time after time to induce her to answer me, but she again gave way to tears and added no more than: 'I don't really remember anything of my youth.' Of this, anyhow, there can be no doubt; on a certain day the young man Feng and the kidnapper met, said the money was paid down; but as the kidnapper happened to be intoxicated, Ying Lien exclaimed, as she sighed: 'My punishment has this day been consummated!' Later on again, when she heard that young Feng would, after three days, have her taken over to his house, she once more underwent a change and put on such a sorrowful look that, unable to brook the sight of it, I waited till the kidnapper went out, when I again told my wife to go and cheer her by representing to her that this Mr. Feng's fixed purpose to wait for a propitious day, on which to come and take her over, was ample proof that he would not look upon her as a servant-girl. 'Furthermore,' (explained my wife to her), 'he is a sort of person exceedingly given to fast habits, and has at home ample means to live upon, so that if, besides, with his extreme aversion to women, he actually purchases you now, at a fancy price, you should be able to guess the issue, without any explanation. You have to bear suspense only for two or three days, and what need is there to be sorrowful and dejected?' After these assurances, she became somewhat composed, flattering herself that she would from henceforth have a home of her own.

"But who would believe that the world is but full of disappointments! On the succeeding day, it came about that the kidnapper again sold her to the Hsüeh family! Had he disposed of her to any other party, no harm would anyhow have resulted; but this young gentleman Hsüeh, who is nicknamed by all, 'the Foolish and overbearing Prince,' is the most perverse and passionate being in the whole world. What is more, he throws money away as if it were dust. The day on which he gave the thrashing with blows like falling leaves and flowing water, he dragged (*lit.* pull alive, drag dead) Ying Lien away more dead than alive, by sheer force, and no one, even up to this date, is aware whether she be among the dead or the living. This young Feng had a spell of empty happiness; for (not only) was his wish not fulfilled, but on the contrary he spent money and lost his life; and was not this a lamentable case?"

When Yü-ts'un heard this account he also heaved a sigh. "This was indeed," he observed, "a retribution in store for them! Their encounter was likewise not accidental; for had it been, how was it that this Feng Yüan took a fancy to Ying Lien?

"This Ying Lien had, during all these years, to endure much harsh treatment from the hands of the kidnapper, and had, at length, obtained the means of escape; and being besides full of warm feeling, had he actually made her his wife, and had they come together, the event would certainly have been happy; but, as luck would have it, there occurred again this contretemps.

"This Hsüeh is, it is true, more laden with riches and honours than Feng was, but when we bear in mind what kind of man he is he certainly, with his large bevy of handmaids, and his licentious and inordinate habits, cannot ever be held equal to Feng Yüan, who had set his heart upon one person! This may appositely be termed a fantastic sentimental destiny, which, by a strange coincidence, befell a couple consisting of an ill-fated young fellow and girl! But why discuss third parties? The only thing now is how to decide this case, so as to put things right."

"Your worship," remarked the Retainer smiling, "displayed, in years gone by, such great intelligence and decision, and how is it that today you, on the contrary, become a person without any resources! Your servant has heard that the promotion of your worship to fill up this office is due to the exertions of the Chia and Wang families; and as this Hsüeh P'an is a relative of the Chia mansion, why doesn't your worship take your craft along with the stream, and bring, by the performance of a kindness, this case to an issue, so that you may again in days to come, be able to go and face the two Dukes Chia and Wang?"

"What you suggest," replied Yü-ts'un, "is, of course, right enough; but this case involves a human life, and honoured as I have been, by His Majesty the Emperor, by a restoration to office, and selection to an appointment, how can I at the very moment, when I may strain all my energies to show my gratitude, by reason of a private consideration, set the laws at nought? This is a thing which I really haven't the courage to do."

"What your worship says is naturally right and proper," remarked the Retainer at these words, smiling sarcastically, "but at the present stage of the world, such things cannot be done. Haven't you heard the saying of a man of old to the effect that great men take action suitable to the times. 'He who presses,' he adds, 'towards what is auspicious and avoids what is inauspicious is a perfect man.' From what your worship says, not only you couldn't, by any display of zeal, repay your obligation to His Majesty, but, what is more, your own life you will find it difficult to preserve. There are still three more considerations necessary to insure a safe settlement."

Yü-ts'un drooped his head for a considerable time.

"What is there in your idea to be done?" he at length inquired.

"Your servant," responded the Retainer, "has already devised a most excellent plan. It's this: To-morrow, when your Lordship sits in court, you should, merely for form's sake, make much ado, by despatching letters and issuing warrants for the arrest of the culprits. The murderer will naturally not be forthcoming; and as the plaintiffs will be strong in their displeasure, you will of course have some members of the clan of the Hsüeh family, together with a few servants and others, taken into custody, and examined under torture, when your servant will be behind the scenes to bring matters to a settlement, by bidding them report that the victim had succumbed to a sudden ailment, and by urging the whole number of the kindred, as well as the headmen of the place, to hand in a declaration to that effect. Your Worship can aver that you understand perfectly how to write charms in dust, and conjure the spirit; having had an altar, covered with dust, placed in the court, you should bid the military and people to come and look on to their heart's content. Your Worship can give out that the divining spirit has declared: 'that the deceased, Feng Yüan, and Hsüeh P'an had been enemies in a former life, that having now met in the narrow road, their destinies were consummated; that Hsüeh P'an has, by this time, contracted some indescribable disease and perished from the effects of the persecution of the spirit of Feng.' That as the calamity had originated entirely from the action of the kidnapper, exclusive of dealing with the kidnapper according to law, the rest need not be interfered with, and so on. Your servant will be in the background to speak to the kidnapper and urge him to make a full confession; and when people find that the response of the divining spirit harmonizes with the statements of the kidnapper, they will, as a matter of course, entertain no suspicion.

"The Hsüeh family have plenty of money, so that if your Worship adjudicates that they should pay five hundred, they can afford it, or one thousand will also be within their means; and this sum can be handed to the Feng family to meet the outlay of burning incense and burial expenses. The Feng family are, besides, people of not much consequence, and (the fuss made by them) being simply for money, they too will, when they have got the cash in hand, have nothing more to say. But may it please your worship to consider carefully this plan and see what you think of it?"

"It isn't a safe course! It isn't a safe course!" Yü-ts'un observed as he smiled. "Let me further think and deliberate; and possibly by succeeding in suppressing public criticism, the matter might also be settled."

These two closed their consultation by a fixed determination, and the next day, when he sat in judgment, he marked off a whole company of the plaintiffs as well as of the accused, as were mentioned by name, and had them brought before him. Yü-ts'un examined them with additional minuteness, and discovered in point of fact, that the inmates of the Feng family were extremely few, that they merely relied upon this charge with the idea of obtaining some compensation for joss-sticks and burials; and that the Hsüeh family, presuming on their prestige and confident of patronage, had been obstinate in the refusal to make any mutual concession, with the result that confusion had supervened, and that no decision had been arrived at.

Following readily the bent of his feelings, Yü-ts'un disregarded the laws, and adjudicated this suit in a random way; and as the Feng family came in for a considerable sum, with which to meet the expense for incense and the funeral, they had, after all, not very much to say (in the way of objections.)

With all despatch, Yü-ts'un wrote and forwarded two letters, one to Chia Cheng, and the other to Wang Tzu-t'eng, at that time commander-in-chief of a Metropolitan Division, simply informing them: that the case, in which their worthy nephew was concerned, had come to a close, and that there was no need for them to give way to any extreme solicitude.

This case had been settled through the exclusive action of the young priest of the Hu Lu temple, now an official Retainer; and Yü-ts'un, apprehending, on the other hand, lest he might in the presence of others, divulge the circumstances connected with the days gone by, when he was in a state of penury, naturally felt very unhappy in his mind. But at a later period, he succeeded, by ultimately finding in him some shortcoming, and deporting him to a far-away place, in setting his fears at rest.

But we will put Yü-ts'un on one side, and refer to the young man Hsüeh, who purchased Ying Lien, and assaulted Feng Yuan to death.

He too was a native of Chin Ling and belonged to a family literary during successive generations; but this young Hsüeh had recently, when of tender age, lost his father, and his widowed mother out of pity for his being the only male issue and a fatherless child, could not help doating on him and indulging him to such a degree, that when he, in course of time, grew up to years of manhood, he was good for nothing.

In their home, furthermore, was the wealth of a millionaire, and they were, at this time, in receipt of an income from His Majesty's privy purse, for the purvey of various articles.

This young Hsüeh went at school under the name of P'an. His style was Wen Ch'i. His natural habits were extravagant; his language haughty and supercilious. He had, of course, also been to school, but all he knew was a limited number of characters, and those not well. The whole day long, his sole delight was in cock-fighting and horse-racing, rambling over hills and doing the sights.

Though a Purveyor, by Imperial appointment, he had not the least idea of anything relating to matters of business or of the world. All he was good for was: to take advantage of the friendships enjoyed by his grandfather in days of old, to present himself at the Board of Revenue to perfunctorily sign his name and to draw the allowance and rations; while the rest of his affairs he, needless to say, left his partners and old servants of the family to manage for him.

His widowed mother, a Miss Wang, was the youngest sister of Wang Tzu-t'eng, whose present office was that of Commander-in-Chief of a Metropolitan Division; and was, with Madame Wang, the spouse of Chia Cheng, of the Jung Kuo Mansion, sisters born of one mother. She was, in this year, more or less forty years of age and had only one son: this Hsüeh P'an.

She also had a daughter, who was two years younger than Hsüeh P'an, and whose infant name was Pao Ch'ai. She was beautiful in appearance, and elegant and refined in deportment. In days gone by, when her father lived, he was extremely fond of this girl, and had her read books and study characters, so that, as compared with her brother, she was actually a hundred times his superior. Having become aware, ever since her father's death, that her brother could not appease the anguish of her mother's heart, she at once dispelled all thoughts of books, and gave her sole mind to needlework, to the menage and other such concerns, so as to be able to participate in her mother's sorrow, and to bear the fatigue in lieu of her.

As of late the Emperor on the Throne held learning and propriety in high esteem, His Majesty called together and singled out talent and ability, upon which he deigned to display exceptional grace and favour. Besides the number called forth from private life and chosen as Imperial secondary wives, the daughters of families of hereditary official status and renown were without exception, reported by name to the authorities, and communicated to the Board, in anticipation of the selection for maids in waiting to the Imperial Princesses and daughters of Imperial Princes in their studies, and for filling up the offices of persons of eminence, to urge them to become excellent.

Ever since the death of Hsüeh P'an's father, the various assistants, managers and partners, and other employes in the respective provinces, perceiving how youthful Hsüeh P'an was in years, and how much he lacked worldly experience, readily availed themselves of the time to begin swindling and defrauding. The business, carried on in various different places in the capital, gradually also began to fall off and to show a deficit.

Hsüeh P'an had all along heard that the capital was the *one* place for gaieties, and was just entertaining the idea of going on a visit, when he eagerly jumped at the opportunity (that presented itself,) first of all to escort his sister, who was going to wait for the selection, in the second place to see his relatives, and in the third to enter personally the capital, (professedly) to settle up long-standing accounts, and to make arrangements for new outlays, but, in reality, with the sole purpose of seeing the life and splendour of the metropolis.

He therefore, had, at an early period, got ready his baggage and small luggage, as well as the presents for relatives and friends, things of every description of local production, presents in acknowledgment of favours received, and other such effects, and he was about to choose a day to start on his journey when unexpectedly he came in the way of the kidnapper who offered Ying Lien for sale. As soon as Hsüeh P'an saw how *distinguée* Ying Lien was in her appearance, he formed the resolution of buying her; and when he encountered Feng Yüan, come with the object of depriving him of her, he in the assurance of superiority, called his sturdy menials together, who set upon Feng Yüan and beat him to death. Forthwith collecting all the affairs of the household, and entrusting them one by one to the charge of some members of the clan and several elderly servants of the family, he promptly took his mother, sister and others and after all started on his distant journey, while the charge of homicide he, however, treated as child's play, flattering himself that if he spent a few filthy pieces of money, there was no doubt as to its settlement.

He had been on his journey how many days, he had not reckoned, when, on a certain day, as they were about to enter the capital, he furthermore heard that his maternal uncle, Wang Tzu-t'eng, had been raised to the rank of Supreme Governor of nine provinces, and had been honoured with an Imperial command to leave the capital and inspect the frontiers.

Hsüeh P'an was at heart secretly elated. "I was just lamenting," he thought, "that on my visit to the capital, I would have my maternal uncle to exercise control over me, and that I wouldn't be able to gambol and frisk to my heart's content, but now that he is leaving the capital, on promotion, it's evident that Heaven accomplishes man's wishes."

As he consequently held consultation with his mother; "Though we have," he argued, "several houses of our own in the capital, yet for these last ten years or so, there has been no one to live in them, and the people charged with the looking after them must unavoidably have stealthily rented them to some one or other. It's therefore needful to let servants go ahead to sweep and get the place in proper order, before we can very well go ourselves."

"What need is there to go to such trouble?" retorted his mother; "the main object of our present visit to the capital is first of all to pay our respects to our relatives and friends; and it is, either at your elder uncle's, my brother's place, or at your other uncle's, my sister's husband's home, both of which families' houses are extremely spacious, that we can put up provisionally, and by and bye, at our ease, we can send servants to make our house tidy. Now won't this be a considerable saving of trouble?"

"My uncle, your brother," suggested Hsüeh P'an, "has just been raised to an appointment in an outside province, so that, of course, in his house, things must be topsy-turvey, on account of his departure; and should we betake ourselves, like a hive of bees and a long trail, to him for shelter; won't we appear very inconsiderate?"

"Your uncle," remarked his mother, "is, it is true, going on promotion, but there's besides the house of your aunt, my sister. What is more, during these last few years from both your uncle's and aunt's have, time after time, been sent messages, and letters forwarded, asking us to come over; and now that we've come, is it likely, though your uncle is busy with his preparations to start on his journey, that your aunt of the Chia family won't do all she can to press us to stay? Besides, were we to have our house got ready in a scramble, won't it make people think it strange? I however know your idea very well that were we kept to stay at your uncle's and aunt's, you won't escape being under strict restraint, unlike what would be the case were we to live in our own house, as you would be free then to act as you please! Such being the case, go, on your own account, and choose some place to take up your quarters in, while I myself, who have been separated from your aunt and cousins for these several years, would however like to stay with them for a few days; and I'll go along with your sister and look up your aunt at her home. What do you say; will this suit you or not?"

Hsüeh P'an, upon hearing his mother speak in this strain, knew well enough that he could not bring her round from her determination; and he had no help but to issue the necessary directions to the servants to make straight for the Jung Kuo mansion. Madame Wang had by this time already come to know that in the lawsuit, in which Hsüeh P'an was concerned, Chia Yü-ts'un had fortunately intervened and lent his good offices, and was at length more composed in her mind. But when she again saw that her eldest brother had been advanced to a post on the frontier, she was just deploring that, deprived of the intercourse of the relatives of her mother's family, how doubly lonely she would feel; when, after the lapse of a few days, some one of the household brought the unexpected announcement that "our lady, your sister, has, with the young gentleman, the young lady and her whole household, entered the capital and have dismounted from their vehicles outside the main entrance." This news so delighted madame Wang that she rushed out, with a few attendants, to greet them in the large Entrance Hall, and brought Mrs. Hsüeh and the others into her house.

The two sisters were now reunited, at an advanced period of their lives, so that mixed feelings of sorrow and joy thronged together, but on these it is, of course, needless to dilate.

After conversing for a time on what had occurred, subsequent to their separation, madame Wang took them to pay their obeisance to dowager lady Chia. They then handed over the various kinds of presents and indigenous articles, and after the whole family had been introduced, a banquet was also spread to greet the guests.

Hsüeh P'an, having paid his respects to Chia Cheng and Chia Lien, was likewise taken to see Chia She, Chia Chen and the other members.

Chia Cheng sent a messenger to tell madame Wang that "'aunt' Hsüeh had already seen many springs and autumns, while their nephew was of tender age, with no experience, so that there was every fear, were he to live outside, that something would again take place. In the South-east corner of our compound," (he sent word,) "there are in the Pear Fragrance Court, over ten apartments, all of which are vacant and lying idle; and were we to tell the servants to sweep them, and invite 'aunt' Hsüeh and the young gentleman and lady to take up their quarters there, it would be an extremely wise thing."

Madame Wang had in fact been entertaining the wish to keep them to live with them, when dowager lady Chia also sent some one to say that, "Mrs. Hsüeh should be asked to put up in the mansion in order that a greater friendliness should exist between them all."

Mrs. Hsüeh herself had all along been desirous to live in one place with her relatives, so as to be able to keep a certain check over her son, fearing that, if they lived in a separate house outside, the natural bent of his habits would run riot, and that some calamity would be brought on; and she therefore, there and then, expressed her sense of appreciation, and accepted the invitation. She further privately told madame Wang in clear terms, that every kind of daily expense and general contribution would have to be entirely avoided and withdrawn as that would be the only thing to justify her to make any protracted stay. And madame Wang aware that she had, in her home, no difficulty in this line, promptly in fact complied with her wishes.

From this date it was that "aunt" Hsüeh and her children took up their quarters in the Pear Fragrance Court.

This Court of Pear Fragrance had, we must explain, been at one time used as a place for the quiet retirement of the Duke Jung in his advanced years. It was on a small scale, but ingeniously laid out. There were, at least, over ten structures. The front halls and the back houses were all in perfect style. There was a separate door giving on to the street, and the people of the household of Hsüeh P'an used this door to go in and out. At the south-west quarter, there was also a side door, which communicated with a narrow roadway. Beyond this narrow road, was the eastern court of madame Wang's principal apartment; so that every day, either after her repast, or in the evening, Mrs. Hsüeh would readily come over and converse, on one thing and another, with dowager lady Chia, or have a chat with madame Wang; while Pao-ch'ai came together, day after day, with Tai yü, Ying-ch'un, her sisters and the other girls, either to read, to play chess, or to do needlework, and the pleasure which they derived was indeed perfect.

Hsüeh P'an however had all along from the first instance, been loth to live in the Chia mansion, as he dreaded that with the discipline enforced by his uncle, he would not be able to be his own master; but his mother had made up her mind so positively to remain there, and what was more, every one in the Chia mansion was most pressing in their efforts to keep them, that there was no alternative for him but to take up his quarters temporarily there, while he at the same time directed servants to go and sweep the apartments of their own house, with a view that they should move into them when they were ready.

But, contrary to expectation, after they had been in their quarters for not over a month, Hsüeh P'an came to be on intimate relations with all the young men among the kindred of the Chia mansion, the half of whom were extravagant in their habits, so that great was, of course, his delight to frequent them. To-day, they would come together to drink wine; the next day to look at flowers. They even assembled to gamble, to dissipate and to go everywhere and anywhere; leading, with all their enticements, Hsüeh P'an so far astray, that he became far worse, by a hundred times, than he was hitherto.

Although it must be conceded that Chia Cheng was in the education of his children quite correct, and in the control of his family quite systematic, yet in the first place, the clan was so large and the members so numerous, that he was unable to attend to the entire supervision; and, in the second place, the head of the family, at this period, was Chia Chen, who, as the eldest grandchild of the Ning mansion, had likewise now come into the inheritance of the official status, with the result that all matters connected with the clan devolved upon his sole and exclusive control. In the third place, public as well as private concerns were manifold and complex, and being a man of negligent disposition, he estimated ordinary affairs of so little consequence that any respite from his official duties he devoted to no more than the study of books and the playing of chess.

Furthermore, this Pear Fragrance Court was separated by two rows of buildings from his quarters and was also provided with a separate door opening into the street, so that, being able at their own heart's desire to go out and to come in, these several young fellows could well indulge their caprices, and gratify the bent of their minds.

Hence it was that Hsüeh P'an, in course of time gradually extinguished from his memory every idea of shifting their quarters.

But what transpired, on subsequent days, the following chapter will explain.

CHAPTER V.

The spirit of Chia Pao-yü visits the confines of the Great Void.
The Monitory Vision Fairy expounds, in ballads, the Dream of the Red
Chamber.

Having in the fourth Chapter explained, to some degree, the circumstances attending the settlement of the mother and children of the Hsüeh family in the Jung mansion, and other incidental matters, we will now revert to Lin Tai-yü.

Ever since her arrival in the Jung mansion, dowager lady Chia showed her the highest sympathy and affection, so that in everything connected with sleeping, eating, rising and accommodation she was on the same footing as Pao-yü; with the result that Ying Ch'un, Hsi Ch'un and T'an Ch'un, her three granddaughters, had after all to take a back seat. In fact, the intimate and close friendliness and love which sprung up between the two persons Pao-yü and Tai-yü, was, in the same degree, of an exceptional kind, as compared with those existing between the others. By daylight they were wont to walk together, and to sit together. At night, they would desist together, and rest together. Really it was a case of harmony in language and concord in ideas, of the consistency of varnish or of glue, (a close friendship), when at this unexpected juncture there came this girl, Hsüeh Pao-ch'ai, who, though not very much older in years (than the others), was, nevertheless, in manner so correct, and in features so beautiful that the consensus of opinion was that Tai-yü herself could not come up to her standard.

What is more, in her ways Pao-Ch'ai was so full of good tact, so considerate and accommodating, so unlike Tai-yü, who was supercilious, self-confident, and without any regard for the world below, that the natural consequence was that she soon completely won the hearts of the lower classes. Even the whole number of waiting-maids would also for the most part, play and joke with Pao-ch'ai. Hence it was that Tai-yü fostered, in her heart, considerable feelings of resentment, but of this however Pao-ch'ai had not the least inkling.

Pao-yü was, likewise, in the prime of his boyhood, and was, besides, as far as the bent of his natural disposition was concerned, in every respect absurd and perverse; regarding his cousins, whether male or female, one and all with one common sentiment, and without any distinction whatever between the degrees of distant or close relationship. Sitting and sleeping, as he now was under the same roof with Tai-yü in dowager lady Chia's suite of rooms, he naturally became comparatively more friendly with her than with his other cousins; and this friendliness led to greater intimacy and this intimacy once established, rendered unavoidable the occurrence of the blight of harmony from unforeseen slight pretexts.

These two had had on this very day, for some unknown reason, words between them more or less unfriendly, and Tai-yü was again sitting all alone in her room, giving way to tears. Pao-yü was once more within himself quite conscience-smitten for his ungraceful remarks, and coming forward, he humbly made advances, until, at length, Tai-yü little by little came round.

As the plum blossom, in the eastern part of the garden of the Ning mansion, was in full bloom, Chia Chen's spouse, Mrs. Yu, made preparations for a collation, (purposing) to send invitations to dowager lady Chia, mesdames Hsing, and Wang, and the other members of the family, to come and admire the flowers; and when the day arrived the first thing she did was to take Chia Jung and his wife, the two of them, and come and ask them round in person. Dowager lady Chia and the other inmates crossed over after their early meal; and they at once promenaded the Hui Fang (Concentrated Fragrance) Garden. First tea was served, and next wine; but the entertainment was no more than a family banquet of the kindred of the two mansions of Ning and Jung, so that there was a total lack of any novel or original recreation that could be put on record.

After a little time, Pao-yü felt tired and languid and inclined for his midday siesta. "Take good care," dowager lady Chia enjoined some of them, "and stay with him, while he rests for a while, when he can come back;" whereupon Chia Jung's wife, Mrs. Ch'in, smiled and said with eagerness: "We got ready in here a room for uncle Pao, so let your venerable ladyship set your mind at ease. Just hand him over to my charge, and he will be quite safe. Mothers and sisters," she continued, addressing herself to Pao-yü's nurses and waiting maids, "invite uncle Pao to follow me in here."

Dowager lady Chia had always been aware of the fact that Mrs. Ch'in was a most trustworthy person, naturally courteous and scrupulous, and in every action likewise so benign and gentle; indeed the most estimable among the whole number of her great grandsons' wives, so that when she saw her about to go and attend to Pao-yü, she felt that, for a certainty, everything would be well.

Mrs. Ch'in, there and then, led away a company of attendants, and came into the rooms inside the drawing room. Pao-yü, upon raising his head, and catching sight of a picture hung on the upper wall, representing a human figure, in perfect style, the subject of which was a portrait of Yen Li, speedily felt his heart sink within him.

There was also a pair of scrolls, the text of which was:

A thorough insight into worldly matters arises from knowledge;
A clear perception of human nature emanates from literary lore.

On perusal of these two sentences, albeit the room was sumptuous and beautifully laid out, he would on no account remain in it. "Let us go at once," he hastened to observe, "let us go at once."

Mrs. Ch'in upon hearing his objections smiled. "If this," she said, "is really not nice, where are you going? if you won't remain here, well then come into my room."

Pao-yü nodded his head and gave a faint grin.

"Where do you find the propriety," a nurse thereupon interposed, "of an uncle going to sleep in the room of a nephew's wife?"

"Ai ya!" exclaimed Mrs. Ch'in laughing, "I don't mind whether he gets angry or not (at what I say); but how old can he be as to reverentially shun all these things? Why my brother was with me here last month; didn't you see him? he's, true enough, of the same age as uncle Pao, but were the two of them to stand side by side, I suspect that he would be much higher in stature."

"How is it," asked Pao-yü, "that I didn't see him? Bring him along and let me have a look at him!"

"He's separated," they all ventured as they laughed, "by a distance of twenty or thirty li, and how can he be brought along? but you'll see him some day."

As they were talking, they reached the interior of Mrs. Ch'in's apartments. As soon as they got in, a very faint puff of sweet fragrance was wafted into their nostrils. Pao-yü readily felt his eyes itch and his bones grow weak. "What a fine smell!" he exclaimed several consecutive times.

Upon entering the apartments, and gazing at the partition wall, he saw a picture the handiwork of T'ang Po-hu, consisting of Begonias drooping in the spring time; on either side of which was one of a pair of scrolls, written by Ch'in Tai-hsü, a Literary Chancellor of the Sung era, running as follows:

A gentle chill doth circumscribe the dreaming man, because the spring
is cold.
The fragrant whiff, which wafts itself into man's nose, is the perfume
of wine!

On the table was a mirror, one which had been placed, in days of yore, in the Mirror Palace of the Emperor Wu Tse-t'ien. On one side stood a gold platter, in which Fei Yen, who lived in the Ch'ao state, used to stand and dance. In this platter, was laid a quince, which An Lu-shan had flung at the Empress T'ai Chen, inflicting a wound on her breast. In the upper part of the room, stood a divan ornamented with gems, on which the Emperor's daughter, Shou Ch'ang, was wont to sleep, in the Han Chang Palace Hanging, were curtains embroidered with strings of pearls, by T'ung Ch'ang, the Imperial Princess.

"It's nice in here, it's nice in here," exclaimed Pao-yü with a chuckle.

"This room of mine," observed Mrs. Ch'in smilingly, "is I think, good enough for even spirits to live in!" and, as she uttered these words, she with her own hands, opened a gauze coverlet, which had been washed by Hsi Shih, and removed a bridal pillow, which had been held in the arms of Hung Niang. Instantly, the nurses attended to Pao-yü, until he had laid down comfortably; when they quietly dispersed, leaving only the four waiting maids: Hsi Jen, Ch'iu Wen, Ch'ing Wen and She Yueh to keep him company.

"Mind be careful, as you sit under the eaves," Mrs. Ch'in recommended the young waiting maids, "that the cats do not start a fight!"

Pao-yü then closed his eyes, and, little by little, became drowsy, and fell asleep.

It seemed to him just as if Mrs. Ch'in was walking ahead of him. Forthwith, with listless and unsettled step, he followed Mrs. Ch'in to some spot or other, where he saw carnation-like railings, jade-like steps, verdant trees and limpid pools—a spot where actually no trace of any human being could be met with, where of the shifting mundane dust little had penetrated.

Pao-yü felt, in his dream, quite delighted. "This place," he mused, "is pleasant, and I may as well spend my whole lifetime in here!

though I may have to lose my home, I'm quite ready for the sacrifice, for it's far better being here than being flogged, day after day, by father, mother, and teacher."

While he pondered in this erratic strain, he suddenly heard the voice of some human being at the back of the rocks, giving vent to this song:

Like scattering clouds doth fleet a vernal dream;
The transient flowers pass like a running stream;
Maidens and youths bear this, ye all, in mind;
In useless grief what profit will ye find?

Pao-yü perceived that the voice was that of a girl. The song was barely at an end, when he soon espied in the opposite direction, a beautiful girl advancing with majestic and elastic step; a girl quite unlike any ordinary mortal being. There is this poem, which gives an adequate description of her:

Lo she just quits the willow bank; and sudden now she issues from the
flower-bedecked house;
As onward alone she speeds, she startles the birds perched in the trees, by the pavilion; to which as she draws nigh, her shadow flits by the verandah!
Her fairy clothes now flutter in the wind! a fragrant perfume like unto musk or olea is wafted in the air; Her apparel lotus-like is sudden wont to move; and the jingle of her ornaments strikes the ear.
Her dimpled cheeks resemble, as they smile, a vernal peach; her kingfisher coiffure is like a cumulus of clouds; her lips part cherry-like; her pomegranate-like teeth conceal a fragrant breath.
Her slender waist, so beauteous to look at, is like the skipping snow wafted by a gust of wind; the sheen of her pearls and kingfisher trinkets abounds with splendour, green as the feathers of a duck, and yellow as the plumes of a goose;
Now she issues to view, and now is hidden among the flowers; beautiful
she is when displeased, beautiful when in high spirits; with lissome step, she treads along the pond, as if she soars on wings or sways in the air.
Her eyebrows are crescent moons, and knit under her smiles; she speaks, and yet she seems no word to utter; her lotus-like feet with ease pursue their course; she stops, and yet she seems still

to be in motion; the charms of her figure all vie with ice in purity, and in splendour with precious gems; Lovely is her brilliant attire, so full of grandeur and refined grace.
Loveable her countenance, as if moulded from some fragrant substance,
or carved from white jade; elegant is her person, like a phoenix, dignified like a dragon soaring high.
What is her chastity like? Like a white plum in spring with snow nestling in its broken skin; Her purity? Like autumn orchids bedecked with dewdrops.
Her modesty? Like a fir-tree growing in a barren plain; Her comeliness? Like russet clouds reflected in a limpid pool.
Her gracefulness? Like a dragon in motion wriggling in a stream; Her refinement? Like the rays of the moon shooting on to a cool river.
Sure is she to put Hsi Tzu to shame! Bound to put Wang Ch'iang to the
blush! What a remarkable person! Where was she born? and whence
does she come?
One thing is true that in Fairy-land there is no second like her! that in the Purple Courts of Heaven there is no one fit to be her peer!
Forsooth, who can it be, so surpassingly beautiful!

Pao-yü, upon realising that she was a fairy, was much elated; and with eagerness advanced and made a bow.

"My divine sister," he ventured, as he put on a smile. "I don't know whence you come, and whither you are going. Nor have I any idea what this place is, but I make bold to entreat that you would take my hand and lead me on."

"My abode," replied the Fairy, "is above the Heavens of Divested Animosities, and in the ocean of Discharged Sorrows. I'm the Fairy of Monitory Vision, of the cave of Drooping Fragrance, in the mount of Emitted Spring, within the confines of the Great Void. I preside over the voluptuous affections and sensual debts among the mortal race, and supervise in the dusty world, the envies of women and the lusts of man. It's because I've recently come to hear that the retribution for voluptuousness extends up to this place, that I betake myself here in order to find suitable opportunities of disseminating mutual affections. My encounter with you now is also not a matter of accident! This spot is not distant from my confines. I have nothing much there besides a cup of the tender buds of tea plucked by my own hands, and a pitcher of luscious wine, fermented by me as well as several spritelike singing and dancing maidens of great proficiency, and twelve ballads of spiritual song, recently completed, on the Dream of the Red Chamber; but won't you come along with me for a stroll?"

Pao-yü, at this proposal, felt elated to such an extraordinary degree that he could skip from joy, and there and then discarding from his mind all idea of where Mrs. Ch'in was, he readily followed the Fairy.

They reached some spot, where there was a stone tablet, put up in a horizontal position, on which were visible the four large characters: "The confines of the Great Void," on either side of which was one of a pair of scrolls, with the two antithetical sentences:

When falsehood stands for truth, truth likewise becomes false;
When naught be made to aught, aught changes into naught!

Past the Portal stood the door of a Palace, and horizontally, above this door, were the four large characters: "The Sea of Retribution, the Heaven of Love." There were also a pair of scrolls, with the inscription in large characters:

Passion, alas! thick as the earth, and lofty as the skies, from ages past to the present hath held incessant sway;
How pitiful your lot! ye lustful men and women envious, that your voluptuous debts should be so hard to pay!

Pao-yü, after perusal, communed with his own heart. "Is it really so!" he thought, "but I wonder what implies the passion from old till now, and what are the voluptuous debts! Henceforward, I must enlighten myself!"

Pao-yü was bent upon this train of thoughts when he unwittingly attracted several evil spirits into his heart, and with speedy step he followed in the track of the fairy, and entered two rows of doors when he perceived that the Lateral Halls were, on both sides, full of tablets and scrolls, the number of which he could not in one moment ascertain. He however discriminated in numerous places the inscriptions: The Board of Lustful Love; the Board of contracted grudges; The Board of Matutinal sobs; the Board of nocturnal tears; the Board of vernal affections; and the Board of autumnal anguish.

After he had perused these inscriptions, he felt impelled to turn round and address the Fairy. "May I venture to trouble my Fairy," he said, "to take me along for a turn into the interior of each of these Boards? May I be allowed, I wonder, to do so?"

"Inside each of these Boards," explained the Fairy, "are accumulated the registers with the records of all women of the whole world; of those who have passed away, as well as of those who have not as yet come into it, and you, with your mortal eyes and human body, could not possibly be allowed to know anything in anticipation."

But would Pao-yü, upon hearing these words, submit to this decree? He went on to implore her permission again and again, until the Fairy casting her eye upon the tablet of the board in front of her observed, "Well, all right! you may go into this board and reap some transient pleasure."

Pao-yü was indescribably joyous, and, as he raised his head, he perceived that the text on the tablet consisted of the three characters: the Board of Ill-fated lives; and that on each side was a scroll with the inscription:

Upon one's self are mainly brought regrets in spring and autumn gloom;
A face, flowerlike may be and moonlike too; but beauty all for whom?

Upon perusal of the scroll Pao-yü was, at once, the more stirred with admiration; and, as he crossed the door, and reached the interior, the only things that struck his eye were about ten large presses, the whole number of which were sealed with paper slips; on every one of these slips, he perceived that there were phrases peculiar to each province.

Pao-yü was in his mind merely bent upon discerning, from the rest, the slip referring to his own native village, when he espied, on the other side, a slip with the large characters: "the Principal Record of the Twelve Maidens of Chin Ling."

"What is the meaning," therefore inquired Pao-yü, "of the Principal Record of the Twelve Maidens of Chin Ling?"

"As this is the record," explained the Fairy, "of the most excellent and prominent girls in your honourable province, it is, for this reason, called the Principal Record."

"I've often heard people say," observed Pao-yü, "that Chin Ling is of vast extent; and how can there only be twelve maidens in it! why, at present, in our own family alone, there are more or less several hundreds of young girls!"

The Fairy gave a faint smile. "Through there be," she rejoined, "so large a number of girls in your honourable province, those only of any note have been selected and entered in this record. The two presses, on the two sides, contain those who are second best; while, for all who remain, as they are of the ordinary run, there are, consequently, no registers to make any entry of them in."

Pao-yü upon looking at the press below, perceived the inscription: "Secondary Record of the twelve girls of Chin Ling;" while again in another press was inscribed: "Supplementary Secondary Record of the Twelve girls of Chin Ling." Forthwith stretching out his hand, Pao-yü opened first the doors of the press, containing the "supplementary secondary Record," extracted a volume of the registers, and opened it. When he came to examine it, he saw on the front page a representation of something, which, though bearing no resemblance to a human being, presented, at the same time, no similitude to scenery; consisting simply of huge blotches made with ink. The whole paper was full of nothing else but black clouds and turbid mists, after which appeared the traces of a few characters, explaining that—

A cloudless moon is rare forsooth to see,
And pretty clouds so soon scatter and flee!
Thy heart is deeper than the heavens are high,
Thy frame consists of base ignominy!
Thy looks and clever mind resentment will provoke,
And thine untimely death vile slander will evoke!
A loving noble youth in vain for love will yearn.

After reading these lines, Pao-yü looked below, where was pictured a bouquet of fresh flowers and a bed covered with tattered matting. There were also several distiches running as follows:

Thy self-esteem for kindly gentleness is but a fancy vain!
Thy charms that they can match the olea or orchid, but thoughts inane!
While an actor will, envious lot! with fortune's smiles be born,
A youth of noble birth will, strange to say, be luckless and forlorn.

Pao-yü perused these sentences, but could not unfold their meaning, so, at once discarding this press, he went over and opened the door of the press of the "Secondary Records" and took out a book, in which, on examination, he found a representation of a twig of Olea fragrans. Below, was a pond, the water of which was parched up and the mud dry, the lotus flowers decayed, and even the roots dead. At the back were these lines:

The lotus root and flower but one fragrance will give;
How deep alas! the wounds of thy life's span will be;
What time a desolate tree in two places will live,
Back to its native home the fragrant ghost will flee!

Pao-yü read these lines, but failed to understand what they meant. He then went and fetched the "Principal Record," and set to looking it over. He saw on the first page a picture of two rotten trees, while on these trees was suspended a jade girdle. There was also a heap of snow, and under this snow was a golden hair-pin. There were in addition these four lines in verse:

Bitter thy cup will be, e'en were the virtue thine to stop the loom,
Thine though the gift the willow fluff to sing, pity who will thy doom?
High in the trees doth hang the girdle of white jade,
And lo! among the snow the golden pin is laid!

To Pao-yü the meaning was again, though he read the lines over, quite unintelligible. He was, about to make inquiries, but he felt convinced that the Fairy would be both to divulge the decrees of Heaven; and though intent upon discarding the book, he could not however tear himself away from it. Forthwith, therefore, he prosecuted a further perusal of what came next, when he caught sight of a picture of a bow. On this bow hung a citron. There was also this ode:

Full twenty years right and wrong to expound will be thy fate!
What place pomegranate blossoms come in bloom will face the Palace Gate!
The third portion of spring, of the first spring in beauty short will fall!
When tiger meets with hare thou wilt return to sleep perennial.

Further on, was also a sketch of two persons flying a kite; a broad expanse of sea, and a large vessel; while in this vessel was a girl, who screened her face bedewed with tears. These four lines were likewise visible:

Pure and bright will be thy gifts, thy purpose very high;
But born thou wilt be late in life and luck be passed by;
At the tomb feast thou wilt repine tearful along the stream,
East winds may blow, but home miles off will be, even in dream.

After this followed a picture of several streaks of fleeting clouds, and of a creek whose waters were exhausted, with the text:

Riches and honours too what benefit are they?
In swaddling clothes thou'lt be when parents pass away;
The rays will slant, quick as the twinkle of an eye;
The Hsiang stream will recede, the Ch'u clouds onward fly!

Then came a picture of a beautiful gem, which had fallen into the mire, with the verse:

Thine aim is chastity, but chaste thou wilt not be;
Abstraction is thy faith, but void thou may'st not see;

Thy precious, gemlike self will, pitiful to say,
Into the mundane mire collapse at length some day.

A rough sketch followed of a savage wolf, in pursuit of a beautiful girl, trying to pounce upon her as he wished to devour her. This was the burden of the distich:

Thy mate is like a savage wolf prowling among the hills;
His wish once gratified a haughty spirit his heart fills!
Though fair thy form like flowers or willows in the golden moon,
Upon the yellow beam to hang will shortly be its doom.

Below, was an old temple, in the interior of which was a beautiful person, just in the act of reading the religious manuals, as she sat all alone; with this inscription:

In light esteem thou hold'st the charms of the three springs for their short-liv'd fate;
Thine attire of past years to lay aside thou chang'st, a Taoist dress to don;
How sad, alas! of a reputed house and noble kindred the scion,
Alone, behold! she sleeps under a glimmering light, an old idol for mate.

Next in order came a hill of ice, on which stood a hen-phoenix, while under it was this motto:

When time ends, sure coincidence, the phoenix doth alight;
The talents of this human form all know and living see,
For first to yield she kens, then to control, and third genial to be;
But sad to say, things in Chin Ling are in more sorry plight.

This was succeeded by a representation of a desolate village, and a dreary inn. A pretty girl sat in there, spinning thread. These were the sentiments affixed below:

When riches will have flown will honours then avail?
When ruin breaks your home, e'en relatives will fail!
But sudden through the aid extended to Dame Liu,
A friend in need fortune will make to rise for you.

Following these verses, was drawn a pot of Orchids, by the side of which, was a beautiful maiden in a phoenix-crown and cloudy mantle (bridal dress); and to this picture was appended this device:

What time spring wanes, then fades the bloom of peach as well as plum!
Who ever can like a pot of the olea be winsome!
With ice thy purity will vie, vain their envy will be!
In vain a laughing-stock people will try to make of thee.

At the end of this poetical device, came the representation of a lofty edifice, on which was a beauteous girl, suspending herself on a beam to commit suicide; with this verse:

Love high as heav'n, love ocean-wide, thy lovely form will don;
What time love will encounter love, license must rise wanton;
Why hold that all impiety in Jung doth find its spring,
The source of trouble, verily, is centred most in Ning.

Pao-yü was still bent upon prosecuting his perusal, when the Fairy perceiving that his intellect was eminent and bright, and his natural talents quickwitted, and apprehending lest the decrees of heaven should be divulged, hastily closed the Book of Record, and addressed herself to Pao-yü. "Come along with me," she said smiling, "and see some wonderful scenery. What's the need of staying here and beating this gourd of ennui?"

In a dazed state, Pao-yü listlessly discarded the record, and again followed in the footsteps of the Fairy. On their arrival at the back, he saw carnation portières, and embroidered curtains, ornamented pillars, and carved eaves. But no words can adequately give an idea of the vermilion apartments glistening with splendour, of the floors garnished with gold, of the snow reflecting lustrous windows, of the palatial mansions made of gems. He also saw fairyland flowers, beautiful and fragrant, and extraordinary vegetation, full of perfume. The spot was indeed elysian.

He again heard the Fairy observe with a smiling face: "Come out all of you at once and greet the honoured guest!"

These words were scarcely completed, when he espied fairies walk out of the mansion, all of whom were, with their dangling lotus sleeves, and their fluttering feather habiliments, as comely as spring flowers, and as winsome as the autumn moon. As soon as they caught sight of Pao-yü, they all, with one voice, resentfully reproached the Monitory Vision Fairy. "Ignorant as to who the honoured guest could be," they argued, "we hastened to come out to offer our greetings simply because you, elder sister, had told us that, on this day, and at this very time, there would be sure to come on a visit, the spirit of the younger sister of Chiang Chu. That's the reason why we've been waiting for ever so long; and now why do you, in lieu of her, introduce this vile object to contaminate the confines of pure and spotless maidens?"

As soon as Pao-yü heard these remarks, he was forthwith plunged in such a state of consternation that he would have retired, but he found it impossible to do so. In fact, he felt the consciousness of the foulness and corruption of his own nature quite intolerable. The Monitory Vision Fairy promptly took Pao-yü's hand in her own, and turning towards her younger sisters, smiled and explained: "You, and all of you, are not aware of the why and wherefore. To-day I did mean to have gone to the Jung mansion to fetch Chiang Chu, but as I went by the Ning mansion, I unexpectedly came across the ghosts of the two dukes of Jung and Ning, who addressed me in this wise: 'Our family has, since the dynasty established itself on the Throne, enjoyed merit and fame, which pervaded many ages, and riches and honours transmitted from generation to generation. One hundred years have already elapsed, but this good fortune has now waned, and this propitious luck is exhausted; so much so that they could not be retrieved! Our sons and grandsons may be many, but there is no one among them who has the means to continue the family estate, with the exception of our kindred grandson, Pao-yü alone, who, though perverse in disposition and wayward by nature, is nevertheless intelligent and quick-witted and qualified in a measure to give effect to our hopes. But alas! the good fortune of our family is entirely decayed, so that we fear there is no person to incite him to enter the right way! Fortunately you worthy fairy come at an unexpected moment, and we venture to trust that you will, above all things, warn him against the foolish indulgence of inordinate desire, lascivious affections and other such things, in the hope that he may, at your instigation, be able to escape the snares of those girls who will allure him with their blandishments, and to enter on the right track; and we two brothers will be ever grateful.'

"On language such as this being addressed to me, my feelings of commiseration naturally burst forth; and I brought him here, and bade him, first of all, carefully peruse the records of the whole lives of the maidens in his family, belonging to the three grades, the upper, middle and lower, but as he has not yet fathomed the import, I have consequently led him into this place to experience the vision of drinking, eating, singing and licentious love, in the hope, there is no saying, of his at length attaining that perception."

Having concluded these remarks, she led Pao-yü by the hand into the apartment, where he felt a whiff of subtle fragrance, but what it was that reached his nostrils he could not tell.

To Pao-yü's eager and incessant inquiries, the Fairy made reply with a sardonic smile. "This perfume," she said, "is not to be found in the world, and how could you discern what it is? This is made of the essence of the first sprouts of rare herbs, growing on all hills of fame and places of superior excellence, admixed with the oil of every species of splendid shrubs in precious groves, and is called the marrow of Conglomerated Fragrance."

At these words Pao-yü was, of course, full of no other feeling than wonder.

The whole party advanced and took their seats, and a young maidservant presented tea, which Pao-yü found of pure aroma, of excellent flavour and of no ordinary kind. "What is the name of this tea?" he therefore asked; upon which the Fairy explained. "This tea," she added, "originates from the Hills of Emitted Spring and the Valley of Drooping Fragrance, and is, besides, brewed in the night dew, found on spiritual plants and divine leaves. The name of this tea is 'one thousand red in one hole.'"

At these words Pao-yü nodded his head, and extolled its qualities. Espying in the room lutes, with jasper mountings, and tripods, inlaid with gems, antique paintings, and new poetical works, which were to be seen everywhere, he felt more than ever in a high state of delight. Below the windows, were also shreds of velvet sputtered about and a toilet case stained with the traces of time and smudged with cosmetic; while on the partition wall was likewise suspended a pair of scrolls, with the inscription:

A lonesome, small, ethereal, beauteous nook!
What help is there, but Heaven's will to brook?

Pao-yü having completed his inspection felt full of admiration, and proceeded to ascertain the names and surnames of the Fairies. One was called the Fairy of Lustful Dreams; another "the High Ruler of Propagated Passion;" the name of one was "the Golden Maiden of Perpetuated Sorrow;" of another the "Intelligent Maiden of Transmitted Hatred." (In fact,) the respective Taoist appellations were not of one and the same kind.

In a short while, young maid-servants came in and laid the table, put the chairs in their places, and spread out wines and eatables. There were actually crystal tankards overflowing with luscious wines, and amber glasses full to the brim with pearly strong liquors. But still less need is there to give any further details about the sumptuousness of the refreshments.

Pao-yü found it difficult, on account of the unusual purity of the bouquet of the wine, to again restrain himself from making inquiries about it.

"This wine," observed the Monitory Dream Fairy, "is made of the twigs of hundreds of flowers, and the juice of ten thousands of trees, with the addition of must composed of unicorn marrow, and yeast prepared with phoenix milk. Hence the name of 'Ten thousand Beauties in one Cup' was given to it."

Pao-yü sang its incessant praise, and, while he sipped his wine, twelve dancing girls came forward, and requested to be told what songs they were to sing.

"Take," suggested the Fairy, "the newly-composed Twelve Sections of the Dream of the Red Chamber, and sing them."

The singing girls signified their obedience, and forthwith they lightly clapped the castagnettes and gently thrummed the virginals. These were the words which they were heard to sing:

> At the time of the opening of the heavens and the laying out of the earth chaos prevailed.

They had just sung this one line when the Fairy exclaimed: "This ballad is unlike the ballads written in the dusty world whose purport is to hand down remarkable events, in which the distinction of scholars, girls, old men and women, and fools is essential, and in which are furthermore introduced the lyrics of the Southern and Northern Palaces. These fairy songs consist either of elegaic effusions on some person or impressions of some occurrence or other, and are impromptu songs readily set to the music of wind or string instruments, so that any one who is not cognisant of their gist cannot appreciate the beauties contained in them. So you are not likely, I fear, to understand this lyric with any clearness; and unless you first peruse the text and then listen to the ballad, you will, instead of pleasure, feel as if you were chewing wax (devoid of any zest)."

After these remarks, she turned her head round, and directed a young maid-servant to fetch the text of the Dream of the Red Chamber, which she handed to Pao-yü, who took it over; and as he followed the words with his eyes, with his ears he listened to the strains of this song:

Preface of the Bream of the Red Chamber.—When the Heavens were opened and earth was laid out chaos prevailed! What was the germ of love? It arises entirely from the strength of licentious love.

What day, by the will of heaven, I felt wounded at heart, and what time I was at leisure, I made an attempt to disburden my sad heart; and with this object in view I indited this Dream of the Bed Chamber, on the subject of a disconsolate gold trinket and an unfortunate piece of jade.

Waste of a whole Lifetime. All maintain that the match between gold and jade will be happy. All I can think of is the solemn oath contracted in days gone by by the plant and stone! Vain will I gaze upon the snow, Hsüeh, [Pao-ch'ai], pure as crystal and lustrous like a gem of the eminent priest living among the hills! Never will I forget the noiseless Fairy Grove, Lin [Tai-yü], beyond the confines of the mortal world! Alas! now only have I come to believe that human happiness is incomplete; and that a couple may be bound by the ties of wedlock for life, but that after all their hearts are not easy to lull into contentment.

Vain knitting of the brows. The one is a spirit flower of Fairyland; the other is a beautiful jade without a blemish. Do you maintain that their union will not be remarkable? Why how then is it that he has come to meet her again in this existence? If the union will you say, be strange, how is it then that their love affair will be but empty words? The one in her loneliness will give way to useless sighs. The other in vain will yearn and crave. The one will be like the reflection of the moon in water; the other like a flower reflected in a mirror. Consider, how many drops of tears can there be in the eyes? and how could they continue to drop from autumn to winter and from spring to flow till summer time?

But to come to Pao-yü. After he had heard these ballads, so diffuse and vague, he failed to see any point of beauty in them; but the plaintive melody of the sound was nevertheless sufficient to drive away his spirit and exhilarate his soul. Hence it was that he did not make any inquiries about the arguments, and that he did not ask about the matter treated, but simply making these ballads the means for the time being of dispelling melancholy, he therefore went on with the perusal of what came below.

Despicable Spirit of Death! You will be rejoicing that glory is at its height when hateful death will come once again, and with eyes wide with horror, you will discard all things, and dimly and softly the fragrant spirit will waste and dissolve! You will yearn for native home, but distant will be the way, and lofty the mountains. Hence it is that you will betake yourself in search of father and mother, while they lie under the influence of a dream, and hold discourse with them. "Your child," you will say, "has already trodden the path of death! Oh my parents, it behoves you to speedily retrace your steps and make good your escape!"

Separated from Relatives. You will speed on a journey of three thousand li at the mercy of wind and rain, and tear yourself from all your family ties and your native home! Your fears will be lest anguish should do any harm to your parents in their failing years! "Father and mother," you will bid them, "do not think with any anxiety of your child. From ages past poverty as well as success have both had a fixed destiny; and is it likely that separation and reunion are not subject to predestination? Though we may now be far apart in two different places, we must each of us try and preserve good cheer. Your abject child has, it is true, gone from home, but abstain from distressing yourselves on her account!"

Sorrow in the midst of Joy. While wrapped as yet in swaddling clothes, father and mother, both alas! will depart, and dwell though you will in that mass of gauze, who is there who will know how to spoil you with any fond attention? Born you will be fortunately with ample moral courage, and high-minded and boundless resources, for your parents will not have, in the least, their child's secret feelings at heart! You will be like a moon appearing to view when the rain holds up, shedding its rays upon the Jade Hall; or a gentle breeze (wafting its breath upon it). Wedded to a husband, fairy like fair and accomplished, you will enjoy a happiness enduring as the earth and perennial as the Heavens! and you will be the means of snapping asunder the bitter fate of your youth! But, after all, the clouds will scatter in Kao T'ang and the waters of the Hsiang river will get parched! This is the inevitable destiny of dissolution and continuance which prevails in the mortal world, and what need is there to indulge in useless grief?

Intolerable to the world. Your figure will be as winsome as an olea fragrans; your talents as ample as those of a Fairy! You will by nature be so haughty that of the whole human race few will be like you! You will look upon a meat diet as one of dirt, and treat splendour as coarse and loathsome! And yet you will not be aware that your high notions will bring upon you the excessive hatred of man! You will be very eager in your desire after chastity, but the human race will despise you! Alas, you will wax old in that antique temple hall under a faint light, where you will waste ungrateful for beauty, looks and freshness! But after all you will still be worldly, corrupt and unmindful of your vows; just like a spotless white jade you will be whose fate is to fall into the mire! And what need will there be for the grandson of a prince or the son of a duke to deplore that his will not be the good fortune (of winning your affections)?

The Voluptuary. You will resemble a wolf in the mountains! a savage beast devoid of all human feeling! Regardless in every way of the obligations of days gone by, your sole pleasure will be in the indulgence of haughtiness, extravagance, licentiousness and dissolute habits! You will be inordinate in your conjugal affections, and look down upon the beautiful charms of the child of a marquis, as if they were cat-tail rush or willow; trampling upon the honourable daughter of a ducal mansion, as if she were one of the common herd. Pitiful to say, the fragrant spirit and beauteous ghost will in a year softly and gently pass away!

The Perception that all things are transient like flowers. You will look lightly upon the three springs and regard the blush of the peach and the green of the willow as of no avail. You will beat out the fire of splendour, and treat solitary retirement as genial! What is it that you say about the delicate peaches in the heavens (marriage) being excellent, and the petals of the almond in the clouds being plentiful (children)? Let him who has after all seen one of them, (really a mortal being) go safely through the autumn, (wade safely through old age), behold the people in the white Poplar village groan and sigh; and the spirits under the green maple whine and moan! Still more wide in expanse than even the heavens is the dead vegetation which covers the graves! The moral is this, that the burden of man is poverty one day and affluence another; that bloom in spring, and decay in autumn, constitute the doom of vegetable life! In the same way, this calamity of birth and the visitation of death, who is able to escape? But I have heard it said that there grows in the western quarter a tree called the P'o So (Patient Bearing) which bears the fruit of Immortal life!

The bane of Intelligence. Yours will be the power to estimate, in a thorough manner, the real motives of all things, as yours will be intelligence of an excessive degree; but instead (of reaping any benefit) you will cast the die of your own existence! The heart of your previous life is already reduced to atoms, and when you shall have died, your nature will have been intelligent to no purpose! Your home will be in easy circumstances; your family will enjoy comforts; but your connexions will, at length, fall a prey to death, and the inmates of your family scatter, each one of you speeding in a different direction, making room for others! In vain, you will have harassed your mind with cankering thoughts for half a lifetime; for it will be just as if you had gone through the confused mazes of a dream on the third watch! Sudden a crash (will be heard) like the fall of a spacious palace, and a dusky gloominess (will supervene) such as is caused by a lamp about to spend itself! Alas! a spell of happiness will be suddenly (dispelled by) adversity! Woe is man in the world! for his ultimate doom is difficult to determine!

Leave behind a residue of happiness! Hand down an excess of happiness; hand down an excess of happiness! Unexpectedly you will come across a benefactor! Fortunate enough your mother, your own mother, will have laid by a store of virtue and secret meritorious actions! My advice to you, mankind, is to relieve the destitute and succour the distressed! Do not resemble those who will harp after lucre and show themselves unmindful of the ties of relationship: that wolf-like maternal uncle of yours and that impostor of a brother! True it is that addition and subtraction, increase and decrease, (reward and punishment,) rest in the hands of Heaven above!

Splendour at last. Loving affection in a mirror will be still more ephemeral than fame in a dream. That fine splendour will fleet how soon! Make no further allusion to embroidered curtain, to bridal coverlet; for though you may come to wear on your head a pearl-laden coronet, and, on your person, a jacket ornamented with phoenixes, yours will not nevertheless be the means to atone for the short life (of your husband)! Though the saying is that mankind should not have, in their old age, the burden of poverty to bear, yet it is also essential that a store of benevolent deeds should be laid up for the benefit of sons and grandsons! (Your son) may come to be dignified in appearance and wear on his head the official tassel, and on his chest may be suspended the gold seal resplendent in lustre; he may be imposing in his majesty, and he may rise high in status and emoluments, but the dark and dreary way which leads to death is short! Are the generals and ministers who have been from ages of old still in the flesh, forsooth? They exist only in a futile name handed down to posterity to reverence!

Death ensues when things propitious reign! Upon the ornamented beam will settle at the close of spring the fragrant dust! Your reckless indulgence of licentious love and your naturally moonlike face will soon be the source of the ruin of a family. The decadence of the family estate will emanate entirely from Ching; while the wane of the family affairs will be entirely attributable to the fault of Ning! Licentious love will be the main reason of the long-standing grudge.

The flying birds each perch upon the trees! The family estates of those in official positions will fade! The gold and silver of the rich and honoured will be scattered! those who will have conferred benefit will, even in death, find the means of escape! those devoid of human feelings will reap manifest retribution! Those indebted for a life will make, in due time, payment with their lives; those indebted for tears have already (gone) to exhaust their tears! Mutual injuries will be revenged in no light manner! Separation and reunion will both alike be determined by predestination! You wish to know why your life will be short; look into your previous existence! Verily, riches and honours, which will come with old age, will likewise be a question of chance!

Those who will hold the world in light esteem will retire within the gate of abstraction; while those who will be allured by enticement will have forfeited their lives (The Chia family will fulfil its destiny) as surely as birds take to the trees after they have exhausted all they had to eat, and which as they drop down will pile up a hoary, vast and lofty heap of dust, (leaving) indeed a void behind!

When the maidens had finished the ballads, they went on to sing the "Supplementary Record;" but the Monitory Vision Fairy, perceiving the total absence of any interest in Pao-yü, heaved a sigh. "You silly brat!" she exclaimed. "What! haven't you, even now, attained perception!"

"There's no need for you to go on singing," speedily observed Pao-yü, as he interrupted the singing maidens; and feeling drowsy and dull, he pleaded being under the effects of wine, and begged to be allowed to lie down.

The Fairy then gave orders to clear away the remains of the feast, and escorted Pao-yü to a suite of female apartments, where the splendour of such objects as were laid out was a thing which he had not hitherto seen. But what evoked in him wonder still more intense, was the sight, at an early period, of a girl seated in the room, who, in the freshness of her beauty and winsomeness of her charms, bore some resemblance to Pao-ch'ai, while, in elegance and comeliness, on the other hand, to Tai-yu.

While he was plunged in a state of perplexity, the Fairy suddenly remarked: "All those female apartments and ladies' chambers in so many wealthy and honourable families in the world are, without exception, polluted by voluptuous opulent puppets and by all that bevy of profligate girls. But still more despicable are those from old till now numberless dissolute roués, one and all of whom maintain that libidinous affections do not constitute lewdness; and who try, further, to prove that licentious love is not tantamount to lewdness. But all these arguments are mere apologies for their shortcomings, and a screen for their pollutions; for if libidinous affection be lewdness, still more does the perception of licentious love constitute lewdness. Hence it is that the indulgence of sensuality and the gratification of licentious affection originate entirely from a relish of lust, as well as from a hankering after licentious love. Lo you, who are the object of my love, are the most lewd being under the heavens from remote ages to the present time!"

Pao-yü was quite dumbstruck by what he heard, and hastily smiling, he said by way of reply: "My Fairy labours under a misapprehension. Simply because of my reluctance to read my books my parents have, on repeated occasions, extended to me injunction and reprimand, and would I have the courage to go so far as to rashly plunge in lewd habits? Besides, I am still young in years, and have no notion what is implied by lewdness!"

"Not so!" exclaimed the Fairy; "lewdness, although one thing in principle is, as far as meaning goes, subject to different constructions; as is exemplified by those in the world whose heart is set upon lewdness. Some delight solely in faces and figures; others find insatiable pleasure in singing and dancing; some in dalliance and raillery; others in the incessant indulgence of their lusts; and these regret that all the beautiful maidens under the heavens cannot minister to their short-lived pleasure. These several kinds of persons are foul objects steeped skin and all in lewdness. The lustful love, for instance, which has sprung to life and taken root in your natural affections, I and such as myself extend to it the character of an abstract lewdness; but abstract lewdness can be grasped by the mind, but cannot be transmitted by the mouth; can be fathomed by the spirit, but cannot be divulged in words. As you now are imbued with this desire only in the abstract, you are certainly well fit to be a trustworthy friend in (Fairyland) inner apartments, but, on the path of the mortal world, you will inevitably be misconstrued and defamed; every mouth will ridicule you; every eye will look down upon you with contempt. After meeting recently your worthy ancestors, the two Dukes of Ning and Jung, who opened their hearts and made their wishes known to me with such fervour, (but I will not have you solely on account of the splendour of our inner apartments look down despisingly upon the path of the world), I consequently led you along, my son, and inebriated you with luscious wines, steeped you in spiritual tea, and admonished you with excellent songs, bringing also here a young sister of mine, whose infant name is Chien Mei, and her style K'o Ching, to be given to you as your wedded wife. To-night, the time will be propitious and suitable for the immediate consummation of the union, with the express object of letting you have a certain insight into the fact that if the condition of the abode of spirits within the confines of Fairyland be still so (imperfect), how much the more so should be the nature of the affections which prevail in the dusty world; with the intent that from this time forth you should positively break loose from bondage, perceive and amend your former disposition, devote your attention to the works of Confucius and Mencius, and set your steady purpose upon the principles of morality."

Having ended these remarks, she initiated him into the mysteries of licentious love, and, pushing Pao-yü into the room, she closed the door, and took her departure all alone. Pao-yü in a dazed state complied with the admonitions given him by the Fairy, and the natural result was, of course, a violent flirtation, the circumstances of which it would be impossible to recount.

When the next day came, he was by that time so attached to her by ties of tender love and their conversation was so gentle and full of charm that he could not brook to part from K'o Ching. Hand-in-hand, the two of them therefore, went out for a stroll, when they unexpectedly reached a place, where nothing else met their gaze than thorns and brambles, which covered the ground, and a wolf and a tiger walking side by side. Before them stretched the course of a black stream, which obstructed their progress; and over this stream there was, what is more, no bridge to enable one to cross it.

While they were exercising their minds with perplexity, they suddenly espied the Fairy coming from the back in pursuit of them. "Desist at once," she exclaimed, "from making any advance into the stream; it is urgent that you should, with all speed, turn your faces round!"

Pao-yü lost no time in standing still. "What is this place?" he inquired.

"This is the Ford of Enticement," explained the Fairy. "Its depth is ten thousand chang; its breadth is a thousand li; in its stream there are no boats or paddles by means of which to effect a passage. There is simply a raft, of which Mu Chu-shih directs the rudder, and which Hui Shih chen punts with the poles. They receive no compensation in the shape of gold or silver, but when they come across any one whose destiny it is to cross, they ferry him over. You now have by accident strolled as far as here, and had you fallen into the stream you would have rendered quite useless the advice and admonition which I previously gave you."

These words were scarcely concluded, when suddenly was heard from the midst of the Ford of Enticement, a sound like unto a peal of thunder, whereupon a whole crowd of gobblins and sea-urchins laid hands upon Pao-yü and dragged him down.

This so filled Pao-yü with consternation that he fell into a perspiration as profuse as rain, and he simultaneously broke forth and shouted, "Rescue me, K'o Ching!"

These cries so terrified Hsi Jen and the other waiting-maids, that they rushed forward, and taking Pao-yü in their arms, "Don't be afraid, Pao-yü," they said, "we are here."

But we must observe that Mrs. Ch'in was just inside the apartment in the act of recommending the young waiting-maids to be mindful that the cats and dogs did not start a fight, when she unawares heard Pao-yü, in his dream, call her by her infant name. In a melancholy mood she therefore communed within herself, "As far as my infant name goes, there is, in this establishment, no one who has any idea what it is, and how is it that he has come to know it, and that he utters it in his dream?" And she was at this period unable to fathom the reason. But, reader, listen to the explanations given in the chapter which follows.

CHAPTER VI.

Chia Pao-yü reaps his first experience in licentious love.
Old Goody Liu pays a visit to the Jung Kuo Mansion.

Mrs. Ch'in, to resume our narrative, upon hearing Pao-yü call her in his dream by her infant name, was at heart very exercised, but she did not however feel at liberty to make any minute inquiry.

Pao-yü was, at this time, in such a dazed state, as if he had lost something, and the servants promptly gave him a decoction of lungn-gan. After he had taken a few sips, he forthwith rose and tidied his clothes.

Hsi Jen put out her hand to fasten the band of his garment, and as soon as she did so, and it came in contact with his person, it felt so icy cold to the touch, covered as it was all over with perspiration, that she speedily withdrew her hand in utter surprise.

"What's the matter with you?" she exclaimed.

A blush suffused Pao-yü's face, and he took Hsi Jen's hand in a tight grip. Hsi Jen was a girl with all her wits about her; she was besides a couple of years older than Pao-yü and had recently come to know something of the world, so that at the sight of his state, she to a great extent readily accounted for the reason in her heart. From modest shame, she unconsciously became purple in the face, and not venturing to ask another question she continued adjusting his clothes. This task accomplished, she followed him over to old lady Chia's apartments; and after a hurry-scurry meal, they came back to this side, and Hsi Jen availed herself of the absence of the nurses and waiting-maids to hand Pao-yü another garment to change.

"Please, dear Hsi Jen, don't tell any one," entreated Pao-yü, with concealed shame.

"What did you dream of?" inquired Hsi Jen, smiling, as she tried to stifle her blushes, "and whence comes all this perspiration?"

"It's a long story," said Pao-yü, "which only a few words will not suffice to explain."

He accordingly recounted minutely, for her benefit, the subject of his dream. When he came to where the Fairy had explained to him the mysteries of love, Hsi Jen was overpowered with modesty and covered her face with her hands; and as she bent down, she gave way to a fit of laughter. Pao-yü had always been fond of Hsi Jen, on account of her gentleness, pretty looks and graceful and elegant manner, and he forthwith expounded to her all the mysteries he had been taught by the Fairy.

Hsi Jen was, of course, well aware that dowager lady Chia had given her over to Pao-yü, so that her present behaviour was likewise no transgression. And subsequently she secretly attempted with Pao-yü a violent flirtation, and lucky enough no one broke in upon them during their tête-à-tête. From this date, Pao-yü treated Hsi Jen with special regard, far more than he showed to the other girls, while Hsi Jen herself was still more demonstrative in her attentions to Pao-yü. But for a time we will make no further remark about them.

As regards the household of the Jung mansion, the inmates may, on adding up the total number, not have been found many; yet, counting the high as well as the low, there were three hundred persons and more. Their affairs may not have been very numerous, still there were, every day, ten and twenty matters to settle; in fact, the household resembled, in every way, ravelled hemp, devoid even of a clue-end, which could be used as an introduction.

Just as we were considering what matter and what person it would be best to begin writing of, by a lucky coincidence suddenly from a distance of a thousand li, a person small and insignificant as a grain of mustard seed happened, on account of her distant relationship with the Jung family, to come on this very day to the Jung mansion on a visit. We shall therefore readily commence by speaking of this family, as it after all affords an excellent clue for a beginning.

The surname of this mean and humble family was in point of fact Wang. They were natives of this district. Their ancestor had filled a minor office in the capital, and had, in years gone by, been acquainted with lady Feng's grandfather, that is madame Wang's father. Being covetous of the influence and affluence of the Wang family, he consequently joined ancestors with them, and was recognised by them as a nephew.

At that time, there were only madame Wang's eldest brother, that is lady Feng's father, and madame Wang herself, who knew anything of these distant relations, from the fact of having followed their parents to the capital. The rest of the family had one and all no idea about them.

This ancestor had, at this date, been dead long ago, leaving only one son called Wang Ch'eng. As the family estate was in a state of ruin, he once more moved outside the city walls and settled down in his native village. Wang Ch'eng also died soon after his father, leaving a son, known in his infancy as Kou Erh, who married a Miss Liu, by whom he had a son called by the infant name of Pan Erh, as well as a daughter, Ch'ing Erh. His family consisted of four, and he earned a living from farming.

As Kou Erh was always busy with something or other during the day and his wife, dame Liu, on the other hand, drew the water, pounded the rice and attended to all the other domestic concerns, the brother and sister, Ch'ing Erh and Pan Erh, the two of them, had no one to look after them. (Hence it was that) Kou Erh brought over his mother-in-law, old goody Liu, to live with them.

This goody Liu was an old widow, with a good deal of experience. She had besides no son round her knees, so that she was dependent for her maintenance on a couple of acres of poor land, with the result that when her son-in-law received her in his home, she naturally was ever willing to exert heart and mind to help her daughter and her son-in-law to earn their living.

This year, the autumn had come to an end, winter had commenced, and the weather had begun to be quite cold. No provision had been made in the household for the winter months, and Kou Erh was, inevitably, exceedingly exercised in his heart. Having had several cups of wine to dispel his distress, he sat at home and tried to seize upon every trifle to give vent to his displeasure. His wife had not the courage to force herself in his way, and hence goody Liu it was who encouraged him, as she could not bear to see the state of the domestic affairs.

"Don't pull me up for talking too much," she said; "but who of us country people isn't honest and open-hearted? As the size of the bowl we hold, so is the quantity of the rice we eat. In your young days, you were dependent on the support of your old father, so that eating and drinking became quite a habit with you; that's how, at the present time, your resources are quite uncertain; when you had money, you looked ahead, and didn't mind behind; and now that you have no money, you blindly fly into huffs. A fine fellow and a capital hero you have made! Living though we now be away from the capital, we are after all at the feet of the Emperor; this city of Ch'ang Ngan is strewn all over with money, but the pity is that there's no one able to go and fetch it away; and it's no use your staying at home and kicking your feet about."

"All you old lady know," rejoined Kou Erh, after he had heard what she had to say, "is to sit on the couch and talk trash! Is it likely you would have me go and play the robber?"

"Who tells you to become a robber?" asked goody Liu. "But it would be well, after all, that we should put our heads together and devise some means; for otherwise, is the money, pray, able of itself to run into our house?"

"Had there been a way," observed Kou Erh, smiling sarcastically, "would I have waited up to this moment? I have besides no revenue collectors as relatives, or friends in official positions; and what way could we devise? 'But even had I any, they wouldn't be likely, I fear, to pay any heed to such as ourselves!"

"That, too, doesn't follow," remarked goody Liu; "the planning of affairs rests with man, but the accomplishment of them rests with Heaven. After we have laid our plans, we may, who can say, by relying on the sustenance of the gods, find some favourable occasion. Leave it to me, I'll try and devise some lucky chance for you people! In years gone by, you joined ancestors with the Wang family of Chin Ling, and twenty years back, they treated you with consideration; but of late, you've been so high and mighty, and not condescended to go and bow to them, that an estrangement has arisen. I remember how in years gone by, I and my daughter paid them a visit. The second daughter of the family was really so pleasant and knew so well how to treat people with kindness, and without in fact any high airs! She's at present the wife of Mr. Chia, the second son of the Jung Kuo mansion; and I hear people say that now that she's advanced in years, she's still more considerate to the poor, regardful of the old, and very fond of preparing vegetable food for the bonzes and performing charitable deeds. The head of the Wang mansion has, it is true, been raised to some office on the frontier, but I hope that this lady Secunda will anyhow notice us. How is it then that you don't find your way as far as there; for she may possibly remember old times, and some good may, no one can say, come of it? I only wish that she would display some of her kind-heartedness, and pluck one hair from her person which would be, yea thicker than our waist."

"What you suggest, mother, is quite correct," interposed Mrs. Liu, Kou Erh's wife, who stood by and took up the conversation, "but with such mouth and phiz as yours and mine, how could we present ourselves before her door? Why I fear that the man at her gate won't also like to go and announce us! and we'd better not go and have our mouths slapped in public!"

Kou Erh, who would have thought it, prized highly both affluence and fame, so that when he heard these remarks, he forthwith began to feel at heart a little more at ease. When he furthermore heard what his wife had to say, he at once caught up the word as he smiled.

"Old mother," he rejoined; "since that be your idea, and what's more, you have in days gone by seen this lady on one occasion, why shouldn't you, old lady, start to-morrow on a visit to her and first ascertain how the wind blows!"

"Ai Ya!" exclaimed old Goody, "It may very well be said that the marquis' door is like the wide ocean! what sort of thing am I? why the servants of that family wouldn't even recognise me! even were I to go, it would be on a wild goose chase."

"No matter about that," observed Kou Erh; "I'll tell you a good way; you just take along with you, your grandson, little Pan Erh, and go first and call upon Chou Jui, who is attached to that household; and when once you've seen him, there will be some little chance. This Chou Jui, at one time, was connected with my father in some affair or other, and we were on excellent terms with him."

"That I too know," replied goody Liu, "but the thing is that you've had no dealings with him for so long, that who knows how he's disposed towards us now? this would be hard to say. Besides, you're a man, and with a mouth and phiz like that of yours, you couldn't, on any account, go on this errand. My daughter is a young woman, and she too couldn't very well go and expose herself to public gaze. But by my sacrificing this old face of mine, and by going and knocking it (against the wall) there may, after all, be some benefit and all of us might reap profit."

That very same evening, they laid their plans, and the next morning before the break of day, old goody Liu speedily got up, and having performed her toilette, she gave a few useful hints to Pan Erh; who, being a child of five or six years of age, was, when he heard that he was to be taken into the city, at once so delighted that there was nothing that he would not agree to.

Without further delay, goody Liu led off Pan Erh, and entered the city, and reaching the Ning Jung street, she came to the main entrance of the Jung mansion, where, next to the marble lions, were to be seen a crowd of chairs and horses. Goody Liu could not however muster the courage to go by, but having shaken her clothes, and said a few more seasonable words to Pan Erh, she subsequently squatted in front of the side gate, whence she could see a number of servants, swelling out their chests, pushing out their stomachs, gesticulating with their hands and kicking their feet about, while they were seated at the main entrance chattering about one thing and another.

Goody Liu felt constrained to edge herself forward. "Gentlemen," she ventured, "may happiness betide you!"

The whole company of servants scrutinised her for a time. "Where do you come from?" they at length inquired.

"I've come to look up Mr. Chou, an attendant of my lady's," remarked goody Liu, as she forced a smile; "which of you, gentlemen, shall I trouble to do me the favour of asking him to come out?"

The servants, after hearing what she had to say, paid, the whole number of them, no heed to her; and it was after the lapse of a considerable time that they suggested: "Go and wait at a distance, at the foot of that wall; and in a short while, the visitors, who are in their house, will be coming out."

Among the party of attendants was an old man, who interposed,

"Don't baffle her object," he expostulated; "why make a fool of her?" and turning to goody Liu: "This Mr. Chou," he said, "is gone south: his house is at the back row; his wife is anyhow at home; so go round this way, until you reach the door, at the back street, where, if you will ask about her, you will be on the right track."

Goody Liu, having expressed her thanks, forthwith went, leading Pan Erh by the hand, round to the back door, where she saw several pedlars resting their burdens. There were also those who sold things to eat, and those who sold playthings and toys; and besides these, twenty or thirty boys bawled and shouted, making quite a noise.

Goody Liu readily caught hold of one of them. "I'd like to ask you just a word, my young friend," she observed; "there's a Mrs. Chou here; is she at home?"

"Which Mrs. Chou?" inquired the boy; "we here have three Mrs. Chous; and there are also two young married ladies of the name of Chou. What are the duties of the one you want, I wonder ?"

"She's a waiting-woman of my lady," replied goody Liu.

"It's easy to get at her," added the boy; "just come along with me."

Leading the way for goody Liu into the backyard, they reached the wall of a court, when he pointed and said, "This is her house.—Mother Chou!" he went on to shout with alacrity; "there's an old lady who wants to see you."

Chou Jui's wife was at home, and with all haste she came out to greet her visitor. "Who is it?" she asked.

Goody Liu advanced up to her. "How are you," she inquired, "Mrs. Chou?"

Mrs. Chou looked at her for some time before she at length smiled and replied, "Old goody Liu, are you well? How many years is it since we've seen each other; tell me, for I forget just now; but please come in and sit."

"You're a lady of rank," answered goody Liu smiling, as she walked along, "and do forget many things. How could you remember such as ourselves?"

With these words still in her mouth, they had entered the house, whereupon Mrs. Chou ordered a hired waiting-maid to pour the tea. While they were having their tea she remarked, "How Pan Erh has managed to grow!" and then went on to make inquiries on the subject of various matters, which had occurred after their separation.

"To-day," she also asked of goody Liu, "were you simply passing by? or did you come with any express object?"

"I've come, the fact is, with an object!" promptly replied goody Liu; "(first of all) to see you, my dear sister-in-law; and, in the second place also, to inquire after my lady's health. If you could introduce me to see her for a while, it would be better; but if you can't, I must readily borrow your good offices, my sister-in-law, to convey my message."

Mr. Chou Jui's wife, after listening to these words, at once became to a great extent aware of the object of her visit. Her husband had, however, in years gone by in his attempt to purchase some land, obtained considerably the support of Kou Erh, so that when she, on this occasion, saw goody Liu in such a dilemma, she could not make up her mind to refuse her wish. Being in the second place keen upon making a display of her own respectability, she therefore said smilingly:

"Old goody Liu, pray compose your mind! You've come from far off with a pure heart and honest purpose, and how can I ever not show you the way how to see this living Buddha? Properly speaking, when people come and guests arrive, and verbal messages have to be given, these matters are not any of my business, as we all here have each one kind of duties to carry out. My husband has the special charge of the rents of land coming in, during the two seasons of spring and autumn, and when at leisure, he takes the young gentlemen out of doors, and then his business is done. As for myself, I have to accompany my lady and young married ladies on anything connected with out-of-doors; but as you are a relative of my lady and have besides treated me as a high person and come to me for help, I'll, after all, break this custom and deliver your message. There's only one thing, however, and which you, old lady, don't know. We here are not what we were five years before. My lady now doesn't much worry herself about anything; and it's entirely lady Secunda who looks after the menage. But who do you presume is this lady Secunda? She's the niece of my lady, and the daughter of my master, the eldest maternal uncle of by-gone days. Her infant name was Feng Ko."

"Is it really she?" inquired promptly goody Liu, after this explanation. "Isn't it strange? what I said about her years back has come out quite correct; but from all you say, shall I to-day be able to see her?"

"That goes without saying," replied Chou Jui's wife; "when any visitors come now-a-days, it's always lady Feng who does the honours and entertains them, and it's better to-day that you should see her for a while, for then you will not have walked all this way to no purpose."

"O mi to fu!" exclaimed old goody Liu; "I leave it entirely to your convenience, sister-in-law."

"What's that you're saying?" observed Chou Jui's wife. "The proverb says: 'Our convenience is the convenience of others.' All I have to do is to just utter one word, and what trouble will that be to me."

Saying this, she bade the young waiting maid go to the side pavilion, and quietly ascertain whether, in her old ladyship's apartment, table had been laid.

The young waiting-maid went on this errand, and during this while, the two of them continued a conversation on certain irrelevant matters.

"This lady Feng," observed goody Liu, "can this year be no older than twenty, and yet so talented as to manage such a household as this! the like of her is not easy to find!"

"Hai! my dear old goody," said Chou Jui's wife, after listening to her, "it's not easy to explain; but this lady Feng, though young in years, is nevertheless, in the management of affairs, superior to any man. She has now excelled the others and developed the very features of a beautiful young woman. To say the least, she has ten thousand eyes in her heart, and were they willing to wager their mouths, why ten men gifted with eloquence couldn't even outdo her! But by and bye, when you've seen her, you'll know all about her! There's only this thing, she can't help being rather too severe in her treatment of those below her."

While yet she spake, the young waiting-maid returned. "In her venerable lady's apartment," she reported, "repast has been spread, and already finished; lady Secunda is in madame Wang's chamber."

As soon as Chou Jui's wife heard this news, she speedily got up and pressed goody Liu to be off at once. "This is," she urged, "just the hour for her meal, and as she is free we had better first go and wait for her; for were we to be even one step too late, a crowd of servants will come with their reports, and it will then be difficult to speak to her; and after her siesta, she'll have still less time to herself."

As she passed these remarks, they all descended the couch together. Goody Liu adjusted their dresses, and, having impressed a few more words of advice on Pan Erh, they followed Chou Jui's wife through winding passages to Chia Lien's house. They came in the first instance into the side pavilion, where Chou Jui's wife placed old goody Liu to wait a little, while she herself went ahead, past the screen-wall and into the entrance of the court.

Hearing that lady Feng had not come out, she went in search of an elderly waiting-maid of lady Feng, P'ing Erh by name, who enjoyed her confidence, to whom Chou Jui's wife first recounted from beginning to end the history of old goody Liu.

"She has come to-day," she went on to explain, "from a distance to pay her obeisance. In days gone by, our lady used often to meet her, so that, on this occasion, she can't but receive her; and this is why I've brought her in! I'll wait here for lady Feng to come down, and explain everything to her; and I trust she'll not call me to task for officious rudeness."

P'ing Erh, after hearing what she had to say, speedily devised the plan of asking them to walk in, and to sit there pending (lady Feng's arrival), when all would be right.

Chou Jui's wife thereupon went out and led them in. When they ascended the steps of the main apartment, a young waiting-maid raised a red woollen portière, and as soon as they entered the hall, they smelt a whiff of perfume as it came wafted into their faces: what the scent was they could not discriminate; but their persons felt as if they were among the clouds.

The articles of furniture and ornaments in the whole room were all so brilliant to the sight, and so vying in splendour that they made the head to swim and the eyes to blink, and old goody Liu did nothing else the while than nod her head, smack her lips and invoke Buddha.

Forthwith she was led to the eastern side into the suite of apartments, where was the bedroom of Chia Lien's eldest daughter. P'ing Erh, who was standing by the edge of the stove-couch, cast a couple of glances at old goody Liu, and felt constrained to inquire how she was, and to press her to have a seat.

Goody Liu, noticing that P'ing Erh was entirely robed in silks, that she had gold pins fixed in her hair, and silver ornaments in her coiffure, and that her countenance resembled a flower or the moon (in beauty), readily imagined her to be lady Feng, and was about to address her as my lady; but when she heard Mrs. Chou speak to her as Miss P'ing, and P'ing Erh promptly address Chou Jui's wife as Mrs. Chou, she eventually became aware that she could be no more than a waiting-maid of a certain respectability.

She at once pressed old goody Liu and Pan Erh to take a seat on the stove-couch. P'ing Erh and Chou Jui's wife sat face to face, on the edges of the couch. The waiting-maids brought the tea. After they had partaken of it, old goody Liu could hear nothing but a "lo tang, lo tang" noise, resembling very much the sound of a bolting frame winnowing flour, and she could not resist looking now to the East, and now to the West. Suddenly in the great Hall, she espied, suspended on a pillar, a box at the bottom of which hung something like the weight of a balance, which incessantly wagged to and fro.

"What can this thing be?" communed goody Liu in her heart, "What can be its use?" While she was aghast, she unexpectedly heard a sound of "tang" like the sound of a golden bell or copper cymbal, which gave her quite a start. In a twinkle of the eyes followed eight or nine consecutive strokes; and she was bent upon inquiring what it was, when she caught sight of several waiting-maids enter in a confused crowd. "Our lady has come down!" they announced.

P'ìng Erh, together with Chou Jui's wife, rose with all haste. "Old goody Liu," they urged, "do sit down and wait till it's time, when we'll come and ask you in."

Saying this, they went out to meet lady Feng.

Old goody Liu, with suppressed voice and ear intent, waited in perfect silence. She heard at a distance the voices of some people laughing, whereupon about ten or twenty women, with rustling clothes and petticoats, made their entrance, one by one, into the hall, and thence into the room on the other quarter. She also detected two or three women, with red-lacquered boxes in their hands, come over on this part and remain in waiting.

"Get the repast ready!" she heard some one from the offside say.

The servants gradually dispersed and went out; and there only remained in attendance a few of them to bring in the courses. For a long time, not so much as the caw of a crow could be heard, when she unexpectedly perceived two servants carry in a couch-table, and lay it on this side of the divan. Upon this table were placed bowls and plates, in proper order replete, as usual, with fish and meats; but of these only a few kinds were slightly touched.

As soon as Pan Erh perceived (all these delicacies), he set up such a noise, and would have some meat to eat, but goody Liu administered to him such a slap, that he had to keep away.

Suddenly, she saw Mrs. Chou approach, full of smiles, and as she waved her hand, she called her. Goody Liu understood her meaning, and at once pulling Pan Erh off the couch, she proceeded to the centre of the Hall; and after Mrs. Chou had whispered to her again for a while, they came at length with slow step into the room on this side, where they saw on the outside of the door, suspended by brass hooks, a deep red flowered soft portière. Below the window, on the southern side, was a stove-couch, and on this couch was spread a crimson carpet. Leaning against the wooden partition wall, on the east side, stood a chain-embroidered back-cushion and a reclining pillow. There was also spread a large watered satin sitting cushion with a gold embroidered centre, and on the side stood cuspidores made of silver.

Lady Feng, when at home, usually wore on her head a front-piece of dark martin à la Chao Chün, surrounded with tassels of strung pearls. She had on a robe of peach-red flowered satin, a short pelisse of slate-blue stiff silk, lined with squirrel, and a jupe of deep red foreign crepe, lined with ermine. Resplendent with pearl-powder and with cosmetics, she sat in there, stately and majestic, with a small brass poker in her hands, with which she was stirring the ashes of the hand-stove. P'ing Erh stood by the side of the couch, holding a very small lacquered tea-tray. In this tray was a small tea-cup with a cover. Lady Feng neither took any tea, nor did she raise her head, but was intent upon stirring the ashes of the hand-stove.

"How is it you haven't yet asked her to come in?" she slowly inquired; and as she spake, she turned herself round and was about to ask for some tea, when she perceived that Mrs. Chou had already introduced the two persons and that they were standing in front of her.

She forthwith pretended to rise, but did not actually get up, and with a face radiant with smiles, she ascertained about their health, after which she went in to chide Chou Jui's wife. "Why didn't you tell me they had come before?" she said.

Old goody Liu was already by this time prostrated on the ground, and after making several obeisances, "How are you, my lady?" she inquired.

"Dear Mrs. Chou," lady Feng immediately observed, "do pull her up, and don't let her prostrate herself! I'm yet young in years and don't know her much; what's more, I've no idea what's the degree of the relationship between us, and I daren't speak directly to her."

"This is the old lady about whom I spoke a short while back," speedily explained Mrs. Chou.

Lady Feng nodded her head assentingly.

By this time old goody Liu had taken a seat on the edge of the stove-couch. As for Pan Erh, he had gone further, and taken refuge behind her back; and though she tried, by every means, to coax him to come forward and make a bow, he would not, for the life of him, consent.

"Relatives though we be," remarked lady Feng, as she smiled, "we haven't seen much of each other, so that our relations have been quite distant. But those who know how matters stand will assert that you all despise us, and won't often come to look us up; while those mean people, who don't know the truth, will imagine that we have no eyes to look at any one."

Old goody Liu promptly invoked Buddha. "We are at home in great straits," she pleaded, "and that's why it wasn't easy for us to manage to get away and come! Even supposing we had come as far as this, had we not given your ladyship a slap on the mouth, those gentlemen would also, in point of fact, have looked down upon us as a mean lot."

"Why, language such as this," exclaimed lady Feng smilingly, "cannot help making one's heart full of displeasure! We simply rely upon the reputation of our grandfather to maintain the status of a penniless official; that's all! Why, in whose household is there anything substantial? we are merely the denuded skeleton of what we were in days of old, and no more! As the proverb has it: The Emperor himself has three families of poverty-stricken relatives; and how much more such as you and I?"

Having passed these remarks, she inquired of Mrs. Chou, "Have you let madame know, yes or no?"

"We are now waiting," replied Mrs. Chou, "for my lady's orders."

"Go and have a look," said lady Feng; "but, should there be any one there, or should she be busy, then don't make any mention; but wait until she's free, when you can tell her about it and see what she says."

Chou Jui's wife, having expressed her compliance, went off on this errand. During her absence, lady Feng gave orders to some servants to take a few fruits and hand them to Pan Erh to eat; and she was inquiring about one thing and another, when there came a large number of married women, who had the direction of affairs in the household, to make their several reports.

P'ing Erh announced their arrival to lady Feng, who said: "I'm now engaged in entertaining some guests, so let them come back again in the evening; but should there be anything pressing then bring it in and I'll settle it at once."

P'ing Erh left the room, but she returned in a short while. "I've asked them," she observed, "but as there's nothing of any urgency, I told them to disperse." Lady Feng nodded her head in token of approval, when she perceived Chou Jui's wife come back. "Our lady," she reported, as she addressed lady Feng, "says that she has no leisure to-day, that if you, lady Secunda, will entertain them, it will come to the same thing; that she's much obliged for their kind attention in going to the trouble of coming; that if they have come simply on a stroll, then well and good, but that if they have aught to say, they should tell you, lady Secunda, which will be tantamount to their telling her."

"I've nothing to say," interposed old goody Liu. "I simply come to see our elder and our younger lady, which is a duty on my part, a relative as I am."

"Well, if there's nothing particular that you've got to say, all right," Mrs. Chou forthwith added, "but if you do have anything, don't hesitate telling lady Secunda, and it will be just as if you had told our lady."

As she uttered these words, she winked at goody Liu. Goody Liu understood what she meant, but before she could give vent to a word, her face got scarlet, and though she would have liked not to make any mention of the object of her visit, she felt constrained to suppress her shame and to speak out.

"Properly speaking," she observed, "this being the first time I see you, my lady, I shouldn't mention what I've to say, but as I come here from far off to seek your assistance, my old friend, I have no help but to mention it."

She had barely spoken as much as this, when she heard the youths at the inner-door cry out: "The young gentleman from the Eastern Mansion has come."

Lady Feng promptly interrupted her. "Old goody Liu," she remarked, "you needn't add anything more." She, at the same time, inquired, "Where's your master, Mr. Jung?" when became audible the sound of footsteps along the way, and in walked a young man of seventeen or eighteen. His appearance was handsome, his person slender and graceful. He had on light furs, a girdle of value, costly clothes and a beautiful cap.

At this stage, goody Liu did not know whether it was best to sit down or to stand up, neither could she find anywhere to hide herself.

"Pray sit down," urged lady Feng, with a laugh; "this is my nephew!' Old goody Liu then wriggled herself, now one way, and then another, on to the edge of the couch, where she took a seat.

"My father," Chia Jung smilingly ventured, "has sent me to ask a favour of you, aunt. On some previous occasion, our grand aunt gave you, dear aunt, a stove-couch glass screen, and as to-morrow father has invited some guests of high standing, he wishes to borrow it to lay it out for a little show; after which he purposes sending it back again."

"You're late by a day," replied lady Feng. "It was only yesterday that I gave it to some one."

Chia Jung, upon hearing this, forthwith, with giggles and smiles, made, near the edge of the couch, a sort of genuflexion. "Aunt," he went on, "if you don't lend it, father will again say that I don't know how to speak, and I shall get another sound thrashing. You must have pity upon your nephew, aunt."

"I've never seen anything like this," observed lady Feng sneeringly; "the things belonging to the Wang family are all good, but where have you put all those things of yours? the only good way is that you shouldn't see anything of ours, for as soon as you catch sight of anything, you at once entertain a wish to carry it off."

"Pray, aunt," entreated Chia Jung with a smile, "do show me some compassion."

"Mind your skin!" lady Feng warned him, "if you do chip or spoil it in the least."

She then bade P'ing Erh take the keys of the door of the upstairs room and send for several trustworthy persons to carry it away.

Chia Jung was so elated that his eyebrows dilated and his eyes smiled. "I've brought myself," he added, with vehemence, "some men to take it away; I won't let them recklessly bump it about."

Saying this, he speedily got up and left the room.

Lady Feng suddenly bethought herself of something, and turning towards the window, she called out, "Jung Erh, come back." Several servants who stood outside caught up her words: "Mr. Jung," they cried, "you're requested to go back;" whereupon Chia Jung turned round and retraced his steps; and with hands drooping respectfully against his sides, he stood ready to listen to his aunt's wishes.

Lady Feng was however intent upon gently sipping her tea, and after a good long while of abstraction, she at last smiled: "Never mind," she remarked; "you can go. But come after you've had your evening meal, and I'll then tell you about it. Just now there are visitors here; and besides, I don't feel in the humour."

Chia Jung thereupon retired with gentle step.

Old goody Liu, by this time, felt more composed in body and heart. "I've to-day brought your nephew," she then explained, "not for anything else, but because his father and mother haven't at home so much as anything to eat; the weather besides is already cold, so that I had no help but to take your nephew along and come to you, old friend, for assistance!"

As she uttered these words, she again pushed Pan Erh forward. "What did your father at home tell you to say?" she asked of him; "and what did he send us over here to do? Was it only to give our minds to eating fruit?"

Lady Feng had long ago understood what she meant to convey, and finding that she had no idea how to express herself in a decent manner, she readily interrupted her with a smile. "You needn't mention anything," she observed, "I'm well aware of how things stand;" and addressing herself to Mrs. Chou, she inquired, "Has this old lady had breakfast, yes or no?"

Old goody Liu hurried to explain. "As soon as it was daylight," she proceeded, "we started with all speed on our way here, and had we even so much as time to have any breakfast?"

Lady Feng promptly gave orders to send for something to eat. In a short while Chou Jui's wife had called for a table of viands for the guests, which was laid in the room on the eastern side, and then came to take goody Liu and Pan Erh over to have their repast.

"My dear Mrs. Chou," enjoined lady Feng, "give them all they want, as I can't attend to them myself;" which said, they hastily passed over into the room on the eastern side.

Lady Feng having again called Mrs. Chou, asked her: "When you first informed madame about them, what did she say?" "Our Lady observed," replied Chou Jui's wife, "that they don't really belong to the same family; that, in former years, their grandfather was an official at the same place as our old master; that hence it came that they joined ancestors; that these few years there hasn't been much intercourse (between their family and ours); that some years back, whenever they came on a visit, they were never permitted to go empty-handed, and that as their coming on this occasion to see us is also a kind attention on their part, they shouldn't be slighted. If they've anything to say," (our lady continued), "tell lady Secunda to do the necessary, and that will be right."

"Isn't it strange!" exclaimed lady Feng, as soon as she had heard the message; "since we are all one family, how is it I'm not familiar even with so much as their shadow?"

While she was uttering these words, old goody Liu had had her repast and come over, dragging Pan Erh; and, licking her lips and smacking her mouth, she expressed her thanks.

Lady Feng smiled. "Do pray sit down," she said, "and listen to what I'm going to tell you. What you, old lady, meant a little while back to convey, I'm already as much as yourself well acquainted with! Relatives, as we are, we shouldn't in fact have waited until you came to the threshold of our doors, but ought, as is but right, to have attended to your needs. But the thing is that, of late, the household affairs are exceedingly numerous, and our lady, advanced in years as she is, couldn't at a moment, it may possibly be, bethink herself of you all! What's more, when I took over charge of the management of the menage, I myself didn't know of all these family connections! Besides, though to look at us from outside everything has a grand and splendid aspect, people aren't aware that large establishments have such great hardships, which, were we to recount to others, they would hardly like to credit as true. But since you've now come from a great distance, and this is the first occasion that you open your mouth to address me, how can I very well allow you to return to your home with empty hands! By a lucky coincidence our lady gave, yesterday, to the waiting-maids, twenty taels to make clothes with, a sum which they haven't as yet touched, and if you don't despise it as too little, you may take it home as a first instalment, and employ it for your wants."

When old goody Liu heard the mention made by lady Feng of their hardships, she imagined that there was no hope; but upon hearing her again speak of giving her twenty taels, she was exceedingly delighted, so much so that her eyebrows dilated and her eyes gleamed with smiles.

"We too know," she smilingly remarked, "all about difficulties! but the proverb says, 'A camel dying of leanness is even bigger by much than a horse!' No matter what those distresses may be, were you yet to pluck one single hair from your body, my old friend, it would be stouter than our own waist."

Chou Jui's wife stood by, and on hearing her make these coarse utterances, she did all she could to give her a hint by winking, and make her desist. Lady Feng laughed and paid no heed; but calling P'ing Erh, she bade her fetch the parcel of money, which had been given to them the previous day, and to also bring a string of cash; and when these had been placed before goody Liu's eyes: "This is," said lady Feng, "silver to the amount of twenty taels, which was for the time given to these young girls to make winter clothes with; but some other day, when you've nothing to do, come again on a stroll, in evidence of the good feeling which should exist between relatives. It's besides already late, and I don't wish to detain you longer and all for no purpose; but, on your return home, present my compliments to all those of yours to whom I should send them."

As she spake, she stood up. Old goody Liu gave utterance to a thousand and ten thousand expressions of gratitude, and taking the silver and cash, she followed Chou Jui's wife on her way to the outhouses. "Well, mother dear," inquired Mrs. Chou, "what did you think of my lady that you couldn't speak; and that whenever you opened your mouth it was all 'your nephew.' I'll make just one remark, and I don't mind if you do get angry. Had he even been your kindred nephew, you should in fact have been somewhat milder in your language; for that gentleman, Mr. Jung, is her kith and kin nephew, and whence has appeared such another nephew of hers (as Pan Erh)?"

Old goody Liu smiled. "My dear sister-in-law," she replied, "as I gazed upon her, were my heart and eyes, pray, full of admiration or not? and how then could I speak as I should?"

As they were chatting, they reached Chou Jui's house. They had been sitting for a while, when old goody Liu produced a piece of silver, which she was purposing to leave behind, to be given to the young servants in Chou Jui's house to purchase fruit to eat; but how could Mrs. Chou satiate her eye with such a small piece of silver? She was determined in her refusal to accept it, so that old goody Liu, after assuring her of her boundless gratitude, took her departure out of the back gate she had come in from.

Reader, you do not know what happened after old goody Liu left, but listen to the explanation which will be given in the next chapter.

CHAPTER VII.

Presentation of artificial flowers made in the Palace.
Chia Lien disports himself with Hsi-feng.
Pao-yü meets Ch'in Chung at a family party.

To resume our narrative. Chou Jui's wife having seen old goody Liu off, speedily came to report the visit to madame Wang; but, contrary to her expectation, she did not find madame Wang in the drawing-room; and it was after inquiring of the waiting-maids that she eventually learnt that she had just gone over to have a chat with "aunt" Hsüeh. Mrs. Chou, upon hearing this, hastily went out by the eastern corner door, and through the yard on the east, into the Pear Fragrance Court.

As soon as she reached the entrance, she caught sight of madame Wang's waiting-maid, Chin Ch'uan-erh, playing about on the terrace steps, with a young girl, who had just let her hair grow. When they saw Chou Jui's wife approach, they forthwith surmised that she must have some message to deliver, so they pursed up their lips and directed her to the inner-room. Chou Jui's wife gently raised the curtain-screen, and upon entering discovered madame Wang, in voluble conversation with "aunt" Hsüeh, about family questions and people in general.

Mrs. Chou did not venture to disturb them, and accordingly came into the inner room, where she found Hsüeh Pao-ch'ai in a house dress, with her hair simply twisted into a knot round the top of the head, sitting on the inner edge of the stove-couch, leaning on a small divan table, in the act of copying a pattern for embroidery, with the waiting-maid Ying Erh. When she saw her enter, Pao Ch'ai hastily put down her pencil, and turning round with a face beaming with smiles, "Sister Chou," she said, "take a seat."

Chou Jui's wife likewise promptly returned the smile.

"How is my young lady?" she inquired, as she sat down on the edge of the couch. "I haven't seen you come over on the other side for two or three days! Has Mr. Pao-yü perhaps given you offence?"

"What an idea!" exclaimed Pao Ch'ai, with a smile. "It's simply that I've had for the last couple of days my old complaint again, and that I've in consequence kept quiet all this time, and looked after myself."

"Is that it?" asked Chou Jui's wife; "but after all, what rooted kind of complaint are you subject to, miss? you should lose really no time in sending for a doctor to diagnose it, and give you something to make you all right. With your tender years, to have an organic ailment is indeed no trifle!"

Pao Ch'ai laughed when she heard these remarks.

"Pray," she said, "don't allude to this again; for this ailment of mine I've seen, I can't tell you, how many doctors; taken no end of medicine and spent I don't know how much money; but the more we did so, not the least little bit of relief did I see. Lucky enough, we eventually came across a bald-pated bonze, whose speciality was the cure of nameless illnesses. We therefore sent for him to see me, and he said that I had brought this along with me from the womb as a sort of inflammatory virus, that luckily I had a constitution strong and hale so that it didn't matter; and that it would be of no avail if I took pills or any medicines. He then told me a prescription from abroad, and gave me also a packet of a certain powder as a preparative, with a peculiar smell and strange flavour. He advised me, whenever my complaint broke out, to take a pill, which would be sure to put me right again. And this has, after all, strange to say, done me a great deal of good."

"What kind of prescription is this one from abroad, I wonder," remarked Mrs. Chou; "if you, miss, would only tell me, it would be worth our while bearing it in mind, and recommending it to others: and if ever we came across any one afflicted with this disease, we would also be doing a charitable deed."

"You'd better not ask for the prescription," rejoined Pao Ch'ai smiling. "Why, its enough to wear one out with perplexity! the necessaries and ingredients are few, and all easy to get, but it would be difficult to find the lucky moment! You want twelve ounces of the pollen of the white peone, which flowers in spring, twelve ounces of the pollen of the white summer lily, twelve ounces of the pollen of the autumn hibiscus flower, and twelve ounces of the white plum in bloom in the winter. You take the four kinds of pollen, and put them in the sun, on the very day of the vernal equinox of the succeeding year to get dry, and then you mix them with the powder and pound them well together. You again want twelve mace of water, fallen on 'rain water' day….."

"Good gracious!" exclaimed Mrs. Chou promptly, as she laughed. "From all you say, why you want three years' time! and what if no rain falls on 'rain water' day! What would one then do?"

"Quite so!" Pao Ch'ai remarked smilingly; "how can there be such an opportune rain on that very day! but to wait is also the best thing, there's nothing else to be done. Besides, you want twelve mace of dew, collected on 'White Dew' day, and twelve mace of the hoar frost, gathered on 'Frost Descent' day, and twelve mace of snow, fallen on 'Slight Snow' day! You next take these four kinds of waters and mix them with the other ingredients, and make pills of the size of a lungngan. You keep them in an old porcelain jar, and bury them under the roots of some flowers; and when the ailment betrays itself, you produce it and take a pill, washing it down with two candareens of a yellow cedar decoction."

"O-mi-to-fu!" cried Mrs. Chou, when she heard all this, bursting out laughing. "It's really enough to kill one! you might wait ten years and find no such lucky moments!"

"Fortunate for me, however," pursued Pao Ch'ai, "in the course of a year or two, after the bonze had told me about this prescription, we got all the ingredients; and, after much trouble, we compounded a supply, which we have now brought along with us from the south to the north; and lies at present under the pear trees."

"Has this medicine any name or other of its own?" further inquired Mrs. Chou.

"It has a name," replied Pao Ch'ai; "the mangy-headed bonze also told it me; he called it 'cold fragrance' pill."

Chou Jui's wife nodded her head, as she heard these words. "What do you feel like after all when this complaint manifests itself?" she went on to ask.

"Nothing much," replied Pao Ch'ai; "I simply pant and cough a bit; but after I've taken a pill, I get over it, and it's all gone."

Mrs. Chou was bent upon making some further remark, when madame Wang was suddenly heard to enquire, "Who is in here?"

Mrs. Chou went out hurriedly and answered; and forthwith told her all about old goody Liu's visit. Having waited for a while, and seeing that madame Wang had nothing to say, she was on the point of retiring, when "aunt" Hsueh unexpectedly remarked smiling: "Wait a bit! I've something to give you to take along with you."

And as she spoke, she called for Hsiang Ling. The sound of the screen-board against the sides of the door was heard, and in walked the waiting-maid, who had been playing with Chin Ch'uan-erh. "Did my lady call?" she asked.

"Bring that box of flowers," said Mrs. Hsueh.

Hsiang Ling assented, and brought from the other side a small embroidered silk box.

"These," explained "aunt" Hsüeh, "are a new kind of flowers, made in the palace. They consist of twelve twigs of flowers of piled gauze. I thought of them yesterday, and as they will, the pity is, only get old, if uselessly put away, why not give them to the girls to wear them in their hair! I meant to have sent them over yesterday, but I forgot all about them. You come to-day most opportunely, and if you will take them with you, I shall have got them off my hands. To the three young ladies in your family give two twigs each, and of the six that will remain give a couple to Miss Lin, and the other four to lady Feng."

"Better keep them and give them to your daughter Pao Ch'ai to wear," observed madame Wang, "and have done with it; why think of all the others?"

"You don't know, sister," replied "aunt" Hsüeh, "what a crotchety thing Pao Ch'ai is! she has no liking for flower or powder."

With these words on her lips, Chou Jui's wife took the box and walked out of the door of the room. Perceiving that Chin Ch'uan-erh was still sunning herself outside, Chou Jui's wife asked her: "Isn't this Hsiang Ling, the waiting-maid that we've often heard of as having been purchased just before the departure of the Hsüeh family for the capital, and on whose account there occurred some case of manslaughter or other?"

"Of course it's she," replied Chin Ch'uan. But as they were talking, they saw Hsiang Ling draw near smirkingly, and Chou Jui's wife at once seized her by the hand, and after minutely scrutinizing her face for a time, she turned round to Chin Ch'uan-erh and smiled. "With these features she really resembles slightly the style of lady Jung of our Eastern Mansion."

"So I too maintain!" said Chin Ch'uan-erh.

Chou Jui's wife then asked Hsiang Ling, "At what age did you enter this family? and where are your father and mother at present?" and also inquired, "In what year of your teens are you? and of what place are you a native?"

But Hsiang Ling, after listening to all these questions, simply nodded her head and replied, "I can't remember."

When Mrs. Chou and Chin Ch'uan-erh heard these words, their spirits changed to grief, and for a while they felt affected and wounded at heart; but in a short time, Mrs. Chou brought the flowers into the room at the back of madame Wang's principal apartment.

The fact is that dowager lady Chia had explained that as her granddaughters were too numerous, it would not be convenient to crowd them together in one place, that Pao-yü and Tai-yü should only remain with her in this part to break her loneliness, but that Ying Ch'un, T'an Ch'un, and Hsi Ch'un, the three of them, should move on this side in the three rooms within the antechamber, at the back of madame lady Wang's quarters; and that Li Wan should be told off to be their attendant and to keep an eye over them.

Chou Jui's wife, therefore, on this occasion came first to these rooms as they were on her way, but she only found a few waiting-maids assembled in the antechamber, waiting silently to obey a call.

Ying Ch'un's waiting-maid, Ssu Chi, together with Shih Shu, T'an Ch'un's waiting-maid, just at this moment raised the curtain, and made their egress, each holding in her hand a tea-cup and saucer; and Chou Jui's wife readily concluding that the young ladies were sitting together also walked into the inner room, where she only saw Ying Ch'un and T'an Ch'un seated near the window, in the act of playing chess. Mrs. Chou presented the flowers and explained whence they came, and what they were.

The girls forthwith interrupted their game, and both with a curtsey, expressed their thanks, and directed the waiting-maids to put the flowers away.

Mrs. Chou complied with their wishes (and handing over the flowers); "Miss Hsi Ch'un," she remarked, "is not at home; and possibly she's over there with our old lady."

"She's in that room, isn't she?" inquired the waiting-maids.

Mrs. Chou at these words readily came into the room on this side, where she found Hsi Ch'un, in company with a certain Chih Neng, a young nun of the "moon reflected on water" convent, talking and laughing together. On seeing Chou Jui's wife enter, Hsi Ch'un at once asked what she wanted, whereupon Chou Jui's wife opened the box of flowers, and explained who had sent them.

"I was just telling Chih Neng," remarked Hsi Ch'un laughing, "that I also purpose shortly shaving my head and becoming a nun; and strange enough, here you again bring me flowers; but supposing I shave my head, where can I wear them?"

They were all very much amused for a time with this remark, and His Ch'un told her waiting-maid, Ju Hua, to come and take over the flowers.

"What time did you come over?" then inquired Mrs. Chou of Chih Neng. "Where is that bald-pated and crotchety superior of yours gone?"

"We came," explained Chih Neng, "as soon as it was day; after calling upon madame Wang, my superior went over to pay a visit in the mansion of Mr. Yü, and told me to wait for her here."

"Have you received," further asked Mrs. Chou, "the monthly allowance for incense offering due on the fifteenth or not?"

"I can't say," replied Chih Neng.

"Who's now in charge of the issue of the monthly allowances to the various temples?" interposed Hsi Ch'un, addressing Mrs. Chou, as soon as she heard what was said.

"It's Yü Hsin," replied Chou Jui's wife, "who's intrusted with the charge."

"That's how it is," observed Hsi Ch'un with a chuckle; "soon after the arrival of the Superior, Yü Hsin's wife came over and kept on whispering with her for some time; so I presume it must have been about this allowance."

Mrs. Chou then went on to bandy a few words with Chih Neng, after which she came over to lady Feng's apartments. Proceeding by a narrow passage, she passed under Li Wan's back windows, and went along the wall ornamented with creepers on the west. Going out of the western side gate, she entered lady Feng's court, and walked over into the Entrance Hall, where she only found the waiting-girl Feng Erh, sitting on the doorsteps of lady Feng's apartments.

When she caught sight of Mrs. Chou approaching, she at once waved her hand, bidding her go to the eastern room. Chou Jui's wife understood her meaning, and hastily came on tiptoe to the chamber on the east, where she saw a nurse patting lady Feng's daughter to sleep.

Mrs. Chou promptly asked the nurse in a low tone of voice: "Is the young lady asleep at this early hour? But if even she is I must wake her up."

The nurse nodded her head in assent, but as these inquiries were being made, a sound of laughter came from over the other side, in which lady Feng's voice could be detected; followed, shortly after, by the sound of a door opening, and out came P'ing Erh, with a large brass basin in her hands, which she told Feng Erh to fill with water and take inside.

P'ing Erh forthwith entered the room on this side, and upon perceiving Chou Jui's wife: "What have you come here again for, my old lady?" she readily inquired.

Chou Jui's wife rose without any delay, and handed her the box. "I've come," said she, "to bring you a present of flowers."

Upon hearing this, P'ing Erh opened the box, and took out four sprigs, and, turning round, walked out of the room. In a short while she came from the inner room with two sprigs in her hand, and calling first of all Ts'ai Ming, she bade her take the flowers over to the mansion on the other side and present them to "madame" Jung, after which she asked Mrs. Chou to express her thanks on her return.

Chou Jui's wife thereupon came over to dowager lady Chia's room on this side of the compound, and as she was going through the Entrance Hall, she casually came, face to face, with her daughter, got up in gala dress, just coming from the house of her mother-in-law.

"What are you running over here for at this time?" promptly inquired Mrs. Chou.

"Have you been well of late, mother?" asked her daughter. "I've been waiting for ever so long at home, but you never come out! What's there so pressing that has prevented you from returning home? I waited till I was tired, and then went on all alone, and paid my respects to our venerable lady; I'm now, on my way to inquire about our lady Wang. What errand haven't you delivered as yet, ma; and what is it you're holding?"

"Ai! as luck would have it," rejoined Chou Jui's wife smilingly, "old goody Liu came over to-day, so that besides my own hundred and one duties, I've had to run about here and there ever so long, and all for her! While attending to these, Mrs. Hsueh came across me, and asked me to take these flowers to the young ladies, and I've been at it up to this very moment, and haven't done yet! But coming at this time, you must surely have something or other that you want me to do for you! what's it?"

"Really ma, you're quick at guessing!" exclaimed her daughter with a smile; "I'll tell you what it's all about. The day before yesterday, your son-in-law had a glass of wine too many, and began altercating with some person or other; and some one, I don't know why, spread some evil report, saying that his antecedents were not clear, and lodged a charge against him at the Yamen, pressing the authorities to deport him to his native place. That's why I've come over to consult with you, as to whom we should appeal to, to do us this favour of helping us out of our dilemma!"

"I knew at once," Mrs. Chou remarked after listening, "that there was something wrong; but this is nothing hard to settle! Go home and wait for me and I'll come straightway, as soon as I've taken these flowers to Miss Lin; our madame Wang and lady Secunda have both no leisure (to attend to you now,) so go back and wait for me! What's the use of so much hurry!"

Her daughter, upon hearing this, forthwith turned round to go back, when she added as she walked away, "Mind, mother, and make haste."

"All right," replied Chou Jui's wife, "of course I will; you are young yet, and without experience, and that's why you are in this flurry."

As she spoke, she betook herself into Tai-yü's apartments. Contrary to her expectation Tai-yü was not at this time in her own room, but in Pao-yü's; where they were amusing themselves in trying to solve the "nine strung rings" puzzle. On entering Mrs. Chou put on a smile. "'Aunt' Hsüeh," she explained, "has told me to bring these flowers and present them to you to wear in your hair."

"What flowers?" exclaimed Pao-yü. "Bring them here and let me see them."

As he uttered these words, he readily stretched out his hands and took them over, and upon opening the box and looking in, he discovered, in fact, two twigs of a novel and artistic kind of artificial flowers, of piled gauze, made in the palace.

Tai-yü merely cast a glance at them, as Pao-yü held them. "Have these flowers," she inquired eagerly, "been sent to me alone, or have all the other girls got some too?"

"Each one of the young ladies has the same," replied Mrs. Chou; "and these two twigs are intended for you, miss."

Tai-yü forced a smile. "Oh! I see," she observed. "If all the others hadn't chosen, even these which remain over wouldn't have been given to me."

Chou Jui's wife did not utter a word in reply.

"Sister Chou, what took you over on the other side?" asked Pao-yü.

"I was told that our madame Wang was over there," explained Mrs. Chou, "and as I went to give her a message, 'aunt' Hsüeh seized the opportunity to ask me to bring over these flowers."

"What was cousin Pao Ch'ai doing at home?" asked Pao-yü. "How is it she's not even been over for these few days?"

"She's not quite well," remarked Mrs. Chou.

When Pao-yü heard this news, "Who'll go," he speedily ascertained of the waiting-maids, "and inquire after her? Tell her that cousin Lin and I have sent round to ask how our aunt and cousin are getting on! ask her what she's ailing from and what medicines she's taking, and explain to her that I know I ought to have gone over myself, but that on my coming back from school a short while back, I again got a slight chill; and that I'll go in person another day."

While Pao-yü was yet speaking, Hsi Hsüeh volunteered to take the message, and went off at once; and Mrs. Chou herself took her leave without another word.

Mrs. Chou's son-in-law was, in fact, Leng Tzu-hsing, the intimate friend of Yü-ts'un. Having recently become involved with some party in a lawsuit, on account of the sale of some curios, he had expressly charged his wife to come and sue for the favour (of a helping hand). Chou Jui's wife, relying upon her master's prestige, did not so much as take the affair to heart; and having waited till evening, she simply went over and requested lady Feng to befriend her, and the matter was forthwith ended.

When the lamps were lit, lady Feng came over, after having disrobed herself, to see madame Wang. "I've already taken charge," she observed, "of the things sent round to-day by the Chen family. As for the presents from us to them, we should avail ourselves of the return of the boats, by which the fresh delicacies for the new year were forwarded, to hand them to them to carry back."

Madame Wang nodded her head in token of approval.

"The birthday presents," continued lady Feng, "for lady Ling Ngan, the mother of the Earl of Ling Ngan, have already been got together, and whom will you depute to take them over?"

"See," suggested madame Wang, "who has nothing to do; let four maids go and all will be right! why come again and ask me?"

"Our eldest sister-in-law Chen," proceeded lady Feng, "came over to invite me to go to-morrow to their place for a little change. I don't think there will be anything for me to do to-morrow."

"Whether there be or not," replied madame Wang, "it doesn't matter; you must go, for whenever she comes with an invitation, it includes us, who are your seniors, so that, of course, it isn't such a pleasant thing for you; but as she doesn't ask us this time, but only asks you, it's evident that she's anxious that you should have a little distraction, and you mustn't disappoint her good intention. Besides it's certainly right that you should go over for a change."

Lady Feng assented, and presently Li Wan, Ying Ch'un and the other cousins, likewise paid each her evening salutation and retired to their respective rooms, where nothing of any notice transpired.

The next day lady Feng completed her toilette, and came over first to tell madame Wang that she was off, and then went to say good-bye to dowager lady Chia; but when Pao-yü heard where she was going, he also wished to go; and as lady Feng had no help but to give in, and to wait until he had changed his clothes, the sister and brother-in-law got into a carriage, and in a short while entered the Ning mansion.

Mrs. Yu, the wife of Chia Chen, and Mrs. Ch'in, the wife of Mr. Chia Jung, the two sisters-in-law, had, along with a number of maids, waiting-girls, and other servants, come as far as the ceremonial gate to receive them, and Mrs. Yu, upon meeting lady Feng, for a while indulged, as was her wont, in humorous remarks, after which, leading Pao-yü by the hand, they entered the drawing room and took their seats, Mrs. Ch'in handed tea round.

"What have you people invited me to come here for?" promptly asked lady Feng; "if you have anything to present me with, hand it to me at once, for I've other things to attend to."

Mrs. Yu and Mrs. Ch'in had barely any time to exchange any further remarks, when several matrons interposed, smilingly: "Had our lady not come to-day, there would have been no help for it, but having come, you can't have it all your own way."

While they were conversing about one thing and another, they caught sight of Chia Jung come in to pay his respects, which prompted Pao-yü to inquire, "Isn't my elder brother at home to-day?"

"He's gone out of town to-day," replied Mrs. Yu, "to inquire after his grandfather. You'll find sitting here," she continued, "very dull, and why not go out and have a stroll?"

"A strange coincidence has taken place to-day," urged Mrs. Ch'in, with a smile; "some time back you, uncle Pao, expressed a wish to see my brother, and to-day he too happens to be here at home. I think he's in the library; but why not go and see for yourself, uncle Pao?"

Pao-yü descended at once from the stove-couch, and was about to go, when Mrs. Yu bade the servants to mind and go with him. "Don't you let him get into trouble," she enjoined. "It's a far different thing when he comes over under the charge of his grandmother, when he's all right."

"If that be so," remarked lady Feng, "why not ask the young gentleman to come in, and then I too can see him. There isn't, I hope, any objection to my seeing him?"

"Never mind! never mind!" observed Mrs. Yu, smilingly; "it's as well that you shouldn't see him. This brother of mine is not, like the boys of our Chia family, accustomed to roughly banging and knocking about. Other people's children are brought up politely and properly, and not in this vixenish style of yours. Why, you'd ridicule him to death!"

"I won't laugh at him then, that's all," smiled lady Feng; "tell them to bring him in at once."

"He's shy," proceeded Mrs. Ch'in, "and has seen nothing much of the world, so that you are sure to be put out when you see him, sister."

"What an idea!" exclaimed lady Feng. "Were he even No Cha himself, I'd like to see him; so don't talk trash; if, after all, you don't bring him round at once, I'll give you a good slap on the mouth."

"I daren't be obstinate," answered Mrs. Ch'in smiling; "I'll bring him round!"

In a short while she did in fact lead in a young lad, who, compared with Pao-yü, was somewhat more slight but, from all appearances, superior to Pao-yü in eyes and eyebrows, (good looks), which were so clear and well-defined, in white complexion and in ruddy lips, as well as graceful appearance and pleasing manners. He was however bashful and timid, like a girl.

In a shy and demure way, he made a bow to lady Feng and asked after her health.

Lady Feng was simply delighted with him. "You take a low seat next to him!" she ventured laughingly as she first pushed Pao-yü back. Then readily stooping forward, she took this lad by the hand and asked him to take a seat next to her. Presently she inquired about his age, his studies and such matters, when she found that at school he went under the name of Ch'in Chung.

The matrons and maids in attendance on lady Feng, perceiving that this was the first time their mistress met Ch'in Chung, (and knowing) that she had not at hand the usual presents, forthwith ran over to the other side and told P'ing Erh about it.

P'ing Erh, aware of the close intimacy that existed between lady Feng and Mrs. Ch'in, speedily took upon herself to decide, and selecting a piece of silk, and two small gold medals, (bearing the wish that he should attain) the highest degree, the senior wranglership, she handed them to the servants who had come over, to take away.

Lady Feng, however, explained that her presents were too mean by far, but Mrs. Ch'in and the others expressed their appreciation of them; and in a short time the repast was over, and Mrs. Yu, lady Feng and Mrs. Ch'in played at dominoes, but of this no details need be given; while both Pao-yü and Ch'in Chung sat down, got up and talked, as they pleased.

Since he had first glanced at Ch'in Chung, and seen what kind of person he was, he felt at heart as if he had lost something, and after being plunged in a dazed state for a time, he began again to give way to foolish thoughts in his mind.

"There are then such beings as he in the world!" he reflected. "I now see there are! I'm however no better than a wallowing pig or a mangy cow! Despicable destiny! why was I ever born in this household of a marquis and in the mansion of a duke? Had I seen the light in the home of some penniless scholar, or poverty-stricken official, I could long ago have enjoyed the communion of his friendship, and I would not have lived my whole existence in vain! Though more honourable than he, it is indeed evident that silk and satins only serve to swathe this rotten trunk of mine, and choice wines and rich meats only to gorge the filthy drain and miry sewer of this body of mine! Wealth! and splendour! ye are no more than contaminated with pollution by me!"

Ever since Ch'in Chung had noticed Pao-yü's unusual appearance, his sedate deportment, and what is more, his hat ornamented with gold, and his dress full of embroidery, attended by beautiful maids and handsome youths, he did not indeed think it a matter of surprise that every one was fond of him.

"Born as I have had the misfortune to be," he went on to commune within himself, "in an honest, though poor family, how can I presume to enjoy his companionship! This is verily a proof of what a barrier poverty and wealth set between man and man. What a serious misfortune is this too in this mortal world!"

In wild and inane ideas of the same strain, indulged these two youths!

Pao-yü by and by further asked of him what books he was reading, and Ch'in Chung, in answer to these inquiries, told him the truth. A few more questions and answers followed; and after about ten remarks, a greater intimacy sprang up between them.

Tea and fruits were shortly served, and while they were having their tea, Pao-yü suggested, "We two don't take any wine, and why shouldn't we have our fruit served on the small couch inside, and go and sit there, and thus save you all the trouble?"

The two of them thereupon came into the inner apartment to have their tea; and Mrs. Ch'in attended to the laying out of fruit and wines for lady Feng, and hurriedly entered the room and hinted to Pao-yü: "Dear uncle Pao, your nephew is young, and should he happen to say anything disrespectful, do please overlook it, for my sake, for though shy, he's naturally of a perverse and wilful disposition, and is rather given to having his own way."

"Off with you!" cried Pao-yü laughing; "I know it all." Mrs. Ch'in then went on to give a bit of advice to her brother, and at length came to keep lady Feng company. Presently lady Feng and Mrs. Yu sent another servant to tell Pao-yü that there was outside of everything they might wish to eat and that they should mind and go and ask for it; and Pao-yü simply signified that they would; but his mind was not set upon drinking or eating; all he did was to keep making inquiries of Ch'in Chung about recent family concerns.

Ch'in Chung went on to explain that his tutor had last year relinquished his post, that his father was advanced in years and afflicted with disease, and had multifarious public duties to preoccupy his mind, so that he had as yet had no time to make arrangements for another tutor, and that all he did was no more than to keep up his old tasks; that as regards study, it was likewise necessary to have the company of one or two intimate friends, as then only, by dint of a frequent exchange of ideas and opinions, one could arrive at progress; and Pao-yü gave him no time to complete, but eagerly urged, "Quite so! But in our household, we have a family school, and those of our kindred who have no means sufficient to engage the services of a tutor are at liberty to come over for the sake of study, and the sons and brothers of our relatives are likewise free to join the class. As my own tutor went home last year, I am now also wasting my time doing nothing; my father's intention was that I too should have gone over to this school, so that I might at least temporarily keep up what I have already read, pending the arrival of my tutor next year, when I could again very well resume my studies alone at home. But my grandmother raised objections; maintaining first of all, that the boys who attend the family classes being so numerous, she feared we would be sure to be up to mischief, which wouldn't be at all proper; and that, in the second place, as I had been ill for some time, the matter should be dropped, for the present. But as, from what you say, your worthy father is very much exercised on this score, you should, on your return, tell him all about it, and come over to our school. I'll also be there as your schoolmate; and as you and I will reap mutual benefit from each other's companionship, won't it be nice!"

"When my father was at home the other day," Ch'in Chung smiled and said, "he alluded to the question of a tutor, and explained that the free schools were an excellent institution. He even meant to have come and talked matters over with his son-in-law's father about my introduction, but with the urgent concerns here, he didn't think it right for him to come about this small thing, and make any trouble. But if you really believe that I might be of use to you, in either grinding the ink, or washing the slab, why shouldn't you at once make the needful arrangements, so that neither you nor I may idle our time? And as we shall be able to come together often and talk matters over, and set at the same time our parents' minds at ease, and to enjoy the pleasure of friendship, won't it be a profitable thing!"

"Compose your mind!" suggested Pao-yü. "We can by and by first of all, tell your brother-in-law, and your sister as well as sister-in-law Secunda Lien; and on your return home to-day, lose no time in explaining all to your worthy father, and when I get back, I'll speak to my grandmother; and I can't see why our wishes shouldn't speedily be accomplished."

By the time they had arrived at this conclusion, the day was far advanced, and the lights were about to be lit; and they came out and watched them once more for a time as they played at dominoes. When they came to settle their accounts Mrs. Ch'in and Mrs. Yu were again the losers and had to bear the expense of a theatrical and dinner party; and while deciding that they should enjoy this treat the day after the morrow, they also had the evening repast.

Darkness having set in, Mrs. Yu gave orders that two youths should accompany Mr. Ch'in home. The matrons went out to deliver the directions, and after a somewhat long interval, Ch'in Chung said goodbye and was about to start on his way.

"Whom have you told off to escort him?" asked Mrs. Yu.

"Chiao Ta," replied the matrons, "has been told to go, but it happens that he's under the effects of drink and making free use again of abusive language."

Mrs. Yu and Mrs. Chin remonstrated. "What's the use," they said, "of asking him? that mean fellow shouldn't be chosen, but you will go again and provoke him."

"People always maintain," added lady Feng, "that you are far too lenient. But fancy allowing servants in this household to go on in this way; why, what will be the end of it?"

"You don't mean to tell me," observed Mrs. Yu, "that you don't know this Chiao Ta? Why, even the gentlemen one and all pay no heed to his doings! your eldest brother, Chia Cheng, he too doesn't notice him. It's all because when he was young he followed our ancestor in three or four wars, and because on one occasion, by extracting our senior from the heap of slain and carrying him on his back, he saved his life. He himself suffered hunger and stole food for his master to eat; they had no water for two days; and when he did get half a bowl, he gave it to his master, while he himself had sewage water. He now simply presumes upon the sentimental obligations imposed by these services. When the seniors of the family still lived, they all looked upon him with exceptional regard; but who at present ventures to interfere with him? He is also advanced in years, and doesn't care about any decent manners; his sole delight is wine; and when he gets drunk, there isn't a single person whom he won't abuse. I've again and again told the stewards not to henceforward ask Chiao Ta to do any work whatever, but to treat him as dead and gone; and here he's sent again to-day."

"How can I not know all about this Chiao Ta?" remarked lady Feng; "but the secret of all this trouble is, that you won't take any decisive step. Why not pack him off to some distant farm, and have done with him?" And as she spoke, "Is our carriage ready?" she went on to inquire.

"All ready and waiting," interposed the married women.

Lady Feng also got up, said good-bye, and hand in hand with Pao-yü, they walked out of the room, escorted by Mrs. Yu and the party, as far as the entrance of the Main Hall, where they saw the lamps shedding a brilliant light and the attendants all waiting on the platforms. Chiao Ta, however, availing himself of Chia Chen's absence from home, and elated by wine, began to abuse the head steward Lai Erh for his injustice.

"You bully of the weak and coward with the strong," he cried, "when there's any pleasant charge, you send the other servants, but when it's a question of seeing any one home in the dark, then you ask me, you disorderly clown! a nice way you act the steward, indeed! Do you forget that if Mr. Chiao Ta chose to raise one leg, it would be a good deal higher than your head! Remember please, that twenty years ago, Mr. Chiao Ta wouldn't even so much as look at any one, no matter who it was; not to mention a pack of hybrid creatures like yourselves!"

While he went on cursing and railing with all his might, Chia Jung appeared walking by lady Feng's carriage. All the servants having tried to hush him and not succeeding, Chia Jung became exasperated; and forthwith blew him up for a time. "Let some one bind him up," he cried, "and tomorrow, when he's over the wine, I'll call him to task, and we'll see if he won't seek death."

Chiao Ta showed no consideration for Chia Jung. On the contrary, he shouted with more vigour. Going up to Chia Jung: "Brother Jung," he said, "don't put on the airs of a master with Chiao Ta. Not to speak of a man such as you, why even your father and grandfather wouldn't presume to display such side with Chiao Ta. Were it not for Chiao Ta, and him alone, where would your office, honours, riches and dignity be? Your ancestor, whom I brought back from the jaws of death, heaped up all this estate, but up to this very day have I received no thanks for the services I rendered! on the contrary, you come here and play the master; don't say a word more, and things may come right; but if you do, I'll plunge the blade of a knife white in you and extract it red."

Lady Feng, from inside the carriage, remarked to Chia Jung: "Don't you yet pack off this insolent fellow! Why, if you keep him in your house, won't he be a source of mischief? Besides, were relatives and friends to hear about these things, won't they have a laugh at our expense, that a household like ours should be so devoid of all propriety?"

Chia Jung assented. The whole band of servants finding that Chiao Ta was getting too insolent had no help but to come up and throw him over, and binding him up, they dragged him towards the stables. Chiao Ta abused even Chia Chen with still more vehemence, and shouted in a boisterous manner. "I want to go," he cried, "to the family Ancestral Temple and mourn my old master. Who would have ever imagined that he would leave behind such vile creatures of descendants as you all, day after day indulging in obscene and incestuous practices, 'in scraping of the ashes' and in philandering with brothers-in-law. I know all about your doings; the best thing is to hide one's stump of an arm in one's sleeve!" (wash one's dirty clothes at home).

The servants who stood by, upon hearing this wild talk, were quite at their wits' end, and they at once seized him, tied him up, and filled his mouth to the fullest extent with mud mixed with some horse refuse.

Lady Feng and Chia Jung heard all he said from a distance, but pretended not to hear; but Pao-yü, seated in the carriage as he was, also caught this extravagant talk and inquired of lady Feng: "Sister, did you hear him say something about 'scraping of the ashes?' What's it?"

"Don't talk such rubbish!" hastily shouted lady Feng; "it was the maudlin talk of a drunkard! A nice boy you are! not to speak of your listening, but you must also inquire! wait and I'll tell your mother and we'll see if she doesn't seriously take you to task."

Pao-yü was in such a state of fright that he speedily entreated her to forgive him. "My dear sister," he craved, "I won't venture again to say anything of the kind"

"My dear brother, if that be so, it's all right!" rejoined lady Feng reassuringly; "on our return we'll speak to her venerable ladyship and ask her to send some one to arrange matters in the family school, and invite Ch'in Chung to come to school for his studies."

While yet this conversation was going on, they arrived at the Jung Mansion.

Reader, do you wish to know what follows? if you do, the next chapter will unfold it.

CHAPTER VIII.

By a strange coincidence, Chia Pao-yü becomes acquainted with the golden clasp.

In an unexpected meeting, Hsüeh Pao-ch'ai sees the jade of spiritual perception.

Pao-yü and lady Feng, we will now explain, paid, on their return home, their respects to all the inmates, and Pao-yü availed himself of the first occasion to tell dowager lady Chia of his wish that Ch'in Chung should come over to the family school. "The presence for himself of a friend as schoolmate would," he argued, "be fitly excellent to stir him to zeal," and he went on to speak in terms of high praise of Ch'in Chung, his character and his manners, which most of all made people esteem him.

Lady Feng besides stood by him and backed his request. "In a day or two," she added, "Ch'in Chung will be coming to pay his obeisance to your venerable ladyship."

This bit of news greatly rejoiced the heart of dowager lady Chia, and lady Feng likewise did not let the opportunity slip, without inviting the old lady to attend the theatrical performance to come off the day after the morrow. Dowager lady Chia was, it is true, well on in years, but was, nevertheless, very fond of enjoyment, so that when the day arrived and Mrs. Yu came over to invite her round, she forthwith took madame Wang, Lin Tai-yü, Pao-yü and others along and went to the play.

It was about noon, when dowager lady Chia returned to her apartments for her siesta; and madame Wang, who was habitually partial to a quiet life, also took her departure after she had seen the old lady retire. Lady Feng subsequently took the seat of honour; and the party enjoyed themselves immensely till the evening, when they broke up.

But to return to Pao-yü. Having accompanied his grandmother Chia back home, and waited till her ladyship was in her midday sleep, he had in fact an inclination to return to the performance, but he was afraid lest he should be a burden to Mrs. Ch'in and the rest and lest they should not feel at ease. Remembering therefore that Pao Ch'ai had been at home unwell for the last few days, and that he had not been to see her, he was anxious to go and look her up, but he dreaded that if he went by the side gate, at the back of the drawing-room, he would be prevented by something or other, and fearing, what would be making matters worse, lest he should come across his father, he consequently thought it better to go on his way by a detour. The nurses and waiting-maids thereupon came to help him to change his clothes; but they saw him not change, but go out again by the second door. These nurses and maids could not help following him out; but they were still under the impression that he was going over to the other mansion to see the theatricals. Contrary to their speculations, upon reaching the entrance hall, he forthwith went to the east, then turned to the north, and walking round by the rear of the hall, he happened to come face to face with two of the family companions, Mr. Ch'an Kuang, and Mr. Tan T'ing-jen. As soon as they caught sight of Pao-yü, they both readily drew up to him, and as they smiled, the one put his arm round his waist, while the other grasped him by the hand.

"Oh divine brother!" they both exclaimed, "this we call dreaming a pleasant dream, for it's no easy thing to come across you!"

While continuing their remarks they paid their salutations, and inquired after his health; and it was only after they had chatted for ever so long, that they went on their way. The nurse called out to them and stopped them, "Have you two gentlemen," she said, "come out from seeing master?"

They both nodded assent. "Your master," they explained, "is in the Meng P'o Chai small library having his siesta; so that you can go through there with no fear."

As they uttered these words, they walked away.

This remark also evoked a smile from Pao-yü, but without further delay he turned a corner, went towards the north, and came into the Pear Fragrance Court, where, as luck would have it, he met the head manager of the Household Treasury, Wu Hsin-teng, who, in company with the head of the granary, Tai Liang, and several other head stewards, seven persons in all, was issuing out of the Account Room.

On seeing Pao-yü approaching, they, in a body, stood still, and hung down their arms against their sides. One of them alone, a certain butler, called Ch'ien Hua, promptly came forward, as he had not seen Pao-yü for many a day, and bending on one knee, paid his respects to Pao-yü. Pao-yü at once gave a smile and pulled him up.

"The day before yesterday," smiled all the bystanders, "we were somewhere together and saw some characters written by you, master Secundus, in the composite style. The writing is certainly better than it was before! When will you give us a few sheets to stick on the wall?"

"Where did you see them?" inquired Pao-yü, with a grin.

"They are to be found in more than one place," they replied, "and every one praises them very much, and what's more, asks us for a few."

"They are not worth having," observed Pao-yü smilingly; "but if you do want any, tell my young servants and it will be all right."

As he said these words, he moved onwards. The whole party waited till he had gone by, before they separated, each one to go his own way.

But we need not dilate upon matters of no moment, but return to Pao-yü.

On coming to the Pear Fragrance Court, he entered, first, into "aunt" Hsüeh's room, where he found her getting some needlework ready to give to the waiting-maids to work at. Pao-yü forthwith paid his respects to her, and "aunt" Hsüeh, taking him by the hand, drew him towards her and clasped him in her embrace.

"With this cold weather," she smilingly urged, "it's too kind of you, my dear child, to think of coming to see me; come along on the stove-couch at once!—Bring some tea," she continued, addressing the servants, "and make it as hot as it can be!"

"Isn't Hsüeh P'an at home?" Pao-yü having inquired: "He's like a horse without a halter," Mrs. Hsüeh remarked with a sigh; "he's daily running here and there and everywhere, and nothing can induce him to stay at home one single day."

"Is sister (Pao Ch'ai) all right again?" asked Pao-yü. "Yes," replied Mrs. Hsüeh, "she's well again. It was very kind of you two days ago to again think of her, and send round to inquire after her. She's now in there, and you can go and see her. It's warmer there than it's here; go and sit with her inside, and, as soon as I've put everything away, I'll come and join you and have a chat."

Pao-yü, upon hearing this, jumped down with alacrity from the stove-couch, and walked up to the door of the inner room, where he saw hanging a portière somewhat the worse for use, made of red silk. Pao-yü raised the portière and making one step towards the interior, he found Pao Ch'ai seated on the couch, busy over some needlework. On the top of her head was gathered, and made into a knot, her chevelure, black as lacquer, and glossy like pomade. She wore a honey-coloured wadded robe, a rose-brown short-sleeved jacket, lined with the fur of the squirrel of two colours: the "gold and silver;" and a jupe of leek-yellow silk. Her whole costume was neither too new, neither too old, and displayed no sign of extravagance.

Her lips, though not rouged, were naturally red; her eyebrows, though not pencilled, were yet blue black; her face resembled a silver basin, and her eyes, juicy plums. She was sparing in her words, chary in her talk, so much so that people said that she posed as a simpleton. She was quiet in the acquittal of her duties and scrupulous as to the proper season for everything. "I practise simplicity," she would say of herself.

"How are you? are you quite well again, sister?" inquired Pao-yü, as he gazed at her; whereupon Pao Ch'ai raised her head, and perceiving Pao-yü walk in, she got up at once and replied with a smile, "I'm all right again; many thanks for your kindness in thinking of me."

While uttering this, she pressed him to take a seat on the stove-couch, and as he sat down on the very edge of the couch, she told Ying Erh to bring tea and asked likewise after dowager lady Chia and lady Feng. "And are all the rest of the young ladies quite well?" she inquired.

Saying this she scrutinised Pao-yü, who she saw had a head-dress of purplish-gold twisted threads, studded with precious stones. His forehead was bound with a gold circlet, representing two dragons, clasping a pearl. On his person he wore a light yellow, archery-sleeved jacket, ornamented with rampant dragons, and lined with fur from the ribs of the silver fox; and was clasped with a dark sash, embroidered with different-coloured butterflies and birds. Round his neck was hung an amulet, consisting of a clasp of longevity, a talisman of recorded name, and, in addition to these, the precious jade which he had had in his mouth at the time of his birth.

"I've daily heard every one speak of this jade," said Pao Ch'ai with a smile, "but haven't, after all, had an opportunity of looking at it closely, but anyhow to-day I must see it."

As she spoke, she drew near. Pao-yü himself approached, and taking it from his neck, he placed it in Pao Ch'ai's hand. Pao Ch'ai held it in her palm. It appeared to her very much like the egg of a bird, resplendent as it was like a bright russet cloud; shiny and smooth like variegated curd and covered with a net for the sake of protection.

Readers, you should know that this was the very block of useless stone which had been on the Ta Huang Hills, and which had dropped into the Ch'ing Keng cave, in a state of metamorphosis. A later writer expresses his feelings in a satirical way as follows:

Nü Wo's fusion of stones was e'er a myth inane,
But from this myth hath sprung fiction still more insane!
Lost is the subtle life, divine, and real!—gone!
Assumed, mean subterfuge! foul bags of skin and bone!
Fortune, when once adverse, how true! gold glows no more!
In evil days, alas! the jade's splendour is o'er!
Bones, white and bleached, in nameless hill-like mounds are flung,
Bones once of youths renowned and maidens fair and young.

The rejected stone has in fact already given a record of the circumstances of its transformation, and the inscription in seal characters, engraved upon it by the bald-headed bonze, and below will now be also appended a faithful representation of it; but its real size is so very diminutive, as to allow of its being held by a child in his mouth while yet unborn, that were it to have been drawn in its exact proportions, the characters would, it is feared, have been so insignificant in size, that the beholder would have had to waste much of his eyesight, and it would besides have been no pleasant thing.

While therefore its shape has been adhered to, its size has unavoidably been slightly enlarged, to admit of the reader being able, conveniently, to peruse the inscription, even by very lamplight, and though he may be under the influence of wine.

These explanations have been given to obviate any such sneering remarks as: "What could be, pray, the size of the mouth of a child in his mother's womb, and how could it grasp such a large and clumsy thing?"

On the face of the jade was written:

Precious Gem of Spiritual Perception.
If thou wilt lose me not and never forget me,
Eternal life and constant luck will be with thee!

On the reverse was written:

1 To exorcise evil spirits and the accessory visitations; 2 To cure predestined sickness; 3 To prognosticate weal and woe.

Pao Ch'ai having looked at the amulet, twisted it again to the face, and scrutinising it closely, read aloud:

If thou wilt lose me not and never forget me,
Eternal life and constant luck will be with thee!

She perused these lines twice, and, turning round, she asked Ying Erh laughingly: "Why don't you go and pour the tea? what are you standing here like an idiot!"

"These two lines which I've heard," smiled Ying Erh, "would appear to pair with the two lines on your necklet, miss!"

"What!" eagerly observed Pao-yü with a grin, when he caught these words, "are there really eight characters too on your necklet, cousin? do let me too see it."

"Don't listen to what she says," remarked Pao Ch'ai, "there are no characters on it."

"My dear cousin," pleaded Pao-yü entreatingly, "how is it you've seen mine?"

Pao Ch'ai was brought quite at bay by this remark of his, and she consequently added, "There are also two propitious phrases engraved on this charm, and that's why I wear it every day. Otherwise, what pleasure would there be in carrying a clumsy thing."

As she spoke, she unfastened the button, and produced from inside her crimson robe, a crystal-like locket, set with pearls and gems, and with a brilliant golden fringe. Pao-yü promptly received it from her, and upon minute examination, found that there were in fact four characters on each side; the eight characters on both sides forming two sentences of good omen. The similitude of the locket is likewise then given below. On the face of the locket is written:

"Part not from me and cast me not away;"

And on the reverse:

"And youth, perennial freshness will display!"

Pao-yü examined the charm, and having also read the inscription twice over aloud, and then twice again to himself, he said as he smiled, "Dear cousin, these eight characters of yours form together with mine an antithetical verse."

"They were presented to her," ventured Ying Erh, "by a mangy-pated bonze, who explained that they should be engraved on a golden trinket...."

Pao Ch'ai left her no time to finish what she wished to say, but speedily called her to task for not going to bring the tea, and then inquired of Pao-yü "Where he had come from?"

Pao-yü had, by this time, drawn quite close to Pao Ch'ai, and perceived whiff after whiff of some perfume or other, of what kind he could not tell. "What perfume have you used, my cousin," he forthwith asked, "to fumigate your dresses with? I really don't remember smelling any perfumery of the kind before."

"I'm very averse," replied Pao Ch'ai blandly, "to the odour of fumigation; good clothes become impregnated with the smell of smoke."

"In that case," observed Pao-yü, "what scent is it?"

"Yes, I remember," Pao Ch'ai answered, after some reflection; "it's the scent of the 'cold fragrance' pills which I took this morning."

"What are these cold fragrance pills," remarked Pao-yü smiling, "that they have such a fine smell? Give me, cousin, a pill to try."

"Here you are with your nonsense again," Pao Ch'ai rejoined laughingly; "is a pill a thing to be taken recklessly?"

She had scarcely finished speaking, when she heard suddenly some one outside say, "Miss Lin is come;" and shortly Lin Tai-yü walked in in a jaunty manner.

"Oh, I come at a wrong moment!" she exclaimed forthwith, smirking significantly when she caught sight of Pao-yü.

Pao-yü and the rest lost no time in rising and offering her a seat, whereupon Pao Ch'ai added with a smile, "How can you say such things?"

"Had I known sooner," continued Tai-yü, "that he was here, I would have kept away."

"I can't fathom this meaning of yours," protested Pao Ch'ai.

"If one comes," Tai-yü urged smiling, "then all come, and when one doesn't come, then no one comes. Now were he to come to-day, and I to come to-morrow, wouldn't there be, by a division of this kind, always some one with you every day? and in this way, you wouldn't feel too lonely, nor too crowded. How is it, cousin, that you didn't understand what I meant to imply?"

"Is it snowing?" inquired Pao-yü, upon noticing that she wore a cloak made of crimson camlet, buttoning in front.

"It has been snowing for some time," ventured the matrons, who were standing below. "Fetch my wrapper!" Pao-yü remarked, and Tai-yü readily laughed. "Am I not right? I come, and, of course, he must go at once."

"Did I ever mention that I was going?" questioned Pao-yü; "I only wish it brought to have it ready when I want it."

"It's a snowy day," consequently remarked Pao-yü's nurse, dame Li, "and we must also look to the time, but you had better remain here and amuse yourself with your cousin. Your aunt has, in there, got ready tea and fruits. I'll tell the waiting-maid to go and fetch your wrapper and the boys to return home." Pao-yü assented, and nurse Li left the room and told the boys that they were at liberty to go.

By this time Mrs. Hsüeh had prepared tea and several kinds of nice things and kept them all to partake of those delicacies. Pao-yü, having spoken highly of some goose feet and ducks' tongues he had tasted some days before, at his eldest sister-in-law's, Mrs. Yu's, "aunt" Hsüeh promptly produced several dishes of the same kind, made by herself, and gave them to Pao-yü to try. "With a little wine," added Pao-yü with a smile, "they would be first rate."

Mrs. Hsüeh thereupon bade the servants fetch some wine of the best quality; but dame Li came forward and remonstrated. "My lady," she said, "never mind the wine."

Pao-yü smilingly pleaded: "My nurse, I'll take just one cup and no more."

"It's no use," nurse Li replied, "were your grandmother and mother present, I wouldn't care if you drank a whole jar. I remember the day when I turned my eyes away but for a moment, and some ignorant fool or other, merely with the view of pandering for your favour, gave you only a drop of wine to drink, and how this brought reproaches upon me for a couple of days. You don't know, my lady, you have no idea of his disposition! it's really dreadful; and when he has had a little wine he shows far more temper. On days when her venerable ladyship is in high spirits, she allows him to have his own way about drinking, but he's not allowed to have wine on any and every day; and why should I have to suffer inside and all for nothing at all?"

"You antiquated thing!" replied Mrs. Hsüeh laughing, "set your mind at ease, and go and drink your own wine! I won't let him have too much, and should even the old lady say anything, let the fault be mine."

Saying this, she asked a waiting-maid to take nurse Li along with her and give her also a glass of wine so as to keep out the cold air.

When nurse Li heard these words, she had no alternative but to go for a time with all the others and have some wine to drink.

"The wine need not be warmed: I prefer it cold!" Pao-yü went on to suggest meanwhile.

"That won't do," remonstrated Mrs. Hsüeh; "cold wine will make your hand tremble when you write."

"You have," interposed Pao Ch'ai smiling, "the good fortune, cousin Pao-yü, of having daily opportunities of acquiring a knowledge of every kind of subject, and yet don't you know that the properties of wine are mostly heating? If you drink wine warm, its effects soon dispel, but if you drink it cold, it at once congeals in you; and as upon your intestines devolves the warming of it, how can you not derive any harm? and won't you yet from this time change this habit of yours? leave off at once drinking that cold wine."

Pao-yü finding that the words he had heard contained a good deal of sense, speedily put down the cold wine, and having asked them to warm it, he at length drank it.

Tai-yü was bent upon cracking melon seeds, saying nothing but simply pursing up her lips and smiling, when, strange coincidence, Hsüeh Yen, Tai-yü's waiting-maid, walked in and handed her mistress a small hand-stove.

"Who told you to bring it?" ascertained Tai-yü grinningly. "I'm sorry to have given whoever it is the trouble; I'm obliged to her. But did she ever imagine that I would freeze to death?"

"Tzu Chuan was afraid," replied Hsüeh Yen, "that you would, miss, feel cold, and she asked me to bring it over."

Tai-yü took it over and held it in her lap. "How is it," she smiled, "that you listen to what she tells you, but that you treat what I say, day after day, as so much wind blowing past your ears! How is it that you at once do what she bids you, with even greater alacrity than you would an imperial edict?"

When Pao-yü heard this, he felt sure in his mind that Tai-yü was availing herself of this opportunity to make fun of him, but he made no remark, merely laughing to himself and paying no further notice. Pao Ch'ai, again, knew full well that this habit was a weak point with Tai-yü, so she too did not go out of her way to heed what she said.

"You've always been delicate and unable to stand the cold," interposed "aunt" Hsüeh, "and is it not a kind attention on their part to have thought of you?"

"You don't know, aunt, how it really stands," responded Tai-yü smilingly; "fortunately enough, it was sent to me here at your quarters; for had it been in any one else's house, wouldn't it have been a slight upon them? Is it forsooth nice to think that people haven't so much as a hand-stove, and that one has fussily to be sent over from home? People won't say that the waiting-maids are too officious, but will imagine that I'm in the habit of behaving in this offensive fashion."

"You're far too punctilious," remarked Mrs. Hsüeh, "as to entertain such notions! No such ideas as these crossed my mind just now."

While they were conversing, Pao-yü had taken so much as three cups of wine, and nurse Li came forward again to prevent him from having any more. Pao-yü was just then in a state of exultation and excitement, (a state) enhanced by the conversation and laughter of his cousins, so that was he ready to agree to having no more! But he was constrained in a humble spirit to entreat for permission. "My dear nurse," he implored, "I'll just take two more cups and then have no more."

"You'd better be careful," added nurse Li, "your father is at home to-day, and see that you're ready to be examined in your lessons."

When Pao-yü heard this mention, his spirits at once sank within him, and gently putting the wine aside, he dropped his head upon his breast.

Tai-yü promptly remonstrated. "You've thrown cold water," she said, "over the spirits of the whole company; why, if uncle should ask to see you, well, say that aunt Hsüeh detained you. This old nurse of yours has been drinking, and again makes us the means of clearing her muddled head!"

While saying this, she gave Pao-yü a big nudge with the intent of stirring up his spirits, adding, as she addressed him in a low tone of voice: "Don't let us heed that old thing, but mind our own enjoyment."

Dame Li also knew very well Tai-yü's disposition, and therefore remarked: "Now, Miss Lin, don't you urge him on; you should after all, give him good advice, as he may, I think, listen to a good deal of what you say to him."

"Why should I urge him on?" rejoined Lin Tai-yü, with a sarcastic smile, "nor will I trouble myself to give him advice. You, old lady, are far too scrupulous! Old lady Chia has also time after time given him wine, and if he now takes a cup or two more here, at his aunt's, lady Hsüeh's house, there's no harm that I can see. Is it perhaps, who knows, that aunt is a stranger in this establishment, and that we have in fact no right to come over here to see her?"

Nurse Li was both vexed and amused by the words she had just heard. "Really," she observed, "every remark this girl Lin utters is sharper than a razor! I didn't say anything much!"

Pao Ch'ai too could not suppress a smile, and as she pinched Tai-yü's cheek, she exclaimed, "Oh the tongue of this frowning girl! one can neither resent what it says, nor yet listen to it with any gratification!"

"Don't be afraid!" Mrs. Hsüeh went on to say, "don't be afraid; my son, you've come to see me, and although I've nothing good to give you, you mustn't, through fright, let the trifle you've taken lie heavy on your stomach, and thus make me uneasy; but just drink at your pleasure, and as much as you like, and let the blame fall on my shoulders. What's more, you can stay to dinner with me, and then go home; or if you do get tipsy, you can sleep with me, that's all."

She thereupon told the servants to heat some more wine. "I'll come," she continued, "and keep you company while you have two or three cups, after which we'll have something to eat!"

It was only after these assurances that Pao-yü's spirits began at length, once more to revive, and dame Li then directed the waiting-maids what to do. "You remain here," she enjoined, "and mind, be diligent while I go home and change; when I'll come back again. Don't allow him," she also whispered to "aunt" Hsüeh, "to have all his own way and drink too much."

Having said this, she betook herself back to her quarters; and during this while, though there were two or three nurses in attendance, they did not concern themselves with what was going on. As soon as they saw that nurse Li had left, they likewise all quietly slipped out, at the first opportunity they found, while there remained but two waiting-maids, who were only too glad to curry favour with Pao-yü. But fortunately "aunt" Hsüeh, by much coaxing and persuading, only let him have a few cups, and the wine being then promptly cleared away, pickled bamboo shoots and chicken-skin soup were prepared, of which Pao-yü drank with relish several bowls full, eating besides more than half a bowl of finest rice congee.

By this time, Hsüeh Pao Ch'ai and Lin Tai-yü had also finished their repast; and when Pao-yü had drunk a few cups of strong tea, Mrs. Hsüeh felt more easy in her mind. Hsüeh Yen and the others, three or four of them in all, had also had their meal, and came in to wait upon them.

"Are you now going or not?" inquired Tai-yü of Pao-yü.

Pao-yü looked askance with his drowsy eyes. "If you want to go," he observed, "I'll go with you."

Tai-yü hearing this, speedily rose. "We've been here nearly the whole day," she said, "and ought to be going back."

As she spoke the two of them bade good-bye, and the waiting-maids at once presented a hood to each of them.

Pao-yü readily lowered his head slightly and told a waiting-maid to put it on. The girl promptly took the hood, made of deep red cloth, and shaking it out of its folds, she put it on Pao-yü's head.

"That will do," hastily exclaimed Pao-yü. "You stupid thing! gently a bit; is it likely you've never seen any one put one on before? let me do it myself."

"Come over here, and I'll put it on for you," suggested Tai-yü, as she stood on the edge of the couch. Pao-yü eagerly approached her, and Tai-yü carefully kept the cap, to which his hair was bound, fast down, and taking the hood she rested its edge on the circlet round his forehead. She then raised the ball of crimson velvet, which was as large as a walnut, and put it in such a way that, as it waved tremulously, it should appear outside the hood. These arrangements completed she cast a look for a while at what she had done. "That's right now," she added, "throw your wrapper over you!"

When Pao-yü caught these words, he eventually took the wrapper and threw it over his shoulders.

"None of your nurses," hurriedly interposed aunt Hsüeh, "are yet come, so you had better wait a while."

"Why should we wait for them?" observed Pao-yü. "We have the waiting-maids to escort us, and surely they should be enough."

Mrs. Hsüeh finding it difficult to set her mind at ease deputed two married women to accompany the two cousins; and after they had both expressed (to these women) their regret at having troubled them, they came straightway to dowager lady Chia's suite of apartments.

Her venerable ladyship had not, as yet, had her evening repast. Hearing that they had been at Mrs. Hsüeh's, she was extremely pleased; but noticing that Pao-yü had had some wine, she gave orders that he should be taken to his room, and put to bed, and not be allowed to come out again.

"Do take good care of him," she therefore enjoined the servants, and when suddenly she bethought herself of Pao-yü's attendants, "How is it," she at once inquired of them all, "that I don't see nurse Li here?"

They did not venture to tell her the truth, that she had gone home, but simply explained that she had come in a few moments back, and that they thought she must have again gone out on some business or other.

"She's better off than your venerable ladyship," remarked Pao-yü, turning round and swaying from side to side. "Why then ask after her? Were I rid of her, I believe I might live a little longer."

While uttering these words, he reached the door of his bedroom, where he saw pen and ink laid out on the writing table.

"That's nice," exclaimed Ch'ing Wen, as she came to meet him with a smile on her face, "you tell me to prepare the ink for you, but though when you get up, you were full of the idea of writing, you only wrote three characters, when you discarded the pencil, and ran away, fooling me, by making me wait the whole day! Come now at once and exhaust all this ink before you're let off."

Pao-yü then remembered what had taken place in the morning. "Where are the three characters I wrote?" he consequently inquired, smiling.

"Why this man is tipsy," remarked Ch'ing Wen sneeringly. "As you were going to the other mansion, you told me to stick them over the door. I was afraid lest any one else should spoil them, as they were being pasted, so I climbed up a high ladder and was ever so long in putting them up myself; my hands are even now numb with cold."

"Oh I forgot all about it," replied Pao-yü grinning, "if your hands are cold, come and I'll rub them warm for you."

Promptly stretching out his hand, he took those of Ch'ing Wen in his, and the two of them looked at the three characters, which he recently had written, and which were pasted above the door. In a short while, Tai-yü came.

"My dear cousin," Pao-yü said to her smilingly, "tell me without any prevarication which of the three characters is the best written?"

Tai-yü raised her head and perceived the three characters: Red, Rue, Hall. "They're all well done," she rejoined, with a smirk, "How is it you've written them so well? By and bye you must also write a tablet for me."

"Are you again making fun of me?" asked Pao-yü smiling; "what about sister Hsi Jen?" he went on to inquire.

Ch'ing Wen pouted her lips, pointing towards the stove-couch in the inner room, and, on looking in, Pao-yü espied Hsi Jen fast asleep in her daily costume.

"Well," Pao-yü observed laughing, "there's no harm in it, but its rather early to sleep. When I was having my early meal, on the other side," he proceeded, speaking to Ch'ing Wen, "there was a small dish of dumplings, with bean-curd outside; and as I thought you would like to have some, I asked Mrs. Yu for them, telling her that I would keep them, and eat them in the evening; I told some one to bring them over, but have you perchance seen them?"

"Be quick and drop that subject," suggested Ch'ing Wen; "as soon as they were brought over, I at once knew they were intended for me; as I had just finished my meal, I put them by in there, but when nurse Li came she saw them. 'Pao-yü,' she said, 'is not likely to eat them, so I'll take them and give them to my grandson.' And forthwith she bade some one take them over to her home."

While she was speaking, Hsi Hsüeh brought in tea, and Pao-yü pressed his cousin Lin to have a cup.

"Miss Lin has gone long ago," observed all of them, as they burst out laughing, "and do you offer her tea?"

Pao-yü drank about half a cup, when he also suddenly bethought himself of some tea, which had been brewed in the morning. "This morning," he therefore inquired of Hsi Hsüeh, "when you made a cup of maple-dew tea, I told you that that kind of tea requires brewing three or four times before its colour appears; and how is that you now again bring me this tea?"

"I did really put it by," answered Hsi Hsüeh, "but nurse Li came and drank it, and then went off."

Pao-yü upon hearing this, dashed the cup he held in his hand on the ground, and as it broke into small fragments, with a crash, it spattered Hsi Hsüeh's petticoat all over.

"Of whose family is she the mistress?" inquired Pao-yü of Hsi Hsüeh, as he jumped up, "that you all pay such deference to her. I just simply had a little of her milk, when I was a brat, and that's all; and now she has got into the way of thinking herself more high and mighty than even the heads of the family! She should be packed off, and then we shall all have peace and quiet."

Saying this, he was bent upon going, there and then, to tell dowager lady Chia to have his nurse driven away.

Hsi Jen was really not asleep, but simply feigning, with the idea, when Pao-yü came, to startle him in play. At first, when she heard him speak of writing, and inquire after the dumplings, she did not think it necessary to get up, but when he flung the tea-cup on the floor, and got into a temper, she promptly jumped up and tried to appease him, and to prevent him by coaxing from carrying out his threat.

A waiting-maid sent by dowager lady Chia came in, meanwhile, to ask what was the matter.

"I had just gone to pour tea," replied Hsi Jen, without the least hesitation, "and I slipped on the snow and fell, while the cup dropped from my hand and broke. Your decision to send her away is good," she went on to advise Pao-yü, "and we are all willing to go also; and why not avail yourself of this opportunity to dismiss us in a body? It will be for our good, and you too on the other hand, needn't perplex yourself about not getting better people to come and wait on you!"

When Pao-yü heard this taunt, he had at length not a word to say, and supported by Hsi Jen and the other attendants on to the couch, they divested him of his clothes. But they failed to understand the drift of what Pao-yü kept on still muttering, and all they could make out was an endless string of words; but his eyes grew heavier and drowsier, and they forthwith waited upon him until he went to sleep; when Hsi Jen unclasped the jade of spiritual perception, and rolling it up in a handkerchief, she lay it under the mattress, with the idea that when he put it on the next day it should not chill his neck.

Pao-yü fell sound asleep the moment he lay his head on the pillow. By this time nurse Li and the others had come in, but when they heard that Pao-yü was tipsy, they too did not venture to approach, but gently made inquiries as to whether he was asleep or not. On hearing that he was, they took their departure with their minds more at ease.

The next morning the moment Pao-yü awoke, some one came in to tell him that young Mr. Jung, living in the mansion on the other side, had brought Ch'in Chung to pay him a visit.

Pao-yü speedily went out to greet them and to take them over to pay their respects to dowager lady Chia. Her venerable ladyship upon perceiving that Ch'in Chung, with his handsome countenance, and his refined manners, would be a fit companion for Pao-yü in his studies, felt extremely delighted at heart; and having readily detained him to tea, and kept him to dinner, she went further and directed a servant to escort him to see madame Wang and the rest of the family.

With the fond regard of the whole household for Mrs. Ch'in, they were, when they saw what a kind of person Ch'in Chung was, so enchanted with him, that at the time of his departure, they all had presents to give him; even dowager lady Chia herself presented him with a purse and a golden image of the God of Learning, with a view that it should incite him to study and harmony.

"Your house," she further advised him, "is far off, and when it's cold or hot, it would be inconvenient for you to come all that way, so you had better come and live over here with me. You'll then be always with your cousin Pao-yü, and you won't be together, in your studies, with those fellow-pupils of yours who have no idea what progress means."

Ch'in Chung made a suitable answer to each one of her remarks, and on his return home he told everything to his father.

His father, Ch'in Pang-yeh, held at present the post of Secretary in the Peking Field Force, and was well-nigh seventy. His wife had died at an early period, and as she left no issue, he adopted a son and a daughter from a foundling asylum.

But who would have thought it, the boy also died, and there only remained the girl, known as Kó Ch'ing in her infancy, who when she grew up, was beautiful in face and graceful in manners, and who by reason of some relationship with the Chia family, was consequently united by the ties of marriage (to one of the household).

Ch'in Pang-yeh was in his fiftieth year when he at length got this son. As his tutor had the previous year left to go south, he remained at home keeping up his former lessons; and (his father) had been just thinking of talking over the matter with his relatives of the Chia family, and sending his son to the private school, when, as luck would have it, this opportunity of meeting Pao-yü presented itself.

Knowing besides that the family school was under the direction of the venerable scholar Chia Tai-ju, and hoping that by joining his class, (his son) might advance in knowledge and by these means reap reputation, he was therefore intensely gratified. The only drawbacks were that his official emoluments were scanty, and that both the eyes of everyone in the other establishment were set upon riches and honours, so that he could not contribute anything short of the amount (given by others); but his son's welfare throughout life was a serious consideration, and he, needless to say, had to scrape together from the East and to collect from the West; and making a parcel, with all deference, of twenty-four taels for an introduction present, he came along with Ch'in Chung to Tai-ju's house to pay their respects. But he had to wait subsequently until Pao-yü could fix on an auspicious date on which they could together enter the school.

As for what happened after they came to school, the next chapter will divulge.

CHAPTER IX.

Chia Cheng gives good advice to his wayward son.
Li Kuei receives a reprimand.
Chia Jui and Li Kuei rebuke the obstinate youths!
Ming Yen causes trouble in the school-room.

But to return to our story. Mr. Ch'in, the father, and Ch'in Chung, his son, only waited until the receipt, by the hands of a servant, of a letter from the Chia family about the date on which they were to go to school. Indeed, Pao-yü was only too impatient that he and Ch'in Chung should come together, and, without loss of time, he fixed upon two days later as the day upon which they were definitely to begin their studies, and he despatched a servant with a letter to this effect.

On the day appointed, as soon as it was daylight, Pao-yü turned out of bed. Hsi Jen had already by that time got books, pencils and all writing necessaries in perfect readiness, and was sitting on the edge of the bed in a moping mood; but as soon as she saw Pao-yü approach, she was constrained to wait upon him in his toilette and ablutions.

Pao-yü, noticing how despondent she was, made it a point to address her. "My dear sister," he said, "how is it you aren't again yourself? Is it likely that you bear me a grudge for being about to go to school, because when I leave you, you'll all feel dull?"

Hsi Jen smiled. "What an ideal" she replied. "Study is a most excellent thing, and without it a whole lifetime is a mere waste, and what good comes in the long run? There's only one thing, which is simply that when engaged in reading your books, you should set your mind on your books; and that you should think of home when not engaged in reading. Whatever you do, don't romp together with them, for were you to meet our master, your father, it will be no joke! Although it's asserted that a scholar must strain every nerve to excel, yet it's preferable that the tasks should be somewhat fewer, as, in the first place, when one eats too much, one cannot digest it; and, in the second place, good health must also be carefully attended to. This is my view on the subject, and you should at all times consider it in practice."

While Hsi Jen gave utterance to a sentence, Pao-yü nodded his head in sign of approval of that sentence. Hsi Jen then went on to speak. "I've also packed up," she continued, "your long pelisse, and handed it to the pages to take it over; so mind, when it's cold in the school-room, please remember to put on this extra clothing, for it's not like home, where you have people to look after you. The foot-stove and hand-stove, I've also sent over; and urge that pack of lazy-bones to attend to their work, for if you say nothing, they will be so engrossed in their frolics, that they'll be loth to move, and let you, all for nothing, take a chill and ruin your constitution."

"Compose your mind," replied Pao-yü; "when I go out, I know well enough how to attend to everything my own self. But you people shouldn't remain in this room, and mope yourselves to death; and it would be well if you would often go over to cousin Lin's for a romp."

While saying this, he had completed his toilette, and Hsi Jen pressed him to go and wish good morning to dowager lady Chia, Chia Cheng, madame Wang, and the other members of the family.

Pao-yü, after having gone on to give a few orders to Ch'ing Wen and She Yueh, at length left his apartments, and coming over, paid his obeisance to dowager lady Chia. Her venerable Ladyship had likewise, as a matter of course, a few recommendations to make to him, which ended, he next went and greeted madame Wang; and leaving again her quarters, he came into the library to wish Chia Cheng good morning.

As it happened, Chia Cheng had on this day returned home at an early hour, and was, at this moment, in the library, engaged in a friendly chat with a few gentlemen, who were family companions. Suddenly perceiving Pao-yü come in to pay his respects, and report that he was about to go to school, Chia Cheng gave a sardonic smile. "If you do again," he remarked, "make allusions to the words going to school, you'll make even me blush to death with shame! My advice to you is that you should after all go your own way and play; that's the best thing for you; and mind you don't pollute with dirt this floor by standing here, and soil this door of mine by leaning against it!"

The family companions stood up and smilingly expostulated.

"Venerable Sir," they pleaded, "why need you be so down upon him? Our worthy brother is this day going to school, and may in two or three years be able to display his abilities and establish his reputation. He will, beyond doubt, not behave like a child, as he did in years gone past. But as the time for breakfast is also drawing nigh, you should, worthy brother, go at once."

When these words had been spoken, two among them, who were advanced in years, readily took Pao-yü by the hand, and led him out of the library.

"Who are in attendance upon Pao-yü?" Chia Cheng having inquired, he heard a suitable reply, "We, Sir!" given from outside; and three or four sturdy fellows entered at an early period and fell on one knee, and bowed and paid their obeisance.

When Chia Cheng came to scrutinise who they were, and he recognised Li Kuei, the son of Pao-yü's nurse, he addressed himself to him. "You people," he said, "remain waiting upon him the whole day long at school, but what books has he after all read? Books indeed! why, he has read and filled his brains with a lot of trashy words and nonsensical phrases, and learnt some ingenious way of waywardness. Wait till I have a little leisure, and I'll set to work, first and foremost, and flay your skin off, and then settle accounts with that good-for-nothing!"

This threat so terrified Li Kuei that he hastily fell on both his knees, pulled off his hat, knocked his head on the ground, and gave vent to repeated assenting utterances: "Oh, quite so, Sir! Our elder brother Mr. Pao has," he continued, "already read up to the third book of the Book of Odes, up to where there's something or other like: 'Yiu, Yiu, the deer bleat; the lotus leaves and duckweed.' Your servant wouldn't presume to tell a lie!"

As he said this, the whole company burst out into a boisterous fit of laughter, and Chia Cheng himself could not also contain his countenance and had to laugh. "Were he even," he observed, "to read thirty books of the Book of Odes, it would be as much an imposition upon people and no more, as (when the thief) who, in order to steal the bell, stops up his own ears! You go and present my compliments to the gentleman in the schoolroom, and tell him, from my part, that the whole lot of Odes and old writings are of no use, as they are subjects for empty show; and that he should, above all things, take the Four Books, and explain them to him, from first to last, and make him know them all thoroughly by heart,—that this is the most important thing!"

Li Kuei signified his obedience with all promptitude, and perceiving that Chia Cheng had nothing more to say, he retired out of the room.

During this while, Pao-yü had been standing all alone outside in the court, waiting quietly with suppressed voice, and when they came out he at once walked away in their company.

Li Kuei and his companions observed as they shook their clothes, "Did you, worthy brother, hear what he said that he would first of all flay our skins off! People's servants acquire some respectability from the master whom they serve, but we poor fellows fruitlessly wait upon you, and are beaten and blown up in the bargain. It would be well if we were, from henceforward, to be treated with a certain amount of regard."

Pao-yü smiled, "Dear Brother," he added, "don't feel aggrieved; I'll invite you to come round to-morrow!"

"My young ancestor," replied Li Kuei, "who presumes to look forward to an invitation? all I entreat you is to listen to one or two words I have to say, that's all."

As they talked they came over once more to dowager lady Chia's on this side.

Ch'in Chung had already arrived, and the old lady was first having a chat with him. Forthwith the two of them exchanged salutations, and took leave of her ladyship; but Pao-yü, suddenly remembering that he had not said good-bye to Tai-yü, promptly betook himself again to Tai-yü's quarters to do so.

Tai-yü was, at this time, below the window, facing the mirror, and adjusting her toilette. Upon hearing Pao-yü mention that he was on his way to school, she smiled and remarked, "That's right! you're now going to school and you'll be sure to reach the lunar palace and pluck the olea fragrans; but I can't go along with you."

"My dear cousin," rejoined Pao-yü, "wait for me to come out from school, before you have your evening meal; wait also until I come to prepare the cosmetic of rouge."

After a protracted chat, he at length tore himself away and took his departure.

"How is it," interposed Tai-yü, as she once again called out to him and stopped him, "that you don't go and bid farewell to your cousin Pao Ch'ai?"

Pao-yü smiled, and saying not a word by way of reply he straightway walked to school, accompanied by Ch'in Chung.

This public school, which it must be noticed was also not far from his quarters, had been originally instituted by the founder of the establishment, with the idea that should there be among the young fellows of his clan any who had not the means to engage a tutor, they should readily be able to enter this class for the prosecution of their studies; that all those of the family who held official position should all give (the institution) pecuniary assistance, with a view to meet the expenses necessary for allowances to the students; and that they were to select men advanced in years and possessed of virtue to act as tutors of the family school.

The two of them, Ch'in Chung and Pao-yü, had now entered the class, and after they and the whole number of their schoolmates had made each other's acquaintance, their studies were commenced. Ever since this time, these two were wont to come together, go together, get up together, and sit together, till they became more intimate and close. Besides, dowager lady Chia got very fond of Ch'in Chung, and would again and again keep him to stay with them for three and five days at a time, treating him as if he were one of her own great-grandsons. Perceiving that in Ch'in Chung's home there was not much in the way of sufficiency, she also helped him in clothes and other necessaries; and scarcely had one or two months elapsed before Ch'in Chung got on friendly terms with every one in the Jung mansion.

Pao-yü was, however, a human being who could not practise contentment and observe propriety; and as his sole delight was to have every caprice gratified, he naturally developed a craving disposition. "We two, you and I, are," he was also wont secretly to tell Ch'in Chung, "of the same age, and fellow-scholars besides, so that there's no need in the future to pay any regard to our relationship of uncle and nephew; and we should treat each other as brothers or friends, that's all."

Ch'in Chung at first (explained that) he could not be so presumptuous; but as Pao-yü would not listen to any such thing, but went on to address him as brother and to call him by his style Ch'ing Ch'ing, he had likewise himself no help, but to begin calling him, at random, anything and anyhow.

There were, it is true, a large number of pupils in this school, but these consisted of the sons and younger brothers of that same clan, and of several sons and nephews of family connections. The proverb appositely describes that there are nine species of dragons, and that each species differs; and it goes of course without saying that in a large number of human beings there were dragons and snakes, confusedly admixed, and that creatures of a low standing were included.

Ever since the arrival of the two young fellows, Ch'in Chung and Pao-yü, both of whom were in appearance as handsome as budding flowers, and they, on the one hand, saw how modest and genial Ch'in

Chung was, how he blushed before he uttered a word, how he was timid and demure like a girl, and on the other hand, how that Pao-yü was naturally proficient in abasing and demeaning himself, how he was so affable and good-natured, considerate in his temperament and so full of conversation, and how that these two were, in consequence, on such terms of intimate friendship, it was, in fact, no matter of surprise that the whole company of fellow-students began to foster envious thoughts, that they, behind their backs, passed on their account, this one one disparaging remark and that one another, and that they insinuated slanderous lies against them, which extended inside as well as outside the school-room.

Indeed, after Hsüeh P'an had come over to take up his quarters in madame Wang's suite of apartments, he shortly came to hear of the existence of a family school, and that this school was mainly attended by young fellows of tender years, and inordinate ideas were suddenly aroused in him. While he therefore fictitiously gave out that he went to school, [he was as irregular in his attendance as the fisherman] who catches fish for three days, and suns his nets for the next two; simply presenting his school-fee gift to Chia Tai-jui and making not the least progress in his studies; his sole dream being to knit a number of familiar friendships. Who would have thought it, there were in this school young pupils, who, in their greed to obtain money, clothes and eatables from Hsüeh P'an, allowed themselves to be cajoled by him, and played tricks upon; but on this topic, it is likewise superfluous to dilate at any length.

There were also two lovable young scholars, relatives of what branch of the family is not known, and whose real surnames and names have also not been ascertained, who, by reason of their good and winsome looks, were, by the pupils in the whole class, given two nicknames, to one that of "Hsiang Lin," "Fragrant Love," and to the other "Yü Ai," "Precious Affection." But although every one entertained feelings of secret admiration for them, and had the wish to take liberties with the young fellows, they lived, nevertheless, one and all, in such terror of Hsüeh P'an's imperious influence, that they had not the courage to come forward and interfere with them.

As soon as Ch'in Chung and Pao-yü had, at this time, come to school, and they had made the acquaintance of these two fellow-pupils, they too could not help becoming attached to them and admiring them, but as they also came to know that they were great friends of Hsüeh P'an, they did not, in consequence, venture to treat them lightly, or to be unseemly in their behaviour towards them. Hsiang Lin and Yü

Ai both kept to themselves the same feelings, which they fostered for Ch'in Chung and Pao-yü, and to this reason is to be assigned the fact that though these four persons nurtured fond thoughts in their hearts there was however no visible sign of them. Day after day, each one of them would, during school hours, sit in four distinct places: but their eight eyes were secretly linked together; and, while indulging either in innuendoes or in double entendres, their hearts, in spite of the distance between them, reflected the whole number of their thoughts.

But though their outward attempts were devoted to evade the detection of other people's eyes, it happened again that, while least expected, several sly lads discovered the real state of affairs, with the result that the whole school stealthily frowned their eyebrows at them, winked their eyes at them, or coughed at them, or raised their voices at them; and these proceedings were, in fact, not restricted to one single day.

As luck would have it, on this day Tai-jui was, on account of business, compelled to go home; and having left them as a task no more than a heptameter line for an antithetical couplet, explaining that they should find a sentence to rhyme, and that the following day when he came back, he would set them their lessons, he went on to hand the affairs connected with the class to his elder grandson, Chia Jui, whom he asked to take charge.

Wonderful to say Hsüeh P'an had of late not frequented school very often, not even so much as to answer the roll, so that Ch'in Chung availed himself of his absence to ogle and smirk with Hsiang Lin; and these two pretending that they had to go out, came into the back court for a chat.

"Does your worthy father at home mind your having any friends?" Ch'in Chung was the first to ask. But this sentence was scarcely ended, when they heard a sound of coughing coming from behind. Both were taken much aback, and, speedily turning their heads round to see, they found that it was a fellow-scholar of theirs, called Chin Jung.

Hsiang Lin was naturally of somewhat hasty temperament, so that with shame and anger mutually impelling each other, he inquired of him, "What's there to cough at? Is it likely you wouldn't have us speak to each other?"

"I don't mind your speaking," Chin Jung observed laughing; "but would you perchance not have me cough? I'll tell you what, however; if you have anything to say, why not utter it in intelligible language? Were you allowed to go on in this mysterious manner, what strange doings would you be up to? But I have sure enough found you out, so what's the need of still prevaricating? But if you will, first of all, let me partake of a share in your little game, you and I can hold our tongue and utter not a word. If not, why the whole school will begin to turn the matter over."

At these words, Ch'in Chung and Hsiang Lin were so exasperated that their blood rushed up to their faces. "What have you found out?" they hastily asked.

"What I have now detected," replied Chin Jung smiling, "is the plain truth!" and saying this he went on to clap his hands and to call out with a loud voice as he laughed: "They have moulded some nice well-baked cakes, won't you fellows come and buy one to eat!" (These two have been up to larks, won't you come and have some fun!)

Both Ch'in Chung and Hsiang Lin felt resentful as well as fuming with rage, and with hurried step they went in, in search of Chia Jui, to whom they reported Chin Jung, explaining that Chin Jung had insulted them both, without any rhyme or reason.

The fact is that this Chia Jui was, in an extraordinary degree, a man with an eye to the main chance, and devoid of any sense of propriety. His wont was at school to take advantage of public matters to serve his private interest, and to bring pressure upon his pupils with the intent that they should regale him. While subsequently he also lent his countenance to Hsüeh P'an, scheming to get some money or eatables out of him, he left him entirely free to indulge in disorderly behaviour; and not only did he not go out of his way to hold him in check, but, on the contrary, he encouraged him, infamous though he was already, to become a bully, so as to curry favour with him.

But this Hsüeh P'an was, by nature, gifted with a fickle disposition; to-day, he would incline to the east, and to-morrow to the west, so that having recently obtained new friends, he put Hsiang Lin and Yü Ai aside. Chin Jung too was at one time an intimate friend of his, but ever since he had acquired the friendship of the two lads, Hsiang Lin and Yü Ai, he forthwith deposed Chin Jung. Of late, he had already come to look down upon even Hsiang Lin and Yü Ai, with the result that Chia Jui as well was deprived of those who could lend him support, or stand by him; but he bore Hsüeh P'an no grudge, for wearying with old friends, as soon as he found new ones, but felt angry that Hsiang Lin and Yü Ai had not put in a word on his behalf with Hsüeh P'an. Chia Jui, Chin Jung and in fact the whole crowd of them were, for this reason, just harbouring a jealous grudge against these two, so that when he saw Ch'in Chung and Hsiang Lin come on this occasion and lodge a complaint against Chin Jung, Chia Jui readily felt displeasure creep into his heart; and, although he did not venture to call Ch'in Chung to account, he nevertheless made an example of Hsiang Lin. And instead (of taking his part), he called him a busybody and denounced him in much abusive language, with the result that Hsiang Lin did not, contrariwise, profit in any way, but brought displeasure upon himself. Even Ch'in Chung grumbled against the treatment, as each of them resumed their places.

Chin Jung became still more haughty, and wagging his head and smacking his lips, he gave vent to many more abusive epithets; but as it happened that they also reached Yü Ai's ears, the two of them, though seated apart, began an altercation in a loud tone of voice.

Chin Jung, with obstinate pertinacity, clung to his version. "Just a short while back," he said, "I actually came upon them, as they were indulging in demonstrations of intimate friendship in the back court. These two had resolved to be one in close friendship, and were eloquent in their protestations, mindful only in persistently talking their trash, but they were not aware of the presence of another person."

But his language had, contrary to all expectations, given, from the very first, umbrage to another person, and who do you, (gentle reader,) imagine this person to have been?

This person was, in fact, one whose name was Chia Se; a grandson likewise of a main branch of the Ning mansion. His parents had died at an early period, and he had, ever since his youth, lived with Chia Chen. He had at this time grown to be sixteen years of age, and was, as compared with Chia Jung, still more handsome and good looking. These two cousins were united by ties of the closest intimacy, and were always together, whether they went out or stayed at home.

The inmates of the Ning mansion were many in number, and their opinions of a mixed kind; and that whole bevy of servants, devoid as they were of all sense of right, solely excelled in the practice of inventing stories to backbite their masters; and this is how some mean person or other again, who it was is not known, insinuated slanderous and opprobrious reports (against Chia Se). Chia Chen had, presumably, also come to hear some unfavourable criticisms (on his account), and having, of course, to save himself from odium and suspicion, he had, at this juncture, after all, to apportion him separate quarters, and to bid Chia Se move outside the Ning mansion, where he went and established a home of his own to live in.

This Chia Se was handsome as far as external appearances went, and intelligent withal in his inward natural gifts, but, though he nominally came to school, it was simply however as a mere blind; for he treated, as he had ever done, as legitimate occupations, such things as cock fighting, dog-racing and visiting places of easy virtue. And as, above, he had Chia Chen to spoil him by over-indulgence; and below, there was Chia Jung to stand by him, who of the clan could consequently presume to run counter to him?

Seeing that he was on the closest terms of friendship with Chia Jung, how could he reconcile himself to the harsh treatment which he now saw Ch'in Chung receive from some persons? Being now bent upon pushing himself forward to revenge the injustice, he was, for the time, giving himself up to communing with his own heart. "Chin Jung, Chia Jui and the rest are," he pondered, "friends of uncle Hsüeh, but I too am on friendly terms with him, and he with me, and if I do come forward and they tell old Hsüeh, won't we impair the harmony which exists between us? and if I don't concern myself, such idle tales make, when spoken, every one feel uncomfortable; and why shouldn't I now devise some means to hold them in check, so as to stop their mouths, and prevent any loss of face!"

Having concluded this train of thought, he also pretended that he had to go out, and, walking as far as the back, he, with low voice, called to his side Ming Yen, the page attending upon Pao-yü in his studies, and in one way and another, he made use of several remarks to egg him on.

This Ming Yen was the smartest of Pao-yü's attendants, but he was also young in years and lacked experience, so that he lent a patient ear to what Chia Se had to say about the way Chin Jung had insulted Ch'in Chung. "Even your own master, Pao-yü," (Chia Se added), "is involved, and if you don't let him know a bit of your mind, he will next time be still more arrogant."

This Ming Yen was always ready, even with no valid excuse, to be insolent and overbearing to people, so that after hearing the news and being furthermore instigated by Chia Se, he speedily rushed into the schoolroom and cried out "Chin Jung;" nor did he address him as Mr. Chin, but merely shouted "What kind of fellow is this called Chin?"

Chia Se presently shuffled his feet, while he designedly adjusted his dress and looked at the rays of the sun. "It's time," he observed and walking forthwith, first up to Chia Jui, he explained to him that he had something to attend to and would like to get away a little early; and as Chia Jui did not venture to stop him, he had no alternative but to let him have his way and go.

During this while, Ming Yen had entered the room and promptly seizing Chin Jung in a grip: "What we do, whether proper or improper," he said, "doesn't concern you! It's enough anyway that we don't defile your father! A fine brat you are indeed, to come out and meddle with your Mr. Ming!"

These words plunged the scholars of the whole class in such consternation that they all wistfully and absently looked at him.

"Ming Yen," hastily shouted out Chia Jui, "you're not to kick up a rumpus."

Chin Jung was so full of anger that his face was quite yellow. "What a subversion of propriety! a slave and a menial to venture to behave in this manner! I'll just simply speak to your master," he exclaimed as he readily pushed his hands off and was about to go and lay hold of Pao-yü to beat him.

Ch'in Chung was on the point of turning round to leave the room, when with a sound of 'whiff' which reached him from behind, he at once caught sight of a square inkslab come flying that way. Who had thrown it he could not say, but it struck the desk where Chia Lan and Chia Chün were seated.

These two, Chia Lan and Chia Chün, were also the great-grandsons of a close branch of the Jung mansion. This Chia Chün had been left fatherless at an early age, and his mother doated upon him in an unusual manner, and it was because at school he was on most friendly terms with Chia Lan, that these two sat together at the same desk. Who would have believed that Chia Chün would, in spite of being young in years, have had an extremely strong mind, and that he would be mostly up to mischief without the least fear of any one. He watched with listless eye from his seat Chin Jung's friends stealthily assist Chin Jung, as they flung an inkslab to strike Ming Yen, but when, as luck would have it, it hit the wrong mark, and fell just in front of him, smashing to atoms the porcelain inkslab and water bottle, and smudging his whole book with ink, Chia Chün was, of course, much incensed, and hastily gave way to abuse. "You consummate pugnacious criminal rowdies! why, doesn't this amount to all of you taking a share in the fight!" And as he uttered this abuse, he too forthwith seized an inkslab, which he was bent upon flinging.

Chia Lan was one who always tried to avoid trouble, so that he lost no time in pressing down the inkslab, while with all the words his mouth could express, he tried to pacify him, adding "My dear brother, it's no business of yours and mine."

Chia Chün could not repress his resentment; and perceiving that the inkslab was held down, he at once laid hold of a box containing books, which he flung in this direction; but being, after all, short of stature, and weak of strength, he was unable to send it anywhere near the mark; so that it dropped instead when it got as far as the desk belonging to Pao-yü and Ch'in Chung, while a dreadful crash became audible as it fell smash on the table. The books, papers, pencils, inkslabs, and other writing materials were all scattered over the whole table; and Pao-yü's cup besides containing tea was itself broken to pieces and the tea spilt.

Chia Chün forthwith jumped forward with the intent of assailing the person who had flung the inkslab at the very moment that Chin Jung took hold of a long bamboo pole which was near by; but as the space was limited, and the pupils many, how could he very well brandish a long stick? Ming Yen at an early period received a whack, and he shouted wildly, "Don't you fellows yet come to start a fight."

Pao-yü had, besides, along with him several pages, one of whom was called Sao Hung, another Ch'u Yo, another Mo Yü. These three were naturally up to every mischief, so that with one voice, bawling boisterously, "You children of doubtful mothers, have you taken up arms?" Mo Yü promptly took up the bar of a door; while Sao Hung and Ch'u Yo both laid hold of horsewhips, and they all rushed forward like a hive of bees.

Chia Jui was driven to a state of exasperation; now he kept this one in check, and the next moment he reasoned with another, but who would listen to his words? They followed the bent of their inclinations and stirred up a serious disturbance.

Of the whole company of wayward young fellows, some there were who gave sly blows for fun's sake; others there were who were not gifted with much pluck and hid themselves on one side; there were those too who stood on the tables, clapping their hands and laughing immoderately, shouting out: "Go at it."

The row was, at this stage, like water bubbling over in a cauldron, when several elderly servants, like Li Kuei and others, who stood outside, heard the uproar commence inside, and one and all came in with all haste and united in their efforts to pacify them. Upon asking "What's the matter?" the whole bevy of voices shouted out different versions; this one giving this account, while another again another story. But Li Kuei temporised by rebuking Ming Yen and others, four in all, and packing them off.

Ch'in Chung's head had, at an early period, come into contact with Chin Jung's pole and had had the skin grazed off. Pao-yü was in the act of rubbing it for him, with the overlap of his coat, but realising that the whole lot of them had been hushed up, he forthwith bade Li Kuei collect his books.

"Bring my horse round," he cried; "I'm going to tell Mr. Chia Tai-ju that we have been insulted. I won't venture to tell him anything else, but (tell him I will) that having come with all propriety and made our report to Mr. Chia Jui, Mr. Chia Jui instead (of helping us) threw the fault upon our shoulders. That while he heard people abuse us, he went so far as to instigate them to beat us; that Ming Yen seeing others insult us, did naturally take our part; but that they, instead (of desisting,) combined together and struck Ming Yen and even broke open Ch'in Chung's head. And that how is it possible for us to continue our studies in here?"

"My dear sir," replied Li Kuei coaxingly, "don't be so impatient! As Mr. Chia Tai-ju has had something to attend to and gone home, were you now, for a trifle like this, to go and disturb that aged gentleman, it will make us, indeed, appear as if we had no sense of propriety: my idea is that wherever a thing takes place, there should it be settled; and what's the need of going and troubling an old man like him. This is all you, Mr. Chia Jui, who is to blame; for in the absence of Mr. Chia Tai-ju, you, sir, are the head in this school, and every one looks to you to take action. Had all the pupils been at fault, those who deserved a beating should have been beaten, and those who merited punishment should have been punished! and why did you wait until things came to such a pass, and didn't even exercise any check?"

"I blew them up," pleaded Chia Jui, "but not one of them would listen."

"I'll speak out, whether you, worthy sir, resent what I'm going to say or not," ventured Li Kuei. "It's you, sir, who all along have after all had considerable blame attached to your name; that's why all these young men wouldn't hear you! Now if this affair is bruited, until it reaches Mr. Chia Tai-ju's ears, why even you, sir, will not be able to escape condemnation; and why don't you at once make up your mind to disentangle the ravelled mess and dispel all trouble and have done with it!"

"Disentangle what?" inquired Pao-yü; "I shall certainly go and make my report."

"If Chin Jung stays here," interposed Ch'in Chung sobbing, "I mean to go back home."

"Why that?" asked Pao-yü. "Is it likely that others can safely come and that you and I can't? I feel it my bounden duty to tell every one everything at home so as to expel Chin Jung. This Chin Jung," he went on to inquire as he turned towards Lei Kuei, "is the relative or friend of what branch of the family?"

Li Kuei gave way to reflection and then said by way of reply: "There's no need whatever for you to raise this question; for were you to go and report the matter to the branch of the family to which he belongs, the harmony which should exist between cousins will be still more impaired."

"He's the nephew of Mrs. Huang, of the Eastern mansion," interposed Ming Yen from outside the window. "What a determined and self-confident fellow he must be to even come and bully us; Mrs. Huang is his paternal aunt! That mother of yours is only good for tossing about like a millstone, for kneeling before our lady Lien, and begging for something to pawn. I've no eye for such a specimen of mistress."

"What!" speedily shouted Li Kuei, "does this son of a dog happen to know of the existence of all these gnawing maggots?" (these disparaging facts).

Pao-yü gave a sardonic smile. "I was wondering whose relative he was," he remarked; "is he really sister-in-law Huang's nephew? well, I'll go at once and speak to her."

As he uttered these words, his purpose was to start there and then, and he called Ming Yen in, to come and pack up his books. Ming Yen walked in and put the books away. "Master," he went on to suggest, in an exultant manner, "there's no need for you to go yourself to see her; I'll go to her house and tell her that our old lady has something to ask of her. I can hire a carriage to bring her over, and then, in the presence of her venerable ladyship, she can be spoken to; and won't this way save a lot of trouble?"

"Do you want to die?" speedily shouted Li Kuei; "mind, when you go back, whether right or wrong, I'll first give you a good bumping, and then go and report you to our master and mistress, and just tell them that it's you, and only you, who instigated Mr. Pao-yü! I've succeeded, after ever so much trouble, in coaxing them, and mending matters to a certain extent, and now you come again to continue a new plan. It's you who stirred up this row in the school-room; and not to speak of your finding, as would have been the proper course, some way of suppressing it, there you are instead still jumping into the fire."

Ming Yen, at this juncture, could not muster the courage to utter a sound. By this time Chia Jui had also apprehended that if the row came to be beyond clearing up, he himself would likewise not be clear of blame, so that circumstances compelled him to pocket his grievances and to come and entreat Ch'in Chung as well as to make apologies to Pao-yü. These two young fellows would not at first listen to his advances, but Pao-yü at length explained that he would not go and report the occurrence, provided only Chin Jung admitted his being in the wrong. Chin Jung refused, at the outset, to agree to this, but he ultimately could find no way out of it, as Chia Jui himself urged him to make some temporising apology.

Li Kuei and the others felt compelled to tender Chin Jung some good advice: "It's you," they said, "who have given rise to the disturbance, and if you don't act in this manner, how will the matter ever be brought to an end?" so that Chin Jung found it difficult to persist in his obstinacy, and was constrained to make a bow to Ch'in Chung.

Pao-yü was, however, not yet satisfied, but would insist upon his knocking his head on the ground, and Chia Jui, whose sole aim was to temporarily smother the affair, quietly again urged Chin Jung, adding that the proverb has it: "That if you keep down the anger of a minute, you will for a whole life-time feel no remorse."

Whether Chin Jung complied or not to his advice is not known, but the following chapter will explain.

CHAPTER X.

Widow Chin, prompted by a desire to reap advantage, puts up temporarily with an insult.
Dr. Chang in discussing Mrs. Chin's illness minutely exhausts its origin.

We will now resume our story. As the persons against Chin Jung were so many and their pressure so great, and as, what was more, Chia Jui urged him to make amends, he had to knock his head on the ground before Ch'in Chung. Pao-yü then gave up his clamorous remonstrances and the whole crowd dispersed from school.

Chin Jung himself returned home all alone, but the more he pondered on the occurrence, the more incensed he felt. "Ch'in Chung," he argued, "is simply Chia Jung's young brother-in-law, and is no son or grandson of the Chia family, and he too joins the class and prosecutes his studies on no other footing than that of mine; but it's because he relies upon Pao-yü's friendship for him that he has no eye for any one. This being the case, he should be somewhat proper in his behaviour, and there would be then not a word to say about it! He has besides all along been very mystical with Pao-yü, imagining that we are all blind, and have no eyes to see what's up! Here he goes again to-day and mixes with people in illicit intrigues; and it's all because they happened to obtrude themselves before my very eyes that this rumpus has broken out; but of what need I fear?"

His mother, née Hu, hearing him mutter; "Why meddle again," she explained, "in things that don't concern you? I had endless trouble in getting to speak to your paternal aunt; and your aunt had, on the other hand, a thousand and one ways and means to devise, before she could appeal to lady Secunda, of the Western mansion; and then only it was that you got this place to study in. Had we not others to depend upon for your studies, would we have in our house the means sufficient to engage a teacher? Besides, in other people's school, tea and eatables are all ready and found; and these two years that you've been there for your lessons, we've likewise effected at home a great saving in what would otherwise have been necessary for your eating and use. Something has been, it's true, economised; but you have further a liking for spick and span clothes. Besides, it's only through your being there to study, that you've come to know Mr. Hsüeh! that Mr. Hsüeh, who has even in one year given us so much pecuniary assistance as seventy and eighty taels! And now you would go and raise a row in this school-room! why, if we were bent upon finding such another place, I tell you plainly, and once for all, that we would find it more difficult than if we tried to scale the heavens! Now do quietly play for a while, and then go to sleep, and you'll be ever so much better for it then."

Chin Jung thereupon stifled his anger and held his tongue; and, after a short while, he in fact went to sleep of his own accord.

The next day he again went to school, and no further comment need be made about it; but we will go on to explain that a young lady related to her had at one time been given in marriage to a descendant (of the eldest branch) of the Chia family, (whose names were written) with the jade radical, Chia Huang by name; but how could the whole number of members of the clan equal in affluence and power the two mansions of Ning and Jung? This fact goes, as a matter of course, without saying. The Chia Huang couple enjoyed some small income; but they also went, on frequent occasions, to the mansions of Ning and Jung to pay their respects; and they knew likewise so well how to adulate lady Feng and Mrs. Yu, that lady Feng and Mrs. Yu would often grant them that assistance and support which afforded them the means of meeting their daily expenses.

It just occurred on this occasion that the weather was clear and fine, and that there happened, on the other hand, to be nothing to attend to at home, so forthwith taking along with her a matron, (Mrs. Chia Huang) got into a carriage and came over to see widow Chin and her nephew. While engaged in a chat, Chin Jung's mother accidentally broached the subject of the affair, which had transpired in the school-room of the Chia mansion on the previous day, and she gave, for the benefit of her young sister-in-law, a detailed account of the whole occurrence from beginning to end.

This Mrs. Huang would not have had her temper ruffled had she not come to hear what had happened; but having heard about it, anger sprung from the very depths of her heart. "This fellow, Ch'in Chung," she exclaimed, "is a relative of the Chia family, but is it likely that Jung Erh isn't, in like manner, a relative of the Chia family; and when relatives are many, there's no need to put on airs! Besides, does his conduct consist, for the most part, of anything that would make one get any face? In fact, Pao-yü himself shouldn't do injury to himself by condescending to look at him. But, as things have come to this pass, give me time and I'll go to the Eastern mansion and see our lady Chen and then have a chat with Ch'in Chung's sister, and ask her to decide who's right and who's wrong!"

Chin Jung's mother upon hearing these words was terribly distressed. "It's all through my hasty tongue," she observed with vehemence, "that I've told you all, sister-in-law: but please, sister, give up at once the idea of going over to say anything about it! Don't trouble yourself as to who is in the right, and who is in the wrong; for were any unpleasantness to come out of it, how could we here stand on our legs? and were we not to stand on our legs, not only would we never be able to engage a tutor, but the result will be, on the contrary, that for his own person will be superadded many an expense for eatables and necessaries."

"What do I care about how many?" replied Mrs. Huang; "wait till I've spoken about it, and we'll see what will be the result." Nor would she accede to her sister-in-law's entreaties, but bidding, at the same time, the matron look after the carriage, she got into it, and came over to the Ning Mansion.

On her arrival at the Ning Mansion, she entered by the eastern side gate, and dismounting from the carriage, she went in to call on Mrs. Yu, the spouse of Chia Chen, with whom she had not the courage to put on any high airs; but gently and quietly she made inquiries after her health, and after passing some irrelevant remarks, she ascertained: "How is it I don't see lady Jung to-day?"

"I don't know," replied Mrs. Yu, "what's the matter with her these last few days; but she hasn't been herself for two months and more; and the doctor who was asked to see her declares that it is nothing connected with any happy event. A couple of days back, she felt, as soon as the afternoon came, both to move, and both even to utter a word; while the brightness of her eyes was all dimmed; and I told her, 'You needn't stick to etiquette, for there's no use for you to come in the forenoon and evening, as required by conventionalities; but what you must do is, to look after your own health. Should any relative come over, there's also myself to receive them; and should any of the senior generation think your absence strange, I'll explain things for you, if you'll let me.'

"I also advised brother Jung on the subject: 'You shouldn't,' I said, 'allow any one to trouble her; nor let her be put out of temper, but let her quietly attend to her health, and she'll get all right. Should she fancy anything to eat, just come over here and fetch it; for, in the event of anything happening to her, were you to try and find another such a wife to wed, with such a face and such a disposition, why, I fear, were you even to seek with a lantern in hand, there would really be no place where you could discover her. And with such a temperament and deportment as hers, which of our relatives and which of our elders don't love her?' That's why my heart has been very distressed these two days! As luck would have it early this morning her brother turned up to see her, but who would have fancied him to be such a child, and so ignorant of what is proper and not proper to do? He saw well enough that his sister was not well; and what's more all these matters shouldn't have been recounted to her; for even supposing he had received the gravest offences imaginable, it behoved him anyhow not to have broached the subject to her! Yesterday, one would scarcely believe it, a fight occurred in the school-room, and some pupil or other who attends that class, somehow insulted him; besides, in this business, there were a good many indecent and improper utterances, but all these he went and told his sister! Now, sister-in-law, you are well aware that though (our son Jung's) wife talks and laughs when she sees people, that she is nevertheless imaginative and withal too sensitive, so that no matter what she hears, she's for the most part bound to brood over it for three days and five nights, before she loses sight of it, and it's from this excessive sensitiveness that this complaint of hers arises. Today, when she heard that some one had insulted her brother, she felt both vexed and angry; vexed that those fox-like, cur-like friends of his had moved right and wrong, and intrigued with this one and deluded that one; angry that her brother had, by not learning anything profitable, and not having his mind set upon study, been the means of bringing about a row at school; and on account of this affair, she was so upset that she did not even have her early meal. I went over a short while back and consoled her for a time, and likewise gave her brother a few words of advice; and after having packed off that brother of hers to the mansion on the other side, in search of Pao-yü, and having stood by and seen her have half a bowl of birds' nests soup, I at length came over. Now, sister-in-law, tell me, is my heart sore or not? Besides, as there's nowadays no good doctor, the mere thought of her complaint makes my heart feel as if it were actually pricked with needles! But do you and yours, perchance, know of any good practitioner?"

Mrs. Chin had, while listening to these words, been, at an early period, so filled with concern that she cast away to distant lands the reckless rage she had been in recently while at her sister-in-law's house, when she had determined to go and discuss matters over with Mrs. Ch'in. Upon hearing Mrs. Yu inquire of her about a good doctor, she lost no time in saying by way of reply: "Neither have we heard of any one speak of a good doctor; but from the account I've just heard of Mrs. Ch'in's illness, it may still, there's no saying, be some felicitous ailment; so, sister-in-law, don't let any one treat her recklessly, for were she to be treated for the wrong thing, the result may be dreadful!"

"Quite so!" replied Mrs. Yu.

But while they were talking, Chia Chen came in from out of doors, and upon catching sight of Mrs. Chin; "Isn't this Mrs. Huang?" he inquired of Mrs. Yu; whereupon Mrs. Chin came forward and paid her respects to Chia Chen.

"Invite this lady to have her repast here before she goes," observed Chia Chen to Mrs. Yu; and as he uttered these words he forthwith walked into the room on the off side.

The object of Mrs. Chin's present visit had originally been to talk to Mrs. Ch'in about the insult which her brother had received from the hands of Ch'in Chung, but when she heard that Mrs. Ch'in was ill, she did not have the courage to even so much as make mention of the object of her errand. Besides, as Chia Chen and Mrs. Yu had given her a most cordial reception, her resentment was transformed into pleasure, so that after a while spent in a further chat about one thing and another, she at length returned to her home.

It was only after the departure of Mrs. Chin that Chia Chen came over and took a seat. "What did she have to say for herself during this visit to-day?" he asked of Mrs. Yu.

"She said nothing much," replied Mrs. Yu. "When she first entered the room, her face bore somewhat of an angry look, but, after a lengthy chat and as soon as mention of our son's wife's illness was made, this angered look after all gradually abated. You also asked me to keep her for the repast, but, having heard that our son's wife was so ill she could not very well stay, so that all she did was to sit down, and after making a few more irrelevant remarks, she took her departure. But she had no request to make. To return however now to the illness of Jung's wife, it's urgent that you should find somewhere a good doctor to diagnose it for her; and whatever you do, you should lose no time. The whole body of doctors who at present go in and out of our household, are they worth having? Each one of them listens to what the patient has to say of the ailment, and then, adding a string of flowery sentences, out he comes with a long rigmarole; but they are exceedingly diligent in paying us visits; and in one day, three or four of them are here at least four and five times in rotation! They come and feel her pulse, they hold consultation together, and write their prescriptions, but, though she has taken their medicines, she has seen no improvement; on the contrary, she's compelled to change her clothes three and five times each day, and to sit up to see the doctor; a thing which, in fact, does the patient no good."

"This child too is somewhat simple," observed Chia Chen; "for what need has she to be taking off her clothes, and changing them for others? And were she again to catch a chill, she would add something more to her illness; and won't it be dreadful! The clothes may be no matter how fine, but what is their worth, after all? The health of our child is what is important to look to! and were she even to wear out a suit of new clothes a-day, what would that too amount to? I was about to tell you that a short while back, Feng Tzu-ying came to see me, and, perceiving that I had somewhat of a worried look, he asked me what was up; and I told him that our son's wife was not well at all, that as we couldn't get any good doctor, we couldn't determine with any certainty, whether she was in an interesting condition, or whether she was suffering from some disease; that as we could neither tell whether there was any danger or not, my heart was, for this reason, really very much distressed. Feng Tzu-ying then explained that he knew a young doctor who had made a study of his profession, Chang by surname, and Yu-shih by name, whose learning was profound to a degree; who was besides most proficient in the principles of medicine, and had the knack of discriminating whether a patient would live or die; that this year he had come to the capital to purchase an official rank for his son, and that he was now living with him in his house. In view of these circumstances, not knowing but that if, perchance, the case of our daughter-in-law were placed in his hands, he couldn't avert the danger, I readily despatched a servant, with a card of mine, to invite him to come; but the hour to-day being rather late, he probably won't be round, but I believe he's sure to be here to-morrow. Besides, Feng-Tzu-ying was also on his return home, to personally entreat him on my behalf, so that he's bound, when he has asked him, to come and see her. Let's therefore wait till Dr. Chang has been here and seen her, when we can talk matters over!"

Mrs. Yu was very much cheered when she heard what was said. "The day after to-morrow," she felt obliged to add, "is again our senior's, Mr. Chia Ching's birthday, and how are we to celebrate it after all?"

"I've just been over to our Senior's and paid my respects," replied Chia Chen, "and further invited the old gentleman to come home, and receive the congratulations of the whole family.

"'I'm accustomed,' our Senior explained, 'to peace and quiet, and have no wish to go over to that worldly place of yours; for you people are certain to have published that it's my birthday, and to entertain the design to ask me to go round to receive the bows of the whole lot of you. But won't it be better if you were to give the "Record of Meritorious Acts," which I annotated some time ago, to some one to copy out clean for me, and have it printed? Compared with asking me to come, and uselessly receive the obeisances of you all, this will be yea even a hundred times more profitable! In the event of the whole family wishing to pay me a visit on any of the two days, to-morrow or the day after to-morrow, if you were to stay at home and entertain them in proper style, that will be all that is wanted; nor will there be any need to send me anything! Even you needn't come two days from this; and should you not feel contented at heart, well, you had better bow your head before me to-day before you go. But if you do come again the day after to-morrow, with a lot of people to disturb me, I shall certainly be angry with you.' After what he said, I will not venture to go and see him two days hence; but you had better send for Lai Sheng, and bid him get ready a banquet to continue for a couple of days."

Mrs. Yu, having asked Chia Jung to come round, told him to direct Lai Sheng to make the usual necessary preparations for a banquet to last for a couple of days, with due regard to a profuse and sumptuous style.

"You go by-and-by," (she advised him), "in person to the Western Mansion and invite dowager lady Chia, mesdames Hsing and Wang, and your sister-in-law Secunda lady Lien to come over for a stroll. Your father has also heard of a good doctor, and having already sent some one to ask him round, I think that by to-morrow he's sure to come; and you had better tell him, in a minute manner, the serious symptoms of her ailment during these few days."

Chia Jung having signified his obedience to each of her recommendations, and taken his leave, was just in time to meet the youth coming back from Feng Tzu-ying's house, whither he had gone a short while back to invite the doctor round.

"Your slave," he consequently reported, "has just been with a card of master's to Mr. Feng's house and asked the doctor to come. 'The gentleman here,' replied the doctor, 'has just told me about it; but to-day, I've had to call on people the whole day, and I've only this moment come home; and I feel now my strength (so worn out), that I couldn't really stand any exertion. In fact were I even to get as far as the mansion, I shouldn't be in a fit state to diagnose the pulses! I must therefore have a night's rest, but, to-morrow for certain, I shall come to the mansion. My medical knowledge,' he went on to observe, 'is very shallow, and I don't deserve the honour of such eminent recommendation; but as Mr. Feng has already thus spoken of me in your mansion, I can't but present myself. It will be all right if in anticipation you deliver this message for me to your honourable master; but as for your worthy master's card, I cannot really presume to keep it.' It was again at his instance that I've brought it back; but, Sir, please mention this result for me (to master)."

Chia Jung turned back again, and entering the house delivered the message to Chia Chen and Mrs. Yu; whereupon he walked out, and, calling Lai Sheng before him, he transmitted to him the orders to prepare the banquet for a couple of days.

After Lai Sheng had listened to the directions, he went off, of course, to get ready the customary preparations; but upon these we shall not dilate, but confine ourselves to the next day.

At noon, a servant on duty at the gate announced that the Doctor Chang, who had been sent for, had come, and Chia Chen conducted him along the Court into the large reception Hall, where they sat down; and after they had partaken of tea, he broached the subject.

"Yesterday," he explained, "the estimable Mr. Feng did me the honour to speak to me of your character and proficiency, venerable doctor, as well as of your thorough knowledge of medicine, and I, your mean brother, was filled with an immeasurable sense of admiration!"

"Your Junior," remonstrated Dr. Chang, "is a coarse, despicable and mean scholar and my knowledge is shallow and vile! but as worthy Mr. Feng did me the honour yesterday of telling me that your family, sir, had condescended to look upon me, a low scholar, and to favour me too with an invitation, could I presume not to obey your commands? But as I cannot boast of the least particle of real learning, I feel overburdened with shame!"

"Why need you be so modest?" observed Chia Chen; "Doctor, do please walk in at once to see our son's wife, for I look up, with full reliance, to your lofty intelligence to dispel my solicitude!"

Chia Jung forthwith walked in with him. When they reached the inner apartment, and he caught sight of Mrs. Ch'in, he turned round and asked Chia Jung, "This is your honourable spouse, isn't it?"

"Yes, it is," assented Chia Jung; "but please, Doctor, take a seat, and let me tell you the symptoms of my humble wife's ailment, before her pulse be felt. Will this do?"

"My mean idea is," remarked the Doctor, "that it would, after all, be better that I should begin by feeling her pulse, before I ask you to inform me what the source of the ailment is. This is the first visit I pay to your honourable mansion; besides, I possess no knowledge of anything; but as our worthy Mr. Feng would insist upon my coming over to see you, I had in consequence no alternative but to come. After I have now made a diagnosis, you can judge whether what I say is right or not, before you explain to me the phases of the complaint during the last few days, and we can deliberate together upon some prescription; as to the suitableness or unsuitableness of which your honourable father will then have to decide, and what is necessary will have been done."

"Doctor," rejoined Chia Jung, "you are indeed eminently clear sighted; all I regret at present is that we have met so late! But please, Doctor, diagnose the state of the pulse, so as to find out whether there be hope of a cure or not; if a cure can be effected, it will be the means of allaying the solicitude of my father and mother."

The married women attached to that menage forthwith presented a pillow; and as it was being put down for Mrs. Ch'in to rest her arm on, they raised the lower part of her sleeve so as to leave her wrist exposed. The Doctor thereupon put out his hand and pressed it on the pulse of the right hand. Regulating his breath (to the pulsation) so as to be able to count the beatings, he with due care and minuteness felt the action for a considerable time, when, substituting the left hand, he again went through the same operation.

"Let us go and sit outside," he suggested, after he had concluded feeling her pulses. Chia Jung readily adjourned, in company with the Doctor, to the outer apartment, where they seated themselves on the stove-couch. A matron having served tea; "Please take a cup of tea, doctor," Chia Jung observed. When tea was over, "Judging," he inquired, "Doctor, from the present action of the pulses, is there any remedy or not?"

"The action of the pulse, under the forefinger, on the left hand of your honorable spouse," proceeded the Doctor, "is deep and agitated; the left hand pulse, under the second finger, is deep and faint. The pulse, under the forefinger, of the right hand, is gentle and lacks vitality. The right hand pulse, under my second finger, is superficial, and has lost all energy. The deep and agitated beating of the forepulse of the left hand arises from the febrile state, due to the weak action of the heart. The deep and delicate condition of the second part of the pulse of the left wrist, emanates from the sluggishness of the liver, and the scarcity of the blood in that organ. The action of the forefinger pulse, of the right wrist, is faint and lacks strength, as the breathing of the lungs is too weak. The second finger pulse of the right wrist is superficial and devoid of vigour, as the spleen must be affected injuriously by the liver. The weak action of the heart, and its febrile state, should be the natural causes which conduce to the present irregularity in the catamenia, and insomnia at night; the poverty of blood in the liver, and the sluggish condition of that organ must necessarily produce pain in the ribs; while the overdue of the catamenia, the cardiac fever, and debility of the respiration of the lungs, should occasion frequent giddiness in the head, and swimming of the eyes, the certain recurrence of perspiration between the periods of 3 to 5 and 5 to 7, and the sensation of being seated on board ship. The obstruction of the spleen by the liver should naturally create distaste for liquid or food, debility of the vital energies and prostration of the four limbs. From my diagnosis of these pulses, there should exist these various symptoms, before (the pulses and the symptoms can be said) to harmonise. But should perchance (any doctor maintain) that this state of the pulses imports a felicitous event, your servant will not presume to give an ear to such an opinion!"

A matron, who was attached as a personal attendant (to Mrs. Ch'in,) and who happened to be standing by interposed: "How could it be otherwise?" she ventured. "In real truth, Doctor, you speak like a supernatural being, and there's verily no need for us to say anything! We have now, ready at hand, in our household, a good number of medical gentlemen, who are in attendance upon her, but none of these are proficient enough to speak in this positive manner. Some there are who say that it's a genital complaint; others maintain that it's an organic disease. This doctor explains that there is no danger: while another, again, holds that there's fear of a crisis either before or after the winter solstice; but there is, in one word, nothing certain said by them. May it please you, sir, now to favour us with your clear directions."

"This complaint of your lady's," observed the Doctor, "has certainly been neglected by the whole number of doctors; for had a treatment with certain medicines been initiated at the time of the first occurrence of her habitual sickness, I cannot but opine that, by this time, a perfect cure would have been effected. But seeing that the organic complaint has now been, through neglect, allowed to reach this phase, this calamity was, in truth, inevitable. My ideas are that this illness stands, as yet, a certain chance of recovery, (three chances out of ten); but we will see how she gets on, after she has had these medicines of mine. Should they prove productive of sleep at night, then there will be added furthermore two more chances in the grip of our hands. From my diagnosis, your lady is a person, gifted with a preëminently excellent, and intelligent disposition; but an excessive degree of intelligence is the cause of frequent contrarieties; and frequent contrarieties give origin to an excessive amount of anxious cares. This illness arises from the injury done, by worrying and fretting, to the spleen, and from the inordinate vigour of the liver; hence it is that the relief cannot come at the proper time and season. Has not your lady, may I ask, heretofore at the period of the catamenia, suffered, if indeed not from anaemia, then necessarily from plethora? Am I right in assuming this or not?"

"To be sure she did," replied the matron; "but she has never been subject to anaemia, but to a plethora, varying from either two to three days, and extending, with much irregularity, to even ten days."

"Quite so!" observed the Doctor, after hearing what she had to say, "and this is the source of this organic illness! Had it in past days been treated with such medicine as could strengthen the heart, and improve the respiration, would it have reached this stage? This has now overtly made itself manifest in an ailment originating from the paucity of water and the vigour of fire; but let me make use of some medicines, and we'll see how she gets on!"

There and then he set to work and wrote a prescription, which he handed to Chia Jung, the purpose of which was: Decoction for the improvement of respiration, the betterment of the blood, and the restoration of the spleen. Ginseng, Atractylodes Lancea; Yunnan root; Prepared Ti root; Aralia edulis; Peony roots; Levisticum from Sze Ch'uan; Sophora tormentosa; Cyperus rotundus, prepared with rice; Gentian, soaked in vinegar; Huai Shan Yao root; Real "O" glue; Carydalis Ambigua; and Dried liquorice. Seven Fukien lotus seeds, (the cores of which should be extracted,) and two large zizyphi to be used as a preparative.

"What exalted intelligence!" Chia Jung, after perusing it, exclaimed. "But I would also ask you, Doctor, to be good enough to tell me whether this illness will, in the long run, endanger her life or not?"

The Doctor smiled. "You, sir, who are endowed with most eminent intelligence (are certain to know) that when a human illness has reached this phase, it is not a derangement of a day or of a single night; but after these medicines have been taken, we shall also have to watch the effect of the treatment! My humble opinion is that, as far as the winter of this year goes, there is no fear; in fact, after the spring equinox, I entertain hopes of a complete cure."

Chia Jung was likewise a person with all his wits about him, so that he did not press any further minute questions.

Chia Jung forthwith escorted the Doctor and saw him off, and taking the prescription and the diagnosis, he handed them both to Chia Chen for his perusal, and in like manner recounted to Chia Chen and Mrs. Yu all that had been said on the subject.

"The other doctors have hitherto not expressed any opinions as positive as this one has done," observed Mrs. Yu, addressing herself to Chia Chen, "so that the medicines to be used are, I think, surely the right ones!"

"He really isn't a man," rejoined Chia Chen, "accustomed to give much of his time to the practice of medicine, in order to earn rice for his support: and it's Feng Tzu-ying, who is so friendly with us, who is mainly to be thanked for succeeding, after ever so much trouble, in inducing him to come. But now that we have this man, the illness of our son's wife may, there is no saying, stand a chance of being cured. But on that prescription of his there is ginseng mentioned, so you had better make use of that catty of good quality which was bought the other day."

Chia Jung listened until the conversation came to a close, after which he left the room, and bade a servant go and buy the medicines, in order that they should be prepared and administered to Mrs. Ch'in.

What was the state of Mrs. Ch'in's illness, after she partook of these medicines, we do not know; but, reader, listen to the explanation given in the chapter which follows.

CHAPTER XI.

In honour of Chia Ching's birthday, a family banquet is spread in the Ning Mansion.
At the sight of Hsi-feng, Chia Jui entertains feelings of licentious love.

We will now explain, in continuation of our story, that on the day of Chia Ching's birthday, Chia Chen began by getting ready luscious delicacies and rare fruits, which he packed in sixteen spacious present boxes, and bade Chia Jung take them, along with the servants belonging to the household, over to Chia Ching.

Turning round towards Chia Jung: "Mind," he said, "that you observe whether your grandfather be agreeable or not, before you set to work and pay your obeisance! 'My father,' tell him, 'has complied with your directions, venerable senior, and not presumed to come over; but he has at home ushered the whole company of the members of the family (into your apartments), where they all paid their homage facing the side of honour.'"

After Chia Jung had listened to these injunctions, he speedily led off the family domestics, and took his departure. During this interval, one by one arrived the guests. First came Chia Lien and Chia Se, who went to see whether the seats in the various places (were sufficient). "Is there to be any entertainment or not?" they also inquired.

"Our master," replied the servants, "had, at one time, intended to invite the venerable Mr. Chia Ching to come and spend this day at home, and hadn't for this reason presumed to get up any entertainment. But when the other day he came to hear that the old gentleman was not coming, he at once gave us orders to go in search of a troupe of young actors, as well as a band of musicians, and all these people are now engaged making their preparations on the stage in the garden."

Next came, in a group, mesdames Hsing and Wang, lady Feng and Pao-yü, followed immediately after by Chia Chen and Mrs. Yu; Mrs. Yu's mother having already arrived and being in there in advance of her. Salutations were exchanged between the whole company, and they pressed one another to take a seat. Chia Chen and Mrs. Yu both handed the tea round.

"Our venerable lady," they explained, as they smiled, "is a worthy senior; while our father is, on the other hand, only her nephew; so that on a birthday of a man of his age, we should really not have had the audacity to invite her ladyship; but as the weather, at this time, is cool, and the chrysanthemums, in the whole garden, are in luxuriant blossom, we have requested our venerable ancestor to come for a little distraction, and to see the whole number of her children and grandchildren amuse themselves. This was the object we had in view, but, contrary to our expectations, our worthy senior has not again conferred upon us the lustre of her countenance."

Lady Feng did not wait until madame Wang could open her mouth, but took the initiative to reply. "Our venerable lady," she urged, "had, even so late as yesterday, said that she meant to come; but, in the evening, upon seeing brother Pao eating peaches, the mouth of the old lady once again began to water, and after partaking of a little more than the half of one, she had, about the fifth watch, to get out of bed two consecutive times, with the result that all the forenoon to-day, she felt her body considerably worn out. She therefore bade me inform our worthy senior that it was utterly impossible for her to come to-day; adding however that, if there were any delicacies, she fancied a few kinds, but that they should be very tender."

When Chia Chen heard these words, he smiled. "Our dowager lady," he replied, "is, I argued, so fond of amusement that, if she doesn't come to-day, there must, for a certainty, be some valid reason; and that's exactly what happens to be the case."

"The other day I heard your eldest sister explain," interposed madame Wang, "that Chia Jung's wife was anything but well; but what's after all the matter with her?"

"She has," observed Mrs. Yu, "contracted this illness verily in a strange manner! Last moon at the time of the mid-autumn festival, she was still well enough to be able to enjoy herself, during half the night, in company with our dowager lady and madame Wang. On her return, she continued in good health, until after the twentieth, when she began to feel more and more languid every day, and loth, likewise, to eat anything; and this has been going on for well-nigh half a month and more; she hasn't besides been anything like her old self for two months."

"May she not," remarked madame Hsing, taking up the thread of the conversation, "be ailing for some happy event?"

But while she was uttering these words, some one from outside announced: "Our senior master, second master and all the gentlemen of the family have come, and are standing in the Reception Hall!" Whereupon Chia Chen and Chia Lien quitted the apartment with hurried step; and during this while, Mrs. Yu reiterated how that some time ago a doctor had also expressed the opinion that she was ailing for a happy event, but that the previous day, had come a doctor, recommended by Feng Tzu-ying—a doctor, who had from his youth up made medicine his study, and was very proficient in the treatment of diseases,—who asserted, after he had seen her, that it was no felicitous ailment, but that it was some grave complaint. "It was only yesterday," (she explained,) "that he wrote his prescription; and all she has had is but one dose, and already to-day the giddiness in the head is considerably better; as regards the other symptoms they have as yet shown no marked improvement."

"I maintain," remarked lady Feng, "that, were she not quite unfit to stand the exertion, would she in fact, on a day like this, be unwilling to strain every nerve and come round."

"You saw her," observed Mrs. Yu, "on the third in here; how that she bore up with a violent effort for ever so long, but it was all because of the friendship that exists between you two, that she still longed for your society, and couldn't brook the idea of tearing herself away."

When lady Feng heard these words, her eyes got quite red, and after a time she at length exclaimed: "In the Heavens of a sudden come wind and rain; while with man, in a day and in a night, woe and weal survene! But with her tender years, if for a complaint like this she were to run any risk, what pleasure is there for any human being to be born and to sojourn in the world?"

She was just speaking, when Chia Jung walked into the apartment; and after paying his respects to madame Hsing, madame Wang, and lady Feng, he then observed to Mrs. Yu: "I have just taken over the eatables to our venerable ancestor; and, at the same time, I told him that my father was at home waiting upon the senior, and entertaining the junior gentlemen of the whole family, and that in compliance with grandfather's orders, he did not presume to go over. The old gentleman was much delighted by what he heard me say, and having signified that that was all in order, bade me tell father and you, mother, to do all you can in your attendance upon the senior gentlemen and ladies, enjoining me to entertain, with all propriety, my uncles, aunts, and my cousins. He also went on to urge me to press the men to cut, with all despatch, the blocks for the Record of Meritorious Deeds, and to print ten thousand copies for distribution. All these messages I have duly delivered to my father, but I must now be quick and go out, so as to send the eatables for the elder as well as for the younger gentlemen of the entire household."

"Brother Jung Erh," exclaimed lady Feng, "wait a moment. How is your wife getting on? how is she, after all, to-day?"

"Not well," replied Chia Jung. "But were you, aunt, on your return to go in and see her, you will find out for yourself."

Chia Jung forthwith left the room. During this interval, Mrs. Yu addressed herself to mesdames Hsing and Wang; "My ladies," she asked, "will you have your repast in here, or will you go into the garden for it? There are now in the garden some young actors engaged in making their preparations?"

"It's better in here," madame Wang remarked, as she turned towards madame Hsing.

Mrs. Yu thereupon issued directions to the married women and matrons to be quick in serving the eatables. The servants, in waiting outside the door, with one voice signified their obedience; and each of them went off to fetch what fell to her share. In a short while, the courses were all laid out, and Mrs. Yu pressed mesdames Hsing and Wang, as well as her mother, into the upper seats; while she, together with lady Feng and Pao-yü, sat at a side table.

"We've come," observed mesdames Hsing and Wang, "with the original idea of paying our congratulations to our venerable senior on the occasion of his birthday; and isn't this as if we had come for our own birthdays?"

"The old gentleman," answered lady Feng, "is a man fond of a quiet life; and as he has already consummated a process of purification, he may well be looked upon as a supernatural being, so that the purpose to which your ladyships have given expression may be considered as manifest to his spirit, upon the very advent of the intention."

As this sentence was uttered the whole company in the room burst out laughing. Mrs. Yu's mother, mesdames Hsing and Wang, and lady Feng having one and all partaken of the banquet, rinsed their mouths and washed their hands, which over, they expressed a wish to go into the garden.

Chia Jung entered the room. "The senior gentlemen," he said to Mrs. Yu, "as well as all my uncles and cousins, have finished their repast; but the elder gentleman Mr. Chia She, who excused himself on the score of having at home something to attend to, and Mr. Secundus (Chia Cheng), who is not partial to theatrical performances and is always afraid that people will be too boisterous in their entertainments, have both of them taken their departure. The rest of the family gentlemen have been taken over by uncle Secundus Mr. Lien, and Mr. Se, to the other side to listen to the play. A few moments back Prince Nan An, Prince Tung P'ing, Prince Hsi Ning, Prince Pei Ching, these four Princes, with Niu, Duke of Chen Kuo, and five other dukes, six in all, and Shih, Marquis of Chung Ching, and other seven, in all eight marquises, sent their messengers with their cards and presents. I have already told father all about it; but before I did so, the presents were put away in the counting room, the lists of presents were all entered in the book, and the 'received with thanks' cards were handed to the respective messengers of the various mansions; the men themselves were also tipped in the customary manner, and all of them were kept to have something to eat before they went on their way. But, mother, you should invite the two ladies, your mother and my aunt, to go over and sit in the garden."

"Just so!" observed Mrs. Yu, "but we've only now finished our repast, and were about to go over."

"I wish to tell you, madame," interposed lady Feng, "that I shall go first and see brother Jung's wife and then come and join you."

"All right," replied madame Wang; "we should all have been fain to have paid her a visit, did we not fear lest she should look upon our disturbing her with displeasure, but just tell her that we would like to know how she is getting on!"

"My dear sister," remarked Mrs. Yu, "as our son's wife has a ready ear for all you say, do go and cheer her up, (and if you do so,) it will besides set my own mind at ease; but be quick and come as soon as you can into the garden."

Pao-yü being likewise desirous to go along with lady Feng to see lady Ch'in, madame Wang remarked, "Go and see her just for a while, and then come over at once into the garden; (for remember) she is your nephew's wife, (and you couldn't sit in there long)."

Mrs. Yu forthwith invited mesdames Wang and Hsing, as well as her own mother, to adjourn to the other side, and they all in a body walked into the garden of Concentrated Fragrance; while lady Feng and Pao-yü betook themselves, in company with Chia Jung, over to this side.

Having entered the door, they with quiet step walked as far as the entrance of the inner chamber. Mrs. Ch'in, upon catching sight of them, was bent upon getting up; but "Be quick," remonstrated lady Feng, "and give up all idea of standing up; for take care your head will feel dizzy."

Lady Feng hastened to make a few hurried steps forward and to grasp Mrs. Ch'in's hand in hers. "My dear girl!" she exclaimed; "How is it that during the few days I've not seen you, you have grown so thin?"

Readily she then took a seat on the rug, on which Mrs. Ch'in was seated, while Pao-yü, after inquiring too about her health, sat in the chair on the opposite side.

"Bring the tea in at once," called out Chia Jung, "for aunt and uncle Secundus have not had any tea in the drawing room."

Mrs. Ch'in took lady Feng's hand in her own and forced a smile. "This is all due to my lack of good fortune; for in such a family as this, my father and mother-in-law treat me just as if I were a daughter of their own flesh and blood! Besides, your nephew, (my husband,) may, it is true, my dear aunt, be young in years, but he is full of regard for me, as I have regard for him, and we have had so far no misunderstanding between us! In fact, among the senior generation, as well as that of the same age as myself, in the whole clan, putting you aside, aunt, about whom no mention need be made, there is not one who has not ever had anything but love for me, and not one who has not ever shown me anything but kindness! But since I've fallen ill with this complaint, all my energy has even every bit of it been taken out of me, so that I've been unable to show to my father and mother-in-law any mark of filial attention, yea so much as for one single day and to you, my dear aunt, with all this affection of yours for me, I have every wish to be dutiful to the utmost degree, but, in my present state, I'm really not equal to it; my own idea is, that it isn't likely that I shall last through this year."

Pao-yü kept, while (she spoke,) his eyes fixed intently upon a picture on the opposite side, representing some begonias drooping in the spring time, and upon a pair of scrolls, with this inscription written by Ch'in Tai-hsü:

A gentle chill doth circumscribe the dreaming man because the spring
is cold!

The fragrant whiff which wafts itself into man's nose, is the perfume of wine!

And he could not help recalling to mind his experiences at the time when he had fallen asleep in this apartment, and had, in his dream, visited the confines of the Great Void. He was just plunged in a state of abstraction, when he heard Mrs. Ch'in give utterance to these sentiments, which pierced his heart as if they were ten thousand arrows, (with the result that) tears unwittingly trickled from his eyes.

Lady Feng perceiving him in tears felt it extremely painful within herself to bear the sight; but she was on pins and needles lest the patient should detect their frame of mind, and feel, instead (of benefit), still more sore at heart, which would not, after all, be quite the purpose of her visit; which was to afford her distraction and consolation. "Pao-yü," she therefore exclaimed, "you are like an old woman! Ill, as she is, simply makes her speak in this wise, and how ever could things come to such a pass! Besides, she is young in years, so that after a short indisposition, her illness will get all right!" "Don't," she said as she turned towards Mrs. Ch'in, "give way to silly thoughts and idle ideas! for by so doing won't you yourself be aggravating your ailment?"

"All that her sickness in fact needs," observed Chia Jung, "is, that she should be able to take something to eat, and then there will be nothing to fear."

"Brother Pao," urged lady Feng, "your mother told you to go over, as soon as you could, so that don't stay here, and go on in the way you're doing, for you after all incite this lady also to feel uneasy at heart. Besides, your mother over there is solicitous on your account." "You had better go ahead with your uncle Pao," she consequently continued, addressing herself to Chia Jung, "while I sit here a little longer."

When Chia Jung heard this remark, he promptly crossed over with Pao-yü into the garden of Concentrated Fragrance, while lady Feng went on both to cheer her up for a time, and to impart to her, in an undertone, a good deal of confidential advice.

Mrs. Yu had despatched servants, on two or three occasions, to hurry lady Feng, before she said to Mrs. Ch'in: "Do all you can to take good care of yourself, and I'll come and see you again. You're bound to get over this illness; and now, in fact, that you've come across that renowned doctor, you have really nothing more to fear."

"He might," observed Mrs. Ch'in as she smiled, "even be a supernatural being and succeed in healing my disease, but he won't be able to remedy my destiny; for, my dear aunt, I feel sure that with this complaint of mine, I can do no more than drag on from day to day."

"If you encourage such ideas," remonstrated lady Feng, "how can this illness ever get all right? What you absolutely need is to cast away all these notions, and then you'll improve. I hear moreover that the doctor asserts that if no cure be effected, the fear is of a change for the worse in spring, and not till then. Did you and I moreover belong to a family that hadn't the means to afford any ginseng, it would be difficult to say how we could manage to get it; but were your father and mother-in-law to hear that it's good for your recovery, why not to speak of two mace of ginseng a day, but even two catties will be also within their means! So mind you do take every care of your health! I'm now off on my way into the garden."

"Excuse me, my dear aunt," added Mrs. Ch'in, "that I can't go with you; but when you have nothing to do, I entreat you do come over and see me! and you and I can sit and have a long chat."

After lady Feng had heard these words, her eyes unwillingly got quite red again. "When I'm at leisure I shall, of course," she rejoined, "come often to see you;" and forthwith leading off the matrons and married women, who had come over with her, as well as the women and matrons of the Ning mansion, she passed through the inner part of the house, and entered, by a circuitous way, the side gate of the park, when she perceived: yellow flowers covering the ground; white willows flanking the slopes; diminutive bridges spanning streams, resembling the Jo Yeh; zigzag pathways (looking as if) they led to the steps of Heaven; limpid springs dripping from among the rocks; flowers hanging from hedges emitting their fragrance, as they were flapped by the winds; red leaves on the tree tops swaying to and fro; groves picture-like, half stripped of foliage; the western breeze coming with sudden gusts, and the wail of the oriole still audible; the warm sun shining with genial rays, and the cicada also adding its chirp: structures, visible to the gaze at a distance in the South-east, soaring high on various sites and resting against the hills; three halls, visible near by on the North-west, stretching in one connected line, on the bank of the stream; strains of music filling the pavilion, imbued with an unwonted subtle charm; and maidens in fine attire penetrating the groves, lending an additional spell to the scene.

Lady Feng, while engaged in contemplating the beauties of the spot, advanced onwards step by step. She was plunged in a state of ecstasy, when suddenly, from the rear of the artificial rockery, egressed a person, who approached her and facing her said, "My respects to you, sister-in-law."

Lady Feng was so startled by this unexpected appearance that she drew back. "Isn't this Mr. Jui?" she ventured.

"What! sister-in-law," exclaimed Chia Jui, "don't you recognise even me?"

"It isn't that I didn't recognise you," explained lady Feng, "but at the sudden sight of you, I couldn't conceive that it would possibly be you, sir, in this place!"

"This was in fact bound to be," replied Chia Jui; "for there's some subtle sympathy between me and you, sister-in-law. Here I just stealthily leave the entertainment, in order to revel for a while in this solitary place when, against every expectation, I come across you, sister-in-law; and isn't this a subtle sympathy?"

As he spoke, he kept his gaze fixed on lady Feng, who being an intelligent person, could not but arrive, at the sight of his manner, at the whole truth in her surmises. "It isn't to be wondered at," she consequently observed, as she smiled hypocritically, "that your eldest brother should make frequent allusion to your qualities! for after seeing you on this occasion, and hearing you utter these few remarks, I have readily discovered what an intelligent and genial person you are! I am just now on my way to join the ladies on the other side, and have no leisure to converse with you; but wait until I've nothing to attend to, when we can meet again."

"I meant to have gone over to your place and paid my respects to you, sister-in-law," pleaded Chia Jui, "but I was afraid lest a person of tender years like yourself mightn't lightly receive any visitors!"

Lady Feng gave another sardonic smile. "Relatives," she continued, "of one family, as we are, what need is there to say anything of tender years?"

After Chia Jui had heard these words, he felt his heart swell within him with such secret joy that he was urged to reflect: "I have at length to-day, when least I expected it, obtained this remarkable encounter with her!"

But as the display of his passion became still more repulsive, lady Feng urged him to go. "Be off at once," she remarked, "and join the entertainment; for mind, if they find you out, they will mulct you in so many glasses of wine!"

By the time this suggestion had reached Chia Jui's ears, half of his body had become stiff like a log of wood; and as he betook himself away, with lothful step, he turned his head round to cast glances at her.

Lady Feng purposely slackened her pace; and when she perceived that he had gone a certain distance, she gave way to reflection. "This is indeed," she thought, "knowing a person, as far as face goes, and not as heart! Can there be another such a beast as he! If he really continues to behave in this manner, I shall soon enough compass his death, with my own hands, and he'll then know what stuff I'm made of."

Lady Feng, at this juncture moved onward, and after turning round a chain of hillocks, she caught sight of two or three matrons coming along with all speed. As soon as they espied lady Feng they put on a smile. "Our mistress," they said, "perceiving that your ladyship was not forthcoming, has been in a great state of anxiety, and bade your servants come again to request you to come over.

"Is your mistress," observed lady Feng, "so like a quick-footed demon?"

While lady Feng advanced leisurely, she inquired, "How many plays have been recited?" to which question one of the matrons replied, "They have gone through eight or nine." But while engaged in conversation, they had already reached the back door of the Tower of Celestial Fragrance, where she caught sight of Pao-yü playing with a company of waiting-maids and pages. "Brother Pao," lady Feng exclaimed, "don't be up to too much mischief!" "The ladies are all sitting upstairs," interposed one of the maids. "Please, my lady, this is the way up."

At these words lady Feng slackened her pace, raised her dress, and walked up the stairs, where Mrs. Yu was already at the top of the landing waiting for her.

"You two," remarked Mrs. Yu, smiling, "are so friendly, that having met you couldn't possibly tear yourself away to come. You had better to-morrow move over there and take up your quarters with her and have done; but sit down and let me, first of all, present you a glass of wine."

Lady Feng speedily drew near mesdames Hsing and Wang, and begged permission to take a seat; while Mrs. Yu brought the programme, and pressed lady Feng to mark some plays.

"The senior ladies occupy the seats of honour," remonstrated lady Feng, "and how can I presume to choose?"

"We, and our relative by marriage, have selected several plays," explained mesdames Hsing and Wang, "and it's for you now to choose some good ones for us to listen to."

Standing up, lady Feng signified her obedience; and taking over the programme, and perusing it from top to bottom, she marked off one entitled, the "Return of the Spirit," and another called "Thrumming and Singing;" after which she handed back the programme, observing, "When they have done with the 'Ennoblement of two Officers,' which they are singing just at present, it will be time enough to sing these two."

"Of course it will," retorted madame Wang, "but they should get it over as soon as they can, so as to allow your elder Brother and your Sister-in-law to have rest; besides, their hearts are not at ease."

"You senior ladies don't come often," expostulated Mrs. Yu, "and you and I will derive more enjoyment were we to stay a little longer; it's as yet early in the day!"

Lady Feng stood up and looked downstairs. "Where have all the gentlemen gone to?" she inquired.

"The gentlemen have just gone over to the Pavilion of Plenteous Effulgence," replied a matron, who stood by; "they have taken along with them ten musicians and gone in there to drink their wine."

"It wasn't convenient for them," remarked lady Feng, "to be over here; but who knows what they have again gone to do behind our backs?"

"Could every one," interposed Mrs. Yu, "resemble you, a person of such propriety!"

While they indulged in chatting and laughing, the plays they had chosen were all finished; whereupon the tables were cleared of the wines, and the repast was served. The meal over, the whole company adjourned into the garden, and came and sat in the drawing-room. After tea, they at length gave orders to get ready the carriages, and they took their leave of Mrs. Yu's mother. Mrs. Yu, attended by all the secondary wives, servants, and married women, escorted them out, while Chia Chen, along with the whole bevy of young men, stood by the vehicles, waiting in a group for their arrival.

After saluting mesdames Hsing and Wang, "Aunts," they said, "you must come over again to-morrow for a stroll."

"We must be excused," observed madame Wang, "we've sat here the whole day to-day, and are, after all, feeling quite tired; besides, we shall need to have some rest to-morrow."

Both of them thereupon got into their carriages and took their departure, while Chia Jui still kept a fixed gaze upon lady Feng; and it was after Chia Chen had gone in that Li Kuei led round the horse, and that Pao-yü mounted and went off, following in the track of mesdames Hsing and Wang.

Chia Chen and the whole number of brothers and nephews belonging to the family had, during this interval, partaken of their meal, and the whole party at length broke up. But in like manner, all the inmates of the clan and the guests spent on the morrow another festive day, but we need not advert to it with any minuteness.

After this occasion, lady Feng came in person and paid frequent visits to Mrs. Ch'in; but as there were some days on which her ailment was considerably better, and others on which it was considerably worse, Chia Chen, Mrs. Yu, and Chia Jung were in an awful state of anxiety.

Chia Jui, it must moreover be noticed, came over, on several instances, on a visit to the Jung mansion; but it invariably happened that he found that lady Feng had gone over to the Ning mansion.

This was just the thirtieth of the eleventh moon, the day on which the winter solstice fell; and the few days preceding that season, dowager lady Chia, madame Wang and lady Feng did not let one day go by without sending some one to inquire about Mrs. Ch'in; and as the servants, on their return, repeatedly reported that, during the last few days, neither had her ailment aggravated, nor had it undergone any marked improvement, madame Wang explained to dowager lady Chia, that as a complaint of this nature had reached this kind of season without getting any worse, there was some hope of recovery.

"Of course there is!" observed the old lady; "what a dear child she is! should anything happen to her, won't it be enough to make people die from grief!" and as she spake she felt for a time quite sore at heart. "You and she," continuing, she said to lady Feng, "have been friends for ever so long; to-morrow is the glorious first (and you can't go), but after to-morrow you should pay her a visit and minutely scrutinise her appearance: and should you find her any better, come and tell me on your return! Whatever things that dear child has all along a fancy for, do send her round a few even as often as you can by some one or other!"

Lady Feng assented to each of her recommendations; and when the second arrived, she came, after breakfast, to the Ning mansion to see how Mrs. Ch'in was getting on; and though she found her none the worse, the flesh all over her face and person had however become emaciated and parched up. She readily sat with Mrs. Ch'in for a long while, and after they had chatted on one thing and another, she again reiterated the assurances that this illness involved no danger, and distracted her for ever so long.

"Whether I get well or not," observed Mrs. Ch'in, "we'll know in spring; now winter is just over, and I'm anyhow no worse, so that possibly I may get all right; and yet there's no saying; but, my dear sister-in-law, do press our old lady to compose her mind! yesterday, her ladyship sent me some potato dumplings, with minced dates in them, and though I had two, they seem after all to be very easily digested!"

"I'll send you round some more to-morrow," lady Feng suggested; "I'm now going to look up your mother-in-law, and will then hurry back to give my report to our dowager lady."

"Please, sister-in-law," Mrs. Ch'in said, "present my best respects to her venerable ladyship, as well as to madame Wang."

Lady Feng signified that she would comply with her wishes, and, forthwith leaving the apartment, she came over and sat in Mrs. Yu's suite of rooms.

"How do you, who don't see our son's wife very often, happen to find her?" inquired Mrs. Yu.

Lady Feng drooped her head for some time. "There's no help," she ventured, "for this illness! but you should likewise make every subsequent preparation, for it would also be well if you could scour it away."

"I've done so much as to secretly give orders," replied Mrs. Yu, "to get things ready; but for that thing (the coffin), there's no good timber to be found, so that it will have to be looked after by and by."

Lady Feng swallowed hastily a cup of tea, and after a short chat, "I must be hurrying back," she remarked, "to deliver my message to our dowager lady!"

"You should," urged Mrs. Yu, "be sparse in what you tell her lady ship so as not to frighten an old person like her!"

"I know well enough what to say," replied lady Feng.

Without any further delay, lady Feng then sped back. On her arrival at home she looked up the old lady. "Brother Jung's wife," she explained, "presents her compliments, and pays obeisance to your venerable ladyship; she says that she's much better, and entreats you, her worthy senior, to set your mind at ease! That as soon as she's a little better she will come and prostrate herself before your ladyship."

"How do you find her?" inquired dowager lady Chia.

"For the present there's nothing to fear," continued lady Feng; "for her mien is still good."

After the old lady had heard these words, she was plunged for a long while in deep reflection; and as she turned towards lady Feng,

"Go and divest yourself of your toilette," she said, "and have some rest."

Lady Feng in consequence signified her obedience, and walked away, returning home after paying madame Wang a visit. P'ing Erh helped lady Feng to put on the house costume, which she had warmed by the fire, and lady Feng eventually took a seat and asked "whether there was anything doing at home?"

P'ing Erh then brought the tea, and after going over to hand the cup: "There's nothing doing," she replied; "as regards the interest on the three hundred taels, Wang Erh's wife has brought it in, and I've put it away. Besides this, Mr. Jui sent round to inquire if your ladyship was at home or not, as he meant to come and pay his respects and to have a chat."

"Heng!" exclaimed lady Feng at these words. "Why should this beast compass his own death? we'll see when he comes what is to be done."

"Why is this Mr. Jui so bent upon coming?' P'ing Erh having inquired, lady Feng readily gave her an account of how she had met him in the course of the ninth moon in the Ning mansion, and of what had been said by him.

"What a mangy frog to be bent upon eating the flesh of a heavenly goose!" ejaculated P'ing Erh. "A stupid and disorderly fellow with no conception of relationship, to harbour such a thought! but we'll make him find an unnatural death!"

"Wait till he comes," added lady Feng, "when I feel certain I shall find some way."

What happened, however, when Chia Jui came has not, as yet, been ascertained, but listen, reader, to the explanation given in the next chapter.

CHAPTER XII.

Wang Hsi-feng maliciously lays a trap for Chia Jui, under pretence that his affection is reciprocated.
Chia T'ien-hsiang gazes at the face of the mirror of Voluptuousness.

Lady Feng, it must be noticed in continuation of our narrative, was just engaged in talking with P'ing Erh, when they heard some one announce that Mr. Jui had come. Lady Feng gave orders that he should be invited to step in, and Chia Jui perceiving that he had been asked to walk in was at heart elated at the prospect of seeing her.

With a face beaming with smiles, Lady Feng inquired again and again how he was; and, with simulated tenderness she further pressed him to take a seat and urged him to have a cup of tea.

Chia Jui noticed how still more voluptuous lady Feng looked in her present costume, and, as his eyes burnt with love, "How is it," he inquired, "that my elder brother Secundus is not yet back?"

"What the reason is I cannot tell," lady Feng said by way of reply.

"May it not be," Chia Jui smilingly insinuated, "that some fair damsel has got hold of him on the way, and that he cannot brook to tear himself from her to come home?"

"That makes it plain that there are those among men who fall in love with any girl they cast their eyes on," hinted lady Feng.

"Your remarks are, sister-in-law, incorrect, for I'm none of this kind!" Chia Jui explained smirkingly.

"How many like you can there be!" rejoined lady Feng with a sarcastic smile; "in ten, not one even could be picked out!"

When Chia Jui heard these words, he felt in such high glee that he rubbed his ears and smoothed his cheeks. "My sister-in-law," he continued, "you must of course be extremely lonely day after day."

"Indeed I am," observed lady Feng, "and I only wish some one would come and have a chat with me to break my dull monotony."

"I daily have ample leisure," Chia Jui ventured with a simper, "and wouldn't it be well if I came every day to dispel your dulness, sister-in-law?"

"You are simply fooling me," exclaimed lady Feng laughing. "It isn't likely you would wish to come over here to me?"

"If in your presence, sister-in-law, I utter a single word of falsehood, may the thunder from heaven blast me!" protested Chia Jui. "It's only because I had all along heard people say that you were a dreadful person, and that you cannot condone even the slightest shortcoming committed in your presence, that I was induced to keep back by fear; but after seeing you, on this occasion, so chatty, so full of fun and most considerate to others, how can I not come? were it to be the cause of my death, I would be even willing to come!"

"You're really a clever person," lady Feng observed sarcastically. "And oh so much superior to both Chia Jung and his brother! Handsome as their presence was to look at, I imagined their minds to be full of intelligence, but who would have thought that they would, after all, be a couple of stupid worms, without the least notion of human affection!"

The words which Chia Jui heard, fell in so much the more with his own sentiments, that he could not restrain himself from again pressing forward nearer to her; and as with eyes strained to give intentness to his view, he gazed at lady Feng's purse: "What rings have you got on?" he went on to ask.

"You should be a little more deferential," remonstrated lady Feng in a low tone of voice, "so as not to let the waiting-maids detect us."

Chia Jui withdrew backward with as much alacrity as if he had received an Imperial decree or a mandate from Buddha.

"You ought to be going!" lady Feng suggested, as she gave him a smile.

"Do let me stay a while longer," entreated Chia Jui, "you are indeed ruthless, my sister-in-law."

But with gentle voice did lady Feng again expostulate. "In broad daylight," she said, "with people coming and going, it is not really convenient that you should abide in here; so you had better go, and when it's dark and the watch is set, you can come over, and quietly wait for me in the corridor on the Eastern side!"

At these words, Chia Jui felt as if he had received some jewel or precious thing. "Don't make fun of me!" he remarked with vehemence. "The only thing is that crowds of people are ever passing from there, and how will it be possible for me to evade detection?"

"Set your mind at ease!" lady Feng advised; "I shall dismiss on leave all the youths on duty at night; and when the doors, on both sides, are closed, there will be no one else to come in!"

Chia Jui was delighted beyond measure by the assurance, and with impetuous haste, he took his leave and went off; convinced at heart of the gratification of his wishes. He continued, up to the time of dusk, a prey to keen expectation; and, when indeed darkness fell, he felt his way into the Jung mansion, availing himself of the moment, when the doors were being closed, to slip into the corridor, where everything was actually pitch dark, and not a soul to be seen going backwards or forwards.

The door leading over to dowager lady Chia's apartments had already been put under key, and there was but one gate, the one on the East, which had not as yet been locked. Chia Jui lent his ear, and listened for ever so long, but he saw no one appear. Suddenly, however, was heard a sound like "lo teng," and the east gate was also bolted; but though Chia Jui was in a great state of impatience, he none the less did not venture to utter a sound. All that necessity compelled him to do was to issue, with quiet steps, from his corner, and to try the gates by pushing; but they were closed as firmly as if they had been made fast with iron bolts; and much though he may, at this juncture, have wished to find his way out, escape was, in fact, out of the question; on the south and north was one continuous dead wall, which, even had he wished to scale, there was nothing which he could clutch and pull himself up by.

This room, besides, was one the interior (of which was exposed) to the wind, which entered through (the fissure) of the door; and was perfectly empty and bare; and the weather being, at this time, that of December, and the night too very long, the northerly wind, with its biting gusts, was sufficient to penetrate the flesh and to cleave the bones, so that the whole night long he had a narrow escape from being frozen to death; and he was yearning, with intolerable anxiety for the break of day, when he espied an old matron go first and open the door on the East side, and then come in and knock at the western gate.

Chia Jui seeing that she had turned her face away, bolted out, like a streak of smoke, as he hugged his shoulders with his hands (from intense cold.) As luck would have it, the hour was as yet early, so that the inmates of the house had not all got out of bed; and making his escape from the postern door, he straightaway betook himself home, running back the whole way.

Chia Jui's parents had, it must be explained, departed life at an early period, and he had no one else, besides his grandfather Tai-ju, to take charge of his support and education. This Tai-ju had, all along, exercised a very strict control, and would not allow Chia Jui to even make one step too many, in the apprehension that he might gad about out of doors drinking and gambling, to the neglect of his studies.

Seeing, on this unexpected occasion, that he had not come home the whole night, he simply felt positive, in his own mind, that he was certain to have run about, if not drinking, at least gambling, and dissipating in houses of the demi-monde up to the small hours; but he never even gave so much as a thought to the possibility of a public scandal, as that in which he was involved. The consequence was that during the whole length of the night he boiled with wrath.

Chia Jui himself, on the other hand, was (in such a state of trepidation) that he could wipe the perspiration (off his face) by handfuls; and he felt constrained on his return home, to have recourse to deceitful excuses, simply explaining that he had been at his eldest maternal uncle's house, and that when it got dark, they kept him to spend the night there.

"Hitherto," remonstrated Tai-ju, "when about to go out of doors, you never ventured to go, on your own hook, without first telling me about it, and how is it that yesterday you surreptitiously left the house? for this offence alone you deserve a beating, and how much more for the lie imposed upon me."

Into such a violent fit of anger did he consequently fly that laying hands on him, he pulled him over and administered to him thirty or forty blows with a cane. Nor would he allow him to have anything to eat, but bade him remain on his knees in the court conning essays; impressing on his mind that he would not let him off, before he had made up for the last ten days' lessons.

Chia Jui had in the first instance, frozen the whole night, and, in the next place, came in for a flogging. With a stomach, besides, gnawed by the pangs of hunger, he had to kneel in a place exposed to drafts reading the while literary compositions, so that the hardships he had to endure were of manifold kinds.

Chia Jui's infamous intentions had at this junction undergone no change; but far from his thoughts being even then any idea that lady Feng was humbugging him, he seized, after the lapse of a couple of days, the first leisure moments to come again in search of that lady.

Lady Feng pretended to bear him a grudge for his breach of faith, and Chia Jui was so distressed that he tried by vows and oaths (to establish his innocence.) Lady Feng perceiving that he had, of his own accord, fallen into the meshes of the net laid for him, could not but devise another plot to give him a lesson and make him know what was right and mend his ways.

With this purpose, she gave him another assignation. "Don't go over there," she said, "to-night, but wait for me in the empty rooms giving on to a small passage at the back of these apartments of mine. But whatever you do, mind don't be reckless."

"Are you in real earnest?" Chia Jui inquired.

"Why, who wants to play with you?" replied lady Feng; "if you don't believe what I say, well then don't come!"

"I'll come, I'll come, yea I'll come, were I even to die!" protested Chia Jui.

"You should first at this very moment get away!" lady Feng having suggested, Chia Jui, who felt sanguine that when evening came, success would for a certainty crown his visit, took at once his departure in anticipation (of his pleasure.)

During this interval lady Feng hastily set to work to dispose of her resources, and to add to her stratagems, and she laid a trap for her victim; while Chia Jui, on the other hand, was until the shades of darkness fell, a prey to incessant expectation.

As luck would have it a relative of his happened to likewise come on that very night to their house and to only leave after he had dinner with them, and at an hour of the day when the lamps had already been lit; but he had still to wait until his grandfather had retired to rest before he could, at length with precipitate step, betake himself into the Jung mansion.

Straightway he came into the rooms in the narrow passage, and waited with as much trepidation as if he had been an ant in a hot pan. He however waited and waited, but he saw no one arrive; he listened but not even the sound of a voice reached his ear. His heart was full of intense fear, and he could not restrain giving way to surmises and suspicion. "May it not be," he thought, "that she is not coming again; and that I may have once more to freeze for another whole night?"

While indulging in these erratic reflections, he discerned some one coming, looking like a black apparition, who Chia Jui readily concluded, in his mind, must be lady Feng; so that, unmindful of distinguishing black from white, he as soon as that person arrived in front of him, speedily clasped her in his embrace, like a ravenous tiger pouncing upon its prey, or a cat clawing a rat, and cried: "My darling sister, you have made me wait till I'm ready to die."

As he uttered these words, he dragged the comer, in his arms, on to the couch in the room; and while indulging in kisses and protestations of warm love, he began to cry out at random epithets of endearment.

Not a sound, however, came from the lips of the other person; and Chia Jui had in the fulness of his passion, exceeded the bounds of timid love and was in the act of becoming still more affectionate in his protestations, when a sudden flash of a light struck his eye, by the rays of which he espied Chia Se with a candle in hand, casting the light round the place, "Who's in this room?" he exclaimed.

"Uncle Jui," he heard some one on the couch explain, laughing, "was trying to take liberties with me!"

Chia Jui at one glance became aware that it was no other than Chia Jung; and a sense of shame at once so overpowered him that he could find nowhere to hide himself; nor did he know how best to extricate himself from the dilemma. Turning himself round, he made an attempt to make good his escape, when Chia Se with one grip clutched him in his hold.

"Don't run away," he said; "sister-in-law Lien has already reported your conduct to madame Wang; and explained that you had tried to make her carry on an improper flirtation with you; that she had temporised by having recourse to a scheme to escape your importunities, and that she had imposed upon you in such a way as to make you wait for her in this place. Our lady was so terribly incensed, that she well-nigh succumbed; and hence it is that she bade me come and catch you! Be quick now and follow me, and let us go and see her."

After Chia Jui had heard these words, his very soul could not be contained within his body.

"My dear nephew," he entreated, "do tell her that it wasn't I; and I'll show you my gratitude to-morrow in a substantial manner."

"Letting you off," rejoined Chia Se, "is no difficult thing; but how much, I wonder, are you likely to give? Besides, what you now utter with your lips, there will be no proof to establish; so you had better write a promissory note."

"How could I put what happened in black and white on paper?" observed Chia Jui.

"There's no difficulty about that either!" replied Chia Se; "just write an account of a debt due, for losses in gambling, to some one outside; for payment of which you had to raise funds, by a loan of a stated number of taels, from the head of the house; and that will be all that is required."

"This is, in fact, easy enough!" Chia Jui having added by way of answer; Chia Se turned round and left the room; and returning with paper and pencils, which had been got ready beforehand for the purpose, he bade Chia Jui write. The two of them (Chia Jung and Chia Se) tried, the one to do a good turn, and the other to be perverse in his insistence; but (Chia Jui) put down no more than fifty taels, and appended his signature.

Chia Se pocketed the note, and endeavoured subsequently to induce Chia Jung to come away; but Chia Jung was, at the outset, obdurate and unwilling to give in, and kept on repeating; "To-morrow, I'll tell the members of our clan to look into your nice conduct!"

These words plunged Chia Jui in such a state of dismay, that he even went so far as to knock his head on the ground; but, as Chia Se was trying to get unfair advantage of him though he had at first done him a good turn, he had to write another promissory note for fifty taels, before the matter was dropped.

Taking up again the thread of the conversation, Chia Se remarked, "Now when I let you go, I'm quite ready to bear the blame! But the gate at our old lady's over there is already bolted, and Mr. Chia Cheng is just now engaged in the Hall, looking at the things which have arrived from Nanking, so that it would certainly be difficult for you to pass through that way. The only safe course at present is by the back gate; but if you do go by there, and perchance meet any one, even I will be in for a mess; so you might as well wait until I go first and have a peep, when I'll come and fetch you! You couldn't anyhow conceal yourself in this room; for in a short time they'll be coming to stow the things away, and you had better let me find a safe place for you."

These words ended, he took hold of Chia Jui, and, extinguishing again the lantern, he brought him out into the court, feeling his way up to the bottom of the steps of the large terrace. "It's safe enough in this nest," he observed, "but just squat down quietly and don't utter a sound; wait until I come back before you venture out."

Having concluded this remark, the two of them (Chia Se and Chia Jung) walked away; while Chia Jui was, all this time, out of his senses, and felt constrained to remain squatting at the bottom of the terrace stairs. He was about to consider what course was open for him to adopt, when he heard a noise just over his head; and, with a splash, the contents of a bucket, consisting entirely of filthy water, was emptied straight down over him from above, drenching, as luck would have it, his whole person and head.

Chia Jui could not suppress an exclamation. "Ai ya!" he cried, but he hastily stopped his mouth with his hands, and did not venture to give vent to another sound. His whole head and face were a mass of filth, and his body felt icy cold. But as he shivered and shook, he espied Chia Se come running. "Get off," he shouted, "with all speed! off with you at once!"

As soon as Chia Jui returned to life again, he bolted with hasty strides, out of the back gate, and ran the whole way home. The night had already reached the third watch, so that he had to knock at the door for it to be opened.

"What's the matter?" inquired the servants, when they saw him in this sorry plight; (an inquiry) which placed him in the necessity of making some false excuse. "The night was dark," he explained, "and my foot slipped and I fell into a gutter."

Saying this, he betook himself speedily to his own apartment; and it was only after he had changed his clothes and performed his ablutions, that he began to realise that lady Feng had made a fool of him. He consequently gave way to a fit of wrath; but upon recalling to mind the charms of lady Feng's face, he felt again extremely aggrieved that he could not there and then clasp her in his embrace, and as he indulged in these wild thoughts and fanciful ideas, he could not the whole night long close his eyes.

From this time forward his mind was, it is true, still with lady Feng, but he did not have the courage to put his foot into the Jung mansion; and with Chia Jung and Chia Se both coming time and again to dun him for the money, he was likewise full of fears lest his grandfather should come to know everything.

His passion for lady Feng was, in fact, already a burden hard to bear, and when, moreover, the troubles of debts were superadded to his tasks, which were also during the whole day arduous, he, a young man of about twenty, as yet unmarried, and a prey to constant cravings for lady Feng, which were difficult to gratify, could not avoid giving way, to a great extent, to such evil habits as exhausted his energies. His lot had, what is more, been on two occasions to be frozen, angered and to endure much hardship, so that with the attacks received time and again from all sides, he unconsciously soon contracted an organic disease. In his heart inflammation set in; his mouth lost the sense of taste; his feet got as soft as cotton from weakness; his eyes stung, as if there were vinegar in them. At night, he burnt with fever. During the day, he was repeatedly under the effects of lassitude. Perspiration was profuse, while with his expectorations of phlegm, he brought up blood.

The whole number of these several ailments came upon him, before the expiry of a year, (with the result that) in course of time, he had not the strength to bear himself up. Of a sudden, he would fall down, and with his eyes, albeit closed, his spirit would be still plunged in confused dreams, while his mouth would be full of nonsense and he would be subject to strange starts.

Every kind of doctor was asked to come in, and every treatment had recourse to; and, though of such medicines as cinnamon, aconitum seeds, turtle shell, ophiopogon, Yü-chü herb, and the like, he took several tens of catties, he nevertheless experienced no change for the better; so that by the time the twelfth moon drew once again to an end, and spring returned, this illness had become still more serious.

Tai-ju was very much concerned, and invited doctors from all parts to attend to him, but none of them could do him any good. And as later on, he had to take nothing else but decoctions of pure ginseng, Tai-ju could not of course afford it. Having no other help but to come over to the Jung mansion, and make requisition for some, Madame Wang asked lady Feng to weigh two taels of it and give it to him. "The other day," rejoined lady Feng, "not long ago, when we concocted some medicine for our dowager lady, you told us, madame, to keep the pieces that were whole, to present to the spouse of General Yang to make physic with, and as it happens it was only yesterday that I sent some one round with them."

"If there's none over here in our place," suggested madame Wang, "just send a servant to your mother-in-law's, on the other side, to inquire whether they have any. Or it may possibly be that your elder brother-in-law Chen, over there, might have a little. If so, put all you get together, and give it to them; and when he shall have taken it, and got well and you shall have saved the life of a human being, it will really be to the benefit of you all."

Lady Feng acquiesced; but without directing a single person to institute any search, she simply took some refuse twigs, and making up a few mace, she despatched them with the meagre message that they had been sent by madame Wang, and that there was, in fact, no more; subsequently reporting to madame Wang that she had asked for and obtained all there was and that she had collected as much as two taels, and forwarded it to them.

Chia Jui was, meanwhile, very anxious to recover his health, so that there was no medicine that he would not take, but the outlay of money was of no avail, for he derived no benefit.

On a certain day and at an unexpected moment, a lame Taoist priest came to beg for alms, and he averred that he had the special gift of healing diseases arising from grievances received, and as Chia Jui happened, from inside, to hear what he said, he forthwith shouted out: "Go at once, and bid that divine come in and save my life!" while he reverentially knocked his head on the pillow.

The whole bevy of servants felt constrained to usher the Taoist in; and Chia Jui, taking hold of him with a dash, "My Buddha!" he repeatedly cried out, "save my life!"

The Taoist heaved a sigh. "This ailment of yours," he remarked, "is not one that could be healed with any medicine; I have a precious thing here which I'll give you, and if you gaze at it every day, your life can be saved!"

When he had done talking, he produced from his pouch a looking-glass which could reflect a person's face on the front and back as well. On the upper part of the back were engraved the four characters: "Precious Mirror of Voluptuousness." Handing it over to Chia Jui: "This object," he proceeded, "emanates from the primordial confines of the Great Void and has been wrought by the Monitory Dream Fairy in the Palace of Unreality and Spirituality, with the sole intent of healing the illnesses which originate from evil thoughts and improper designs. Possessing, as it does, the virtue of relieving mankind and preserving life, I have consequently brought it along with me into the world, but I only give it to those intelligent preëminent and refined princely men to set their eyes on. On no account must you look at the front side; and you should only gaze at the back of it; this is urgent, this is expedient! After three days, I shall come and fetch it away; by which time, I'm sure, it will have made him all right."

These words finished, he walked away with leisurely step, and though all tried to detain him, they could not succeed.

Chia Jui received the mirror. "This Taoist," he thought, "would seem to speak sensibly, and why should I not look at it and try its effect?" At the conclusion of these thoughts, he took up the Mirror of Voluptuousness, and cast his eyes on the obverse side; but upon perceiving nought else than a skeleton standing in it, Chia Jui sustained such a fright that he lost no time in covering it with his hands and in abusing the Taoist. "You good-for-nothing!" he exclaimed, "why should you frighten me so? but I'll go further and look at the front and see what it's like."

While he reflected in this manner, he readily looked into the face of the mirror, wherein he caught sight of lady Feng standing, nodding her head and beckoning to him. With one gush of joy, Chia Jui felt himself, in a vague and mysterious manner, transported into the mirror, where he held an affectionate tête-à-tête with lady Feng. Lady Feng escorted him out again. On his return to bed, he gave vent to an exclamation of "Ai yah!" and opening his eyes, he turned the glass over once more; but still, as hitherto, stood the skeleton in the back part.

Chia Jui had, it is true, experienced all the pleasant sensations of a tête-à-tête, but his heart nevertheless did not feel gratified; so that he again turned the front round, and gazed at lady Feng, as she still waved her hand and beckoned to him to go. Once more entering the mirror, he went on in the same way for three or four times, until this occasion, when just as he was about to issue from the mirror, he espied two persons come up to him, who made him fast with chains round the neck, and hauled him away. Chia Jui shouted. "Let me take the mirror and I'll come along." But only this remark could he utter, for it was forthwith beyond his power to say one word more. The servants, who stood by in attendance, saw him at first still holding the glass in his hand and looking in, and then, when it fell from his grasp, open his eyes again to pick it up, but when at length the mirror dropped, and he at once ceased to move, they in a body came forward to ascertain what had happened to him. He had already breathed his last. The lower part of his body was icy-cold; his clothes moist from profuse perspiration. With all promptitude they changed him there and then, and carried him to another bed.

Tai-ju and his wife wept bitterly for him, to the utter disregard of their own lives, while in violent terms they abused the Taoist priest. "What kind of magical mirror is it?" they asked. "If we don't destroy this glass, it will do harm to not a few men in the world!"

Having forthwith given directions to bring fire and burn it, a voice was heard in the air to say, "Who told you to look into the face of it? You yourselves have mistaken what is false for what is true, and why burn this glass of mine?"

Suddenly the mirror was seen to fly away into the air; and when Tai-ju went out of doors to see, he found no one else than the limping Taoist, shouting, "Who is he who wishes to destroy the Mirror of Voluptuousness?" While uttering these words, he snatched the glass, and, as all eyes were fixed upon him, he moved away lissomely, as if swayed by the wind.

Tai-ju at once made preparations for the funeral and went everywhere to give notice that on the third day the obsequies would commence, that on the seventh the procession would start to escort the coffin to the Iron Fence Temple, and that on the subsequent day, it would be taken to his original home.

Not much time elapsed before all the members of the Chia family came, in a body, to express their condolences. Chia She, of the Jung Mansion, presented twenty taels, and Chia Cheng also gave twenty taels. Of the Ning Mansion, Chia Chen likewise contributed twenty taels. The remainder of the members of the clan, of whom some were poor and some rich, and not equally well off, gave either one or two taels, or three or four, some more, some less. Among strangers, there were also contributions, respectively presented by the families of his fellow-scholars, amounting, likewise, collectively to twenty or thirty taels.

The private means of Tai-ju were, it is true, precarious, but with the monetary assistance he obtained, he anyhow performed the funeral rites with all splendour and éclat.

But who would have thought it, at the close of winter of this year, Lin Ju-hai contracted a serious illness, and forwarded a letter, by some one, with the express purpose of fetching Lin Tai-yü back. These tidings, when they reached dowager lady Chia, naturally added to the grief and distress (she already suffered), but she felt compelled to make speedy preparations for Tai-yü's departure. Pao-yü too was intensely cut up, but he had no alternative but to defer to the affection of father and daughter; nor could he very well place any hindrance in the way.

Old lady Chia, in due course, made up her mind that she would like Chia Lien to accompany her, and she also asked him to bring her back again along with him. But no minute particulars need be given of the manifold local presents and of the preparations, which were, of course, everything that could be wished for in excellence and perfectness. Forthwith the day for starting was selected, and Chia Lien, along with Lin Tai-yü, said good-bye to all the members of the family, and, followed by their attendants, they went on board their boats, and set out on their journey for Yang Chou.

But, Reader, should you have any wish to know fuller details, listen to the account given in the subsequent Chapter.

CHAPTER XIII.

Ch'in K'o-ch'ing dies, and Chia Jung is invested with the rank of military officer to the Imperial Body-guard.
Wang Hsi-feng lends her help in the management of the Jung Kuo Mansion.

Lady Feng, it must be added, in prosecuting our narrative, was ever since Chia Lien's departure to accompany Tai-yü to Yang Chou, really very dejected at heart; and every day, when evening came, she would, after simply indulging in a chat and a laugh with P'ing Erh, turn in, in a heedless frame of mind, for the night.

In the course of the night of this day, she had been sitting with P'ing Erh by lamp-light clasping the hand-stove; and weary of doing her work of embroidery, she had at an early hour, given orders to warm the embroidered quilt, and both had gone to bed; and as she was bending her fingers, counting the progress of the journey, and when they should be arriving, unexpectedly, the third watch struck.

P'ing Erh had already fallen fast asleep; and lady Feng was feeling at length her sleepy eyes slightly dose, when she faintly discerned Mrs. Ch'in walk in from outside.

"My dear sister-in-law," she said as she smiled, "sleep in peace; I'm on my way back to-day, and won't even you accompany me just one stage? But as you and I have been great friends all along, I cannot part from you, sister-in-law, and have therefore come to take my leave of you. There is, besides, a wish of mine, which isn't yet accomplished; and if I don't impart it to you, it isn't likely that telling any one else will be of any use."

Lady Feng could not make out the sense of the words she heard. "What wish is it you have?" she inquired, "do tell me, and it will be safe enough with me."

"You are, my dear sister-in-law, a heroine among women," observed Mrs. Ch'in, "so much so that those famous men, with sashes and official hats, cannot excel you; how is it that you're not aware of even a couple of lines of common adages, of that trite saying, 'when the moon is full, it begins to wane; when the waters are high, they must overflow?' and of that other which says that 'if you ascend high, heavy must be your fall.' Our family has now enjoyed splendour and prosperity for already well-nigh a century, but a day comes when at the height of good fortune, calamity arises; and if the proverb that 'when the tree falls, the monkeys scatter,' be fulfilled, will not futile have been the reputation of culture and old standing of a whole generation?"

Lady Feng at these words felt her heart heavy, and overpowered by intense awe and veneration.

"The fears you express are well founded," she urgently remarked, "but what plan is there adequate to preserve it from future injury?"

"My dear sister-in-law," rejoined Mrs. Ch'in with a sardonic smile, "you're very simple indeed! When woe has reached its climax, weal supervenes. Prosperity and adversity, from days of yore up to the present time, now pass away, and now again revive, and how can (prosperity) be perpetuated by any human exertion? But if now, we could in the time of good fortune, make provision against any worldly concerns, which might arise at any season of future adversity, we might in fact prolong and preserve it. Everything, for instance, is at present well-regulated; but there are two matters which are not on a sure footing, and if such and such suitable action could be adopted with regard to these concerns, it will, in subsequent days, be found easy to perpetuate the family welfare in its entity."

"What matters are these?" inquired lady Feng.

"Though at the graves of our ancestors," explained Mrs. Ch'in, "sacrifices and oblations be offered at the four seasons, there's nevertheless no fixed source of income. In the second place, the family school is, it is true, in existence; but it has no definite grants-in-aid. According to my views, now that the times are prosperous, there's, as a matter of course, no lack of offerings and contributions; but by and bye, when reverses set in, whence will these two outlays be met from? Would it not be as well, and my ideas are positive on this score, to avail ourselves of the present time, when riches and honours still reign, to establish in the immediate vicinity of our ancestral tombs, a large number of farms, cottages, and estates, in order to enable the expenditure for offerings and grants to entirely emanate from this source? And if the household school were also established on this principle, the old and young in the whole clan can, after they have, by common consent, determined upon rules, exercise in days to come control, in the order of the branches, over the affairs connected with the landed property, revenue, ancestral worship and school maintenance for the year (of their respective term.) Under this rotatory system, there will likewise be no animosities; neither will there be any mortgages, or sales, or any of these numerous malpractices; and should any one happen to incur blame, his personal effects can be confiscated by Government. But the properties, from which will be derived the funds for ancestral worship, even the officials should not be able to appropriate, so that when reverses do supervene, the sons and grandsons of the family may be able to return to their homes, and prosecute their studies, or go in for farming. Thus, while they will have something to fall back upon, the ancestral worship will, in like manner, be continued in perpetuity. But, if the present affluence and splendour be looked upon as bound to go on without intermission, and with no thought for the day to come, no enduring plan be after all devised, presently, in a little while, there will, once again, transpire a felicitous occurrence of exceptional kind, which, in point of fact, will resemble the splendour of oil scorched on a violent fire, or fresh flowers decorated with brocades. You should bear in mind that it will also be nothing more real than a transient pageant, nothing but a short-lived pleasure! Whatever you do, don't forget the proverb, that 'there's no banquet, however sumptuous, from which the guests do not disperse;' and unless you do, at an early date, take precautions against later evils, regret will, I apprehend, be of no avail."

"What felicitous occurrence will take place?" lady Feng inquired with alacrity.

"The decrees of Heaven cannot be divulged; but as I have been very friendly with you, sister-in-law, for so long, I will present you, before I take my leave, with two lines, which it behoves you to keep in mind," rejoined Mrs. Ch'in, as she consequently proceeded to recite what follows:

The three springs, when over, all radiance will wane;
The inmates to seek each a home will be fain.

Lady Feng was bent upon making further inquiries, when she heard a messenger at the second gate strike the "cloudy board" four consecutive blows. It was indeed the announcement of a death; and it woke up lady Feng with a start. A servant reported that lady Jung of the eastern mansion was no more.

Lady Feng was so taken aback that a cold perspiration broke out all over her person, and she fell for a while into vacant abstraction. But she had to change her costume, with all possible haste, and to come over to madame Wang's apartments.

By this time, all the members of the family were aware of the tidings, and there was not one of them who did not feel disconsolate; one and all of them were much wounded at heart. The elder generation bethought themselves of the dutiful submission which she had all along displayed; those of the same age as herself reflected upon the friendship and intimacy which had ever existed with her; those younger than her remembered her past benevolence. Even the servants of the household, whether old or young, looked back upon her qualities of sympathy with the poor, pity of the destitute, affection for the old, and consideration for the young; and not one of them all was there who did not mourn her loss, and give way to intense grief.

But these irrelevant details need not be dilated upon; suffice it to confine ourselves to Pao-yü.

Consequent upon Lin Tai-yü's return home, he was left to his own self and felt very lonely. Neither would he go and disport himself with others; but with the daily return of dusk, he was wont to retire quietly to sleep.

On this day, while he was yet under the influence of a dream, he heard the announcement of Mrs. Ch'in's death, and turning himself round quickly he crept out of bed, when he felt as if his heart had been stabbed with a sword. With a sudden retch, he straightway expectorated a mouthful of blood, which so frightened Hsi Jen and the rest that they rushed forward and supported him.

"What is the matter?" they inquired, and they meant also to go and let dowager lady Chia know, so as to send for a doctor, but Pao-yü dissuaded them.

"There's no need of any flurry; it's nothing at all," he said, "it's simply that the fire of grief has attacked the heart, and that the blood did not circulate through the arteries."

As he spoke, he speedily raised himself up, and, after asking for his clothes and changing, he came over to see dowager lady Chia. His wish was to go at once to the other side; and Hsi Jen, though feeling uneasy at heart, seeing the state of mind he was in, did not again hinder him, as she felt constrained to let him please himself.

When old lady Chia saw that he was bent upon going: "The breath is just gone out of the body," she consequently remonstrated, "and that side is still sullied. In the second place it's now dark, and the wind is high; so you had better wait until to-morrow morning, when you will be in ample time."

Pao-yü would not agree to this, and dowager lady Chia gave orders to get the carriage ready, and to depute a few more attendants and followers to go with him. Under this escort he went forward and straightway arrived in front of the Ning mansion, where they saw the main entrance wide open, the lamps on the two sides giving out a light as bright as day, and people coming and going in confused and large numbers; while the sound of weeping inside was sufficient to shake the mountains and to move the hills.

Pao-yü dismounted from the carriage; and with hurried step, walked into the apartment, where the coffin was laid. He gave vent to bitter tears for a few minutes, and subsequently paid his salutations to Mrs. Yu. Mrs. Yu, as it happened, had just had a relapse of her old complaint of pains in the stomach and was lying on her bed.

He eventually came out again from her chamber to salute Chia Chen, just at the very moment that Chia Tai-ju, Chia Tai-hsiu, Chia Ch'ih, Chiao Hsiao, Chia Tun, Chia She, Chia Cheng, Chia Tsung, Chia Pin, Chia Hsing, Chia Kuang, Chia Shen, Chia Ch'iung, Chia Lin, Chia Se, Chia Ch'ang, Chia Ling, Chia Yün, Chia Ch'in, Chia Chen, Chia P'ing, Chia Tsao, Chia Heng, Chia Fen, Chia Fang, Chia Lan, Chia Chun, Chia Chih and the other relatives of the families had likewise arrived in a body.

Chia Chen wept so bitterly that he was like a man of tears. "Of the whole family, whether young or old, distant relatives or close friends," he was just explaining to Chia Tai-ju and the rest, "who did not know that this girl was a hundred times better than even our son? but now that her spirit has retired, it's evident that this elder branch of the family will be cut off and that there will be no survivor."

While he gave vent to these words, he again burst into tears, and the whole company of relatives set to work at once to pacify him. "She has already departed this life," they argued, "and tears are also of no avail, besides the pressing thing now is to consult as to what kind of arrangements are to be made."

Chia Chen clapped his hands. "What arrangements are to be made!" he exclaimed; "nothing is to be done, but what is within my means."

As they conversed, they perceived Ch'in Yeh and Ch'in Chung, as well as several relations of Mrs. Yu, arrive, together with Mrs. Yu's sisters; and Chia Chen forthwith bade Chia Ch'ung, Chia Shen, Chia Lin and Chia Se, the four of them, to go and entertain the guests; while he, at the same time, issued directions to go and ask the Astrologer of the Imperial Observatory to come and choose the days for the ceremonies.

(This Astrologer) decided that the coffin should remain in the house for seven times seven days, that is forty-nine days; that after the third day, the mourning rites should be begun and the formal cards should be distributed; that all that was to be done during these forty-nine days was to invite one hundred and eight Buddhist bonzes to perform, in the main Hall, the High Confession Mass, in order to ford the souls of departed relatives across the abyss of suffering, and afterwards to transmute the spirit (of Mrs. Ch'in); that, in addition, an altar should be erected in the Tower of Heavenly Fragrance, where nine times nine virtuous Taoist priests should, for nineteen days, offer up prayers for absolution from punishment, and purification from retribution. That after these services, the tablet should be moved into the Garden of Concentrated Fragrance, and that in the presence of the tablet, fifteen additional eminent bonzes and fifteen renowned Taoist Priests should confront the altar and perform meritorious deeds every seven days.

The news of the death of the wife of his eldest grandson reached Chia Ching; but as he himself felt sure that, at no distant date, he would ascend to the regions above, he was loth to return again to his home, and so expose himself to the contamination of the world, as to completely waste the meritorious excellence acquired in past days. For this reason, he paid no heed to the event, but allowed Chia Chen a free hand to accomplish the necessary preparations.

Chia Chen, to whom we again revert, was fond of display and extravagance, so that he found, on inspection of coffins, those few made of pine-wood unsuitable to his taste; when, strange coincidence, Hsüeh P'an came to pay his visit of condolence, and perceiving that Chia Chen was in quest of a good coffin: "In our establishment," he readily suggested, "we have a lot of timber of some kind or other called Ch'iang wood, which comes from the T'ieh Wang Mount, in Huang Hai; and which made into coffins will not rot, not for ten thousand years. This lot was, in fact, brought down, some years back, by my late father; and had at one time been required by His Highness I Chung, a Prince of the royal blood; but as he became guilty of some mismanagement, it was, in consequence, not used, and is still lying stored up in our establishment; and another thing besides is that there's no one with the means to purchase it. But if you do want it, you should come and have a look at it."

Chia Chen, upon hearing this, was extremely delighted, and gave orders that the planks should be there and then brought over. When the whole family came to inspect them, they found those for the sides and the bottom to be all eight inches thick, the grain like betel-nut, the smell like sandal-wood or musk, while, when tapped with the hand, the sound emitted was like that of precious stones; so that one and all agreed in praising the timber for its remarkable quality.

"What is their price?" Chia Chen inquired with a smile.

"Even with one thousand taels in hand," explained Hsüeh P'an laughingly, "I feel sure you wouldn't find any place, where you could buy the like. Why ask about price? if you just give the workmen a few taels for their labour, it will be quite sufficient."

Chia Chen, at these words, lost no time in giving expression to profuse assurances of gratitude, and was forthwith issuing directions that the timber should be split, sawn and made up, when Chia Cheng proffered his advice. "Such articles shouldn't," he said, "be, in my idea, enjoyed by persons of the common run; it would be quite ample if the body were placed in a coffin made of pine of the best quality."

But Chia Chen would not listen to any suggestion.

Suddenly he further heard that Mrs. Ch'in's waiting-maid, Jui Chu by name, had, after she had become alive to the fact that her mistress had died, knocked her head against a post, and likewise succumbed to the blows. This unusual occurrence the whole clan extolled in high terms; and Chia Chen promptly directed that, with regard to ceremonies, she should be treated as a granddaughter, and that the body should, after it had been placed in the coffin, be also deposited in the Hall of Attained Immortality, in the Garden of Concentrated Fragrance.

There was likewise a young waiting-maid, called Pao Chu, who, as Mrs. Ch'in left no issue, was willing to become an adopted child, and begged to be allowed to undertake the charge of dashing the mourning bowl, and accompanying the coffin; which pleased Chia Chen so much that he speedily transmitted orders that from that time forth Pao Chu should be addressed by all as 'young miss.'

Pao Chu, after the rites of an unmarried daughter, mourned before the coffin to such an unwonted degree, as if bent upon snapping her own life; while the members of the entire clan, as well as the inmates of the Mansions, each and all, readily observed, in their conduct, the established mourning usages, without of course any transgression or confusion.

"Chia Jung," pondered Chia Chen, "has no higher status than that of graduate by purchase, and were this designation written on the funeral streamer, it will not be imposing, and, in point of fact, the retinue will likewise be small." He therefore was exceedingly unhappy, in his own mind, when, as luck would have it, on this day, which was the fourth day of the first seven, Tai Ch'üan, a eunuch of the Palace of High Renown, whose office was that of Palace Overseer, first prepared sacrificial presents, which he sent round by messengers, and next came himself in an official chair, preceded by criers beating the gong, to offer sacrificial oblations.

Chia Chen promptly received him, and pressed him into a seat; and when they adjourned into the Hall of the Loitering Bees, tea was presented.

Chia Chen had already arrived at a fixed purpose, so that he seized an opportunity to tell him of his wish to purchase an office for Chia Jung's advancement.

Tai Ch'üan understood the purport of his remark. "It is, I presume," he added smilingly, "that the funeral rites should be a little more sumptuous."

"My worthy sir," eagerly rejoined Chia Chen, "your surmise on that score is perfectly correct."

"The question," explained Tai Ch'üan, "comes up at an opportune moment; for there is just at present a good vacancy. Of the three hundred officers who at present constitute the Imperial Body Guard, there are two wanting. Yesterday marquis Hsiang Yang's third brother came to appeal to me with one thousand five hundred taels of ready money, which he brought over to my house. You know the friendship of old standing which exists between him and me, so that, placing other considerations aside, I without a second thought, assented for his father's sake. But there still remains another vacancy, which, who would have thought it, fat general Feng, of Yung Hsing, asked to purchase for his son; but I have had no time to give him an answer. Besides, as our child wants to purchase it, you had better at once write a statement of his antecedents."

Chia Chen lost no time in bidding some one write the statement on red paper, which Tai Ch'üan found, on perusal, to record that Chia Jung was a graduate, by purchase, of the District of Chiang Ning, of the Ying T'ien Prefecture, in Chiang Nan; that Chia Tai-hua, his great grandfather, had been Commander-in-Chief of the Metropolitan Camp, and an hereditary general of the first class, with the prefix of Spiritual Majesty; that his grandfather Chia Ching was a metropolitan graduate of the tripos in the Ping Ch'en year; and that his father Chia Chen had inherited a rank of nobility of the third degree, and was a general, with the prefix of Majestic Intrepidity.

Tai Ch'üan, after perusal, turned his hand behind him and passed (the statement) to a constant attendant of his, to put away: "Go back," he enjoined him, "and give it to His Excellency Mr. Chao, at the head of the Board of Revenue, and tell him, that I present him my compliments, and would like him to draw up a warrant for subaltern of the Imperial Body Guard of the fifth grade, and to also issue a commission; that he should take the particulars from this statement and fill them up; and that to-morrow I'll come and have the money weighed and sent over."

The young attendant signified his obedience, and Tai Ch'üan thereupon took his leave. Chia Chen did all he could to detain him, but with no success; so that he had no alternative but to escort him as far as the entrance of the Mansion. As he was about to mount into his chair, Chia Chen inquired, "As regards the money, shall I go and pay it into the Board, or am I to send it to the Board of Eunuchs?"

"If you were to go and pay it at the Board," observed Tai Ch'üan; "you are sure to suffer loss; so that it would be better if you just weighed exactly one thousand taels and sent them over to my place; for then an end will be put to all trouble."

Chia Chen was incessant in his expression of gratitude. "When the period of mourning has expired," he consequently added, "I shall lead in person, my despicable eldest son to your mansion, to pay our obeisance, and express our thanks."

They then parted company, but close upon this, were heard again the voices of runners. It was, in fact, the spouse of Shih Ting, the marquis of Chung Ching, who was just arriving. Shih Hsiang-yun, mesdames Wang, and Hsing, lady Feng and the rest came out at once, to greet her, and lead her into the Main Building; when they further saw the sacrificial presents of the three families, of the marquis of Chin Hsiang, the marquis of Ch'uan Ning, and the earl of Shou Shan, likewise spread out in front of the tablet.

In a short while, these three noblemen descended from their chairs, and Chia Chen received them in the Large Hall. In like manner all the relatives and friends arrived in such quick succession, one coming, another going, that it is impossible to remember even so much as their number. One thing need be said that during these forty-nine days the street on which the Ning Kuo mansion stood, was covered with a sheet of white, formed by the people, coming and going; and thronged with clusters of flowers, as the officials came and went.

At the instance of Chia Chen, Chia Jung, the next day donned his gala dress and went over for his papers; and on his return the articles in use in front of the coffin, as well as those belonging to the cortege and other such things, were all regulated by the rules prescribed for an official status of the fifth degree; while, on the tablet and notice alike the inscription consisted of: Spirit of lady Ch'in, (by marriage) of the Chia mansion, and by patent a lady of the fifth rank (of the titles of honour).

The main entrance of the Garden of Concentrated Fragrance, adjoining the street, was opened wide; and on both sides were raised sheds for the musicians, and two companies of players, dressed in blue, discoursed music at the proper times; while one pair after another of the paraphernalia was drawn out so straight as if cut by a knife or slit by an axe. There were also two large carmine boards, carved with gilt inscriptions, erected outside the gate; the designations in bold characters on the upper sides being: Guard of the Imperial Antechamber, charged with the protection of the Inner Palace and Roads, in the Red Prohibited City.

On the opposite side, facing each other, rose, high above the ground, two altars for the services of the Buddhist and Taoist priests, while a placard bore the inscription in bold type: Funeral Obsequies of lady Ch'in, (by marriage) of the Chia mansion, by patent a lady of the fifth rank, consort of the eldest grandson of the hereditary duke of Ning Kuo, and guard of the Imperial Antechamber, charged with the protection of the Inner Palace and Roads in the Red Prohibited City. We, Wan Hsü, by Heaven's commands charged with the perennial preservation of perfect peace in the Kingdom of the Four Continents, as well as of the lands contained therein, Head Controller of the School of Void and Asceticism, and Superior in Chief (of the Buddhist hierarchy); and Yeh Sheng, Principal Controller, since the creation, of the Disciples of Perfect Excellence and Superior in Chief (of the Taoist priesthood), and others, having in a reverent spirit purified ourselves by abstinence, now raise our eyes up to Heaven, prostrate ourselves humbly before Buddha, and devoutly pray all the Chia Lans, Chieh Tis, Kung Ts'aos and other divinities to extend their sacred bounties, and from afar to display their spiritual majesty, during the forty-nine days (of the funeral rites), for the deliverance from judgment and the absolution from retribution (of the spirit of lady Ch'in), so that it may enjoy a peaceful and safe passage, whether by sea or by land; and other such prayers to this effect, which are in fact not worth the trouble of putting on record.

Chia Chen had, it is true, all his wishes gratified; but, as his wife was laid up in the inner chambers, with a relapse of her old complaint, and was not in a fit state to undertake the direction of the ceremonies, he was very much distressed lest, when the high officials (and their wives) came and went, there should occur any breach of the prescribed conventionalities, which he was afraid would evoke ridicule. Hence it was that he felt in low spirits; but while he was plunged in solicitude Pao-yü, who happened to be close by, readily inquired, "Everything may be safely looked upon as being satisfactorily settled, and why need you, elder brother, still be so full of concern?"

Chia Chen forthwith explained to him how it was that in the ladies' apartments there was no one (to do the honours), but Pao-yü at these words smiled: "What difficulty is there about it?" he remarked; "I'll recommend some one to take temporary charge of the direction of things for you during the month, and I can guarantee that everything will be properly carried out."

"Who is it?" Chia Chen was quick to ask; but as Pao-yü perceived that there were still too many relatives and friends seated around, he did not feel as if he could very well speak out; so that he went up to Chia Chen and whispered a couple of remarks in his ear.

Chia Chen's joy knew no bounds when he heard this suggestion. "Everything will indeed be properly carried out," he added laughingly; "but I must now be going at once."

With these words, he drew Pao-yü along, and taking leave of the whole number of visitors, they forthwith came into the drawing rooms.

This day was luckily not a grand occasion, so that few relatives and friends had come. In the inner apartments there were only a small number of ladies of close kinship. Mesdames Hsing and Wang, and lady Feng, and the women of the whole household, were entertaining the guests, when they heard a servant announce that Mr. Chia Chen had come. (This announcement) took the whole body of ladies and young ladies so much by surprise, that, with a rushing sound, they tried to hide in the back rooms; but they were not quick enough (to effect their escape).

Lady Feng alone composedly stood up. Chia Chen was himself at this time rather unwell, and being also very much cut up, he entered the room shuffling along, propping himself up with a staff.

"You are not well?" therefore remarked madame Hsing and the others, "and you've had besides so much to attend to during these consecutive days, that what you require is rest to get all right; and why do you again come over?"

Chia Chen was, as he leant on his staff, straining every nerve to bend his body so as to fall on his knees and pay his respects to them, and express his sense of obligation for the trouble they had taken, when madame Hsing and the other ladies hastily called Pao-yü to raise him up, bidding a servant move a chair for him to sit on. Chia Chen would not take a seat; but making an effort to return a smile, "Your nephew," he urged, "has come over, as there's a favour that I want to ask of my two aunts as well as of my eldest cousin."

"What is it?" promptly inquired madame Hsing and the rest.

"My aunts," Chia Chen replied with all haste, "you surely are aware that your grandson's wife is now no more; your nephew's wife is also laid up unwell, and, as I see that things in the inner apartments are really not what they should properly be, I would trouble my worthy eldest cousin to undertake in here the direction of affairs for a month; and if she does, my mind will be set at ease."

Madame Hsing smiled. "Is it really about this that you've come?" she asked; "your eldest cousin is at present staying with your aunt Secunda, and all you have to do is to speak to her and it will be all right."

"How ever could a mere child like her," speedily remonstrated madame Wang, "carry out all these matters? and shouldn't she manage things properly, she will, on the contrary, make people laugh, so it would therefore be better that you should trouble some one else."

"What your ideas are, aunt," rejoined Chia Chen smiling, "your nephew has guessed; you're afraid lest my eldest cousin should have to bear fatigue and annoyance; for as to what you say, that she cannot manage things, why my eldest cousin has, from her youth up, ever been in her romping and playing so firm and decided; and now that she has entered the married estate, and has the run of affairs in that mansion, she must have reaped so much the more experience, and have become quite an old hand! I've been thinking these last few days that outside my eldest cousin, there's no one else who could come to my help; and, aunt, if you don't do it for the face of your nephew and your nephew's wife, do it, at least, for the affection you bore to her who is no more."

While he uttered these words tears trickled down his face. The fears that madame Wang inwardly entertained were that lady Feng had no experience in funeral matters, and she apprehended, that if she was not equal to managing them, she would incur the ridicule of others; but when she now heard Chia Chen make the appeal in such a disconsolate mood, she relented considerably in her resolution. But as she turned her eyes towards lady Feng (to ascertain her wishes), she saw that she was plunged in abstraction.

Lady Feng had all along found the greatest zest in taking the initiative in everything, with the idea of making a display of her abilities, so that when she perceived how earnest Chia Chen was in his entreaties, she had, at an early period, made up her mind to give a favourable reply. Seeing besides madame Wang show signs of relenting, she readily turned round and said to her, "My elder cousin has made his appeal in such a solicitous way that your ladyship should give your consent and have done with it."

"Do you think you are equal to the task?" inquired madame Wang in a whisper.

"What's there that I couldn't be equal to?" replied lady Feng; "for urgent matters outside, my cousin may be said to have already made full provision; and all there is to be done is to keep an eye over things inside. But should there occur anything that I don't know, I can ask you, madame, and it will be right."

Madame Wang perceiving the reasonableness of what she heard her say, uttered not a word, and when Chia Chen saw that lady Feng had assented; "How much you do attend to I don't mind," he observed, forcing another smile, "but I must, in any case, entreat you, cousin, to assume the onerous charge. As a first step I'll pay my obeisance to you in here, and when everything has been finished, I shall then come over into that mansion to express my thanks."

With these words still on his lips, he made a low bow, but lady Feng had scarcely had time to return the compliment, before Chia Chen had directed a servant to fetch the warrant of the Ning mansion, which he bade Pao-yü hand over to lady Feng.

"Cousin," he added, "take whatever steps you think best; and if you want anything, all you have to do is to simply send for it with this, and there will even be no use to consult me. The only thing I must ask you is, not to be too careful in order to save me expense, for the main consideration is that things should be handsomely done. In the second place, it will be well if you were also to treat servants here in the same way as in the other mansion, and not be too scrupulous in the fear that any one might take offence. Outside these two concerns, there's nothing else to disturb my mind."

Lady Feng did not venture to take over the warrant at once, but merely turned round to ascertain what were madame Wang's wishes.

"In view of the reason brother Chen advances," madame Wang rejoined, "you had better assume the charge at once and finish with it; don't, however, act on your own ideas; but when there's aught to be done, be careful and send some one to consult your cousin's wife, ever so little though it be on the subject."

Pao-yü had already taken over the warrant from Chia Chen's grasp, and forcibly handed it to lady Feng, "Will you, cousin," he went on to question, "take up your quarters here or will you come every day? should you cross over, day after day, it will be ever so much more fatiguing for you, so that I shall speedily have a separate court got ready for you in here, where you, cousin, can put up for these several days and be more comfortable."

"There's no need," replied lady Feng smiling; "for on that side they can't do without me; and it will be better if I were to come daily."

"Do as you like," Chia Chen observed; and after subsequently passing a few more irrelevant remarks, he at length left the room.

After a time, the lady relatives dispersed, and madame Wang seized the opportunity to inquire of lady Feng, "What do you purpose doing to-day?"

"You had better, please madame, go back," urged lady Feng, "for I must first of all find out some clue before I can go home."

Madame Wang, upon hearing these words, returned to her quarters, in advance, in company with madame Hsing, where we will leave them.

Lady Feng meanwhile came into a colonnade, which enclosed a suite of three apartments, and taking a seat, she gave way to reflection. "The first consideration," she communed within herself, "is that the household is made up of mixed elements, and things might be lost; the second is that the preparations are under no particular control, with the result that, when the time comes, the servants might shirk their duties; the third is that the necessary expenditure being great, there will be reckless disbursements and counterfeit receipts; the fourth, that with the absence of any distinction in the matter of duties, whether large or small, hardship and ease will be unequally shared; and the fifth, that the servants being arrogant, through leniency, those with any self-respect will not brook control, while those devoid of 'face' will not be able to improve their ways."

These five were, in point of fact, usages in vogue in the Ning mansion. But as you are unable, reader, to ascertain here how lady Feng set things right, listen to the explanations given in the following chapter.

CHAPTER XIV.

Lin Ju-hai dies in the City of Yang Chou.
Chia Pao-yü meets the Prince of Pei Ching on the way.

When Lai Sheng, be it noticed in continuing our story, the major-domo in the Ning Kuo mansion, came to hear that from inside an invitation had been extended to lady Feng to act as deputy, he summoned together his co-workers and other servants. "Lady Secunda, of the western mansion," he harangued them, "has now been asked to take over the control of internal affairs; and should she come we must, when we apply for anything, or have anything to say, be circumspect in our service; we should all every day come early and leave late; and it's better that we should exert ourselves during this one month and take rest after it's over. We mustn't throw away our old 'face,' for she's well known to be an impetuous thing, with a soured face and a hard heart, who, when angry, knows no distinction of persons."

The whole company unanimously admitted that he was right; and one of their number too observed smilingly, "It's but right that for the inner apartments, we should, in fact, get her to come and put things in proper order, as everything is very much what it should not be."

But while he uttered these words, they saw Lai Wang's wife coming, with an indent in hand, to fetch paper for the supplications and prayers, the amount of which was mentioned on the order; and they one and all hastened to press her into a seat, and to help her to a cup of tea; while a servant was told to fetch the quantity of paper required. (When it was brought,) Lai Wang carried it in his arms and came, the whole way with his wife, as far as the ceremonial gate; when he, at length, delivered it over to her and she clasped it, and walked into the room all alone.

Lady Feng issued prompt directions to Ts'ai Ming to prepare a register; and sending, there and then, for Lai Sheng's wife, she asked her to submit, for her perusal, the roll with the servants' names. She furthermore fixed upon an early hour of the following day to convene the domestics and their wives in the mansion, in order that they should receive their orders; but, after cursorily glancing over the number of entries in the list, and making a few inquiries of Lai Sheng's wife, she soon got into her curricle, and went home.

On the next day, at six and two quarters, she speedily came over. The matrons and married women of the Ning Kuo mansion assembled together, as soon as they heard of her arrival; but, perceiving lady Feng, assisted by Lai Sheng's wife, engaged in apportioning the duties of each servant, they could not presume to intrude, but remained outside the window listening to what was going on.

"As I've been asked to take over the charge," they heard lady Feng explain to Lai Sheng's wife, "I'm, needless to say, sure to incur the displeasure of you all, for I can't compare with your mistress, who has such a sweet temper, and allows you to have your own way. But saying nothing more of those ways, which prevailed hitherto among your people in this mansion, you must now do as I tell you; for on the slightest disregard of my orders, I shall, with no discrimination between those who may be respectable and those who may not be, clearly and distinctly call all alike to account."

Having concluded these remarks, she went on to order Ts'ai Ming to read the roll; and, as their names were uttered, one by one was called in, and passed under inspection. After this inspection, which was got over in a short time, she continued giving further directions. "These twenty," she said "should be divided into two companies; ten in each company, whose sole daily duties should be to attend inside to the guests, coming and going, and to serve tea for them; while with any other matters, they needn't have anything to do. These other twenty should also be divided into two companies, whose exclusive duties will be, day after day, to look after the tea and eatables of the relatives of our family; and these too will have no business to concern themselves with outside matters. These forty will again be divided into two companies, who will have nothing else to look to than to remain in front of the coffin and offer incense, renew the oil, hang up the streamers, watch the coffin, offer sacrifices of rice, and oblations of tea, and mourn with the mourners; and neither need they mind anything outside these duties. These four servants will be specially attached to the inner tea-rooms to look after cups, saucers and the tea articles generally; and in the event of the loss of any single thing, the four of them will have to make it good between them. These other four servants will have the sole charge of the articles required for eatables and wine; and should any get mislaid compensation will have likewise to be made by them. These eight servants will only have to attend to taking over the sacrificial offerings; while these eight will have nothing more to see to beyond keeping an eye over the lamps, oil, candles and paper wanted everywhere. I'll have a whole supply served out and handed to you eight to by and by apportion to the various places, in quantities which I will determine. These thirty servants are each day, by rotation, to keep watch everywhere during the night, looking after the gates and windows, taking care of the fires and candles, and sweeping the grounds; while the servants, who remain, are to be divided for duty in the houses and rooms, each one having charge of a particular spot. And beginning from the tables, chairs and curios in each place, up to the very cuspidors and brooms, yea even to each blade of grass or sprout of herb, which may be there, the servants looking after this part will be called upon to make good anything that may be either mislaid or damaged. You, Lai Sheng's wife, will every day have to exercise general supervision and inspection; and should there be those who be lazy, any who may gamble, drink, fight or wrangle, come at once and report the matter to me; and you mustn't show any leniency, for if I come to find it out, I shall have no regard to the good old name of three or four generations, which you may enjoy. You now all have your fixed duties, so that whatever batch of you after this acts contrary to these orders, I shall simply have something to say to that batch and to no one else. The servants, who have all along been in my service, carry watches on their persons, and things, whether large or small, are invariably done at a fixed time. But, in any case, you also have clocks in your master's rooms, so that at 6.30, I shall come and read the roll, and at ten you'll have breakfast. Whenever there is any indent of any permits to be made or any report to be submitted, it should be done at 11.30 a.m. and no later. At 7 p.m., after the evening paper has been burnt, I shall come to each place in person to hold an inspection; and on my return, the servants on watch for the night will hand over the keys. The next day, I shall again come over at 6.30 in the morning; and needless to say we must all do the best we can for these few days; and when the work has been finished your master is sure to recompense you."

When she had done speaking, she went on to give orders that tea, oil, candles, feather dusters, brooms and other necessaries should be issued, according to the fixed quantities. She also had furniture, such as table-covers, antimacassars, cushions, rugs, cuspidors, stools and the like brought over and distributed; while, at the same time, she took up the pencil and made a note of the names of the persons in charge of the various departments, and of the articles taken over by the respective servants, in entries remarkable for the utmost perspicacity.

The whole body of servants received their charge and left; but they all had work to go and attend to; not as in former times, when they were at liberty to select for themselves what was convenient to do, while the arduous work, which remained over, no one could be found to take in hand. Neither was it possible for them in the various establishments to any longer avail themselves of the confusion to carelessly mislay things. In fact, visitors came and guests left, but everything after all went off quietly, unlike the disorderly way which prevailed hitherto, when there was no clue to the ravel; and all such abuses as indolence, and losses, and the like were completely eradicated.

Lady Feng, on her part, (perceiving) the weight her influence had in enjoining the observance of her directions, was in her heart exceedingly delighted. But as she saw, that Chia Chen was, in consequence of Mrs. Yu's indisposition, even so much the more grieved as to take very little to drink or to eat, she daily, with her own hands, prepared, in the other mansion, every kind of fine congee and luscious small dishes, which she sent over, in order that he might be tempted to eat.

And Chia Lien had likewise given additional directions that every day the finest delicacies should be taken into the ante-chamber, for the exclusive use of lady Feng.

Lady Feng was not one to shirk exertion and fatigue, so that, day after day, she came over at the proper time, called the roll, and managed business, sitting all alone in the ante-chamber, and not congregating with the whole bevy of sisters-in-law. Indeed, even when relatives or visitors came or went, she did not go to receive them, or see them off.

This day was the thirty-fifth day, the very day of the fifth seven, and the whole company of bonzes had just (commenced the services) for unclosing the earth, and breaking Hell open; for sending a light to show the way to the departed spirit; for its being admitted to an audience by the king of Hell; for arresting all the malicious devils, as well as for soliciting the soul-saving Buddha to open the golden bridge and to lead the way with streamers. The Taoist priests were engaged in reverently reading the prayers; in worshipping the Three Pure Ones and in prostrating themselves before the Gemmy Lord. The disciples of abstraction were burning incense, in order to release the hungered spirits, and were reading the water regrets manual. There was also a company of twelve nuns of tender years, got up in embroidered dresses, and wearing red shoes, who stood before the coffin, silently reading all the incantations for the reception of the spirit (from the lower regions,) with the result that the utmost bustle and stir prevailed.

Lady Feng, well aware that not a few guests would call on this day, was quick to get out of bed at four sharp, to dress her hair and perform her ablutions. After having completed every arrangement for the day, she changed her costume, washed her hands, and swallowed a couple of mouthfuls of milk. By the time she had rinsed her mouth, it was exactly 6.30; and Lai Wang's wife, at the head of a company of servants, had been waiting a good long while, when lady Feng appeared in front of the Entrance Hall, mounted her carriage and betook herself, preceded by a pair of transparent horn lanterns, on which were written, in large type, the three characters, Jung Kuo mansion, to the main entrance gate of the Ning Household. The door lanterns shed brilliant rays from where they were suspended; while on either side the lanterns, of uniform colours, propped upright, emitted a lustrous light as bright as day.

The servants of the family, got up in their mourning clothes, covered the ground far and wide like a white sheet. They stood drawn in two rows, and requested that the carriage should drive up to the main entrance. The youths retired, and all the married women came forward, and raising the curtain of the carriage, lady Feng alighted; and as with one arm she supported herself on Feng Erh, two married women, with lanterns in their hands, lighted the way. Pressed round by the servants, lady Feng made her entry. The married women of the Ning mansion advanced to greet her, and to pay their respects; and this over, lady Feng, with graceful bearing, entered the Garden of Concentrated Fragrance. Ascending the Spirit Hall, where the tablet was laid, the tears, as soon as she caught sight of the coffin, trickled down her eyes like pearls whose string had snapped; while the youths in the court, and their number was not small, stood in a reverent posture, with their arms against their sides, waiting to burn the paper. Lady Feng uttered one remark, by way of command: "Offer the tea and burn the paper!" when the sound of two blows on the gong was heard and the whole band struck up together. A servant had at an early period placed a large armchair in front of the tablet, and lady Feng sat down, and gave way to loud lamentations. Promptly all those, who stood inside or outside, whether high or low, male or female, took up the note, and kept on wailing and weeping until Chia Chen and Mrs. Yu, after a time, sent a message to advise her to withhold her tears; when at length lady Feng desisted.

Lai Wang's wife served the tea; and when she had finished rinsing her mouth, lady Feng got up; and, taking leave of all the members of the clan, she walked all alone into the ante-chamber, where she ascertained, in the order of their names, the number of the servants of every denomination in there. They were all found to be present, with the exception of one, who had failed to appear, whose duties consisted in receiving and escorting the relatives and visitors. Orders were promptly given to summon him, and the man appeared in a dreadful fright. "What!" exclaimed lady Feng, as she forced a smile, "is it you who have been remiss? Is it because you're more respectable than they that you don't choose to listen to my words?"

"Your servant," he pleaded, "has come at an early hour every day; and it's only to-day that I come late by one step; and I entreat your ladyship to forgive this my first offence."

While yet he spoke, she perceived the wife of Wang Hsing, of the Jung Kuo mansion, come forward and pop her head in to see what was going on; but lady Feng did not let this man go, but went on to inquire of Wang Hsing's wife what she had come for.

Wang Hsing's wife drew near. "I've come," she explained, "to get an order, so as to obtain some thread to make tassels for the carriages and chairs." Saying this, she produced the permit and handed it up, whereupon lady Feng directed Ts'ai Ming to read the contents aloud. "For two large, sedan chairs," he said, "four small sedan chairs and four carriages, are needed in all so many large and small tassels, each tassel requiring so many catties of beads and thread."

Lady Feng finding, after she had heard what was read, that the numbers (and quantities) corresponded, forthwith bade Ts'ai Ming make the proper entry; and when the order from the Jung Kuo mansion had been fetched, and thrown at her, Wang Hsing's wife took her departure.

Lady Feng was on the very point of saying something, when she espied four managers of the Jung Kuo mansion walk in; all of whom wanted permits to indent for stores. Having asked them to read out the list of what they required, she ascertained that they wanted four kinds of articles in all. Drawing attention to two items: "These entries," she remarked, "are wrong; and you had better go again and make out the account clearly, and then come and fetch a permit."

With these words, she flung down the requisitions, and the two men went their way in lower spirits than when they had come.

Lady Feng then caught sight of the wife of Chang Ts'ai standing by, and asked her what was her business, whereupon Chang Ts'ai's wife promptly produced an indent. "The covers of the carriages and sedan chairs," she reported, "have just been completed, and I've come to fetch the amount due to the tailors for wages."

Lady Feng, upon hearing her explanation, took over the indent, and directed Ts'ai Ming to enter the items in the book. After Wang Hsing had handed over the money, and obtained the receipt of the accountant, duly signed, which tallied with the payment, he subsequently walked away in company with Chang Ts'ai's wife. Lady Feng simultaneously proceeded to give orders that another indent should be read, which was for money to purchase paper with to paste on the windows of Pao-yü's outer school-room, the repairs to which had been brought to completion, and as soon as lady Feng heard the nature of the application, she there and then gave directions that the permit should be taken over and an entry made, and that the money should be issued after Chang Ts'ai's wife had delivered everything clearly.

"If to-morrow he were to come late," lady Feng then remarked, "and if the day after, I were to come late; why by and by there'll be no one here at all! I should have liked to have let you off, but if I be lenient with you on this first instance, it will be hard for me, on the occurrence of another offence, to exercise any control over the rest. It's much better therefore that I should settle accounts with you."

The moment she uttered these words, she put on a serious look, and gave orders that he should be taken out and administered twenty blows with the bamboo. When the servants perceived that lady Feng was in an angry mood, they did not venture to dilly-dally, but dragged him out, and gave him the full number of blows; which done, they came in to report that the punishment had been inflicted.

Lady Feng likewise threw down the Ning Mansion order and exclaimed, addressing herself to Lai Sheng: "Cut him a month's wages and rice! and tell them all to disperse, and have done with it!"

All the servants at length withdrew to attend to their respective duties, while the man too, who had been flogged, walked away, as he did all he could to conceal his shame and stifle his tears. About this time arrived and went, in an incessant stream, servants from both the Jung and Ning mansions, bent upon applying for permits and returning permits, and with one by one again did lady Feng settle accounts. And, as in due course, the inmates of the Ning mansion came to know how terrible lady Feng was, each and all were ever since so wary and dutiful that they did not venture to be lazy.

But without going into further details on this subject, we shall now return to Pao-yü. Seeing that there were a lot of people about and fearing lest Ch'in Chung might receive some offence, he lost no time in coming along with him to sit over at lady Feng's. Lady Feng was just having her repast, and upon seeing them arrive: "Your legs are long enough, and couldn't you have come somewhat quicker!" she laughingly observed.

"We've had our rice, thanks," replied Pao-yü.

"Have you had it," inquired lady Feng, "outside here, or over on the other side?"

"Would we eat anything with all that riff-raff?" exclaimed Pao-yü; "we've really had it over there; in fact, I now come after having had mine with dowager lady Chia."

As he uttered these words, they took their seats. Lady Feng had just finished her meal, when a married woman from the Ning mansion came to get an order to obtain an advance of money to purchase incense and lanterns with.

"I calculated," observed lady Feng, "that you would come to-day to make requisition, but I was under the impression that you had forgotten; had you really done so you would certainly have had to get them on your own account, and I would have been the one to benefit."

"Didn't I forget? I did," rejoined the married woman as she smiled; "and it's only a few minutes back that it came to my mind; had I been one second later I wouldn't have been in time to get the things."

These words ended, she took over the order and went off. Entries had, at the time to be made in the books, and orders to be issued, and Ch'in Chung was induced to interpose with a smirk, "In both these mansions of yours, such orders are alike in use; but were any outsider stealthily to counterfeit one and to abscond, after getting the money, what could ever be done?"

"In what you say," replied lady Feng, "you take no account of the laws of the land."

"How is it that from our house, no one comes to get any orders or to obtain anything?" Pao-yü having inquired: "At the time they come to fetch them," rejoined lady Feng, "you're still dreaming; but let me ask you one thing, when will you two at last begin your evening course of studies?"

"Oh, I wish we were able to begin our studies this very day," Pao-yü added; "that would be the best thing, but they're very slow in putting the school-room in order, so that there's no help for it!"

Lady Feng laughed. "Had you asked me," she remarked, "I can assure you it would have been ready quick enough."

"You too would have been of no use," observed Pao-yü, "for it will certainly be ready by the time they ought to finish it in."

"But in order that they should do the work," suggested lady Feng, "it's also necessary that they should have the material, they can't do without them; and if I don't give them any permits, it will be difficult to obtain them."

Pao-yü at these words readily drew near to lady Feng, and there and then applied for the permits. "My dear sister," he added, "do give them the permits to enable them to obtain the material and effect the repairs."

"I feel quite sore from fatigue," ventured lady Feng, "and how can I stand your rubbing against me? but compose your mind. They have this very day got the paper, and gone to paste it; and would they, for whatever they need, have still waited until they had been sent for? they are not such fools after all!"

Pao-yü would not believe it, and lady Feng at once called Ts'ai Ming to look up the list, which she handed for Pao-yü's inspection; but while they were arguing a servant came in to announce that Chao Erh, who had gone to Su Chow, had returned, and lady Feng all in a flurry directed that he should be asked to walk in. Chao Erh bent one knee and paid his obeisance.

"Why have you come back?" lady Feng readily inquired.

"Mr. Secundus (Chia Lien)," he reported, "sent me back to tell you that Mr. Lin (our dowager lady's) son-in-law, died on the third of the ninth moon; that Master Secundus is taking Miss Lin along with him to escort the coffin of Mr. Lin as far as Su Chow; and that they hope to be back some time about the end of the year. Master despatched me to come and announce the news, to bring his compliments, and to crave our old lady's instructions as well as to see how you are getting on in my lady's home. He also bade me take back to him a few long fur pelisses."

"Have you seen any one else besides me?" lady Feng inquired.

"I've seen every one," rejoined Chao Erh; and withdrew hastily at the conclusion of this remark, out of the apartment, while lady Feng turned towards Pao-yü with a smile and said, "Your cousin Lin can now live in our house for ever."

"Poor thing!" exclaimed Pao-yü. "I presume that during all these days she has wept who knows how much;" and saying this he wrinkled his brow and heaved a deep sigh.

Lady Feng saw Chao Erh on his return, but as she could not very well, in the presence of third persons, make minute inquiries after Chia Lien, she had to continue a prey to inward solicitude till it was time to go home, for, not having got through what she had to do, she was compelled to wait patiently until she went back in the evening, when she again sent word for Chao Erh to come in, and asked him with all minuteness whether the journey had been pleasant throughout, and for full particulars. That very night, she got in readiness the long pelisses, which she herself, with the assistance of P'ing Erh, packed up in a bundle; and after careful thought as to what things he would require, she put them in the same bundle and committed them to Chao Erh's care. She went on to solicitously impress upon Chao Erh to be careful in his attendance abroad. "Don't provoke your master to wrath," she said, "and from time to time do advise him not to drink too much wine; and don't entice him to make the acquaintance of any low people; for if you do, when you come back I will cut your leg off."

The preparations were hurriedly and confusedly completed; and it was already the fourth watch of the night when she went to sleep. But soon again the day dawned, and after hastily performing her toilette and ablutions, she came over to the Ning Mansion.

As Chia Chen realised that the day for escorting the body away was drawing nigh, he in person went out in a curricle, along with geomancers, to the Temple of the Iron Fence to inspect a suitable place for depositing the coffin. He also, point by point, enjoined the resident managing-bonze, Se K'ung, to mind and get ready brand-new articles of decoration and furniture, and to invite a considerable number of bonzes of note to be at hand to lend their services for the reception of the coffin.

Se K'ung lost no time in getting ready the evening meal, but Chia Chen had, in fact, no wish for any tea or rice; and, as the day was far advanced and he was not in time to enter the city, he had, after all, to rest during that night as best he could in a "chaste" room in the temple. The next morning, as soon as it was day, he hastened to come into the city and to make every preparation for the funeral. He likewise deputed messengers to proceed ahead to the Temple of the Iron Fence to give, that very night, additional decorative touches to the place where the coffin was to be deposited, and to get ready tea and all the other necessaries, for the use of the persons who would be present at the reception of the coffin.

Lady Feng, seeing that the day was not far distant, also apportioned duties and made provision for everything beforehand with circumspect care; while at the same time she chose in the Jung mansion, such carriages, sedan chairs and retinue as were to accompany the cortege, in attendance upon madame Wang, and gave her mind furthermore to finding a place where she herself could put up in at the time of the funeral. About this very time, it happened that the consort of the Duke Shan Kuo departed this life, and that mesdames Wang and Hsing had likewise to go and offer sacrifices, and to follow the burial procession; that the birthday occurred of the consort of Prince Hsi An; that presents had to be forwarded on the occasion of this anniversary; and that the consort of the Duke of Chen Kuo gave birth to a first child, a son, and congratulatory gifts had, in like manner, to be provided. Besides, her uterine brother Wang Jen was about to return south, with all his family, and she had too to write her home letters, to send her reverent compliments to her father and mother, as well as to get the things ready that were to be taken along. There was also Ying Ch'un, who had contracted some illness, and the doctor had every day to be sent for, and medicines to be administered, the notes of the doctor to be looked after, consisting of the bulletins of the diagnosis and the prescriptions, with the result that the various things that had to be attended to by lady Feng were so manifold that it would, indeed, be difficult to give an exhaustive idea of them.

In addition to all this, the day for taking the coffin away was close at hand, so that lady Feng was so hard pressed for time that she had even no desire for any tea to drink or anything to eat, and that she could not sit or rest in peace. As soon as she put her foot into the Ning mansion, the inmates of the Jung mansion would follow close upon her heels; and the moment she got back into the Jung mansion, the servants again of the Ning mansion would follow her about. In spite however of this great pressure, lady Feng, whose natural disposition had ever been to try and excel, was urged to strain the least of her energies, as her sole dread was lest she should incur unfavourable criticism from any one; and so excellent were the plans she devised, that every one in the clan, whether high or low, readily conceded her unlimited praise.

On the night of this day, the body had to be watched, and in the inner suite of apartments two companies of young players as well as jugglers entertained the relatives, friends and other visitors during the whole of the night. Mrs. Yu was still laid up in the inside room, so that the whole task of attending to and entertaining the company devolved upon lady Feng alone, who had to look after everything; for though there were, in the whole clan, many sisters-in-law, some there were too bashful to speak, others too timid to stand on their feet; while there were also those who were not accustomed to meeting company; and those likewise who were afraid of people of high estate and shy of officials. Of every kind there were, but the whole number of them could not come up to lady Feng's standard, whose deportment was correct and whose speech was according to rule. Hence it was that she did not even so much as heed any of that large company, but gave directions and issued orders, adopting any course of action which she fancied, just as if there were no bystander.

The whole night, the lanterns emitted a bright light and the fires brilliant rays; while guests were escorted on their way out and officials greeted on their way in; but of this hundredfold bustle and stir nothing need, of course, be said.

The next morning at the dawn of day, and at a propitious moment, sixty-four persons, dressed all alike in blue, carried the coffin, preceded by a streamer with the record in large characters: Coffin of lady Ch'in, a lady of the fifth degree, (by marriage) of the Chia mansion, deceased at middle age, consort of the grandson of the Ning Kuo Duke with the first rank title of honour, (whose status is) a guard of the Imperial antechamber, charged with the protection of the Inner Palace and Roads in the Red Prohibited City.

The various paraphernalia and ornaments were all brand-new, hurriedly made for the present occasion, and the uniform lustrous brilliancy they shed was sufficient to dazzle the eyes.

Pao-chu, of course, observed the rites prescribed for unmarried daughters, and dashed the bowl and walked by the coffin, as she gave way to most bitter lamentations.

At that time, among the officials who escorted the funeral procession, were Niu Chi-tsung, the grandson of the Chen Kuo duke, who had now inherited the status of earl of the first degree; Liu Fang, the grandson of Liu Piao, duke of Li Kuo, who had recently inherited the rank of viscount of the first class; Ch'en Jui-wen, a grandson of Ch'en Yi, duke of Ch'i Kuo, who held the hereditary rank of general of the third degree, with the prefix of majestic authority; Ma Shang, the grandson of Ma K'uei, duke of Chih Kuo, by inheritance general of the third rank with the prefix of majesty afar; Hou Hsiao-keng, an hereditary viscount of the first degree, grandson of the duke of Hsiu Kuo, Hou Hsiao-ming by name; while the death of the consort of the duke of Shan Kuo had obliged his grandson Shih Kuang-chu to go into mourning so that he could not be present. These were the six families which had, along with the two households of Jung and Ning, been, at one time, designated the eight dukes.

Among the rest, there were besides the grandson of the Prince of Nan An; the grandson of the Prince of Hsi An; Shih Ting, marquis of Chung Ching; Chiang Tzu-ning, an hereditary baron of the second grade, grandson of the earl of P'ing Yuan; Hsieh K'un, an hereditary baron of the second order and Captain of the Metropolitan camp, grandson of the marquis of Ting Ch'ang: Hsi Chien-hui, an hereditary baron of the second rank, a grandson of the marquis of Nang Yang; Ch'in Liang, in command of the Five Cities, grandson of the marquis of Ching T'ien. The remainder were Wei Chi, the son of the earl of Chin Hsiang; Feng Tzu-ying, the son of a general, whose prefix was supernatural martial spirit; Ch'en Yeh-chün, Wei Jo-lan and others, grandsons and sons of princes who could not be enumerated.

In the way of ladies, there were also in all about ten large official sedan chairs full of them, thirty or forty private chairs, and including the official and non-official chairs, and carriages containing inmates of the household, there must have been over a hundred and ten; so that with the various kinds of paraphernalia, articles of decoration and hundreds of nick-nacks, which preceded, the vast expanse of the cortege covered a continuous line extending over three or four li.

They had not been very long on their way, when they reached variegated sheds soaring high by the roadside, in which banquets were spread, feasts laid out, and music discoursed in unison. These were the viatory sacrificial offerings contributed by the respective families. The first shed contained the sacrificial donations of the mansion of the Prince of Tung P'ing; the second shed those of the Prince of Nan An; the third those of the Prince of Hsi Ning, and the fourth those of the Prince of Pei Ching.

Indeed of these four Princes, the reputation enjoyed in former days by the Prince of Pei Ching had been the most exalted, and to this day his sons and grandsons still succeeded to the inheritance of the princely dignity. The present incumbent of the Princedom of Pei Ching, Shih Jung, had not as yet come of age, but he was gifted with a presence of exceptional beauty, and with a disposition condescending and genial. At the demise, recently, of the consort of the eldest grandson of the mansion of Ning Kuo, he, in consideration of the friendship which had formerly existed between the two grandfathers, by virtue of which they had been inseparable, both in adversity as well as in prosperity, treating each other as if they had not been of different surnames, was consequently induced to pay no regard to princely dignity or to his importance, but having like the others paid, on the previous day, his condolences and presented sacrificial offerings, he had further now raised a shed wherein to offer libations. Having directed every one of his subordinate officers to remain in this spot in attendance, he himself went at the fifth watch to court, and when he acquitted himself of his public duties he forthwith changed his attire for a mourning costume, and came along, in an official sedan chair, preceded by gongs and umbrellas. Upon reaching the front of the shed the chair was deposited on the ground, and as his subordinate officers pressed on either side and waited upon him, neither the military nor the populace, which composed the mass of people, ventured to make any commotion. In a short while, the long procession of the Ning mansion became visible, spreading far and wide, covering in its course from the north, the whole ground like a silver mountain. At an early hour, the forerunners, messengers and other attendants on the staff of the Ning mansion apprised Chia Chen (of the presence of the sheds), and Chia Chen with all alacrity gave orders that the foremost part of the cortege should halt. Attended by Chia She and Chia Chen, the three of them came with hurried step to greet (the Prince of Pei Ching), whom they saluted with due ceremony. Shih Jung, who was seated in his sedan chair, made a bow and returned their salutations with a smile, proceeding to address them and to treat them, as he had done hitherto, as old friends, without any airs of self-importance.

"My daughter's funeral has," observed Chia Chen, "put your Highness to the trouble of coming, an honour which we, though noble by birth, do not deserve."

Shih Jung smiled. "With the terms of friendship," he added, "which have existed for so many generations (between our families), is there any need for such apologies?"

Turning his head round there and then, he gave directions to the senior officer of his household to preside at the sacrifices and to offer libations in his stead; and Chia She and the others stood together on one side and made obeisance in return, and then came in person again and gave expression to their gratitude for his bounty.

Shih Jung was most affable and complaisant. "Which is the gentleman," he inquired of Chia Chen, "who was born with a piece of jade in his mouth? I've long had a wish to have the pleasure of seeing him, and as he's sure to be on the spot on an occasion like this, why shouldn't you invite him to come round?"

Chia Chen speedily drew back, and bidding Pao-yü change his mourning clothes, he led him forward and presented him.

Pao-yü had all along heard that Shih Jung was a worthy Prince, perfect in ability as well as in appearance, pleasant and courteous, not bound down by any official custom or state rite, so that he had repeatedly felt a keen desire to meet him. With the sharp control, however, which his father exercised over him, he had not been able to gratify his wish. But on this occasion, he saw on the contrary that he came to call him, and it was but natural that he should be delighted. Whilst advancing, he scrutinised Shih Jung with the corner of his eye, who, seated as he was in the sedan chair, presented an imposing sight.

But, reader, what occurred on his approach is not yet known, but listen to the next chapter, which will divulge it.

CHAPTER XV.

Lady Peng, née Wang, exercises her authority in the Iron Fence Temple.

Ch'in Ching-ch'ing (Ch'ing Chung) amuses himself in the Man-t'ou (Bread) nunnery.

But we shall now resume our story. When Pao-yü raised his eyes, he noticed that Shih Jung, Prince of Pei Ching, wore on his head a princely cap with pure white tassels and silvery feathers, that he was appareled in a white ceremonial robe, (with a pattern representing) the toothlike ripple of a river and the waters of the sea, embroidered with five-clawed dragons; and that he was girded with a red leather belt, inlaid with white jade. That his face was like a beauteous gem; that his eyes were like sparkling stars; and that he was, in very truth, a human being full of graceful charms.

Pao-yü hastily pressed forward and made a reverent obeisance, and Shih Jung lost no time in extending his arms from inside the sedan-chair, and embracing him. At a glance, he saw that Pao-yü had on his head a silver cap, to which the hair was attached, that he had, round his forehead, a flap on which were embroidered a couple of dragons issuing from the sea, that he wore a white archery-sleeved robe, ornamented with dragons, and that his waist was encircled by a silver belt, inlaid with pearls; that his face resembled vernal flowers and that his eyes were like drops of lacquer.

Shih Jung smiled. "Your name is," he said, "no trumped-up story; for you, verily, resemble a precious gem; but where's the valuable trinket you had in your mouth?" he inquired.

As soon as Pao-yü heard this inquiry, he hastened to produce the jade from inside his clothes and to hand it over to Shih Jung. Shih Jung minutely examined it; and having also read the motto on it, he consequently ascertained whether it was really efficacious or not.

"It's true that it's said to be," Pao-yü promptly explained, "but it hasn't yet been put to the test."

Shih Jung extolled it with unbounded praise, and, as he did so, he set the variegated tassels in proper order, and, with his own hands, attached it on to Pao-yü's neck. Taking also his hand in his, he inquired of Pao-yü what was his age? and what books he was reading at present, to each of which questions Pao-yü gave suitable answer.

Shih Jung perceiving the perspicacity of his speech and the propriety of his utterances, simultaneously turned towards Chia Chen and observed with a smile on his face: "Your worthy son is, in very truth, like the young of a dragon or like the nestling of a phoenix! and this isn't an idle compliment which I, a despicable prince, utter in your venerable presence! But how much more glorious will be, in the future, the voice of the young phoenix than that of the old phoenix, it isn't easy to ascertain."

Chia Chen forced a smile: "My cur-like son," he replied, "cannot presume to such bountiful praise and golden commendation; but if, by the virtue of your Highness' excess of happiness, he does indeed realise your words, he will be a source of joy to us all!"

"There's one thing, however," continued Shih Jung; "with the excellent abilities which your worthy scion possesses, he's sure, I presume, to be extremely loved by her dowager ladyship, (his grandmother), and by all classes. But for young men of our age it's a great drawback to be doated upon, for with over-fondness, we cannot help utterly frustrating the benefits of education. When I, a despicable prince, was young, I walked in this very track, and I presume that your honourable son cannot likewise but do the same. By remaining at home, your worthy scion will find it difficult to devote his attention to study; and he will not reap any harm, were he to come, at frequent intervals, to my humble home; for though my deserts be small, I nevertheless enjoy the great honour of the acquaintance of all the scholars of note in the Empire, so that, whenever any of them visit the capital, not one of them is there who does not lower his blue eyes upon me. Hence it is that in my mean abode, eminent worthies rendezvous; and were your esteemed son to come, as often as he can, and converse with them and meet them, his knowledge would, in that case, have every opportunity of making daily strides towards improvement."

Chia Chen speedily bent his body and expressed his acquiescence, by way of reply; whereupon Shih Jung went further, and taking off from his wrist a chaplet of pearls, he presented it to Pao-yü.

"This is the first time we meet," he observed. "Our meeting was so unexpected that I have no suitable congratulatory present to offer you. This was conferred upon me by His Majesty, and is a string of chaplet-pearls, scented with Ling Ling, which will serve as a temporary token of respectful congratulations."

Pao-yü hastened to receive it from his hands, and turning round, he reverently presented it to Chia Chen. Chia Chen and Pao-yü jointly returned thanks; and forthwith Chia She, Chia Chen and the rest came forward in a body, and requested the Prince to turn his chair homewards.

"The departed," expostulated Shih Jung, "has already ascended the spiritual regions, and is no more a mortal being in this dusty world exposed to vicissitude like you and I. Although a mean prince like me has been the recipient of the favour of the Emperor, and has undeservedly been called to the princely inheritance, how could I presume to go before the spiritual hearse and return home?"

Chia She and the others, perceiving how persistent he was in his refusal had no course but to take their leave, express their sense of gratitude and to rejoin the cortege. They issued orders to their servants to stop the band, and to hush the music, and making the procession go by, they at length left the way clear for Shih Jung to prosecute his way.

But we will now leave him and resume our account of the funeral of the Ning mansion. All along its course the road was plunged in unusual commotion. As soon as they reached the city gates Chia She, Chia Cheng, Chia Chen, and the others again received donations from all their fellow officers and subordinates, in sacrificial sheds erected by their respective families, and after they returned thanks to one after another, they eventually issued from the city walls, and proceeded eventually along the highway, in the direction of the Temple of the Iron Fence.

Chia Chen, at this time, went, together with Chia Jung, up to all their seniors, and pressed them to get into their sedan chairs, and to ride their horses; and Chia She and all of the same age as himself were consequently induced to mount into their respective carriages or chairs. Chia Chen and those of the same generation were likewise about to ride their horses, when lady Feng, through her solicitude on Pao-yü's account, gave way to fears lest now that they had reached the open country, he should do as he pleased, and not listen to the words of any of the household, and lest Chia Chen should not be able to keep him in check; and, as she dreaded that he might go astray, she felt compelled to bid a youth call him to her; and Pao-yü had no help but to appear before her curricle.

"My dear brother," lady Feng remarked smiling, "you are a respectable person, and like a girl in your ways, and shouldn't imitate those monkeys on horseback! do get down and let both you and I sit together in this carriage; and won't that be nice?"

At these words, Pao-yü readily dismounted and climbed up into the carriage occupied by lady Feng; and they both talked and laughed, as they continued their way.

But not a long time elapsed before two men, on horseback, were seen approaching from the opposite direction. Coming straight up to lady Feng's vehicle they dismounted, and said, as they leaned on the sides of her carriage, "There's a halting place here, and will it not please your ladyship to have a rest and change?"

Lady Feng directed them to ask the two ladies Hsing and Wang what they would like to do, and the two men explained: "These ladies have signified that they had no desire to rest, and they wish your ladyship to suit your convenience."

Lady Feng speedily issued orders that they should have a rest, before they prosecuted their way, and the servant youth led the harnessed horses through the crowd of people and came towards the north, while Pao-yü, from inside the carriage, urgently asked that Mr. Ch'in should be requested to come.

Ch'in Chung was at this moment on horseback following in the track of his father's carriage, when unexpectedly he caught sight of Pao-yü's page, come at a running pace and invite him to have some refreshment. Ch'in Chung perceived from a distance that the horse, which Pao-yü had been riding, walked behind lady Feng's vehicle, as it went towards the north, with its saddle and bridles all piled up, and readily concluding that Pao-yü must be in the same carriage with that lady, he too turned his horse and came over in haste and entered, in their company, the door of a farm-house.

This dwelling of the farmer's did not contain many rooms so that the women and girls had nowhere to get out of the way; and when the village lasses and country women perceived the bearing and costumes of lady Feng, Pao-yü, and Ch'in Chung, they were inclined to suspect that celestial beings had descended into the world.

Lady Feng entered a thatched house, and, in the first place, asked Pao-yü and the rest to go out and play. Pao-yü took the hint, and, along with Ch'in Chung, he led off the servant boys and went to romp all over the place.

The various articles in use among the farmers they had not seen before, with the result that after Pao-yü had inspected them, he thought them all very strange; but he could neither make out their names nor their uses. But among the servant boys, there were those who knew, and they explained to them, one after another, what they were called, as well as what they were for. As Pao-yü, after this explanation, nodded his head; "It isn't strange," he said, "that an old writer has this line in his poetical works, 'Who can realise that the food in a bowl is, grain by grain, all the fruit of labour.' This is indeed so!" As he spoke, they had come into another house; and at the sight of a spinning wheel on a stove-bed, they thought it still more strange and wonderful, but the servant boys again told them that it was used for spinning the yarn to weave cloth with, and Pao-yü speedily jumping on to the stove-bed, set to work turning the wheel for the sake of fun, when a village lass of about seventeen or eighteen years of age came forward, and asked them not to meddle with it and spoil it.

The servant boys promptly stopped her interference; but Pao-yü himself desisted, as he added: "It's because I hadn't seen one before that I came to try it for fun."

"You people can't do it," rejoined the lass, "let me turn it for you to see."

Ch'in Chung secretly pulled Pao-yü and remarked, "It's great fun in this village!" but Pao-yü gave him a nudge and observed, "If you talk nonsense again, I'll beat you." Watching intently, as he uttered these words, the village girl who started reeling the thread, and presented, in very truth, a pretty sight. But suddenly an old woman from the other side gave a shout. "My girl Secunda, come over at once;" and the lass discarded the spinning-wheel and hastily went on her way.

Pao-yü was the while feeling disappointed and unhappy, when he espied a servant, whom lady Feng had sent, come and call them both in. Lady Feng had washed her hands and changed her costume; and asked him whether he would change or not, and Pao-yü, having replied "No! it doesn't matter after all if I don't change," the female attendants served tea, cakes and fruits and also poured the scented tea. Lady Feng and the others drank their tea, and waiting until they had put the various articles by, and made all the preparations, they promptly started to get into their carriages. Outside, Wang Erh had got ready tips and gave them to the people of the farm, and the farm women and all the inmates went up to them to express their gratitude; but when Pao-yü came to look carefully, he failed to see anything of the lass who had reeled the thread. But they had not gone far before they caught sight of this girl Secunda coming along with a small child in her arms, who, they concluded, was her young brother, laughing and chatting, in company with a few young girls.

Pao-yü could not suppress the voice of love, but being seated in the carriage, he was compelled to satisfy himself by following her with his eyes. Soon however the vehicle sped on as rapidly as a cloud impelled by the wind, so that when he turned his head round, there was already no vestige to be seen of her; but, while they were bandying words, they had unexpectedly overtaken the great concourse of the cortege.

Likewise, at an early stage men were stationed ahead, with Buddhist drums and gold cymbals, with streamers, and jewelled coverings; and the whole company of bonzes, belonging to the Iron Fence Temple, had already been drawn out in a line by the sides of the road. In a short while, they reached the interior of the temple, where additional sacrifices were offered and Buddhistic services performed; and where altars had again been erected to burn incense on. The coffin was deposited in a side room of the inner court; and Pao Chu got ready a bedroom in which she could keep her watch.

In the outer apartments, Chia Chen did the honours among the whole party of relatives and friends, some of whom asked to be allowed to stay for their meals, while others at this stage took their leave. And after they had one by one returned thanks, the dukes, marquises, earls, viscounts and barons, each in respective batches, (got up to go,) and they kept on leaving from between 1 and 3 p.m. before they had finally all dispersed.

In the inner Chambers, the ladies were solely entertained and attended to by lady Feng. First to make a move were the consorts of officials; and noon had also come, by the time the whole party of them had taken their departure. Those that remained were simply a few relatives of the same clan and others like them, who eventually left after the completion of the three days' rationalistic liturgies.

The two ladies Hsing and Wang, well aware at this time that lady Feng could on no account return home, desired to enter the city at once; and madame Wang wanted to take Pao-yü home; but Pao-yü, who had, on an unexpected occasion, come out into the country, entertained, of course, no wish to go back; and he would agree to nothing else than to stay behind with lady Feng, so that madame Wang had no alternative but to hand him over to her charge and to start.

This Temple of the Iron Fence had, in fact, been erected in days gone by, at the expense of the two dukes Ning and Jung; and there still remained up to these days, acres of land, from which were derived the funds for incense and lights for such occasions, on which the coffins of any members, old or young, (who died) in the capital, had to be deposited in this temple; and the inner and outer houses, in this compound were all kept in readiness and good order, for the accommodation of those who formed part of the cortège.

At this time, as it happened, the descendants mustered an immense crowd, and among them were poor and rich of various degrees, or with likes and dislikes diametrically opposed. There were those, who, being in straitened circumstances at home, and easily contented, readily took up their quarters in the temple. And there were those with money and position, and with extravagant ideas, who maintained that the accommodation in the temple was not suitable, and, of course, went in search of additional quarters, either in country houses, or in convents, where they could have their meals and retire, after the ceremonies were over.

On the occasion of Mrs. Ch'in's funeral, all the members of the clan put up temporarily in the Iron Fence Temple; lady Feng alone looked down upon it as inconvenient, and consequently despatched a servant to go and tell Ch'ing Hsü, a nun in the Bread Convent, to empty two rooms for her to go and live in.

This Bread Convent had at one time been styled the Shui Yueh nunnery (water moon); but as good bread was made in that temple, it gave rise to this nickname.

This convent was not very distant from the Temple of the Iron Fence, so that as soon as the bonzes brought their functions to a close, and the sacrifice of evening was offered, Chia Chen asked Chia Jung to request lady Feng to retire to rest; and as lady Feng perceived that there still remained several sisters-in-law to keep company to the female relatives, she readily, of her own accord, took leave of the whole party, and, along with Pao-yü and Ch'in Chung, came to the Water Moon Convent.

Ch'in Yeh, it must be noticed, was advanced in years and a victim to many ailments, so that he was unable to remain in the temple long, and he bade Ch'in Chung tarry until the coffin had been set in its resting place, with the result that Ch'in Chung came along, at the same time as lady Feng and Pao-yü, to the Water Moon Convent, where Ch'ing Hsü appeared, together with two neophytes, Chih Shan and Chih Neng, to receive them. After they had exchanged greetings, lady Feng and the others entered the "chaste" apartments to change their clothes and wash their hands; and when they had done, as she perceived how much taller in stature Chih Neng had grown and how much handsomer were her features, she felt prompted to inquire, "How is it that your prioress and yourselves haven't been all these days as far as our place?"

"It's because during these days we haven't had any time which we could call our own," explained Ch'ing Hsü. "Owing to the birth of a son in Mr. Hu's mansion, dame Hu sent over about ten taels and asked that we should invite several head-nuns to read during three days the service for the churching of women, with the result that we've been so very busy and had so little leisure, that we couldn't come over to pay our respects to your ladyship."

But leaving aside the old nun, who kept lady Feng company, we will now return to the two lads Pao-yü and Ch'in Chung. They were up to their pranks in the main building of the convent, when seeing Chih Neng come over: "Here's Neng Erh," Pao-yü exclaimed with a smile.

"Why notice a creature like her?" remarked Ch'in Chung; to which Pao-yü rejoined laughingly: "Don't be sly! why then did you the other day, when you were in the old lady's rooms, and there was not a soul present, hold her in your arms? and do you want to fool me now?"

"There was nothing of the kind," observed Ch'in Chung smiling.

"Whether there was or not," replied Pao-yü, "doesn't concern me; but if you will stop her and tell her to pour a cup of tea and bring it to me to drink, I'll then keep hands off."

"This is indeed very strange!" Ch'in Chung answered laughing; "do you fear that if you told her to pour you one, that she wouldn't; and what need is there that I should tell her?"

"If I ask her," Pao-yü observed, "to pour it, she wouldn't be as ready as she would were you to tell her about it."

Ch'in Chung had no help but to speak. "Neng Erh!" he said, "bring a cup of tea."

This Neng Erh had, since her youth, been in and out of the Jung mansion, so that there was no one that she did not know; and she had also, time after time, romped and laughed with Pao-yü and Ch'in Chung. Being now grown up she gradually came to know the import of love, and she readily took a fancy to Ch'in Chung, who was an amorous being. Ch'in Chung too returned her affection, on account of her good looks; and, although he and she had not had any very affectionate tête-à-têtes, they had, however, long ago come to understand each other's feelings and wishes.

Chih Neng walked away and returned after having poured the tea.

"Give it to me," Ch'in Chung cried out smirkingly; while Pao-yü likewise shouted: "Give it to me."

Chih Neng compressed her lips and sneeringly rejoined, "Are you going to have a fight even over a cup of tea? Is it forsooth likely that there's honey in my hand?"

Pao-yü was the first to grasp and take over the cup, but while drinking it, he was about to make some inquiry, when he caught sight of Chih Shan, who came and called Chih Neng away to go and lay the plates with fruit on the table. Not much time elapsed before she came round to request the two lads to go and have tea and refreshments; but would they eat such things as were laid before them? They simply sat for a while and came out again and resumed their play.

Lady Feng too stayed for a few moments, and then returned, with the old nun as her escort, into the "unsullied" rooms to lie down. By this time, all the matrons and married women discovered that there was nothing else to be done, and they dispersed in succession, retiring each to rest. There only remained in attendance several young girls who enjoyed her confidence, and the old nun speedily availed herself of the opportunity to speak. "I've got something," she said, "about which I mean to go to your mansion to beg of madame Wang; but I'll first request you, my lady, to tell me how to set to work."

"What's it?" ascertained lady Feng.

"O-mi-to-fu!" exclaimed the old nun, "It's this; in days gone by, I first lived in the Ch'ang An district. When I became a nun and entered the monastery of Excellent Merit, there lived, at that time, a subscriber, Chang by surname, a very wealthy man. He had a daughter, whose infant name was Chin Ko; the whole family came in the course of that year to the convent I was in, to offer incense, and as luck would have it they met Li Ya-nei, a brother of a secondary wife of the Prefect of the Ch'ang An Prefecture. This Li Ya-nei fell in love at first sight with her, and would wed Chin Ko as his wife. He sent go-betweens to ask her in marriage, but, contrary to his expectations, Chin Ko had already received the engagement presents of the son of the ex-Major of the Ch'ang An Prefecture. The Chang family, on the other hand, were afraid that if they withdrew from the match, the Major would not give up his claim, and they therefore replied that she was already promised to another. But, who would have thought it, this Mr. Li was seriously bent upon marrying the young lady. But while the Chang family were at a loss what plan to devise, and both parties were in a dilemma, the family of the Major came unexpectedly to hear of the news; and without even looking thoroughly into the matter, they there and then had recourse to insult and abuse. 'Is a girl,' they insinuated, 'to be promised to the sons of several families!' And obstinately refusing to allow the restitution of the betrothal presents, they at once had recourse to litigation and brought an action (against the girl's people.) That family was at their wits' end, and had no alternative but to find some one to go to the capital to obtain means of assistance; and, losing all patience, they insisted upon the return of the presents. I believe that the present commander of the troops at Ch'ang An, Mr. Yün, is on friendly terms with your honourable family, and could one solicit madame Wang to put in a word with Mr. Chia Cheng to send a letter and ask Mr. Yün to speak to that Major, I have no fear that he will not agree. Should (your ladyship) be willing to take action, the Chang family are even ready to present all they have, though it may entail the ruin of their estate."

"This affair is, it's true, of no great moment," lady Feng replied smiling, after hearing this appeal; "but the only thing is that madame Wang does no longer attend to matters of this nature."

"If madame doesn't heed them," suggested the old nun, "you, my lady, can safely assume the direction."

"I'm neither in need of any money to spend," added lady Feng with a smirk, "nor do I undertake such matters!"

These words did not escape Ching Hsü's ear; they scattered to the winds her vain hopes. After a minute or so she heaved a sigh.

"What you say may be true enough," she remarked; "but the Chang family are also aware that I mean to come and make my appeal to your mansion; and were you now not to manage this affair, the Chang family having no idea that the lack of time prevents any steps being taken and that no importance is attached to their presents, it will appear, on the contrary, as if there were not even this little particle of skill in your household."

At these words lady Feng felt at once inspirited. "You've known of old," she added, "that I've never had any faith in anything concerning retribution in the Court of Judgment in the unseen or in hell; and that whatever I say that I shall do, that I do; tell them therefore to bring three thousand taels; and I shall then remedy this grievance of theirs."

The old nun upon hearing this remark was so exceedingly delighted, that she precipitately exclaimed, "They've got it, they've got it! there will be no difficulty about it."

"I'm not," lady Feng went on to add, "like those people, who afford help and render assistance with an eye to money; these three thousand taels will be exclusively devoted for the travelling expenses of those youths, who will be sent to deliver messages and for them to make a few cash for their trouble; but as for me I don't want even so much as a cash. In fact I'm able at this very moment to produce as much as thirty thousand taels."

The old nun assented with alacrity, and said by way of reply, "If that be so, my lady, do display your charitable bounty at once to-morrow and bring things to an end."

"Just see," remarked lady Feng, "how hard pressed I am; which place can do without me? but since I've given you my word, I shall, needless to say, speedily bring the matter to a close."

"A small trifle like this," hinted the old nun, "would, if placed in the hands of any one else, flurry her to such an extent that she would be quite at a loss what to do; but in your hands, my lady, even if much more were superadded, it wouldn't require as much exertion as a wave of your hand. But the proverb well says: 'that those who are able have much to do;' for madame Wang, seeing that your ladyship manages all concerns, whether large or small, properly, has still more shoved the burden of everything on your shoulders, my lady; but you should, it's but right, also take good care of your precious health."

This string of flattery pleased lady Feng more and more, so that heedless of fatigue she went on to chat with still greater zest.

But, thing unthought of, Ch'in Chung availed himself of the darkness, as well as of the absence of any one about, to come in quest of Chih Neng. As soon as he reached the room at the back, he espied Chih Neng all alone inside washing the tea cups; and Ch'in Chung forthwith seized her in his arms and implanted kisses on her cheek. Chih Neng got in a dreadful state, and stamping her feet, cried, "What are you up to?" and she was just on the point of shouting out, when Ch'in Chung rejoined: "My dear girl! I'm nearly dead from impatience, and if you don't again to-day accept my advances, I shall this very moment die on this spot."

"What you're bent upon," added Chih Neng, "can't be effected; not unless you wait until I've left this den and parted company from these people, when it will be safe enough."

"This is of course easy enough!" remonstrated Ch'in Chung; "but the distant water cannot extinguish the close fire!"

As he spoke, with one puff, he put out the light, plunging the whole room in pitch darkness; and seizing Chih Neng, he pushed her on to the stove-couch and started a violent love affair. Chih Neng could not, though she strained every nerve, escape his importunities; nor could she very well shout, so that she felt compelled to humour him; but while he was in the midst of his ecstatic joy, they perceived a person walk in, who pressed both of them down, without uttering even so much as a sound, and plunged them both in such a fright that their very souls flew away and their spirits wandered from their bodies; and it was after the third party had burst out laughing with a spurting sound that they eventually became aware that it was Pao-yü; when, springing to his feet impetuously, Ch'in Chung exclaimed full of resentment, "What's this that you're up to!"

"If you get your monkey up," retorted Pao-yü, "why, then let you and I start bawling out;" which so abashed Chih Neng that she availed herself of the gloomy light to make her escape; while Pao-yü had dragged Ch'in Chung out of the room and asked, "Now then, do you still want to play the bully!"

"My dear fellow," pleaded Ch'in Chung smilingly, "whatever you do don't shout out and let every one know; and all you want, I'll agree to."

"We needn't argue just now," Pao-yü observed with a grin; "wait a while, and when all have gone to sleep, we can minutely settle accounts together."

Soon it was time to ease their clothes, and go to bed; and lady Feng occupied the inner room; Ch'in Chung and Pao-yü the outer; while the whole ground was covered with matrons of the household, who had spread their bedding, and sat watching. As lady Feng entertained fears that the jade of Spiritual Perception might be lost, she waited until Pao-yü fell asleep, when having directed a servant to bring it to her, she placed it under the side of her own pillow.

What accounts Pao-yü settled with Ch'in Chung cannot be ascertained; and as in the absence of any positive proof what is known is based upon surmises, we shall not venture to place it on record.

Nothing worth noticing occurred the whole night; but the next day, as soon as the morning dawned, dowager lady Chia and madame Wang promptly despatched servants to come and see how Pao-yü was getting on; and to tell him likewise to put on two pieces of extra clothing, and that if there was nothing to be done it would be better for him to go back.

But was it likely that Pao-yü would be willing to go back? Besides Ch'in Chung, in his inordinate passion for Chih Neng, instigated Pao-yü to entreat lady Feng to remain another day. Lady Feng pondered in her own mind that, although the most important matters connected with the funeral ceremonies had been settled satisfactorily, there were still a few minor details, for which no provision had been made, so that could she avail herself of this excuse to remain another day would she not win from Chia Chen a greater degree of approbation, in the second place, would she not be able further to bring Ch'ing Hsü's business to an issue, and, in the third place, to humour Pao-yü's wish? In view of these three advantages, which would accrue, "All that I had to do, I have done," she readily signified to Pao-yü, "and if you be bent upon running about in here, you'll unavoidably place me in still greater trouble; so that we must for certain start homewards tomorrow."

"My dear cousin, my own dear cousin," urgently entreated Pao-yü, when he heard these words, "let's stay only this one day, and tomorrow we can go back without fail."

They actually spent another night there, and lady Feng availed herself of their stay to give directions that the case which had been entrusted to her the previous day by the old nun should be secretly communicated to Lai Wang Erh. Lai Wang's mind grasped the import of all that was said to him, and, having entered the city with all despatch, he went in search of the gentleman, who acted as secretary (in Mr. Yün's office), pretending that he had been directed by Mr. Chia Lien to come and ask him to write a letter and to send it that very night to the Ch'ang An magistrate. The distance amounted to no more than one hundred li, so that in the space of two days everything was brought to a satisfactory settlement. The general, whose name was Yün Kuang, had been for a long time under obligations to the Chia family, so that he naturally could not refuse his co-operation in such small trifles. When he had handed his reply, Wang Erh started on his way back; where we shall leave him and return to lady Feng.

Having spent another day, she on the morrow took leave of the old nun, whom she advised to come to the mansion after the expiry of three days to fetch a reply.

Ch'in Chung and Chih Neng could not, by any means, brook the separation, and they secretly agreed to a clandestine assignation; but to these details we need not allude with any minuteness; sufficient to say that they had no alternative but to bear the anguish and to part.

Lady Feng crossed over again to the temple of the Iron Fence and ascertained how things were progressing. But as Pao Chu was obstinate in her refusal to return home, Chia Chen found himself under the necessity of selecting a few servants to act as her companions. But the reader must listen to what is said in the next chapter by way of explanation.

CHAPTER XVI.

Chia Yuan-ch'un is, on account of her talents, selected to enter the Feng Ts'ao Palace.

Ch'in Ching-ch'ing departs, in the prime of life, by the yellow spring road.

But we must now return to the two lads, Ch'in Chung and Pao-yü. After they had passed, along with lady Feng from the Temple of the Iron Fence, whither she had gone to see how things were getting on, they entered the city in their carriages. On their arrival at home, they paid their obeisance to dowager lady Chia, madame Wang and the other members of the family, whence they returned to their own quarters, where nothing worth mentioning transpired during the night.

On the next day, Pao-yü perceiving that the repairs to the outer schoolroom had been completed, settled with Ch'in Chung that they should have evening classes. But as it happened that Ch'in Chung, who was naturally of an extremely delicate physique, caught somewhat of a chill in the country and clandestinely indulged, besides, in an intimacy with Chih Neng, which unavoidably made him fail to take good care of himself, he was, shortly after his return, troubled with a cough and a feverish cold, with nausea for drink and food, and fell into such an extremely poor state of health that he simply kept indoors and nursed himself, and was not in a fit condition to go to school. Pao-yü's spirits were readily damped, but as there was likewise no remedy he had no other course than to wait until his complete recovery, before he could make any arrangements.

Lady Feng had meanwhile received a reply from Yün Kuang, in which he informed her that everything had been satisfactorily settled, and the old nun apprised the Chang family that the major had actually suppressed his indignation, hushed his complaints, and taken back the presents of the previous engagement. But who would have ever anticipated that a father and mother, whose hearts were set upon position and their ambition upon wealth, could have brought up a daughter so conscious of propriety and so full of feeling as to seize the first opportunity, after she had heard that she had been withdrawn from her former intended, and been promised to the Li family, to stealthily devise a way to commit suicide, by means of a handkerchief. The son of the Major, upon learning that Chin Ko had strangled herself, there and then jumped into the river and drowned himself, as he too was a being full of love. The Chang and Li families were, sad to relate, very much cut up, and, in very truth, two lives and money had been sacrificed all to no use.

Lady Feng, however, during this while, quietly enjoyed the three thousand taels, and madame Wang did not have even so much as the faintest idea of the whole matter. But ever since this occasion, lady Feng's audacity acquired more and more strength; and the actions of this kind, which she, in after days, performed, defy enumeration.

One day, the very day on which Chia Cheng's birthday fell, while the members of the two households of Ning and Jung were assembled together offering their congratulations, and unusual bustle and stir prevailed, a gatekeeper came in, at quite an unexpected moment, to announce that Mr. Hsia, Metropolitan Head Eunuch of the six palaces, had come with the special purpose of presenting an edict from his Majesty; a bit of news which plunged Chia She, Chia Cheng and the whole company into great consternation, as they could not make out what was up. Speedily interrupting the theatrical performance, they had the banquet cleared, and the altar laid out with incense, and opening the centre gate they fell on their knees to receive the edict.

Soon they caught sight of the head eunuch, Hsia Ping-chung, advancing on horseback, and besides himself, a considerable retinue of eunuchs. The eunuch Hsia did not, in fact, carry any mandate or present any decree; but straightway advancing as far as the main hall, he dismounted, and, with a face beaming with smiles, he walked into the Hall and took his stand on the southern side.

"I have had the honour," he said, "of receiving a special order to at once summon Chia Cheng to present himself at Court and be admitted in His Majesty's presence in the Lin Ching Hall."

When he had delivered this message, he did not so much as take any tea, but forthwith mounted his horse and took his leave.

Chia Cheng and the others could not even conceive what omen this summons implied, but he had no alternative but to change his clothes with all haste and to present himself at Court, while dowager lady Chia and the inmates of the whole household were, in their hearts, a prey to such perplexity and uncertainty that they incessantly despatched messengers on flying steeds to go and bring the news.

After the expiry of four hours, they suddenly perceived Lai Ta and three or four other butlers run in, quite out of breath, through the ceremonial gate and report the glad tidings. "We have received," they added, "our master's commands, to hurriedly request her venerable ladyship to take madame Wang and the other ladies into the Palace, to return thanks for His Majesty's bounty;" and other words to the same purport.

Dowager lady Chia was, at this time, standing, with agitated heart, under the verandah of the Large Hall waiting for tidings, whilst the two ladies, mesdames Hsing and Wang, Mrs. Yu, Li Wan, lady Feng, Ying Ch'un and her sisters, even up to Mrs. Hsüeh and the rest, were congregated in one place ascertaining what was the news. Old lady Chia likewise called Lai Ta in and minutely questioned him as to what had happened. "Your servants," replied Lai Ta, "simply stood waiting outside the Lin Chuang gate, so that we were in total ignorance of what was going on inside, when presently the Eunuch Hsia came out and imparted to us the glad tidings; telling us that the eldest of the young ladies in our household had been raised, by His Majesty, to be an overseer in the Feng Ts'ao Palace, and that he had, in addition, conferred upon her the rank of worthy and virtuous secondary consort. By and by, Mr. Chia Cheng came out and also told us the same thing. Master is now gone back again to the Eastern Palace, whither he requests your venerable ladyship to go at once and offer thanks for the Imperial favour."

When old lady Chia and the other members of the family heard these tidings they were at length reassured in their minds, and so elated were they all in one moment that joy was visible in their very faces. Without loss of time, they commenced to don the gala dresses suitable to their rank; which done, old lady Chia led the way for the two ladies, mesdames Hsing and Wang, as well as for Mrs. Yu; and their official chairs, four of them in all, entered the palace like a trail of fish; while Chia She and Chia Chen, who had likewise changed their clothes for their court dress, took Chia Se and Chia Jung along and proceeded in attendance upon dowager lady Chia.

Indeed, of the two households of Ning and Jung, there was not one, whether high or low, woman or man, who was not in a high state of exultation, with the exception of Pao-yü, who behaved just as if the news had not reached his ears; and can you, reader, guess why? The fact is that Chih Neng, of the Water Moon Convent, had recently entered the city in a surreptitious manner in search of Ch'in Chung; but, contrary to expectation, her visit came to be known by Ch'in Yeh, who drove Chih Neng away and laid hold of Ch'in Chung and gave him a flogging. But this outburst of temper of his brought about a relapse of his old complaint, with the result that in three or five days, he, sad to say, succumbed. Ch'in Chung had himself ever been in a delicate state of health and had besides received a caning before he had got over his sickness, so that when he now saw his aged father pass away from the consequences of a fit of anger, he felt, at this stage, so full of penitence and distress that the symptoms of his illness were again considerably aggravated. Hence it was that Pao-yü was downcast and unhappy at heart, and that nothing could, in spite of the promotion of Yuan Ch'un by imperial favour, dispel the depression of his spirits.

Dowager lady Chia and the rest in due course offered thanks and returned home, the relatives and friends came to present their congratulations, great stir and excitement prevailed during these few days in the two mansions of Ning and Jung, and every one was in high glee; but he alone looked upon everything as if it were nothing; taking not the least interest in anything; and as this reason led the whole family to sneer at him, the result was that he got more and more doltish.

Luckily, however, Chia Lien and Tai-yü were on their way back, and had despatched messengers, in advance, to announce the news that they would be able to reach home the following day, so that when Pao-yü heard the tidings, he was at length somewhat cheered. And when he came to institute minute inquiries, he eventually found out: "that Chia Yü-ts'un was also coming to the capital to have an audience with His Majesty, that it was entirely because Wang Tzu-t'eng had repeatedly laid before the Throne memorials recommending him that he was coming on this occasion to wait in the metropolis for a vacancy which he could fill up; that as he was a kinsman of Chia Lien's, acknowledging the same ancestors as he did, and he stood, on the other hand, with Tai-yü, in the relationship of tutor and pupil, he was in consequence following the same road and coming as their companion; that Lin Ju-hai had already been buried in the ancestral vault, and that every requirement had been attended to with propriety; that Chia Lien, on this voyage to the capital, would, had he progressed by the ordinary stages, have been over a month before he could reach home, but that when he came to hear the good news about Yuan Ch'un, he pressed on day and night to enter the capital; and that the whole journey had been throughout, in every respect, both pleasant and propitious."

But Pao-yü merely ascertained whether Tai-yü was all right, and did not even so much as trouble his mind with the rest of what he heard; and he remained on the tiptoe of expectation, till noon of the morrow; when, in point of fact, it was announced that Mr. Lien, together with Miss Lin, had made their entrance into the mansion. When they came face to face, grief and joy vied with each other; and they could not help having a good cry for a while; after which followed again expressions of sympathy and congratulations; while Pao-yü pondered within himself that Tai-yü had become still more surpassingly handsome.

Tai-yü had also brought along with her a good number of books, and she promptly gave orders that the sleeping rooms should be swept, and that the various nicknacks should be put in their proper places. She further produced a certain quantity of paper, pencils and other such things, and distributed them among Pao Ch'ai, Ying Ch'un, Pao-yü and the rest; and Pao-yü also brought out, with extreme care, the string of Ling-ling scented beads, which had been given to him by the Prince of Pei Ching, and handed them, in his turn, to Tai-yü as a present.

"What foul man has taken hold of them?" exclaimed Tai-yü. "I don't want any such things;" and as she forthwith dashed them down, and would not accept them, Pao-yü was under the necessity of taking them back. But for the time being we will not allude to them, but devote our attention to Chia Lien.

Having, after his arrival home, paid his salutations to all the inmates, he retired to his own quarters at the very moment that lady Feng had multifarious duties to attend to, and had not even a minute to spare; but, considering that Chia Lien had returned from a distant journey, she could not do otherwise than put by what she had to do, and to greet him and wait on him.

"Imperial uncle," she said, in a jocose manner, when she realised that there was no outsider present in the room, "I congratulate you! What fatigue and hardship you, Imperial uncle, have had to bear throughout the whole journey, your humble servant heard yesterday, when the courier sent ahead came and announced that Your Highness would this day reach this mansion. I have merely got ready a glass of mean wine for you to wipe down the dust with, but I wonder, whether Your Highness will deign to bestow upon it the lustre of your countenance, and accept it."

Chia Lien smiled. "How dare I presume to such an honour," he added by way of rejoinder; "I'm unworthy of such attention! Many thanks, many thanks."

P'ing Erh and the whole company of waiting-maids simultaneously paid their obeisance to him, and this ceremony concluded, they presented tea. Chia Lien thereupon made inquiries about the various matters, which had transpired in their home after his departure, and went on to thank lady Feng for all the trouble she had taken in the management of them.

"How could I control all these manifold matters," remarked lady Feng; "my experience is so shallow, my speech so dull and my mind so simple, that if any one showed me a club, I would mistake it for a pin. Besides, I'm so tender-hearted that were any one to utter a couple of glib remarks, I couldn't help feeling my heart give way to compassion and sympathy. I've had, in addition, no experience in any weighty questions; my pluck is likewise so very small that when madame Wang has felt in the least displeased, I have not been able to close my eyes and sleep. Urgently did I more than once resign the charge, but her ladyship wouldn't again agree to it; maintaining, on the contrary, that my object was to be at ease, and that I was not willing to reap experience. Leaving aside that she doesn't know that I take things so much to heart, that I can scoop the perspiration in handfuls, that I daren't utter one word more than is proper, nor venture to recklessly take one step more than I ought to, you know very well which of the women servants, in charge of the menage in our household, is easy to manage! If ever I make the slightest mistake, they laugh at me and poke fun at me; and if I incline a little one way, they show their displeasure by innuendoes; they sit by and look on, they use every means to do harm, they stir up trouble, they stand by on safe ground and look on and don't give a helping hand to lift any one they have thrown over, and they are, one and all of them, old hands in such tricks. I'm moreover young in years and not able to keep people in check, so that they naturally don't show any regard for me! What is still more ridiculous is that after the death of Jung Erh's wife in that mansion, brother Chen, time and again, begged madame Wang, on his very knees, to do him the favour to ask me to lend him a hand for several days. I repeatedly signified my refusal, but her ladyship gave her consent in order to oblige him, so that I had no help but to carry out her wish; putting, as is my wont, everything topsy-turvey, and making matters worse than they were; with the result that brother Chen up to this day bears me a grudge and regrets having asked for my assistance. When you see him to-morrow, do what you can to excuse me by him. 'Young as she is,' tell him, 'and without experience of the world, who ever could have instigated Mr. Chia Cheng to make such a mistake as to choose her.'"

While they were still chatting, they heard people talking in the outer apartments, and lady Feng speedily inquired who it was. P'ing Erh entered the room to reply. "Lady Hsüeh," she said, "has sent sister Hsiang Ling over to ask me something; but I've already given her my answer and sent her back."

"Quite so," interposed Chia Lien with a smile. "A short while ago I went to look up Mrs. Hsüeh and came face to face with a young girl, whose features were supremely perfect, and as I suspected that, in our household, there was no such person, I asked in the course of conversation, Mrs. Hsüeh about her, and found out eventually that this was the young waiting-maid they had purchased on their way to the capital, Hsiang Ling by name, and that she had after all become an inmate of the household of that big fool Hsüeh. Since she's had her hair dressed as a married woman she does look so much more pre-eminently beautiful! But that big fool Hsüeh has really brought contamination upon her."

"Ai!" exclaimed lady Feng, "here you are back from a trip to Suchow and Hang Chow, where you should have seen something of the world! and have you still an eye as envious and a heart so covetous? Well, if you wish to bestow your love on her, there's no difficulty worth speaking of. I'll take P'ing Erh over and exchange her for her; what do you say to that? that old brother Hsüeh is also one of those men, who, while eating what there is in the bowl, keeps an eye on what there is in the pan! For the last year or so, as he couldn't get Hsiang Ling to be his, he made ever so many distressing appeals to Mrs. Hsüeh; and Mrs. Hsüeh while esteeming Hsiang Ling's looks, though fine, as after all a small matter, (thought) her deportment and conduct so far unlike those of other girls, so gentle and so demure that almost the very daughters of masters and mistresses couldn't attain her standard, that she therefore went to the trouble of spreading a banquet, and of inviting guests, and in open court, and in the legitimate course, she gave her to him for a secondary wife. But half a month had scarcely elapsed before he looked upon her also as a good-for-nothing person as he did upon a large number of them! I can't however help feeling pity for her in my heart."

Scarcely had she time to conclude what she had to say when a youth, on duty at the second gate, transmitted the announcement that Mr. Chia Cheng was in the Library waiting for Mr. Secundus. At these words, Chia Lien speedily adjusted his clothes, and left the apartment; and during his absence, lady Feng inquired of P'ing Erh what Mrs.

Hsüeh wanted a few minutes back, that she sent Hsiang Ling round in such a hurry.

"What Hsiang Ling ever came?" replied P'ing Erh. "I simply made use of her name to tell a lie for the occasion. Tell me, my lady, (what's come to) Wang Erh's wife? why she's got so bad that there's even no common sense left in her!" Saying this she again drew near lady Feng's side, and in a soft tone of voice, she continued: "That interest of yours, my lady, she doesn't send later, nor does she send it sooner; but she must send it round the very moment when master Secundus is at home! But as luck would have it, I was in the hall, so that I came across her; otherwise, she would have walked in and told your ladyship, and Mr. Secundus would naturally have come to know about it! And our master would, with that frame of mind of his, have fished it out and spent it, had the money even been at the bottom of a pan full of oil! and were he to have heard that my lady had private means, would he not have been still more reckless in spending? Hence it was that, losing no time in taking the money over, I had to tell her a few words which, who would have thought, happened to be overheard by your ladyship; that's why, in the presence of master Secundus, I simply explained that Hsiang Ling had come!"

These words evoked a smile from lady Feng. "Mrs. Hsueh, I thought to myself," she observed, "knows very well that your Mr. Secundus has come, and yet, regardless of propriety, she, instead (of keeping her at home), sends some one over from her inner rooms! and it was you after all, you vixen, playing these pranks!"

As she uttered this remark, Chia Lien walked in, and lady Feng issued orders to serve the wine and the eatables, and husband and wife took their seats opposite to each other; but notwithstanding that lady Feng was very partial to drink, she nevertheless did not have the courage to indulge her weakness, but merely partook of some to keep him company. Chia Lien's nurse, dame Chao, entered the room, and Chia Lien and lady Feng promptly pressed her to have a glass of wine, and bade her sit on the stove-couch, but dame Chao was obstinate in her refusal. P'ing Erh and the other waiting-maids had at an early hour placed a square stool next to the edge of the couch, where was likewise a small footstool, and on this footstool dame Chao took a seat, whereupon Chia Lien chose two dishes of delicacies from the table, which he handed her to place on the square stool for her own use.

"Dame Chao," lady Feng remarked, "couldn't very well bite through that, for mind it might make her teeth drop! This morning," she therefore asked of P'ing Erh, "I suggested that that shoulder of pork stewed with ham was so tender as to be quite the thing to be given to dame Chao to eat; and how is it you haven't taken it over to her? But go at once and tell them to warm it and bring it in! Dame Chao," she went on, "just you taste this Hui Ch'üan wine brought by your foster-son."

"I'll drink it," replied dame Chao, "but you, my lady, must also have a cup: what's there to fear? the one thing to guard against is any excess, that's all! But I've now come over, not for any wine or eatables; on the contrary, there's a serious matter, which I would ask your ladyship to impress on your mind, and to show me some regard, for this master of ours is only good to utter fine words, but when the time (to act) does come, he forgets all about us! As I have had the good fortune to nurse him in his infancy and to bring him up to this age, 'I too have grown old in years,' I said to him, 'and all that belong to me are those two sons, and do look upon them with some particular favour!' With any one else I shouldn't have ventured to open my mouth, but him I anyway entreated time and again on several occasions. His assent was of course well and good, but up to this very moment he still withholds his help. Now besides from the heavens has dropped such a mighty piece of good luck; and in what place will there be no need of servants? that's why I come to tell you, my lady, as is but right, for were I to depend upon our master, I fear I shall even die of starvation."

Lady Feng laughed. "You'd better," she suggested, "put those two elder foster brothers of his both under my charge! But you've nursed that foster-son from his babyhood, and don't you yet know that disposition of his, how that he takes his skin and flesh and sticks it, (not on the body of a relative), but, on the contrary, on that of an outsider and stranger? (to Chia Lien.) Which of those foster brothers whom you have now discarded, isn't clearly better than others? and were you to have shown them some favour and consideration, who would have ventured to have said 'don't?' Instead of that, you confer benefits upon thorough strangers, and all to no purpose whatever! But these words of mine are also incorrect, eh? for those whom we regard as strangers you, contrariwise, will treat just as if they were relatives!"

At these words every one present in the room burst out laughing; even nurse Chao could not repress herself; and as she invoked Buddha,—"In very truth," she exclaimed, "in this room has sprung up a kind-hearted person! as regards relatives and strangers, such foolish distinctions aren't drawn by our master; and it's simply because he's full of pity and is tenderhearted that he can't put off any one who gives vent to a few words of entreaty, and nothing else!"

"That's quite it!" rejoined lady Feng smiling sarcastically, "to those whom he looks upon as relatives, he's kindhearted, but with me and his mother he's as hard as steel."

"What you say, my lady, is very considerate," remarked nurse Chao, "and I'm really so full of delight that I'll have another glass of good wine! and, if from this time forward, your ladyship will act as you think best, I'll have then nothing to be sorry for!"

Chia Lien did not at this juncture feel quite at his ease, but he could do no more than feign a smile. "You people," he said, "should leave off talking nonsense, and bring the eatables at once and let us have our meal, as I have still to go on the other side and see Mr. Chia Chen, to consult with him about business."

"To be sure you have," ventured lady Feng, "and you shouldn't neglect your legitimate affairs; but what did Mr. Chia Chen tell you when he sent for you just a while back?"

"It was about the visit (of Yuan Ch'un) to her parents," Chia Lien explained.

"Has after all permission for the visit been granted?" lady Feng inquired with alacrity.

"Though not quite granted," Chia Lien replied joyously, "it's nevertheless more or less an accomplished fact."

"This is indeed evidence of the great bounty of the present Emperor!" lady Feng observed smirkingly; "one doesn't hear in books, or see in plays, written from time to time, any mention of such an instance, even so far back as the days of old!"

Dame Chao took up again the thread of the conversation. "Indeed it's so!" she interposed; "But I'm in very truth quite stupid from old age, for I've heard every one, high and low, clamouring during these few days, something or other about 'Hsing Ch'in' or no 'Hsing Ch'in,' but I didn't really pay any heed to it; and now again, here's something more about this 'Hsing Ch'in,' but what's it all about, I wonder?"

"The Emperor at present on the Throne," explained Chia Lien, "takes into consideration the feelings of his people. In the whole world, there is (in his opinion), no more essential thing than filial piety; maintaining that the feelings of father, mother, son and daughter are indiscriminately subject to one principle, without any distinction between honorable and mean. The present Emperor himself day and night waits upon their majesties his Father and the Empress Dowager, and yet cannot, in the least degree, carry out to the full his ideal of filial piety. The secondary consorts, meritorious persons and other inmates of the Palace, he remembered, had entered within its precincts many years back, casting aside fathers and mothers, so how could they not help thinking of them? Besides, the fathers and mothers, who remain at home must long for their daughters, of whom they cannot get even so much as a glimpse, and if, through this solicitude, they were to contract any illness, the harmony of heaven would also be seriously impaired, so for this reason, he memorialised the Emperor, his father, and the Empress Dowager that every month, on the recurrence of the second and sixth days, permission should be accorded to the relatives of the imperial consorts to enter the palace and make application to see their daughters. The Emperor, his father, and Empress Dowager were, forthwith, much delighted by this representation, and eulogised, in high terms, the piety and generosity of the present Emperor, his regard for the will of heaven and his research into the nature of things. Both their sacred Majesties consequently also issued a decree to the effect: that the entrance of the relatives of the imperial consorts into the Palace could not but interfere with the dignity of the state, and the rules of conventional rites, but that as the mothers and daughters could not gratify the wishes of their hearts, Their Majesties would, after all, show a high proof of expedient grace, and issue a special command that: 'exclusive of the generous bounty, by virtue of which the worthy relations of the imperial consorts could enter the palace on the second and sixth days, any family, having extensive accommodation and separate courts suitable for the cantonment of the imperial body-guard, could, without any detriment, make application to the Inner Palace, for the entrance of the imperial chair into the private residences, to the end that the personal feelings of relations might be gratified, and that they should collectively enjoy the bliss of a family reunion.' After the issue of this decree, who did not leap from grateful joy! The father of the honourable secondary consort Chou has now already initiated works, in his residence, for the repairs to the separate courts necessary for the visiting party. Wu T'ien-yu too, the father of Wu, the distinguished consort, has likewise gone outside the city walls in search of a suitable plot of ground; and don't these amount to well-nigh accomplished facts?"

"O-mi-to-fu!" exclaimed dame Chao. "Is it really so? but from what you say, our family will also be making preparations for the reception of the eldest young lady!"

"That goes without saying," added Chia Lien, "otherwise, for what purpose could we be in such a stir just now?"

"It's of course so!" interposed lady Feng smiling, "and I shall now have an opportunity of seeing something great of the world. My misfortune is that I'm young by several years; for had I been born twenty or thirty years sooner, all these old people wouldn't really be now treating me contemptuously for not having seen the world! To begin with, the Emperor Tai Tsu, in years gone by, imitated the old policy of Shun, and went on a tour, giving rise to more stir than any book could have ever produced; but I happen to be devoid of that good fortune which could have enabled me to come in time."

"Ai ya, ya!" ejaculated dame Chao, "such a thing is rarely met with in a thousand years! I was old enough at that time to remember the occurrence! Our Chia family was then at Ku Su, Yangchow and all along that line, superintending the construction of ocean vessels, and the repairs to the seaboard. This was the only time in which preparations were made for the reception of the Emperor, and money was lavished in quantities as great as the billowing waters of the sea!"

This subject once introduced, lady Feng took up the thread of the conversation with vehemence. "Our Wang family," she said, "did also make preparations on one occasion. At that time my grandfather was in sole charge of all matters connected with tribute from various states, as well as with general levées, so that whenever any foreigners arrived, they all came to our house to be entertained, while the whole of the goods, brought by foreign vessels from the two Kuang provinces, from Fukien, Yunnan and Chekiang, were the property of our family."

"Who isn't aware of these facts?" ventured dame Chao; "there is up to this day a saying that, 'in the eastern sea, there was a white jade bed required, and the dragon prince came to request Mr. Wang of Chin Ling (to give it to him)!' This saying relates to your family, my lady, and remains even now in vogue. The Chen family of Chiang Nan has recently held, oh such a fine old standing! it alone has entertained the Emperor on four occasions! Had we not seen these things with our own eyes, were we to tell no matter whom, they wouldn't surely ever believe them! Not to speak of the money, which was as plentiful as mud, all things, whether they were to be found in the world or not, were they not heaped up like hills, and collected like the waters of the sea? But with the four characters representing sin and pity they didn't however trouble their minds."

"I've often heard," continued lady Feng, "my eldest uncle say that things were in such a state, and how couldn't I believe? but what surprises me is how it ever happened that this family attained such opulence and honour!"

"I'll tell your ladyship and all in one sentence," replied nurse Chao. "Why they simply took the Emperor's money and spent it for the

Emperor's person, that's all! for what family has such a lot of money as to indulge in this useless extravagance?"

While they were engaged in this conversation, a servant came a second time, at the instance of madame Wang, to see whether lady Feng had finished her meal or not; and lady Feng forthwith concluding that there must be something waiting for her to attend to, hurriedly rushed through her repast. She had just rinsed her mouth and was about to start when the youths, on duty at the second gate, also reported that the two gentlemen, Mr. Chia Jung and Mr. Chia Se, belonging to the Eastern mansion, had arrived.

Chia Lien had, at length, rinsed his mouth; but while P'ing Erh presented a basin for him to wash his hands, he perceived the two young men walk in, and readily inquired of them what they had to say.

Lady Feng was, on account (of their arrival), likewise compelled to stay, and she heard Chia Jung take the lead and observe: "My father has sent me to tell you, uncle, that the gentlemen, have already decided that the whole extent of ground, starting from the East side, borrowing (for the occasion) the flower garden of the Eastern mansion, straight up to the North West, had been measured and found to amount in all to three and a half li; that it will be suitable for the erection of extra accommodation for the visiting party; that they have already commissioned an architect to draw a plan, which will be ready by to-morrow; that as you, uncle, have just returned home, and must unavoidably feel fatigued, you need not go over to our house, but that if you have anything to say you should please come tomorrow morning, as early as you can, and consult verbally with him."

"Thank uncle warmly," Chia Lien rejoined smilingly, "for the trouble he has taken in thinking of me; I shall, in that case, comply with his wishes and not go over. This plan is certainly the proper one, for while trouble will thus be saved, the erection of the quarters will likewise be an easy matter; for had a distinct plot to be selected and to be purchased, it would involve far greater difficulties. What's more, things wouldn't, after all, be what they properly should be. When you get back, tell your father that this decision is the right one, and that should the gentlemen have any further wish to introduce any change in their proposals, it will rest entirely with my uncle to prevent them, as it's on no account advisable to go and cast one's choice on some other plot; that to-morrow as soon as it's daylight, I'll come and pay my respects to uncle, when we can enter into further details in our deliberations!"

Chia Jung hastily signified his assent by several yes's, and Chia Se also came forward to deliver his message. "The mission to Ku Su," he explained, "to find tutors, to purchase servant girls, and to obtain musical instruments, and theatrical properties and the like, my uncle has confided to me; and as I'm to take along with me the two sons of a couple of majordomos, and two companions of the family, besides, Tan P'ing-jen and Pei Ku-hsiu, he has, for this reason, enjoined me to come and see you, uncle."

Upon hearing this, Chia Lien scrutinised Chia Se. "What!" he asked, "are you able to undertake these commissions? These matters are, it's true, of no great moment; but there's something more hidden in them!"

Chia Se smiled. "The best thing I can do," he remarked, "will be to execute them in my novice sort of way, that's all."

Chia Jung was standing next to lady Feng, out of the light of the lamp, and stealthily pulled the lapel of her dress. Lady Feng understood the hint, and putting on a smiling expression, "You are too full of fears!" she interposed. "Is it likely that our uncle Chen doesn't, after all, know better than we do what men to employ, that you again give way to apprehensions that he isn't up to the mark! but who are those who are, in every respect, up to the mark? These young fellows have grown up already to this age, and if they haven't eaten any pork, they have nevertheless seen a pig run. If Mr. Chen has deputed him to go, he is simply meant to sit under the general's standard; and do you imagine, forsooth, that he has, in real earnest, told him to go and bargain about the purchase money, and to interview the brokers himself? My own idea is that (the choice) is a very good one."

"Of course it is!" observed Chia Lien; "but it isn't that I entertain any wish to be factious; my only object is to devise some plan or other for him. Whence will," he therefore went on to ask, "the money required for this purpose come from?"

"A little while ago the deliberations reached this point," rejoined Chia Se; "and Mr. Lai suggested that there was no necessity at all to take any funds from the capital, as the Chen family, in Chiang Nan, had still in their possession Tls. 50,000 of our money. That he would to-morrow write a letter of advice and a draft for us to take along, and that we should, first of all, obtain cash to the amount of Tls. 30,000, and let the balance of Tls. 20,000 remain over, for the purchase of painted lanterns, and coloured candles, as well as for the outlay for every kind of portieres, banners, curtains and streamers."

Chia Lien nodded his head. "This plan is first-rate!" he added.

"Since that be so," observed lady Feng, as she addressed herself to Chia Se, "I've two able and reliable men; and if you would take them with you, to attend to these matters, won't it be to your convenience?"

Chia Se forced a smile. "I was just on the point," he rejoined, "of asking you, aunt, for the loan of two men, so that this suggestion is a strange coincidence."

As he went on to ascertain what were their names, lady Feng inquired what they were of nurse Chao. But nurse Chao had, by this time, become quite dazed from listening to the conversation, and P'ing Erh had to give her a push, as she smiled, before she returned to consciousness. "The one," she hastened to reply, "is called Chao T'ien-liang and the other Chao T'ien-tung."

"Whatever you do," suggested lady Feng, "don't forget them; but now I'm off to look after my duties."

With these words, she left the room, and Chia Jung promptly followed her out, and with gentle voice he said to her: "Of whatever you want, aunt, issue orders that a list be drawn up, and I'll give it to my brother to take with him, and he'll carry out your commissions according to the list."

"Don't talk nonsense!" replied lady Feng laughing; "I've found no place, as yet, where I could put away all my own things; and do the stealthy practices of you people take my fancy?"

As she uttered these words she straightway went her way.

Chia Se, at this time, likewise, asked Chia Lien: "If you want anything (in the way of curtains), I can conveniently have them woven for you, along with the rest, and bring them as a present to you."

"Don't be in such high glee!" Chia Lien urged with a grin, "you've but recently been learning how to do business, and have you come first and foremost to excel in tricks of this kind? If I require anything, I'll of course write and tell you, but we needn't talk about it."

Having finished speaking, he dismissed the two young men; and, in quick succession, servants came to make their business reports, not limited to three and five companies, but as Chia Lien felt exhausted, he forthwith sent word to those on duty at the second gate not to allow any one at all to communicate any reports, and that the whole crowd should wait till the next day, when he would give his mind to what had to be done.

Lady Feng did not come to retire to rest till the third watch; but nothing need be said about the whole night.

The next morning, at an early hour, Chia Lien got up and called on Chia She and Chia Cheng; after which, he came over to the Ning Kuo mansion; when, in company with the old major-domos and other servants, as well as with several old family friends and companions, he inspected the grounds of the two mansions, and drew plans of the palatial buildings (for the accommodation of the Imperial consort and her escort) on her visit to her parents; deliberating at the same time, on the subject of the works and workmen.

From this day the masons and workmen of every trade were collected to the full number; and the articles of gold, silver, copper, and pewter, as well as the earth, timber, tiles, and bricks, were brought over, and carried in, in incessant supplies. In the first place, orders were issued to the workmen to demolish the wall and towers of the garden of Concentrated Fragrance, and extend a passage to connect in a straight line with the large court in the East of the Jung mansion; for the whole extent of servants' quarters on the Eastern side of the Jung mansion had previously been pulled down.

The two residences of Ning and Jung were, in these days, it is true, divided by a small street, which served as a boundary line, and there was no communication between them, but this narrow passage was also private property, and not in any way a government street, so that they could easily be connected, and as in the garden of Concentrated Fragrance, there was already a stream of running water, which had been introduced through the corner of the Northern wall, there was no further need now of going to the trouble of bringing in another. Although the rockeries and trees were not sufficient, the place where Chia She lived, was an old garden of the Jung mansion, so that the bamboos, trees, and rockeries in that compound, as well as the arbours, railings and other such things could all be very well removed to the front; and by these means, these two grounds, situated as they were besides so very near to each other, could, by being thrown into one, conduce to the saving of considerable capital and labour; for, in spite of some deficiency, what had to be supplied did not amount to much. And it devolved entirely upon a certain old Hu, a man of note, styled Shan Tzu-yeh, to deliberate upon one thing after another, and to initiate its construction.

Chia Cheng was not up to these ordinary matters, so that it fell to Chia She, Chia Chen, Chia Lien, Lai Ta, Lai Sheng, Lin Chih-hsiao, Wu Hsin-teng, Chan Kuang, Ch'eng Jih-hsing and several others to allot the sites, to set things in order, (and to look after) the heaping up of rockeries, the digging of ponds, the construction of two-storied buildings, the erection of halls, the plantation of bamboos and the cultivation of flowers, everything connected with the improvement of the scenery devolving, on the other hand, upon Shan Tzu-yeh to make provision for, and after leaving Court, he would devote such leisure moments as he had to merely going everywhere to give a look at the most important spots, and to consult with Chia She and the others; after which he troubled his mind no more with anything. And as Chia She did nothing else than stay at home and lie off, whenever any matter turned up, trifling though it may have been as a grain of mustard seed or a bean, Chia Chen and his associates had either to go and report it in person or to write a memorandum of it. Or if he had anything to say, he sent for Chia Lien, Lai Ta and others to come and receive his instructions. Chia Jung had the sole direction of the manufacture of the articles in gold and silver; and as for Chia Se, he had already set out on his journey to Ku Su. Chia Chen, Lai Ta and the rest had also to call out the roll with the names of the workmen, to superintend the works and other duties relative thereto, which could not be recorded by one pen alone; sufficient to say that a great bustle and stir prevailed, but to this subject we shall not refer for a time, but allude to Pao-yü.

As of late there were in the household concerns of this magnitude to attend to, Chia Cheng did not come to examine him in his lessons, so that he was, of course, in high spirits, but, as unfortunately Ch'in Chung's complaint became, day by day, more serious, he was at the same time really so very distressed at heart on his account, that enjoyment was for him out of the question.

On this day, he got up as soon as it was dawn, and having just combed his hair and washed his face and hands, he was bent upon going to ask dowager lady Chia to allow him to pay a visit to Ch'in Chung, when he suddenly espied Ming Yen peep round the curtain-wall at the second gate, and then withdraw his head. Pao-yü promptly walked out and inquired what he was up to.

"Mr. Ch'in Chung," observed Ming Yen, "is not well at all."

Pao-yü at these words was quite taken aback. "It was only yesterday," he hastily added, "that I saw him, and he was still bright and cheery; and how is it that he's anything but well now?"

"I myself can't explain," replied Ming Yen; "but just a few minutes ago an old man belonging to his family came over with the express purpose of giving me the tidings."

Upon hearing this news, Pao-yü there and then turned round and told dowager lady Chia; and the old lady issued directions to depute some trustworthy persons to accompany him. "Let him go," (she said), "and satisfy his feelings towards his fellow-scholar; but as soon as he has done, he must come back; and don't let him tarry too long."

Pao-yü with hurried step left the room and came and changed his clothes. But as on his arrival outside, the carriage had not as yet been got ready, he fell into such a state of excitement, that he went round and round all over the hall in quite an erratic manner. In a short while, after pressure had been brought to bear, the carriage arrived, and speedily mounting the vehicle, he drove up to the door of Ch'in Chung's house, followed by Li Kuei, Ming Yen and the other servants. Everything was quiet. Not a soul was about. Like a hive of bees they flocked into the house, to the astonishment of two distant aunts, and of several male cousins of Ch'in Chung, all of whom had no time to effect their retreat.

Ch'in Chung had, by this time, had two or three fainting fits, and had already long ago been changed his mat. As soon as Pao-yü realised the situation, he felt unable to repress himself from bursting forth aloud. Li Kuei promptly reasoned with him. "You shouldn't go on in this way," he urged, "you shouldn't. It's because Mr. Ch'in is so weak that lying flat on the stove-couch naturally made his bones feel uncomfortable; and that's why he has temporarily been removed down here to ease him a little. But if you, sir, go on in this way, will you not, instead of doing him any good, aggravate his illness?"

At these words, Pao-yü accordingly restrained himself, and held his tongue; and drawing near, he gazed at Ch'in Chung's face, which was as white as wax, while with closed eyes, he gasped for breath, rolling about on his pillow.

"Brother Ching," speedily exclaimed Pao-yü, "Pao-yü is here!" But though he shouted out two or three consecutive times, Ch'in Chung did not heed him.

"Pao-yü has come!" Pao-yü went on again to cry. But Ch'in Chung's spirit had already departed from his body, leaving behind only a faint breath of superfluous air in his lungs.

He had just caught sight of a number of recording devils, holding a warrant and carrying chains, coming to seize him, but Ch'in Chung's soul would on no account go along with them; and remembering how that there was in his home no one to assume the direction of domestic affairs, and feeling concerned that Chih Neng had as yet no home, he consequently used hundreds of arguments in his entreaties to the recording devils; but alas! these devils would, none of them, show him any favour. On the contrary, they heaped invectives upon Ch'in Chung.

"You're fortunate enough to be a man of letters," they insinuated, "and don't you know the common saying that: 'if the Prince of Hell call upon you to die at the third watch, who can presume to retain you, a human being, up to the fifth watch?' In our abode, in the unseen, high as well as low, have all alike a face made of iron, and heed not selfish motives; unlike the mortal world, where favouritism and partiality prevail. There exist therefore many difficulties in the way (to our yielding to your wishes)."

While this fuss was going on, Ch'in Chung's spirit suddenly grasped the four words, "Pao-yü has come," and without loss of time, it went on again to make further urgent appeals. "Gentlemen, spiritual deputies," it exclaimed; "show me a little mercy and allow me to return to make just one remark to an intimate friend of mine, and I'll be back again."

"What intimate friend is this again?" the devils observed with one voice.

"I'm not deceiving you, gentlemen," rejoined Ch'in Chung; "it's the grandson of the duke of Jung Kuo, whose infant name is Pao-yü."

The Decider of life was, at first, upon hearing these words, so seized with dismay that he vehemently abused the devils sent on the errand.

"I told you," he shouted, "to let him go back for a turn; but you would by no means comply with my words! and now do you wait until he has summoned a man of glorious fortune and prosperous standing to at last desist?"

When the company of devils perceived the manner of the Decider of life, they were all likewise so seized with consternation that they bustled with hand and feet; while with hearts also full of resentment: "You, sir," they replied, "were at one time such a terror, formidable as lightning; and are you not forsooth able to listen with equanimity to the two sounds of 'Pao-yü?' our humble idea is that mortal as he is, and immortal as we are, it wouldn't be to our credit if we feared him!"

But whether Ch'in Chung, after all, died or survived, the next chapter will explain.

CHAPTER XVII.

In the Ta Kuan Garden, (Broad Vista,) the merits of Pao-yü are put to
the test, by his being told to write devices for scrolls and tablets.
Yuan Ch'un returns to the Jung Kuo mansion, on a visit to her parents,
and offers her congratulations to them on the feast of lanterns, on the fifteenth of the first moon.

Ch'in Chung, to resume our story, departed this life, and Pao-yü went on so unceasingly in his bitter lamentations, that Li Kuei and the other servants had, for ever so long, an arduous task in trying to comfort him before he desisted; but on his return home he was still exceedingly disconsolate.

Dowager lady Chia afforded monetary assistance to the amount of several tens of taels; and exclusive of this, she had sacrificial presents likewise got ready. Pao-yü went and paid a visit of condolence to the family, and after seven days the funeral and burial took place, but there are no particulars about them which could be put on record.

Pao-yü, however, continued to mourn (his friend) from day to day, and was incessant in his remembrance of him, but there was likewise no help for it. Neither is it known after how many days he got over his grief.

On this day, Chia Chen and the others came to tell Chia Cheng that the works in the garden had all been reported as completed, and that Mr. Chia She had already inspected them. "It only remains," (they said), "for you, sir, to see them; and should there possibly be anything which is not proper, steps will be at once taken to effect the alterations, so that the tablets and scrolls may conveniently be written."

After Chia Cheng had listened to these words, he pondered for a while. "These tablets and scrolls," he remarked, "present however a difficult task. According to the rites, we should, in order to obviate any shortcoming, request the imperial consort to deign and compose them; but if the honourable consort does not gaze upon the scenery with her own eyes, it will also be difficult for her to conceive its nature and indite upon it! And were we to wait until the arrival of her highness, to request her to honour the grounds with a visit, before she composes the inscriptions, such a wide landscape, with so many pavilions and arbours, will, without one character in the way of a motto, albeit it may abound with flowers, willows, rockeries, and streams, nevertheless in no way be able to show off its points of beauty to advantage."

The whole party of family companions, who stood by, smiled. "Your views, remarkable sir," they ventured, "are excellent; but we have now a proposal to make. Tablets and scrolls for every locality cannot, on any account, be dispensed with, but they could not likewise, by any means, be determined upon for good! Were now, for the time being, two, three or four characters fixed upon, harmonising with the scenery, to carry out, for form's sake, the idea, and were they provisionally utilised as mottoes for the lanterns, tablets and scrolls, and hung up, pending the arrival of her highness, and her visit through the grounds, when she could be requested to decide upon the devices, would not two exigencies be met with satisfactorily?"

"Your views are perfectly correct," observed Chia Cheng, after he had heard their suggestion; "and we should go to-day and have a look at the place so as then to set to work to write the inscriptions; which, if suitable, can readily be used; and, if unsuitable, Yü-ts'un can then be sent for, and asked to compose fresh ones."

The whole company smiled. "If you, sir, were to compose them to-day," they ventured, "they are sure to be excellent; and what need will there be again to wait for Yü-ts'un!"

"You people are not aware," Chia Cheng added with a smiling countenance, "that I've been, even in my young days, very mediocre in the composition of stanzas on flowers, birds, rockeries and streams; and that now that I'm well up in years and have moreover the fatigue and trouble of my official duties, I've become in literary compositions like these, which require a light heart and gladsome mood, still more inapt. Were I even to succeed in composing any, they will unavoidably be so doltish and forced that they would contrariwise be instrumental in making the flowers, trees, garden and pavilions, through their demerits, lose in beauty, and present instead no pleasing feature."

"This wouldn't anyhow matter," remonstrated all the family companions, "for after perusing them we can all decide upon them together, each one of us recommending those he thinks best; which if excellent can be kept, and if faulty can be discarded; and there's nothing unfeasible about this!"

"This proposal is most apposite," rejoined Chia Cheng. "What's more, the weather is, I rejoice, fine to-day; so let's all go in a company and have a look."

Saying this, he stood up and went forward, at the head of the whole party; while Chia Chen betook himself in advance into the garden to let every one know of their coming. As luck would have it, Pao-yü—for he had been these last few days thinking of Ch'in Chung and so ceaselessly sad and wounded at heart, that dowager lady Chia had frequently directed the servants to take him into the new garden to play—made his entrance just at this very time, and suddenly became aware of the arrival of Chia Chen, who said to him with a smile, "Don't you yet run away as fast as you can? Mr. Chia Cheng will be coming in a while."

At these words, Pao-yü led off his nurse and the youths, and rushed at once out of the garden, like a streak of smoke; but as he turned a corner, he came face to face with Chia Cheng, who was advancing towards that direction, at the head of all the visitors; and as he had no time to get out of the way, the only course open to him was to stand on one side.

Chia Cheng had, of late, heard the tutor extol him by saying that he displayed special ability in rhyming antithetical lines, and that although he did not like to read his books, he nevertheless possessed some depraved talents, and hence it was that he was induced at this moment to promptly bid him follow him into the garden, with the intent of putting him to the test.

Pao-yü could not make out what his object was, but he was compelled to follow. As soon as they reached the garden gate, and he caught sight of Chia Chen, standing on one side, along with several managers: "See that the garden gate is closed for a time," Chia Cheng exclaimed, "for we'll first see the outside and then go in."

Chia Chen directed a servant to close the gate, and Chia Cheng first looked straight ahead of him towards the gate and espied on the same side as the main entrance a suite of five apartments. Above, the cylindrical tiles resembled the backs of mud eels. The doors, railings, windows, and frames were all finely carved with designs of the new fashion, and were painted neither in vermilion nor in white colours.

The whole extent of the walls was of polished bricks of uniform colour; while below, the white marble on the terrace and steps was engraved with western foreign designs; and when he came to look to the right and to the left, everything was white as snow. At the foot of the white-washed walls, tiger-skin pebbles were, without regard to pattern, promiscuously inserted in the earth in such a way as of their own selves to form streaks. Nothing fell in with the custom of gaudiness and display so much in vogue, so that he naturally felt full of delight; and, when he forthwith asked that the gate should be thrown open, all that met their eyes was a long stretch of verdant hills, which shut in the view in front of them.

"What a fine hill, what a pretty hill!" exclaimed all the companions with one voice.

"Were it not for this one hill," Chia Cheng explained, "whatever scenery is contained in it would clearly strike the eye, as soon as one entered into the garden, and what pleasure would that have been?"

"Quite so," rejoined all of them. "But without large hills and ravines in one's breast (liberal capacities), how could one attain such imagination!"

After the conclusion of this remark, they cast a glance ahead of them, and perceived white rugged rocks looking, either like goblins, or resembling savage beasts, lying either crossways, or in horizontal or upright positions; on the surface of which grew moss and lichen with mottled hues, or parasitic plants, which screened off the light; while, slightly visible, wound, among the rocks, a narrow pathway like the intestines of a sheep.

"If we were now to go and stroll along by this narrow path," Chia Cheng suggested, "and to come out from over there on our return, we shall have been able to see the whole grounds."

Having finished speaking, he asked Chia Chen to lead the way; and he himself, leaning on Pao-yü, walked into the gorge with leisurely step. Raising his head, he suddenly beheld on the hill a block of stone, as white as the surface of a looking-glass, in a site which was, in very deed, suitable to be left for an inscription, as it was bound to meet the eye.

"Gentlemen," Chia Cheng observed, as he turned his head round and smiled, "please look at this spot. What name will it be fit to give it?"

When the company heard his remark, some maintained that the two words "Heaped verdure" should be written; and others upheld that the device should be "Embroidered Hill." Others again suggested:

"Vying with the Hsiang Lu;" and others recommended "the small Chung Nan." And various kinds of names were proposed, which did not fall short of several tens.

All the visitors had been, it must be explained, aware at an early period of the fact that Chia Cheng meant to put Pao-yü's ability to the test, and for this reason they merely proposed a few combinations in common use. But of this intention, Pao-yü himself was likewise cognizant.

After listening to the suggestions, Chia Cheng forthwith turned his head round and bade Pao-yü think of some motto.

"I've often heard," Pao-yü replied, "that writers of old opine that it's better to quote an old saying than to compose a new one; and that an old engraving excels in every respect an engraving of the present day. What's more, this place doesn't constitute the main hill or the chief feature of the scenery, and is really no site where any inscription should be put, as it no more than constitutes the first step in the inspection of the landscape. Won't it be well to employ the exact text of an old writer consisting of 'a tortuous path leading to a secluded (nook).' This line of past days would, if inscribed, be, in fact, liberal to boot."

After listening to the proposed line, they all sang its praise. "First-rate! excellent!" they cried, "the natural talents of your second son, dear friend, are lofty; his mental capacity is astute; he is unlike ourselves, who have read books but are simple fools."

"You shouldn't," urged Chia Cheng smilingly, "heap upon him excessive praise; he's young in years, and merely knows one thing which he turns to the use of ten purposes; you should laugh at him, that's all; but we can by and by choose some device."

As he spoke, he entered the cave, where he perceived beautiful trees with thick foliage, quaint flowers in lustrous bloom, while a line of limpid stream emanated out of a deep recess among the flowers and trees, and oozed down through the crevice of the rock. Progressing several steps further in, they gradually faced the northern side, where a stretch of level ground extended far and wide, on each side of which soared lofty buildings, intruding themselves into the skies, whose carved rafters and engraved balustrades nestled entirely among the depressions of the hills and the tops of the trees. They lowered their eyes and looked, and beheld a pure stream flowing like jade, stone steps traversing the clouds, a balustrade of white marble encircling the pond in its embrace, and a stone bridge with three archways, the animals upon which had faces disgorging water from their mouths. A pavilion stood on the bridge, and in this pavilion Chia Chen and the whole party went and sat.

"Gentlemen," he inquired, "what shall we write about this?"

"In the record," they all replied, "of the 'Drunken Old Man's Pavilion,' written in days of old by Ou Yang, appears this line: 'There is a pavilion pinioned-like,' so let us call this 'the pinioned-like pavilion,' and finish."

"Pinioned-like," observed Chia Cheng smiling, "is indeed excellent; but this pavilion is constructed over the water, and there should, after all, be some allusion to the water in the designation. My humble opinion is that of the line in Ou Yang's work, '(the water) drips from between the two peaks,' we should only make use of that single word 'drips.'"

"First-rate!" rejoined one of the visitors, "capital! but what would really be appropriate are the two characters 'dripping jadelike.'"

Chia Chen pulled at his moustache, as he gave way to reflection; after which, he asked Pao-yü to also propose one himself.

"What you, sir, suggested a while back," replied Pao-yü, "will do very well; but if we were now to sift the matter thoroughly, the use of the single word 'drip' by Ou Yang, in his composition about the Niang spring, would appear quite apposite; while the application, also on this occasion, to this spring, of the character 'drip' would be found not quite suitable. Moreover, seeing that this place is intended as a separate residence (for the imperial consort), on her visit to her parents, it is likewise imperative that we should comply with all the principles of etiquette, so that were words of this kind to be used, they would besides be coarse and inappropriate; and may it please you to fix upon something else more recondite and abstruse."

"What do you, gentlemen, think of this argument?" Chia Cheng remarked sneeringly. "A little while ago, when the whole company devised something original, you observed that it would be better to quote an old device; and now that we have quoted an old motto, you again maintain that it's coarse and inappropriate! But you had better give us one of yours."

"If two characters like 'dripping jadelike' are to be used," Pao-yü explained, "it would be better then to employ the two words 'Penetrating Fragrance,' which would be unique and excellent, wouldn't they?"

Chia Cheng pulled his moustache, nodded his head and did not utter a word; whereupon the whole party hastily pressed forward with one voice to eulogize Pao-yü's acquirements as extraordinary.

"The selection of two characters for the tablet is an easy matter," suggested Chia Cheng, "but now go on and compose a pair of antithetical phrases with seven words in each."

Pao-yü cast a glance round the four quarters, when an idea came into his head, and he went on to recite:

The willows, which enclose the shore, the green borrow from three bamboos;
On banks apart, the flowers asunder grow, yet one perfume they give.

Upon hearing these lines, Chia Cheng gave a faint smile, as he nodded his head, whilst the whole party went on again to be effusive in their praise. But forthwith they issued from the pavilions, and crossed the pond, contemplating with close attention each elevation, each stone, each flower, or each tree. And as suddenly they raised their heads, they caught sight, in front of them, of a line of white wall, of numbers of columns, and beautiful cottages, where flourished hundreds and thousands of verdant bamboos, which screened off the rays of the sun.

"What a lovely place!" they one and all exclaimed.

Speedily the whole company penetrated inside, perceiving, as soon as they had entered the gate, a zigzag arcade, below the steps of which was a raised pathway, laid promiscuously with stones, and on the furthest part stood a diminutive cottage with three rooms, two with doors leading into them and one without. Everything in the interior, in the shape of beds, teapoys, chairs and tables, were made to harmonise with the space available. Leading out of the inner room of the cottage was a small door from which, as they egressed, they found a back-court with lofty pear trees in blossom and banana trees, as well as two very small retiring back-courts. At the foot of the wall, unexpectedly became visible an aperture where was a spring, for which a channel had been opened scarcely a foot or so wide, to enable it to run inside the wall. Winding round the steps, it skirted the buildings until it reached the front court, where it coiled and curved, flowing out under the bamboos.

"This spot," observed Chia Cheng full of smiles, "is indeed pleasant! and could one, on a moonlight night, sit under the window and study, one would not spend a whole lifetime in vain!"

As he said this, he quickly cast a glance at Pao-yü, and so terrified did Pao-yü feel that he hastily drooped his head. The whole company lost no time in choosing some irrelevant talk to turn the conversation, and two of the visitors prosecuted their remarks by adding that on the tablet, in this spot, four characters should be inscribed.

"Which four characters?" Chia Cheng inquired, laughingly.

"The bequeathed aspect of the river Ch'i!" suggested one of them.

"It's commonplace," observed Chia Cheng.

Another person recommended "the remaining vestiges of the Chü Garden."

"This too is commonplace!" replied Chia Cheng.

"Let brother Pao-yü again propound one!" interposed Chia Chen, who stood by.

"Before he composes any himself," Chia Cheng continued, "his wont is to first discuss the pros and cons of those of others; so it's evident that he's an impudent fellow!"

"He's most reasonable in his arguments," all the visitors protested, "and why should he be called to task?"

"Don't humour him so much!" Chia Cheng expostulated. "I'll put up for to-day," he however felt constrained to tell Pao-yü, "with your haughty manner, and your rubbishy speech, so that after you have, to begin with, given us your opinion, you may next compose a device. But tell me, are there any that will do among the mottoes suggested just now by all the gentlemen?"

"They all seem to me unsuitable!" Pao-yü did not hesitate to say by way of reply to this question.

Chia Cheng gave a sardonic smile. "How all unsuitable?" he exclaimed.

"This," continued Pao-yü, "is the first spot which her highness will honour on her way, and there should be inscribed, so that it should be appropriate, something commending her sacred majesty. But if a tablet with four characters has to be used, there are likewise devices ready at hand, written by poets of old; and what need is there to compose any more?"

"Are forsooth the devices 'the river Ch'i and the Chu Garden' not those of old authors?" insinuated Chia Cheng.

"They are too stiff," replied Pao-yü. "Would not the four characters: 'a phoenix comes with dignified air,' be better?"

With clamorous unanimity the whole party shouted: "Excellent:" and Chia Cheng nodding his head; "You beast, you beast!" he ejaculated, "it may well be said about you that you see through a thin tube and have no more judgment than an insect! Compose another stanza," he consequently bade him; and Pao-yü recited:

In the precious tripod kettle, tea is brewed, but green is still the smoke!

O'er is the game of chess by the still window, but the fingers are yet cold.

Chia Cheng shook his head. "Neither does this seem to me good!" he said; and having concluded this remark he was leading the company out, when just as he was about to proceed, he suddenly bethought himself of something.

"The several courts and buildings and the teapoys, sideboards, tables and chairs," he added, "may be said to be provided for. But there are still all those curtains, screens and portieres, as well as the furniture, nicknacks and curios; and have they too all been matched to suit the requirements of each place?"

"Of the things that have to be placed about," Chia Chen explained, a good number have, at an early period, been added, and of course when the time comes everything will be suitably arranged. As for the curtains, screens, and portieres, which have to be hung up, I heard yesterday brother Lien say that they are not as yet complete, that when the works were first taken in hand, the plan of each place was drawn, the measurements accurately calculated and some one despatched to attend to the things, and that he thought that yesterday half of them were bound to come in.

Chia Cheng, upon hearing this explanation, readily remembered that with all these concerns Chia Chen had nothing to do; so that he speedily sent some one to go and call Chia Lien.

Having arrived in a short while, "How many sorts of things are there in all?" Chia Cheng inquired of him. "Of these how many kinds have by this time been got ready? and how many more are short?"

At this question, Chia Lien hastily produced, from the flaps of his boot, a paper pocket-book, containing a list, which he kept inside the tops of his boot. After perusing it and reperusing it, he made suitable reply. "Of the hundred and twenty curtains," he proceeded, "of stiff spotted silks, embroidered with dragons in relief, and of the curtains large and small, of every kind of damask silk, eighty were got yesterday, so that there still remain forty of them to come. The two portieres were both received yesterday; and besides these, there are the two hundred red woollen portieres, two hundred portieres of Hsiang Fei bamboo; two hundred door-screens of rattan, with gold streaks, and of red lacquered bamboo; two hundred portieres of black lacquered rattan; two hundred door-screens of variegated thread-netting with clusters of flowers. Of each of these kinds, half have come in, but the whole lot of them will be complete no later than autumn. Antimacassars, table-cloths, flounces for the beds, and cushions for the stools, there are a thousand two hundred of each, but these likewise are ready and at hand."

As he spoke, they proceeded outwards, but suddenly they perceived a hill extending obliquely in such a way as to intercept the passage; and as they wound round the curve of the hill faintly came to view a line of yellow mud walls, the whole length of which was covered with paddy stalks for the sake of protection, and there were several hundreds of apricot trees in bloom, which presented the appearance of being fire, spurted from the mouth, or russet clouds, rising in the air. Inside this enclosure, stood several thatched cottages. Outside grew, on the other hand, mulberry trees, elms, mallows, and silkworm oaks, whose tender shoots and new twigs, of every hue, were allowed to bend and to intertwine in such a way as to form two rows of green fence. Beyond this fence and below the white mound, was a well, by the side of which stood a well-sweep, windlass and such like articles; the ground further down being divided into parcels, and apportioned into fields, which, with the fine vegetables and cabbages in flower, presented, at the first glance, the aspect of being illimitable.

"This is," Chia Cheng observed chuckling, "the place really imbued with a certain amount of the right principle; and laid out, though it has been by human labour, yet when it strikes my eye, it so moves my heart, that it cannot help arousing in me the wish to return to my native place and become a farmer. But let us enter and rest a while."

As he concluded these words, they were on the point of walking in, when they unexpectedly discerned a stone, outside the trellis gate, by the roadside, which had also been left as a place on which to inscribe a motto.

"Were a tablet," argued the whole company smilingly, "put up high in a spot like this, to be filled up by and by, the rustic aspect of a farm would in that case be completely done away with; and it will be better, yea far better to erect this slab on the ground, as it will further make manifest many points of beauty. But unless a motto could be composed of the same excellence as that in Fan Shih-hu's song on farms, it will not be adequate to express its charms!"

"Gentlemen," observed Chia Cheng, "please suggest something."

"A short while back," replied the whole company, "your son, venerable brother, remarked that devising a new motto was not equal to quoting an old one, and as sites of this kind have been already exhausted by writers of days of old, wouldn't it be as well that we should straightway call it the 'apricot blossom village?' and this will do splendidly."

When Chia Cheng heard this remark, he smiled and said, addressing himself to Chia Chen: "This just reminds me that although this place is perfect in every respect, there's still one thing wanting in the shape of a wine board; and you had better then have one made to-morrow on the very same pattern as those used outside in villages; and it needn't be anything gaudy, but hung above the top of a tree by means of bamboos."

Chia Chen assented. "There's no necessity," he went on to explain, "to keep any other birds in here, but only to rear a few geese, ducks, fowls and such like; as in that case they will be in perfect keeping with the place."

"A splendid idea!" Chia Cheng rejoined, along with all the party.

"'Apricot blossom village' is really first-rate," continued Chia Cheng as he again addressed himself to the company; "but the only thing is that it encroaches on the real designation of the village; and it will be as well to wait (until her highness comes), when we can request her to give it a name."

"Certainly!" answered the visitors with one voice; "but now as far as a name goes, for mere form, let us all consider what expressions will be suitable to employ."

Pao-yü did not however give them time to think; nor did he wait for Chia Cheng's permission, but suggested there and then: "In old poetical works there's this passage: 'At the top of the red apricot tree hangs the flag of an inn,' and wouldn't it be advisable, on this occasion, to temporarily adopt the four words: 'the sign on the apricot tree is visible'?"

"'Is visible' is excellent," suggested the whole number of them, "and what's more it secretly accords with the meaning implied by 'apricot blossom village.'"

"Were the two words 'apricot blossom' used for the name of the village, they would be too commonplace and unsuitable;" added Pao-yü with a sardonic grin, "but there's another passage in the works of a poet of the T'ang era: 'By the wooden gate near the water the corn-flower emits its fragrance;' and why not make use of the motto 'corn fragrance village,' which will be excellent?"

When the company heard his proposal, they, with still greater vigour, unanimously combined in crying out "Capital!" as they clapped their hands.

Chia Cheng, with one shout, interrupted their cries, "You ignorant child of wrath!" he ejaculated; "how many old writers can you know, and how many stanzas of ancient poetical works can you remember, that you will have the boldness to show off in the presence of all these experienced gentlemen? (In allowing you to give vent to) all the nonsense you uttered my object was no other than to see whether your brain was clear or muddled; and all for fun's sake, that's all; and lo, you've taken things in real earnest!"

Saying this, he led the company into the interior of the hall with the mallows. The windows were pasted with paper, and the bedsteads made of wood, and all appearance of finery had been expunged, and Chia Cheng's heart was naturally much gratified; but nevertheless, scowling angrily at Pao-yü, "What do you think of this place?" he asked.

When the party heard this question, they all hastened to stealthily give a nudge to Pao-yü, with the express purpose of inducing him to say it was nice; but Pao-yü gave no ear to what they all urged. "It's by far below the spot," he readily replied, "designated 'a phoenix comes with dignified air.'"

"You ignorant stupid thing!" exclaimed Chia Cheng at these words; "what you simply fancy as exquisite, with that despicable reliance of yours upon luxury and display, are two-storied buildings and painted pillars! But how can you know anything about this aspect so pure and unobtrusive, and this is all because of that failing of not studying your books!"

"Sir," hastily answered Pao-yü, "your injunctions are certainly correct; but men of old have often made allusion to 'natural;' and what is, I wonder, the import of these two characters?"

The company had perceived what a perverse mind Pao yü possessed, and they one and all were much surprised that he should be so silly beyond the possibility of any change; and when now they heard the question he asked, about the two characters representing "natural," they, with one accord, speedily remarked, "Everything else you understand, and how is it that on the contrary you don't know what 'natural' implies? The word 'natural' means effected by heaven itself and not made by human labour."

"Well, just so," rejoined Pao-yü; "but the farm, which is laid out in this locality, is distinctly the handiwork of human labour; in the distance, there are no neighbouring hamlets; near it, adjoin no wastes; though it bears a hill, the hill is destitute of streaks; though it be close to water, this water has no spring; above, there is no pagoda nestling in a temple; below, there is no bridge leading to a market; it rises abrupt and solitary, and presents no grand sight! The palm would seem to be carried by the former spot, which is imbued with the natural principle, and possesses the charms of nature; for, though bamboos have been planted in it, and streams introduced, they nevertheless do no violence to the works executed. 'A natural landscape,' says, an ancient author in four words; and why? Simply because he apprehended that what was not land, would, by forcible ways, be converted into land; and that what was no hill would, by unnatural means, be raised into a hill. And ingenious though these works might be in a hundred and one ways, they cannot, after all, be in harmony."...

But he had no time to conclude, as Chia Cheng flew into a rage. "Drive him off," he shouted; (but as Pao-yü) was on the point of going out, he again cried out: "Come back! make up," he added, "another couplet, and if it isn't clear, I'll for all this give you a slap on your mouth."

Pao-yü had no alternative but to recite as follows:

A spot in which the "Ko" fibre to bleach, as the fresh tide doth swell the waters green!

A beauteous halo and a fragrant smell the man encompass who the cress
did pluck!

Chia Cheng, after this recital, nodded his head. "This is still worse!" he remarked, but as he reproved him, he led the company outside, and winding past the mound, they penetrated among flowers, and wending their steps by the willows, they touched the rocks and lingered by the stream. Passing under the trellis with yellow roses, they went into the shed with white roses; they crossed by the pavilion with peonies, and walked through the garden, where the white peony grew; and entering the court with the cinnamon roses, they reached the island of bananas. As they meandered and zigzagged, suddenly they heard the rustling sound of the water, as it came out from a stone cave, from the top of which grew parasitic plants drooping downwards, while at its bottom floated the fallen flowers.

"What a fine sight!" they all exclaimed; "what beautiful scenery!"

"Gentlemen," observed Chia Cheng, "what name do you propose for this place?"

"There's no further need for deliberation," the company rejoined; "for this is just the very spot fit for the three words 'Wu Ling Spring.'"

"This too is matter-of-fact!" Chia Cheng objected laughingly, "and likewise antiquated."

"If that won't do," the party smiled, "well then what about the four characters implying 'An old cottage of a man of the Ch'in dynasty?'"

"This is still more exceedingly plain!" interposed Pao-yü. "'The old cottage of a man of the Ch'in dynasty' is meant to imply a retreat from revolution, and how will it suit this place? Wouldn't the four characters be better denoting 'an isthmus with smart weed, and a stream with flowers'?"

When Chia Cheng heard these words, he exclaimed: "You're talking still more stuff and nonsense?" and forthwith entering the grotto, Chia Cheng went on to ask of Chia Chen, "Are there any boats or not?"

"There are to be," replied Chia Chen, "four boats in all from which to pick the lotus, and one boat for sitting in; but they haven't now as yet been completed."

"What a pity!" Chia Cheng answered smilingly, "that we cannot go in."

"But we could also get into it by the tortuous path up the hill," Chia Chen ventured; and after finishing this remark, he walked ahead to show the way, and the whole party went over, holding on to the creepers, and supporting themselves by the trees, when they saw a still larger quantity of fallen leaves on the surface of the water, and the stream itself, still more limpid, gently and idly meandering along on its circuitous course. By the bank of the pond were two rows of weeping willows, which, intermingling with peach and apricot trees, screened the heavens from view, and kept off the rays of the sun from this spot, which was in real truth devoid of even a grain of dust.

Suddenly, they espied in the shade of the willows, an arched wooden bridge also reveal itself to the eye, with bannisters of vermilion colour. They crossed the bridge, and lo, all the paths lay open before them; but their gaze was readily attracted by a brick cottage spotless and cool-looking; whose walls were constructed of polished bricks, of uniform colour; (whose roof was laid) with speckless tiles; and whose enclosing walls were painted; while the minor slopes, which branched off from the main hill, all passed along under the walls on to the other side.

"This house, in a site like this, is perfectly destitute of any charm!" added Chia Cheng.

And as they entered the door, abruptly appeared facing them, a large boulder studded with holes and soaring high in the skies, which was surrounded on all four sides by rocks of every description, and completely, in fact, hid from view the rooms situated in the compound. But of flowers or trees, there was not even one about; and all that was visible were a few strange kinds of vegetation; some being of the creeper genus, others parasitic plants, either hanging from the apex of the hill, or inserting themselves into the base of the rocks; drooping down even from the eaves of the house, entwining the pillars, and closing round the stone steps. Or like green bands, they waved and flapped; or like gold thread, they coiled and bent, either with seeds resembling cinnabar, or with blossoms like golden olea; whose fragrance and aroma could not be equalled by those emitted by flowers of ordinary species.

"This is pleasant!" Chia Cheng could not refrain from saying; "the only thing is that I don't know very much about flowers."

"What are here are lianas and ficus pumila!" some of the company observed.

"How ever can the liana and the ficus have such unusual scent?" questioned Chia Cheng.

"Indeed they aren't!" interposed Pao-yü. "Among all these flowers, there are also ficus and liana, but those scented ones are iris, ligularia, and 'Wu' flowers; that kind consist, for the most part, of 'Ch'ih' flowers and orchids; while this mostly of gold-coloured dolichos. That species is the hypericum plant, this the 'Yü Lu' creeper. The red ones are, of course, the purple rue; the green ones consist for certain, of the green 'Chih' plant; and, to the best of my belief, these various plants are mentioned in the 'Li Sao' and 'Wen Hsuan.' These rare plants are, some of them called something or other like 'Huo Na' and 'Chiang Hui;' others again are designated something like 'Lun Tsu' and 'Tz'u Feng;' while others there are whose names sound like 'Shih Fan,' 'Shui Sung' and 'Fu Liu,' which together with other species are to be found in the 'Treatise about the Wu city' by Tso T'ai-chung. There are also those which go under the appellation of 'Lu T'i,' or something like that; while there are others that are called something or other like 'Tan Chiao,' 'Mi Wu' and 'Feng Lien;' reference to which is made in the 'Treatise on the Shu city.' But so many years have now elapsed, and the times have so changed (since these treatises were written), that people, being unable to discriminate (the real names) may consequently have had to appropriate in every case such names as suited the external aspect, so that they may, it is quite possible, have gradually come to be called by wrong designations."

But he had no time to conclude; for Chia Cheng interrupted him. "Who has ever asked you about it?" he shouted; which plunged Pao-yü into such a fright, that he drew back, and did not venture to utter another word.

Chia Cheng perceiving that on both sides alike were covered passages resembling outstretched arms, forthwith continued his steps and entered the covered way, when he caught sight, at the upper end, of a five-roomed building, without spot or blemish, with folding blinds extending in a connected line, and with corridors on all four sides; (a building) which with its windows so green, and its painted walls, excelled, in spotless elegance, the other buildings they had seen before, to which it presented such a contrast.

Chia Cheng heaved a sigh. "If one were able," he observed, "to boil his tea and thrum his lyre in here, there wouldn't even be any need for him to burn any more incense. But the execution of this structure is so beyond conception that you must, gentlemen, compose something nice and original to embellish the tablet with, so as not to render such a place of no effect!"

"There's nothing so really pat," suggested the company smiling; "as 'the orchid-smell-laden breeze' and 'the dew-bedecked epidendrum!"

"These are indeed the only four characters," rejoined Chia Cheng, "that could be suitably used; but what's to be said as far as the scroll goes?"

"I've thought of a couplet," interposed one of the party, "which you'll all have to criticise, and put into ship-shape; its burden is this:

"The musk-like epidendrum smell enshrouds the court, where shines the
sun with oblique beams;
The iris fragrance is wafted over the isle illumined by the moon's
clear rays."

"As far as excellence is concerned, it's excellent," observed the whole party, "but the two words representing 'with oblique beams' are not felicitous."

And as some one quoted the line from an old poem:

The angelica fills the court with tears, what time the sun doth slant.

"Lugubrious, lugubrious!" expostulated the company with one voice.

Another person then interposed. "I also have a couplet, whose merits you, gentlemen, can weigh; it runs as follows:

"Along the three pathways doth float the Yü Hui scented breeze!
The radiant moon in the whole hall shines on the gold orchid!"

Chia Cheng tugged at his moustache and gave way to meditation. He was just about also to suggest a stanza, when, upon suddenly raising his head, he espied Pao-yü standing by his side, too timid to give vent to a single sound.

"How is it," he purposely exclaimed, "that when you should speak, you contrariwise don't? Is it likely that you expect some one to request you to confer upon us the favour of your instruction?"

"In this place," Pao-yü rejoined at these words, "there are no such things as orchids, musk, resplendent moon or islands; and were one to begin quoting such specimens of allusions, to scenery, two hundred couplets could be readily given without, even then, having been able to exhaust the supply!"

"Who presses your head down," Chia Cheng urged, "and uses force that you must come out with all these remarks?"

"Well, in that case," added Pao-yü, "there are no fitter words to put on the tablet than the four representing: 'The fragrance pure of the ligularia and iris.' While the device on the scroll might be:

"Sung is the nutmeg song, but beauteous still is the sonnet!
Near the T'u Mei to sleep, makes e'en a dream with fragrance full!"

"This is," laughed Chia Cheng sneeringly, "an imitation of the line:

"A book when it is made of plaintain leaves, the writing green is also bound to be!

"So that there's nothing remarkable about it."

"Li T'ai-po, in his work on the Phoenix Terrace," protested the whole party, "copied, in every point, the Huang Hua Lou. But what's essential is a faultless imitation. Now were we to begin to criticise minutely the couplet just cited, we would indeed find it to be, as compared with the line 'A book when it is made of plantain leaves,' still more elegant and of wider application!"

"What an idea?" observed Chia Cheng derisively.

But as he spoke, the whole party walked out; but they had not gone very far before they caught sight of a majestic summer house, towering high peak-like, and of a structure rising loftily with storey upon storey; and completely locked in as they were on every side they were as beautiful as the Jade palace. Far and wide, road upon road coiled and wound; while the green pines swept the eaves, the jady epidendrum encompassed the steps, the animals' faces glistened like gold, and the dragons' heads shone resplendent in their variegated hues.

"This is the Main Hall," remarked Chia Cheng; "the only word against it is that there's a little too much finery."

"It should be so," rejoined one and all, "so as to be what it's intended to be! The imperial consort has, it is true, an exalted preference for economy and frugality, but her present honourable position requires the observance of such courtesies, so that (finery) is no fault."

As they made these remarks and advanced on their way the while, they perceived, just in front of them, an archway project to view, constructed of jadelike stone; at the top of which the coils of large dragons and the scales of small dragons were executed in perforated style.

"What's the device to be for this spot?" inquired Chia Cheng.

"It should be 'fairy land,'" suggested all of them, "so as to be apposite!"

Chia Cheng nodded his head and said nothing. But as soon as Pao-yü caught sight of this spot something was suddenly aroused in his heart and he began to ponder within himself. "This place really resembles something that I've seen somewhere or other." But he could not at the moment recall to mind what year, moon, or day this had happened.

Chia Cheng bade him again propose a motto; but Pao-yü was bent upon thinking over the details of the scenery he had seen on a former occasion, and gave no thought whatever to this place, so that the whole company were at a loss what construction to give to his silence, and came simply to the conclusion that, after the bullying he had had to put up with for ever so long, his spirits had completely vanished, his talents become exhausted and his speech impoverished; and that if he were harassed and pressed, he might perchance, as the result of anxiety, contract some ailment or other, which would of course not be a suitable issue, and they lost no time in combining together to dissuade Chia Cheng.

"Never mind," they said, "to-morrow will do to compose some device; let's drop it now."

Chia Cheng himself was inwardly afraid lest dowager lady Chia should be anxious, so that he hastily remarked as he forced a smile. "You beast, there are, after all, also occasions on which you are no good! but never mind! I'll give you one day to do it in, and if by to-morrow you haven't been able to compose anything, I shall certainly not let you off. This is the first and foremost place and you must exercise due care in what you write."

Saying this, he sallied out, at the head of the company, and cast another glance at the scenery.

Indeed from the time they had entered the gate up to this stage, they had just gone over five or six tenths of the whole ground, when it happened again that a servant came and reported that some one had arrived from Mr. Yü-'ts'un's to deliver a message. "These several places (which remain)," Chia Cheng observed with a smile, "we have no time to pass under inspection; but we might as well nevertheless go out at least by that way, as we shall be able, to a certain degree, to have a look at the general aspect."

With these words, he showed the way for the family companions until they reached a large bridge, with water entering under it, looking like a curtain made of crystal. This bridge, the fact is, was the dam, which communicated with the river outside, and from which the stream was introduced into the grounds.

"What's the name of this water-gate?" Chia Cheng inquired.

"This is," replied Pao-yü, "the main stream of the Hsin Fang river, and is therefore called the Hsin Fang water-gate."

"Nonsense!" exclaimed Chia Cheng. "The two words Hsin Fang must on no account be used!"

And as they speedily advanced on their way, they either came across elegant halls, or thatched cottages; walls made of piled-up stone, or gates fashioned of twisted plants; either a secluded nunnery or Buddhist fane, at the foot of some hill; or some unsullied houses, hidden in a grove, tenanted by rationalistic priestesses; either extensive corridors and winding grottoes; or square buildings, and circular pavilions. But Chia Cheng had not the energy to enter any of these places, for as he had not had any rest for ever so long, his legs felt shaky and his feet weak.

Suddenly they also discerned ahead of them a court disclose itself to view.

"When we get there," Chia Cheng suggested, "we must have a little rest." Straightway as he uttered the remark, he led them in, and winding round the jade-green peach-trees, covered with blossom, they passed through the bamboo fence and flower-laden hedge, which were twisted in such a way as to form a circular, cavelike gateway, when unexpectedly appeared before their eyes an enclosure with white-washed walls, in which verdant willows drooped in every direction.

Chia Cheng entered the gateway in company with the whole party. Along the whole length of both sides extended covered passages, connected with each other; while in the court were laid out several rockeries. In one quarter were planted a number of banana trees; on the opposite stood a plant of begonia from Hsi Fu. Its appearance was like an open umbrella. The gossamer hanging (from its branches) resembled golden threads. The corollas (seemed) to spurt out cinnabar.

"What a beautiful flower! what a beautiful flower!" ejaculated the whole party with one voice; "begonias are verily to be found; but never before have we seen anything the like of this in beauty."

"This is called the maiden begonia and is, in fact, a foreign species," Chia Cheng observed. "There's a homely tradition that it is because it emanates from the maiden kingdom that its flowers are most prolific; but this is likewise erratic talk and devoid of common sense."

"They are, after all," rejoined the whole company, "so unlike others (we have seen), that what's said about the maiden kingdom is, we are inclined to believe, possibly a fact."

"I presume," interposed Pao-yü, "that some clever bard or poet, (perceiving) that this flower was red like cosmetic, delicate as if propped up in sickness, and that it closely resembled the nature of a young lady, gave it, consequently, the name of maiden! People in the world will propagate idle tales, all of which are unavoidably treated as gospel!"

"We receive (with thanks) your instructions; what excellent explanation!" they all remarked unanimously, and as they expressed these words, the whole company took their seats on the sofas under the colonnade.

"Let's think of some original text or other for a motto," Chia Cheng having suggested, one of the companions opined that the two characters: "Banana and stork" would be felicitous; while another one was of the idea that what would be faultless would be: "Collected splendour and waving elegance!"

"'Collected splendour and waving elegance' is excellent," Chia Cheng observed addressing himself to the party; and Pao-yü himself, while also extolling it as beautiful, went on to say: "There's only one thing however to be regretted!"

"What about regret?" the company inquired.

"In this place," Pao-yü explained, "are set out both bananas as well as begonias, with the intent of secretly combining in them the two properties of red and green; and if mention of one of them be made, and the other be omitted, (the device) won't be good enough for selection."

"What would you then suggest?" Chia Cheng asked.

"I would submit the four words, 'the red (flowers) are fragrant, the green (banana leaves) like jade,' which would render complete the beauties of both (the begonias and bananas)."

"It isn't good! it isn't good!" Chia Cheng remonstrated as he shook his head; and while passing this remark, he conducted the party into the house, where they noticed that the internal arrangements effected differed from those in other places, as no partitions could, in fact, be discerned. Indeed, the four sides were all alike covered with boards carved hollow with fretwork, (in designs consisting) either of rolling clouds and hundreds of bats; or of the three friends of the cold season of the year, (fir, bamboo and almond); of scenery and human beings, or of birds or flowers; either of clusters of decoration, or of relics of olden times; either of ten thousand characters of happiness or of ten thousand characters of longevity. The various kinds of designs had been all carved by renowned hands, in variegated colours, inlaid with gold, and studded with precious gems; while on shelf upon shelf were either arranged collections of books, or tripods were laid out; either pens and inkslabs were distributed about, or vases with flowers set out, or figured pots were placed about; the designs of the shelves being either round or square; or similar to sunflowers or banana leaves; or like links, half overlapping each other. And in very truth they resembled bouquets of flowers or clusters of tapestry, with all their fretwork so transparent. Suddenly (the eye was struck) by variegated gauzes pasted (on the wood-work), actually forming small windows; and of a sudden by fine thin silks lightly overshadowing (the fretwork) just as if there were, after all, secret doors. The whole walls were in addition traced, with no regard to symmetry, with outlines of the shapes of curios and nick-nacks in imitation of lutes, double-edged swords, hanging bottles and the like, the whole number of which, though (apparently) suspended on the walls, were all however on a same level with the surface of the partition walls.

"What fine ingenuity!" they all exclaimed extollingly; "what a labour they must have been to carry out!"

Chia Cheng had actually stepped in; but scarcely had they reached the second stage, before the whole party readily lost sight of the way by which they had come in. They glanced on the left, and there stood a door, through which they could go. They cast their eyes on the right, and there was a window which suddenly impeded their progress. They went forward, but there again they were obstructed by a bookcase. They turned their heads round, and there too stood windows pasted with transparent gauze and available door-ways: but the moment they came face to face with the door, they unexpectedly perceived that a whole company of people had likewise walked in, just in front of them, whose appearance resembled their own in every respect. But it was only a mirror. And when they rounded the mirror, they detected a still larger number of doors.

"Sir," Chia Chen remarked with a grin; "if you'll follow me out through this door, we'll forthwith get into the back-court; and once out of the back-court, we shall be, at all events, nearer than we were before."

Taking the lead, he conducted Chia Cheng and the whole party round two gauze mosquito houses, when they verily espied a door through which they made their exit, into a court, replete with stands of cinnamon roses. Passing round the flower-laden hedge, the only thing that spread before their view was a pure stream impeding their advance. The whole company was lost in admiration. "Where does this water again issue from?" they cried.

Chia Chen pointed to a spot at a distance. "Starting originally," he explained, "from that water-gate, it runs as far as the mouth of that cave, when from among the hills on the north-east side, it is introduced into that village, where again a diverging channel has been opened and it is made to flow in a south-westerly direction; the whole volume of water then runs to this spot, where collecting once more in one place, it issues, on its outward course, from beneath that wall."

"It's most ingenious!" they one and all exclaimed, after they had listened to him; but, as they uttered these words, they unawares realised that a lofty hill obstructed any further progress. The whole party felt very hazy about the right road. But "Come along after me," Chia Chen smilingly urged, as he at once went ahead and showed the way, whereupon the company followed in his steps, and as soon as they turned round the foot of the hill, a level place and broad road lay before them; and wide before their faces appeared the main entrance.

"This is charming! this is delightful!" the party unanimously exclaimed, "what wits must have been ransacked, and ingenuity attained, so as to bring things to this extreme degree of excellence!"

Forthwith the party egressed from the garden, and Pao-yü's heart anxiously longed for the society of the young ladies in the inner quarters, but as he did not hear Chia Cheng bid him go, he had no help but to follow him into the library. But suddenly Chia Cheng bethought himself of him. "What," he said, "you haven't gone yet! the old lady will I fear be anxious on your account; and is it pray that you haven't as yet had enough walking?"

Pao-yü at length withdrew out of the library. On his arrival in the court, a page, who had been in attendance on Chia Cheng, at once pressed forward, and took hold of him fast in his arms. "You've been lucky enough," he said, "to-day to have been in master's good graces! just a while back when our old mistress despatched servants to come on several occasions and ask after you, we replied that master was pleased with you; for had we given any other answer, her ladyship would have sent to fetch you to go in, and you wouldn't have had an opportunity of displaying your talents. Every one admits that the several stanzas you recently composed were superior to those of the whole company put together; but you must, after the good luck you've had to-day, give us a tip!"

"I'll give each one of you a tiao," Pao-yü rejoined smirkingly.

"Who of us hasn't seen a tiao?" they all exclaimed, "let's have that purse of yours, and have done with it!"

Saying this, one by one advanced and proceeded to unloosen the purse, and to unclasp the fan-case; and allowing Pao-yü no time to make any remonstrance, they stripped him of every ornament in the way of appendage which he carried about on his person. "Whatever we do let's escort him home!" they shouted, and one after another hustled round him and accompanied him as far as dowager lady Chia's door.

Her ladyship was at this moment awaiting his arrival, so that when she saw him walk in, and she found out that (Chia Cheng) had not bullied him, she felt, of course, extremely delighted. But not a long interval elapsed before Hsi Jen came to serve the tea; and when she perceived that on his person not one of the ornaments remained, she consequently smiled and inquired: "Have all the things that you had on you been again taken away by these barefaced rascals?"

As soon as Lin Tai-yü heard this remark, she crossed over to him and saw at a glance that not one single trinket was, in fact, left. "Have you also given them," she felt constrained to ask, "the purse that I gave you? Well, by and by, when you again covet anything of mine, I shan't let you have it."

After uttering these words, she returned into her apartment in high dudgeon, and taking the scented bag, which Pao-yü had asked her to make for him, and which she had not as yet finished, she picked up a pair of scissors, and instantly cut it to pieces.

Pao-yü noticing that she had lost her temper, came after her with hurried step, but the bag had already been cut with the scissors; and as Pao-yü observed how extremely fine and artistic this scented bag was, in spite of its unfinished state, he verily deplored that it should have been rent to pieces for no rhyme or reason. Promptly therefore unbuttoning his coat, he produced from inside the lapel the purse, which had been fastened there. "Look at this!" he remarked as he handed it to Tai-yü; "what kind of thing is this! have I given away to any one what was yours?" Lin Tai-yü, upon seeing how much he prized it as to wear it within his clothes, became alive to the fact that it was done with intent, as he feared lest any one should take it away; and as this conviction made her sorry that she had been so impetuous as to have cut the scented bag, she lowered her head and uttered not a word.

"There was really no need for you to have cut it," Pao-yü observed; "but as I know that you're loth to give me anything, what do you say to my returning even this purse?"

With these words, he threw the purse in her lap and walked off; which vexed Tai-yü so much the more that, after giving way to tears, she took up the purse in her hands to also destroy it with the scissors, when Pao-yü precipitately turned round and snatched it from her grasp.

"My dear cousin," he smilingly pleaded, "do spare it!" and as Tai-yü dashed down the scissors and wiped her tears: "You needn't," she urged, "be kind to me at one moment, and unkind at another; if you wish to have a tiff, why then let's part company!" But as she spoke, she lost control over her temper, and, jumping on her bed, she lay with her face turned towards the inside, and set to work drying her eyes.

Pao-yü could not refrain from approaching her. "My dear cousin, my own cousin," he added, "I confess my fault!"

"Go and find Pao-yü!" dowager lady Chia thereupon gave a shout from where she was in the front apartment, and all the attendants explained that he was in Miss Lin's room.

"All right, that will do! that will do!" her ladyship rejoined, when she heard this reply; "let the two cousins play together; his father kept him a short while back under check, for ever so long, so let him have some distraction. But the only thing is that you mustn't allow them to have any quarrels." To which the servants in a body expressed their obedience.

Tai-yü, unable to put up with Pao-yü's importunity, felt compelled to rise. "Your object seems to be," she remarked, "not to let me have any rest. If it is, I'll run away from you." Saying which, she there and then was making her way out, when Pao-yü protested with a face full of smiles: "Wherever you go, I'll follow!" and as he, at the same time, took the purse and began to fasten it on him, Tai-yü stretched out her hand, and snatching it away, "You say you don't want it," she observed, "and now you put it on again! I'm really much ashamed on your account!" And these words were still on her lips when with a sound of Ch'ih, she burst out laughing.

"My dear cousin," Pao-yü added, "to-morrow do work another scented bag for me!"

"That too will rest upon my good pleasure," Tai-yü rejoined.

As they conversed, they both left the room together and walked into madame Wang's suite of apartments, where, as luck would have it, Pao-ch'ai was also seated.

Unusual commotion prevailed, at this time, over at madame Wang's, for the fact is that Chia Se had already come back from Ku Su, where he had selected twelve young girls, and settled about an instructor, as well as about the theatrical properties and the other necessaries. And as Mrs. Hsüeh had by this date moved her quarters into a separate place on the northeast side, and taken up her abode in a secluded and quiet house, (madame Wang) had had repairs of a distinct character executed in the Pear Fragrance Court, and then issued directions that the instructor should train the young actresses in this place; and casting her choice upon all the women, who had, in days of old, received a training in singing, and who were now old matrons with white hair, she bade them have an eye over them and keep them in order. Which done, she enjoined Chia Se to assume the chief control of all matters connected with the daily and monthly income and outlay, as well as of the accounts of all articles in use of every kind and size.

Lin Chih-hsiao also came to report: "that the twelve young nuns and Taoist girls, who had been purchased after proper selection, had all arrived, and that the twenty newly-made Taoist coats had also been received. That there was besides a maiden, who though devoted to asceticism, kept her chevelure unshaved; that she was originally a denizen of Suchow, of a family whose ancestors were also people of letters and official status; that as from her youth up she had been stricken with much sickness, (her parents) had purchased a good number of substitutes (to enter the convent), but all with no relief to her, until at last this girl herself entered the gate of abstraction when she at once recovered. That hence it was that she grew her hair, while she devoted herself to an ascetic life; that she was this year eighteen years of age, and that the name given to her was Miao Yü; that her father and mother were, at this time, already dead; that she had only by her side, two old nurses and a young servant girl to wait upon her; that she was most proficient in literature, and exceedingly well versed in the classics and canons; and that she was likewise very attractive as far as looks went; that having heard that in the city of Ch'ang-an, there were vestiges of Kuan Yin and relics of the canons inscribed on leaves, she followed, last year, her teacher (to the capital). She now lives," he said, "in the Lao Ni nunnery, outside the western gate; her teacher was a great expert in prophetic divination, but she died in the winter of last year, and her dying words were that as it was not suitable for (Miao Yü) to return to her native place, she should await here, as something in the way of a denouement was certain to turn up; and this is the reason why she hasn't as yet borne the coffin back to her home!"

"If such be the case," madame Wang readily suggested, "why shouldn't we bring her here?"

"If we are to ask her," Lin Chih-hsiao's wife replied, "she'll say that a marquis' family and a duke's household are sure, in their honourable position, to be overbearing to people; and I had rather not go."

"As she's the daughter of an official family," madame Wang continued, "she's bound to be inclined to be somewhat proud; but what harm is there to our sending her a written invitation to ask her to come!"

Lin Chih-hsiao's wife assented; and leaving the room, she made the secretary write an invitation and then went to ask Miao Yü. The next day servants were despatched, and carriages and sedan chairs were got ready to go and bring her over.

What subsequently transpired is not as yet known, but, reader, listen to the account given in the following chapter.

CHAPTER XVIII.

His Majesty shows magnanimous bounty.
The Imperial consort Yuan pays a visit to her parents.
The happiness of a family gathering.
Pao-yü displays his polished talents.

But let us resume our story. A servant came, at this moment, to report that for the works in course of execution, they were waiting for gauze and damask silk to paste on various articles, and that they requested lady Feng to go and open the depôt for them to take the gauze and silk, while another servant also came to ask lady Feng to open the treasury for them to receive the gold and silver ware. And as Madame Wang, the waiting-maids and the other domestics of the upper rooms had all no leisure, Pao-ch'ai suggested: "Don't let us remain in here and be in the way of their doing what there is to be done, and of going where they have to go," and saying this, she betook herself, escorted by Pao-yü and the rest, into Ying Ch'un's rooms.

Madame Wang continued day after day in a great state of flurry and confusion, straight up to within the tenth moon, by which time every arrangement had been completed, and the overseers had all handed in a clear statement of their accounts. The curios and writing materials, wherever needed, had all already been laid out and everything got ready, and the birds (and animals), from the stork, the deer and rabbits to the chickens, geese and the like, had all been purchased and handed over to be reared in the various localities in the garden; and over at Chia Se's, had also been learnt twenty miscellaneous plays, while a company of young nuns and Taoist priestesses had likewise the whole number of them, mastered the intonation of Buddhist classics and incantations.

Chia Cheng after this, at length, was slightly composed in mind, and cheerful at heart; and having further invited dowager lady Chia and other inmates to go into the garden, he deliberated with them on, and made arrangements for, every detail in such a befitting manner that not the least trifle remained for which suitable provision had not been made; and Chia Cheng eventually mustered courage to indite a memorial, and on the very day on which the memorial was presented, a decree was received fixing upon the fifteenth day of the first moon of the ensuing year, the very day of the Shang Yuan festival, for the honourable consorts to visit their homes.

Upon the receipt of this decree, with which the Chia family was honoured, they had still less leisure, both by day as well as by night; so much so that they could not even properly observe the new year festivities. But in a twinkle of the eye, the festival of the full moon of the first moon drew near; and beginning from the eighth day of the first moon, eunuchs issued from the palace and inspected beforehand the various localities, the apartments in which the imperial consort was to change her costume; the place where she would spend her leisure moments; the spot where she would receive the conventionalities; the premises where the banquets would be spread; the quarters where she would retire for rest.

There were also eunuchs who came to assume the patrol of the grounds and the direction of the defences; and they brought along with them a good many minor eunuchs, whose duty it was to look after the safety of the various localities, to screen the place with enclosing curtains, to instruct the inmates and officials of the Chia mansion whither to go out and whence to come in from, what side the viands should be brought in from, where to report matters, and in the observance of every kind of etiquette; and for outside the mansion, there were, on the other hand, officers from the Board of Works, and a superintendent of the Police, of the "Five Cities," in charge of the sweeping of the streets and roads, and the clearing away of loungers. While Chia She and the others superintended the workmen in such things as the manufacture of flowered lanterns and fireworks.

The fourteenth day arrived and everything was in order; but on this night, one and all whether high or low, did not get a wink of sleep; and when the fifteenth came, every one, at the fifth watch, beginning from dowager lady Chia and those who enjoyed any official status, appeared in full gala dress, according to their respective ranks. In the garden, the curtains were, by this time, flapping like dragons, the portieres flying about like phoenixes with variegated plumage. Gold and silver glistened with splendour. Pearls and precious gems shed out their brilliant lustre. The tripod censers burnt the Pai-ho incense. In the vases were placed evergreens. Silence and stillness prevailed, and not a man ventured so much as to cough.

Chia She and the other men were standing outside the door giving on to the street on the west; and old lady Chia and the other ladies were outside the main entrance of the Jung mansion at the head of the street, while at the mouth of the lane were placed screens to rigorously obstruct the public gaze. They were unable to bear the fatigue of any further waiting when, at an unexpected moment, a eunuch arrived on horseback, and Chia Cheng went up to meet him, and ascertained what tidings he was the bearer of.

"It's as yet far too early," rejoined the eunuch, "for at one o'clock (her highness) will have her evening repast, and at two she has to betake herself to the Palace of Precious Perception to worship Buddha. At five, she will enter the Palace of Great Splendour to partake of a banquet, and to see the lanterns, after which, she will request His Majesty's permission; so that, I'm afraid, it won't be earlier than seven before they set out."

Lady Feng's ear caught what was said. "If such be the case," she interposed, "may it please your venerable ladyship, and you, my lady, to return for a while to your apartments, and wait; and if you come when it's time you'll be here none too late."

Dowager lady Chia and the other ladies immediately left for a time and suited their own convenience, and as everything in the garden devolved upon lady Feng to supervise, she ordered the butlers to take the eunuchs and give them something to eat and drink; and at the same time, she sent word that candles should be brought in and that the lanterns in the various places should be lit.

But unexpectedly was heard from outside the continuous patter of horses running, whereupon about ten eunuchs hurried in gasping and out of breath. They clapped their hands, and the several eunuchs (who had come before), understanding the signal, and knowing that the party had arrived, stood in their respective positions; while Chia She, at the head of all the men of the clan, remained at the western street door, and dowager lady Chia, at the head of the female relatives of the family, waited outside the principal entrance to do the honours.

For a long interval, everything was plunged in silence and quiet; when suddenly two eunuchs on horseback were espied advancing with leisurely step. Reaching the western street gate, they dismounted, and, driving their horses beyond the screens, they forthwith took their stand facing the west. After another long interval, a second couple arrived, and went likewise through the same proceedings. In a short time, drew near about ten couples, when, at length, were heard the gentle strains of music, and couple by couple advanced with banners, dragons, with fans made with phoenix feathers, and palace flabella of pheasant plumes; and those besides who carried gold-washed censers burning imperial incense. Next in order was brought past a state umbrella of golden yellow, with crooked handle and embroidered with seven phoenixes; after which quickly followed the crown, robe, girdle and shoes.

There were likewise eunuchs, who took a part in the procession, holding scented handkerchiefs and embroidered towels, cups for rinsing the mouth, dusters and other such objects; and company after company went past, when, at the rear, approached with stately step eight eunuchs carrying an imperial sedan chair, of golden yellow, with a gold knob and embroidered with phoenixes.

Old lady Chia and the other members of the family hastily fell on their knees, but a eunuch came over at once to raise her ladyship and the rest; and the imperial chair was thereupon carried through the main entrance, the ceremonial gate and into a court on the eastern side, at the door of which stood a eunuch, who prostrated himself and invited (her highness) to dismount and change her costume.

Having forthwith carried her inside the gate, the eunuchs dispersed; and only the maids-of-honour and ladies-in-waiting ushered Yuan Ch'un out of the chair, when what mainly attracted her eye in the park was the brilliant lustre of the flowered lamps of every colour, all of which were made of gauze or damask, and were beautiful in texture, and out of the common run; while on the upper side was a flat lantern with the inscription in four characters, "Regarded (by His Majesty's) benevolence and permeated by his benefits."

Yuan Ch'un entered the apartment and effected the necessary changes in her toilette; after which, she again egressed, and, mounting her chair, she made her entry into the garden, when she perceived the smoke of incense whirling and twirling, and the reflection of the flowers confusing the eyes. Far and wide, the rays of light, shed by the lanterns, intermingled their brilliancy, while, from time to time, fine strains of music sounded with clamorous din. But it would be impossible to express adequately the perfect harmony in the aspect of this scene, and the grandeur of affluence and splendour.

The imperial consort of the Chia family, we must now observe, upon catching sight, from the interior of her chair, of the picture presented within as well as without the confines of this garden, shook her head and heaved a sigh. "What lavish extravagance! What excessive waste!" she soliloquised.

But of a sudden was again seen a eunuch who, on his knees, invited her to get into a boat; and the Chia consort descended from the chair and stepped into the craft, when the expanse of a limpid stream met her gaze, whose grandeur resembled that of the dragon in its listless course. The stone bannisters, on each side, were one mass of airtight lanterns, of every colour, made of crystal or glass, which threw out a light like the lustre of silver or the brightness of snow.

The willow, almond and the whole lot of trees, on the upper side, were, it is true, without blossom and leaves; but pongee and damask silks, paper and lustring had been employed, together with rice-paper, to make flowers of, which had been affixed on the branches. Upon each tree were suspended thousands of lanterns; and what is more, the lotus and aquatic plants, the ducks and water fowl in the pond had all, in like manner, been devised out of conches and clams, plumes and feathers. The various lanterns, above and below, vied in refulgence. In real truth, it was a crystal region, a world of pearls and precious stones. On board the boat were also every kind of lanterns representing such designs as are used on flower-pots, pearl-laden portieres, embroidered curtains, oars of cinnamon wood, and paddles of magnolia, which need not of course be minutely described.

They entered a landing with a stone curb; and on this landing was erected a flat lantern upon which were plainly visible the four characters the "Persicary beach and flower-laden bank." But, reader, you have heard how that these four characters "the persicary beach and the flower-laden bank," the motto "a phoenix comes with dignified air," and the rest owe one and all their origin to the unexpected test to which Chia Cheng submitted, on a previous occasion, Pao-yü's literary abilities; but how did it come about that they were actually adopted?

You must remember that the Chia family had been, generation after generation, given to the study of letters, so that it was only natural that there should be among them one or two renowned writers of verses; for how could they ever resemble the families of such upstarts, who only employ puerile expressions as a makeshift to get through what they have to do? But the why and the wherefore must be sought in the past. The consort, belonging to the Chia mansion, had, before she entered the palace, been, from her infancy, also brought up by dowager lady Chia; and when Pao-yü was subsequently added to the family, she was the eldest sister and Pao-yü the youngest child. The Chia consort, bearing in mind how that she had, when her mother was verging on old age, at length obtained this younger brother, she for this reason doated upon him with single love; and as they were besides companions in their attendance upon old lady Chia, they were inseparable for even a moment. Before Pao-yü had entered school, and when three or four years of age, he had already received oral instruction from the imperial spouse Chia from the contents of several books and had committed to memory several thousands of characters, for though they were only sister and brother, they were like mother and child. And after she had entered the Palace, she was wont time and again to have letters taken out to her father and her cousins, urgently recommending them to be careful with his bringing up, that if they were not strict, he could not possibly become good for anything, and that if they were immoderately severe, there was the danger of something unpropitious befalling him, with the result, moreover, that his grandmother would be stricken with sorrow; and this solicitude on his account was never for an instant lost sight of by her.

Hence it was that Chia Cheng having, a few days back, heard his teacher extol him for his extreme abilities, he forthwith put him to the test on the occasion of their ramble through the garden. And though (his compositions) were not in the bold style of a writer of note, yet they were productions of their own family, and would, moreover, be instrumental, when the Chia consort had her notice attracted by them, and come to know that they were devised by her beloved brother, in also not rendering nugatory the anxious interest which she had ever entertained on his behalf, and he, therefore, purposely adopted what had been suggested by Pao-yü; while for those places, for which on that day no devices had been completed, a good number were again subsequently composed to make up what was wanted.

After the Chia consort had, for we shall now return to her, perused the four characters, she gave a smile. "The two words 'flower-laden bank,'" she said, "are really felicitous, so what use was there for 'persicary beach?'"

When the eunuch in waiting heard this observation, he promptly jumped off the craft on to the bank, and at a flying pace hurried to communicate it to Chia Cheng, and Chia Cheng instantly effected the necessary alteration.

By this time the craft had reached the inner bank, and leaving the boat, and mounting into her sedan chair, she in due course contemplated the magnificent Jade-like Palace; the Hall of cinnamon wood, lofty and sublime; and the marble portals with the four characters in bold style: the "Precious confines of heavenly spirits," which the Chia consort gave directions should be changed for the four words denoting: "additional Hall (for the imperial consort) on a visit to her parents." And forthwith making her entrance into the travelling lodge her gaze was attracted by torches burning in the court encompassing the heavens, fragments of incense strewn on the ground, fire-like trees and gem-like flowers, gold-like windows and jade-like bannisters. But it would be difficult to give a full account of the curtains, which rolled up (as fine as a) shrimp's moustache; of the carpets of other skins spread on the floor; of the tripods exhaling the fragrant aroma of the brain of the musk deer; of the screens in a row resembling fans made of pheasant tails. Indeed, the gold-like doors and the windows like jade were suggestive of the abode of spirits; while the halls made of cinnamon wood and the palace of magnolia timber, of the very homes of the imperial secondary consorts.

"Why is it," the Chia consort inquired, "that there is no tablet in this Hall?"

The eunuch in waiting fell on his knees. "This is the main Hall," he reverently replied, "and the officials, outside the palace, did not presume to take upon themselves to suggest any motto."

The Chia consort shook her head and said not a word; whereupon the eunuch, who acted as master of ceremonies, requested Her Majesty to ascend the throne and receive homage. The band stationed on the two flights of steps struck up a tune, while two eunuchs ushered Chia She, Chia Cheng and the other members on to the moonlike stage, where they arranged themselves in order and ascended into the hall, but when the ladies-in-waiting transmitted her commands that the homage could be dispensed with, they at once retraced their footsteps.

(The master of the ceremonies), in like manner led forward the dowager lady of the Jung Kuo mansion, as well as the female relatives, from the steps on the east side, on to the moon-like stage; where they were placed according to their ranks. But the maids-of-honour again commanded that they should dispense with the ceremony, so they likewise promptly withdrew.

After tea had been thrice presented, the Chia consort descended the Throne, and the music ceased. She retired into a side room to change her costume, and the private chairs were then got ready for her visit to her parents. Issuing from the garden, she came into the main quarters belonging to dowager lady Chia, where she was bent upon observing the domestic conventionalities, when her venerable ladyship, and the other members of the family, prostrated themselves in a body before her, and made her desist. Tears dropped down from the eyes of the Chia consort as (she and her relatives) mutually came forward, and greeted each other, and as with one hand she grasped old lady Chia, and with the other she held madame Wang, the three had plenty in their hearts which they were fain to speak about; but, unable as each one of them was to give utterance to their feelings, all they did was to sob and to weep, as they kept face to face to each other; while madame Hsing, widow Li Wan, Wang Hsi-feng, and the three sisters: Ying Ch'un, T'an Ch'un, and Hsi Ch'un, stood aside in a body shedding tears and saying not a word.

After a long time, the Chia consort restrained her anguish, and forcing a smile, she set to work to reassure old lady Chia and madame Wang. "Having in days gone by," she urged, "been sent to that place where no human being can be seen, I have to-day after extreme difficulty returned home; and now that you ladies and I have been reunited, instead of chatting or laughing we contrariwise give way to incessant tears! But shortly, I shall be gone, and who knows when we shall be able again to even see each other!"

When she came to this sentence, they could not help bursting into another tit of crying; and Madame Hsing hastened to come forward, and to console dowager lady Chia and the rest. But when the Chia consort resumed her seat, and one by one came again, in turn, to exchange salutations, they could not once more help weeping and sobbing for a time.

Next in order, were the managers and servants of the eastern and western mansions to perform their obeisance in the outer pavilion; and after the married women and waiting-maids had concluded their homage, the Chia consort heaved a sigh. "How many relatives," she observed, "there are all of whom, alas! I may not see."

"There are here now," madame Wang rejoined with due respect, "kindred with outside family names, such as Mrs. Hsüeh, née Wang, Pao-ch'ai, and Tai-yü waiting for your commands; but as they are distant relatives, and without official status, they do not venture to arrogate to themselves the right of entering into your presence." But the Chia consort issued directions that they should be invited to come that they should see each other; and in a short while, Mrs. Hsüeh and the other relatives walked in, but as they were on the point of performing the rites, prescribed by the state, she bade them relinquish the observance so that they came forward, and each, in turn, alluded to what had transpired during the long separation.

Pao Ch'in also and a few other waiting-maids, whom the Chia consort had originally taken along with her into the palace, knocked their heads before dowager lady Chia, but her ladyship lost no time in raising them up, and in bidding them go into a separate suite of rooms to be entertained; and as for the retainers, eunuchs as well as maids-of-honour, ladies-in-waiting and every attendant, there were needless to say, those in the two places, the Ning mansion and Chia She's residence, to wait upon them; there only remained three or four young eunuchs to answer the summons.

The mother and daughter and her cousins conversed for some time on what had happened during the protracted separation, as well as on domestic affairs and their private feelings, when Chia Cheng likewise advanced as far as the other side of the portiere, and inquired after her health, and the Chia consort from inside performed the homage and other conventionalities (due to her parent).

"The families of farmers," she further went on to say to her father, "feed on salted cabbage, and clothe in cotton material; but they readily enjoy the happiness of the relationships established by heaven! We, however, relatives though we now be of one bone and flesh, are, with all our affluence and honours, living apart from each other, and deriving no happiness whatsoever!"

Chia Cheng, on his part endeavoured, to restrain his tears. "I belonged," he rejoined, "to a rustic and poor family; and among that whole number of pigeons and pheasants, how could I have imagined that I would have obtained the blessing of a hidden phoenix! Of late all for the sake of your honourable self, His Majesty, above, confers upon us his heavenly benefits; while we, below, show forth the virtue of our ancestors! And it is mainly because the vital principle of the hills, streams, sun, and moon, and the remote virtue of our ancestors have been implanted in you alone that this good fortune has attained me Cheng and my wife! Moreover, the present emperor, bearing in mind the great bounty shewn by heaven and earth in promoting a ceaseless succession, has vouchsafed a more generous act of grace than has ever been displayed from old days to the present. And although we may besmear our liver and brain in the mire, how could we show our gratitude, even to so slight a degree as one ten-thousandth part. But all I can do is, in the daytime, to practise diligence, vigilance at night, and loyalty in my official duties. My humble wish is that His Majesty, my master, may live ten thousand years and see thousands of autumns, so as to promote the welfare of all mankind in the world! And you, worthy imperial consort, must, on no account, be mindful of me Cheng and my wife, decrepid as we are in years. What I would solicit more than anything is that you should be more careful of yourself, and that you should be diligent and reverential in your service to His Majesty, with the intent that you may not prove ungrateful of his affectionate regard and bountiful grace."

The Chia consort, on the other hand, enjoined "that much as it was expedient to display zeal, in the management of state matters, it behoved him, when he had any leisure, to take good care of himself, and that he should not, whatever he did, give way to solicitude on her behalf." And Chia Cheng then went on to say "that the various inscriptions in the park over the pavilions, terraces, halls and residences had been all composed by Pao-yü, and, that in the event of there being one or two that could claim her attention, he would be happy if it would please her to at once favour him with its name." Whereupon the imperial consort Yüan, when she heard that Pao-yü could compose verses, forthwith exclaimed with a smile: "He has in very truth made progress!"

After Chia Cheng had retired out of the hall, the Chia consort made it a point to ask: "How is it that I do not see Pao-yü?" and dowager lady Chia explained: "An outside male relative as he is, and without official rank, he does not venture to appear before you of his own accord."

"Bring him in!" the imperial consort directed; whereupon a young eunuch ushered Pao-yü in. After he had first complied with the state ceremonies, she bade him draw near to her, and taking his hand, she held it in her lap, and, as she went on to caress his head and neck, she smiled and said: "He's grown considerably taller than he was before;" but she had barely concluded this remark, when her tears ran down as profuse as rain. Mrs. Yu, lady Feng, and the rest pressed forward. "The banquet is quite ready," they announced, "and your highness is requested to favour the place with your presence."

The imperial consort Yuan stood up and asking Pao-yü to lead the way, she followed in his steps, along with the whole party, and betook herself on foot as far as the entrance of the garden gate, whence she at once espied, in the lustre shed by the lanterns, every kind of decorations. Entering the garden, they first passed the spots with the device "a phoenix comes with dignified air," "the red (flowers are) fragrant and the green (banana leaves like) jade!" "the sign on the apricot tree is visible," "the fragrance pure of the ligularia and iris," and other places; and ascending the towers they walked up the halls, forded the streams and wound round the hills; contemplating as they turned their gaze from side to side, each place arranged in a different style, and each kind of article laid out in unique designs. The Chia consort expressed her admiration in most profuse eulogiums, and then went on to advise them: "that it was not expedient to indulge in future in such excessive extravagance and that all these arrangements were over and above what should have been done."

Presently they reached the main pavilion, where she commanded that they could dispense with the rites and take their seats. A sumptuous banquet was laid out, at which dowager lady Chia and the other ladies occupied the lower seats and entertained each other, while Mrs. Yu, widow Li Wan, lady Feng and the rest presented the soup and handed the cups. The Imperial consort Yuan subsequently directed that the pencils and inkslabs should be brought, and with her own hands she opened the silken paper. She chose the places she liked, and conferred upon them a name; and devising a general designation for the garden, she called it the Ta Kuan garden (Broad vista), while for the tablet of the main pavilion the device she composed ran as follows: "Be mindful of the grace and remember the equity (of His Majesty);" with this inscription on the antithetical scrolls:

Mercy excessive Heaven and earth display,
And it men young and old hail gratefully;
From old till now they pour their bounties great
Those rich gifts which Cathay and all states permeate.

Changing also the text: "A phoenix comes with dignified air for the Hsiao Hsiang Lodge."

"The red (flowers are) fragrant and the green (banana leaves like) jade," she altered into "Happy red and joyful green"; bestowing upon the place the appellation of the I Hung court (joyful red). The spot where "the fragrance pure of the ligularia and iris," was inscribed, she called "the ligularia and the 'Wu' weed court;" and where was "the sign in the apricot tree is visible," she designated "the cottage in the hills where dolichos is bleached." The main tower she called the Broad Vista Tower. The lofty tower facing the east, she designated "the variegated and flowery Hall;" bestowing on the line of buildings, facing the west, the appellation of "the Hall of Occult Fragrance;" and besides these figured such further names as: "the Hall of peppery wind," "the Arbour of lotus fragrance," "the Islet of purple caltrop," "the Bank of golden lotus," and the like. There were also tablets with four characters such as: "the peach blossom and the vernal rain;" "the autumnal wind prunes the Eloecocca," "the artemisia leaves and the night snow," and other similar names which could not all be placed on record. She furthermore directed that such tablets as were already put up, should not be dismounted, and she forthwith took the lead and composed an heptameter stanza, the burden of which was:

Hills it enclasps, embraces streams, with skill it is laid out:
What task the grounds to raise! the works to start and bring about!
Of scenery in heaven and amongst men store has been made;
The name Broad Vista o'er the fragrant park should be engraved.

When she had finished writing, she observed smilingly, as she addressed herself to all the young ladies: "I have all along lacked the quality of sharpness and never besides been good at verses; as you, sisters, and all of you have ever been aware; but, on a night like this I've been fain to do my best, with the object of escaping censure, and of not reflecting injustice on this scenery and nothing more. But some other day when I've got time, be it ever so little, I shall deem it my duty to make up what remains by inditing a record of the Broad Vista Garden, as well as a song on my visit to my parents and other such literary productions in memory of the events of this day. You sisters and others must, each of you, in like manner compose a stanza on the motto on each tablet, expressing your sentiments, as you please, without being restrained by any regard for my meagre ability. Knowing as I do besides that Pao-yü is, indeed, able to write verses, I feel the more delighted! But among his compositions, those I like the best are those in the two places, 'the Hsiao Hsiang Lodge,' and 'the court of Heng and Wu;' and next those of 'the Joyful red court,' and 'the cottage in the hills, where the dolichos is bleached.' As for grand sites like these four, there should be found some out-of-the-way expressions to insert in the verses so that they should be felicitous. The antithetical lines composed by you, (Pao-yü), on a former occasion are excellent, it is true; but you should now further indite for each place, a pentameter stanza, so that by allowing me to test you in my presence, you may not show yourself ungrateful for the trouble I have taken in teaching you from your youth up."

Pao-yü had no help but to assent, and descending from the hall, he went off all alone to give himself up to reflection.

Of the three Ying Ch'un, T'an Ch'un, and Hsi Ch'un, T'an Ch'un must be considered to have also been above the standard of her sisters, but she, in her own estimation, imagined it, in fact, difficult to compete with Hsüeh Pao-ch'ai and Lin Tai-yü. With no alternative however than that of doing her best, she followed the example of all the rest with the sole purpose of warding off criticism. And Li Wan too succeeded, after much exertion, in putting together a stanza.

The consort of the Chia family perused in due order the verses written by the young ladies, the text of which is given below.

The lines written by Ying Ch'un on the tablet of "Boundless spirits and blissful heart" were:

A park laid out with scenery surpassing fine and rare!
Submissive to thy will, on boundless bliss bashful I write!
Who could believe that yonder scenes in this world found a share!
Will not thy heart be charmed on thy visit by the sight?

These are the verses by T'an Ch'un on the tablet of "All nature vies in splendour":

Of aspect lofty and sublime is raised a park of fame!
Honoured with thy bequest, my shallow lore fills me with shame.
No words could e'er amply exhaust the beauteous skill,
For lo! in very truth glory and splendour all things fill!

Thus runs Hsi Ch'un's stanza on the tablet of the "Conception of literary compositions":

The hillocks and the streams crosswise beyond a thousand li extend!
The towers and terraces 'midst the five-coloured clouds lofty ascend!
In the resplendent radiance of both sun and moon the park it lies!
The skill these scenes to raise the skill e'en essays to conceive
outvies!

The lines composed by Li Wan on the tablet "grace and elegance," consisted of:

The comely streams and hillocks clear, in double folds, embrace;
E'en Fairyland, forsooth, transcend they do in elegance and grace!
The "Fragrant Plant" the theme is of the ballad fan, green-made.
Like drooping plum-bloom flap the lapel red and the Hsiang gown.
From prosperous times must have been handed down those pearls and
jade.
What bliss! the fairy on the jasper terrace will come down!
When to our prayers she yields, this glorious park to contemplate,
No mortal must e'er be allowed these grounds to penetrate.

The ode by Hsüeh Pao-ch'ai on the tablet of "Concentrated Splendour and Accumulated auspiciousness" was:

Raised on the west of the Imperial city, lo! the park stored with
fragrant smell,
Shrouded by Phoebe's radiant rays and clouds of good omen, in wondrous
glory lies!
The willows tall with joy exult that the parrots their nests have

shifted from the dell.
The bamboo groves, when laid, for the phoenix with dignity to come, were meant to rise.
The very eve before the Empress' stroll, elegant texts were ready and affixed.
If even she her parents comes to see, how filial piety supreme must be!
When I behold her beauteous charms and talents supernatural, with awe
transfixed,
One word, to utter more how can I troth ever presume, when shame overpowers me.

The distich by Lin Tai-yü on the tablet of "Spiritual stream outside the world," ran thus:

Th' imperial visit doth enhance joy and delight.
This fairy land from mortal scenes what diff'rent sight!
The comely grace it borrows of both hill and stream;
And to the landscape it doth add a charm supreme.
The fumes of Chin Ku wine everything permeate;
The flowers the inmate of the Jade Hall fascinate.
The imperial favour to receive how blessed our lot!
For oft the palace carriage will pass through this spot.

The Chia consort having concluded the perusal of the verses, and extolled them for a time: "After all," she went on to say with a smile, "those composed by my two cousins, Hsüeh Pao-ch'ai and Lin Tai-yü, differ in excellence from those of all the rest; and neither I, stupid as I am, nor my sisters can attain their standard."

Lin Tao-yü had, in point of fact, made up her mind to display, on this evening, her extraordinary abilities to their best advantage, and to put down every one else, but contrary to her expectations the Chia consort had expressed her desire that no more than a single stanza should be written on each tablet, so that unable, after all, to disregard her directions by writing anything in excess, she had no help but to compose a pentameter stanza, in an offhand way, merely with the intent of complying with her wishes.

Pao-yü had by this time not completed his task. He had just finished two stanzas on the Hsiao Hsiang Lodge and the Heng Wu garden, and was just then engaged in composing a verse on the "Happy red Court." In his draft figured a line: "The (leaves) of jade-like green in spring are yet rolled up," which Pao-ch'ai stealthily observed as she turned her eyes from side to side; and availing herself of the very first moment, when none of the company could notice her, she gave him a nudge. "As her highness," she remarked, "doesn't relish the four characters, representing the red (flowers are) fragrant, and the green (banana leaves) like jade, she changed them, just a while back, for 'the joyful red and gladsome green;' and if you deliberately now again employ these two words 'jade-like green,' won't it look as if you were bent upon being at variance with her? Besides, very many are the old books, in which the banana leaves form the theme, so you had better think of another line and substitute it and have done with it!"

When Pao-yü heard the suggestion made by Pao-ch'ai, he speedily replied, as he wiped off the perspiration: "I can't at all just at present call to mind any passage from the contents of some old book."

"Just simply take," proposed Pao-ch'ai smilingly, "the character jade in jade-like green and change it into the character wax, that's all."

"Does 'green wax,'" Pao-yü inquired, "come out from anywhere?"

Pao-ch'ai gently smacked her lips and nodded her head as she laughed. "I fear," she said, "that if, on an occasion like to-night, you show no more brains than this, by and by when you have to give any answers in the golden hall, to the questions (of the examiner), you will, really, forget (the very first four names) of Chao, Oh'ien, Sun and Li (out of the hundred)! What, have you so much as forgotten the first line of the poem by Han Yü, of the T'ang dynasty, on the Banana leaf:

"Cold is the candle and without a flame, the green wax dry?"

On hearing these words, Pao-yü's mind suddenly became enlightened. "What a fool I am!" he added with a simper; "I couldn't for the moment even remember the lines, ready-made though they were and staring at me in my very eyes! Sister, you really can be styled my teacher, little though you may have taught me, and I'll henceforward address you by no other name than 'teacher,' and not call you 'sister' any more!"

"Don't you yet hurry to go on," Pao-ch'ai again observed in a gentle tone of voice sneeringly, "but keep on calling me elder sister and younger sister? Who's your sister? that one over there in a yellow coat is your sister!"

But apprehending, as she bandied these jokes, lest she might be wasting his time, she felt constrained to promptly move away; whereupon Pao-yü continued the ode he had been working at, and brought it to a close, writing in all three stanzas.

Tai-yü had not had so far an opportunity of making a display of her ability, and was feeling at heart in a very dejected mood; but when she perceived that Pao-yü was having intense trouble in conceiving what he had to write, and she found, upon walking up to the side of the table, that he had only one stanza short, that on "the sign on the apricot tree is visible," she consequently bade him copy out clean the first three odes, while she herself composed a stanza, which she noted down on a slip of paper, rumpled up into a ball, and threw just in front of Pao-yü.

As soon as Pao-yü opened it and glanced at it, he realised that it was a hundred times better than his own three stanzas, and transcribing it without loss of time, in a bold writing, he handed up his compositions.

On perusal, the Chia Consort read what follows. By Pao-yü, on: "A phoenix comes with dignified air:"

The bamboos just now don that jadelike grace,
Which worthy makes them the pheasant to face;
Each culm so tender as if to droop fain,
Each one so verdant, in aspect so cool,
The curb protects, from the steps wards the pool.
The pervious screens the tripod smell restrain.
The shadow will be strewn, mind do not shake
And (Hsieh) from her now long fine dream (awake)!

On "the pure fragrance of the Ligularia and Iris Florentina:"

Hengs and Wus the still park permeate;
The los and pis their sweet perfume enhance;
And supple charms the third spring flowers ornate;
Softly is wafted one streak of fragrance!
A light mist doth becloud the tortuous way!
With moist the clothes bedews, that verdure cold!
The pond who ever sinuous could hold?
Dreams long and subtle, dream the household Hsieh.

On "the happy red and joyful green:"

Stillness pervades the deep pavilion on a lengthy day.
The green and red, together matched, transcendent grace display.
Unfurled do still remain in spring the green and waxlike leaves.
No sleep yet seeks the red-clad maid, though night's hours be
far-spent,
But o'er the rails lo, she reclines, dangling her ruddy sleeves;
Against the stone she leans shrouded by taintless scent,
And stands the quarter facing whence doth blow the eastern wind!
Her lord and master must look up to her with feelings kind.

On "the sign on the apricot tree is visible:"

The apricot tree sign to drink wayfarers doth invite;
A farm located on a hill, lo! yonder strikes the sight!
And water caltrops, golden lotus, geese, as well as flows,
And mulberry and elm trees which afford rest to swallows.
That wide extent of spring leeks with verdure covers the ground;
And o'er ten li the paddy blossom fragrance doth abound.
In days of plenty there's a lack of dearth and of distress,
And what need then is there to plough and weave with such briskness?

When the Chia consort had done with the perusal, excessive joy filled her heart. "He has indeed made progress!" she exclaimed, and went on to point at the verses on "the sign on the apricot tree," as being the crowning piece of the four stanzas. In due course, she with her own hands changed the motto "a cottage in the hills where dolichos is bleached" into "the paddy-scented village;" and bidding also T'an Ch'un to take the several tens of stanzas written then, and to transcribe them separately on ornamented silk paper, she commanded a eunuch to send them to the outer quarters. And when Chia Cheng and the other men perused them, one and all sung their incessant praise, while Chia Cheng, on his part, sent in some complimentary message, with regard to her return home on a visit.

Yuan Ch'un went further and gave orders that luscious wines, a ham and other such presents should be conferred upon Pao-yü, as well as upon Chia Lan. This Chia Lan was as yet at this time a perfect youth without any knowledge of things in general, so that all that he could do was to follow the example of his mother, and imitate his uncle in performing the conventional rites.

At the very moment that Chia Se felt unable, along with a company of actresses, to bear the ordeal of waiting on the ground floor of the two-storied building, he caught sight of a eunuch come running at a flying pace. "The composition of verses is over," he said, "so quick give me the programme;" whereupon Chia Se hastened to present the programme as well as a roll of the names of the twelve girls. And not a long interval elapsed before four plays were chosen; No. 1 being the Imperial Banquet; No. 2 Begging (the weaver goddess) for skill in needlework; No. 3 The spiritual match; and No. 4 the Parting spirit. Chia Se speedily lent a hand in the getting up, and the preparations for the performance, and each of the girls sang with a voice sufficient to split the stones and danced in the manner of heavenly spirits; and though their exterior was that of the characters in which they were dressed up for the play, their acting nevertheless represented, in a perfect manner, both sorrow as well as joy. As soon as the performance was brought to a close, a eunuch walked in holding a golden salver containing cakes, sweets, and the like, and inquired who was Ling Kuan; and Chia Se readily concluding that these articles were presents bestowed upon Ling Kuan, made haste to take them over, as he bade Ling Kuan prostrate herself.

"The honourable consort," the eunuch further added, "directs that Ling Kuan, who is the best actress of the lot, should sing two more songs; any two will do, she does not mind what they are."

Chia Se at once expressed his obedience, and felt constrained to urge Ling Kuan to sing the two ballads entitled: "The walk through the garden" and "Frightened out of a dream." But Ling Kuan asserted that these two ballads had not originally been intended for her own role; and being firm in her refusal to accede and insisting upon rendering the two songs "The Mutual Promise" and "The Mutual Abuse," Chia Se found it hard to bring her round, and had no help but to let her have her own way. The Chia consort was so extremely enchanted with her that she gave directions that she should not be treated harshly, and that this girl should receive a careful training, while besides the fixed number of presents, she gave her two rolls of palace silk, two purses, gold and silver ingots, and presents in the way of eatables.

Subsequently, when the banquet had been cleared, and she once more prosecuted her visit through those places to which she had not been, she quite accidentally espied the Buddhist Temple encircled by hills, and promptly rinsing her hands, she walked in and burnt incense and worshipped Buddha. She also composed the device for a tablet, "a humane boat on the (world's) bitter sea," and went likewise so far as to show special acts of additional grace to a company of ascetic nuns and Taoist priestesses.

A eunuch came in a short while and reverently fell on his knees. "The presents are all in readiness," he reported, "and may it please you to inspect them and to distribute them, in compliance with custom;" and presented to her a list, which the Chia consort perused from the very top throughout without raising any objection, and readily commanding that action should be taken according to the list, a eunuch descended and issued the gifts one after another. The presents for dowager lady Chia consisted, it may be added, of two sceptres, one of gold, the other of jade, with "may your wishes be fulfilled" inscribed on them; a staff made of lign-aloes; a string of chaplet beads of Chia-nan fragrant wood; four rolls of imperial satins with words "Affluence and honours" and Perennial Spring (woven in them); four rolls of imperial silk with Perennial Happiness and Longevity; two shoes of purple gold bullion, representing a pen, an ingot and "as you like;" and ten silver ingots with the device "Felicitous Blessings." While the two shares for madame Hsing and madame Wang were only short of hers by the sceptres and staffs, four things in all. Chia She, Chia Cheng and the others had each apportioned to him a work newly written by the Emperor, two boxes of superior ink, and gold and silver cups, two pairs of each; their other gifts being identical with those above. Pao-ch'ai, Tai-yü, all the sisters and the rest were assigned each a copy of a new book, a fine slab and two pair of gold and silver ornaments of a novel kind and original shape; Pao-yü likewise receiving the same presents. Chia Lan's gifts consisted of two necklets, one of gold, the other of silver, and of two pair of gold ingots. Mrs. Yu, widow Li Wan, lady Feng and the others had each of them, four ingots of gold and silver; and, in the way of keepsakes, four pieces of silk. There were, in addition, presents consisting of twenty-four pieces of silk and a thousand strings of good cash to be allotted to the nurses, and waiting-maids, in the apartments of dowager lady Chia, madame Wang and of the respective sisters; while Chia Chen, Chia Lien, Chia Huan, Chia Jung and the rest had, every one, for presents, a piece of silk, and a pair of gold and silver ingots.

As regards the other gifts, there were a hundred rolls of various coloured silks, a thousand ounces of pure silver, and several bottles of imperial wine, intended to be bestowed upon all the men-servants of the mansions, on the East and the West, as well as upon those who had been in the garden overseeing works, arranging the decorations, and in waiting to answer calls, and upon those who looked after the theatres and managed the lanterns. There being, besides, five hundred strings of pure cash for the cooks, waiters, jugglers and hundreds of actors and every kind of domestic.

The whole party had finished giving expression to their thanks for her bounty, when the managers and eunuchs respectfully announced: "It is already a quarter to three, and may it please your Majesty to turn back your imperial chariot;" whereupon, much against her will, the Chia consort's eyes brimmed over, and she once more gave vent to tears. Forcing herself however again to put on a smile, she clasped old lady Chia's and madame Wang's hands, and could not bring herself to let them go; while she repeatedly impressed upon their minds: that there was no need to give way to any solicitude, and that they should take good care of their healths; that the grace of the present emperor was so vast, that once a month he would grant permission for them to enter the palace and pay her a visit. "It is easy enough for us to see each other," (she said,) "and why should we indulge in any excess of grief? But when his majesty in his heavenly generosity allows me another time to return home, you shouldn't go in for such pomp and extravagance."

Dowager lady Chia and the other inmates had already cried to such an extent that sobs choked their throats and they could with difficulty give utterance to speech. But though the Chia consort could not reconcile herself to the separation, the usages in vogue in the imperial household could not be disregarded or infringed, so that she had no alternative but to stifle the anguish of her heart, to mount her chariot, and take her departure.

The whole family experienced meanwhile a hard task before they succeeded in consoling the old lady and madame Wang and in supporting them away out of the garden. But as what follows is not ascertained, the next chapter will disclose it.

CHAPTER XIX.

In the vehemence of her feelings, Hua (Hsi Jen) on a quiet evening admonishes Pao-yü.
While (the spell) of affection continues unbroken, Pao-yü, on a still day, perceives the fragrance emitted from Tai-yü's person.

The Chia consort, we must now go on to explain, returned to the Palace, and the next day, on her appearance in the presence of His Majesty, she thanked him for his bounty and gave him furthermore an account of her experiences on her visit home. His Majesty's dragon countenance was much elated, and he also issued from the privy store coloured satins, gold and silver and such like articles to be presented to Chia Cheng and the other officials in the various households of her relatives. But dispensing with minute details about them, we will now revert to the two mansions of Jung and Ning.

With the extreme strain on mind and body for successive days, the strength of one and all was, in point of fact, worn out and their respective energies exhausted. And it was besides after they had been putting by the various decorations and articles of use for two or three days, that they, at length, got through the work.

Lady Feng was the one who had most to do, and whose responsibilities were greatest. The others could possibly steal a few leisure moments and retire to rest, while she was the sole person who could not slip away. In the second place, naturally anxious as she was to excel and both to fall in people's estimation, she put up with the strain just as if she were like one of those who had nothing to attend to. But the one who had the least to do and had the most leisure was Pao-yü.

As luck would have it on this day, at an early hour, Hsi Jen's mother came again in person and told dowager lady Chia that she would take Hsi Jen home to drink a cup of tea brewed in the new year and that she would return in the evening. For this reason Pao-yü was only in the company of all the waiting-maids, throwing dice, playing at chess and amusing himself. But while he was in the room playing with them with a total absence of zest, he unawares perceived a few waiting-maids arrive, who informed him that their senior master Mr. Chen, of the Eastern Mansion, had come to invite him to go and see a theatrical performance, and the fireworks, which were to be let off.

Upon hearing these words, Pao-yü speedily asked them to change his clothes; but just as he was ready to start, presents of cream, steamed with sugar, arrived again when least expected from the Chia Consort, and Pao-yü recollecting with what relish Hsi Jen had partaken of this dish on the last occasion forthwith bid them keep it for her; while he went himself and told dowager lady Chia that he was going over to see the play.

The plays sung over at Chia Chen's consisted, who would have thought it, of "Ting L'ang recognises his father," and "Huang Po-ying deploys the spirits for battle," and in addition to these, "Sung Hsing-che causes great commotion in the heavenly palace;" "Ghiang T'ai-kung kills the general and deifies him," and other such like. Soon appeared the spirits and devils in a confused crowd on the stage, and suddenly also became visible the whole band of sprites and goblins, among which were some waving streamers, as they went past in a procession, invoking Buddha and burning incense. The sound of the gongs and drums and of shouts and cries were audible at a distance beyond the lane; and in the whole street, one and all extolled the performance as exceptionally grand, and that the like could never have been had in the house of any other family.

Pao-yü, noticing that the commotion and bustle had reached a stage so unbearable to his taste, speedily betook himself, after merely sitting for a little while, to other places in search of relaxation and fun. First of all, he entered the inner rooms, and after spending some time in chatting and laughing with Mrs. Yu, the waiting-maids, and secondary wives, he eventually took his departure out of the second gate; and as Mrs. Yu and her companions were still under the impression that he was going out again to see the play, they let him speed on his way, without so much as keeping an eye over him.

Chia Chen, Chia Lien, Hsúeh P'an and the others were bent upon guessing enigmas, enforcing the penalties and enjoying themselves in a hundred and one ways, so that even allowing that they had for a moment noticed that he was not occupying his seat, they must merely have imagined that he had gone inside and not, in fact, worried their minds about him. And as for the pages, who had come along with Pao-yü, those who were a little advanced in years, knowing very well that Pao-yü would, on an occasion like the present, be sure not to be going before dusk, stealthily therefore took advantage of his absence, those, who could, to gamble for money, and others to go to the houses of relatives and friends to drink of the new year tea, so that what with gambling and drinking the whole bevy surreptitiously dispersed, waiting for dusk before they came back; while those, who were younger, had all crept into the green rooms to watch the excitement; with the result that Pao-yü perceiving not one of them about bethought himself of a small reading room, which existed in previous days on this side, in which was suspended a picture of a beauty so artistically executed as to look life-like. "On such a bustling day as this," he reasoned, "it's pretty certain, I fancy, that there will be no one in there; and that beautiful person must surely too feel lonely, so that it's only right that I should go and console her a bit." With these thoughts, he hastily betook himself towards the side-house yonder, and as soon as he came up to the window, he heard the sound of groans in the room. Pao-yü was really quite startled. "What!" (he thought), "can that beautiful girl, possibly, have come to life!" and screwing up his courage, he licked a hole in the paper of the window and peeped in. It was not she, however, who had come to life, but Ming Yen holding down a girl and likewise indulging in what the Monitory Dream Fairy had taught him.

"Dreadful!" exclaimed Pao-yü, aloud, unable to repress himself, and, stamping one of his feet, he walked into the door to the terror of both of them, who parting company, shivered with fear, like clothes that are being shaken. Ming Yen perceiving that it was Pao-yü promptly fell on his knees and piteously implored for pardon.

"What! in broad daylight! what do you mean by it? Were your master Mr. Chen to hear of it, would you die or live?" asked Pao-yü, as he simultaneously cast a glance at the servant-girl, who although not a beauty was anyhow so spick and span, and possessed besides a few charms sufficient to touch the heart. From shame, her face was red and her ears purple, while she lowered her head and uttered not a syllable.

Pao-yü stamped his foot. "What!" he shouted, "don't you yet bundle yourself away!"

This simple remark suggested the idea to the girl's mind who ran off, as if she had wings to fly with; but as Pao-yü went also so far as to go in pursuit of her, calling out: "Don't be afraid, I'm not one to tell anyone," Ming Yen was so exasperated that he cried, as he went after them, "My worthy ancestor, this is distinctly telling people about it."

"How old is that servant girl?" Pao-yü having asked; "She's, I expect, no more than sixteen or seventeen," Ming Yen rejoined.

"Well, if you haven't gone so far as to even ascertain her age," Pao-yü observed, "you're sure to know still less about other things; and it makes it plain enough that her acquaintance with you is all vain and futile! What a pity! what a pity!"

He then went on to enquire what her name was; and "Were I," continued Ming Yen smiling, "to tell you about her name it would involve a long yarn; it's indeed a novel and strange story! She relates that while her mother was nursing her, she dreamt a dream and obtained in this dream possession of a piece of brocaded silk, on which were designs, in variegated colours, representing opulence and honour, and a continuous line of the character Wan; and that this reason accounts for the name of Wan Erh, which was given her."

"This is really strange!" Pao-yü exclaimed with a grin, after lending an ear to what he had to say; "and she is bound, I think, by and by to have a good deal of good fortune!"

These words uttered, he plunged in deep thought for a while, and Ming Yen having felt constrained to inquire: "Why aren't you, Mr. Secundus, watching a theatrical performance of this excellent kind?" "I had been looking on for ever so long," Pao-yü replied, "until I got quite weary; and had just come out for a stroll, when I happened to meet you two. But what's to be done now?"

Ming Yen gave a faint smile. "As there's no one here to know anything about it," he added, "I'll stealthily take you, Mr. Secundus, for a walk outside the city walls; and we'll come back shortly, before they've got wind of it."

"That won't do," Pao-yü demurred, "we must be careful, or else some beggar might kidnap us away; besides, were they to come to hear of it, there'll be again a dreadful row; and isn't it better that we should go to some nearer place, from which we could, after all, return at once?"

"As for some nearer place," Ming Yen observed; "to whose house can we go? It's really no easy matter!"

"My idea is," Pao-yü suggested with a smirk, "that we should simply go, and find sister Hua, and see what she's up to at home."

"Yes! Yes!" Ming Yen replied laughingly; "the fact is I had forgotten all about her home; but should it reach their ears," he continued, "they'll say that it was I who led you, Mr. Secundus, astray, and they'll beat me!"

"I'm here for you!" Pao-yü having assured him; Ming Yen at these words led the horses round, and the two of them speedily made their exit by the back gate. Luckily Hsi Jen's house was not far off. It was no further than half a li's distance, so that in a twinkle they had already reached the front of the door, and Ming Yen was the first to walk in and to call for Hsi Jen's eldest brother Hua Tzu-fang.

Hsi Jen's mother had, on this occasion, united in her home Hsi Jen, several of her sister's daughters, as well as a few of her nieces, and they were engaged in partaking of fruits and tea, when they heard some one outside call out, "Brother Hua." Hua Tzu-fang lost no time in rushing out; and upon looking and finding that it was the two of them, the master and his servant, he was so taken by surprise that his fears could not be set at rest. Promptly, he clasped Pao-yü in his arms and dismounted him, and coming into the court, he shouted out at the top of his voice: "Mr. Pao has come." The other persons heard the announcement of his arrival, with equanimity, but when it reached Hsi Jen's ears, she truly felt at such a loss to fathom the object of his visit that issuing hastily out of the room, she came to meet Pao-yü, and as she laid hold of him: "Why did you come?" she asked.

"I felt awfully dull," Pao-yü rejoined with a smile, "and came to see what you were up to."

Hsi Jen at these words banished, at last, all anxiety from her mind. "You're again up to your larks," she observed, "but what's the aim of your visit? Who else has come along with him?" she at the same time went on to question Ming Yen.

"All the others know nothing about it!" explained Ming Yen exultingly; "only we two do, that's all."

When Hsi Jen heard this remark, she gave way afresh to solicitous fears: "This is dreadful!" she added; "for were you to come across any one from the house, or to meet master; or were, in the streets, people to press against you, or horses to collide with you, as to make (his horse) shy, and he were to fall, would that too be a joke? The gall of both of you is larger than a peck measure; but it's all you, Ming Yen, who has incited him, and when I go back, I'll surely tell the nurses to beat you."

Ming Yen pouted his mouth. "Mr. Secundus," he pleaded, "abused me and beat me, as he bade me bring him here, and now he shoves the blame on my shoulders! 'Don't let us go,' I suggested; 'but if you do insist, well then let us go and have done.'"

Hua Tzu-fang promptly interceded. "Let things alone," he said; "now that they're already here, there's no need whatever of much ado.

The only thing is that our mean house with its thatched roof is both so crammed and so filthy that how could you, sir, sit in it!"

Hsi Jen's mother also came out at an early period to receive him, and Hsi Jen pulled Pao-yü in. Once inside the room, Pao-yü perceived three or five girls, who, as soon as they caught sight of him approaching, all lowered their heads, and felt so bashful that their faces were suffused with blushes. But as both Hua Tzu-fang and his mother were afraid that Pao-yü would catch cold, they pressed him to take a seat on the stove-bed, and hastened to serve a fresh supply of refreshments, and to at once bring him a cup of good tea.

"You needn't be flurrying all for nothing," Hsi Jen smilingly interposed; "I, naturally, should know; and there's no use of even laying out any fruits, as I daren't recklessly give him anything to eat."

Saying this, she simultaneously took her own cushion and laid it on a stool, and after Pao-yü took a seat on it, she placed the footstove she had been using, under his feet; and producing, from a satchet, two peach-blossom-scented small cakes, she opened her own hand-stove and threw them into the fire; which done, she covered it well again and placed it in Pao-yü's lap. And eventually, she filled her own tea-cup with tea and presented it to Pao-yü, while, during this time, her mother and sister had been fussing about, laying out in fine array a tableful of every kind of eatables.

Hsi Jen noticed that there were absolutely no things that he could eat, but she felt urged to say with a smile: "Since you've come, it isn't right that you should go empty away; and you must, whether the things be good or bad, taste a little, so that it may look like a visit to my house!"

As she said this, she forthwith took several seeds of the fir-cone, and cracking off the thin skin, she placed them in a handkerchief and presented them to Pao-yü. But Pao-yü, espying that Hsi Jen's two eyes were slightly red, and that the powder was shiny and moist, quietly therefore inquired of Hsi Jen, "Why do you cry for no rhyme or reason?"

"Why should I cry?" Hsi Jen laughed; "something just got into my eyes and I rubbed them." By these means she readily managed to evade detection; but seeing that Pao-yü wore a deep red archery-sleeved pelisse, ornamented with gold dragons, and lined with fur from foxes' ribs and a grey sable fur surtout with a fringe round the border. "What! have you," she asked, "put on again your new clothes for? specially to come here? and didn't they inquire of you where you were going?"

"I had changed," Pao-yü explained with a grin, "as Mr. Chen had invited me to go over and look at the play."

"Well, sit a while and then go back;" Hsi Jen continued as she nodded her head; "for this isn't the place for you to come to!"

"You'd better be going home now," Pao-yü suggested smirkingly; "where I've again kept something good for you."

"Gently," smiled Hsi Jen, "for were you to let them hear, what figure would we cut?" And with these, words, she put out her hand and unclasping from Pao-yü's neck the jade of Spiritual Perception, she faced her cousins and remarked exultingly. "Here! see for yourselves; look at this and learn! When I repeatedly talked about it, you all thought it extraordinary, and were anxious to have a glance at it; to-day, you may gaze on it with all your might, for whatever precious thing you may by and by come to see will really never excel such an object as this!"

When she had finished speaking, she handed it over to them, and after they had passed it round for inspection, she again fastened it properly on Pao-yü's neck, and also bade her brother go and hire a small carriage, or engage a small chair, and escort Pao-yü back home.

"If I see him back," Hua Tzu-fang remarked, "there would be no harm, were he even to ride his horse!"

"It isn't because of harm," Hsi Jen replied; "but because he may come across some one from the house."

Hua Tzu-fang promptly went and bespoke a small chair; and when it came to the door, the whole party could not very well detain him, and they of course had to see Pao-yü out of the house; while Hsi Jen, on the other hand, snatched a few fruits and gave them to Ming Yen; and as she at the same time pressed in his hand several cash to buy crackers with to let off, she enjoined him not to tell any one as he himself would likewise incur blame.

As she uttered these words, she straightway escorted Pao-yü as far as outside the door, from whence having seen him mount into the sedan chair, she dropped the curtain; whereupon Ming Yen and her brother, the two of them, led the horses and followed behind in his wake. Upon reaching the street where the Ning mansion was situated, Ming Yen told the chair to halt, and said to Hua Tzu-fang, "It's advisable that I should again go, with Mr. Secundus, into the Eastern mansion, to show ourselves before we can safely betake ourselves home; for if we don't, people will suspect!"

Hua Tzu-fang, upon hearing that there was good reason in what he said, promptly clasped Pao-yü out of the chair and put him on the horse, whereupon after Pao-yü smilingly remarked: "Excuse me for the trouble I've surely put you to," they forthwith entered again by the back gate; but putting aside all details, we will now confine ourselves to Pao-yü.

After he had walked out of the door, the several waiting-maids in his apartments played and laughed with greater zest and with less restraint. Some there were who played at chess, others who threw the dice or had a game of cards; and they covered the whole floor with the shells of melon-seeds they were cracking, when dame Li, his nurse, happened to come in, propping herself on a staff, to pay her respects and to see Pao-yü, and perceiving that Pao-yü was not at home and that the servant-girls were only bent upon romping, she felt intensely disgusted. "Since I've left this place," she therefore exclaimed with a sigh, "and don't often come here, you've become more and more unmannerly; while the other nurse does still less than ever venture to expostulate with you; Pao-yü is like a candlestick eighty feet high, shedding light on others, and throwing none upon himself! All he knows is to look down upon people as being filthy; and yet this is his room and he allows you to put it topsy-turvey, and to become more and more unmindful of decorum!"

These servant-girls were well aware that Pao-yü was not particular in these respects, and that in the next place nurse Li, having pleaded old age, resigned her place and gone home, had nowadays no control over them, so that they simply gave their minds to romping and joking, and paid no heed whatever to her. Nurse Li however still kept on asking about Pao-yü, "How much rice he now ate at one meal? and at what time he went to sleep?" to which questions, the servant-girls replied quite at random; some there being too who observed: "What a dreadful despicable old thing she is!"

"In this covered bowl," she continued to inquire, "is cream, and why not give it to me to eat?" and having concluded these words, she took it up and there and then began eating it.

"Be quick, and leave it alone!" a servant-girl expostulated, "that, he said, was kept in order to be given to Hsi Jen; and on his return, when he again gets into a huff, you, old lady, must, on your own motion, confess to having eaten it, and not involve us in any way as to have to bear his resentment."

Nurse Li, at these words, felt both angry and ashamed. "I can't believe," she forthwith remarked, "that he has become so bad at heart! Not to speak of the milk I've had, I have, in fact every right to even something more expensive than this; for is it likely that he holds Hsi

Jen dearer than myself? It can't forsooth be that he doesn't bear in mind how that I've brought him up to be a big man, and how that he has eaten my blood transformed into milk and grown up to this age! and will be because I'm now having a bowl of milk of his be angry on that score! I shall, yes, eat it, and we'll see what he'll do! I don't know what you people think of Hsi Jen, but she was a lowbred girl, whom I've with my own hands raised up! and what fine object indeed was she!"

As she spoke, she flew into a temper, and taking the cream she drank the whole of it.

"They don't know how to speak properly!" another servant-girl interposed sarcastically, "and it's no wonder that you, old lady, should get angry! Pao-yü still sends you, venerable dame, presents as a proof of his gratitude, and is it possible that he will feel displeased for such a thing like this?"

"You girls shouldn't also pretend to be artful flatterers to cajole me!" nurse Li added; "do you imagine that I'm not aware of the dismissal, the other day, of Hsi Hsüeh, on account of a cup of tea? and as it's clear enough that I've incurred blame, I'll come by and by and receive it!"

Having said this, she went off in a dudgeon, but not a long interval elapsed before Pao-yü returned, and gave orders to go and fetch Hsi Jen; and perceiving Ching Ling reclining on the bed perfectly still: "I presume she's ill," Pao-yü felt constrained to inquire, "or if she isn't ill, she must have lost at cards."

"Not so!" observed Chiu Wen; "she had been a winner, but dame Li came in quite casually and muddled her so that she lost; and angry at this she rushed off to sleep."

"Don't place yourselves," Pao-yü smiled, "on the same footing as nurse Li, and if you were to let her alone, everything will be all right."

These words were still on his lips when Hsi Jen arrived. After the mutual salutations, Hsi Jen went on to ask of Pao-yü: "Where did you have your repast? and what time did you come back?" and to present likewise, on behalf of her mother and sister, her compliments to all the girls, who were her companions. In a short while, she changed her costume and divested herself of her fineries, and Pao-yü bade them fetch the cream.

"Nurse Li has eaten it," the servant-girls rejoined, and as Pao-yü was on the point of making some remark Hsi Jen hastened to interfere, laughing the while; "Is it really this that you had kept for me? many thanks for the trouble; the other day, when I had some, I found it very toothsome, but after I had partaken of it, I got a pain in the stomach, and was so much upset, that it was only after I had brought it all up that I felt all right. So it's as well that she has had it, for, had it been kept here, it would have been wasted all for no use! What I fancy are dry chestnuts; and while you clean a few for me, I'll go and lay the bed!"

Pao-yü upon hearing these words credited them as true, so that he discarded all thought of the cream and fetched the chestnuts, which he, with his own hands, selected and pealed. Perceiving at the same time that none of the party were present in the room, he put on a smile and inquired of Hsi Jen: "Who were those persons dressed in red to day?"

"They're my two cousins on my mother's side," Hsi Jen explained, and hearing this, Pao-yü sang their praise as he heaved a couple of sighs.

"What are you sighing for?" Hsi Jen remarked. "I know the secret reasons of your heart; it's I fancy because she isn't fit to wear red!"

"It isn't that," Pao-yü protested smilingly, "it isn't that; if such a person as that isn't good enough to be dressed in red, who would forsooth presume to wear it? It's because I find her so really lovely! and if we could, after all, manage to get her into our family, how nice it would be then!"

Hsi Jen gave a sardonic smile. "That it's my own fate to be a slave doesn't matter, but is it likely that the destiny of even my very relatives could be to become one and all of them bond servants? But you should certainly set your choice upon some really beautiful girl, for she would in that case be good enough to enter your house."

"Here you are again with your touchiness!" Pao-yü eagerly exclaimed smiling, "if I said that she should come to our house, does it necessarily imply that she should be a servant? and wouldn't it do were I to mention that she should come as a relative!"

"That too couldn't exalt her to be a fit match for you!" rejoined Hsi Jen; but Pao-yü being loth to continue the conversation, simply busied himself with cleaning the chestnuts.

"How is it you utter not a word?" Hsi Jen laughed; "I expect it's because I just offended you by my inconsiderate talk! But if by and by you have your purpose fixed on it, just spend a few ounces of silver to purchase them with, and bring them in and have done!"

"How would you have one make any reply?" Pao-yü smilingly rejoined; "all I did was to extol her charms; for she's really fit to have been born in a deep hall and spacious court as this; and it isn't for such foul things as myself and others to contrariwise spend our days in this place!"

"Though deprived of this good fortune," Hsi Jen explained, "she's nevertheless also petted and indulged and the jewel of my maternal uncle and my aunt! She's now seventeen years of age, and everything in the way of trousseau has been got ready, and she's to get married next year."

Upon hearing the two words "get married," he could not repress himself from again ejaculating: "Hai hai!" but while he was in an unhappy frame of mind, he once more heard Hsi Jen remark as she heaved a sigh: "Ever since I've come here, we cousins haven't all these years been able to get to live together, and now that I'm about to return home, they, on the other hand, will all be gone!"

Pao-yü, realising that there lurked in this remark some meaning or other, was suddenly so taken aback that dropping the chestnuts, he inquired: "How is it that you now want to go back?"

"I was present to-day," Hsi Jen explained, "when mother and brother held consultation together, and they bade me be patient for another year, and that next year they'll come up and redeem me out of service!"

Pao-yü, at these words, felt the more distressed. "Why do they want to redeem you?" he consequently asked.

"This is a strange question!" Hsi Jen retorted, "for I can't really be treated as if I were the issue born in this homestead of yours! All the members of my family are elsewhere, and there's only myself in this place, so that how could I end my days here?"

"If I don't let you go, it will verily be difficult for you to get away!" Pao-yü replied.

"There has never been such a principle of action!" urged Hsi Jen; "even in the imperial palace itself, there's a fixed rule, by which possibly every certain number of years a selection (of those who have to go takes place), and every certain number of years a new batch enters; and there's no such practice as that of keeping people for ever; not to speak of your own home."

Pao-yü realised, after reflection, that she, in point of fact, was right, and he went on to observe: "Should the old lady not give you your release, it will be impossible for you to get off."

"Why shouldn't she release me?" Hsi Jen questioned. "Am I really so very extraordinary a person as to have perchance made such an impression upon her venerable ladyship and my lady that they will be positive in not letting me go? They may, in all likelihood, give my family some more ounces of silver to keep me here; that possibly may come about. But, in truth, I'm also a person of the most ordinary run, and there are many more superior to me, yea very many! Ever since my youth up, I've been in her old ladyship's service; first by waiting upon Miss Shih for several years, and recently by being in attendance upon you for another term of years; and now that our people will come to redeem me, I should, as a matter of right, be told to go. My idea is that even the very redemption money won't be accepted, and that they will display such grace as to let me go at once. And, as for being told that I can't be allowed to go as I'm so diligent in my service to you, that's a thing that can on no account come about! My faithful attendance is an obligation of my duties, and is no exceptional service! and when I'm gone you'll again have some other faithful attendant, and it isn't likely that when I'm no more here, you'll find it impracticable to obtain one!"

After Pao-yü had listened to these various arguments, which proved the reasonableness of her going and the unreasonableness of any detention, he felt his heart more than ever a prey to distress. "In spite of all you say," he therefore continued, "the sole desire of my heart is to detain you; and I have no doubt but that the old lady will speak to your mother about it; and if she were to give your mother ample money, she'll, of course, not feel as if she could very well with any decency take you home!"

"My mother won't naturally have the audacity to be headstrong!" Hsi Jen ventured, "not to speak besides of the nice things, which may be told her and the lots of money she may, in addition, be given; but were she even not to be paid any compliments, and not so much as a single cash given her, she won't, if you set your mind upon keeping me here, presume not to comply with your wishes, were it also against my inclination. One thing however; our family would never rely upon prestige, and trust upon honorability to do anything so domineering as this! for this isn't like anything else, which, because you take a fancy to it, a hundred per cent profit can be added, and it obtained for you! This action can be well taken if the seller doesn't suffer loss! But in the present instance, were they to keep me back for no rhyme or reason, it would also be of no benefit to yourself; on the contrary, they would be instrumental in keeping us blood relatives far apart; a thing the like of which, I feel positive that dowager lady Chia and my lady will never do!"

After lending an ear to this argument, Pao-yü cogitated within himself for a while. "From what you say," he then observed, "when you say you'll go, it means that you'll go for certain!"

"Yes, that I'll go for certain," Hsi Jen rejoined.

"Who would have anticipated," Pao-yü, after these words, mused in his own heart, "that a person like her would have shown such little sense of gratitude, and such a lack of respect! Had I," he then remarked aloud with a sigh, "been aware, at an early date, that your whole wish would have been to go, I wouldn't, in that case, have brought you over! But when you're away, I shall remain alone, a solitary spirit!"

As he spoke, he lost control over his temper, and, getting into bed, he went to sleep.

The fact is that when Hsi Jen had been at home, and she heard her mother and brother express their intention of redeeming her back, she there and then observed that were she even at the point of death, she would not return home. "When in past days," she had argued, "you had no rice to eat, there remained myself, who was still worth several taels; and hadn't I urged you to sell me, wouldn't I have seen both father and mother die of starvation under my very eyes? and you've now had the good fortune of selling me into this place, where I'm fed and clothed just like a mistress, and where I'm not beaten by day, nor abused by night! Besides, though now father be no more, you two have anyhow by putting things straight again, so adjusted the family estate that it has resumed its primitive condition. And were you, in fact, still in straitened circumstances, and you could by redeeming me back, make again some more money, that would be well and good; but the truth is that there's no such need, and what would be the use for you to redeem me at such a time as this? You should temporarily treat me as dead and gone, and shouldn't again recall any idea of redeeming me!"

Having in consequence indulged in a loud fit of crying, her mother and brother resolved, when they perceived her in this determined frame of mind, that for a fact there was no need for her to come out of service. What is more they had sold her under contract until death, in the distinct reliance that the Chia family, charitable and generous a family as it was, would, possibly, after no more than a few entreaties, make them a present of her person as well as the purchase money. In the second place, never had they in the Chia mansion ill-used any of those below; there being always plenty of grace and little of imperiousness. Besides, the servant-girls, who acted as personal attendants in the apartments of the old as well as of the young, were treated so far unlike the whole body of domestics in the household that the daughters even of an ordinary and penniless parentage could not have been so looked up to. And these considerations induced both the mother as well as her son to at once dispel the intention and not to redeem her, and when Pao-yü had subsequently paid them an unexpected visit, and the two of them (Pao-yü and Hsi Jen) were seen to be also on such terms, the mother and her son obtained a clearer insight into their relations, and still one more burden (which had pressed on their mind) fell to the ground, and as besides this was a contingency, which they had never reckoned upon, they both composed their hearts, and did not again entertain any idea of ransoming her.

It must be noticed moreover that Hsi Jen had ever since her youth not been blind to the fact that Pao-yü had an extraordinary temperament, that he was self-willed and perverse, far even in excess of all young lads, and that he had, in addition, a good many peculiarities and many unspeakable defects. And as of late he had placed such reliance in the fond love of his grandmother that his father and mother even could not exercise any extreme control over him, he had become so much the more remiss, dissolute, selfish and unconcerned, not taking the least pleasure in what was proper, that she felt convinced, whenever she entertained the idea of tendering him advice, that he would not listen to her. On this day, by a strange coincidence, came about the discussion respecting her ransom, and she designedly made use, in the first instance, of deception with a view to ascertain his feelings, to suppress his temper, and to be able subsequently to extend to him some words of admonition; and when she perceived that Pao-yü had now silently gone to sleep, she knew that his feelings could not brook the idea of her return and that his temper had already subsided. She had never had, as far as she was concerned, any desire of eating chestnuts, but as she feared lest, on account of the cream, some trouble might arise, which might again lead to the same results as when Hsi Hsüeh drank the tea, she consequently made use of the pretence that she fancied chestnuts, in order to put off Pao-yü from alluding (to the cream) and to bring the matter speedily to an end. But telling forthwith the young waiting-maids to take the chestnuts away and eat them, she herself came and pushed Pao-yü; but at the sight of Pao-yü with the traces of tears on his face, she at once put on a smiling expression and said: "What's there in this to wound your heart? If you positively do wish to keep me, I shall, of course, not go away!"

Pao-yü noticed that these words contained some hidden purpose, and readily observed: "Do go on and tell me what else I can do to succeed in keeping you here, for of my own self I find it indeed difficult to say how!"

"Of our friendliness all along," Hsi Jen smilingly rejoined, "there's naturally no need to speak; but, if you have this day made up your mind to retain me here, it isn't through this friendship that you'll succeed in doing so. But I'll go on and mention three distinct conditions, and, if you really do accede to my wishes, you'll then have shown an earnest desire to keep me here, and I won't go, were even a sword to be laid on my neck!"

"Do tell me what these conditions are," Pao-yü pressed her with alacrity, as he smiled, "and I'll assent to one and all. My dear sister, my own dear sister, not to speak of two or three, but even two or three hundred of them I'm quite ready to accept. All I entreat you is that you and all of you should combine to watch over me and take care of me, until some day when I shall be transformed into flying ashes; but flying ashes are, after all, not opportune, as they have form and substance and they likewise possess sense, but until I've been metamorphosed into a streak of subtle smoke. And when the wind shall have with one puff dispelled me, all of you then will be unable to attend to me, just as much as I myself won't be able to heed you. You will, when that time comes, let me go where I please, as I'll let you speed where you choose to go!"

These words so harassed Hsi Jen that she hastened to put her hand over his mouth. "Speak decently," she said; "I was on account of this just about to admonish you, and now here you are uttering all this still more loathsome trash."

"I won't utter these words again," Pao-yü eagerly added.

"This is the first fault that you must change," Hsi Jen replied.

"I'll amend," Pao-yü observed, "and if I say anything of the kind again you can wring my mouth; but what else is there?"

"The second thing is this," Hsi Jen explained; "whether you really like to study or whether you only pretend to like study is immaterial; but you should, when you are in the presence of master, or in the presence of any one else, not do nothing else than find fault with people and make fun of them, but behave just as if you were genuinely fond of study, so that you shouldn't besides provoke your father so much to anger, and that he should before others have also a chance of saying something! 'In my family,' he reflects within himself, 'generation after generation has been fond of books, but ever since I've had you, you haven't accomplished my expectations, and not only is it that you don't care about reading books,'—and this has already filled his heart with anger and vexation,—'but both before my face and behind my back, you utter all that stuff and nonsense, and give those persons, who have, through their knowledge of letters, attained high offices, the nickname of the "the salaried worms." You also uphold that there's no work exclusive (of the book where appears) "fathom spotless virtue;" and that all other books consist of foolish compilations, which owe their origin to former authors, who, unable themselves to expound the writings of Confucius, readily struck a new line and invented original notions.' Now with words like these, how can one wonder if master loses all patience, and if he does from time to time give you a thrashing! and what do you make other people think of you?"

"I won't say these things again," Pao-yü laughingly protested, "these are the reckless and silly absurdities of a time when I was young and had no idea of the height of the heavens and the thickness of the earth; but I'll now no more repeat them. What else is there besides?"

"It isn't right that you should sneer at the bonzes and vilify the Taoist priests, nor mix cosmetics or prepare rouge," Hsi Jen continued; "but there's still another thing more important, you shouldn't again indulge the bad habits of licking the cosmetic, applied by people on their lips, nor be fond of (girls dressed) in red!"

"I'll change in all this," Pao-yü added by way of rejoinder; "I'll change in all this; and if there's anything more be quick and tell me."

"There's nothing more," Hsi Jen observed; "but you must in everything exercise a little more diligence, and not indulge your caprices and allow your wishes to run riot, and you'll be all right. And should you comply to all these things in real earnest, you couldn't carry me out, even in a chair with eight bearers."

"Well, if you do stay in here long enough," Pao-yü remarked with a smile, "there's no fear as to your not having an eight-bearer-chair to sit in!"

Hsi Jen gave a sardonic grin. "I don't care much about it," she replied; "and were I even to have such good fortune, I couldn't enjoy such a right. But allowing I could sit in one, there would be no pleasure in it!"

While these two were chatting, they saw Ch'iu Wen walk in. "It's the third watch of the night," she observed, "and you should go to sleep. Just a few moments back your grandmother lady Chia and our lady sent a nurse to ask about you, and I replied that you were asleep."

Pao-yü bade her fetch a watch, and upon looking at the time, he found indeed that the hand was pointing at ten; whereupon rinsing his mouth again and loosening his clothes, he retired to rest, where we will leave him without any further comment.

The next day, Hsi Jen got up as soon as it was dawn, feeling her body heavy, her head sore, her eyes swollen, and her limbs burning like fire. She managed however at first to keep up, an effort though it was, but as subsequently she was unable to endure the strain, and all she felt disposed to do was to recline, she therefore lay down in her clothes on the stove-couch. Pao-yü hastened to tell dowager lady Chia, and the doctor was sent for, who, upon feeling her pulse and diagnosing her complaint, declared that there was nothing else the matter with her than a chill, which she had suddenly contracted, that after she had taken a dose or two of medicine, it would be dispelled, and that she would be quite well. After he had written the prescription and taken his departure, some one was despatched to fetch the medicines, which when brought were properly decocted. As soon as she had swallowed a dose, Pao-yü bade her cover herself with her bed-clothes so as to bring on perspiration; while he himself came into Tai-yü's room to look her up. Tai-yü was at this time quite alone, reclining on her bed having a midday siesta, and the waiting-maids having all gone out to attend to whatever they pleased, the whole room was plunged in stillness and silence. Pao-yü raised the embroidered soft thread portiere and walked in; and upon espying Tai-yü in the room fast asleep, he hurriedly approached her and pushing her: "Dear cousin," he said, "you've just had your meal, and are you asleep already?" and he kept on calling "Tai-yü" till he woke her out of her sleep.

Perceiving that it was Pao-yü, "You had better go for a stroll," Tai-yü urged, "for the day before yesterday I was disturbed the whole night, and up to this day I haven't had rest enough to get over the fatigue. My whole body feels languid and sore."

"This languor and soreness," Pao-yü rejoined, "are of no consequence; but if you go on sleeping you'll be feeling very ill; so I'll try and distract you, and when we've dispelled this lassitude, you'll be all right."

Tai-yü closed her eyes. "I don't feel any lassitude," she explained, "all I want is a little rest; and you had better go elsewhere and come back after romping about for a while."

"Where can I go?" Pao-yü asked as he pushed her. "I'm quite sick and tired of seeing the others."

At these words, Tai-yü burst out laughing with a sound of Ch'ih. "Well! since you wish to remain here," she added, "go over there and sit down quietly, and let's have a chat."

"I'll also recline," Pao-yü suggested.

"Well, then, recline!" Tai-yü assented.

"There's no pillow," observed Pao-yü, "so let us lie on the same pillow."

"What nonsense!" Tai-yü urged, "aren't those pillows outside? get one and lie on it."

Pao-yü walked into the outer apartment, and having looked about him, he returned and remarked with a smile: "I don't want those, they may be, for aught I know, some dirty old hag's."

Tai-yü at this remark opened her eyes wide, and as she raised herself up: "You're really," she exclaimed laughingly, "the evil star of my existence! here, please recline on this pillow!" and as she uttered these words, she pushed her own pillow towards Pao-yü, and, getting up she went and fetched another of her own, upon which she lay her head in such a way that both of them then reclined opposite to each other. But Tai-yü, upon turning up her eyes and looking, espied on Pao-yü's cheek on the left side of his face, a spot of blood about the size of a button, and speedily bending her body, she drew near to him, and rubbing it with her hand, she scrutinised it closely. "Whose nail," she went on to inquire, "has scratched this open?"

Pao-yü with his body still reclining withdrew from her reach, and as he did so, he answered with a smile: "It isn't a scratch; it must, I presume, be simply a drop, which bespattered my cheek when I was just now mixing and clarifying the cosmetic paste for them."

Saying this, he tried to get at his handkerchief to wipe it off; but Tai-yü used her own and rubbed it clean for him, while she observed: "Do you still give your mind to such things? attend to them you may; but must you carry about you a placard (to make it public)? Though uncle mayn't see it, were others to notice it, they would treat it as a strange occurrence and a novel bit of news, and go and tell him to curry favour, and when it has reached uncle's ear, we shall all again not come out clean, and provoke him to anger."

Pao-yü did not in the least heed what she said, being intent upon smelling a subtle scent which, in point of fact, emanated from Tai-yü's sleeve, and when inhaled inebriated the soul and paralysed the bones. With a snatch, Pao-yü laid hold of Tai-yü's sleeve meaning to see what object was concealed in it; but Tai-yü smilingly expostulated: "At such a time as this," she said, "who keeps scents about one?"

"Well, in that case," Pao-yü rejoined with a smirking face, "where does this scent come from?"

"I myself don't know," Tai-yü replied; "I presume it must be, there's no saying, some scent in the press which has impregnated the clothes."

"It doesn't follow," Pao-yü added, as he shook his head; "the fumes of this smell are very peculiar, and don't resemble the perfume of scent-bottles, scent-balls, or scented satchets!"

"Is it likely that I have, like others, Buddhistic disciples," Tai-yü asked laughing ironically, "or worthies to give me novel kinds of scents? But supposing there is about me some peculiar scent, I haven't, at all events, any older or younger brothers to get the flowers, buds, dew, and snow, and concoct any for me; all I have are those common scents, that's all."

"Whenever I utter any single remark," Pao-yü urged with a grin, "you at once bring up all these insinuations; but unless I deal with you severely, you'll never know what stuff I'm made of; but from henceforth I'll no more show you any grace!"

As he spoke, he turned himself over, and raising himself, he puffed a couple of breaths into both his hands, and hastily stretching them out, he tickled Tai-yü promiscuously under her armpits, and along both sides. Tai-yü had never been able to stand tickling, so that when Pao-yü put out his two hands and tickled her violently, she forthwith giggled to such an extent that she could scarcely gasp for breath. "If you still go on teasing me," she shouted, "I'll get angry with you!"

Pao-yü then kept his hands off, and as he laughed, "Tell me," he asked, "will you again come out with all those words or not?"

"I daren't do it again," Tai-yü smiled and adjusted her hair; adding with another laugh: "I may have peculiar scents, but have you any 'warm' scents?"

Pao-yü at this question, could not for a time unfold its meaning: "What 'warm' scent?" he therefore asked.

Tai-yü nodded her head and smiled deridingly. "How stupid! what a fool!" she sighed; "you have jade, and another person has gold to match with you, and if some one has 'cold' scent, haven't you any 'warm' scent as a set-off?"

Pao-yü at this stage alone understood the import of her remark.

"A short while back you craved for mercy," Pao-yü observed smilingly, "and here you are now going on talking worse than ever;" and as he spoke he again put out his hands.

"Dear cousin," Tai-yü speedily implored with a smirk, "I won't venture to do it again."

"As for letting you off," Pao-yü remarked laughing, "I'll readily let you off, but do allow me to take your sleeve and smell it!" and while uttering these words, he hastily pulled the sleeve, and pressing it against his face, kept on smelling it incessantly, whereupon Tai-yü drew her hand away and urged: "You must be going now!"

"Though you may wish me to go, I can't," Pao-yü smiled, "so let us now lie down with all propriety and have a chat," laying himself down again, as he spoke, while Tai-yü likewise reclined, and covered her face with her handkerchief. Pao-yü in a rambling way gave vent to a lot of nonsense, which Tai-yü did not heed, and Pao-yü went on to inquire: "How old she was when she came to the capital? what sights and antiquities she saw on the journey? what relics and curiosities there were at Yang Chou? what were the local customs and the habits of the people?"

Tai-yü made no reply; and Pao-yü fearing lest she should go to sleep, and get ill, readily set to work to beguile her to keep awake. "Ai yah!" he exclaimed, "at Yang Chou, where your official residence is, has occurred a remarkable affair; have you heard about it?"

Tai-yü perceiving that he spoke in earnest, that his words were correct and his face serious, imagined that what he referred to was a true story, and she therefore inquired what it was?

Pao-yü upon hearing her ask this question, forthwith suppressed a laugh, and, with a glib tongue, he began to spin a yarn. "At Yang Chou," he said, "there's a hill called the Tai hill; and on this hill stands a cave called the Lin Tzu."

"This must all be lies," Tai-yü answered sneeringly, "as I've never before heard of such a hill."

"Under the heavens many are the hills and rivers," Pao-yü rejoined, "and how could you know them all? Wait until I've done speaking, when you will be free to express your opinion!"

"Go on then," Tai-yü suggested, whereupon Pao-yü prosecuted his raillery. "In this Lin Tzu cave," he said, "there was once upon a time a whole swarm of rat-elves. In some year or other and on the seventh day of the twelfth moon, an old rat ascended the throne to discuss matters. 'Tomorrow,' he argued, 'is the eighth of the twelfth moon, and men in the world will all be cooking the congee of the eighth of the twelfth moon. We have now in our cave a short supply of fruits of all kinds, and it would be well that we should seize this opportunity to steal a few and bring them over.' Drawing a mandatory arrow, he handed it to a small rat, full of aptitude, to go forward on a tour of inspection. The young rat on his return reported that he had already concluded his search and inquiries in every place and corner, and that in the temple at the bottom of the hill alone was the largest stock of fruits and rice. 'How many kinds of rice are there?' the old rat ascertained, 'and how many species of fruits?' 'Rice and beans,' the young rat rejoined, 'how many barns-full there are, I can't remember; but in the way of fruits there are five kinds: 1st, red dates; 2nd, chestnuts; 3rd, ground nuts; 4th, water caltrops, and 5th, scented taros.' At this report the old rat was so much elated that he promptly detailed rats to go forth; and as he drew the mandatory arrow, and inquired who would go and steal the rice, a rat readily received the order and went off to rob the rice. Drawing another mandatory arrow, he asked who would go and abstract the beans, when once more a rat took over the arrow and started to steal the beans; and one by one subsequently received each an arrow and started on his errand. There only remained the scented taros, so that picking again a mandatory arrow, he ascertained who would go and carry away the taros: whereupon a very puny and very delicate rat was heard to assent. 'I would like,' he said, 'to go and steal the scented taros.' The old rat and all the swarm of rats, upon noticing his state, feared that he would not be sufficiently expert, and apprehending at the same time that he was too weakly and too devoid of energy, they one and all would not allow him to proceed. 'Though I be young in years and though my frame be delicate,' the wee rat expostulated, 'my devices are unlimited, my talk is glib and my designs deep and farseeing; and I feel convinced that, on this errand, I shall be more ingenious in pilfering than any of them.' 'How could you be more ingenious than they?' the whole company of rats asked. 'I won't,' explained the young rat, 'follow their example, and go straight to work and steal, but by simply shaking my body, and transforming myself, I shall metamorphose myself into a taro, and roll myself among the heap of taros, so that people will not be able to detect me, and to hear me; whereupon I shall stealthily, by means of the magic art of dividing my body into many, begin the removal, and little by little transfer the whole lot away, and will not this be far more ingenious than any direct pilfering or forcible abstraction?' After the whole swarm of rats had listened to what he had to say, they, with one voice, exclaimed: 'Excellent it is indeed, but what is this art of metamorphosis we wonder? Go forth you may, but first transform yourself and let us see you.' At these words the young rat laughed. 'This isn't a hard task!' he observed, 'wait till I transform myself.'

"Having done speaking, he shook his body and shouted out 'transform,' when he was converted into a young girl, most beauteous and with a most lovely face.

"'You've transformed yourself into the wrong thing,' all the rats promptly added deridingly; 'you said that you were to become a fruit, and how is it that you've turned into a young lady?'

"The young rat in its original form rejoined with a sneering smile: 'You all lack, I maintain, experience of the world; what you simply are aware of is that this fruit is the scented taro, but have no idea that the young daughter of Mr. Lin, of the salt tax, is, in real truth, a genuine scented taro.'"

Tai-yü having listened to this story, turned herself round and raising herself, she observed laughing, while she pushed Pao-yü: "I'll take that mouth of yours and pull it to pieces! Now I see that you've been imposing upon me."

With these words on her lips, she readily gave him a pinch, and Pao-yü hastened to plead for mercy. "My dear cousin," he said, "spare me; I won't presume to do it again; and it's when I came to perceive this perfume of yours, that I suddenly bethought myself of this old story."

"You freely indulge in abusing people," Tai-yü added with a smile, "and then go on to say that it's an old story."

But hardly had she concluded this remark before they caught sight of Pao-ch'ai walk in. "Who has been telling old stories?" she asked with a beaming face; "do let me also hear them."

Tai-yü pressed her at once into a seat. "Just see for yourself who else besides is here!" she smiled; "he goes in for profuse abuses and then maintains that it's an old story!"

"Is it indeed cousin Pao-yü?" Pao-ch'ai remarked. "Well, one can't feel surprised at his doing it; for many have ever been the stories stored up in his brain. The only pity is that when he should make use of old stories, he invariably forgets them! To-day, he can easily enough recall them to mind, but in the stanza of the other night on the banana leaves, when he should have remembered them, he couldn't after all recollect what really stared him in the face! and while every one else seemed so cool, he was in such a flurry that he actually perspired! And yet, at this moment, he happens once again to have a memory!"

At these words, Tai-yü laughed. "O-mi-to-fu!" she exclaimed. "You are indeed my very good cousin! But you've also (to Pao-yü) come across your match. And this makes it clear that requital and retribution never fail or err."

She had just reached this part of her sentence, when in Pao-yü's rooms was heard a continuous sound of wrangling; but as what transpired is not yet known, the ensuing chapter will explain.

CHAPTER XX.

Wang Hsi-feng with earnest words upbraids Mrs. Chao's jealous notions. Lin Tai-yü uses specious language to make sport of Shih Hsiang-yün's querulous tone of voice.

But to continue. Pao-yü was in Tai yü's apartments relating about the rat-elves, when Pao-ch'ai entered unannounced, and began to gibe Pao-yü, with trenchant irony: how that on the fifteenth of the first moon, he had shown ignorance of the allusion to the green wax; and the three of them then indulged in that room in mutual poignant satire, for the sake of fun. Pao-yü had been giving way to solicitude lest Tai-yü should, by being bent upon napping soon after her meal, be shortly getting an indigestion, or lest sleep should, at night, be completely dispelled, as neither of these things were conducive to the preservation of good health, when luckily Pao-ch'ai walked in, and they chatted and laughed together; and when Lin Tai-yü at length lost all inclination to dose, he himself then felt composed in his mind. But suddenly they heard clamouring begin in his room, and after they had all lent an ear and listened, Lin Tai-yü was the first to smile and make a remark. "It's your nurse having a row with Hsi Jen!" she said. "Hsi Jen treats her well enough, but that nurse of yours would also like to keep her well under her thumb; she's indeed an old dotard;" and Pao-yü was anxious to go over at once, but Pao-ch'ai laid hold of him and kept him back, suggesting: "It's as well that you shouldn't wrangle with your nurse, for she's quite stupid from old age; and it's but fair, on the contrary, that you should bear with her a little."

"I know all about that!" Pao-yü rejoined. But having concluded this remark, he walked into his room, where he discovered nurse Li, leaning on her staff, standing in the centre of the floor, abusing Hsi Jen, saying: "You young wench! how utterly unmindful you are of your origin! It's I who've raised you up, and yet, when I came just now, you put on high airs and mighty side, and remained reclining on the stove-couch! You saw me well enough, but you paid not the least heed to me! Your whole heart is set upon acting like a wily enchantress to befool Pao-yü; and you so impose upon Pao-yü that he doesn't notice me, but merely lends an ear to what you people have to say! You're no more than a low girl bought for a few taels and brought in here; and will it ever do that you should be up to your mischievous tricks in this room? But whether you like it or not, I'll drag you out from this, and give you to some mean fellow, and we'll see whether you will still behave like a very imp, and cajole people or not?"

Hsi Jen was, at first, under the simple impression that the nurse was wrath for no other reason than because she remained lying down, and she felt constrained to explain that "she was unwell, that she had just succeeded in perspiring, and that having had her head covered, she hadn't really perceived the old lady;" but when she came subsequently to hear her mention that she imposed upon Pao-yü, and also go so far as to add that she would be given to some mean fellow, she unavoidably experienced both a sense of shame and injury, and found it impossible to restrain herself from beginning to cry.

Pao-yü had, it is true, caught all that had been said, but unable with any propriety to take notice of it, he thought it his duty to explain matters for her. "She's ill," he observed, "and is taking medicines; and if you don't believe it," he went on, "well then ask the rest of the servant-girls."

Nurse Li at these words flew into a more violent dudgeon. "Your sole delight is to screen that lot of sly foxes!" she remarked, "and do you pay any notice to me? No, none at all! and whom would you like me to go and ask; who's it that doesn't back you? and who hasn't been dismounted from her horse by Hsi Jen? I know all about it; but I'll go with you and explain all these matters to our old mistress and my lady; for I've nursed you till I've brought you to this age, and now that you don't feed on milk, you thrust me on one side, and avail yourself of the servant-girls, in your wish to browbeat me."

As she uttered this remark, she too gave way to tears, but by this time, Tai-yü and Pao-ch'ai had also come over, and they set to work to reassure her. "You, old lady," they urged, "should bear with them a little, and everything will be right!" And when nurse Li saw these two arrive, she hastened to lay bare her grievances to them; and taking up the question of the dismissal in days gone by, of Hsi Hsüeh, for having drunk some tea, of the cream eaten on the previous day, and other similar matters, she spun a long, interminable yarn.

By a strange coincidence lady Feng was at this moment in the upper rooms, where she had been making up the account of losses and winnings, and upon hearing at the back a continuous sound of shouting and bustling, she readily concluded that nurse Li's old complaint was breaking forth, and that she was finding fault with Pao-yü's servants. But she had, as luck would have it, lost money in gambling on this occasion, so that she was ready to visit her resentment upon others. With hurried step, she forthwith came over, and laying hold of nurse Li, "Nurse," she said smiling, "don't lose your temper, on a great festival like this, and after our venerable lady has just gone through a day in excellent spirits! You're an old dame, and should, when others get up a row, still do what is right and keep them in proper order; and aren't you, instead of that, aware what good manners imply, that you will start vociferating in this place, and make our dowager lady full of displeasure? Tell me who's not good, and I'll beat her for you; but be quick and come along with me over to my quarters, where a pheasant which they have roasted is scalding hot, and let us go and have a glass of wine!" And as she spoke, she dragged her along and went on her way. "Feng Erh," she also called, "hold the staff for your old lady Li, and the handkerchief to wipe her tears with!" While nurse Li walked along with lady Feng, her feet scarcely touched the ground, as she kept on saying: "I don't really attach any value to this decrepid existence of mine! and I had rather disregard good manners, have a row and lose face, as it's better, it seems to me, than to put up with the temper of that wench!"

Behind followed Pao-ch'ai and Tai-yü, and at the sight of the way in which lady Feng dealt with her, they both clapped their hands, and exclaimed, laughing, "What piece of luck that this gust of wind has come, and dragged away this old matron!" while Pao-yü nodded his head to and fro and soliloquised with a sigh: "One can neither know whence originates this score; for she will choose the weak one to maltreat; nor can one see what girl has given her offence that she has come to be put in her black books!"

Scarcely had he ended this remark, before Ch'ing Wen, who stood by, put in her word. "Who's gone mad again?" she interposed, "and what good would come by hurting her feelings? But did even any one happen to hurt her, she would have pluck enough to bear the brunt, and wouldn't act so improperly as to involve others!"

Hsi Jen wept, and as she, did so, she drew Pao-yü towards her: "All through my having aggrieved an old nurse," she urged, "you've now again given umbrage, entirely on my account, to this crowd of people; and isn't this still enough for me to bear but must you also go and drag in third parties?"

When Pao-yü realised that to this sickness of hers, had also been superadded all these annoyances, he promptly stifled his resentment, suppressed his voice and consoled her so far as to induce her to lie down again to perspire. And when he further noticed how scalding like soup and burning like fire she was, he himself watched by her, and reclining by her side, he tried to cheer her, saying: "All you must do is to take good care of your ailment; and don't give your mind to those trifling matters, and get angry."

"Were I," Hsi Jen smiled sardonically, "to lose my temper over such concerns, would I be able to stand one moment longer in this room? The only thing is that if she goes on, day after day, doing nothing else than clamour in this manner, how can she let people get along? But you rashly go and hurt people's feelings for our sakes; but they'll bear it in mind, and when they find an opportunity, they'll come out with what's easy enough to say, but what's not pleasant to hear, and how will we all feel then?"

While her mouth gave utterance to these words, she could not stop her tears from running; but fearful, on the other hand, lest Pao-yü should be annoyed, she felt compelled to again strain every nerve to repress them. But in a short while, the old matrons employed for all sorts of duties, brought in some mixture of two drugs; and, as Pao-yü noticed that she was just on the point of perspiring, he did not allow her to get up, but readily taking it up to her, she immediately swallowed it, with her head still on her pillow; whereupon he gave speedy directions to the young servant-maids to lay her stove-couch in order.

"Whether you mean to have anything to eat or not," Hsi Jen advised, "you should after all sit for a time with our old mistress and our lady, and have a romp with the young ladies; after which you can come back again; while I, by quietly keeping lying down, will also feel the better."

When Pao-yü heard this suggestion, he had no help but to accede, and, after she had divested herself of her hair-pins and earrings, and he saw her lie down, he betook himself into the drawing-rooms, where he had his repast with old lady Chia. But the meal over, her ladyship felt still disposed to play at cards with the nurses, who had looked after the household for many years; and Pao-yü, bethinking himself of Hsi Jen, hastened to return to his apartments; where seeing that Hsi Jen was drowsily falling asleep, he himself would have wished to go to bed, but the hour was yet early. And as about this time Ch'ing Wen, I Hsia,

Ch'in Wen, Pi Hen had all, in their desire of getting some excitement, started in search of Yüan Yang, Hu Po and their companions, to have a romp with them, and he espied She Yüeh alone in the outer room, having a game of dominoes by lamp-light, Pao-yü inquired full of smiles: "How is it you don't go with them?"

"I've no money," She Yüeh replied.

"Under the bed," continued Pao-yü, "is heaped up all that money, and isn't it enough yet for you to lose from?"

"Had we all gone to play," She Yüeh added, "to whom would the charge of this apartment have been handed over? That other one is sick again, and the whole room is above, one mass of lamps, and below, full of fire; and all those old matrons, ancient as the heavens, should, after all their exertions in waiting upon you from morning to night, be also allowed some rest; while the young servant girls, on the other hand, have likewise been on duty the whole day long, and shouldn't they even at this hour be left to go and have some distraction? and that's why I am in here on watch."

When Pao-yü heard these words, which demonstrated distinctly that she was another Hsi Jen, he consequently put on a smile and remarked: "I'll sit in here, so you had better set your mind at ease and go!"

"Since you remain in here, there's less need for me to go," resumed She Yüeh, "for we two can chat and play and laugh; and won't that be nice?"

"What can we two do? it will be awfully dull! but never mind," Pao-yü rejoined; "this morning you said that your head itched, and now that you have nothing to do, I may as well comb it for you."

"Yes! do so!" readily assented She Yüeh, upon catching what he suggested; and while still speaking, she brought over the dressing-case containing a set of small drawers and looking-glass, and taking off her ornaments, she dishevelled her hair; whereupon Pao-yü picked up the fine comb and passed it repeatedly through her hair; but he had only combed it three or five times, when he perceived Ch'ing Wen hurriedly walk in to fetch some money. As soon as she caught sight of them both: "You haven't as yet drunk from the marriage cup," she said with a smile full of irony, "and have you already put up your hair?"

"Now that you've come, let me also comb yours for you," Pao-yü continued.

"I'm not blessed with such excessive good fortune!" Ch'ing Wen retorted, and as she uttered these words, she took the money, and forthwith dashing the portiere after her, she quitted the room.

Pao-yü stood at the back of She Yüeh, and She Yüeh sat opposite the glass, so that the two of them faced each other in it, and Pao-yü readily observed as he gazed in the glass, "In the whole number of rooms she's the only one who has a glib tongue!"

She Yüeh at these words hastily waved her hand towards the inside of the glass, and Pao-yü understood the hint; and suddenly a sound of "hu" was heard from the portiere, and Ch'ing Wen ran in once again.

"How have I got a glib tongue?" she inquired; "it would be well for us to explain ourselves."

"Go after your business, and have done," She Yüeh interposed laughingly; "what's the use of your coming and asking questions of people?"

"Will you also screen him?" Ch'ing Wen smiled significantly; "I know all about your secret doings, but wait until I've got back my capital, and we'll then talk matters over!"

With this remark still on her lips, she straightway quitted the room, and during this while, Pao-yü having finished combing her hair, asked She Yüeh to quietly wait upon him, while he went to sleep, as he would not like to disturb Hsi Jen.

Of the whole night there is nothing to record. But the next day, when he got up at early dawn, Hsi Jen had already perspired, during the night, so that she felt considerably lighter and better; but limiting her diet to a little rice soup, she remained quiet and nursed herself, and Pao-yü was so relieved in mind that he came, after his meal, over on this side to his aunt Hsüeh's on a saunter. The season was the course of the first moon, and the school was shut up for the new year holidays; while in the inner chambers the girls had put by their needlework, and were all having a time of leisure, and hence it was that when Chia Huan too came over in search of distraction, he discovered Pao-ch'ai, Hsiang Ling, Ying Erh, the three of them, in the act of recreating themselves by playing at chess. Chia Huan, at the sight of them, also wished to join in their games; and Pao-ch'ai, who had always looked upon him with, in fact, the same eye as she did Pao-yü, and with no different sentiment of any kind, pressed him to come up, upon hearing that he was on this occasion desirous to play; and, when he had seated himself together with them, they began to gamble, staking each time a pile of ten cash. The first time, he was the winner, and he felt supremely elated at heart, but as it happened that he subsequently lost in several consecutive games he soon became a prey to considerable distress. But in due course came the game in which it was his turn to cast the dice, and, if in throwing, he got seven spots, he stood to win, but he was likewise bound to be a winner were he to turn up six; and when Ying Erh had turned up three spots and lost, he consequently took up the dice, and dashing them with spite, one of them settled at five; and, as the other reeled wildly about, Ying Erh clapped her hands, and kept on shouting, "one spot;" while Chia Huan at once gazed with fixed eye and cried at random: "It's six, it's seven, it's eight!" But the dice, as it happened, turned up at one spot, and Chia Huan was so exasperated that putting out his hand, he speedily made a snatch at the dice, and eventually was about to lay hold of the money, arguing that it was six spot. But Ying Erh expostulated, "It was distinctly an ace," she said. And as Pao-ch'ai noticed how distressed Chia Huan was, she forthwith cast a glance at Ying Erh and observed: "The older you get, the less manners you have! Is it likely that gentlemen will cheat you? and don't you yet put down the money?"

Ying Erh felt her whole heart much aggrieved, but as she heard Pao-ch'ai make these remarks, she did not presume to utter a sound, and as she was under the necessity of laying down the cash, she muttered to herself: "This one calls himself a gentleman, and yet cheats us of these few cash, for which I myself even have no eye! The other day when I played with Mr. Pao-yü, he lost ever so many, and yet he did not distress himself! and what remained of the cash were besides snatched away by a few servant-girls, but all he did was to smile, that's all!"

Pao-ch'ai did not allow her time to complete what she had to say, but there and then called her to account and made her desist; whereupon Chia Huan exclaimed: "How can I compare with Pao-yü; you all fear him, and keep on good terms with him, while you all look down upon me for not being the child of my lady." And as he uttered these words, he at once gave way to tears.

"My dear cousin," Pao-ch'ai hastened to advise him, "leave off at once language of this kind, for people will laugh at you;" and then went on to scold Ying Erh, when Pao-yü just happened to come in. Perceiving him in this plight, "What is the matter?" he asked; but Chia Huan had not the courage to say anything.

Pao-ch'ai was well aware of the custom, which prevailed in their family, that younger brothers lived in respect of the elder brothers, but she was not however cognisant of the fact that Pao-yü would not that any one should entertain any fear of him. His idea being that elder as well as younger brothers had, all alike, father and mother to admonish them, and that there was no need for any of that officiousness, which, instead of doing good gave, on the contrary, rise to estrangement. "Besides," (he reasoned,) "I'm the offspring of the primary wife, while he's the son of the secondary wife, and, if by treating him as leniently as I have done, there are still those to talk about me, behind my back, how could I exercise any control over him?" But besides these, there were other still more foolish notions, which he fostered in his mind; but what foolish notions they were can you, reader, guess? As a result of his growing up, from his early youth, among a crowd of girls, of whom, in the way of sister, there was Yüan Ch'un, of cousins, from his paternal uncle's side, there were Ying Ch'un, and Hsi Ch'un, and of relatives also there were Shih Hsiang-yün, Lin Tai-yü, Hsüeh Pao-ch'ai and the rest, he, in due course, resolved in his mind that the divine and unsullied virtue of Heaven and earth was only implanted in womankind, and that men were no more than feculent dregs and foul dirt. And for this reason it was that men were without discrimination, considered by him as so many filthy objects, which might or might not exist; while the relationships of father, paternal uncles, and brothers, he did not however presume to disregard, as these were among the injunctions bequeathed by the holy man, and he felt bound to listen to a few of their precepts. But to the above causes must be assigned the fact that, among his brothers, he did no more than accomplish the general purport of the principle of human affections; bearing in mind no thought whatever that he himself was a human being of the male sex, and that it was his duty to be an example to his younger brothers. And this is why Chia Huan and the others entertained no respect for him, though in their veneration for dowager lady Chia, they yielded to him to a certain degree.

Pao-ch'ai harboured fears lest, on this occasion, Pao-yü should call him to book, and put him out of face, and she there and then lost no time in taking Chia Huan's part with a view to screening him.

"In this felicitous first moon what are you blubbering for?" Pao-yü inquired, "if this place isn't nice, why then go somewhere else to play. But from reading books, day after day, you've studied so much that you've become quite a dunce. If this thing, for instance, isn't good, that must, of course, be good, so then discard this and take up that, but is it likely that by sticking to this thing and crying for a while that it will become good? You came originally with the idea of reaping some fun, and you've instead provoked yourself to displeasure, and isn't it better then that you should be off at once."

Chia Huan upon hearing these words could not but come back to his quarters; and Mrs. Chao noticing the frame of mind in which he was felt constrained to inquire: "Where is it that you've been looked down upon by being made to fill up a hole, and being trodden under foot?"

"I was playing with cousin Pao-ch'ai," Chia Huan readily replied, "when Ying Erh insulted me, and deprived me of my money, and brother Pao-yü drove me away."

"Ts'ui!" exclaimed Mrs. Chao, "who bade you (presume so high) as to get up into that lofty tray? You low and barefaced thing! What place is there that you can't go to and play; and who told you to run over there and bring upon yourself all this shame?"

As she spoke, lady Feng was, by a strange coincidence, passing outside under the window; so that every word reached her ear, and she speedily asked from outside the window: "What are you up to in this happy first moon? These brothers are, really, but mere children, and will you just for a slight mistake, go on preaching to him! what's the use of coming out with all you've said? Let him go wherever he pleases; for there are still our lady and Mr. Chia Cheng to keep him in order. But you go and sputter him with your gigantic mouth; he's at present a master, and if there be anything wrong about him, there are, after all, those to rate him; and what business is that of yours? Brother Huan, come out with you, and follow me and let us go and enjoy ourselves."

Chia Huan had ever been in greater fear and trembling of lady Feng, than of madame Wang, so that when her summons reached his ear, he hurriedly went out, while Mrs. Chao, on the other hand, did not venture to breathe a single word.

"You too," resumed lady Feng, addressing Chia Huan; "are a thing devoid of all natural spirit! I've often told you that if you want to eat, drink, play, or laugh, you were quite free to go and play with whatever female cousin, male cousin, or sister-in-law you choose to disport yourself with; but you won't listen to my words. On the contrary, you let all these persons teach you to be depraved in your heart, perverse in your mind, to be sly, artful, and domineering; and you've, besides, no respect for your own self, but will go with that low-bred lot! and your perverse purpose is to begrudge people's preferences! But what you've lost are simply a few cash, and do you behave in this manner? How much did you lose?" she proceeded to ask Chia Huan; and Chia Huan, upon hearing this question, felt constrained to obey, by saying something in the way of a reply. "I've lost," he explained, "some hundred or two hundred cash."

"You have," rejoined lady Feng, "the good fortune of being a gentleman, and do you make such a fuss for the loss of a hundred or two hundred cash!" and turning her head round, "Feng Erh," she added, "go and fetch a thousand cash; and as the girls are all playing at the back, take him along to go and play. And if again by and by, you're so mean and deceitful, I shall, first of all, beat you, and then tell some one to report it at school, and won't your skin be flayed for you? All because of this want of respect of yours, your elder cousin is so angry with you that his teeth itch; and were it not that I prevent him, he would hit you with his foot in the stomach and kick all your intestines out! Get away," she then cried; whereupon Chia Huan obediently followed Feng Erh, and taking the money he went all by himself to play with Ying Ch'un and the rest; where we shall leave him without another word.

But to return to Pao-yü. He was just amusing himself and laughing with Pao-ch'ai, when at an unexpected moment, he heard some one announce that Miss Shih had come. At these words, Pao-yü rose, and was at once going off when "Wait," shouted Pao-ch'ai with a smile, "and we'll go over together and see her."

Saying this, she descended from the stove-couch, and came, in company with Pao-yü, to dowager lady Chia's on this side, where they saw Shih Hsiang-yün laughing aloud, and talking immoderately; and upon catching sight of them both, she promptly inquired after their healths, and exchanged salutations.

Lin Tai-yü just happened to be standing by, and having set the question to Pao-yü "Where do you come from?" "I come from cousin Pao-ch'ai's rooms," Pao-yü readily replied.

Tai-yü gave a sardonic smile. "What I maintain is this," she rejoined, "that lucky enough for you, you were detained over there; otherwise, you would long ago have, at once, come flying in here!"

"Am I only free to play with you?" Pao-yü inquired, "and to dispel your ennui! I simply went over to her place for a run, and that quite casually, and will you insinuate all these things?"

"Your words are quite devoid of sense," Tai-yü added; "whether you go or not what's that to me? neither did I tell you to give me any distraction; you're quite at liberty from this time forth not to pay any notice to me!"

Saying this, she flew into a high dudgeon and rushed back into her room; but Pao-yü promptly followed in her footsteps: "Here you are again in a huff," he urged, "and all for no reason! Had I even passed any remark that I shouldn't, you should anyhow have still sat in there, and chatted and laughed with the others for a while; instead of that, you come again to sit and mope all alone!"

"Are you my keeper?" Tai-yü expostulated.

"I couldn't, of course," Pao-yü smiled, "presume to exercise any influence over you; but the only thing is that you are doing your own health harm!"

"If I do ruin my health," Tai-yü rejoined, "and I die, it's my own lookout! what's that to do with you?"

"What's the good," protested Pao-yü, "of talking in this happy first moon of dying and of living?"

"I *will* say die," insisted Tai-yü, "die now, at this very moment! but you're afraid of death; and you may live a long life of a hundred years, but what good will that be!"

"If all we do is to go on nagging in this way," Pao-yü remarked smiling, "will I any more be afraid to die? on the contrary, it would be better to die, and be free!"

"Quite so!" continued Tai-yü with alacrity, "if we go on nagging in this way, it would be better for me to die, and that you should be free of me!"

"I speak of my own self dying," Pao-yü added, "so don't misunderstand my words and accuse people wrongly."

While he was as yet speaking, Pao-ch'ai entered the room: "Cousin Shih is waiting for you;" she said; and with these words, she hastily pushed Pao-yü on, and they walked away.

Tai-yü, meanwhile, became more and more a prey to resentment; and disconsolate as she felt, she shed tears in front of the window. But not time enough had transpired to allow two cups of tea to be drunk, before Pao-yü came back again. At the sight of him, Tai-yü sobbed still more fervently and incessantly, and Pao-yü realising the state she was in, and knowing well enough how arduous a task it would be to bring her round, began to join together a hundred, yea a thousand kinds of soft phrases and tender words to console her. But at an unforeseen moment, and before he could himself open his mouth, he heard Tai-yü anticipate him.

"What have you come back again for?" she asked. "Let me die or live, as I please, and have done! You've really got at present some one to play with you, one who, compared with me, is able to read and able to compose, able to write, to speak, as well as to joke, one too who for fear lest you should have ruffled your temper dragged you away: and what do you return here for now?"

Pao-yü, after listening to all she had to say, hastened to come up to her. "Is it likely," he observed in a low tone of voice, "that an intelligent person like you isn't so much as aware that near relatives can't be separated by a distant relative, and a remote friend set aside an old friend! I'm stupid, there's no gainsaying, but I do anyhow understand what these two sentiments imply. You and I are, in the first place, cousins on my father's sister's side; while sister Pao-ch'ai and I are two cousins on mother's sides, so that, according to the degrees of relationship, she's more distant than yourself. In the second place, you came here first, and we two have our meals at one table and sleep in one bed, having ever since our youth grown up together; while she has only recently come, and how could I ever distance you on her account?"

"Ts'ui!" Tai-yü exclaimed. "Will I forsooth ever make you distance her! who and what kind of person have I become to do such a thing? What (I said) was prompted by my own motives."

"I too," Pao-yü urged, "made those remarks prompted by my own heart's motives, and do you mean to say that your heart can only read the feelings of your own heart, and has no idea whatsoever of my own?"

Tai-yü at these words, lowered her head and said not a word. But after a long interval, "You only know," she continued, "how to feel bitter against people for their action in censuring you: but you don't, after all, know that you yourself provoke people to such a degree, that it's hard for them to put up with it! Take for instance the weather of to-day as an example. It's distinctly very cold, to-day, and yet, how is it that you are so contrary as to go and divest yourself of the pelisse with the bluish breast-fur overlapping the cloth?"

"Why say I didn't wear it?" Pao-yü smilingly observed. "I did, but seeing you get angry I felt suddenly in such a terrible blaze, that I at once took it off!"

Tai-yü heaved a sigh. "You'll by and by catch a cold," she remarked, "and then you'll again have to starve, and vociferate for something to eat!"

While these two were having this colloquy, Hsiang-yün was seen to walk in! "You two, Ai cousin and cousin Lin," she ventured jokingly, "are together playing every day, and though I've managed to come after ever so much trouble, you pay no heed to me at all!"

"It's invariably the rule," Tai-yü retorted smilingly, "that those who have a defect in their speech will insist upon talking; she can't even come out correctly with 'Erh' (secundus) cousin, and keeps on calling him 'Ai' cousin, 'Ai' cousin! And by and by when you play 'Wei

Ch'i' you're sure also to shout out yao, ai, (instead of erh), san; (one, two, three)."

Pao-yü laughed. "If you imitate her," he interposed, "and get into that habit, you'll also begin to bite your tongue when you talk."

"She won't make even the slightest allowance for any one," Hsiang-yün rejoined; "her sole idea being to pick out others' faults. You may readily be superior to any mortal being, but you shouldn't, after all, offend against what's right and make fun of every person you come across! But I'll point out some one, and if you venture to jeer her, I'll at once submit to you."

"Who is it?" Tai-yü vehemently inquired.

"If you do have the courage," Hsiang-yün answered, "to pick out cousin Pao-ch'ai's faults, you then may well be held to be first-rate!"

Tai-yü after hearing these words, gave a sarcastic smile. "I was wondering," she observed, "who it was. Is it indeed she? How could I ever presume to pick out hers?"

Pao-yü allowed her no time to finish, but hastened to say something to interrupt the conversation.

"I couldn't, of course, during the whole of this my lifetime," Hsiang-yün laughed, "attain your standard! but my earnest wish is that by and by should be found for you, cousin Lin, a husband, who bites his tongue when he speaks, so that you should every minute and second listen to 'ai-ya-os!' O-mi-to-fu, won't then your reward be manifest to my eyes!"

As she made this remark, they all burst out laughing heartily, and Hsiang-yün speedily turned herself round and ran away.

But reader, do you want to know the sequel? Well, then listen to the explanation given in the next chapter.

CHAPTER XXI.

The eminent Hsi Jen, with winsome ways, rails at Pao-yü, with a view to exhortation.
The beauteous P'ing Erh, with soft words, screens Chia Lien.

But to resume our story. When Shih Hsiang-yün ran out of the room, she was all in a flutter lest Lin Tai-yü should catch her up; but Pao-yü, who came after her, readily shouted out, "You'll trip and fall. How ever could she come up to you?"

Lin Tai-yü went in pursuit of her as far as the entrance, when she was impeded from making further progress by Pao-yü, who stretched his arms out against the posts of the door.

"Were I to spare Yün Erh, I couldn't live!" Lin Tai-yü exclaimed, as she tugged at his arms. But Hsiang-yün, perceiving that Pao-yü obstructed the door, and surmising that Tai-yü could not come out, speedily stood still. "My dear cousin," she smilingly pleaded, "do let me off this time!"

But it just happened that Pao-ch'ai, who was coming along, was at the back of Hsiang-yün, and with a face also beaming with smiles: "I advise you both," she said, "to leave off out of respect for cousin Pao-yü, and have done."

"I don't agree to that," Tai-yü rejoined; "are you people, pray, all of one mind to do nothing but make fun of me?"

"Who ventures to make fun of you?" Pao-yü observed advisingly; "and hadn't you made sport of her, would she have presumed to have said anything about you?"

While this quartet were finding it an arduous task to understand one another, a servant came to invite them to have their repast, and they eventually crossed over to the front side, and as it was already time for the lamps to be lit, madame Wang, widow Li Wan, lady Feng, Ying Ch'un, T'an Ch'un, Hsi Ch'un and the other cousins, adjourned in a body to dowager lady Chia's apartments on this side, where the whole company spent a while in a chat on irrelevant topics, after which they each returned to their rooms and retired to bed. Hsiang-yün, as of old, betook herself to Tai-yü's quarters to rest, and Pao-yü escorted them both into their apartment, and it was after the hour had already past the second watch, and Hsi Jen had come and pressed him several times, that he at length returned to his own bedroom and went to sleep. The next morning, as soon as it was daylight, he threw his clothes over him, put on his low shoes and came over into Tai-yü's room, where he however saw nothing of the two girls Tzu Chüan and Ts'ui Lu, as there was no one else here in there besides his two cousins, still reclining under the coverlets. Tai-yü was closely wrapped in a quilt of almond-red silk, and lying quietly, with closed eyes fast asleep; while Shih Hsiang-yün, with her handful of shiny hair dragging along the edge of the pillow, was covered only up to the chest, and outside the coverlet rested her curved snow-white arm, with the gold bracelets, which she had on.

At the sight of her, Pao-yü heaved a sigh. "Even when asleep," he soliloquised, "she can't be quiet! but by and by, when the wind will have blown on her, she'll again shout that her shoulder is sore!" With these words, he gently covered her, but Lin Tai-yü had already awoke out of her sleep, and becoming aware that there was some one about, she promptly concluded that it must, for a certainty, be Pao-yü, and turning herself accordingly round, and discovering at a glance that the truth was not beyond her conjectures, she observed: "What have you run over to do at this early hour?" to which question Pao-yü replied: "Do you call this early? but get up and see for yourself!"

"First quit the room," Tai-yü suggested, "and let us get up!"

Pao-yü thereupon made his exit into the ante-chamber, and Tai-yü jumped out of bed, and awoke Hsiang-yün. When both of them had put on their clothes, Pao-yü re-entered and took a seat by the side of the toilet table; whence he beheld Tzu-chüan and Hsüeh Yen walk in and wait upon them, as they dressed their hair and performed their ablutions. Hsiang-yün had done washing her face, and Ts'üi Lü at once took the remaining water and was about to throw it away, when Pao-yü interposed, saying: "Wait, I'll avail myself of this opportunity to wash too and finish with it, and thus save myself the trouble of having again to go over!" Speaking the while, he hastily came forward, and bending his waist, he washed his face twice with two handfuls of water, and when Tzu Chüan went over to give him the scented soap, Pao-yü added: "In this basin, there's a good deal of it, and there's no need of rubbing any more!" He then washed his face with two more handfuls, and forthwith asked for a towel, and Ts'üi Lü exclaimed: "What! have you still got this failing? when will you turn a new leaf?" But Pao-yü paid not so much as any heed to her, and there and then called for some salt, with which he rubbed his teeth, and rinsed his mouth. When he had done, he perceived that Hsiang-yün had already finished combing her hair, and speedily coming up to her, he put on a smile, and said: "My dear cousin, comb my hair for me!"

"This can't be done!" Hsiang-yün objected.

"My dear cousin," Pao-yü continued smirkingly, "how is it that you combed it for me in former times?"

"I've forgotten now how to comb it!" Hsiang-yün replied.

"I'm not, after all, going out of doors," Pao-yü observed, "nor will I wear a hat or frontlet, so that all that need be done is to plait a few queues, that's all!" Saying this, he went on to appeal to her in a thousand and one endearing terms, so that Hsiang-yün had no alternative, but to draw his head nearer to her and to comb one queue after another, and as when he stayed at home he wore no hat, nor had, in fact, any tufted horns, she merely took the short surrounding hair from all four sides, and twisting it into small tufts, she collected it together over the hair on the crown of the head, and plaited a large queue, binding it fast with red ribbon; while from the root of the hair to the end of the queue, were four pearls in a row, below which, in the way of a tip, was suspended a golden pendant.

"Of these pearls there are only three," Hsiang-yün remarked as she went on plaiting; "this isn't one like them; I remember these were all of one kind, and how is it that there's one short?"

"I've lost one," Pao-yü rejoined.

"It must have dropped," Hsiang-yün added, "when you went out of doors, and been picked up by some one when you were off your guard; and he's now, instead of you, the richer for it."

"One can neither tell whether it has been really lost," Tai-yü, who stood by, interposed, smiling the while sarcastically; "nor could one say whether it hasn't been given away to some one to be mounted in some trinket or other and worn!"

Pao-yü made no reply; but set to work, seeing that the two sides of the dressing table were all full of toilet boxes and other such articles, taking up those that came under his hand and examining them. Grasping unawares a box of cosmetic, which was within his reach, he would have liked to have brought it to his lips, but he feared again lest Hsiang-yün should chide him. While he was hesitating whether to do so or not, Hsiang-yün, from behind, stretched forth her arm and gave him a smack, which sent the cosmetic flying from his hand, as she cried out: "You good-for-nothing! when will you mend those weaknesses of yours!" But hardly had she had time to complete this remark, when she caught sight of Hsi Jen walk in, who upon perceiving this state of things, became aware that he was already combed and washed, and she felt constrained to go back and attend to her own coiffure and ablutions. But suddenly, she saw Pao-ch'ai come in and inquire: "Where's cousin Pao-yü gone?"

"Do you mean to say," Hsi Jen insinuated with a sardonic smile, "that your cousin Pao-yü has leisure to stay at home?"

When Pao-ch'ai heard these words, she inwardly comprehended her meaning, and when she further heard Hsi Jen remark with a sigh: "Cousins may well be on intimate terms, but they should also observe some sort of propriety; and they shouldn't night and day romp together; and no matter how people may tender advice it's all like so much wind blowing past the ears." Pao-ch'ai began, at these remarks, to cogitate within her mind: "May I not, possibly, have been mistaken in my estimation of this girl; for to listen to her words, she would really seem to have a certain amount of *savoir faire*!"

Pao-ch'ai thereupon took a seat on the stove-couch, and quietly, in the course of their conversation on one thing and another, she managed to ascertain her age, her native village and other such particulars, and then setting her mind diligently to put, on the sly, her conversation and mental capacity to the test, she discovered how deeply worthy she was to be respected and loved. But in a while Pao-yü arrived, and Pao-ch'ai at once quitted the apartment.

"How is it," Pao-yü at once inquired, "that cousin Pao-ch'ai was chatting along with you so lustily, and that as soon as she saw me enter, she promptly ran away?"

Hsi Jen did not make any reply to his first question, and it was only when he had repeated it that Hsi Jen remarked: "Do you ask me? How can I know what goes on between you two?"

When Pao-yü heard these words, and he noticed that the look on her face was so unlike that of former days, he lost no time in putting on a smile and asking: "Why is it that you too are angry in real earnest?"

"How could I presume to get angry!" Hsi Jen rejoined smiling indifferently; "but you mustn't, from this day forth, put your foot into this room! and as you have anyhow people to wait on you, you shouldn't come again to make use of my services, for I mean to go and attend to our old mistress, as in days of old."

With this remark still on her lips, she lay herself down on the stove-couch and closed her eyes. When Pao-yü perceived the state of mind she was in, he felt deeply surprised and could not refrain from coming forward and trying to cheer her up. But Hsi Jen kept her eyes closed and paid no heed to him, so that Pao-yü was quite at a loss how to act. But espying She Yüeh enter the room, he said with alacrity: "What's up with your sister?"

"Do I know?" answered She Yüeh, "examine your own self and you'll readily know!"

After these words had been heard by Pao-yü, he gazed vacantly for some time, feeling the while very unhappy; but raising himself impetuously: "Well!" he exclaimed, "if you don't notice me, all right, I too will go to sleep," and as he spoke he got up, and, descending from the couch, he betook himself to his own bed and went to sleep. Hsi Jen noticing that he had not budged for ever so long, and that he faintly snored, presumed that he must have fallen fast asleep, so she speedily rose to her feet, and, taking a wrapper, came over and covered him. But a sound of "hu" reached her ear, as Pao-yü promptly threw it off and once again closed his eyes and feigned sleep. Hsi Jen distinctly grasped his idea and, forthwith nodding her head, she smiled coldly. "You really needn't lose your temper! but from this time forth, I'll become mute, and not say one word to you; and what if I do?"

Pao-yü could not restrain himself from rising. "What have I been up to again," he asked, "that you're once more at me with your advice? As far as your advice goes, it's all well and good; but just now without one word of counsel, you paid no heed to me when I came in, but, flying into a huff, you went to sleep. Nor could I make out what it was all about, and now here you are again maintaining that I'm angry. But when did I hear you, pray, give me a word of advice of any kind?"

"Doesn't your mind yet see for itself?" Hsi Jen replied; "and do you still expect me to tell you?"

While they were disputing, dowager lady Chia sent a servant to call him to his repast, and he thereupon crossed over to the front; but after he had hurriedly swallowed a few bowls of rice, he returned to his own apartment, where he discovered Hsi Jen reclining on the outer stove-couch, while She Yüeh was playing with the dominoes by her side. Pao-yü had been ever aware of the intimacy which existed between She Yüeh and Hsi Jen, so that paying not the slightest notice to even She Yüeh, he raised the soft portiere and straightway walked all alone into the inner apartment. She Yüeh felt constrained to follow him in, but Pao-yü at once pushed her out, saying: "I don't venture to disturb you two;" so that She Yüeh had no alternative but to leave the room with a smiling countenance, and to bid two young waiting-maids go in. Pao-yü took hold of a book and read for a considerable time in a reclining position; but upon raising his head to ask for some tea, he caught sight of a couple of waiting-maids, standing below; the one of whom, slightly older than the other, was exceedingly winsome.

"What's your name?" Pao-yü eagerly inquired.

"I'm called Hui Hsiang, (orchid fragrance)," that waiting-maid rejoined simperingly.

"Who gave you this name?" Pao-yü went on to ask.

"I went originally under the name of Yün Hsiang (Gum Sandarac)," added Hui Hsiang, "but Miss Hua it was who changed it."

"You should really be called Hui Ch'i, (latent fragrance), that would be proper; and why such stuff as Hui Hsiang, (orchid fragrance)?"

"How many sisters have you got?" he further went on to ask of her.

"Four," replied Hui Hsiang.

"Which of them are you?" Pao-yü asked.

"The fourth," answered Hui Hsiang.

"By and by you must be called Ssu Erh, (fourth child)," Pao-yü suggested, "for there's no need for any such nonsense as Hui Hsiang (orchid fragrance) or Lan Ch'i (epidendrum perfume.) Which single girl deserves to be compared to all these flowers, without profaning pretty names and fine surnames!"

As he uttered these words, he bade her give him some tea, which he drank; while Hsi Jen and She Yüeh, who were in the outer apartment, had been listening for a long time and laughing with compressed lips.

Pao-yü did not, on this day, so much as put his foot outside the door of his room, but sat all alone sad and dejected, simply taking up his books, in order to dispel his melancholy fit, or diverting himself with his writing materials; while he did not even avail himself of the services of any of the family servants, but simply bade Ssu Erh answer his calls.

This Ssu Erh was, who would have thought it, a girl gifted with matchless artfulness, and perceiving that Pao-yü had requisitioned her services, she speedily began to devise extreme ways and means to inveigle him. When evening came, and dinner was over, Pao-yü's eyes were scorching hot and his ears burning from the effects of two cups of wine that he had taken. Had it been in past days, he would have now had Hsi Jen and her companions with him, and with all their good cheer and laughter, he would have been enjoying himself. But here was he, on this occasion, dull and forlorn, a solitary being, gazing at the lamp with an absolute lack of pleasure. By and by he felt a certain wish to go after them, but dreading that if they carried their point, they would, in the future, come and tender advice still more immoderate, and that, were he to put on the airs of a superior to intimidate them, he would appear to be too deeply devoid of all feeling, he therefore, needless to say, thwarted the wish of his heart, and treated them just as if they were dead. And as anyway he was constrained also to live, alone though he was, he readily looked upon them, for the time being as departed, and did not worry his mind in the least on their account. On the contrary, he was able to feel happy and contented with his own society. Hence it was that bidding Ssu Erh trim the candles and brew the tea, he himself perused for a time the "Nan Hua Ching," and upon reaching the precept: "On thieves," given on some additional pages, the burden of which was: "Therefore by exterminating intuitive wisdom, and by discarding knowledge, highway robbers will cease to exist, and by taking off the jade and by putting away the pearls, pilferers will not spring to existence; by burning the slips and by breaking up the seals, by smashing the measures, and snapping the scales, the result will be that the people will not wrangle; by abrogating, to the utmost degree, wise rules under the heavens, the people will, at length, be able to take part in deliberation. By putting to confusion the musical scale, and destroying fifes and lutes, by deafening the ears of the blind Kuang, then, at last, will the human race in the world constrain his sense of hearing. By extinguishing literary compositions, by dispersing the five colours and by sticking the eyes of Li Chu, then, at length, mankind under the whole sky, will restrain the perception of his eyes. By destroying and eliminating the hooks and lines, by discarding the compasses and squares, and by amputating Kung Chui's fingers, the human race will ultimately succeed in constraining his ingenuity,"—his high spirits, on perusal of this passage, were so exultant that taking advantage of the exuberance caused by the wine, he picked up his pen, for he could not repress himself, and continued the text in this wise: "By burning the flower, (Hua-Hsi Jen) and dispersing the musk, (She Yüeh), the consequence will be that the inmates of the inner chambers will, eventually, keep advice to themselves. By obliterating Pao-ch'ai's supernatural beauty, by reducing to ashes Tai-yü's spiritual perception, and by destroying and extinguishing my affectionate preferences, the beautiful in the inner chambers as well as the plain will then, at length, be put on the same footing. And as they will keep advice to themselves, there will be no fear of any disagreement. By obliterating her supernatural beauty, I shall then have no incentive for any violent affection; by dissolving her spiritual perception, I will have no feelings with which to foster the memory of her talents. The hair-pin, jade, flower and musk (Pao-ch'ai, Tai-yü, Hsi Jen and She Yüeh) do each and all spread out their snares and dig mines, and thus succeed in inveigling and entrapping every one in the world."

At the conclusion of this annex, he flung the pen away, and lay himself down to sleep. His head had barely reached the pillow before he at once fell fast asleep, remaining the whole night long perfectly unconscious of everything straight up to the break of day, when upon waking and turning himself round, he, at a glance, caught sight of no one else than Hsi Jen, sleeping in her clothes over the coverlet.

Pao-yü had already banished from his mind every thought of what had transpired the previous day, so that forthwith giving Hsi Jen a push: "Get up!" he said, "and be careful where you sleep, as you may catch cold."

The fact is that Hsi Jen was aware that he was, without regard to day or night, ever up to mischief with his female cousins; but presuming that if she earnestly called him to account, he would not mend his ways, she had, for this reason, had recourse to tender language to exhort him, in the hope that, in a short while, he would come round again to his better self. But against all her expectations Pao-yü had, after the lapse of a whole day and night, not changed the least in his manner, and as she really was in her heart quite at a loss what to do, she failed to find throughout the whole night any proper sleep. But when on this day, she unexpectedly perceived Pao-yü in this mood, she flattered herself that he had made up his mind to effect a change, and readily thought it best not to notice him. Pao-yü, seeing that she made no reply, forthwith stretched out his hand and undid her jacket; but he had just unclasped the button, when his arm was pushed away by Hsi Jen, who again made it fast herself.

Pao-yü was so much at his wit's ends that he had no alternative but to take her hand and smilingly ask: "What's the matter with you, after all, that I've had to ask you something time after time?"

Hsi Jen opened her eyes wide. "There's nothing really the matter with me!" she observed; "but as you're awake, you surely had better be going over into the opposite room to comb your hair and wash; for if you dilly-dally any longer, you won't be in time."

"Where shall I go over to?" Pao-yü inquired.

Hsi Jen gave a sarcastic grin. "Do you ask me?" she rejoined; "do I know? you're at perfect liberty to go over wherever you like; from this day forth you and I must part company so as to avoid fighting like cocks or brawling like geese, to the amusement of third parties. Indeed, when you get surfeited on that side, you come over to this, where there are, after all, such girls as Fours and Fives (Ssu Erh and Wu Erh) to dance attendance upon you. But such kind of things as ourselves uselessly defile fine names and fine surnames."

"Do you still remember this to-day!" Pao-yü asked with a smirk.

"Hundred years hence I shall still bear it in mind," Hsi Jen protested; "I'm not like you, who treat my words as so much wind blowing by the side of your ears, that what I've said at night, you've forgotten early in the morning."

Pao-yü perceiving what a seductive though angry air pervaded her face found it difficult to repress his feelings, and speedily taking up, from the side of the pillow, a hair-pin made of jade, he dashed it down breaking it into two exclaiming: "If I again don't listen to your words, may I fare like this hair-pin."

Hsi Jen immediately picked up the hair-pin, as she remarked: "What's up with you at this early hour of the morning? Whether you listen or not is of no consequence; and is it worth while that you should behave as you do?"

"How can you know," Pao-yü answered, "the anguish in my heart!"

"Do you also know what anguish means?" Hsi Jen observed laughing; "if you do, then you can judge what the state of my heart is! But be quick and get up, and wash your face and be off!"

As she spoke, they both got out of bed and performed their toilette; but after Pao-yü had gone to the drawing rooms, and at a moment least expected by any one, Tai-yü walked into his apartment. Noticing that Pao-yü was not in, she was fumbling with the books on the table and examining them, when, as luck would have it, she turned up the Chuang Tzu of the previous day. Upon perusing the passage tagged on by Pao-yü, she could not help feeling both incensed and amused. Nor could she restrain herself from taking up the pen and appending a stanza to this effect:

Who is that man, who of his pen, without good rhyme, made use,
A toilsome task to do into the Chuang-tzu text to steal,

Who for the knowledge he doth lack no sense of shame doth feel,
But language vile and foul employs third parties to abuse?

At the conclusion of what she had to write, she too came into the drawing room; but after paying her respects to dowager lady Chia, she walked over to madame Wang's quarters.

Contrary to everybody's expectations, lady Feng's daughter, Ta Chieh Erh, had fallen ill, and a great fuss was just going on as the doctor had been sent for to diagnose her ailment.

"My congratulations to you, ladies," the doctor explained; "this young lady has fever, as she has small-pox; indeed it's no other complaint!"

As soon as madame Wang and lady Feng heard the tidings, they lost no time in sending round to ascertain whether she was getting on all right or not, and the doctor replied: "The symptoms are, it is true, serious, but favourable; but though after all importing no danger, it's necessary to get ready the silkworms and pigs' tails."

When lady Feng received this report, she, there and then, hastened to make the necessary preparations, and while she had the rooms swept and oblations offered to the goddess of small-pox, she, at the same time, transmitted orders to her household to avoid viands fried or roasted in fat, or other such heating things; and also bade P'ing Erh get ready the bedding and clothes for Chia Lien in a separate room, and taking pieces of deep red cotton material, she distributed them to the nurses, waiting-maids and all the servants, who were in close attendance, to cut out clothes for themselves. And having had likewise some apartments outside swept clean, she detained two doctors to alternately deliberate on the treatment, feel the pulse and administer the medicines; and for twelve days, they were not at liberty to return to their homes; while Chia Lien had no help but to move his quarters temporarily into the outer library, and lady Feng and P'ing Erh remained both in daily attendance upon madame Wang in her devotions to the goddess.

Chia Lien, now that he was separated from lady Feng, soon felt disposed to look round for a flame. He had only slept alone for a couple of nights, but these nights had been so intensely intolerable that he had no option than to choose, for the time being, from among the young pages, those who were of handsome appearance, and bring them over to relieve his monotony. In the Jung Kuo mansion, there was, it happened, a cook, a most useless, good-for-nothing drunkard, whose name was To Kuan, in whom people recognised an infirm and a useless husband so that they all dubbed him with the name of To Hun

Ch'ung, the stupid worm To. As the wife given to him in marriage by his father and mother was this year just twenty, and possessed further several traits of beauty, and was also naturally of a flighty and frivolous disposition, she had an extreme penchant for violent flirtations. But To Hun-ch'ung, on the other hand, did not concern himself (with her deportment), and as long as he had wine, meat and money he paid no heed whatever to anything. And for this reason it was that all the men in the two mansions of Ning and Jung had been successful in their attentions; and as this woman was exceptionally fascinating and incomparably giddy, she was generally known by all by the name To Ku Ning (Miss To).

Chia Lien, now that he had his quarters outside, chafed under the pangs of irksome ennui, yet he too, in days gone by, had set his eyes upon this woman, and had for long, watered in the mouth with admiration; but as, inside, he feared his winsome wife, and outside, he dreaded his beloved lads, he had not made any advances. But this To Ku Niang had likewise a liking for Chia Lien, and was full of resentment at the absence of a favourable opportunity; but she had recently come to hear that Chia Lien had shifted his quarters into the outer library, and her wont was, even in the absence of any legitimate purpose, to go over three and four times to entice him on; but though Chia Lien was, in every respect, like a rat smitten with hunger, he could not dispense with holding consultation with the young friends who enjoyed his confidence; and as he struck a bargain with them for a large amount of money and silks, how could they ever not have come to terms (with him to speak on his behalf)? Besides, they were all old friends of this woman, so that, as soon as they conveyed the proposal, she willingly accepted it. When night came To Hun Ch'ung was lying on the couch in a state of drunkenness, and at the second watch, when every one was quiet, Chia Lien at once slipped in, and they had their assignation. As soon as he gazed upon her face, he lost control over his senses, and without even one word of ordinary greeting or commonplace remark, they forthwith, fervently indulged in a most endearing tête-à-tête.

This woman possessed, who could have thought it, a strange natural charm; for, as soon as any one of her lovers came within any close distance of her, he speedily could not but notice that her very tendons and bones mollified, paralysed-like from feeling, so that his was the sensation of basking in a soft bower of love. What is more, her demonstrative ways and free-and-easy talk put even those of a born coquette to shame, with the result that while Chia Lien, at this time, longed to become heart and soul one with her, the woman designedly indulged in immodest innuendoes.

"Your daughter is at home," she insinuated in her recumbent position, "ill with the small-pox, and prayers are being offered to the goddess; and your duty too should be to abstain from love affairs for a couple of days, but on the contrary, by flirting with me, you've contaminated yourself! but, you'd better be off at once from me here!"

"You're my goddess!" gaspingly protested Chia Lien, as he gave way to demonstrativeness; "what do I care about any other goddess!"

The woman began to be still more indelicate in her manner, so that Chia Lien could not refrain himself from making a full exhibition of his warm sentiments. When their tête-à-tête had come to a close, they both went on again to vow by the mountains and swear by the seas, and though they found it difficult to part company and hard to tear themselves away, they, in due course, became, after this occasion, mutual sworn friends. But by a certain day the virus in Ta Chieh's system had become exhausted, and the spots subsided, and at the expiry of twelve days the goddess was removed, and the whole household offered sacrifices to heaven, worshipped the ancestors, paid their vows, burnt incense, exchanged congratulations, and distributed presents. And these formalities observed, Chia Lien once more moved back into his own bedroom and was reunited with lady Feng. The proverb is indeed true which says: "That a new marriage is not equal to a long separation," for there ensued between them demonstrations of loving affection still more numerous than heretofore, to which we need not, of course, refer with any minuteness.

The next day, at an early hour, after lady Feng had gone into the upper rooms, P'ing Erh set to work to put in order the clothes and bedding, which had been brought from outside, when, contrary to her expectation, a tress of hair fell out from inside the pillow-case, as she was intent upon shaking it. P'ing Erh understood its import, and taking at once the hair, she concealed it in her sleeve, and there and then came over into the room on this side, where she produced the hair, and smirkingly asked Chia Lien, "What's this?"

Chia Lien, at the sight of it, lost no time in making a snatch with the idea of depriving her of it; and when P'ing Erh speedily endeavoured to run away, she was clutched by Chia Lien, who put her down on the stove-couch, and came up to take it from her hand.

"You heartless fellow!" P'ing Erh laughingly exclaimed, "I conceal this, with every good purpose, from her knowledge, and come to ask you about it, and you, on the contrary, fly into a rage! But wait till she comes back, and I'll tell her, and we'll see what will happen."

At these words, Chia Lien hastily forced a smile. "Dear girl!" he entreated, "give it to me, and I won't venture again to fly into a passion."

But hardly was this remark finished, when they heard the voice of lady Feng penetrate into the room. As soon as it reached the ear of Chia Lien, he was at a loss whether it was better to let her go or to snatch it away, and kept on shouting, "My dear girl! don't let her know."

P'ing Erh at once rose to her feet; but lady Feng had already entered the room; and she went on to bid P'ing Erh be quick and open a box and find a pattern for madame Wang. P'ing Erh expressed her obedience with alacrity; but while in search of it, lady Feng caught sight of Chia Lien; and suddenly remembering something, she hastened to ask P'ing Erh about it.

"The other day," she observed, "some things were taken out, and have you brought them all in or not?"

"I have!" P'ing Erh assented.

"Is there anything short or not?" lady Feng inquired.

"I've carefully looked at them," P'ing Erh added, "and haven't found even one single thing short."

"Is there anything in excess?" lady Feng went on to ascertain.

P'ing Erh laughed. "It's enough," she rejoined, "that there's nothing short; and how could there really turn out to be anything over and above?"

"That this half month," lady Feng continued still smiling, "things have gone on immaculately it would be hard to vouch; for some intimate friend there may have been, who possibly has left something behind, in the shape of a ring, handkerchief or other such object, there's no saying for certain!"

While these words were being spoken, Chia Lien's face turned perfectly sallow, and, as he stood behind lady Feng, he was intent upon gazing at P'ing Erh, making signs to her (that he was going) to cut her throat as a chicken is killed, (threatening her not to utter a sound) and entreating her to screen him; but P'ing Erh pretended not to notice him, and consequently observed smiling: "How is it that my ideas should coincide with those of yours, my lady; and as I suspected that there may have been something of the kind, I carefully searched all over, but I didn't find even so much as the slightest thing wrong; and if you don't believe me, my lady, you can search for your own self."

"You fool!" lady Feng laughed, "had he any things of the sort, would he be likely to let you and I discover them!"

With these words still on her lips, she took the patterns and went her way; whereupon P'ing Erh pointed at her nose, and shook her head to and fro. "In this matter," she smiled, "how much you should be grateful to me!" A remark which so delighted Chia Lien that his eyebrows distended, and his eyes smiled, and running over, he clasped her in his embrace, and called her promiscuously: "My darling, my pet, my own treasure!"

"This," observed P'ing Erh, with the tress in her hand, "will be my source of power, during all my lifetime! if you treat me kindly, then well and good! but if you behave unkindly, then we'll at once produce this thing!"

"Do put it away, please," Chia Lien entreated smirkingly, "and don't, on an any account, let her know about it!" and as he uttered these words, he noticed that she was off her guard, and, with a snatch, readily grabbed it adding laughingly: "In your hands, it would be a source of woe, so that it's better that I should burn it, and have done with it!" Saying this he simultaneously shoved it down the sides of his boot, while P'ing Erh shouted as she set her teeth close: "You wicked man! you cross the river and then demolish the bridge! but do you imagine that I'll by and by again tell lies on your behalf!"

Chia Lien perceiving how heart-stirring her seductive charms were, forthwith clasped her in his arms, and begged her to be his; but P'ing Erh snatched her hands out of his grasp and ran away out of the room; which so exasperated Chia Lien that as he bent his body, he exclaimed, full of indignation: "What a dreadful niggardly young wench! she actually sets her mind to stir up people's affections with her wanton blandishments, and then, after all, she runs away!"

"If I be wanton, it's my own look-out;" P'ing Erh answered, from outside the window, with a grin, "and who told you to arouse your affections? Do you forsooth mean to imply that my wish is to become your tool? And did she come to know about it would she again ever forgive me?"

"You needn't dread her!" Chia Lien urged; "wait till my monkey is up, and I'll take this jealous woman, and beat her to atoms; and she'll then know what stuff I'm made of. She watches me just as she would watch a thief! and she's only to hobnob with men, and I'm not to say a word to any girl! and if I do say aught to a girl, or get anywhere near one, she must at once give way to suspicion. But with no regard to younger brothers or nephews, to young and old, she prattles and giggles with them, and doesn't entertain any fear that I may be jealous; but henceforward I too won't allow her to set eyes upon any man."

"If she be jealous, there's every reason," P'ing Erh answered, "but for you to be jealous on her account isn't right. Her conduct is really straightforward, and her deportment upright, but your conduct is actuated by an evil heart, so much so that even I don't feel my heart at ease, not to say anything of her."

"You two," continued Chia Lien, "have a mouth full of malicious breath! Everything the couple of you do is invariably proper, while whatever I do is all from an evil heart! But some time or other I shall bring you both to your end with my own hands!"

This sentence was scarcely at an end, when lady Feng walked into the court. "If you're bent upon chatting," she urgently inquired, upon seeing P'ing Erh outside the window, "why don't you go into the room? and what do you mean, instead, by running out, and speaking with the window between?"

Chia Lien from inside took up the string of the conversation. "You should ask her," he said. "It would verily seem as if there were a tiger in the room to eat her up."

"There's not a single person in the room," P'ing Erh rejoined, "and what shall I stay and do with him?"

"It's just the proper thing that there should be no one else! Isn't it?" lady Feng remarked grinning sarcastically.

"Do these words allude to me?" P'ing Erh hastily asked, as soon as she had heard what she said.

Lady Feng forthwith laughed. "If they don't allude to you," she continued, "to whom do they?"

"Don't press me to come out with some nice things!" P'ing Erh insinuated, and, as she spoke, she did not even raise the portiere (for lady Feng to enter), but straightway betook herself to the opposite side.

Lady Feng lifted the portiere with her own hands, and walked into the room. "That girl P'ing Erh," she exclaimed, "has gone mad, and if this hussey does in real earnest wish to try and get the upper hand of me, it would be well for you to mind your skin."

Chia Lien listened to her, as he kept reclining on the couch. "I never in the least knew," he ventured, clapping his hands and laughing, "that P'ing Erh was so dreadful; and I must, after all, from henceforth look up to her with respect!"

"It's all through your humouring her," lady Feng rejoined; "so I'll simply settle scores with you and finish with it."

"Ts'ui!" ejaculated Chia Lien at these words, "because you two can't agree, must you again make a scapegoat of me! Well then, I'll get out of the way of both of you!"

"I'll see where you'll go and hide," lady Feng observed.

"I've got somewhere to go!" Chia Lien added; and with these words, he was about to go, when lady Feng urged: "Don't be off! I have something to tell you."

What it is, is not yet known, but, reader, listen to the account given in the next chapter.

CHAPTER XXII.

Upon hearing the text of the stanza, Pao-yü comprehends the Buddhistic
spells.
While the enigmas for the lanterns are being devised, Chia Cheng is grieved by a prognostic.

Chia Lien, for we must now prosecute our story, upon hearing lady Feng observe that she had something to consult about with him, felt constrained to halt and to inquire what it was about.

"On the 21st," lady Feng explained, "is cousin Hsüeh's birthday, and what do you, after all, purpose doing?"

"Do I know what to do?" exclaimed Chia Lien; "you have made, time and again, arrangements for ever so many birthdays of grown-up people, and do you, really, find yourself on this occasion without any resources?"

"Birthdays of grown-up people are subject to prescribed rules," lady Feng expostulated; "but her present birthday is neither one of an adult nor that of an infant, and that's why I would like to deliberate with you!"

Chia Lien upon hearing this remark, lowered his head and gave himself to protracted reflection. "You're indeed grown dull!" he cried; "why you've a precedent ready at hand to suit your case! Cousin Lin's birthday affords a precedent, and what you did in former years for cousin Lin, you can in this instance likewise do for cousin Hsüeh, and it will be all right."

At these words lady Feng gave a sarcastic smile. "Do you, pray, mean to insinuate," she added, "that I'm not aware of even this! I too had previously come, after some thought, to this conclusion; but old lady Chia explained, in my hearing yesterday, that having made inquiries about all their ages and their birthdays, she learnt that cousin

Hsüeh would this year be fifteen, and that though this was not the birthday, which made her of age, she could anyhow well be regarded as being on the dawn of the year, in which she would gather up her hair, so that our dowager lady enjoined that her anniversary should, as a matter of course, be celebrated, unlike that of cousin Lin."

"Well, in that case," Chia Lien suggested, "you had better make a few additions to what was done for cousin Lin!"

"That's what I too am thinking of," lady Feng replied, "and that's why I'm asking your views; for were I, on my own hook, to add anything you would again feel hurt for my not have explained things to you."

"That will do, that will do!" Chia Lien rejoined laughing, "none of these sham attentions for me! So long as you don't pry into my doings it will be enough; and will I go so far as to bear you a grudge?"

With these words still in his mouth, he forthwith went off. But leaving him alone we shall now return to Shih Hsiang-yün. After a stay of a couple of days, her intention was to go back, but dowager lady Chia said: "Wait until after you have seen the theatrical performance, when you can return home."

At this proposal, Shih Hsiang-yün felt constrained to remain, but she, at the same time, despatched a servant to her home to fetch two pieces of needlework, which she had in former days worked with her own hands, for a birthday present for Pao-ch'ai.

Contrary to all expectations old lady Chia had, since the arrival of Pao-ch'ai, taken quite a fancy to her, for her sedateness and good nature, and as this happened to be the first birthday which she was about to celebrate (in the family) she herself readily contributed twenty taels which, after sending for lady Feng, she handed over to her, to make arrangements for a banquet and performance.

"A venerable senior like yourself," lady Feng thereupon smiled and ventured, with a view to enhancing her good cheer, "is at liberty to celebrate the birthday of a child in any way agreeable to you, without any one presuming to raise any objection; but what's the use again of giving a banquet? But since it be your good pleasure and your purpose to have it celebrated with éclat, you could, needless to say, your own self have spent several taels from the private funds in that old treasury of yours! But you now produce those twenty taels, spoiled by damp and mould, to play the hostess with, with the view indeed of compelling us to supply what's wanted! But hadn't you really been able to contribute any more, no one would have a word to say; but the gold and silver, round as well as flat, have with their heavy weight pressed down the bottom of the box! and your sole object is to harass us and to extort from us. But raise your eyes and look about you; who isn't your venerable ladyship's son and daughter? and is it likely, pray, that in the future there will only be cousin Pao-yü to carry you, our old lady, on his head, up the Wu T'ai Shan? You may keep all these things for him alone! but though we mayn't at present, deserve that anything should be spent upon us, you shouldn't go so far as to place us in any perplexities (by compelling us to subscribe). And is this now enough for wines, and enough for the theatricals?"

As she bandied these words, every one in the whole room burst out laughing, and even dowager lady Chia broke out in laughter while she observed: "Do you listen to that mouth? I myself am looked upon as having the gift of the gab, but why is it that I can't talk in such a wise as to put down this monkey? Your mother-in-law herself doesn't dare to be so overbearing in her speech; and here you are jabber, jabber with me!"

"My mother-in-law," explained lady Feng, "is also as fond of Pao-yü as you are, so much so that I haven't anywhere I could go and give vent to my grievances; and instead of (showing me some regard) you say that I'm overbearing in my speech!"

With these words, she again enticed dowager lady Chia to laugh for a while. The old lady continued in the highest of spirits, and, when evening came, and they all appeared in her presence to pay their obeisance, her ladyship made it a point, while the whole company of ladies and young ladies were engaged in chatting, to ascertain of Pao-ch'ai what play she liked to hear, and what things she fancied to eat.

Pao-ch'ai was well aware that dowager lady Chia, well up in years though she was, delighted in sensational performances, and was partial to sweet and tender viands, so that she readily deferred, in every respect, to those things, which were to the taste of her ladyship, and enumerated a whole number of them, which made the old lady become the more exuberant. And the next day, she was the first to send over clothes, nicknacks and such presents, while madame Wang and lady Feng, Tai-yü and the other girls, as well as the whole number of inmates had all presents for her, regulated by their degree of relationship, to which we need not allude in detail.

When the 21st arrived, a stage of an ordinary kind, small but yet handy, was improvised in dowager lady Chia's inner court, and a troupe of young actors, who had newly made their début, was retained for the nonce, among whom were both those who could sing tunes, slow as well as fast. In the drawing rooms of the old lady were then laid out several tables for a family banquet and entertainment, at which there was not a single outside guest; and with the exception of Mrs. Hsüeh, Shih Hsiang-yün, and Pao-ch'ai, who were visitors, the rest were all inmates of her household.

On this day, Pao-yü failed, at any early hour, to see anything of Lin Tai-yü, and coming at once to her rooms in search of her, he discovered her reclining on the stove-couch. "Get up," Pao-yü pressed her with a smile, "and come and have breakfast, for the plays will commence shortly; but whichever plays you would like to listen to, do tell me so that I may be able to choose them."

Tai-yü smiled sarcastically. "In that case," she rejoined, "you had better specially engage a troupe and select those I like sung for my benefit; for on this occasion you can't be so impertinent as to make use of their expense to ask me what I like!"

"What's there impossible about this?" Pao-yü answered smiling; "well, to-morrow I'll readily do as you wish, and ask them too to make use of what is yours and mine."

As he passed this remark, he pulled her up, and taking her hand in his own, they walked out of the room and came and had breakfast. When the time arrived to make a selection of the plays, dowager lady Chia of her own motion first asked Pao-ch'ai to mark off those she liked; and though for a time Pao-ch'ai declined, yielding the choice to others, she had no alternative but to decide, fixing upon a play called, "the Record of the Western Tour," a play of which the old lady was herself very fond. Next in order, she bade lady Feng choose, and lady Feng, had, after all, in spite of madame Wang ranking before her in precedence, to consider old lady Chia's request, and not to presume to show obstinacy by any disobedience. But as she knew well enough that her ladyship had a penchant for what was exciting, and that she was still more partial to jests, jokes, epigrams, and buffoonery, she therefore hastened to precede (madame Wang) and to choose a play, which was in fact no other than "Liu Erh pawns his clothes."

Dowager lady Chia was, of course, still more elated. And after this she speedily went on to ask Tai-yü to choose. Tai-yü likewise concedingly yielded her turn in favour of madame Wang and the other seniors, to make their selections before her, but the old lady expostulated. "To-day," she said, "is primarily an occasion, on which I've brought all of you here for your special recreation; and we had better look after our own selves and not heed them! For have I, do you imagine, gone to the trouble of having a performance and laying a feast for their special benefit? they're already reaping benefit enough by being in here, listening to the plays and partaking of the banquet, when they have no right to either; and are they to be pressed further to make a choice of plays?"

At these words, the whole company had a hearty laugh; after which, Tai-yü, at length, marked off a play; next in order following Pao-yü, Shih Hsiang-yün, Ying-ch'un, T'an Ch'un, Hsi Ch'un, widow Li Wan, and the rest, each and all of whom made a choice of plays, which were sung in the costumes necessary for each. When the time came to take their places at the banquet, dowager lady Chia bade Pao-ch'ai make another selection, and Pao-ch'ai cast her choice upon the play: "Lu Chih-shen, in a fit of drunkenness stirs up a disturbance up the Wu T'ai mountain;" whereupon Pao-yü interposed, with the remark: "All you fancy is to choose plays of this kind;" to which Pao-ch'ai rejoined, "You've listened to plays all these years to no avail! How could you know the beauties of this play? the stage effect is grand, but what is still better are the apt and elegant passages in it."

"I've always had a dread of such sensational plays as these!" Pao-yü retorted.

"If you call this play sensational," Pao-ch'ai smilingly expostulated, "well then you may fitly be looked upon as being no connoisseur of plays. But come over and I'll tell you. This play constitutes one of a set of books, entitled the 'Pei Tien Peng Ch'un,' which, as far as harmony, musical rests and closes, and tune go, is, it goes without saying, perfect; but there's among the elegant compositions a ballad entitled: 'the Parasitic Plant,' written in a most excellent style; but how could you know anything about it?"

Pao-yü, upon hearing her speak of such points of beauty, hastily drew near to her. "My dear cousin," he entreated, "recite it and let me hear it!" Whereupon Pao-ch'ai went on as follows:

My manly tears I will not wipe away,
But from this place, the scholar's home, I'll stray.
The bonze for mercy I shall thank; under the lotus altar shave my pate;
With Yüan to be the luck I lack; soon in a twinkle we shall separate,
And needy and forlorn I'll come and go, with none to care about my fate.
Thither shall I a suppliant be for a fog wrapper and rain hat; my warrant I shall roll,
And listless with straw shoes and broken bowl, wherever to convert my fate may be, I'll stroll.

As soon as Pao-yü had listened to her recital, he was so full of enthusiasm, that, clapping his knees with his hands, and shaking his head, he gave vent to incessant praise; after which he went on to extol Pao-ch'ai, saying: "There's no book that you don't know."

"Be quiet, and listen to the play," Lin Tai-yü urged; "they haven't yet sung about the mountain gate, and you already pretend to be mad!"

At these words, Hsiang-yün also laughed. But, in due course, the whole party watched the performance until evening, when they broke up. Dowager lady Chia was so very much taken with the young actor, who played the role of a lady, as well as with the one who acted the buffoon, that she gave orders that they should be brought in; and, as she looked at them closely, she felt so much the more interest in them, that she went on to inquire what their ages were. And when the would-be lady (replied) that he was just eleven, while the would-be buffoon (explained) that he was just nine, the whole company gave vent for a time to expressions of sympathy with their lot; while dowager lady Chia bade servants bring a fresh supply of meats and fruits for both of them, and also gave them, besides their wages, two tiaos as a present.

"This lad," lady Feng observed smiling, "is when dressed up (as a girl), a living likeness of a certain person; did you notice it just now?"

Pao-ch'ai was also aware of the fact, but she simply nodded her head assentingly and did not say who it was. Pao-yü likewise expressed his assent by shaking his head, but he too did not presume to speak out. Shih Hsiang-yün, however, readily took up the conversation. "He resembles," she interposed, "cousin Lin's face!" When this remark reached Pao-yü's ear, he hastened to cast an angry scowl at Hsiang-yün, and to make her a sign; while the whole party, upon hearing what had been said, indulged in careful and minute scrutiny of (the lad); and as they all began to laugh: "The resemblance is indeed striking!" they exclaimed.

After a while, they parted; and when evening came Hsiang-yün directed Ts'ui Lü to pack up her clothes.

"What's the hurry?" Ts'ui Lü asked. "There will be ample time to pack up, on the day on which we go!"

"We'll go to-morrow," Hsiang-yün rejoined; "for what's the use of remaining here any longer—to look at people's mouths and faces?"

Pao-yü, at these words, lost no time in pressing forward.

"My dear cousin," he urged; "you're wrong in bearing me a grudge! My cousin Lin is a girl so very touchy, that though every one else distinctly knew (of the resemblance), they wouldn't speak out; and all because they were afraid that she would get angry; but unexpectedly out you came with it, at a moment when off your guard; and how ever couldn't she but feel hurt? and it's because I was in dread that you would give offence to people that I then winked at you; and now here you are angry with me; but isn't that being ungrateful to me? Had it been any one else, would I have cared whether she had given offence to even ten; that would have been none of my business!"

Hsiang-yün waved her hand: "Don't," she added, "come and tell me these flowery words and this specious talk, for I really can't come up to your cousin Lin. If others poke fun at her, they all do so with impunity, while if I say anything, I at once incur blame. The fact is I shouldn't have spoken of her, undeserving as I am; and as she's the daughter of a master, while I'm a slave, a mere servant girl, I've heaped insult upon her!"

"And yet," pleaded Pao-yü, full of perplexity, "I had done it for your sake; and through this, I've come in for reproach. But if it were with an evil heart I did so, may I at once become ashes, and be trampled upon by ten thousands of people!"

"In this felicitous firstmonth," Hsiang-yün remonstrated, "you shouldn't talk so much reckless nonsense! All these worthless despicable oaths, disjointed words, and corrupt language, go and tell for the benefit of those mean sort of people, who in everything take pleasure in irritating others, and who keep you under their thumb! But mind don't drive me to spit contemptuously at you."

As she gave utterance to these words, she betook herself in the inner room of dowager lady Chia's suite of apartments, where she lay down in high dudgeon, and, as Pao-yü was so heavy at heart, he could not help coming again in search of Tai-yü; but strange to say, as soon as he put his foot inside the doorway, he was speedily hustled out of it by Tai-yü, who shut the door in his face.

Pao-yü was once more unable to fathom her motives, and as he stood outside the window, he kept on calling out: "My dear cousin," in a low tone of voice; but Tai-yü paid not the slightest notice to him so that Pao-yü became so melancholy that he drooped his head, and was plunged in silence. And though Hsi Jen had, at an early hour, come to know the circumstances, she could not very well at this juncture tender any advice.

Pao-yü remained standing in such a vacant mood that Tai-yü imagined that he had gone back; but when she came to open the door she caught sight of Pao-yü still waiting in there; and as Tai-yü did not feel justified to again close the door, Pao-yü consequently followed her in.

"Every thing has," he observed, "a why and a wherefore; which, when spoken out, don't even give people pain; but you will rush into a rage, and all without any rhyme! but to what really does it owe its rise?"

"It's well enough, after all, for you to ask me," Tai-yü rejoined with an indifferent smile, "but I myself don't know why! But am I here to afford you people amusement that you will compare me to an actress, and make the whole lot have a laugh at me?"

"I never did liken you to anything," Pao-yü protested, "neither did I ever laugh at you! and why then will you get angry with me?"

"Was it necessary that you should have done so much as made the comparison," Tai-yü urged, "and was there any need of even any laughter from you? why, though you mayn't have likened me to anything, or had a laugh at my expense, you were, yea more dreadful than those who did compare me (to a singing girl) and ridiculed me!"

Pao-yü could not find anything with which to refute the argument he had just heard, and Tai-yü went on to say. "This offence can, anyhow, be condoned; but, what is more, why did you also wink at Yün Erh? What was this idea which you had resolved in your mind? wasn't it perhaps that if she played with me, she would be demeaning herself, and making herself cheap? She's the daughter of a duke or a marquis, and we forsooth the mean progeny of a poor plebeian family; so that, had she diverted herself with me, wouldn't she have exposed herself to being depreciated, had I, perchance, said anything in retaliation? This was your idea wasn't it? But though your purpose was, to be sure, honest enough, that girl wouldn't, however, receive any favours from you, but got angry with you just as much as I did; and though she made me also a tool to do you a good turn, she, on the contrary, asserts that I'm mean by nature and take pleasure in irritating people in everything! and you again were afraid lest she should have hurt my feelings, but, had I had a row with her, what would that have been to you? and had she given me any offence, what concern would that too have been of yours?"

When Pao-yü heard these words, he at once became alive to the fact that she too had lent an ear to the private conversation he had had a short while back with Hsiang-yün: "All because of my, fears," he carefully mused within himself, "lest these two should have a misunderstanding, I was induced to come between them, and act as a mediator; but I myself have, contrary to my hopes, incurred blame and abuse on both sides! This just accords with what I read the other day in the Nan Hua Ching. 'The ingenious toil, the wise are full of care; the good-for-nothing seek for nothing, they feed on vegetables, and roam where they list; they wander purposeless like a boat not made fast!' 'The mountain trees,' the text goes on to say, 'lead to their own devastation; the spring (conduces) to its own plunder; and so on." And the more he therefore indulged in reflection, the more depressed he felt. "Now there are only these few girls," he proceeded to ponder minutely, "and yet, I'm unable to treat them in such a way as to promote perfect harmony; and what will I forsooth do by and by (when there will be more to deal with)!"

When he had reached this point in his cogitations, (he decided) that it was really of no avail to agree with her, so that turning round, he was making his way all alone into his apartments; but Lin Tai-yü, upon noticing that he had left her side, readily concluded that reflection had marred his spirits and that he had so thoroughly lost his temper as to be going without even giving vent to a single word, and she could not restrain herself from feeling inwardly more and more irritated. "After you've gone this time," she hastily exclaimed, "don't come again, even for a whole lifetime; and I won't have you either so much as speak to me!"

Pao-yü paid no heed to her, but came back to his rooms, and laying himself down on his bed, he kept on muttering in a state of chagrin; and though Hsi Jen knew full well the reasons of his dejection, she found it difficult to summon up courage to say anything to him at the moment, and she had no alternative but to try and distract him by means of irrelevant matters. "The theatricals which you've seen to-day," she consequently observed smiling, "will again lead to performances for several days, and Miss Pao-ch'ai will, I'm sure, give a return feast."

"Whether she gives a return feast or not," Pao-yü rejoined with an apathetic smirk, "is no concern of mine!"

When Hsi Jen perceived the tone, so unlike that of other days, with which these words were pronounced: "What's this that you're saying?" she therefore remarked as she gave another smile. "In this pleasant and propitious first moon, when all the ladies and young ladies are in high glee, how is it that you're again in a mood of this sort?"

"Whether the ladies and my cousins be in high spirits or not," Pao-yü replied forcing a grin, "is also perfectly immaterial to me."

"They are all," Hsi Jen added, smilingly, "pleasant and agreeable, and were you also a little pleasant and agreeable, wouldn't it conduce to the enjoyment of the whole company?"

"What about the whole company, and they and I?" Pao-yü urged. "They all have their mutual friendships; while I, poor fellow, all forlorn, have none to care a rap for me."

His remarks had reached this clause, when inadvertently the tears trickled down; and Hsi Jen realising the state of mind he was in, did not venture to say anything further. But as soon as Pao-yü had reflected minutely over the sense and import of this sentence, he could not refrain from bursting forth into a loud fit of crying, and, turning himself round, he stood up, and, drawing near the table, he took up the pencil, and eagerly composed these enigmatical lines:

If thou wert me to test, and I were thee to test,
Our hearts were we to test, and our minds to test,
When naught more there remains for us to test
That will yea very well be called a test,
And when there's naught to put, we could say, to the test,
We will a place set up on which our feet to rest.

After he had finished writing, he again gave way to fears that though he himself could unfold their meaning, others, who came to peruse these lines, would not be able to fathom them, and he also went on consequently to indite another stanza, in imitation of the "Parasitic Plant," which he inscribed at the close of the enigma; and when he had read it over a second time, he felt his heart so free of all concern that forthwith he got into his bed, and went to sleep.

But, who would have thought it, Tai-yü, upon seeing Pao-yü take his departure in such an abrupt manner, designedly made use of the excuse that she was bent upon finding Hsi Jen, to come round and see what he was up to.

"He's gone to sleep long ago!" Hsi Jen replied.

At these words, Tai-yü felt inclined to betake herself back at once; but Hsi Jen smiled and said: "Please stop, miss. Here's a slip of paper, and see what there is on it!" and speedily taking what Pao-yü had written a short while back, she handed it over to Tai-yü to examine. Tai-yü, on perusal, discovered that Pao-yü had composed it, at the spur of the moment, when under the influence of resentment; and she could not help thinking it both a matter of ridicule as well as of regret; but she hastily explained to Hsi Jen: "This is written for fun, and there's nothing of any consequence in it!" and having concluded this remark, she readily took it along with her to her room, where she conned it over in company with Hsiang-yün; handing it also the next day to Pao-ch'ai to peruse. The burden of what Pao-ch'ai read was:

In what was no concern of mine, I should to thee have paid no heed,
For while I humour this, that one to please I don't succeed!
Act as thy wish may be! go, come whene'er thou list; 'tis naught to me.
Sorrow or joy, without limit or bound, to indulge thou art free!
What is this hazy notion about relatives distant or close?
For what purpose have I for all these days racked my heart with woes?
Even at this time when I look back and think, my mind no pleasure knows.

After having finished its perusal, she went on to glance at the Buddhistic stanza, and smiling: "This being," she soliloquised; "has awakened to a sense of perception; and all through my fault, for it's that ballad of mine yesterday which has incited this! But the subtle devices in all these rationalistic books have a most easy tendency to unsettle the natural disposition, and if to-morrow he does actually get up, and talk a lot of insane trash, won't his having fostered this idea owe its origin to that ballad of mine; and shan't I have become the prime of all guilty people?"

Saying this, she promptly tore the paper, and, delivering the pieces to the servant girls, she bade them go at once and burn them.

"You shouldn't have torn it!" Tai-yü remonstrated laughingly. "But wait and I'll ask him about it! so come along all of you, and I vouch I'll make him abandon that idiotic frame of mind and that depraved language."

The three of them crossed over, in point of fact, into Pao-yü's room, and Tai-yü was the first to smile and observe. "Pao-yü, may I ask you something? What is most valuable is a precious thing; and what is most firm is jade, but what value do you possess and what firmness is innate in you?"

But as Pao-yü could not, say anything by way of reply, two of them remarked sneeringly: "With all this doltish bluntness of his will he after all absorb himself in abstraction?" While Hsiang-yün also clapped her hands and laughed, "Cousin Pao has been discomfited."

"The latter part of that apothegm of yours," Tai-yü continued, "says:

"We would then find some place on which our feet to rest.

"Which is certainly good; but in my view, its excellence is not as yet complete! and I should still tag on two lines at its close;" as she proceeded to recite:

"If we do not set up some place on which our feet to rest,
For peace and freedom then it will be best."

"There should, in very truth, be this adjunct to make it thoroughly explicit!" Pao-ch'ai added. "In days of yore, the sixth founder of the Southern sect, Hui Neng, came, when he went first in search of his patron, in the Shao Chou district; and upon hearing that the fifth founder, Hung Jen, was at Huang Mei, he readily entered his service in the capacity of Buddhist cook; and when the fifth founder, prompted by a wish to select a Buddhistic successor, bade his neophytes and all the bonzes to each compose an enigmatical stanza, the one who occupied the upper seat, Shen Hsiu, recited:

"A P'u T'i tree the body is, the heart so like a stand of mirror bright,
On which must needs, by constant careful rubbing, not be left dust to alight!

"And Hui Neng, who was at this time in the cook-house pounding rice, overheard this enigma. 'Excellent, it is excellent,' he ventured, 'but as far as completeness goes it isn't complete;' and having bethought himself of an apothegm: 'The P'u T'i, (an expression for Buddha or intelligence),' he proceeded, 'is really no tree; and the resplendent mirror, (Buddhistic term for heart), is likewise no stand; and as, in fact, they do not constitute any tangible objects, how could they be contaminated by particles of dust?' Whereupon the fifth founder at once took his robe and clap-dish and handed them to him. Well, the text now of this enigma presents too this identical idea, for the simple fact is that those lines full of subtleties of a short while back are not, as yet, perfected or brought to an issue, and do you forsooth readily give up the task in this manner?"

"He hasn't been able to make any reply," Tai-yü rejoined sneeringly, "and must therefore be held to be discomfited; but were he even to make suitable answer now, there would be nothing out of the common about it! Anyhow, from this time forth you mustn't talk about Buddhistic spells, for what even we two know and are able to do, you don't as yet know and can't do; and do you go and concern yourself with abstraction?"

Pao-yü had, in his own mind, been under the impression that he had attained perception, but when he was unawares and all of a sudden subjected to this question by Tai-yü, he soon found it beyond his power to give any ready answer. And when Pao-ch'ai furthermore came out with a religious disquisition, by way of illustration, and this on subjects, in all of which he had hitherto not seen them display any ability, he communed within himself: "If with their knowledge, which is indeed in advance of that of mine, they haven't, as yet, attained perception, what need is there for me now to bring upon myself labour and vexation?"

"Who has, pray," he hastily inquired smilingly, after arriving at the end of his reflections, "indulged in Buddhistic mysteries? what I did amounts to nothing more than nonsensical trash, written, at the spur of the moment, and nothing else."

At the close of this remark all four came to be again on the same terms as of old; but suddenly a servant announced that the Empress (Yüan Ch'un) had despatched a messenger to bring over a lantern-conundrum with the directions that they should all go and guess it, and that after they had found it out, they should each also devise one and send it in. At these words, the four of them left the room with hasty step, and adjourned into dowager lady Chia's drawing room, where they discovered a young eunuch, holding a four-cornered, flat-topped lantern, of white gauze, which had been specially fabricated for lantern riddles. On the front side, there was already a conundrum, and the whole company were vying with each other in looking at it and making wild guesses; when the young eunuch went on to transmit his orders, saying: "Young ladies, you should not speak out when you are guessing; but each one of you should secretly write down the solutions for me to wrap them up, and take them all in together to await her Majesty's personal inspection as to whether they be correct or not."

Upon listening to these words, Pao-ch'ai drew near, and perceived at a glance, that it consisted of a stanza of four lines, with seven characters in each; but though there was no novelty or remarkable feature about it, she felt constrained to outwardly give utterance to words of praise. "It's hard to guess!" she simply added, while she pretended to be plunged in thought, for the fact is that as soon as she had cast her eye upon it, she had at once solved it. Pao-yü, Tai-yü, Hsiang-yün, and T'an-ch'un, had all four also hit upon the answer, and each had secretly put it in writing; and Chia Huan, Chia Lan and the others were at the same time sent for, and every one of them set to work to exert the energies of his mind, and, when they arrived at a guess, they noted it down on paper; after which every individual member of the family made a choice of some object, and composed a riddle, which was transcribed in a large round hand, and affixed on the lantern. This done, the eunuch took his departure, and when evening drew near, he came out and delivered the commands of the imperial consort. "The conundrum," he said, "written by Her Highness, the other day, has been solved by every one, with the exception of Miss Secunda and master Tertius, who made a wrong guess. Those composed by you, young ladies, have likewise all been guessed; but Her Majesty does not know whether her solutions are right or not." While speaking, he again produced the riddles, which had been written by them, among which were those which had been solved, as well as those which had not been solved; and the eunuch, in like manner, took the presents, conferred by the imperial consort, and handed them over to those who had guessed right. To each person was assigned a bamboo vase, inscribed with verses, which had been manufactured for palace use, as well as articles of bamboo for tea; with the exception of Ying-ch'un and Chia Huan, who were the only two persons who did not receive any. But as Ying-ch'un looked upon the whole thing as a joke and a trifle, she did not trouble her mind on that score, but Chia Huan at once felt very disconsolate.

"This one devised by Mr. Tertius," the eunuch was further heard to say, "is not properly done; and as Her Majesty herself has been unable to guess it she commanded me to bring it back, and ask Mr. Tertius what it is about."

After the party had listened to these words, they all pressed forward to see what had been written. The burden of it was this:

The elder brother has horns only eight;
The second brother has horns only two;
The elder brother on the bed doth sit;
Inside the room the second likes to squat.

After perusal of these lines, they broke out, with one voice, into a loud fit of laughter; and Chia Huan had to explain to the eunuch that the one was a pillow, and the other the head of an animal. Having committed the explanation to memory and accepted a cup of tea, the eunuch took his departure; and old lady Chia, noticing in what buoyant spirits Yüan Ch'un was, felt herself so much the more elated, that issuing forthwith directions to devise, with every despatch, a small but ingenious lantern of fine texture in the shape of a screen, and put it in the Hall, she bade each of her grandchildren secretly compose a conundrum, copy it out clean, and affix it on the frame of the lantern; and she had subsequently scented tea and fine fruits, as well as every kind of nicknacks, got ready, as prizes for those who guessed right.

And when Chia Cheng came from court and found the old lady in such high glee he also came over in the evening, as the season was furthermore holiday time, to avail himself of her good cheer to reap some enjoyment. In the upper part of the room seated themselves, at one table dowager lady Chia, Chia Cheng, and Pao-yü; madame Wang, Pao-ch'ai, Tai-yü, Hsiang-yün sat round another table, and Ying-ch'un, Tan-ch'un and Hsi Ch'un the three of them, occupied a separate table, and both these tables were laid in the lower part, while below, all over the floor, stood matrons and waiting-maids for Li Kung-ts'ai and Hsi-feng were both seated in the inner section of the Hall, at another table.

Chia Chen failed to see Chia Lan, and he therefore inquired: "How is it I don't see brother Lan," whereupon the female servants, standing below, hastily entered the inner room and made inquiries of widow Li. "He says," Mrs. Li stood up and rejoined with a smile, "that as your master didn't go just then to ask him round, he has no wish to come!" and when a matron delivered the reply to Chia Cheng; the whole company exclaimed much amused: "How obstinate and perverse his natural disposition is!" But Chia Cheng lost no time in sending Chia Huan, together with two matrons, to fetch Chia Lan; and, on his arrival, dowager lady Chia bade him sit by her side, and, taking a handful of fruits, she gave them to him to eat; after which the party chatted, laughed, and enjoyed themselves.

Ordinarily, there was no one but Pao-yü to say much or talk at any length, but on this day, with Chia Cheng present, his remarks were limited to assents. And as to the rest, Hsiang-yün had, though a young girl, and of delicate physique, nevertheless ever been very fond of talking and discussing; but, on this instance, Chia Cheng was at the feast, so that she also held her tongue and restrained her words. As for Tai-yü she was naturally peevish and listless, and not very much inclined to indulge in conversation; while Pao-ch'ai, who had never been reckless in her words or frivolous in her deportment, likewise behaved on the present occasion in her usual dignified manner. Hence it was that this banquet, although a family party, given for the sake of relaxation, assumed contrariwise an appearance of restraint, and as old lady Chia was herself too well aware that it was to be ascribed to the presence of Chia Cheng alone, she therefore, after the wine had gone round three times, forthwith hurried off Chia Cheng to retire to rest.

No less cognisant was Chia Cheng himself that the old lady's motives in packing him off were to afford a favourable opportunity to the young ladies and young men to enjoy themselves, and that is why, forcing a smile, he observed: "Having to-day heard that your venerable ladyship had got up in here a large assortment of excellent riddles, on the occasion of the spring festival of lanterns, I too consequently prepared prizes, as well as a banquet, and came with the express purpose of joining the company; and why don't you in some way confer a fraction of the fond love, which you cherish for your grandsons and granddaughters, upon me also, your son?"

"When you're here," old lady Chia replied smilingly, "they won't venture to chat or laugh; and unless you go, you'll really fill me with intense dejection! But if you feel inclined to guess conundrums, well, I'll tell you one for you to solve; but if you don't guess right, mind, you'll be mulcted!"

"Of course I'll submit to the penalty," Chia Cheng rejoined eagerly, as he laughed, "but if I do guess right, I must in like manner receive a reward!"

"This goes without saying!" dowager lady Chia added; whereupon she went on to recite:

The monkey's body gently rests on the tree top!

"This refers," she said, "to the name of a fruit."

Chia Cheng was already aware that it was a lichee, but he designedly made a few guesses at random, and was fined several things; but he subsequently gave, at length, the right answer, and also obtained a present from her ladyship.

In due course he too set forth this conundrum for old lady Chia to guess:

Correct its body is in appearance,
Both firm and solid is it in substance;
To words, it is true, it cannot give vent,
But spoken to, it always does assent.

When he had done reciting it, he communicated the answer in an undertone to Pao-yü; and Pao-yü fathoming what his intention was, gently too told his grandmother Chia, and her ladyship finding, after some reflection, that there was really no mistake about it, readily remarked that it was an inkslab.

"After all," Chia Cheng smiled; "Your venerable ladyship it is who can hit the right answer with one guess!" and turning his head round, "Be quick," he cried, "and bring the prizes and present them!" whereupon the married women and waiting-maids below assented with one voice, and they simultaneously handed up the large trays and small boxes.

Old lady Chia passed the things, one by one, under inspection; and finding that they consisted of various kinds of articles, novel and ingenious, of use and of ornament, in vogue during the lantern festival, her heart was so deeply elated that with alacrity she shouted, "Pour a glass of wine for your master!"

Pao-yü took hold of the decanter, while Ying Ch'un presented the cup of wine.

"Look on that screen!" continued dowager lady Chia, "all those riddles have been written by the young ladies; so go and guess them for my benefit!"

Chia Cheng signified his obedience, and rising and walking up to the front of the screen, he noticed the first riddle, which was one composed by the Imperial consort Yüan, in this strain:

The pluck of devils to repress in influence it abounds,
Like bound silk is its frame, and like thunder its breath resounds.
But one report rattles, and men are lo! in fear and dread;
Transformed to ashes 'tis what time to see you turn the head.

"Is this a cracker?" Chia Cheng inquired.

"It is," Pao-yü assented.

Chia Cheng then went on to peruse that of Ying-Ch'un's, which referred to an article of use:

Exhaustless is the principle of heavenly calculations and of human skill;
Skill may exist, but without proper practice the result to find hard yet
will be!
Whence cometh all this mixed confusion on a day so still?
Simply it is because the figures Yin and Yang do not agree.

"It's an abacus," Chia Cheng observed.

"Quite so!" replied Ying Ch'un smiling; after which they also conned the one below, by T'an-ch'un, which ran thus and had something to do with an object:

This is the time when 'neath the stairs the pages their heads raise!
The term of "pure brightness" is the meetest time this thing to make!
The vagrant silk it snaps, and slack, without tension it strays!
The East wind don't begrudge because its farewell it did take!

"It would seem," Chia Cheng suggested, "as if that must be a kite!"

"It is," answered T'an C'h'un; whereupon Chia Cheng read the one below, which was written by Tai-yü to this effect and bore upon some thing:

After the audience, his two sleeves who brings with fumes replete?
Both by the lute and in the quilt, it lacks luck to abide!
The dawn it marks; reports from cock and man renders effete!
At midnight, maids no trouble have a new one to provide!
The head, it glows during the day, as well as in the night!

Its heart, it burns from day to day and 'gain from year to year!
Time swiftly flies and mete it is that we should hold it dear!
Changes might come, but it defies wind, rain, days dark or bright!

"Isn't this a scented stick to show the watch?" Chia Cheng inquired.

"Yes!" assented Pao-yü, speaking on Tai-yü's behalf; and Chia Cheng thereupon prosecuted the perusal of a conundrum, which ran as follows, and referred to an object;

With the South, it sits face to face,
And the North, the while, it doth face;
If the figure be sad, it also is sad,
If the figure be glad, it likewise is glad!

"Splendid! splendid!" exclaimed Chia Cheng, "my guess is that it's a looking-glass. It's excellently done!"

Pao-yü smiled. "It is a looking glass!" he rejoined.

"This is, however, anonymous; whose work is it?" Chia Cheng went on to ask, and dowager lady Chia interposed: "This, I fancy, must have been composed by Pao-yü," and Chia Cheng then said not a word, but continued reading the following conundrum, which was that devised by Pao-ch'ai, on some article or other:

Eyes though it has; eyeballs it has none, and empty 'tis inside!
The lotus flowers out of the water peep, and they with gladness meet,
But when dryandra leaves begin to drop, they then part and divide,
For a fond pair they are, but, united, winter they cannot greet.

When Chia Cheng finished scanning it, he gave way to reflection. "This object," he pondered, "must surely be limited in use! But for persons of tender years to indulge in all this kind of language, would seem to be still less propitious; for they cannot, in my views, be any of them the sort of people to enjoy happiness and longevity!" When his reflections reached this point, he felt the more dejected, and plainly betrayed a sad appearance, and all he did was to droop his head and to plunge in a brown study.

But upon perceiving the frame of mind in which Chia Cheng was, dowager lady Chia arrived at the conclusion that he must be fatigued; and fearing, on the other hand, that if she detained him, the whole party of young ladies would lack the spirit to enjoy themselves, she there and then faced Chia Cheng and suggested: "There's no need really for you to remain here any longer, and you had better retire to rest; and let us sit a while longer; after which, we too will break up!"

As soon as Chia Cheng caught this hint, he speedily assented several consecutive yes's; and when he had further done his best to induce old lady Chia to have a cup of wine, he eventually withdrew out of the Hall. On his return to his bedroom, he could do nothing else than give way to cogitation, and, as he turned this and turned that over in his mind, he got still more sad and pained.

"Amuse yourselves now!" readily exclaimed dowager lady Chia, during this while, after seeing Chia Cheng off; but this remark was barely finished, when she caught sight of Pao-yü run up to the lantern screen, and give vent, as he gesticulated with his hands and kicked his feet about, to any criticisms that first came to his lips. "In this," he remarked, "this line isn't happy; and that one, hasn't been suitably solved!" while he behaved just like a monkey, whose fetters had been let loose.

"Were the whole party after all," hastily ventured Tai-yü, "to sit down, as we did a short while back and chat and laugh; wouldn't that be more in accordance with good manners?"

Lady Feng thereupon egressed from the room in the inner end and interposed her remarks. "Such a being as you are," she said, "shouldn't surely be allowed by Mr. Chia Cheng, an inch or a step from his side, and then you'll be all right. But just then it slipped my memory, for why didn't I, when your father was present, instigate him to bid you compose a rhythmical enigma; and you would, I have no doubt, have been up to this moment in a state of perspiration!"

At these words, Pao-yü lost all patience, and laying hold of lady Feng, he hustled her about for a few moments.

But old lady Chia went on for some time to bandy words with Li Kung-ts'ai, with the whole company of young ladies and the rest, so that she, in fact, felt considerably tired and worn out; and when she heard that the fourth watch had already drawn nigh, she consequently issued directions that the eatables should be cleared away and given to the crowd of servants, and suggested, as she readily rose to her feet, "Let us go and rest! for the next day is also a feast, and we must get up at an early hour; and to-morrow evening we can enjoy ourselves again!" whereupon the whole company dispersed.

But now, reader, listen to the sequel given in the chapter which follows.

CHAPTER XXIII.

Pao-yü and Tai-yü make use of some beautiful passages from the Record
of the Western Side-building to bandy jokes.
The excellent ballads sung in the Peony Pavilion touch the tender heart of Tai-yü.

Soon after the day on which Chia Yuan-ch'un honoured the garden of Broad Vista with a visit, and her return to the Palace, so our story goes, she forthwith desired that T'an-ch'un should make a careful copy, in consecutive order, of the verses, which had been composed and read out on that occasion, in order that she herself should assign them their rank, and adjudge the good and bad. And she also directed that an inscription should be engraved on a stone, in the Broad Vista park, to serve in future years as a record of the pleasant and felicitous event; and Chia Cheng, therefore, gave orders to servants to go far and wide, and select skilful artificers and renowned workmen, to polish the stone and engrave the characters in the garden of Broad Vista; while Chia Chen put himself at the head of Chia Jung, Chia P'ing and others to superintend the work. And as Chia Se had, on the other hand, the control of Wen Kuan and the rest of the singing girls, twelve in all, as well as of their costumes and other properties, he had no leisure to attend to anything else, and consequently once again sent for Chia Ch'ang and Chia Ling to come and act as overseers.

On a certain day, the works were taken in hand for rubbing the stones smooth with wax, for carving the inscription, and tracing it with vermilion, but without entering into details on these matters too minutely, we will return to the two places, the Yu Huang temple and the Ta Mo monastery. The company of twelve young bonzes and twelve young Taoist priests had now moved out of the Garden of Broad Vista, and Chia Cheng was meditating upon distributing them to various temples to live apart, when unexpectedly Chia Ch'in's mother, née Chou,—who resided in the back street, and had been at the time contemplating to pay a visit to Chia Cheng on this side so as to obtain some charge, be it either large or small, for her son to look after, that he too should be put in the way of turning up some money to meet his expenses with,—came, as luck would have it, to hear that some work was in hand in this mansion, and lost no time in driving over in a curricle and making her appeal to lady Feng. And as lady Feng remembered that she had all along not presumed on her position to put on airs, she willingly acceded to her request, and after calling to memory some suitable remarks, she at once went to make her report to madame Wang: "These young bonzes and Taoist priests," she said, "can by no means be sent over to other places; for were the Imperial consort to come out at an unexpected moment, they would then be required to perform services; and in the event of their being scattered, there will, when the time comes to requisition their help, again be difficulties in the way; and my idea is that it would be better to send them all to the family temple, the Iron Fence Temple; and every month all there will be to do will be to depute some one to take over a few taels for them to buy firewood and rice with, that's all, and when there's even a sound of their being required uttered, some one can at once go and tell them just one word 'come,' and they will come without the least trouble!"

Madame Wang gave a patient ear to this proposal, and, in due course, consulted with Chia Cheng.

"You've really," smiled Chia Cheng at these words, "reminded me how I should act! Yes, let this be done!" And there and then he sent for Chia Lien.

Chia Lien was, at the time, having his meal with lady Feng, but as soon as he heard that he was wanted, he put by his rice and was just walking off, when lady Feng clutched him and pulled him back. "Wait a while," she observed with a smirk, "and listen to what I've got to tell you! if it's about anything else, I've nothing to do with it; but if it be about the young bonzes and young Taoists, you must, in this particular matter, please comply with this suggestion of mine," after which, she went on in this way and that way to put him up to a whole lot of hints.

"I know nothing about it," Chia Lien rejoined smilingly, "and as you have the knack you yourself had better go and tell him!"

But as soon as lady Feng heard this remark, she stiffened her head and threw down the chopsticks; and, with an expression on her cheeks, which looked like a smile and yet not a smile, she glanced angrily at

Chia Lien. "Are you speaking in earnest," she inquired, "or are you only jesting?"

"Yün Erh, the son of our fifth sister-in-law of the western porch, has come and appealed to me two or three times, asking for something to look after," Chia Lien laughed, "and I assented and bade him wait; and now, after a great deal of trouble, this job has turned up; and there you are once again snatching it away!"

"Compose your mind," lady Feng observed grinning, "for the Imperial Consort has hinted that directions should be given for the planting, in the north-east corner of the park, of a further plentiful supply of pine and cedar trees, and that orders should also be issued for the addition, round the base of the tower, of a large number of flowers and plants and such like; and when this job turns up, I can safely tell you that Yun Erh will be called to assume control of these works."

"Well if that be really so," Chia Lien rejoined, "it will after all do! But there's only one thing; all I was up to last night was simply to have some fun with you, but you obstinately and perversely wouldn't."

Lady Feng, upon hearing these words, burst out laughing with a sound of Ch'ih, and spurting disdainfully at Chia Lien, she lowered her head and went on at once with her meal; during which time Chia Lien speedily walked away laughing the while, and betook himself to the front, where he saw Chia Cheng. It was, indeed, about the young bonzes, and Chia Lien readily carried out lady Feng's suggestion. "As from all appearances," he continued, "Ch'in Erh has, actually, so vastly improved, this job should, after all, be entrusted to his care and management; and provided that in observance with the inside custom Ch'in Erh were each day told to receive the advances, things will go on all right." And as Chia Cheng had never had much attention to give to such matters of detail, he, as soon as he heard what Chia Lien had to say, immediately signified his approval and assent. And Chia Lien, on his return to his quarters, communicated the issue to lady Feng; whereupon lady Feng at once sent some one to go and notify dame Chou.

Chia Ch'in came, in due course, to pay a visit to Chia Lien and his wife, and was incessant in his expressions of gratitude; and lady Feng bestowed upon him a further favour by giving him, as a first instalment, an advance of the funds necessary for three months' outlay, for which she bade him write a receipt; while Chia Lien filled up a cheque and signed it; and a counter-order was simultaneously issued, and he came out into the treasury where the sum specified for three months' supplies, amounting to three hundred taels, was paid out in pure ingots.

Chia Ch'in took the first piece of silver that came under his hand, and gave it to the men in charge of the scales, with which he told them to have a cup of tea, and bidding, shortly after, a boy-servant take the money to his home, he held consultation with his mother; after which, he hired a donkey for himself to ride on, and also bespoke several carriages, and came to the back gate of the Jung Kuo mansion; where having called out the twenty young priests, they got into the carriages, and sped straightway beyond the city walls, to the Temple of the Iron Fence, where nothing of any note transpired at the time.

But we will now notice Chia Yüan-ch'un, within the precincts of the Palace. When she had arranged the verses composed in the park of Broad Vista in their order of merit, she suddenly recollected that the sights in the garden were sure, ever since her visit through them, to be diligently and respectfully kept locked up by her father and mother; and that by not allowing any one to go in was not an injustice done to this garden? "Besides," (she pondered), "in that household, there are at present several young ladies, capable of composing odes, and able to write poetry, and why should not permission be extended to them to go and take their quarters in it; in order too that those winsome persons might not be deprived of good cheer, and that the flowers and willows may not lack any one to admire them!"

But remembering likewise that Pao-yü had from his infancy grown up among that crowd of female cousins, and was such a contrast to the rest of his male cousins that were he not allowed to move into it, he would, she also apprehended, be made to feel forlorn; and dreading lest his grandmother and his mother should be displeased at heart, she thought it imperative that he too should be permitted to take up his quarters inside, so that things should be put on a satisfactory footing; and directing the eunuch Hsia Chung to go to the Jung mansion and deliver her commands, she expressed the wish that Pao-ch'ai and the other girls should live in the garden and that it should not be kept closed, and urged that Pao-yü should also shift into it, at his own pleasure, for the prosecution of his studies. And Chia Cheng and madame Wang, upon receiving her commands, hastened, after the departure of Hsia Chung, to explain them to dowager lady Chia, and to despatch servants into the garden to tidy every place, to dust, to sweep, and to lay out the portieres and bed-curtains. The tidings were heard by the rest even with perfect equanimity, but Pao-yü was immoderately delighted; and he was engaged in deliberation with dowager lady

Chia as to this necessary and to that requirement, when suddenly they descried a waiting-maid arrive, who announced: "Master wishes to see Pao-yü."

Pao-yü gazed vacantly for a while. His spirits simultaneously were swept away; his countenance changed colour; and clinging to old lady Chia, he readily wriggled her about, just as one would twist the sugar (to make sweetmeats with), and could not, for the very death of him, summon up courage to go; so that her ladyship had no alternative but to try and reassure him. "My precious darling" she urged, "just you go, and I'll stand by you! He won't venture to be hard upon you; and besides, you've devised these excellent literary compositions; and I presume as Her Majesty has desired that you should move into the garden, his object is to give you a few words of advice; simply because he fears that you might be up to pranks in those grounds. But to all he tells you, whatever you do, mind you acquiesce and it will be all right!"

And as she tried to compose him, she at the same time called two old nurses and enjoined them to take Pao-yü over with due care, "And don't let his father," she added, "frighten him!"

The old nurses expressed their obedience, and Pao-yü felt constrained to walk ahead; and with one step scarcely progressing three inches, he leisurely came over to this side. Strange coincidence Chia Cheng was in madame Wang's apartments consulting with her upon some matter or other, and Chin Ch'uan-erh, Ts'ai Yun, Ts'ai Feng, Ts'ai Luan, Hsiu Feng and the whole number of waiting-maids were all standing outside under the verandah. As soon as they caught sight of Pao-yü, they puckered up their mouths and laughed at him; while Chin Ch'uan grasped Pao-yü with one hand, and remarked in a low tone of voice: "On these lips of mine has just been rubbed cosmetic, soaked with perfume, and are you now inclined to lick it or not?" whereupon Ts'ai Yün pushed off Chin Ch'uan with one shove, as she interposed laughingly, "A person's heart is at this moment in low spirits and do you still go on cracking jokes at him? But avail yourself of this opportunity when master is in good cheer to make haste and get in!"

Pao-yü had no help but to sidle against the door and walk in. Chia Cheng and madame Wang were, in fact, both in the inner rooms, and dame Chou raised the portière. Pao-yü stepped in gingerly and perceived Chia Cheng and madame Wang sitting opposite to each other, on the stove-couch, engaged in conversation; while below on a row of chairs sat Ying Ch'un, T'an Ch'un, Hsi Ch'un and Chia Huan; but though all four of them were seated in there only T'an Ch'un, Hsi Ch'un and Chia Huan rose to their feet, as soon as they saw him make his appearance in the room; and when Chia Cheng raised his eyes and noticed Pao-yü standing in front of him, with a gait full of ease and with those winsome looks of his, so captivating, he once again realised what a mean being Chia Huan was, and how coarse his deportment. But suddenly he also bethought himself of Chia Chu, and as he reflected too that madame Wang had only this son of her own flesh and blood, upon whom she ever doated as upon a gem, and that his own beard had already begun to get hoary, the consequence was that he unwittingly stifled, well nigh entirely, the feeling of hatred and dislike, which, during the few recent years he had ordinarily fostered towards Pao-yü. And after a long pause, "Her Majesty," he observed, "bade you day after day ramble about outside to disport yourself, with the result that you gradually became remiss and lazy; but now her desire is that we should keep you under strict control, and that in prosecuting your studies in the company of your cousins in the garden, you should carefully exert your brains to learn; so that if you don't again attend to your duties, and mind your regular tasks, you had better be on your guard!" Pao-yü assented several consecutive yes's; whereupon madame Wang drew him by her side and made him sit down, and while his three cousins resumed the seats they previously occupied: "Have you finished all the pills you had been taking a short while back?" madame Wang inquired, as she rubbed Pao-yü's neck.

"There's still one pill remaining," Pao-yü explained by way of reply.

"You had better," madame Wang added, "fetch ten more pills tomorrow morning; and every day about bedtime tell Hsi Jen to give them to you; and when you've had one you can go to sleep!"

"Ever since you, mother, bade me take them," Pao-yü rejoined, "Hsi Jen has daily sent me one, when I was about to turn in."

"Who's this called Hsi Jen?" Chia Chen thereupon ascertained.

"She's a waiting-maid!" madame Wang answered.

"A servant girl," Chia Cheng remonstrated, "can be called by whatever name one chooses; anything is good enough; but who's it who has started this kind of pretentious name!"

Madame Wang noticed that Chia Cheng was not in a happy frame of mind, so that she forthwith tried to screen matters for Pao-yü, by saying: "It's our old lady who has originated it!"

"How can it possibly be," Chia Cheng exclaimed, "that her ladyship knows anything about such kind of language? It must, for a certainty, be Pao-yü!"

Pao-yü perceiving that he could not conceal the truth from him, was under the necessity of standing up and of explaining; "As I have all along read verses, I remembered the line written by an old poet:

"What time the smell of flowers wafts itself into man, one knows the day is warm.

"And as this waiting-maid's surname was Hua (flower), I readily gave her the name, on the strength of this sentiment."

"When you get back," madame Wang speedily suggested addressing Pao-yü, "change it and have done; and you, sir, needn't lose your temper over such a trivial matter!"

"It doesn't really matter in the least," Chia Cheng continued; "so that there's no necessity of changing it; but it's evident that Pao-yü doesn't apply his mind to legitimate pursuits, but mainly devotes his energies to such voluptuous expressions and wanton verses!" And as he finished these words, he abruptly shouted out: "You brute-like child of retribution! Don't you yet get out of this?"

"Get away, off with you!" madame Wang in like manner hastened to urge; "our dowager lady is waiting, I fear, for you to have her repast!"

Pao-yü assented, and, with gentle step, he withdrew out of the room, laughing at Chin Ch'uan-erh, as he put out his tongue; and leading off the two nurses, he went off on his way like a streak of smoke. But no sooner had he reached the door of the corridor than he espied Hsi Jen standing leaning against the side; who perceiving Pao-yü come back safe and sound heaped smile upon smile, and asked: "What did he want you for?"

"There was nothing much," Pao-yü explained, "he simply feared that I would, when I get into the garden, be up to mischief, and he gave me all sorts of advice;" and, as while he explained matters, they came into the presence of lady Chia, he gave her a clear account, from first to last, of what had transpired. But when he saw that Lin Tai-yü was at the moment in the room, Pao-yü speedily inquired of her: "Which place do you think best to live in?"

Tai-yü had just been cogitating on this subject, so that when she unexpectedly heard Pao-yü's inquiry, she forthwith rejoined with a smile: "My own idea is that the Hsio Hsiang Kuan is best; for I'm fond of those clusters of bamboos, which hide from view the tortuous balustrade and make the place more secluded and peaceful than any other!"

Pao-yü at these words clapped his hands and smiled. "That just meets with my own views!" he remarked; "I too would like you to go and live in there; and as I am to stay in the I Hung Yuan, we two will be, in the first place, near each other; and next, both in quiet and secluded spots."

While the two of them were conversing, a servant came, sent over by Chia Cheng, to report to dowager lady Chia that: "The 22nd of the second moon was a propitious day for Pao-yü and the young ladies to shift their quarters into the garden; that during these few days, servants should be sent in to put things in their proper places and to clean; that Hsueh Pao-ch'ai should put up in the Heng Wu court; that Lin Tai-yü was to live in the Hsiao Hsiang lodge; that Chia Ying-ch'un should move into the Cho Chin two-storied building; that T'an Ch'un should put up in the Ch'iu Yen library; that Hsi Ch'un should take up her quarters in the Liao Feng house; that widow Li should live in the Tao Hsiang village, and that Pao-yü was to live in the I Hung court. That at every place two old nurses should be added and four servant-girls; that exclusive of the nurse and personal waiting-maid of each, there should, in addition, be servants, whose special duties should be to put things straight and to sweep the place; and that on the 22nd, they should all, in a body, move into the garden."

When this season drew near, the interior of the grounds, with the flowers waving like embroidered sashes, and the willows fanned by the fragrant breeze, was no more as desolate and silent as it had been in previous days; but without indulging in any further irrelevant details, we shall now go back to Pao-yü.

Ever since he shifted his quarters into the park, his heart was full of joy, and his mind of contentment, fostering none of those extraordinary ideas, whose tendency could be to give birth to longings and hankerings. Day after day, he simply indulged, in the company of his female cousins and the waiting-maids, in either reading his books, or writing characters, or in thrumming the lute, playing chess, drawing pictures and scanning verses, even in drawing patterns of argus pheasants, in embroidering phoenixes, contesting with them in searching for strange plants, and gathering flowers, in humming poetry with gentle tone, singing ballads with soft voice, dissecting characters, and in playing at mora, so that, being free to go everywhere and anywhere, he was of course completely happy. From his pen emanate four ballads on the times of the four seasons, which, although they could not be looked upon as first-rate, afford anyhow a correct idea of his sentiments, and a true account of the scenery.

The ballad on the spring night runs as follows:

The silken curtains, thin as russet silk, at random are spread out.
The croak of frogs from the adjoining lane but faintly strikes the ear.
The pillow a slight chill pervades, for rain outside the window falls.
The landscape, which now meets the eye, is like that seen in dreams by man.
In plenteous streams the candles' tears do drop, but for whom do they weep?
Each particle of grief felt by the flowers is due to anger against me.
It's all because the maids have by indulgence indolent been made.
The cover over me I'll pull, as I am loth to laugh and talk for long.

This is the description of the aspect of nature on a summer night:

The beauteous girl, weary of needlework, quiet is plunged in a long dream.
The parrot in the golden cage doth shout that it is time the tea to brew.
The lustrous windows with the musky moon like open palace-mirrors look;
The room abounds with fumes of sandalwood and all kinds of imperial scents.
From the cups made of amber is poured out the slippery dew from the lotus.
The banisters of glass, the cool zephyr enjoy flapped by the willow trees.
In the stream-spanning kiosk, the curtains everywhere all at one time do wave.
In the vermilion tower the blinds the maidens roll, for they have made the night's toilette.

The landscape of an autumnal evening is thus depicted:

In the interior of the Chiang Yün house are hushed all clamorous din and noise.
The sheen, which from Selene flows, pervades the windows of carnation gauze.
The moss-locked, streaked rocks shelter afford to the cranes, plunged in sleep.
The dew, blown on the t'ung tree by the well, doth wet the roosting rooks.

Wrapped in a quilt, the maid comes the gold phoenix coverlet to spread.
The girl, who on the rails did lean, on her return drops the kingfisher flowers!
This quiet night his eyes in sleep he cannot close, as he doth long for wine.
The smoke is stifled, and the fire restirred, when tea is ordered to be brewed.

The picture of a winter night is in this strain:

The sleep of the plum trees, the dream of the bamboos the third watch have already reached.
Under the embroidered quilt and the kingfisher coverlet one can't sleep for the cold.
The shadow of fir trees pervades the court, but cranes are all that meet the eye.
Both far and wide the pear blossom covers the ground, but yet the hawk
cannot be heard.
The wish, verses to write, fostered by the damsel with the green sleeves, has waxéd cold.
The master, with the gold sable pelisse, cannot endure much wine.
But yet he doth rejoice that his attendant knows the way to brew the tea.
The newly-fallen snow is swept what time for tea the water must be boiled.

But putting aside Pao-yü, as he leisurely was occupied in scanning some verses, we will now allude to all these ballads. There lived, at that time, a class of people, whose wont was to servilely court the influential and wealthy, and who, upon perceiving that the verses were composed by a young lad of the Jung Kuo mansion, of only twelve or thirteen years of age, had copies made, and taking them outside sang their praise far and wide. There were besides another sort of light-headed young men, whose heart was so set upon licentious and seductive lines, that they even inscribed them on fans and screen-walls, and time and again kept on humming them and extolling them. And to the above reasons must therefore be ascribed the fact that persons came in search of stanzas and in quest of manuscripts, to apply for sketches and to beg for poetical compositions, to the increasing satisfaction of Pao-yü, who day after day, when at home, devoted his time and attention to these extraneous matters. But who would have anticipated that he could ever in his quiet seclusion have become a prey to a spirit of restlessness? Of a sudden, one day he began to feel discontent, finding fault with this and turning up his nose at that; and going in and coming out he was simply full of ennui. And as all the girls in the garden were just in the prime of youth, and at a time of life when, artless and unaffected, they sat and reclined without regard to retirement, and disported themselves and joked without heed, how could they ever have come to read the secrets which at this time occupied a place in the heart of Pao-yü? But so unhappy was Pao-yü within himself that he soon felt loth to stay in the garden, and took to gadding about outside like an evil spirit; but he behaved also the while in an idiotic manner.

Ming Yen, upon seeing him go on in this way, felt prompted, with the idea of affording his mind some distraction, to think of this and to devise that expedient; but everything had been indulged in with surfeit by Pao-yü, and there was only this resource, (that suggested itself to him,) of which Pao-yü had not as yet had any experience. Bringing his reflections to a close, he forthwith came over to a bookshop, and selecting novels, both of old and of the present age, traditions intended for outside circulation on Fei Yen, Ho Te, Wu Tse-t'ien, and Yang Kuei-fei, as well as books of light literature consisting of strange legends, he purchased a good number of them with the express purpose of enticing Pao-yü to read them. As soon as Pao-yü caught sight of them, he felt as if he had obtained some gem or jewel. "But you mustn't," Ming Yen went on to enjoin him, "take them into the garden; for if any one were to come to know anything about them, I shall then suffer more than I can bear; and you should, when you go along, hide them in your clothes!"

But would Pao-yü agree to not introducing them into the garden? So after much wavering, he picked out only several volumes of those whose style was more refined, and took them in, and threw them over the top of his bed for him to peruse when no one was present; while those coarse and very indecent ones, he concealed in a bundle in the outer library.

On one day, which happened to be the middle decade of the third moon, Pao-yü, after breakfast, took a book, the "Hui Chen Chi," in his hand and walked as far as the bridge of the Hsin Fang lock. Seating himself on a block of rock, that lay under the peach trees in that quarter, he opened the Hui Chen Chi and began to read it carefully from the beginning. But just as he came to the passage: "the falling red (flowers) have formed a heap," he felt a gust of wind blow through the trees, bringing down a whole bushel of peach blossoms; and, as they fell, his whole person, the entire surface of the book as well as a large extent of ground were simply bestrewn with petals of the blossoms. Pao-yü was bent upon shaking them down; but as he feared lest they should be trodden under foot, he felt constrained to carry the petals in his coat and walk to the bank of the pond and throw them into the stream. The petals floated on the surface of the water, and, after whirling and swaying here and there, they at length ran out by the Hsin Fang lock. But, on his return under the tree, he found the ground again one mass of petals, and Pao-yü was just hesitating what to do, when he heard some one behind his back inquire, "What are you up to here?" and as soon as Pao-yü turned his head round, he discovered that it was Lin Tai-yü, who had come over carrying on her shoulder a hoe for raking flowers, that on this hoe was suspended a gauze-bag, and that in her hand she held a broom.

"That's right, well done!" Pao-yü remarked smiling; "come and sweep these flowers, and throw them into the water yonder. I've just thrown a lot in there myself!"

"It isn't right," Lin Tai-yü rejoined, "to throw them into the water. The water, which you see, is clean enough here, but as soon as it finds its way out, where are situated other people's grounds, what isn't there in it? so that you would be misusing these flowers just as much as if you left them here! But in that corner, I have dug a hole for flowers, and I'll now sweep these and put them into this gauze-bag and bury them in there; and, in course of many days, they will also become converted into earth, and won't this be a clean way (of disposing of them)?"

Pao-yü, after listening to these words, felt inexpressibly delighted. "Wait!" he smiled, "until I put down my book, and I'll help you to clear them up!"

"What's the book?" Tai-yü inquired.

Pao-yü at this question was so taken aback that he had no time to conceal it. "It's," he replied hastily, "the Chung Yung and the Ta Hsüeh!"

"Are you going again to play the fool with me? Be quick and give it to me to see; and this will be ever so much better a way!"

"Cousin," Pao-yü replied, "as far as you yourself are concerned I don't mind you, but after you've seen it, please don't tell any one else. It's really written in beautiful style; and were you to once begin reading it, why even for your very rice you wouldn't have a thought?"

As he spoke, he handed it to her; and Tai-yü deposited all the flowers on the ground, took over the book, and read it from the very first page; and the more she perused it, she got so much the more fascinated by it, that in no time she had finished reading sixteen whole chapters. But aroused as she was to a state of rapture by the diction, what remained even of the fascination was enough to overpower her senses; and though she had finished reading, she nevertheless continued in a state of abstraction, and still kept on gently recalling the text to mind, and humming it to herself.

"Cousin, tell me is it nice or not?" Pao-yü grinned.

"It is indeed full of zest!" Lin Tai-yü replied exultingly.

"I'm that very sad and very sickly person," Pao-yü explained laughing, "while you are that beauty who could subvert the empire and overthrow the city."

Lin Tai-yü became, at these words, unconsciously crimson all over her cheeks, even up to her very ears; and raising, at the same moment, her two eyebrows, which seemed to knit and yet not to knit, and opening wide those eyes, which seemed to stare and yet not to stare, while her peach-like cheeks bore an angry look and on her thin-skinned face lurked displeasure, she pointed at Pao-yü and exclaimed: "You do deserve death, for the rubbish you talk! without any provocation you bring up these licentious expressions and wanton ballads to give vent to all this insolent rot, in order to insult me; but I'll go and tell uncle and aunt."

As soon as she pronounced the two words "insult me," her eyeballs at once were suffused with purple, and turning herself round she there and then walked away; which filled Pao-yü with so much distress that he jumped forward to impede her progress, as he pleaded: "My dear cousin, I earnestly entreat you to spare me this time! I've indeed said what I shouldn't; but if I had any intention to insult you, I'll throw myself to-morrow into the pond, and let the scabby-headed turtle eat me up, so that I become transformed into a large tortoise. And when you shall have by and by become the consort of an officer of the first degree, and you shall have fallen ill from old age and returned to the west, I'll come to your tomb and bear your stone tablet for ever on my back!"

As he uttered these words, Lin Tai-yü burst out laughing with a sound of "pu ch'ih," and rubbing her eyes, she sneeringly remarked: "I too can come out with this same tune; but will you now still go on talking nonsense? Pshaw! you're, in very truth, like a spear-head, (which looks) like silver, (but is really soft as) wax!"

"Go on, go on!" Pao-yü smiled after this remark; "and what you've said, I too will go and tell!"

"You maintain," Lin Tai-yü rejoined sarcastically, "that after glancing at anything you're able to recite it; and do you mean to say that I can't even do so much as take in ten lines with one gaze?"

Pao-yü smiled and put his book away, urging: "Let's do what's right and proper, and at once take the flowers and bury them; and don't let us allude to these things!"

Forthwith the two of them gathered the fallen blossoms; but no sooner had they interred them properly than they espied Hsi Jen coming, who went on to observe: "Where haven't I looked for you? What! have you found your way as far as this! But our senior master, Mr. Chia She, over there isn't well; and the young ladies have all gone over to pay their respects, and our old lady has asked that you should be sent over; so go back at once and change your clothes!"

When Pao-yü heard what she said, he hastily picked up his books, and saying good bye to Tai-yü, he came along with Hsi Jen, back into his room, where we will leave him to effect the necessary change in his costume. But during this while, Lin Tai-yü was, after having seen Pao-yü walk away, and heard that all her cousins were likewise not in their rooms, wending her way back alone, in a dull and dejected mood, towards her apartment, when upon reaching the outside corner of the wall of the Pear Fragrance court, she caught, issuing from inside the walls, the harmonious strains of the fife and the melodious modulations of voices singing. Lin Tai-yü readily knew that it was the twelve singing-girls rehearsing a play; and though she did not give her mind to go and listen, yet a couple of lines were of a sudden blown into her ears, and with such clearness, that even one word did not escape. Their burden was this:

These troth are beauteous purple and fine carmine flowers, which in this way all round do bloom,
And all together lie ensconced along the broken well, and the dilapidated wall!

But the moment Lin Tai-yü heard these lines, she was, in fact, so intensely affected and agitated that she at once halted and lending an ear listened attentively to what they went on to sing, which ran thus:

A glorious day this is, and pretty scene, but sad I feel at heart!
Contentment and pleasure are to be found in whose family courts?

After overhearing these two lines, she unconsciously nodded her head, and sighed, and mused in her own mind. "Really," she thought, "there is fine diction even in plays! but unfortunately what men in this world simply know is to see a play, and they don't seem to be able to enjoy the beauties contained in them."

At the conclusion of this train of thought, she experienced again a sting of regret, (as she fancied) she should not have given way to such idle thoughts and missed attending to the ballads; but when she once more came to listen, the song, by some coincidence, went on thus:

It's all because thy loveliness is like a flower and like the comely spring,
That years roll swiftly by just like a running stream.

When this couplet struck Tai-yu's ear, her heart felt suddenly a prey to excitement and her soul to emotion; and upon further hearing the words:

Alone you sit in the secluded inner rooms to self-compassion giving way.

—and other such lines, she became still more as if inebriated, and like as if out of her head, and unable to stand on her feet, she speedily stooped her body, and, taking a seat on a block of stone, she minutely pondered over the rich beauty of the eight characters:

It's all because thy loveliness is like a flower and like the comely spring,
That years roll swiftly by just like a running stream.

Of a sudden, she likewise bethought herself of the line:

Water flows away and flowers decay, for both no feelings have.

—which she had read some days back in a poem of an ancient writer, and also of the passage:

When on the running stream the flowers do fall, spring then is past and gone;

—and of:

Heaven (differs from) the human race,

—which also appeared in that work; and besides these, the lines, which she had a short while back read in the Hsi Hiang Chi:

The flowers, lo, fall, and on their course the waters red do flow!
Petty misfortunes of ten thousand kinds (my heart assail!)

both simultaneously flashed through her memory; and, collating them all together, she meditated on them minutely, until suddenly her heart was stricken with pain and her soul fleeted away, while from her eyes trickled down drops of tears. But while nothing could dispel her present state of mind, she unexpectedly realised that some one from behind gave her a tap; and, turning her head round to look, she found that it was a young girl; but who it was, the next chapter will make known.

CHAPTER XXIV.

The drunken Chin Kang makes light of lucre and shows a preference for
generosity.
The foolish girl mislays her handkerchief and arouses mutual thoughts.

But to return to our narrative. Lin Tai-yü's sentimental reflections were the while reeling and ravelling in an intricate maze, when unexpectedly some one from behind gave her a tap, saying: "What are you up to all alone here?" which took Lin Tai-yu so much by surprise that she gave a start, and turning her head round to look and noticing that it was Hsiang Ling and no one else; "You stupid girl!" Lin Tai-yü replied, "you've given me such a fright! But where do you come from at this time?"

Hsiang Ling giggled and smirked. "I've come," she added, "in search of our young lady, but I can't find her anywhere. But your Tzu Chuan is also looking after you; and she says that lady Secunda has sent a present to you of some tea. But you had better go back home and sit down."

As she spoke, she took Tai-yü by the hand, and they came along back to the Hsiao Hsiang Kuan; where lady Feng had indeed sent her two small catties of a new season tea, of superior quality. But Lin Tai-yü sat down, in company with Hsiang Ling, and began to converse on the merits of this tapestry and the fineness of that embroidery; and after they had also had a game at chess, and read a few sentences out of a book, Hsiang Ling took her departure. But we need not speak of either of them, but return now to Pao-yü. Having been found, and brought back home, by Hsi Jen, he discovered Yuan Yang reclining on the bed, in the act of examining Hsi Jen's needlework; but when she perceived Pao-yü arrive, she forthwith remarked: "Where have you been? her venerable ladyship is waiting for you to tell you to go over and pay your obeisance to our Senior master, and don't you still make haste to go and change your clothes and be off!"

Hsi Jen at once walked into the room to fetch his clothes, and Pao-yü sat on the edge of the bed, and pushed his shoes off with his toes; and, while waiting for his boots to put them on, he turned round and perceiving that Yüan Yang, who was clad in a light red silk jacket and a green satin waistcoat, and girdled with a white crepe sash, had her face turned the other way, and her head lowered giving her attention to the criticism of the needlework, while round her neck she wore a collar with embroidery, Pao-yü readily pressed his face against the nape of her neck, and as he sniffed the perfume about it, he did not stay his hand from stroking her neck, which in whiteness and smoothness was not below that of Hsi Jen; and as he approached her, "My dear girl," he said smiling and with a drivelling face, "do let me lick the cosmetic off your mouth!" clinging to her person, as he uttered these words, like twisted sweetmeat.

"Hsi Jen!" cried Yüan Yang at once, "come out and see! You've been with him a whole lifetime, and don't you give him any advice; but let him still behave in this fashion!" Whereupon, Hsi Jen walked out, clasping the clothes, and turning to Pao-yü, she observed, "I advise you in this way and it's no good, I advise you in that way and you don't mend; and what do you mean to do after all? But if you again behave like this, it will then, in fact, be impossible for me to live any longer in this place!"

As she tendered these words of counsel, she urged him to put his clothes on, and, after he had changed, he betook himself, along with Yuan Yang, to the front part of the mansion, and bade good-bye to dowager lady Chia; after which he went outside, where the attendants and horses were all in readiness; but when he was about to mount his steed, he perceived Chia Lien back from his visit and in the act of dismounting; and as the two of them stood face to face, and mutually exchanged some inquiries, they saw some one come round from the side, and say: "My respects to you, uncle Pao-yü!"

When Pao-yü came to look at him, he noticed that this person had an oblong face, that his body was tall and lanky, that his age was only eighteen or nineteen, and that he possessed, in real truth, an air of refinement and elegance; but though his features were, after all, exceedingly familiar, he could not recall to mind to what branch of the family he belonged, and what his name was.

"What are you staring vacantly for?" Chia Lien inquired laughing.

"Don't you even recognise him? He's Yün Erh, the son of our fifth sister-in-law, who lives in the back court!"

"Of course!" Pao-yü assented complacently. "How is it that I had forgotten just now!" And having gone on to ask how his mother was, and what work he had to do at present; "I've come in search of uncle Secundus, to tell him something," Chia Yün replied, as he pointed at Chia Lien.

"You've really improved vastly from what you were before," added Pao-yü smiling; "you verily look just is if you were my son!"

"How very barefaced!" Chia Lien exclaimed as he burst out laughing; "here's a person four or five years your senior to be made your son!"

"How far are you in your teens this year?" Pao-yü inquired with a smile.

"Eighteen!" Chia Yün rejoined.

This Chia Yün was, in real deed, sharp and quick-witted; and when he heard Pao-yü remark that he looked like his son, he readily gave a sarcastic smile and observed, "The proverb is true which says, 'the grandfather is rocked in the cradle while the grandson leans on a staff.' But though old enough in years, I'm nevertheless like a mountain, which, in spite of its height, cannot screen the sun from view. Besides, since my father's death, I've had no one to look after me, and were you, uncle Pao, not to disdain your doltish nephew, and to acknowledge me as your son, it would be your nephew's good fortune!"

"Have you heard what he said?" Chia Lien interposed cynically. "But to acknowledge him as a son is no easy question to settle!" and with these words, he walked in; whereupon Pao-yü smilingly said: "To-morrow when you have nothing to do, just come and look me up; but don't go and play any devilish pranks with them! I've just now no leisure, so come to-morrow, into the library, where I'll have a chat with you for a whole day, and take you into the garden for some fun!"

With this remark still on his lips, he laid hold of the saddle and mounted his horse; and, followed by the whole bevy of pages, he crossed over to Chia She's on this side; where having discovered that Chia She had nothing more the matter with him than a chill which he had suddenly contracted, he commenced by delivering dowager lady Chia's message, and next paid his own obeisance. Chia She, at first, stood up and made suitable answer to her venerable ladyship's inquiries, and then calling a servant, "Take the gentleman," he said, "into my lady's apartment to sit down."

Pao-yü withdrew out of the room, and came by the back to the upper apartment; and as soon as madame Hsing caught sight of him, she, before everything else, rose to her feet and asked after old lady Chia's health; after which, Pao-yü made his own salutation, and madame Hsing drew him on to the stove-couch, where she induced him to take a seat, and eventually inquired after the other inmates, and also gave orders to serve the tea. But scarcely had they had tea, before they perceived Chia Tsung come in to pay his respects to Pao-yü.

"Where could one find such a living monkey as this!" madame Hsing remarked; "is that nurse of yours dead and gone that she doesn't even keep you clean and tidy, and that she lets you go about with those eyebrows of yours so black and that mouth so filthy! you scarcely look like the child of a great family of scholars."

While she spoke, she perceived both Chia Huan and Chia Lan, one of whom was a young uncle and the other his nephew, also advance and present their compliments, and madame Hsing bade the two of them sit down on the chairs. But when Chia Huan noticed that Pao-yü sat on the same rug with madame Hsing, and that her ladyship was further caressing and petting him in every possible manner, he soon felt so very unhappy at heart, that, after sitting for a short time, he forthwith made a sign to Chia Lan that he would like to go; and as Chia Lan could not but humour him, they both got up together to take their leave. But when Pao-yü perceived them rise, he too felt a wish to go back along with them, but madame Hsing remarked smilingly, "You had better sit a while as I've something more to tell you," so that Pao-yü had no alternative but to stay. "When you get back," madame Hsing added, addressing the other two, "present, each one of you, my regards to your respective mothers. The young ladies, your cousins, are all here making such a row that my head is dazed, so that I won't to-day keep you to have your repast here." To which Chia Huan and Chia Lan assented and quickly walked out.

"If it be really the case that all my cousins have come over," Pao-yü ventured with a smirk, "how is it that I don't see them?"

"After sitting here for a while," madame Hsing explained, "they all went at the back; but in what rooms they have gone, I don't know."

"My senior aunt, you said you had something to tell me, Pao-yü observed; what's it, I wonder?"

"What can there possibly be to tell you?" madame Hsing laughed; "it was simply to make you wait and have your repast with the young ladies and then go; but there's also a fine plaything that I'll give you to take back to amuse yourself with."

These two, the aunt and her nephew, were going on with their colloquy when, much to their surprise, it was time for dinner and the young ladies were all invited to come. The tables and chairs were put in their places, and the cups and plates were arranged in proper order; and, after the mother, her daughter and the cousins had finished their meal, Pao-yü bade good-bye to Chia She and returned home in company with all the young ladies; and when they had said good-night to dowager lady Chia, madame Wang and the others, they each went back into their rooms and retired to rest; where we shall leave them without any further comment and speak of Chia Yün's visit to the mansion. As soon as he saw Chia Lien, he inquired what business it was that had turned up, and Chia Lien consequently explained: "The other day something did actually present itself, but as it happened that your aunt had again and again entreated me, I gave it to Chia Ch'in; as she promised me that there would be by and by in the garden several other spots where flowers and trees would be planted; and that when this job did occur, she would, for a certainty, give it to you and finish!"

Chia Yün, upon hearing these words, suggested after a short pause; "If that be so, there's nothing for me to do than to wait; but, uncle, you too mustn't make any allusion beforehand in the presence of aunt to my having come to-day to make any inquiries; for there will really be ample time to speak to her when the job turns up!"

"Why should I allude to it?" Chia Lien rejoined. "Have I forsooth got all this leisure to talk of irrelevant matters! But to-morrow, besides, I've got to go as far as Hsing Yi for a turn, and it's absolutely necessary that I should hurriedly come back the very same day; so off with you now and go and wait; and the day after to-morrow, after the watch has been set, come and ask for news; but mind at any earlier hour, I shan't have any leisure!" With these words, he hastily went at the back to change his clothes. And from the time Chia Yun put his foot out of the door of the Jung Kuo mansion, he was, the whole way homeward, plunged in deep thought; but having bethought himself of some expedient, he straightway wended his steps towards the house of his maternal uncle, Pu Shih-jen. This Pu Shih-jen, it must be explained, kept, at the present date, a shop for the sale of spices. He had just returned home from his shop, and as soon as he noticed Chia Yun, he inquired of him what business brought him there.

"There's something," Chia Yun replied, "in which I would like to crave your assistance, uncle; I'm in need of some baroos camphor and musk, so please, uncle, give me on credit four ounces of each kind, and on the festival of the eighth moon, I'll bring you the amount in full."

Pu Shih-jen gave a sardonic smile. "Don't," he said, "again allude to any such thing as selling on tick! Some time back a partner in our establishment got several ounces of goods for his relatives on credit, and up to this date the bill hasn't as yet been settled; the result being that we've all had to make the amount good, so that we've entered into an agreement that we should no more allow any one to obtain on tick anything on behalf of either relative or friend, and that whoever acted contrary to this resolution should be, at once, fined twenty taels, with which to stand a treat. Besides, the stock of these articles is now short, and were you also to come, with ready money to this our mean shop to buy any, we wouldn't even have as much to give you. The best way therefore is for you to go elsewhere. This is one side of the question; for on the other, you can't have anything above-board in view; and were you to obtain what you want as a loan you would again go and play the giddy dog! But you'll simply say that on every occasion your uncle sees you, he avails himself of it to find fault with you, but a young fellow like you doesn't know what's good and what is bad; and you should, besides, make up your mind to earn a few cash, wherewith to clothe and feed yourself, so that, when I see you, I too may rejoice!"

"What you, uncle, say," Chia Yun rejoined smiling, "is perfectly right; the only thing is that at the time of my father's death, I was likewise so young in years that I couldn't understand anything; but later on, I heard my mother explain how that for everything, it was lucky that you, after all, my uncles, went over to our house and devised the ways and means, and managed the funeral; and is it likely you, uncle, aren't aware of these things? Besides, have I forsooth had a single acre of land or a couple of houses, the value of which I've run through as soon as it came into my hands? An ingenious wife cannot make boiled rice without raw rice; and what would you have me do? It's your good fortune however that you've got to deal with one such as I am, for had it been any one else barefaced and shameless, he would have come, twice every three days, to worry you, uncle, by asking for two pints of rice and two of beans, and you then, uncle, would have had no help for it."

"My dear child," Pu Shih-jen exclaimed, "had I anything that I could call my own, your uncle as I am, wouldn't I feel bound to do something for you? I've day after day mentioned to your aunt that the misfortune was that you had no resources. But should you ever succeed in making up your mind, you should go into that mighty household of yours, and when the gentlemen aren't looking, forthwith pocket your pride and hobnob with those managers, or possibly with the butlers, as you may, even through them, be able to get some charge or other! The other day, when I was out of town, I came across that old Quartus of the third branch of the family, astride of a tall donkey, at the head of four or five carriages, in which were about forty to fifty bonzes and Taoist priests on their way to the family fane, and that man can't lack brains, for such a charge to have fallen to his share!"

Chia Yün, upon hearing these words, indulged in a long and revolting rigmarole, and then got up to take his leave.

"What are you in such a hurry for?" Pu Shih-jen remarked. "Have your meal and then go!"

But this remark was scarcely ended when they heard his wife say: "Are you again in the clouds? When I heard that there was no rice, I bought half a catty of dry rice paste, and brought it here for you to eat; and do you pray now still put on the airs of a well-to-do, and keep your nephew to feel the pangs of hunger?"

"Well, then, buy half a catty more, and add to what there is, that's all," Pu Shih-jen continued; whereupon her mother explained to her daughter, Yin Chieh, "Go over to Mrs. Wang's opposite, and ask her if she has any cash, to lend us twenty or thirty of them; and to-morrow, when they're brought over, we'll repay her."

But while the husband and wife were carrying on this conversation, Chia Yün had, at an early period, repeated several times: "There's no need to go to this trouble," and off he went, leaving no trace or shadow behind. But without passing any further remarks on the husband and wife of the Pu family, we will now confine ourselves to Chia Yün. Having gone in high dudgeon out of the door of his uncle's house, he started straight on his way back home; but while distressed in mind, and preoccupied with his thoughts, he paced on with drooping head, he unexpectedly came into collision with a drunken fellow, who gripped Chia Yün, and began to abuse him, crying: "Are your eyes gone blind, that you come bang against me?"

The tone of voice, when it reached Chia Yün ears, sounded like that of some one with whom he was intimate; and, on careful scrutiny, he found, in fact, that it was his next-door neighbour, Ni Erh. This Ni Erh was a dissolute knave, whose only idea was to give out money at heavy rates of interest and to have his meals in the gambling dens. His sole delight was to drink and to fight.

He was, at this very moment, coming back home from the house of a creditor, whom he had dunned, and was already far gone with drink, so that when, at an unforeseen moment, Chia Yün ran against him, he meant there and then to start a scuffle with him.

"Old Erh!" Chia Yün shouted, "stay your hand; it's I who have hustled against you."

As soon as Ni Erh heard the tone of his voice, he opened wide his drunken eyes and gave him a look; and realising that it was Chia Yün, he hastened to loosen his grasp and to remark with a smile, as he staggered about, "Is it you indeed, master Chia Secundus? where were you off to now?"

"I couldn't tell you!" Chia Yün rejoined; "I've again brought displeasure upon me, and all through no fault of mine."

"Never mind!" urged Ni Erh, "if you're in any trouble you just tell me, and I'll give vent to your spite for you; for in these three streets, and six lanes, no matter who may give offence to any neighbours of mine, of me, Ni Erh, the drunken Chin Kang, I'll wager that I compel that man's family to disperse, and his home to break up!"

"Old Ni, don't lose your temper," Chia Yün protested, "but listen and let me tell you what happened!" After which, he went on to tell Ni Erh the whole affair with Pu Shih-jen. As soon as Ni Erh heard him, he got into a frightful rage; "Were he not," he shouted, a "relative of yours, master Secundus, I would readily give him a bit of my mind! Really resentment will stifle my breath! but never mind! you needn't however distress yourself. I've got here a few taels ready at hand, which, if you require, don't scruple to take; and from such good neighbours as you are, I won't ask any interest upon this money."

With this remark still on his lips, he produced from his pouch a bundle of silver.

"Ni Erh has, it is true, ever been a rogue," Chia Yün reflected in his own mind, "but as he is regulated in his dealings by a due regard to persons, he enjoys, to a great degree, the reputation of generosity; and were I to-day not to accept this favour of his, he'll, I fear, be put to shame; and it won't contrariwise be nice on my part! and isn't it better that I should make use of his money, and by and by I can repay him double, and things will be all right!"

"Old Erh," he therefore observed aloud with a smile, "you're really a fine fellow, and as you've shown me such eminent consideration, how can I presume not to accept your offer! On my return home, I'll write the customary I.O.U., and send it to you, and all will be in order."

Ni Erh gave a broad grin. "It's only fifteen taels and three mace," he answered, "and if you insist upon writing an I.O.U., I won't then lend it to you!"

Chia Yün at these words, took over the money, smiling the while. "I'll readily," he retorted, "comply with your wishes and have done; for what's the use of exasperating you!"

"Well then that will be all right!" Ni Erh laughed; "but the day is getting dark; and I shan't ask you to have a cup of tea or stand you a drink, for I've some small things more to settle. As for me, I'm going over there, but you, after all, should please wend your way homewards; and I shall also request you to take a message for me to my people. Tell them to close the doors and turn in, as I'm not returning home; and that in the event of anything occurring, to bid our daughter come over to-morrow, as soon as it is daylight, to short-legged Wang's house, the horse-dealer's, in search of me!" And as he uttered this remark he walked away, stumbling and hobbling along. But we will leave him without further notice and allude to Chia Yün.

He had, at quite an unexpected juncture, met this piece of luck, so that his heart was, of course, delighted to the utmost degree. "This Ni Erh," he mused, "is really a good enough sort of fellow, but what I dread is that he may have been open-handed in his fit of drunkenness, and that he mayn't, by and by, ask for his money to be paid twice over; and what will I do then? Never mind," he suddenly went on to ponder, "when that job has become an accomplished fact, I shall even have the means to pay him back double the original amount."

Prompted by this resolution, he came over to a money-shop, and when he had the silver weighed, and no discrepancy was discovered in the weight, he was still more elated at heart; and on his way back, he first and foremost delivered Ni Erh's message to his wife, and then returned to his own home, where he found his mother seated all alone on a stove-couch spinning thread. As soon as she saw him enter, she inquired where he had been the whole day long, in reply to which Chia Yün, fearing lest his parent should be angry, forthwith made no allusion to what transpired with Pu Shih-jen, but simply explained that he had been in the western mansion, waiting for his uncle Secundus, Lien. This over, he asked his mother whether she had had her meal or not, and his parent said by way of reply: "I've had it, but I've kept something for you in there," and calling to the servant-maid, she bade her bring it round, and set it before him to eat. But as it was already dark, when the lamps had to be lit, Chia Yün, after partaking of his meal, got ready and turned in.

Nothing of any notice transpired the whole night; but the next day, as soon it was dawn, he got up, washed his face, and came to the main street, outside the south gate, and purchasing some musk from a perfumery shop, he, with rapid stride, entered the Jung Kuo mansion; and having, as a result of his inquiries, found out that Chia Lien had gone out of doors, Chia Yün readily betook himself to the back, in front of the door of Chia Lien's court, where he saw several servant-lads, with immense brooms in their hands, engaged in that place in sweeping the court. But as he suddenly caught sight of Chou Jui's wife appear outside the door, and call out to the young boys; "Don't sweep now, our lady is coming out," Chia Yün eagerly walked up to her and inquired, with a face beaming with smiles: "Where's aunt Secunda going to?"

To this inquiry, Chou Jui's wife explained: "Our old lady has sent for her, and I expect, it must be for her to cut some piece of cloth or other." But while she yet spoke, they perceived a whole bevy of people, pressing round lady Feng, as she egressed from the apartment.

Chia Yün was perfectly aware that lady Feng took pleasure in flattery, and delighted in display, so that hastily dropping his arms, he with all reverence, thrust himself forward and paid his respects to her. But lady Feng did not even so much as turn to look at him with straight eyes; but continued, as hitherto, her way onwards, simply confining herself to ascertaining whether his mother was all right, and adding: "How is it that she doesn't come to our house for a stroll?"

"The thing is," Chia Yün replied, "that she's not well: she, however, often thinks fondly of you, aunt, and longs to see you; but as for coming round, she's quite unable to do so."

"You have, indeed, the knack of telling lies!" lady Feng laughed with irony; "for hadn't I alluded to her, she would never have thought of me!"

"Isn't your nephew afraid," Chia Yün protested smilingly, "of being blasted by lightning to have the audacity of telling lies in the presence of an elder! Even so late as yesterday evening, she alluded to you, aunt! 'Though naturally,' she said, 'of a weak constitution, you had, however, plenty to attend to! that it's thanks to your supremely eminent energies, aunt, that you're, after all, able to manage everything in such a perfect manner; and that had you ever made the slightest slip, there would have long ago crept up, goodness knows, what troubles!'"

As soon as lady Feng heard these words, her whole face beamed with smiles, and she unconsciously halted her steps, while she proceeded to ask: "How is it that, both your mother and yourself, tattle about me behind my back, without rhyme or reason?"

"There's a reason for it," Chia Yün observed, "which is simply this. I've an excellent friend with considerable money of his own at home, who recently kept a perfumery shop; but as he obtained, by purchase, the rank of deputy sub-prefect, he was, the other day, selected for a post in Yunnan, in some prefecture or other unknown to me; whither he has gone together with his family. He even closed this shop of his, and forthwith collecting all his wares, he gave away, what he could give away, and what he had to sell at a discount, was sold at a loss; while such valuable articles, as these, were all presented to relatives or friends; and that's why it is that I came in for some baroos camphor and musk. But I at the time, deliberated with my mother that to sell them below their price would be a pity, and that if we wished to give them as a present to any one, there was no one good enough to use such perfumes. But remembering how you, aunt, had all along in years gone by, even to this day, to spend large bundles of silver, in purchasing such articles, and how, not to speak of this year with an imperial consort in the Palace, what's even required for this dragon boat festival, will also necessitate the addition of hundred times as much as the quantity of previous years, I therefore present them to you, aunt, as a token of my esteem!"

With these words still on his lips, he simultaneously produced an ornamented box, which he handed over to her. And as lady Feng was, at this time, making preparations for presents for the occasion of the dragon boat festival, for which perfumes were obligatory, she, with all promptitude, directed Feng Erh: "Receive Mr. Yün's present and take it home and hand it over to P'ing Erh. To one," she consequently added, "who seems to me so full of discrimination, it isn't a wonder that your uncle is repeatedly alluding, and that he speaks highly of you; how that you talk with all intelligence and that you have experience stored up in your mind."

Chia Yün upon hearing this propitious language, hastily drew near one step, and designedly asked: "Does really uncle often refer to me?"

The moment lady Feng caught this question, she was at once inclined to tell him all about the charge to be entrusted to him, but on second thought, she again felt apprehensive lest she should be looked lightly upon by him, by simply insinuating that she had promptly and needlessly promised him something to do, so soon as she got a little scented ware; and this consideration urged her to once more restrain her tongue, so that she never made the slightest reference even to so much as one word about his having been chosen to look after the works of planting the flowers and trees. And after confining herself to making the first few irrelevant remarks which came to her lips, she hastily betook herself into dowager lady Chia's apartments.

Chia Yün himself did not feel as if he could very well advert to the subject, with the result that he had no alternative but to retrace his steps homewards. But as when he had seen Pao-yü the previous day, he had asked him to go into the outer library and wait for him, he therefore finished his meal and then once again entered the mansion and came over into the I Hsia study, situated outside the ceremonial gate, over at old lady Chia's part of the compound, where he discovered the two lads Ming Yen, whose name had been changed into Pei Ming, and Chu Yo playing at chess, and just arguing about the capture of a castle; and besides them, Yin Ch'uan, Sao Hua, T'iao Yün, Pan Ho, these four or five of them, up to larks, stealing the young birds from the nests under the eaves of the house.

As soon as Chia Yün entered the court, he stamped his foot and shouted, "The monkeys are up to mischief! Here I am, I've come;" and when the company of servant-boys perceived him, they one and all promptly dispersed; while Chia Yün walked into the library, and seating himself at once in a chair, he inquired, "Has your master Secundus, Mr. Pao, come down?"

"He hasn't been down here at all to-day," Pei Ming replied, "but if you, Mr. Secundus, have anything to tell him, I'll go and see what he's up to for you."

Saying this he there and then left the room; and Chia Yün meanwhile gave himself to the inspection of the pictures and nicknacks. But some considerable time elapsed, and yet he did not see him arrive; and noticing besides that the other lads had all gone to romp, he was just plunged in a state of despondency, when he heard outside the door a voice cry out, with winning tone, and tender accents: "My elder brother!"

Chia Yün looked out, and saw that it was a servant-maid of fifteen or sixteen, who was indeed extremely winsome and spruce. As soon however as the maid caught a glimpse of Chia Yün, she speedily turned herself round and withdrew out of sight. But, as luck would have it, it happened that Pei Ming was coming along, and seeing the servant-maid in front of the door, he observed: "Welcome, welcome! I was quite at a loss how to get any news of Pao-yü." And as Chia Yün discerned Pei Ming, he hastily too, ran out in pursuit of him, and ascertained what was up; whereupon Pei Ming returned for answer: "I waited a whole day long, and not a single soul came over; but this girl is attached to master Secundus' (Mr. Pao's) rooms!" and, "My dear girl," he consequently went on to say, "go in and take a message. Say that Mr. Secundus, who lives under the portico, has come!"

The servant-maid, upon hearing these words, knew at once that he was a young gentleman belonging to the family in which she served, and she did not skulk out of sight, as she had done in the first instance; but with a gaze sufficient to kill, she fixed her two eyes upon Chia Yün, when she heard Chia Yün interpose: "What about over the portico and under the portico; you just tell him that Yün Erh is come, that's all."

After a while this girl gave a sarcastic smile. "My idea is," she ventured, "that you, master Secundus, should really, if it so please you, go back, and come again to-morrow; and to-night, if I find time, I'll just put in a word with him!"

"What's this that you're driving at?" Pei Ming then shouted.

And the maid rejoined: "He's not even had a siesta to-day, so that he'll have his dinner at an early hour, and won't come down again in the evening; and is it likely that you would have master Secundus wait here and suffer hunger? and isn't it better than he should return home? The right thing is that he should come to-morrow; for were even by and by some one to turn up, who could take a message, that person would simply acquiesce with the lips, but would he be willing to deliver the message in for you?"

Chia Yün, upon finding how concise and yet how well expressed this girl's remarks had been, was bent upon inquiring what her name was; but as she was a maid employed in Pao-yü's apartments, he did not therefore feel justified in asking the question, and he had no other course but to add, "What you say is quite right, I'll come to-morrow!" and as he spoke, he there and then was making his way outside, when Pei Ming remarked: "I'll go and pour a cup of tea; and master Secundus, have your tea and then go."

Chia Yün turned his head round, as he kept on his way, and said by way of rejoinder: "I won't have any tea; for I've besides something more to attend to!" and while with his lips he uttered these words, he, with his eyes, stared at the servant-girl, who was still standing in there.

Chia Yün wended his steps straightway home; and the next day, he came to the front entrance, where, by a strange coincidence, he met lady Feng on her way to the opposite side to pay her respects. She had just mounted her carriage, but perceiving Chia Yün arrive, she eagerly bade a servant stop him, and, with the window between them, she smiled and observed: "Yün Erh, you're indeed bold in playing your pranks with me! I thought it strange that you should give me presents; but the fact is you had a favour to ask of me; and your uncle told me even yesterday that you had appealed to him!"

Chia Yün smiled. "Of my appeal to uncle, you needn't, aunt, make any mention; for I'm at this moment full of regret at having made it. Had I known, at an early hour, that things would have come to this pass, I would, from the very first, have made my request to you, aunt; and by this time everything would have been settled long ago! But who would have anticipated that uncle was, after all, a man of no worth!"

"Strange enough," lady Feng remarked sneeringly, "when you found that you didn't succeed in that quarter, you came again yesterday in search of me!"

"Aunt, you do my filial heart an injustice," Chia Yün protested; "I never had such a thought; had I entertained any such idea, wouldn't I, aunt, have made my appeal to you yesterday? But as you are now aware of everything, I'll really put uncle on one side, and prefer my request to you; for circumstances compel me to entreat you, aunt, to be so good as to show me some little consideration!"

Lady Feng laughed sardonically. "You people will choose the long road to follow and put me also in a dilemma! Had you told me just one word at an early hour, what couldn't have been brought about? an affair of state indeed to be delayed up to this moment! In the garden, there are to be more trees planted and flowers laid down, and I couldn't think of any person that I could have recommended, and had you spoken before this, wouldn't the whole question have been settled soon enough?"

"Well, in that case, aunt," ventured Chia Yün with a smile, "you had better depute me to-morrow, and have done!"

"This job," continued lady Feng after a pause, "is not, my impression is, very profitable; and if you were to wait till the first moon of next year, when the fireworks, lanterns, and candles will have to be purveyed, I'll depute you as soon as those extensive commissions turn up."

"My dear aunt," pleaded Chia Yün, "first appoint me to this one, and if I do really manage this satisfactorily, you can then commission me with that other!"

"You know in truth how to draw a long thread," lady Feng observed laughing. "But hadn't it been that your uncle had spoken to me on your account, I wouldn't have concerned myself about you. But as I shall cross over here soon after the repast, you had better come at eleven a.m., and fetch the money, for you to enter into the garden the day after to-morrow, and have the flowers planted!"

As she said this, she gave orders to drive the "scented" carriage, and went on her way by the quickest cut; while Chia Yün, who was irrepressibly delighted, betook himself into the I Hsia study, and inquired after Pao-yü. But, who would have thought it, Pao-yü had, at an early hour, gone to the mansion of the Prince of Pei Ching, so that Chia Yün had to sit in a listless mood till noon; and when he found out that lady Feng had returned, he speedily wrote an acknowledgment and came to receive the warrant. On his arrival outside the court, he commissioned a servant to announce him, and Ts'ai Ming thereupon walked out, and merely asking for the receipt, went in, and, after filling in the amount, the year and moon, he handed it over to Chia Yün together with the warrant. Chia Yün received them from him, and as the entry consisted of two hundred taels, his heart was full of exultant joy; and turning round, he hurried to the treasury, where after he had taken over the amount in silver, he returned home and laid the case before his mother, and needless to say, that both the parent and her son were in high spirits. The next day, at the fifth watch, Chia Yun first came in search of Ni Erh, to whom he repaid the money, and then taking fifty taels along with him, he sped outside the western gate to the house of Fang Ch'un, a gardener, to purchase trees, where we will leave him without saying anything more about him.

We will now resume our story with Pao-yü. The day on which he encountered Chia Yün, he asked him to come in on the morrow and have a chat with him, but this invitation was practically the mere formal talk of a rich and well-to-do young man, and was not likely to be so much as borne in mind; and so it was that it readily slipped from his memory. On the evening of the day, however, on which he returned home from the mansion of the Prince Pei Ching, he came, after paying his salutations to dowager lady Chia, madame Wang, and the other inmates, back into the garden; but upon divesting himself of all his fineries, he was just about to have his bath, when, as Hsi Jen had, at the invitation of Hsüeh Pao-ch'ai, crossed over to tie a few knotted buttons, as Ch'in Wen and Pi Hen had both gone to hurry the servants to bring the water, as T'an Yun had likewise been taken home, on account of her mother's illness, and She Yueh, on the other hand, was at present ailing in her quarters, while the several waiting-maids, who were in there besides to attend to the dirty work, and answer the calls, had, surmising that he would not requisition their services, one and all gone out in search of their friends and in quest of their companions, it occurred, contrary to their calculations, that Pao-yü remained this whole length of time quite alone in his apartments; and as it so happened that Pao-yü wanted tea to drink, he had to call two or three times before he at last saw three old matrons walk in. But at the sight of them, Pao-yü hastily waved his hand and exclaimed: "No matter, no matter; I don't want you," whereupon the matrons had no help but to withdraw out of the rooms; and as Pao-yü perceived that there were no waiting-maids at hand, he had to come down and take a cup and go up to the teapot to pour the tea; when he heard some one from behind him observe: "Master Secundus, beware, you'll scorch your hand; wait until I come to pour it!" And as she spoke, she walked up to him, and took the cup from his grasp, to the intense surprise, in fact, of Pao-yü, who inquired: "Where were you that you have suddenly come to give me a start?"

The waiting-maid smiled as she handed him the tea. "I was in the back court," she replied, "and just came in from the back door of the inner rooms; and is it likely that you didn't, sir, hear the sound of my footsteps?"

Pao-yü drank his tea, and as he simultaneously passed the servant-girl under a minute inspection, he found that though she wore several articles of clothing the worse for wear, she was, nevertheless, with that head of beautiful hair, as black as the plumage of a raven, done up in curls, her face so oblong, her figure so slim and elegant, indeed, supremely beautiful, sweet, and spruce, and Pao-yü eagerly inquired: "Are you also a girl attached to this room of mine?"

"I am," rejoined that waiting-maid.

"But since you belong to this room, how is it I don't know you?" Pao-yü added.

When the maid heard these words, she forced a laugh. "There are even many," she explained, "that are strangers to you; and is it only myself? I've never, before this, served tea, or handed water, or brought in anything; nor have I attended to a single duty in your presence, so how could you know me?"

"But why don't you attend to any of those duties that would bring you to my notice?" Pao-yü questioned.

"I too," answered the maid, "find it as difficult to answer such a question. There's however one thing that I must report to you, master Secundus. Yesterday, some Mr. Yün Erh or other came to see you; but as I thought you, sir, had no leisure, I speedily bade Pei Ming tell him to come early to-day. But you unexpectedly went over again to the mansion of the Prince of Pei Ching."

When she had spoken as far as this, she caught sight of Ch'iu Wen and Pi Hen enter the court, giggling and laughing; the two of them carrying between them a bucket of water; and while raising their skirts with one hand, they hobbled along, as the water spurted and plashed. The waiting-maid hastily come out to meet them so as to relieve them of their burden, but Ch'iu Wen and Pi Hen were in the act of standing face to face and finding fault with each other; one saying, "You've wetted my clothes," the other adding, "You've trod on my shoes," and upon, all of a sudden, espying some one walk out to receive the water, and discovering, when they came to see, that it was actually no one else than Hsiao Hung, they were at once both so taken aback that, putting down the bucket, they hurried into the room; and when they looked about and saw that there was no other person inside besides Pao-yü they were at once displeased. But as they were meanwhile compelled to get ready the articles necessary for his bath, they waited until Pao-yü was about to divest himself of his clothes, when the couple of them speedily pulled the door to behind them, as they went out, and walked as far as the room on the opposite side, in search of Hsiao Hung; of whom they inquired: "What were you doing in his room a short while back?"

"When was I ever in the room?" Hsiao Hung replied; "simply because I lost sight of my handkerchief, I went to the back to try and find it, when unexpectedly Mr. Secundus, who wanted tea, called for you sisters; and as there wasn't one even of you there, I walked in and poured a cup for him, and just at that very moment you sisters came back."

"You barefaced, low-bred thing!" cried Ch'iu Wen, turning towards her and spurting in her face. "It was our bounden duty to tell you to go and hurry them for the water, but you simply maintained that you were busy and made us go instead, in order to afford you an opportunity of performing these wily tricks! and isn't this raising yourself up li by li? But don't we forsooth, even so much as come up to you? and you just take that looking-glass and see for yourself, whether you be fit to serve tea and to hand water or not?"

"To-morrow," continued Pi Hea, "I'll tell them that whenever there's anything to do connected with his wanting tea, or asking for water, or with fetching things for him, not one of us should budge, and that *she* alone should be allowed to go, and have done!"

"If this be your suggestion," remarked Ch'iu Wen, "wouldn't it be still better that we should all disperse, and let her reign supreme in this room!"

But while the two of them were up to this trouble, one saying one thing, and another, another, they caught sight of two old nurses walk in to deliver a message from lady Feng; who explained: "To-morrow, someone will bring in gardeners to plant trees, and she bids you keep under more rigorous restraint, and not sun your clothes and petticoats anywhere and everywhere; nor air them about heedlessly; that the artificial hill will, all along, be entirely shut in by screening curtains, and that you mustn't he running about at random."

"I wonder," interposed Ch'iu Wen with alacrity, "who it is that will bring the workmen to-morrow, and supervise the works?"

"Some one or other called Mr. Yün, living at the back portico," the old woman observed.

But Ch'iu Wen and Pi Hen were neither of them acquainted with him, and they went on promiscuously asking further questions on his account, but Hsiao Hung knew distinctly in her mind who it was, and was well aware that it was the person whom she had seen, the previous day, in the outer library.

The surname of this Hsiao Hung had, in fact, been originally Lin, while her infant name had been Hung Yü; but as the word Yü improperly corresponded with the names of Pao-yü and Tai-yü, she was, in due course, simply called Hsiao Hung. She was indeed an hereditary servant of the mansion; and her father had latterly taken over the charge of all matters connected with the farms and farmhouses in every locality. This Hung-yü came, at the age of sixteen, into the mansion, to enter into service, and was attached to the Hung Yuan, where in point of fact she found both a quiet and pleasant home; and when contrary to all expectation, the young ladies as well as Pao-yü, were subsequently permitted to move their quarters into the garden of Broad Vista, it so happened that this place was, moreover, fixed upon by Pao-yü. This Hsiao Hung was, it is true, a girl without any experience, but as she could, to a certain degree, boast of a pretty face, and as, in her own heart, she recklessly fostered the idea of exalting herself to a higher standard, she was ever ready to thrust herself in Pao-yü's way, with a view to showing herself off. But attached to Pao-yü's personal service were a lot of servants, all of whom were glib and specious, so that how could she ever find an opportunity of thrusting herself forward? But contrary to her anticipations, there turned up, eventually on this day, some faint glimmer of hope, but as she again came in for a spell of spiteful abuse from Ch'iu Wen and her companion, her expectations were soon considerably frustrated, and she was just plunged in a melancholy mood, when suddenly she heard the old nurse begin the conversation about Chia Yün, which unconsciously so affected her heart that she hastily returned, quite disconsolate, into her room, and lay herself down on her bed, giving herself quietly to reflection. But while she was racking and torturing her brain and at a moment when she was at a loss what decision to grasp, her ear unexpectedly caught, emanating from outside the window, a faint voice say: "Hsiao Hung, I've picked up your pocket handkerchief in here!" and as soon as Hsiao Hung heard these words, she walked out with hurried step and found that it was no one else than Chia Yün in person; and as Hsiao Hung unwillingly felt her powdered face suffused with brushes: "Where did you pick it up, Mr. Secundus?" she asked.

"Come over," Chia Yün smiled, "and I'll tell you!" And as he uttered these words, he came up and drew her to him; but Hsiao Hung twisted herself round and ran away; but was however tripped over by the step of the door.

Now, reader, do you want to know the sequel? If so the next chapter will explain.

NOTES

[Notes on this edition. The original Chinese novel was written by Cao Xueqin. Another author later added half again as much. H. Bencraft Joly translated only the work of the first author, essentially two-thirds of the whole; the work ends abruptly at the end of volume II as if he intended to go on, but the third volume was never published.

There IS such a word as 'teapoy'; it is NOT 'teapot' and it means a three-legged table. 'Dullness' was consistently spelled 'dulness' and is left thus. 'Decrepit' was consistently spelled 'decrepid' and is left thus. 'Dote, dotes,' etc. was consistently spelled 'doat, doats,' etc. and is left thus. 'License' is spelled once thus and once 'licence.' The word 'speciality' appears only once, and that is the proper British spelling.

Whenever a proper name normally contained an umlaut we attempted to supply it in the instances where it was missing; this was most common with the name Pao-yü. There were also variations of use of apostrophes in proper names, and many were corrected.]

Also from Benediction Books ...

Wandering Between Two Worlds: Essays on Faith and Art
Anita Mathias
Benediction Books, 2007
152 pages
ISBN: 0955373700

Available from www.amazon.com, www.amazon.co.uk

In these wide-ranging lyrical essays, Anita Mathias writes, in lush, lovely prose, of her naughty Catholic childhood in Jamshedpur, India; her large, eccentric family in Mangalore, a sea-coast town converted by the Portuguese in the sixteenth century; her rebellion and atheism as a teenager in her Himalayan boarding school, run by German missionary nuns, St. Mary's Convent, Nainital; and her abrupt religious conversion after which she entered Mother Teresa's convent in Calcutta as a novice. Later rich, elegant essays explore the dualities of her life as a writer, mother, and Christian in the United States-- Domesticity and Art, Writing and Prayer, and the experience of being "an alien and stranger" as an immigrant in America, sensing the need for roots.

About the Author

Anita Mathias is the author of *Wandering Between Two Worlds: Essays on Faith and Art.* She has a B.A. and M.A. in English from Somerville College, Oxford University, and an M.A. in Creative Writing from the Ohio State University, USA. Anita won a National Endowment of the Arts fellowship in Creative Nonfiction in 1997. She lives in Oxford, England with her husband, Roy, and her daughters, Zoe and Irene.

Visit Anita's website
http://www.anitamathias.com,
and Anita's blog
http://dreamingbeneaththespires.blogspot.com, (Dreaming Beneath the Spires).

The Church That Had Too Much
Anita Mathias
Benediction Books, 2010
52 pages
ISBN: 9781849026567

Available from www.amazon.com, www.amazon.co.uk

The Church That Had Too Much was very well-intentioned. She wanted to love God, she wanted to love people, but she was both hampered by her muchness and the abundance of her possessions, and beset by ambition, power struggles and snobbery. Read about the surprising way The Church That Had Too Much began to resolve her problems in this deceptively simple and enchanting fable.

About the Author

Anita Mathias is the author of *Wandering Between Two Worlds: Essays on Faith and Art.* She has a B.A. and M.A. in English from Somerville College, Oxford University, and an M.A. in Creative Writing from the Ohio State University, USA. Anita won a National Endowment of the Arts fellowship in Creative Nonfiction in 1997. She lives in Oxford, England with her husband, Roy, and her daughters, Zoe and Irene.

Visit Anita's website
http://www.anitamathias.com,
and Anita's blog
http://dreamingbeneaththespires.blogspot.com (Dreaming Beneath the Spires).

www.ingramcontent.com/pod-product-compliance
Lightning Source LLC
Chambersburg PA
CBHW030342310726
48979CB00001B/152

* 9 7 8 1 7 8 1 3 9 2 7 6 8 *